PENGUIN

RĀMA THE S

CW00530493

THE AUTHOR of the Rāma story is known only from the content of his work. He was an oral poet speaking a distinct dialect of Sanskrit in the central Gaṅgā region of northern India in about the fifth century BC. He was a man with the traditional outlook of a man, familiar with the interests and pursuits of the warrior class in a small, agriculturally based kingdom within which there was as yet limited social differentiation, still observing an archaic pattern of worship. He was also a perceptive craftsman, skilled and sensitive, whose work was appreciated, emulated and augmented by generations of successors.

It is clear that the text translated in this volume is the product of many minds and many tongues, but what about the original text? Was there one author or many? Was it, in outline, the product of a single composer's mind, or did the story emerge gradually from the coalescence of multiple pre-existent sources? Scholarly opinion is divided.

JOHN BROCKINGTON was educated at Mill Hill School and Corpus Christi College, Oxford. He is emeritus Professor of Sanskrit in the School of Asian Studies (of which he was the first Head) at the University of Edinburgh. His books include *The Sacred Thread* (1981), *Righteous Rāma* (1985), *Hinduism and Christianity* (1992) and *The Sanskrit Epics* (1998). His special area of research is the Sanskrit epics. He is the Secretary General of the International Association of Sanskrit Studies.

MARY BROCKINGTON was educated at Homelands Grammar School, Derby, and St Hilda's College, Oxford. She has edited three volumes of Indological papers and published several articles on the *Rāmāyaṇa*, the *Mahābhārata* and the *Harivaṃśa*, and on traditional tales and early literature in Europe and South Asia. Her research is focused mainly on narrative strategies and on performance.

Rāma the Steadfast

An Early Form of the Rāmāyaṇa

Translated by
JOHN BROCKINGTON *and* MARY BROCKINGTON

PENGUIN BOOKS

PENGUIN CLASSICS

Published by the Penguin Group
Penguin Books Ltd, 80 Strand, London WC2R 0RL, England
Penguin Group (USA) Inc., 375 Hudson Street, New York, New York 10014, USA
Penguin Group (Canada), 90 Eglinton Avenue East, Suite 700, Toronto, Ontario, Canada M4P 2Y3
(a division of Pearson Penguin Canada Inc.)
Penguin Ireland, 25 St Stephen's Green, Dublin 2, Ireland (a division of Penguin Books Ltd)
Penguin Group (Australia), 250 Camberwell Road, Camberwell, Victoria 3124, Australia
(a division of Pearson Australia Group Pty Ltd)
Penguin Books India Pvt Ltd, 11 Community Centre, Panchsheel Park, New Delhi – 110 017, India
Penguin Books (NZ), cnr Airborne and Rosedale Roads, Albany, Auckland 1310, New Zealand
(a division of Pearson New Zealand Ltd)
Penguin Books (South Africa) (Pty) Ltd, 24 Sturdee Avenue, Rosebank, Johannesburg 2196, South Africa

Penguin Books Ltd, Registered Offices: 80 Strand, London WC2R 0RL, England

www.penguin.com

First published in Penguin Classics 2006
1

Set in 10.25/12.25 pt PostScript Adobe Sabon
Typeset by Rowland Phototypesetting Ltd, Bury St Edmunds, Suffolk
Printed in England by Clays Ltd, St Ives plc

ISBN-13: 978-0-140-44744-6
ISBN-10: 0-140-44744-X

‘Journey steadfastly, my son; may your path be safe and free from all danger, and may fortune and prosperity attend your return.’

[2,31.26]

Contents

Acknowledgements

The translators wish to thank various friends and colleagues for support and advice, in particular James L. Fitzgerald and the late Alison Smith. John Brockington also gratefully acknowledges the award of a Leverhulme Research Fellowship which greatly assisted work on this translation.

Introduction

(Readers are warned that elements of the plot are discussed in this Introduction; for necessary background information see the Note to the Reader.)

Rāma, the hero who became God

Ever since about the twelfth century AD the warrior-prince Rāma has been widely recognized and revered in India as God. This understanding did not result from a single, sudden, historical revelation like the birth of Christ or Mohammed; it developed over many centuries, and it will continue to develop. As faith in Rāma's divinity has grown, devotees have turned for spiritual insight and revelation to the tale of his earthly heroism, the tale of Rāma the steadfast mortal hero, of his selfless preservation of his father's integrity, of his quest for his lost wife and his triumphant battle to rescue her.

This tale had by then already been being told, heard and retold for many centuries in a long Sanskrit narrative poem known as the *Rāmāyaṇa* belonging to that diverse category of early literature collectively labelled 'anonymous'. Indian tradition and most Western scholars are united in believing that it was originally composed orally, and transmitted for several centuries by oral recitation, but opinion is divided about the date of composition: Indian tradition would place it several millennia ago, while scholars have proposed various later periods. Based on the language, style and content of the work, we suggest a date of roughly the fifth century BC. The *Mahābhārata*, an even longer Sanskrit narrative poem, probably originated at much the same time. It is the earliest levels of the story that have been translated in this book, that is to say, those passages which can be identified as the work of the original author as augmented by his immediate successors; these passages, detailed in the Note on the Text Translated, which have been identified by careful evaluation of the linguistic evidence, together represent the first stage of development of the tale.

Scholars are in the habit of referring to the *Rāmāyaṇa* and the *Mahābhārata* alike as epics, but their origins are cast in very different genres, and in the case of the *Rāmāyaṇa* the term 'epic' can justifiably be applied only to its later, developed form; the story lying at its heart would in Western literary terms best be classified as a heroic romance, for it is the personal story of the Prince, a lone figure, supported in his adventures only by a younger brother who functions merely as his squire or confidant, and the outcome affects only himself and the individuals he encounters: no wider or national interests are involved. It is the struggle for integrity and happiness of one man, not a war of conquest. Victory for Rāma twice involves transfer of sovereignty merely between 'bad' and 'good' members of the same family, and while defeat for him would be a private grief for those close to him, the destiny of his subjects would be unaffected. In the *Mahābhārata* the situation is quite different: that text chronicles a bitter struggle for sovereignty between two groups of cousins, with the fate of several kingdoms depending on the outcome, and explores the issue of how far it is permissible for the heroes to compromise their integrity in pursuit of their legitimate claim and still remain fit to rule. Indian tradition too distinguishes between the two works, designating the *Rāmāyaṇa* as the *ādikāvya*, 'the first poetic work' or perhaps 'the first work of pure literature', but the *Mahābhārata* commonly as *itihāsa*, 'thus indeed it was', a term roughly equivalent to 'history'. It is the practice in many households for a copy of Rāma's story to be kept in an honoured place, while presence of a *Mahābhārata* text is regarded as unlucky.

From these early origins there developed the more lengthy versions represented by their Critical Editions, so that the *Rāmāyaṇa* with almost 20,000 verses and the *Mahābhārata* with more than three times that number are now among the most extensive literary works in the world. It has long been recognized that these two great narrative poems are central to the whole of Indian culture, exercising an enormous formative influence and doing much to establish the canons of taste. The *Rāmāyaṇa* furnished the plots of many works of classical Sanskrit literature and a much greater number of vernacular adaptations at all levels of society and culture within India and throughout much of Southeast and East Asia. Ample testimony to the text's significance is provided by the wide variety of art forms in which it has been expressed over the centuries. Alongside conventional retellings by storytellers, the tale thrives in puppet plays and in the *Rāmlīlā* (a form of popular dramatic presentation analogous to the Western medieval mystery plays); in the last years of the twentieth century, a long-running nationwide adaptation on Indian television achieved huge popularity and has been repeated on Western channels. Important insights into the popular understanding of the tale can also be gained from non-verbal forms of the story, including temple sculptures and narrative friezes, paintings and dance; in many cases the temple sculptures are the earliest testimonia we have, antedating the manuscript evidence by several centuries.

The original conception of the Rāma story as it emerges in this volume reflects the interests and concerns of the warrior aristocracy (the *kṣatriya* class): Rāma is a martial hero whose actions are accepted without question as necessary and, for that reason, as justified. Later times and different milieux had different values, and new characteristics were attributed to Rāma through the centuries during which the text was expanded and reworked. First he becomes a moral hero, then a regal but still human figure; later he was viewed as the earthly manifestation (*avatāra*) of the god Viṣṇu, finally as God in his own right, with the developed text acquiring the status of holy scripture. The Rāma story has been in a constant state of re-creation, and in the development of many of these later adaptations (though by no means all), the role played by the faith of believers has been crucial. Some of the issues raised by these subsequent developments are explored in Afterthoughts.

What does the story of Rāma tell us?

External sources tell us absolutely nothing about the author of the poem or any of his early successors: names, dates, geographical location, social status, interests, all are unknown. Linguistic evidence, based on comparison with other texts which can be roughly dated, points to a date for the earliest parts of about the fifth century BC, but this is a period about which we have hitherto known little. Yet if we turn to the text translated in this volume we can see a clear picture emerge of the original author and the world in which he lived.

In all probability he was a man resident in the central Gaṅgā basin (English form, Ganges), with only limited knowledge of areas beyond: the focus of the story is the city state of Ayodhyā situated on the river Sarayū, at the heart of the Kosala region, and portrayed as a real place probably to be identified with modern Faizabad on the Gharghara. Apart from this, the geographical horizons of the text are limited. Its early authors and reciters have heard of Videha, the region to the northeast, around modern Darbhanga between the Gaṅgā and the southeast boundary of Nepal; its capital Mithilā, though not itself mentioned, gives Sītā one of her names (Maithilī, 'Princess of Mithilā'), but no part of the story is set there. To the northwest, the grandfather and uncle of Bharata and Śatrughna live at Rājagṛha in the northern Panjab, and we are given a realistic account of the route taken there by messengers sent from Ayodhyā to summon the princes back home after the death of their father. It is noteworthy that on the banks of the Gaṅgā, Rāma, Lakṣmaṇa and Sītā make contact with the Niṣāda tribe, a group whom they treat with respect, not with the contempt of later Indian culture.

Most of the poem, however, details the wanderings of the exiles in a fantasy land, the uncultivated, uncharted forest immediately south of the Gaṅgā. Here live hermits, but here too they encounter monsters, *rākṣasas*, monkeys, bears and vultures, all with human speech and human characteristics, some living in cities, using artefacts like humans, and, by an apparent slip of the teller's memory, occasionally referred to in human terms. The Vindhyas, the east–west chain of mountains dividing northern India off from the peninsula, is the effective limit of the poets' knowledge at this time. The sea is mentioned rarely, and located immediately south of the Vindhyas, but it too is a hostile environment, full of monsters, a barrier between the forest and the enemy's island capital, Laṅkā. Many attempts have been made to identify Laṅkā and Kiṣkindhā, the *vānaras'* city, with real sites on mainland India, and especially to equate Rāvaṇa's kingdom with the island in modern times renamed Śrī Laṅkā, but there is nothing in the first stage of the text to indicate that they are anything more than the product of the storytellers' imaginations, with little help even from travellers' tales.

The Ayodhyā Book portrays a city state, headed by a royal family where primogeniture is the norm and family ties are important, a pattern copied in the non-human societies of Kiṣkindhā and Laṅkā. Rulers regularly have more than one wife, and the importance of a queen's family background in cementing political alliances with marriage ties is shown by the frequency with which women such as Kausalyā, Kaikeyī and Sītā are referred to by names indicating their family. Respect for parents and obedience to them are of the highest importance, but particularly among the humans there is clearly genuine affection too, both between Daśaratha and his sons and between Bharata and his grandfather and uncle; equally genuine is the affection of the people of Ayodhyā for their royal family, with whom they have a direct relationship. The king's court is fairly simple with a council of advisers who take charge in the absence of a monarch, but with no elaborate array of officials. It is the king's duty to protect his subjects in return for their loyalty, and there is some stratification within society, but little significance is attached to the topic. The work is founded on the values of the warrior aristocracy (*kṣatriyas*): devotion to duty, integrity, pride and valour – both physical and spiritual – with brāhmanic values acknowledged but not inappropriately obtrusive. No incongruity is seen in the performance of a sacrifice by the *kṣatriya* Rāma to consecrate the hut Lakṣmaṇa has built for them to live in on Citrakūṭa. If the rigidity of the developed class structure or of four stages of life (from student to renunciant) existed at all by this time, the tellers of the *Rāmāyaṇa* took no interest in them. Women too are accorded rather greater freedom than might be expected, superficially at least, although a wife's duty to be subordinate to her husband is already emphasized. Widows are not yet regarded as inauspicious, but courtesans can convey auspiciousness by their presence on special occasions.

It is clear that various practical forms of learning were well developed, but formal education for young warriors seems to consist only of the necessary instruction in weaponry, alongside knowledge of the Vedas; for a princess a good upbringing means learning the duties of a wife.

Writing, if known at all, is not used to any significant extent for communication; messages are delivered orally, with recognition tokens functioning only to confirm a messenger's credentials. Music figures occasionally as part of city life, but more often in a military context. The one area of learning that appears more prominently than an outsider to the culture might expect is astronomy or astrology (the two are not differentiated); this science had already been well developed in the Vedic period because of its practical importance in regulating the calendar and thus the timing of periodic rituals.

The interest of the early authors was not focused on the activities of merchants or farmers, so economic life and agricultural pursuits are taken for granted. It is clear that agriculture, as at all pre-modern periods of India's history, was the main activity and source of revenue for the king, but there is little mention of the utilitarian cereals which must have been widely grown, nor do we hear much of the cattle that must have been common. The poets and their audience among the warrior aristocracy were obviously more interested in horses and elephants because of their use in battle and hunting, and the considerable number of wild animals mentioned bears testimony to their wide acquaintance with the natural world, as well as close observation and appreciation. Trees are an important part of the landscape, with several different species distinguished, but the plant accorded greatest prestige is the lotus:

beautiful faces are compared to lotus blooms and eyes to lotus petals in shape, while its growth from the slime of the pond and its flowers' ability to shed water symbolize the triumph of purity over impurity.

The food and drink mentioned are basically those typical of a heroic society, and have not yet given way to the pattern typical of later Indian culture. There are frequent references to meat-eating, with Rāma and Lakṣmaṇa often killing game to eat and sometimes for sacrifice. Only the diet of ascetics is vegetarian: fruit and roots gathered from the forest. Similarly, alcoholic drinks do not attract the same opprobrium as later: an episode of drunken hooliganism attributed to the hero's monkey allies is indulgently exploited for its comic value.

Hunting is a favourite pastime for princes, and we find numerous allusions to deer being hunted for sport or food. In hunt and battle alike, at this stage the bow is the standard weapon, often firing a fantastic number of arrows with awesomely fanciful results. Spears and missiles of all kinds are also employed, particularly by the *rākṣasas*, while the monkeys achieve shattering results by ripping up and wielding trees and even mountain-tops. The typical form of combat is a duel fought between two leading warriors, often preceded by the formalized boasting characteristic of single combat in heroic literature generally. The warriors would be expected to be mounted on horse-drawn chariots, but the exigencies of the plot dictate that for most of the story Rāma must fight on foot. This is clearly felt inappropriate for a warrior of his status, and he is eventually supplied with a chariot by supernatural means so that he may fight his supreme enemy on more nearly equal terms.

The religious pattern found in the early *Rāmāyaṇa* is the older pattern of deities and of rituals based on sacrifice leading to heaven, rather than the newer patterns of worship, usually seen as leading to liberation (*mokṣa*), even though they are found in the later parts of the *Mahābhārata*. The gods mentioned or playing any part in the narrative are largely those of the Vedic pantheon. Indra is particularly prominent, both as the leader of the gods and as the performer of various heroic deeds; not surprisingly, therefore, Rāma is most often compared with Indra and receives the help of Indra's charioteer in the final duel at the climax of the battle; this is in marked contrast to the later assimilation of Rāma to Viṣṇu, who hardly appears at all. Yama appears quite often in his role as King of the Dead (a role later to be incompatible with the concept of transmigration, *saṃsāra*); a common formulaic expression refers to dispatching warriors to Yama's realm. Varuṇa too still finds mention, mainly as the Lord of the Ocean, but also in his association with Indra, reflecting an early stage in the relative importance of these two deities. In general, the opposition between gods and anti-gods and their contests for supremacy show a Vedic or immediately post-Vedic pattern, very different from the pattern in later Hinduism.

The commonest rituals mentioned are the morning and evening worship, but sacrifice in general and some individual sacrifices are occasionally mentioned. The narrative requires that funerals take place, but comparatively little attention is paid to their ritual aspect and more to their practicalities.

The various sages who feature in the narrative and offer hospitality to Rāma and his companions also represent an archaic pattern: they are *vānaprastha* hermits, continuing to practise simple rituals and may be accompanied by their wives, not the later *saṃnyāsins*, renunciant ascetics who have abandoned all links with society. Nevertheless, the idea is already present that supernatural powers may be acquired, or even extorted from the gods, by the practice of severely exaggerated forms of asceticism.

Who composed the story of Rāma?

Almost the only thing the text does not tell us about the earliest teller of Rāma's story is his name. He was a poet familiar with the geography of the central Gaṅgā region at a period before the rise there of large-scale monarchies (which culminated in the Maurya dynasty of the fourth to second centuries BC), a time when local chieftains held sway over small, agriculturally based kingdoms within which there was limited social differentiation, a poet familiar with the interests and pursuits of the *kṣatriya* class, for whom warfare and the pleasures of the hunt in the surrounding forest areas were of most importance, a poet speaking a distinct dialect of Sanskrit, probably to some extent regionally based in the Gaṅgā basin but more specifically the language of the *kṣatriya* class, a poet still observing the older pattern of worship and untouched by heterodox trends that were soon to result in the emergence of Buddhism and Jainism, or the development of brāhmanic Hinduism with its rigid social stratification. This poet gives no indication of knowing the *Mahābhārata*, although many passages of that epic refer to *Rāmāyaṇa* episodes: it is to be hoped that *Mahābhārata* linguistic scholarship will one day enable us to judge how far this absence indicates a difference in date or milieu, and how far the *Rāmāyaṇa* poets may have been deliberately avoiding any reference to the other poem. Taken as a whole, the evidence suggests that the Rāma story as first composed about the fifth century BC was then augmented by poets of similar outlook throughout its first stage of development, with the boundary between this stage and the next (a boundary as real as a contour line on a map) very roughly 300 BC.

That this poet was a man there can be no doubt. The sufferings of women characters are portrayed in moving fashion, but these sufferings – whether the grief of Daśaratha's queens, the mourning of Tārā and Mandodarī or the hardships and stoic resistance of Sītā – are all centred on the loss of their menfolk. Women do not direct positive events, but react to them with sweetness, malice, common sense, jealousy, meekness or frivolous desire – the stereotypical attributes of women: more than once a husband dies with the words 'I told you so' ringing in his ears. When disaster is to ensue, it is women who are made to direct the plot: Kaikeyī contrives the banishment and Śūrpaṇakhā's infatuation with Rāma is treated as ludicrous, with no hint that the concerns of either female should be taken seriously; and Sītā's desire for the golden deer and insistence on sending Lakṣmaṇa after Rāma make her responsible for her own capture. Sītā's initial request to accompany Rāma into exile is subject to his consent, and is not merely indispensable to the plot but a useful means by which the author can deflect criticism from his hero for exposing her to the hardships of forest life. The author's main concern is with the men. Only a male author could expect to evoke sympathy for his noble, considerate, thoughtful hero with the utterly self-centred, self-pitying laments he utters when he believes his beloved wife has been captured and probably devoured by a monster, and the misfortune falls on Rāma, not on Sītā. More successful is his treatment of the act of injustice that opens the poem: Daśaratha's granting of Kaikeyī's request to banish Rāma is portrayed as strength rather than as weakness or folly. The king has given his word, and must keep it, no matter how great the personal cost to him, and the cost to the pathetic old man is portrayed in the most moving and convincing terms that outweigh the mild criticism expressed by the citizens and by his far from impartial senior queen, Rāma's mother.

There can be no doubt that the author was a poet of considerable skill and sensitivity, who put great thought and care into planning his plot. The narrative is enclosed within a structured framework designed to enhance the humanity of Rāma and soften the edges of his martial heroism, opening with his capitulation to his wife's pleas to accompany him into exile, and closing with his capitulation to his allies' desire to accompany him back to Ayodhyā; in both cases we are clearly intended to assume that this flagrant disregard of his instructions coincides with his own inner wishes. Within this framework, each Book begins and ends with parallel themes or episodes: in the Ayodhyā Book it is Sītā and the duties of wife; the Forest Book is framed by episodes with sages; the Kiṣkindhā Book moves from despair to despair, before ending on a final note of elation; Beauty opens with Hanumān's search for Sītā and closes with his report of finding her; War begins with Rāma's preparations for the journey to Laṅkā and ends with his preparations for the return journey to Ayodhyā.

Parallelism of structure is echoed by parallelism of theme. The poem is constructed around the relationships within three contrasting families of brothers, the humans, the *vānaras* and the *rākṣasas*, expressed in warm, lively, realistic terms. The humans are characterized by a love and loyalty to each other that overwhelm all feelings of rivalry or resentment, without entirely obliterating them. The situation in Kiṣkindhā parallels that in Ayodhyā, with Vālin and Sugrīva the counterparts of Rāma and Bharata respectively, but the issues of right and wrong are much less clear-cut and suspicion, harshness and distrust rule among the *vānaras*. The *rākṣasas* display virtually no family feeling. Rāvaṇa has already usurped the position of his elder half-brother, and his abduction of Sītā is motivated far less by revenge for his sister's disfigurement or even the slaughter of his brothers and the army commanded by Khara than by his lust for her, a lust that Śūrpaṇakhā recognizes and deliberately excites. The one who has usurped his elder finds himself in turn replaced by his youngest brother, the virtuous Vibhīṣaṇa, a shameful state of affairs in itself. This outcome has been created by the poet to allow Rāma to leave Laṅkā in good hands and return home, for the death of Rāvaṇa and the recovery of Sītā are his only objectives, not the conquest of the city. Nevertheless, the strength of brotherly ties cannot be altogether eliminated, even from these most quarrelsome of families. The dying Vālin begs Sugrīva's forgiveness, awakening in his brother the affection that befits an ally of Rāma and robs Sugrīva of his initial exultation at his brother's death. Even Rāvaṇa exhibits genuine grief at the death of Kumbhakarṇa: his lament is his first display of real emotion in the poem, and has analogies to Rāma's laments when he twice thinks Lakṣmaṇa dead and realizes that he values his faithful brother more than his lost wife.

The author's craftsmanship is apparent throughout. His plot is a series of skilfully contrived surprises which contrasts markedly with the doom-laden inevitability of the *Mahābhārata*. Rāma's uncomplaining acceptance of his exile and his agreement to allow Sītā and Lakṣmaṇa to accompany him, his father's feeble efforts to prevent the fulfilment of his own decree and Bharata's angry attempt to reject the sovereignty his mother has contrived for him set the story in motion, and find their echo at the end in the revelation that Bharata, almost as strong-willed as his elder brother, has only outwardly carried out Rāma's insistence that it is he who should act as king of Ayodhyā, and has in fact been sharing his brother's ascetic life at home – a revelation that sends Rāma hurrying back to Ayodhyā with the promise of the appropriate happy-ever-after ending. It is sad to think that the impact of these beautifully crafted surprises was destined to be blunted by the story's very popularity, so that the twists of plot no longer come as a surprise. So familiar are Indians with the story, from their earliest years, that it is now said that 'Nobody hears the story of Rāma for the first time', a paradox that has contributed both to the fervour of later tellers to embellish the beloved story, and to the need for some way of renewing interest in the well-known plot with elaborations that have gone far towards obscuring or even obliterating the original.

The unobtrusive way in which the author sets the tone of his story provides a further demonstration of his craftsmanship. The first thing we learn about Sītā is her fear of being separated from Rāma, and Rāma's first speech expresses his thoughtfulness for his wife and mother in the midst of his distress. Not until well into the Forest Book does the first *rākṣasa*, Śūrpaṇakhā, participate in the action, but the audience have been prepared for danger from *rākṣasas* from as early as Kausalyā's lament after her son's departure, a peril more emphatically expressed in the opening paragraphs of The Forest.

The narrative is never flat. There is lively dialogue, especially within a family context, and there is the pompous sermon Prahasta directs to the captive Hanumān. Jaṭāyus' speech challenging Rāvaṇa is a masterstroke. Just as the audience's fears and emotions have been roused to fever pitch by Sītā's anguished cries, the sleepy bird delivers a long, slow, moralizing speech exhorting Rāvaṇa to release his captive – a change of pace that represents not so much a release of tension as a maddening increase; readers could skip the passage, but in an oral performance listeners impatient to hear what happens next are compelled to await the pleasure of the teller. The rumbustuous coarseness of the Honey Orchard episode is deftly handled to combine the maximum comedy with the minimum offensiveness, and the fantastic count of monkeys assembled for the siege of Laṅkā and the descriptions of their movements throughout the second half of the text are merely a vivid exaggeration of the impression a real troop of monkeys can give.

Subtle, though, is the progressive disintegration apparent in the morale of Rāvaṇa from the beginning of the War Book as he first ponders the damage Hanumān has caused to Laṅkā, then sees that the *vānara* army has crossed the sea; as his spies Śuka and Sāraṇa report back and show him the army and its leaders in a dramatically visual panoramic display (to which Śārdūla's colourless supplementary report bears no comparison), he begins to feel the first stirrings of doubt about his power to resist.

Disagreements in particular are full of movement and life. When Bharata meets Rāma on Citrakūṭa, he finds his resolve to replace his brother in exile gently but inexorably undermined by arguments playing not on any weak points of his character but on the strong ones, until finally he crumples and agrees to return to Ayodhyā as Rāma's regent. Sītā's rejection of the lovelorn Rāvaṇa's proposition when he shows her around his palace builds up powerfully as patient explanation (as if she were speaking to a simpleton) gradually gives way to confident defiance.

To present the necessarily repetitive series of battles that compose the bulk of the War Book in a way that sustains the audience's interest while whetting their appetite for the climactic final encounter poses a challenge which the author meets in a number of ways. Physical battles are interspersed with episodes of magic, and variety is introduced into the largely episodic and linear construction by Rāma's duel with Makarākṣa, whose attempt to avenge the death of his father Khara recalls the earlier conflict in Daṇḍaka forest. The tone is varied, with the humour of Kumbhakarṇa's grumpiness and Hanumān's decision to bring a whole mountain-peak to ensure he has brought the right healing herb; there is an extensive passage of puns on the names of *vānaras* who Rāvaṇa pretends have been killed; and Rāma taunts Rāvaṇa with biting sarcasm before their final duel. This is the battle for which the audience have been waiting ever since the beginning of the War Book, but even when Rāvaṇa finally takes the field, it is repeatedly put off and then long drawn out, to the extent that the villain's inevitable death, when it comes, shocks by its abrupt finality just as much as Daśaratha's had done. Unlike Vālin, Rāvaṇa is given no opportunity for a dying speech, last-minute repentance or reconciliation with victim, opponent or virtuous brother: he retains his heroic stature and remains a villain to the end, mourned only by his wives. Vibhīṣaṇa is still so bitter that Rāma has to order him to fulfil his fraternal duty and perform the funeral rites.

What happened next?

The heroic tale that formed the core of the *Rāmāyaṇa* was expanded considerably by generations of reciters and redactors, both before and after it was written down (perhaps about the first century AD) by compilers who gathered together differing, sometimes contradictory, treatments, passages or episodes into an increasingly unwieldy text; we have explored the content of some of these developments in Afterthoughts. Most manuscripts were written on palm leaves, some on birch bark. Neither medium is as durable as the skins used in Europe, which would have been unacceptable to Indian sensibilities in the context of growing respect for animals, so manuscripts had to be recopied frequently. The oldest *Rāmāyaṇa* manuscript known dates from AD 1020, but most were copied as late as the seventeenth and eighteenth centuries. The process of writing did not fix the text, and large amounts of modification and additional material continued to be made as manuscripts were copied. Rāma was by now enjoying increasing prestige as an object of veneration, and the scribes were evidently intent on including every scrap of material they could find that could even remotely be considered relevant to his story; the one thing these copyists did not do was deliberately delete anything. The manuscripts were copied in widely different parts of the huge area roughly corresponding to pre-Partition India, and though the language remains Sanskrit, copyists used their local script.

These developments resulted in the emergence of a complex of recensions (groupings of manuscripts according to content and script). To over-simplify the position drastically, we can say that the Southern group is regarded as remaining closer than the Northern to the origins, but it is coming to be recognized that there has been a great deal of cross-fertilization within and between recensions and sub-recensions; much work remains to be done before a clear picture of the main directions of influence emerges.

The search for a text

Under the influence of Western scholarship, towards the end of the nineteenth century certain individual recensions were printed and published; the second half of the twentieth century saw an ambitious project conducted by Indian scholars at Vadodarā (the Westernized spelling 'Baroda' is still often employed); it culminated in the publication of the Critical Edition (listed in Further Reading). Evidence was collated from a wide variety of manuscripts, in the hope of identifying a version of the Rāma story as close as possible to the original, while distinguishing and printing a large amount of later material. It is possible to criticize this project as misguided in that the text it produced may never have existed in precisely that form, and it is legitimate to dispute individual readings, but the achievement of this group of scholars must never be underestimated in providing in readily accessible form the materials that have given a new impetus to *Rāmāyaṇa* scholarship. Most subsequent study takes the Baroda Critical Edition as its base text; a close translation of this text into English (still in progress at the time of writing) was begun soon afterwards by a team of scholars in the United States. Our translation too is based on the relevant portions of the Baroda text.

Transmission of the *Rāmāyaṇa* and *Mahābhārata* in their oral stages had been a different process from transmission of the Vedic texts that preceded them, which in traditional circles still retain their original oral form. Knowledge of Vedic texts was restricted to the brāhmanic class, and the words themselves took on a ritual, even a magic, significance largely unrelated to their semantic meaning. They were handed down verbatim over the centuries without variation, and the reciter's or hearer's understanding of them – or lack of it – was immaterial. The case of the *Rāmāyaṇa* and the *Mahābhārata* has been completely the opposite. They were heroic tales, narratives conceived as entertainment. Both began, and both continued for several centuries, as the preserve of the warrior *kṣatriya* class, before being taken over by brāhman redactors. Meaning, as opposed to sound, has been crucial, and additions and modifications have been freely made. All living languages evolve, and the important point here is that later material, naturally, was composed in the diction and style of the teller's own day, alongside the earlier material that they felt unable to omit. The diction of the *Rāmāyaṇa* did not become relatively fixed until perhaps the Gupta period (fourth to sixth centuries AD), a period of consolidation of the high culture, the best part of a thousand years after the core material had been composed in the fifth century BC. The distance in time, language, ethos, interests and material culture can be compared to that between the Old English heroic narrative *Beowulf* and the eighteenth-century Augustan poet Alexander Pope. As Sanskrit later became less and less a living language, tellings were also composed in the vernaculars, but these authors felt less constrained by the now growing sanctity of the Sanskrit text, and were uninhibited about reworking the story in their own words.

As for the Sanskrit text, most of the material now contained in the first *kāṇḍa* ('Childhood Book') and the last ('Further Book') has long been recognized by scholars not to have been present in the earliest tellings. What has attracted only isolated scholarly attention is the wide divergence in expression throughout the central five Books. This volume is based on a rigorous linguistic analysis of those five core Books, which has identified the passages preserved in the earlier diction. Only these passages appear in this translation, and even they cannot be claimed to be 'original', merely 'the earliest text yet recoverable'.

The content of the poem at this earliest stage is still not entirely straightforward to identify: later passages may consist of insertions of new material, which are relatively easy to remove again; but they may consist of elaborations made to a necessary part of the existing text, which are not. In the latter case it is much more difficult to determine what was there before, a particularly annoying problem since it is the most dramatic points of the narrative that naturally attract the most embellishment.

Linguistic analysis cannot tell us all we should like to know, but it represents an advance on previous research. By revealing much information about the earliest poets, their language, their skill, their horizons, and the customs, material culture and religious pattern with which they were familiar, undistorted by presuppositions conditioned by our knowledge of Hindu beliefs and practices as they were to develop later, it gives scholars the opportunity to follow these clues through the stages of the poem's growth, contributing to a better understanding of the development of Indian culture.

The methodology employed in determining the stages of transmission has been rigorously applied to minimize any element of subjectivity. What it has not done, and should never be expected to have done, is create rigid boundaries between the stages. A certain amount of overlapping must be expected. Composition was a continuous process taking place over several centuries and involving many tellers, so 'earlier', 'later' or simply 'different' styles can be discerned within each stage, as can narrative anomalies or contradictions symptomatic of multiple, continuous authorship. A prime example is the fact that Sītā seems to have forgotten that she believes Rāma to have been killed by the golden deer, but immediately screams for his help and continues to expect him to rescue her, showing no surprise when Hanumān brings her news of him. This and other problems in the Mārīca episode, notably that he claims a previous encounter with Rāma in exile that is not recorded in the text, and that Sītā herself believes Rāvaṇa to have been the decoy deer, imply that the episode as it now appears has been developed from a much simpler original no longer extant.

Similarly, there are two largely incompatible forms of the Kabandha episode. Narrative criteria suggest that episodes such as the history of Dundubhi, and the first fight between Vālin and Sugrīva, may have been composed in the later part of stage 1, while the relatively elaborate style of other passages shows them to be nearing the boundary with the second stage.

Other anomalies are of a different nature, and do not necessarily indicate multiple authorship or a corrupt text. Some, such as the reference to Rāma's battle with Timidhvaja's son, an exploit otherwise unrecorded, may have been devised by the author simply to add colour to the narrative. Rāma appears to know of Daśaratha's death before Bharata tells him of it, for he has already made an offering for the dead; but doings of the Ayodhyā court are clearly common knowledge among the sages, and there is no reason for the author to have narrated such an episode when he gains much greater effect by presenting the discovery as a shock to the queens.

Trivial anomalies abound in the text, but can best be attributed to lapses of memory on the part of the poet, entirely characteristic of an oral work of this length and complexity. As such they have no bearing on the question of authorship. The attentive reader can waste many an hour pointing out that at one point Sumitrā and at another Kaikeyī is described as 'middle mother' of the princes (i.e. the second of Daśaratha's three wives); that discuses appear twice in one list of weapons when Rāvaṇa tries to frighten Sītā into thinking Rāma has been killed; that a number of *rākṣasas* appear to be killed twice if not three times; that Suṣeṇa claims it was Jāmbavān who told Hanumān about the herb mountain when in fact it was Suṣeṇa himself.

It is clear that the text translated in this volume is the product of many minds and many tongues, but what about the original text? Was there one author or many? Was it, in outline, the product of a single composer's mind, or did the story emerge gradually from the coalescence of multiple pre-existent sources? Scholarly opinion is divided.

Most hold that the origins may be traced back to ballads about gods and heroes recited within the context of Vedic rituals and more particularly to the bardic tradition which emerged at the courts of *kṣatriya* chieftains, where stories about the exploits of heroes would naturally be welcome. Eulogies of heroes and cycles of stories about warrior exploits were composed by bards (*sūtas*) who were attached to the courts of chieftains and recited the glorious deeds of their lords for entertainment and on festive occasions. *Sūtas* had first-hand experience of the kind of events they described, for they also acted as charioteers to their masters, in battle or in the hunt. In one view, the next stage was simply the progressive clustering of ballads and similar material around some central theme, the fortunes of a hero or events of particular significance, with such cycles gradually becoming linked together into works with a more complex plot, giving rise to the extant poems, which continued to grow in transmission.

The contrary opinion is that the coherence and careful planning apparent in the core story of the *Rāmāyaṇa* demonstrates it to be the conception of a single creative intelligence – an author – though this conception has subsequently been much obscured by the amplifications and modifications of later generations of redactors. In either case, the nature of the compilers or author, the milieu in which they or he operated, and the interests of the audience addressed, would be the same.

Objective evidence of any precursors of the central Rāma story is lacking. Two characters (Sītā and her father Janaka) bear names which are found in Vedic literature, but there is nothing in the earliest levels of the text to suggest that this is more than a coincidence. Sītā bears the name of a minor Vedic goddess connected with agriculture (the name means 'furrow'), an association which gave rise in later additions to the text of an increasingly fantastic birth-story which made her the daughter of Rāvaṇa or of Daśaratha, cast away and discovered in a furrow by Janaka when that king was ploughing. In the early form of the text there is no hint that she is anything other than the natural-born daughter of Janaka. Nor is there anything apart from their common dynastic name to identify Janaka with the king who had figured in debates presented in the Upaniṣadic texts (sixth century BC onwards). A number of the peripheral characters mentioned even in the early stages (deities, sages and the like), and the allusions sometimes made to stories associated with them, have roots in the earlier Vedic hymns and tales, but their incorporation into the text merely demonstrates that they were still well known to the storytellers and widely enough understood by their audiences to be employed as part of their stock in trade, not that the story of Rāma as such has any pre-history. Nor does any trace remain of any divergent versions of the basic story, such as would be expected to persist in at least some of the countless vernacular retellings, if the *Rāmāyaṇa* was in reality the survivor of an amorphous mass of ballads. Widely different though some of these retellings are, they can all be shown to adapt the same core story, modified according to the peculiar needs of the context. Someone must have composed that core story.

The text itself

The form of the poem echoes the simplicity of the expression. The metre employed is the standard narrative metre, the *śloka*, a simple metre comprising non-rhyming verses of four *pādas* (quarters) of eight syllables each, grouped in pairs. Verses are grouped into units called *sargas*, which vary greatly in length (from in the teens of couplets to over one hundred), with twenty-five to thirty being a rough average; this division probably dates back to the earlier stages of the text, if it is not indeed original, although it has been much obscured in transmission. The *sargas* are grouped into *kāṇḍas*, or Books, varying between about sixty and a hundred and twenty *sargas* long. In its fully-developed form, the poem comprises seven *kāṇḍas*.

Each *śloka* couplet is normally a complete unit and it is unusual for the sense or construction to be carried over into a subsequent verse. Grammatical structure regularly coincides with the four-quarter metrical structure: 2+2 or 3+1 are the usual subdivisions. The greater emphasis often placed on the first and last words of the verse, coupled with a general tautness of expression, can in themselves convey subtleties of meaning best brought out by the intonation and similar interpretative skills of an oral performer.

The diction of this text is vivid and enlivened by alliteration, but direct and uncomplicated when compared with later Sanskrit. It is also distinctive. Around the fifth century BC (at roughly the same time as the *Rāmāyaṇa* was first being composed) the grammarian Pāṇini made a minute description of the language exemplified by the later Vedic texts and spoken by the learned individuals who studied them, a description that soon became prescriptive and is exemplified in classical Sanskrit literature, which reached its height from about the fourth century AD onwards. However, the text here translated shows certain well-defined deviations from this norm, deviations (to a large extent shared with the *Mahābhārata*) that help to establish the language of the *Rāmāyaṇa* as genuinely a variant form, a dialect, distinct both from Vedic and from classical Sanskrit.

In this earliest stage, the use of standard phrases (or 'formulae') conforms to the pattern common in oral, improvised poetry: they aid the reciter, allowing him to build his narrative without too much effort of memorization or improvisation, and aid the audience by refreshing their memory of the main lines of the narrative when they cannot pause or turn back the pages to check something they may have forgotten or misheard. In the text translated, the formulae commonly consist of a character's name plus descriptive adjective (for example, *lakṣmaṇaḥ śubhalakṣaṇaḥ*, 'Fortune-favoured Lakṣmaṇa'), and their use adds vitality to the text, often directing the audience's attention with subtle economy of expression to some factor the teller wishes to emphasize, or to the irony of the situation, in contrast to later stages of transmission when the formulae tend to be applied mechanically and inappositely, a feature which indicates that the technique is breaking down and suggests that the oral style is being imitated in a written work.

The work of the first author of the *Rāmāyaṇa* and his immediate successors, belonging as they did to an age and a culture accurately characterized as 'highly literary, but illiterate', is best judged in the context within which it was composed, that of multi-dimensional oral performance. Its drama inevitably loses much of its force in the single, restrictive medium of the printed page; orally transmitted narratives such as the *Rāmāyaṇa* should never be regarded as works *preserved* by being written down, but rather as works in danger of being *destroyed* by being written down. That this one in some measure survived that danger and was transformed by subsequent generations of admirers into a vibrant, living and still developing work of art in so many different media is testimony to the skill and achievement of those first tellers of the tale of Rāma.

Further Reading

Text and translations

The Vālmīki-Rāmāyaṇa, critically edited for the first time, 7 vols., general editors G. H. Bhatt and U. P. Shah (Baroda: Oriental Institute, 1960–75). The most authoritative text of the *Rāmāyaṇa*, based on the evidence of between 29 and 37 mss for each book. It forms the basis for this translation.

The Rāmāyaṇa of Vālmīki, An Epic of Ancient India, general editor Robert P. Goldman (Princeton: Princeton University Press, 1984–): I, *Bālakāṇḍa*, translated by Robert P. Goldman; II and III, *Ayodhyākāṇḍa* and *Araṇyakāṇḍa*, translated by Sheldon I. Pollock; IV, *Kiṣkindhākāṇḍa*, translated by Rosalind Lefeber; V, *Sundarakāṇḍa*, translated by Robert P. Goldman and Sally J. Sutherland Goldman. When complete, this will be a translation of the whole Critical Edition with full introductions, notes and other scholarly apparatus, aimed at the serious scholar.

Le Rāmāyaṇa, general editors Madeleine Biardeau and Marie-Claude Porcher, translated by Philippe Benoît, Brigitte Pagani, Bernard Parlier, Jean-Michel Péterfalvi and Alain Rebière (Paris: Bibliothèque de la Pléiade, 458, Gallimard, 1999). A recent complete translation of an older recension of the *Rāmāyaṇa*, made directly from the Sanskrit (unlike some renderings into European languages) and worth reading by those competent in French.

Studies of the Vālmīki Rāmāyaṇa

Brockington, John, *Epic Threads: John Brockington on the Sanskrit Epics*, ed. Greg Bailey and Mary Brockington (Delhi: Oxford University Press, 2000). Detailed studies of the language of the *Rāmāyaṇa*, of its interrelationship with the *Mahābhārata* and of its religious aspects.

—, *Righteous Rāma: The Evolution of an Epic* (Delhi: Oxford University Press, 1985). An analysis of the linguistic features of the Critical Edition text, leading to the differentiation of the text into successive stages and to the recognition of changes also in cultural and social aspects over time.

—, *The Sanskrit Epics* (Handbuch der Orientalistik 2.12; Leiden: Brill, 1998). A survey of previous research on both the *Mahābhārata* and the *Rāmāyaṇa* (with full bibliography), including description of the contents and nature of both texts.

Brockington, Mary, 'The art of backwards composition: some narrative techniques in Vālmīki's *Rāmāyaṇa*', in *Composing a tradition: concepts, techniques and relationships*, Proceedings of the First Dubrovnik International Conference on the Sanskrit Epics and Purāṇas, August 1997, ed. Mary Brockington and Peter Schreiner (Zagreb: Croatian Academy of Sciences and Arts, 1999), pp. 99–110. An innovative demonstration of the deliberate and skilful plot construction that can be discerned in the basic narrative.

—, 'Who was the golden deer? narrative inconsistency in the abduction of Sītā', in *2nd International Conference on Indian Studies: Proceedings*, Cracow Indological Studies 3–4 (Kraków: Księgarnia Akademicka, 2003). Notes various anomalies in the narration of this central episode which point to the golden deer having been Rāvaṇa himself, rather than Mārīca, in a simpler and tauter original narrative.

Goldman, Robert P., and Sally J. Sutherland Goldman, *Rāmāyaṇa*, in *The Hindu World*, ed. Sushil Mittal and Gene Thursby (New York and London: Routledge, 2004), pp. 75–96. The most recent survey of the content and nature of the text, including some treatment of later versions.

Collections of articles on various versions of the Rāmāyaṇa

Bose, Mandakranta, ed., *The Rāmāyaṇa Revisited* (New York: Oxford University Press, 2004).

—, *A Varied Optic: Contemporary Studies in the Rāmāyaṇa* (Vancouver: Institute of Asian Research, University of British Columbia, 2000). The variety of the subjects treated in this and the preceding collection of articles illustrates well the diffusion throughout Asia of the Rāma story and its continued popularity.

Richman, Paula, ed., *Many Rāmāyaṇas: The Diversity of a Narrative Tradition in South Asia* (Berkeley: University of California Press, 1991).

—, *Questioning Rāmāyaṇas: A South Asian Tradition* (Berkeley: University of California Press, 2001). The articles in these two collections by some major scholars demonstrate the hold of the story on the Indian consciousness, centring around the variety of forms that it has taken as a result and its use to subvert as well as to uphold traditional social values.

Note to the Reader

The translators hope that you will read this story for enjoyment, with your ears more than with your eyes. It was originally composed to be spoken aloud and heard, not read silently.

You will come across a number of concepts or images familiar to the Western mind that have a very different value in this text: elephants should not be thought of as the cuddly gentle friends from zoo or nursery, but as symbolic of the forces of power, swiftness and destruction. Bulls, elephants and tigers, as symbols of strength, are frequent in formulae to express the idea of excellence, leading to the incongruous expression 'elephant of a monkey'. Cloud imagery evokes neither fluffy cotton-wool wisps, nor dull pale-grey skies, both varieties so familiar to British and to many North American readers, but towering, black, fearful monsoon thunderclouds with torrential, often destructive, rain. Mountains are regularly given a degree of personality or even deified, as is the Ocean. Truth is thought of as an entity with inherent power. Sanskrit repeatedly classifies actions as 'hard' to perform, where English, more pessimistically, thinks of them as 'impossible'.

Another culturally specific feature is the treatment of large numbers. One that has been retained in this translation is 'crore' for ten millions (this is the modern term: the Sanskrit form is *koṭi/koṭī*). Other less frequent terms have been transferred into the Western system, occasionally with some adaptation for the sake of readability when they are obviously just vague large numbers (as in the colloquial use of 'millions').

Without making it unintelligibly literal, we have aimed to keep this translation as close as possible to the text, with all its rich variety of style and expression, and to reproduce natural speech-patterns, bearing in mind that the whole poem, not just the speeches, was designed to be spoken. The original poem was composed in the verse rhythm then natural for telling a narrative; we have attempted to render it in the rhythm now natural for this purpose, continuous prose, but the original 4-*pāda* end-stopped *śloka* structure is still sometimes apparent. Oral performance gave ancient audiences considerable non-verbal clues to understanding the tale which are lacking to modern readers with nothing but words on a page to guide them, so we have occasionally felt it necessary to give our readers a little help to bring out the implicit meaning. Details of metaphors, similes or other items that have been paraphrased to make them meaningful to a modern Western reader can be found in the Notes.

All names, whether proper names or names of flora and fauna, are presented in the standard transliteration used for Sanskrit, whose great advantage is that each sound can be spelled in only one way, and each spelling can represent only one sound. Long vowels (*ā*, *ī*, *ū*) are distinguished from short by the macron (¯); *e*, *ai*, *o* and *au* are always long, since they are diphthongs in origin. The letter *h* always indicates aspiration, even in combinations like *th* and *ph* (to be pronounced as in *goatherd* and *uphill*). A dot below the letter distinguishes retroflex consonants (*ṭ*, *ṭh*, *ḍ*, *ḍh*, *ṇ*), pronounced with the tip of the tongue far back in the mouth, from the dentals (*t*, *th*, *d*, *dh*, *n*) made with the tip of the tongue against the teeth. The retroflex nasal is distinguished as *ṇ*, the gutteral nasal by *ṅ* and the palatal by *ñ*, and in certain contexts nasalization is represented by *ṃ*. There are three sibilants, *s* pronounced as in English *seat*, and *ś* and *ṣ* both approximating to *sh* as in *sheet*. In addition, *c* is always pronounced as in English *church*.

The majority of names end in a vowel. Those ending in a short vowel (*-a*, *-i* and occasionally *-u*) are those of males and those ending in a long vowel (*-ā*, *-ī* and *-ū*) are those of females; so, for example, a *rākṣasī* is a female *rākṣasa*. It is important not to confuse length of vowel with stress in pronunciation: all syllables should be given equal stress. English-speaking readers should be particularly careful not to overstress the second syllable.

Another point that might confuse the unwary is the formation of words denoting 'belonging to': the most frequent instances are patronymics or metronymics, terms meaning 'son of, descendant of' someone (as originally did surnames like Johnson, McDonald, O'Neil, and so on). The first and final syllables of the name may be modified in various ways: a son of Daśaratha is Dāśarathi, the son of Rāvaṇa is Rāvaṇi, Airāvata comes from mount Irāvata, a descendant of Raghu is Rāghava, the daughter of Janaka is Jānakī and the princess from Mithilā is Maithilī. Readers can find these characters identified by both names in the Index/Glossary.

Marginal figures refer the specialist to the Sanskrit text of the Critical Edition (see Further Reading); more precise details can be found in the Note on the Text Translated. Where it has proved impossible to recover the poem's early text, the translators have composed brief bridging passages to explain what has been lost; they are printed in italics within square brackets. The translation is not intended as a crib, so annotation has been kept to a minimum to avoid distracting attention from the story. Unavoidable notes are indicated in the text by superscript numbers, but most of the information that the new reader will need can be found gathered together in Appendix 1 or the Index/Glossary. Appendix 1 should be consulted for all greetings, rituals and other customs puzzling to the modern Western reader; where it may not be immediately apparent that any explanation is needed, an asterisk (*) directs attention to that Appendix. Similarly, names in Sanskrit are normally meaningful and quite often occur in punning combinations; we recommend the reader to consult the Index/Glossary for an explanation of words that have an initial capital letter or are italicized, as well as for more general terms.

Principal Characters

(For genealogical tables see Appendix 2; fuller details can be found in the Index / Glossary.)

Daśaratha, king of Ayodhyā. *Also called Kākutstha, the Rāghava, the Mahārāja*

Kausalyā, senior queen to Daśaratha; mother of Rāma

Kaikeyī, junior queen to Daśaratha; mother of Bharata; daughter of King Aśvapati of Kekaya

Sumitrā, junior queen to Daśaratha; mother of Lakṣmaṇa and Śatrughna

Rāma, son of Daśaratha and Kausalyā; husband of Sītā. *Also called Dāśarathi, pride of the Ikṣvākus, Kākutstha, pride of the Raghus, the Rāghava*

Sītā, wife of Rāma; daughter of King Janaka of Mithilā. *Also called Jānakī, Maithilī, Vaidehī*

Lakṣmaṇa, elder son of Daśaratha and Sumitrā; Rāma's companion. *Also called Dāśarathi, Saumitri, Kākutstha, pride of the Raghus, the Rāghava*

Bharata, son of Daśaratha and Kaikeyī. *Also called Kaikeyī's son, pride of the Ikṣvākus, Kākutstha, the Rāghava*

Śatrughna, younger son of Daśaratha and Sumitrā; Bharata's companion

Sumantra, charioteer to Daśaratha

Vānaras

Sugrīva, king of Kiṣkindhā; husband of Rumā
Vālin, elder brother of Sugrīva; husband of Tārā; father of Aṅgada
Aṅgada, son of Vālin and Tārā
Tārā, wife of Vālin; daughter of Suṣeṇa
Hanumān, monkey captain

Rākṣasas, also called Paulastyas

Rāvaṇa, king of Laṅkā; son of Viśravas. *Also called Daśagrīva*
Dūṣaṇa, Khara, Kumbhakarṇa, Vibhīṣaṇa: four of Rāvaṇa's full brothers
Śūrpaṇakhā, their sister
Vaiśravaṇa, their dispossessed elder half-brother. *Also called Naravāhana, Kubera*
Mandodarī, wife of Rāvaṇa
Indrajit, son of Rāvaṇa. *Also called Rāvaṇi*

RĀMA THE STEADFAST

AYODHYĀ

[Prince Rāma is expecting to be consecrated Young King when he receives devastating news, which he must tell his wife Sītā Vaidehī.]

Rāma was sure that he was pursuing the right course: he was 2,23.1–7
setting out for the wilderness. He took leave of his mother Kausalyā, who gave him her blessing. To the men lining the king's highway the king's son seemed to radiate light, and his goodness stirred the hearts of the people. Of course, poor Vaidehī had heard nothing of all this; her thoughts were fixed on his consecration as Young King. She had performed the rituals she knew were due to the gods and her mind was dwelling in delight on royal duties as she waited for the prince, when Rāma entered his handsome private rooms, embarrassed and unable to meet the gaze of the many excited occupants. Sītā jumped up trembling to see her husband tormented by grief and distraught with anxiety. She looked at his pallid, sweat-stained, impassioned face and sorrow gripped her.

'What's the matter, mighty lord?' she asked. 'Your consecra- 23.7,17
tion is prepared – what's the matter? Never before have I seen your face with no vestige of colour or delight!'

Seeing she was on the point of tears, the pride of the Raghu 23.18–22
dynasty declared, 'Sītā, his majesty – my papa – has banished me to the forest! Jānakī, you were brought up in a good family – you know what's right – you behave properly – just listen to what's overtaken me! My father Daśaratha was once so pleased with his wife Kaikeyī that he promised her two important boons, and the king's always true to his word. Today, with the consecration ceremony planned by the king ready prepared,

she claimed her dues and his integrity forced him to concur. Fourteen years I am to live in Daṇḍaka forest and my father has to install her Bharata as Young King. I've come to see you as I set out for the desolate forest.

23.23–31 'Don't ever talk about me in Bharata's presence, for successful men can't bear hearing others being praised; so don't parade my virtues in front of Bharata. And above all don't ever be a burden to him; making yourself agreeable is the way to ensure you can remain in his presence. It's for me to keep the pledge made by my superior: I'm going to the forest today. Be sensible, be strong. Good lady, with me away among the sages frequenting the forest, you, my sinless wife, will have to take your pleasure in vows and fasts. Get up early and offer due worship to the gods, then pay your respects to my father, King Daśaratha. Once you have performed those duties, Kausalyā my own mother must be the prime object of your consideration because of her age and the torment that will be racking her. Then you should always pay respect to all my stepmothers, for in affection, obedience and pleasure I make no distinction between my mothers. Like brothers or sons you should regard Bharata and Śatrughna, for they are both dearer to me than my life, and you must never displease Bharata: he is the king, and the master both of country and family.'

26.1–19 As she listened to Rāma's words, Sītā's eyes filled with tears. Sadly and gently she replied: 'I must seek the permission* of our elders and go with you. What you consider the hardships of a forest life are attractions to me, so attached am I to you. Separation from you, Rāma, would kill me! With you at my side, Rāghava, not even Śakra lord of the gods could overcome me with his might, but no woman bereft of her husband can go on living, despite all the instructions you've given me. Heroic husband, it is intemperate men that are sure to suffer misfortune from living in a forest; I know that. When I was a girl in my father's house, I heard about life in the forest from a holy mendicant woman in my mother's presence, and I've begged you time and again before now, my lord – I should so love to live in the forest in your company! I entreat you, Rāghava! The moment has come for us to go; life with a forest-wandering hero would suit me. You are pure; I shall gain in purity by following my husband out of my heartfelt affection. To me, my husband is a god. So why don't you want to take me with you? I'm your very own wife, I do what's right, I'm devoted to my husband! Kākutstha, I'm devoted to my husband, I'm faithful for better, for worse, and I'm heartbroken. I'd welcome weal or woe if only you'd take me. I'm grief-stricken. If you refuse to take me to the forest, I'll resort to poison, or fire, or water. I'll kill myself!'

However much she begged to go, the mighty prince would 26.20–22
not consent to take her to the desolate wilderness. Maithilī brooded on his refusal, bathing the earth with the hot tears that flowed from her eyes, but then, while Vaidehī was still pondering how to win him over, the self-possessed Kākutstha assuaged the anger that had taken hold of her.

'I can't leave you behind, Maithilī, when you are determined 27.27–32
to live with me in the forest, any more than a self-respecting man can abandon his good name. But there's a tradition the upright have always followed, wife with thighs shapely as elephants' trunks, and that's the one I'm following today as surely as its lustre follows the sun: that tradition, my full-hipped beauty, is obedience to father and mother, and I would not dare remain alive if I disobeyed their command. My father remains true to his word, and I wish to follow the example his integrity has set me: that's been the tradition since time immemorial. Follow me, my timid wife; we will share in following the tradition. Distribute our treasure among brāhmans and give food to mendicants and beggars; but hurry! Don't be long!' When the queen realized that her husband had agreed to her going too she was delighted and quickly began to make her donations.

When Lakṣmaṇa too approached his radiant brother, stand- 28.1–4
ing before him with hands respectfully raised in supplication, Rāma said, 'Saumitri, who will support Kausalyā or illustrious Sumitrā if you come with me to the forest today? The king in his splendour, the one who should satisfy all desires like Parjanya sending rain on earth, is trapped in the noose of desire. Now that King Aśavapati's daughter has gained control

of the kingdom she'll do nothing to promote the wellbeing of all her wretched co-wives.'

28.5–10 Lakṣmaṇa knew how to coax Rāma, and replied in a soothing voice to eloquent Rāma's words: 'Your power, heroic brother, is enough to ensure that Bharata will pay scrupulous respect to Kausalyā and Sumitrā; we can be certain of that. Kausalyā is of noble birth and has a thousand villages as her own property: she could support a thousand men like me. I will bring my bow and arrows and carry a spade and basket, and walk in front of you to show you the way, continually picking roots and fruit for you, and any other forest produce that's a fit diet for ascetics. You, my lord, can sport on the mountain-sides with Vaidehī while I attend to everything, whether you're awake or asleep.'

28.11 Rāma was happy with his speech and replied, 'Go then Saumitri and take leave of all our friends.'

30.1; When they had joined Vaidehī in donating large amounts of
31.13–17 treasure to brāhmans, the two Rāghavas went with Sītā to take audience with their father. The sight of his son coming in the distance and saluting* gave the king such distress that he sprang at once from his throne surrounded by women. Seeing Rāma, the emperor rushed forward, but before he could reach him the torment of his grief sent him to the floor in a faint. Rāma and the great chariot warrior Lakṣmaṇa flew to his side, but the sorrowful, grief-stricken sovereign was unconscious. A loud jingling of bangles was heard throughout the king's palace as thousands of women suddenly shrieked, 'Alas! Alas for Rāma!' Rāma and Lakṣmaṇa both threw their arms round him and with Sītā's help, weeping they laid him on a couch.

31.18–21 After a moment the king regained consciousness, to be overwhelmed by a sea of sorrow as, with a deferential gesture, Rāma said, 'Mahārāja, lord of us all, I ask your leave.* As I set out for Daṇḍaka Forest, pray give me your blessing. Lakṣmaṇa too asks your leave; Sītā is also coming with me to the forest, despite the many sound arguments I advanced to dissuade them. Rid yourself of grief and send us out with your blessing, Lakṣmaṇa, me and Sītā, as the Lord of Creation did his creatures.'

While the steadfast Rāghava stood awaiting leave to go to live in the forest, the king who ruled the world gazed at him and said, 'Rāghava, I've been tricked into granting a boon to Kaikeyī. You must arrest me and become King of Ayodhyā today.' 31.22–3

Rāma was a pillar of propriety above all. At this suggestion from the monarch he replied to his father with courtesy and a respectful gesture. 'Your lordship shall be Lord of the Earth for a thousand years, your majesty, and I shall live in the forest. You must not lose your integrity on my account.' 31.24–5

'Journey steadfastly, my son; may your path be safe and free from all danger, and may fortune and prosperity attend your return. But it's evening, my son; don't go just yet, not on any account. Spend the night in company with your mother and me, and enjoy every comfort. Tomorrow will be time enough for what you intend.' 31.26–7

Rāma responded to the words he and his brother Lakṣmaṇa heard uttered by his grieving father: 'I shall gain merit* by leaving today: am I to lose it by waiting till tomorrow? To me, an immediate departure is preferable to all comforts. I give up all claim to the earth – land and people – and its abundant goods and grain. Let them be conferred on Bharata. Banish your sadness. Don't give way to tears. Be impassive as the Lord of Streams, the immutable Sea. My desire isn't for kingship or happiness, or even for Maithilī; what I desire, you bull of a man, is for you to maintain your integrity and not break your word.' 31.28–32

That word was burdensome to the descendant of the Ikṣvākus as he issued repeated instructions to Sumantra, punctuated by deep sighs and sobs: 'Quickly, charioteer, get together a troop – a regular army – no expense spared, to escort the Rāghava. Eminent courtesans and merchants of great wealth are to confer auspiciousness upon the prince's army by displaying their wares. Mobilize his retainers too, and use all manner of gifts to entice his heroic fellow-sportsmen: hunting deer and elephants, drinking forest mead and touring round the rivers will make him forget the kingdom. And all the supplies of grain and goods that I own are to be at Rāma's disposal while 32.1–8 he lives in the desolate forest. Meeting sages, sacrificing in holy places and duly rewarding the officiants will add pleasure to his life in the forest. Bharata's strong enough to defend Ayodhyā, but glorious Rāma must be furnished with every comfort.'

32.9–10 Kaikeyī grew alarmed as she heard the Kākutstha's words; her mouth ran dry and her voice cracked. Dismayed and apprehensive, Kaikeyī protested, 'Sir, Bharata is not to inherit a kingdom devoid of its population, empty and unpalatable as the dregs left in a wine cup!'

32.11 The shamelessness of Kaikeyī's malicious pronouncement belied the beauty of her eyes, and King Daśaratha retorted, 'I'm bearing the unwelcome burden you've heaped on me, so why goad me?'

32.12 With redoubled spite Kaikeyī answered the king: 'Your own ancestor Sagara disinherited his eldest son Asamañja, as is well known. You should do the same with this one.'

32.13 'Curse you!' was all King Daśaratha could reply. Everyone present was ashamed, but Kaikeyī treated them with disdain.

32.14–20 Then an aged minister called Siddhārtha, holy and much esteemed by the king, explained to her, 'But Asamañja was a reprobate taking delight in seizing children playing in the street and throwing them into the water of the Sarayū! The citizens were roused to fury at the sight and demanded of the king, "Make your choice, defender of the nation: Asamañja or us!" The king then asked, "What has alarmed you?" and in answer to the king's question the subjects replied: "It's this madman; he gets his kicks from throwing our little sons into the Sarayū when they're out playing, the lunatic!" It was hearing this complaint from his subjects that induced the monarch to abandon his worthless son out of desire to satisfy them; that was why Sagara, that very righteous king, abandoned him. What crime has Rāma committed that he should be disinherited?'

33.1–5 The minister's speech drew a courteous intervention from Rāma. Deferentially he asked Daśaratha, 'Why would I need such a retinue, your majesty, when I've renounced pleasure and the trappings of society to go and live on what I can find in the forest? If a man gives away a fine elephant but won't part with the girth strap, it's useless for him to cherish the rope once his favourite beast is gone. Nor do I need an army, my excellent lord emperor. I'm leaving all that behind. Just let them fetch me some bark-fibre clothes, and a spade and basket, and I'll go off and live my life in the forest for fourteen years.'

The shameless Kaikeyī fetched the bark clothes herself, and 33.6–10
told the Rāghava to put them on in front of the crowd. That tiger of a man took a pair from her, removed his delicate clothing and dressed himself like a sage. Then Lakṣmaṇa too stripped off his finery in front of his father and put on the clothes of an ascetic; but Sītā in her silks was as frightened as a chital deer at a snare when she saw the bark garment meant for her. Overcome with shyness, she sadly picked one up and asked her husband – a husband fit to be king of the *gandharvas* – 'Just how do the forest sages put their bark dresses on?'

Janaka's daughter held a bark wrap up to her throat and 33.11–18
stood there, awkward and ashamed, but Rāma, anxious as always to maintain the proprieties, quickly came up and himself wrapped the bark around Sītā, over her silk. To see the wife of such a husband wearing bark as if she were in *need* of a husband, all the people cried out, 'Shame on you, Daśaratha!' That descendant of Ikṣvāku groaned and said to his wife, 'Kaikeyī, it's not right for Sītā to have to go in *kuśa* grass and bark. Isn't it enough for you to have Rāma exiled? Why must you go on with more and more of these vicious outrages?' He sat with head bowed as his son Rāma made him his farewell speech: 'My righteous lord, here is my noble mother, Kausalyā. She is mature and gracious, and she doesn't reproach you, your majesty; she will be drowned in the depths of grief for the first time in her life now that I am taken from her. You can grant boons; you have a particular responsibility towards her.'

Rāma's words, and the sight of him dressed as a sage, made 34.1–8
the king and all his wives swoon. In the torment of his sorrow he could not look at the Rāghava, and when he did manage to look at him he was still too wretched to reply. After his momentary faint, the grief-stricken Lord of the Earth could think of nothing but Rāma: 'My mighty son!' he wailed. 'I think I must be the one who once injured many people or else robbed them

of their children; that's why this has happened to me. But life cannot leave the body before its time has come, and Kaikeyī's cruelty has not brought death to me. That I should live to see my radiant son standing before me with his delicate garments replaced by ascetic clothes! It's all Kaikeyī's fault, it's her selfish plotting and her deceitfulness that have brought this calamity on our people!' After that his eyes clouded with sobbing. 'Rāma!' he moaned, then could utter no more.

34.9–11 After a moment the Lord of the Earth pulled himself together and, eyes brimming with tears, said to Sumantra: 'Harness a riding chariot with the best steeds, drive it here and take his Royal Highness out of the country. I think the virtuous are allowed so much reward for their virtue when a good man is exiled to the forest by his own father and mother.'

34.12–15 In obedience to the king's command, Sumantra the charioteer came smartly back with a chariot harnessed with fine horses, saluted the prince and motioned him towards the gilded chariot harnessed with the best steeds. Hastily the king summoned his treasurer and gave him fit and proper instructions: 'Be quick and bring Vaidehī enough expensive clothes and fine jewellery to last out the fourteen years.'

34.16–21 He rushed to the treasury, fetched what the king had commanded and handed it all to Sītā. As the woman born to the life of a princess embarked on a life in the forest, she adorned her high-born limbs with those many-hued gems, till the resplendent princess of Videha lit up the palace like the radiant sun lighting up the sky at sunrise. Her mother-in-law flung her arms around her, kissed her and implored the departing Maithilī: 'The whole world condemns wives who have always had the best of everything but then don't honour their husbands in misfortune. You mustn't look down on my son in his exile; for richer, for poorer, let him be your god.'

34.22–31 Sītā recognized the justice and good sense of her mother-in-law's words, respectfully turned to her and replied: 'Of course I will do all you say, noble lady; I have been well taught, and know how I should behave towards my husband. You shouldn't rank me with wicked people, my lady; I'm no more capable of straying from what's right than splendour is of deserting the moon. Without strings a *vīṇā* can make no sound, without wheels a chariot cannot move, without her husband no woman can achieve fulfilment, not even with a hundred children! Some comes from a father, some from a mother, some from a son, but the fulfilment a husband gives is inexhaustible. What woman would not worship her husband?[1] My lady, I've been brought up well. I'm the sort of woman who knows right from wrong. Her husband is a woman's god, so how could I look down on him?' Sıta's words touched Kausalya's pure heart, and she suddenly let fall a tear of sorrow mingled with joy. Rāma implicitly knew what to do: he went up to his mother, the most honoured of the king's wives, and said, 'Mamma, don't be upset, but look after Father. The end of my stay in the forest will soon be here. The nine plus five years will pass while you're asleep and you'll see me back again safe and sound with those I love.'

This advice he gave to his own mother, then he turned and 34.32–5
looked at his three hundred and fifty other mothers, who were also grief-stricken. Daśaratha's son Rāma greeted them respectfully, and piously bade them farewell, asking their forgiveness for any slight or negligence during their life together; they then set to keening like cranes, those wives of the Indra of men, to hear the words of the Rāghava.

Rāma, Sītā and Lakṣmaṇa bowed down to the king's feet, 35.1–8
then sadly and respectfully circumambulated him and took his leave to go. The pious Rāghava was overpowered by grief as he and Sītā said goodbye to his mother. Lakṣmaṇa followed his brother in saying farewell to Kausalyā, then bowed to the feet of Sumitrā, his own mother; as mighty Lakṣmaṇa Saumitri paid her his respects, his weeping mother kissed him and gave him some well-intentioned advice. 'Your devotion to those you love has consigned you to a life in the forest; my son, do not fail your brother Rāma on his journeyings. In weal or in woe, you will do no wrong if you resort to him.[2] It's a universal principle among right-minded people that the younger should be subject to the will of the elder, and the custom of this family has always been to give alms, to undergo initiation for sacrifice, and to lay down their lives in battle.

Think of Rāma as Daśaratha, think of Janaka's daughter as me, and of the wilderness as Ayodhyā: then, my dear son, your journey will be serene.'

35.9–14 Then Sumantra saluted Rāma Kākutstha, and addressed him with deferential courtesy, like Mātali speaking to Indra Vāsava. 'Be so good as to mount the chariot, your Royal Highness. I will drive you quickly wherever you direct me, Rāma, to spend the fourteen years the queen has decreed that you live in the forest.' Shapely Sītā, now fully adorned, climbed joyfully into that sun-bright chariot; then Sumantra loaded up the brothers' battle gear – weapons, armour, shields – and a cooking pot. Seeing all three safely aboard he quickly urged on the horses, famous horses that could go like the rushing wind.

35.15–23 At the Rāghava's departure for his long stay in the forest, confusion settled on the city, army and townspeople alike. The town was in uproar, agitated and perplexed, with a din of horses whinnying and elephants maddened with rage. Then the whole city, young and old, rushed after Rāma in great distress, like someone tormented by the summer heat rushing towards water. They clutched at the chariot's back and sides, gazing at him, choked with sobs and overwhelmed by sorrow. 'Rein in the horses, charioteer!' they begged. 'Slowly, go slowly! Let us see Rāma's face, the face we shall see no more! His mother's heart must be made of iron not to be breaking to see him leave for the forest – he that might be the son of a god! Happy Sītā, to be following her husband like a shadow, delighting in her duty! She won't leave him, any more than the sun's splendour will leave mount Meru. Happy Lakṣmaṇa, to be able to wander about all the time with your brother, him so genial, so godlike! For you, true happiness, true fulfilment, a true stairway to heaven, is to follow him!' At these words they were overcome with sobs of grief.

35.24–34 Then the king came out of the palace with his wives – he desolate, they miserable – insisting he must see his son. Before him the women raised a great wail like the wailing of a herd of females at the capture of a big bull elephant, and the glory of King Kākutstha, the father, was dimmed like the full moon being swallowed up by an eclipsing planet; the king broke down in severe distress. When the men following Rāma saw this they raised a tumultuous uproar. 'Poor Rāma!' cried some. 'Oh, you poor mother!' cried others, and all the inhabitants of the palace wept over the wailing king. Rāma glanced round and saw the despondent, brokenhearted king, and his mother, following them along the road, but knew it was not right for him to be seen staring at them. He saw them trudging along when they should have been in a carriage, used as they were to comfort and undeserving of hardship, but still he urged on the charioteer to greater speed; that tiger of a man could no more bear the distressing sight of his father and mother than an elephant can bear the torment of the goad. Repeatedly he glimpsed his mother Kausalyā running in tears after the chariot, calling out now to Rāma, now to Sītā and Lakṣmaṇa as she darted along. 'Stop!' shouted the king. 'Go on, go on!' ordered the Rāghava, until Sumantra felt trapped between two mill-stones. 'If you get into trouble,' said Rāma 'you can tell the king you didn't hear. A long-drawn-out agony is the worst of all.'

At once the charioteer obeyed Rāma's command, quickening 35.35–7
the pace of the horses and leaving the people behind. The king's subjects did obeisance to Rāma; they had to renounce him, but could not renounce their human feelings nor check the flow of their tears. As for Mahārāja Daśaratha, his ministers tried to console him: 'To bring a man back, don't follow him too far,' they advised.

At such a respectful farewell from that tiger of a man, the 36.1–7
women had filled the inner apartments with the tumult of their grief. 'Where has he gone, that man who was the princely resort and refuge of the leaderless, the weak, the wretched? Where has he gone, that man who could not be ruffled by sorrow, who could not be angered by cursing, who could not be roused to anger, but instead calmed all the angry? Where has he gone, that exalted man, that glorious man, who treats us just the same as his own mother Kausalyā? Where has he gone – consigned to the forest by the king in thrall to cruel Kaikeyī – protector of his own people, protector of the world? The king must be grievously out of his mind to banish to forest life that darling

of the living world, that righteous performer of all pledges, that Rāma!' Like cows bereft of their calves, all those queens wailed in their crushing sorrow and rent the air with their weeping.

36.8–16 The Lord of the Earth, tortured as he was by sorrow for his son, heard the terrible sound of distress coming from the inner apartments, and felt great distress. No offerings made in the fire, no sun to be seen, fodder refused by elephants, calves not suckled by the cows; Triśaṅku and Lohitāṅga, Bṛhaspati and Budha, those malign planets, all stationed close to the moon, constellations shorn of their brilliance, planets without their radiance, the Viśākhās hanging smoky and dim in the heavens: all the people in the city were struck with terror, and thought no more of fun or food. People in the streets had their faces contorted by tears; joy could nowhere be glimpsed, all were filled with sorrow. No cooling breeze blew, the moon did not soothe nor the sun heat the earth; all the world was out of joint. Sons neglected their mothers, husbands their wives, brothers their sisters; all others forgotten, everyone thought only of Rāma, while those who were Rāma's special friends were overcome by the burden of their grief and in their consternation were unable to rise from their couches.

37.1–9 As long as the dust cloud raised by the departing Rāma remained visible, so long could the best of the Ikṣvākus not withdraw his gaze. As long as the king could still see his beloved paragon of a son, so long did he continue craning to see him. When he who could protect the earth could no longer see even the dust raised by Rāma, then distressed and doleful he collapsed on the ground. The lady Kausalyā came to his right arm and Kaikeyī, Bharata's champion, to his left side. The sight of Kaikeyī outraged the king's prudent, upright, disciplined nature, and he declared: 'You wicked woman, Kaikeyī, don't touch me! Get out of my sight! You're neither wife nor relative of mine! And as for your dependants, I am no part of them nor they of me. You have renounced what's right, intent only on your own advantage: now I renounce you. I repent taking your hand to lead you around the marriage fire; I repudiate it all in this world and the next. And if Bharata should feel satisfied when he gains this enduring kingdom for himself, then may none of his funeral offerings ever reach me!'

37.10–18
Queen Kausalyā, haggard with grief, raised the dust-covered overlord of men and led him back. Just as if he had deliberately killed a brāhman, or plunged his hand into a fire, the worthy king shrivelled up at the thought of his son becoming an ascetic; repeatedly he turned back, sinking down in the chariot's tracks. His appearance lost its splendour, like the sun during an eclipse; afflicted by sorrow as he remembered his beloved son, he lamented. When he judged he must have reached the edge of the city, he moaned, 'I can see the tracks left on the road by my son's fine equipage, but I can't see my noble son himself. Surely by now he must have taken refuge at the bottom of some tree; he'll find a log or a stone to lie down on. The poor boy will get up again coated in dirt and sighing, like the bull of a herd of she-elephants rising from a mountain stream. I can imagine men wandering about in the forest watching mighty Rāma, Lord of the World, getting up and walking on as if he had no liege. Kaikeyī, you can have what you want; live on in the kingdom a widow! I cannot bear to go on living without that tiger of a man!'

37.19–27
With this lamentation, and with his subjects thronging around him, the king went back into his matchless city like a man returning from a funeral to a place of mourning. The king gazed on the whole city, its houses and courtyards empty, its markets and shrines closed, its people worn out, enfeebled and tormented with suffering, its highways unoccupied. He could do nothing but think of Rāma and lament as he entered his palace like the sun going behind a cloud; without Rāma, Vaidehī and Lakṣmaṇa the palace was as still as a great lake after Garuḍa has emptied it of snakes. On the king's instructions, the doorkeepers led him quickly to the house of Kausalyā, Rāma's mother. He went into Kausalyā's chamber and slumped on to the bed, his mind in a ferment; stretching out his arms to the son he could still see, the heroic Mahārāja cried loudly, 'Ah! Rāghava! you're deserting me! Happy indeed will those worthy men be who will live to see and embrace Rāma on his return! Kausalyā, hold out your hand to me, please do.

My sight has followed Rāma and not returned, and I can't see you.'

38.1–19 Seeing the Lord of the Earth sunk in sorrow on the bed, sorrowing Kausalyā shared with him her own torment for her son. 'Rāghava, you tiger of a man! Kaikeyī has sown poison with her forked tongue, and now she will be even more energetic, like a snake that has sloughed its skin. Now she's got her own way and had Rāma exiled, that pretty specimen, that snake in the grass will set about making me shake in my shoes all the more. She could have let Rāma live in a house while he was practising his begging; she could even have got all she wanted and more by making him a slave. But now she's had her wish and toppled him from his position, that Kaikeyī, she's sent him out to be picked up by *rākṣasas*, as if he was the portion of a sacrifice left out for them at the right phase of the moon. The mighty hero, that man with the majestic tread of an elephant king, bow in hand, is going into the forest with his wife and Lakṣmaṇa. But what state will the hardships they see reduce them to, now that you've allowed Kaikeyī to consign them to the forest? Delicate as they are, how will the poor things survive on a diet of fruit and roots, stripped of their jewels, banished in their prime? Oh for the happy, the auspicious day, when I might be able to see the Rāghava and his wife and brother! When will Ayodhyā hear that the two heroes have arrived, and become glorious? When will her people be joyful and hang up banners and garlands? When will the city see those two tigers of men come back, and swell with joy like the sea when the moon is full? When will the mighty hero place Sītā before him on the chariot like a bull honouring the dam, and enter the city of Ayodhyā? When will thousands of souls cram the highway to shower parched grain upon my two victorious sons as they enter? When will girls make due offerings of flowers and fruit to the Twice-Born, and circumambulate the city in their delight? When will he come back, that right-minded, godlike young man with the wisdom of maturity, who still caresses me like he did when he was three? Heroic king, I think I must once upon a time have been cruel and sliced the udders off some cows when their calves wanted to drink, for

Kaikeyī to have wrenched away the child of my love, violently, like a lion from a cow. I'm like a mother cow with its young calf, you tiger of a man; without my son, my only son, so noble and accomplished, without my son I have no will to live; I cannot possibly go on living if I can't see my darling, broad-shouldered,[3] mighty son.'

Peerless Kausalyā's lament brought words of wisdom from steadfast Sumitrā. 'Noble lady, your son is the best of men, goodness through and through. Why ever are you lamenting and weeping so wretchedly? Your mighty son has gone, noble lady, he's given up his kingship, only to keep his noble father true to his word. Rāma is steadfast in keeping strictly to what the learned know is the right course; he'll reap its eternal reward after death, will your excellent Rāma, so you needn't ever weep for him. Besides, Lakṣmaṇa is punctilious and exemplary in his behaviour towards him; he is kind to all, a boon companion for high-minded Rāma. Vaidehī follows your son along his path of virtue, accustomed to a life of comfort but well aware of the hardships of forest life. What has your son not achieved already, that lord who flies the banner of worldwide fame for holding fast to his vow of self-control and integrity? The sun will easily recognize how pure and supremely noble Rāma is, and won't dare let its rays burn his limbs, and a pleasant breeze, mild and always gentle, born of the woodland, will do the Rāghava's bidding. Fatherlike, the moon will fold the innocent man in its arms as he sleeps through the night, and will refresh him with the cool touch of its beams. What's more, Brahmā gave that mighty man divine missiles when he saw him kill the *dānava* ruler, Timidhvaja's son, in battle. That bull of a man will soon be made king; Rāma will be sprinkled,* he and the Earth, Vaidehī and Śrī, all three. You wept tears of grief as you watched him leave, but your eyes will soon be wet with tears of joy. Before long you'll be like a bank of monsoon clouds, shedding tears of joy, when you see your son and those he loves greeting you. Your wishes will soon be granted when your son comes back to Ayodhyā and respectfully takes your feet in his gentle grasp.*' 39.1–15

*

40.1–12 Rāma, noble and truly brave, had a devoted following as he set out for life in the forest; they had refused to go home when king and family were forced to turn back, but followed the chariot. The inhabitants of Ayodhyā regarded the illustrious man as an example of all the virtues, and held him dear as the full moon, but despite his subjects' entreaties the Kākutstha upheld his father's integrity and continued towards the forest. With affection Rāma glanced at the people, drinking in the scene with his eyes, then addressed them affectionately, like a father. 'The inhabitants of Ayodhyā will be doing me a personal favour if they make a point of transferring to Bharata any fondness or regard they may have for me, for Kaikeyī's darling is so good-natured that he will fulfil your wishes and confirm your privileges. Young in years but old in wisdom, gentle but resolute, he will calm your fears and make you a fitting lord. He has all the qualities needed of a king; what's more, I approve of his installation as Young King, so let your experts carry out the king's command. It is my wish that this should be performed to save the Mahārāja from suffering distress while I am living in the forest.' The more firmly Daśaratha's son persevered in his duty, the more the subjects longed to have him as their lord, as if the city's populace, tear-stained and dejected, had been bound in a noose that was dragging them after Rāma and Sumitrā's son.

41.1–8 When they reached the charming bank of the Tamasā, the Rāghava glanced at Sītā and said to Saumitri, 'Saumitri, may all go well with you! Night is falling on the forest, the first night of our forest life. Cheer up! Look, the woods seem empty, yet all around are the calls of animals and birds settling to their resting places; but now I'm sure my father's royal capital, the city of Ayodhyā, with all its men and women, will be grieving over our absence. I've no doubt that worthy Bharata will be a comfort to my father and mother, telling them that it's all for the best. As I think over and over about Bharata's lack of malice, I see no need to grieve for my father, Lakṣmaṇa, or even for my mother. You tiger of a man, you've done the right thing in joining me in my wanderings: I shall need your help to protect Vaidehī. It will suit me for tonight, Saumitri, to take nothing but water, even though there's all sorts of forest food to be had.'

With these words to Saumitri, the Rāghava then turned to Sumantra, calling him his good friend, and told him to see to the horses. As the sun was now set, Sumantra hobbled the horses and provided them with ample fodder, then took up his station close by. When the auspicious twilight ritual had been performed, Saumitri and the charioteer saw that night had fallen, and they got a bed ready for Rama, made of the leaves of trees on the bank of the Tamasā; when Rāma saw it, he lay down with his wife and Saumitri. When he saw that his brother and his wife were fast asleep, Lakṣmaṇa sang Rāma's praises to the charioteer. Saumitri kept vigil on the bank of the Tamasā through the night, talking to the charioteer about Rāma's virtues, until the sun rose. 41.9–14

Rāma and his subjects all spent that night close to the Tamasā, its bank teeming with herds of cattle, but when he got up and saw his subjects, Rāma the glorious said to his brother, Fortune-favoured Lakṣmaṇa, 'Saumitri, look at these people sleeping under the trees, moved by no regard for their own homes, but only for us; Lakṣmaṇa, just look at them! These citizens won't give up their resolve. They'll lay down their lives to achieve their goal of persuading us to go back. What we must do is jump into our chariot while they're still asleep, and go on our way undaunted. From now on I don't want any resident of the Ikṣvākus' city to have to sleep among tree roots out of devotion to me. It's for princes to free their citizens from troubles they've brought upon themselves, certainly not themselves to inflict trouble on their townspeople.' 41.15–21

Lakṣmaṇa saw Rāma standing there like rectitude personified, and replied: 'I'm happy with that, my wise brother! Let's get in.' 41.22

The charioteer hastily harnessed the choice horses to the carriage, then reported to Rāma with a salute. Rāma, though, wanted to hoodwink the citizens, so he instructed the charioteer, 'Get into the chariot, driver, and head northwards. Drive fast for a little while, then bring the chariot back again. Take great care to see that the citizens won't know where I'm going.' 41.23–5

41.26–8 The driver did as Rāma said, came back, and showed Rāma to the carriage. Aboard the carriage with his gear, the Rāghava crossed the river Tamasā. It was fast-flowing and turbulent with eddies, but once he was across, the heaven-blessed hero set out along a favourable path, free of thorns and free of all fearsome creatures.

42.1–5 The spirits of the city dwellers following Rāma sank, and they went back disconsolate. As each one reached his own house he was surrounded by his wives and children; then they gave way to tears and their faces were racked with sobs. There was no rejoicing, no merrymaking; no business was done, no merchandise displayed, no cooking in the household; finding the lost, making a fortune, brought no rejoicing; newborn first sons brought no rejoicing even to their mothers. In house after house wailing women, sick with sorrow, scolded their husbands for returning, stabbing them with their words like elephants with goads.

42.6–15 'What's the use of homes or wives or wealth or sons or any pleasures at all, if we can't see the Rāghava? There's only one good man in the world, and that's Lakṣmaṇa! He and Sītā are in the forest, following Kākutstha Rāma to serve him in his wanderings. The streams, the lotus ponds, the lakes, the pure waters where Kākutstha will bathe will be rendered sacred when he plunges in. The charming forest groves, the wide-banked rivers, the mountain-slopes, will furnish Kākutstha with adornment. No grove, no mountain he visits can fail to receive him as a welcome, honoured guest. The mountains will be crowned with all sorts of flowers and decked with posies: in their sympathy for Rāma they'll put on a show of beautiful flowers and fruit for him, in season or out; for him they'll display all their sparkling cascades, and the mountain-top trees will gladden the Rāghava's heart. Where there is Rāma there can be neither fear nor hurt, for he is a mighty hero, and son of Daśaratha. Let's go after the Rāghava, before he gets too far away. Pleasant is the shade of such a noble master's feet: he's the lord of these people, their refuge and their mainstay. We can wait on Sītā, you on the Rāghava.'

Sorrow pained the citizens' wives, and they kept on and on at their husbands: 'The Rāghava will look after your welfare in the forest, and Sītā will look after us women. No one will enjoy living in this dreary place, where everyone's pining away; it's unsettling, it's heartbreaking. If by dishonest means Kaikeyī comes into the kingdom, a kingdom that might as well be kingless, there'd be no point for us in life itself, let alone in sons or wealth. If she can abandon husband and son for the sake of power, who will she stop at, that disgrace to her family, that Kaikeyī? This we swear by our sons: we will never live as servants under Kaikeyī's rule as long as she and we are alive. The Lord of the Earth has seen his son exiled by that pitiless woman; how can he live happily with that unjust criminal as his wife? Now Rāma's exiled, the Lord of the Earth will live no more, and Daśaratha's death is bound to bring ruin. If your merit is exhausted, and you're so useless, stir up a cup of poison and drink it! Go after the Rāghava, or else get lost! It's not right that Rāma and his wife and Lakṣmaṇa should be banished, and that we should be handed over to Bharata like lambs to the slaughter.'[4] Throughout the city its women wailed on, raising an anguished clamour as if they feared the approach of their own death. 42.15–25

Rāma meanwhile, that tiger of a man, made good progress through what was left of the night, mindful of his father's command. Night passed peacefully as he travelled on; in the half light of dawn he performed the appropriate ritual, then plunged beyond the bounds of the realm. He cast his eye over spreading villages and flower-decked forests as he slipped quickly past with his fine horses, hearing the villagers crying out in their homes, 'Confound King Daśaratha for getting himself enslaved by desire! How awful it is that Kaikeyī, that cruel, malicious, malevolent, bitter woman, should violate all decency and stir up this outrage, exiling to life in the forest a prince so righteous, so wise, so compassionate, so tireless!' Hearing the villagers crying out in their homes, the heroic lord of Kosala left the land of Kosala. 43.1–7

The Rāghava crossed the quiet waters of the Vedaśruti river, 43.8–15 then set his face towards Agastya's southern domain. A long time later he crossed the cold waters of the river Gomatī, as it made its way to the sea, its banks thronged with cattle. After the Gomatī, his swift horses bore him across the river Syandikā, which echoed to the sound of peacocks and geese. Rāma pointed out to Vaidehī the land that Manu had once conferred upon Ikṣvāku, showing her how it was prospering amid the surrounding kingdoms. Again and again, in the tones of a frantic goose,[5] that noble bull of a man lamented to the charioteer: 'When shall I come back and hunt through the flower-decked forest beside the Sarayū, in the company of my mother and father? But I mustn't yearn too much for that best of the world's pleasures, so prized by companies of royal sages, the hunt in the Sarayū forest.' And Ikṣvāku's descendant continued to chat genially to the charioteer as he pursued his path.

44.1–8 They crossed the broad and lovely Kosala lands. Then Lakṣmaṇa's mighty brother reached Śṛṅgaverapura, and the Rāghava saw the heavenly Gaṅgā: holy in all three worlds, its auspicious waters innocent of duckweed and attended by sages; echoing to the calls of geese and *sārasas* and the murmurs of sheldrakes, waited on by dolphins, crocodiles and serpents. When he saw its eddying whirlpools, the great warrior told Sumantra the charioteer to halt there. 'Not far from the river,' said the Rāghava, 'is a huge *badam* tree covered with flowering branches. This is where to halt, charioteer.' Lakṣmaṇa and Sumantra assented, and steered the horses towards the *badam*. When they reached the lovely tree, Rāma, the Ikṣvākus' delight, alighted from the chariot with his wife and Lakṣmaṇa. Sumantra got down as well, loosed the fine horses and stood respectfully before Rāma at the foot of the tree.

44.9–15 The king of that region was called Guha. He was the powerful, renowned chief of the Niṣāda tribe, a friend of Rāma, and his equal, and when he heard that Rāma, that tiger of a man, had come to his land, he led his venerable ministers and his family out to find him. Rāma and Saumitri saw the lord of the Niṣādas from some distance away, and went to meet Guha. Guha embraced the Rāghava in distress, saying, 'Rāma, let this land be as Ayodhyā to you. What can I do for you?' He got together all sorts of choice eatables and had them brought quickly with water of welcome,* then said, 'Welcome, you mighty man! The whole earth is yours; we are your servants, and you, sir, the master. That's good! The kingdom is yours to command. All this is for you to eat and enjoy, to drink and to taste; here is fine bedding and fodder for your steeds.'

At Guha's words, the Rāghava replied, 'You delight and 44.16–22
honour us, sir, in all you have done, by coming here on foot and showing us so much affection.' He clasped him in his shapely arms and said, 'Guha, it's good to see you and your family in good health, and enjoying a prosperous kingdom, with wealth and allies. I know you have offered all this to me out of kindness, sir, but I must decline it all. It's not my way to accept gifts. You must now recognize me to be an ascetic, clad in *kuśa* grass, bark cloth and skins, eating fruit and roots, and wandering in the forest in pursuance of the right. I would like some fodder for the horses, but nothing more; that will be demonstration enough of your respect for me. These horses are the pride and joy of my father, King Daśaratha, so if you look after them well, that will be the same as honouring me.'

Guha accordingly ordered his men to bring water and fodder 44.23–6
at once for the horses, but the bark-clad Rāma performed the twilight ritual and would accept no sustenance except water brought personally by Lakṣmaṇa. Lakṣmaṇa bathed his brother's feet as he lay on the ground with his wife, then walked away and stationed himself by the tree. Guha, bow in hand, ever-attentive and watchful, chatted to Saumitri and the charioteer as he kept guard over Rāma.

As honest Lakṣmaṇa Rāghava kept himself awake for his 45.1–7
brother's sake, Guha was distressed by their distress. 'Friend,' he told him, 'I have had this comfortable bed got ready for you. Rest on it in comfort, your Highness, please do. My people and I are all used to roughing it, but you are used to a life of ease. We will keep awake tonight to guard Kākutstha. No one on earth is dearer to me than Rāma, and that's the truth; it's the plain truth, and I'll take my oath on it. He's favoured me with the chance to gain fame throughout the world, and great merit, and mere wealth too. I'm the one to guard my dear

friend Rāma as he sleeps beside Sītā, my bow in my hand and my clan all around. I'm always roaming about in this forest, and there's nothing I don't know about it. We could get the better of even the biggest regular army.'

45.8–22 'We know you're honest and mean well,' replied Lakṣmaṇa, 'and as long as you're guarding us all we shall have nothing to fear. But how can I possibly sleep while Dāśarathi is lying on the ground beside Sītā? How can I take any pleasure in life? He can't be conquered in battle by all the gods and anti-gods put together, but just look at him now, taking his rest beside Sītā on the grass. It took *mantras* and mortifications and all sorts of trouble to produce him,[6] and he's the only one of Daśaratha's sons to compare with him. With him gone off, the king won't survive for long: the earth must soon be widowed. I suppose the exhausted women will have given up all their weeping and wailing by now, sir, and the king's apartment will no longer be filled with their clamour. As for Kausalyā and the king, and my mother too – I can't imagine they will last the night. Even if thought of Śatrughna keeps my mother alive, Kausalyā, who gave birth to this hero, will be destroyed by her great sorrow. Destroyed too will be that city, so replete with loyal citizens, so entrancing to behold, now sharing in the king's affliction. Destroyed will be my father, unable to achieve his oft-expressed desire to appoint Rāma to the kingship. And when the time comes that they've got what they wanted, it's those evil-doers that will purify my dead father the king with all the funeral rituals. My father's capital has lovely squares and buildings, its highways are well planned, its mansions and palaces abundant; it's graced with attractive courtesans, crowded with chariots, horses and elephants, ringing to the sound of trumpets; it's crammed with everything good, it's teeming with happy, prosperous people, it's well provided with parks and gardens, and there are plenty of assemblies and fairs: and they'll be the ones to stroll at ease around my father's capital! If only we could be back in Ayodhyā, with him fit and well and his integrity intact, and our stay in the forest completed!'

So the night passed, with the noble prince lamenting and disconsolate as he stood on guard. 45.23

[*Rāma sends Sumantra back to Ayodhyā with the chariot and bids farewell to Guha. The trio continue their journey on foot, cross the Gaṅgā and again camp beneath a tree.*]

When they had spent the night in peace beneath that great tree, the spotless sun rose and they set out towards the place where Bhāgīrathī Gaṅgā joins the Yamunā. As they plunged into the vast forest, the splendid trio admired on all sides varied scenery and fascinating sights they had never seen before, picking out a safe path between the different kinds of trees. Just as the day was ending, Rāma said to Saumitri, 'Saumitri, see, rising from Prayāga, the smoke that's the banner of Lord Agni; I suppose there's a sage nearby. We must have reached the confluence of the Gaṅgā and the Yamunā, for we can hear the sound of water beating against water. These logs felled by forest-born servants and these different sorts of trees must mean that we've reached Bharadvāja's hermitage.' 48.1–7

Bow in hand, the brothers went on at an easy pace, and just as the sun was setting they reached the junction of the Gaṅgā and Yamunā where the sage lived. The wildlife was alarmed as Rāma approached the hermitage; he went along the path and soon arrived. Now they had reached Bharadvāja's hermitage, the two heroes, accompanied by Sītā, stood at a respectful distance and waited for the sage to emerge. As soon as they saw that the distinguished sage had offered the fire-oblation, Rāma, Saumitri and Sītā greeted him with respect and reverence, and Lakṣmaṇa's older brother introduced themselves. 'Your reverence, we are Rāma and Lakṣmaṇa, sons of Daśaratha, and this is my wife Vaidehī, daughter of Janaka, beautiful, irreproachable, but following me to the austere, desolate wilderness. I have been exiled to the forest by my father, but Saumitri here, my dear younger brother, has followed me, resolute in support of me, his brother. Your reverence, we are carrying out our father's command to go into the austere wilderness, there to practise meritorious behaviour and live on roots and fruit.' 48.8–15

48.16–20 At the wise prince's words, the holy sage offered him a cow* and the water of welcome, honouring Rāma's arrival as he sat surrounded by fellow-sages and wildlife, and welcoming him. Accepting his invitation, the Rāghava sat down, and Bharadvāja addressed him as was fitting. 'At long last, Kākutstha,' he said, 'I see you arrive! I have heard about your undeserved banishment. This lonely place at the confluence of the two great rivers is holy and pleasant too: your Highness could easily live here.'

48.21–3 Rāghava Rāma, ever benevolent, made this courteous reply to Bharadvāja: 'Your reverence, townsmen and country people live near here, and they will come to stare at Vaidehī, and at me too, so I don't think it a good idea to stay here. Can you suggest a good place for a hermitage, your reverence, somewhere deserted, where Janaka's daughter Vaidehī can enjoy the comfort she deserves?'

48.24–30 The great sage Bharadvāja replied pertinently to the Rāghava's polite request. 'Ten *krośas* away, sir, lies a mountain attended by great seers. It is holy and altogether attractive. You could live there. Langurs range over it, and it is the haunt of monkeys and bears. It's like Gandhamādana, and it's called Citrakūṭa. Fixing his gaze on Citrakūṭa's peaks leads a man to contemplate the beautiful rather than the evil. Many a tonsured seer[7] has spent a hundred autumns there and been raised up to heaven by the power of his austerities. I think your highness would enjoy a stay in that deserted spot; alternatively, Rāma, pass your forest-life here with me.' With such a welcome did pious Bharadvāja satisfy the desires of his beloved guests, Rāma, his brother, and his wife.

48.31–3 Now that Rāma had reached the great seer at Prayāga, holy night descended on their lively conversation; when it lifted again, the tiger of a man approached Bharadvāja. The seer was resplendent in his radiance. 'Now that we have spent the night in your hermitage, your reverence,' said Rāma to the upright sage, 'be so good as to give us your blessing to leave.'

48.34–5 Bharadvāja marked the passing of the night, and replied, 'Go forward to Citrakūṭa, with its abundance of honey, roots and fruit. There you will see herds of elephants, Rāghava, and herds of deer roaming in the forest close by.'

With night over, the two invincible princes saluted the great 49.1–6
seer and set off for the mountain. Seeing them go, the great sage went after them, like a father following his sons, and carried on talking to them. 'When you reach the swift Yamunā, make a raft and cross that splendid river. You will come to a great banyan with pale foliage; *siddhas* haunt its many gloomy trunks. No more than a *krośa* from there, Rāma, you will see a dark grove with mingled flame-trees, jujubes and Yamunā bamboos. That's the way I've often travelled to Citrakūṭa; it's pleasant and easy, and avoids forest fires.'

When he had shown them the way, the great seer went back, 49.6–14
leaving Rāma saying to Lakṣmaṇa, 'Saumitri, we must have done good deeds to have met with such kindness from the sage!' They talked it over, then the tigers of men prudently placed Sītā ahead of them and made their way to the Yamunā river. There they fixed logs together to make a sizeable raft, and Lakṣmaṇa cut some to make a comfortable seat for Sītā. Like Śrī herself, she surpassed all belief. She was a little nervous, so Rāma Dāśarathi helped his beloved wife aboard. On the raft they crossed the splendid, swift-flowing river, crowned with waves and lined with trees, then let it go, set off from the Yamunā forest, and found the gloomy banyan with its cool pale foliage. Sītā circumambulated that forest-lord with a respectful gesture, making a wish that she would live to see Kausalyā and the illustrious Sumitrā again, while the brothers Rāma and Lakṣmaṇa went just a *krośa* further and killed a large amount of game fit for them to eat in the Yamunā forest.

Next day, the pride of the Raghus gently woke the sleeping 50.1–4
Lakṣmaṇa. 'Saumitri, hark what sweet songs the forest fauna are sounding! Let's set out; it's time to go, my brave brother!' Lakṣmaṇa threw off sleep the moment he was roused by his brother's words, his tiredness from the wearisome journey all gone. They all got up, touched the river's pure water and continued on the path to Citrakūṭa as the sage had directed.

It was early when Rāma set out with Saumitri, chatting to 50.5–10 the lotus-eyed Sītā as they went. 'Look, Vaidehī, all around the flame-trees are blossoming, garlanded with flowers, ablaze at the passing of winter! Look at the flowering cashews, untended by men but weighed down with fruit and foliage – no need to starve! Lakṣmaṇa, look at all the honey the bees have left hanging from tree after tree: the nests are as big as barrels! That's a moorhen's call, and a peacock answering from some delightful part of the forest, thickly carpeted with flowers! There's the lofty peak of Citrakūṭa, home to elephant herds and alive with birdsong!'

50.11–19 On they walked with Sītā towards that mount of delight, charming Citrakūṭa, until they reached the bird-girt mountain. 'My dear brother,' said Rāma, 'I propose that we make our home here for the present, and here enjoy life. Lakṣmaṇa, old fellow, find some good sturdy logs and let's build a shelter; I like the idea of living here.' Saumitri did as he was asked: the man who could conquer enemies sorted out timber and built a leaf-hut. Then that obedient, resolute man was asked to go and get some blackbuck meat for a sacrifice to inaugurate their hut. Lakṣmaṇa, Sumitrā's mighty son, killed a suitable blackbuck for the offering, then placed it over a sacrificial fire he had kindled. When he saw it was cooked right through and the juices sealed, Lakṣmaṇa said to the Rāghava, that tiger of a man, 'The buck and all its legs are well done, so you can sacrifice to the gods now. You know how, my godlike brother.' Rāma bathed, then carefully applied his skills and experience in chanting and completed the offering to ward off evil.

51.1–6 Guha had stayed talking with Sumantra for a long time, plunged in grief; when Rāma reached the southern bank, he went back to his own home. Sumantra obeyed orders to return; he harnessed the fine horses and set out in the depths of despair for the city of Ayodhyā. Fragrant forests, streams and lakes passed beneath his gaze as he hurried on to villages and towns, then, on the evening of the third day the charioteer saw he had reached a joyless Ayodhyā. The sight of it, so silent and empty-looking, overwhelmed Sumantra with despair; grief flooded over him, and he mused, 'The city and all its elephants, horses, people and officials must have been burnt up by the fire of their grief and sorrow at this calamity to Rāma.'

Engrossed in these thoughts, Sumantra drove quickly 51.6–13
through the city as men rushed up in their hundreds and thousands, asking the charioteer where Rāma was. 'The righteous, noble Rāghava instructed me to return,' he informed them, 'so I have come back and they have crossed the Gaṅgā.' At this news the people's faces were contorted with sobbing; they sighed, they moaned, they cried out for Rāma. He could hear crowd after crowd standing there lamenting, 'We shall perish if we can't see the Rāghava! Never again shall we see Rāma the righteous at presentations, at sacrifices, at weddings, at great ceremonies. Rāma protected the town like a father, devising what was best for us, the people, what would please us, what would do us good.' The whole length of the inner market, he could hear the women, distraught with grief for Rāma, wailing at their windows.

Down the middle of the king's highway Sumantra drove on, 51.14–20
averting his eyes, until he reached King Daśaratha's quarters; there he jumped down and entered the royal palace, passing through seven courtyards thronged with dignitaries. On all sides he could hear the soft voices of Daśaratha's womenfolk, distraught with grief for Rāma: 'The charioteer left with Rāma but has come back without him; whatever will he say to Kausalyā in her sorrow?' they wondered. '"What can't be cured must be endured" maybe, but it'll be hard for Kausalyā to carry on living with her son gone.' He recognized the truth of what the king's women were saying, and walked quickly through the palace that seemed to be aflame with sorrow until he reached the eighth courtyard and saw a light-coloured building. Here sat the king, wretched, suffering and miserable in his sorrow for his son.

Sumantra went up to the Lord of Men, saluted and delivered 51.21–9
the message Rāma had entrusted to him. The king listened in silence, his mind in a whirl, then fell swooning to the ground, weighed down with sorrow for Rāma. As the Lord of the Earth swooned – as the king fell to the ground – the private apartment was rent with women's shrieks and gesticulations; but

Kausalyā, helped by Sumitrā, lifted her fallen lord to his feet. 'Noble sir,' she said, 'this is a messenger come back from the forest, sent by the man who has performed such a difficult feat. Why won't you speak to him? What's the use of being ashamed, Rāghava, now you've done that foul deed? Pull yourself together and act as you should; don't make a bad situation worse. My lord, Kaikeyī's not here, if it's fear of her that's stopping you questioning the charioteer. We can talk to him with confidence.' So much said Kausalyā to the Mahārāja before her words were drowned by tears and she collapsed to the floor, while all the women burst into tears at the sight of their lord, and of Kausalyā weeping so on the ground.

52.1–9 When the king had regained consciousness and recovered from his faint, he called for his old charioteer to give him news of Rāma. The man was greatly distressed – distressed as a newly captured elephant, sighing and brooding like an ill-at-ease tusker; his limbs were smeared with dust, his face was filled with tears, and he was completely and utterly wretched. 'Wherever will the virtuous Rāma live? He can't camp among tree-roots!' wailed the king to his charioteer. 'The Rāghava is used to nothing but the best: what is he going to eat, charioteer? He's the son of a Lord of the Earth: how can he lie on the earth as if it were lordless? Foot soldiers and chariots and elephants used to follow Rāma about: how will he live with the unpeopled forest for his refuge, roamed as it is by wild animals and haunted by black snakes? How did the princes and Vaidehī react to the forest? Sumantra, how did the princes get along on foot with poor delicate Sītā, once they'd got down from the chariot? Oh yes, charioteer, you've done your job; you've watched my sons go into the edge of the forest, like the Aśvins going up the Mandara mountain. What did Rāma say, Sumantra, what did Lakṣmaṇa say, and Maithilī, as they reached the forest? Tell me, charioteer, what was his seat, what was his bed, what was the food of Rāma?'

52.10–17 The charioteer's voice was jerking and constricted by sobs as he answered his sovereign's entreaties. 'Bent on doing what's right, Mahārāja, the Rāghava saluted and bowed, then gave me messages to convey in his name. I was to prostrate myself with due respect before his learned and noble father. I was to enquire after the health of the whole inner apartment, without distinction, and greet them in due order. I was to enquire after his mother Kausalyā's health, reminding her that as Queen, she should care for the King with the respect due to a god. I was to ask after Bharata's health, remind him to behave in a proper manner to all their mothers, and tell the broad-shouldered pride of the Ikṣvāku family, "When you are appointed Young King, remain subordinate to our father as long as he is still the king." As illustrious Rāma was giving me these instructions, Mahārāja, tears streamed down from his copper-coloured, lotus-like eyes.

'Lakṣmaṇa, though, with an angry sigh, wanted to know 52.18–22
what offence could justify the exile of such a prince as Rāma. Whatever the reason he had been banished, whether it was to satisfy someone's greed, or whether it was a boon for someone, it was wrong; but he could see no sense in getting rid of Rāma. In any case, such an abominable act of folly as exiling the Rāghava would raise an outcry. For his part, he could no longer consider the Mahārāja as his father; the Rāghava would be brother, lord, kinsman and father to him. How could anyone in the whole wide world stay loyal to you after this, after you've got rid of the man who is loved by the whole world for the love he shows to the whole world?

'Poor Jānakī, Mahārāja, stood stock still and abstracted, 52.23–5
sighing like one possessed. That glorious princess has never before met misfortune; she wept at their sorrow, but spoke no word to me. Her mouth dried up as she gazed at her husband, then, as she watched me leave, she uttered a sudden sob.

'As Rāma set out for the forest I turned to come back, but 53.1–13
even the horses shed hot tears and refused to start. Weighed down with sadness, I saluted both princes and mounted the chariot to set out, but stayed there with Guha for many days, hoping that Rāma would send for me again. The very trees in your kingdom, Mahārāja, have been weakened by Rāma's misfortune: trees, flowers, shoots and buds are all withered. Nothing crawls about, no wild animals roam; the forest has been stilled, overcome by sorrow for Rāma. In the lotus ponds,

my sovereign, the petals have all closed up, the water has been defiled, the lotuses scorched and the birds and fish have hidden. Flowers born of water, garlands born of dry land, fruits too, all shine no more and have lost their fragrance. As I entered Ayodhyā no one greeted me, only sighed and sighed at not seeing Rāma. Women looked out from mansions, buildings and palaces to see the chariot return, and shrieked, laid low by not seeing Rāma; they gazed at each other in obvious great distress, their wide spotless eyes drowned by a torrent of tears. Rivals, friends and neutrals: I couldn't distinguish between them in their distress. Mahārāja, with its melancholy people and its woebegone elephants and horses, the city wasting away with lamentations and echoing with sighs, joyless and mourning over Rāma's banishment, I see Ayodhyā as the very image of Kausalyā bereft of her son.'

53.14–24 The king responded to his charioteer's words in a voice that was doleful and shaken by sobs. 'It was Kaikeyī who coerced me into acting without the advice of shrewd and experienced counsellors: she was born in evil! she is evil through and through! I consulted no friends, no ministers, no merchants even! I was mad to act so impulsively to please a woman. But perhaps it was Fate that has dealt us this great blow, charioteer, to bring unforeseen destruction on this lineage. Charioteer, if ever I have been good to you, bring Rāma back quickly to me; my life is hastening away. If a word from me would only make the Rāghava turn back! Without Rāma I shan't be able to carry on living a moment longer. Oh, but my broad-shouldered boy must be a long way off by now: quick, drive me in the chariot to see Rāma. Where is that great bowman with the sweet smile,[8] Lakṣmaṇa's older brother? Pray let me live to see him and Sītā. If I can't see Rāma with his copper-coloured eyes, his broad shoulders and his jewelled earrings I shall go to the land of the dead. What worse state could I have reached than not seeing beside me the pride of the Ikṣvāku lineage, the Rāghava? Oh Rāma! Oh Lakṣmaṇa! Oh, poor Vaidehī! You don't know that I'm dying of sorrow, a cast-off. Lady, this sea of sorrow is a hard one for me to come through alive.'

54.1–3 Kausalyā kept writhing about on the floor as if a spirit possessed her, and said feebly to the charioteer, 'Take me to where Kākutstha and Sītā are, and Lakṣmaṇa too, for my life's not worth living here for a moment without them. Turn the chariot round quickly, and take me to the Daṇḍakas as well; then I can follow them, or else go to the land of the dead.'

The charioteer, his voice halting and thick with tears, re- 54.4–18
spectfully comforted the queen. 'Forget your grief and worry,' he said, 'and the sorrow that's harassing you. The Rāghava will shed his distress and survive life in the forest. Dutiful Lakṣmaṇa is following Rāma's footsteps through the forest, with a self-denial worthy of the realms above. Sītā too will feel at home in the deserted forest when she has found somewhere to live; she relies on Rāma, and is not afraid, but puts her trust in him. I didn't notice that Vaidehī was at all depressed, not even a little: she gave me the impression of being used to life in exile. She is enjoying the deserted forests just as she once used to enjoy going to the city parklands. Her face radiant as the young moon, Sītā is like a young girl, enjoying living in the deserted forest; her mind is free from melancholy as she exults in Rāma; her heart is his alone, on him her life depends; Ayodhyā itself would be a wilderness to her without Rāma. Vaidehī wants to know about the villages and towns she's seen along the way; she asks about the course of the rivers and about the different kinds of trees. Vaidehī's moonlike radiance is undimmed by the road, by the rushing wind, by turmoil, by heat. Generous Vaidehī's face, radiant as the full moon, lovely as the lotus, remains undisturbed. She has no lac juice to paint her feet, yet they still look the colour of lac, beautiful as the lotus calyx. Her affection has made her lay aside her ornaments, yet lovely Vaidehī walks along as gracefully as if she were sporting tinkling anklets. She takes no fright at the sight of elephant, lion or tiger in her forest refuge, but takes her refuge in Rāma's arms. No need to grieve for them, nor for yourself, nor even for the king: the fame of this deed will endure in the world for ever.'

With Rāma, darling of all, gone to the forest to maintain his 55.1–19
integrity, Kausalyā was heartbroken and sobbed out to her husband, 'Your great fame may be spread throughout the three

worlds, but the Rāghava is compassionate, generous and courteous. Your majesty, these two sons and Sītā have been brought up to pleasure; now that they're in pain, how will they endure that pain? Certainly, Maithilī is a dainty and beautiful young girl, used to comfort: how will she bear the heat and cold? Almond-eyed Sītā has lived on rich food with tasty sauces: how can she eat a forest diet of wild rice? That irreproachable woman has known only pleasant sounds, singing and music playing: how will she react to the hideous noise of lions tearing at flesh? Where does the mighty, broad-shouldered hero lie down, his burly arm for a pillow? It must be like the lowering of great Indra's standard! When shall I see again Rāma's beautiful face and lovely hair – his face coloured like the lotus, scented like the lotus, altogether like the lotus? My heart must be hard as a diamond, it must be, not to have burst into a thousand pieces at not being able to see him any more. If the Rāghava does come back in fifteen years, he'll have to renounce kingship and treasury: Bharata will be in possession. When a younger brother has been enjoying a kingdom, my lord king, won't the eldest and best of the brothers be sure to spurn it? No tiger will eat another tiger's prey, and this tiger of a man won't dream of touching what someone else has tasted. Sacrificial objects – oblation, *ghī*, rice-cakes, *kuśa* grass, *khadira*-wood stakes – can never be used a second time. Rāma would be too proud to accept a kingdom that was a leftover, like wine that had lost its flavour, or a sacrifice when the *soma* was gone. The Rāghava will no more put up with such an affront than a powerful tiger will allow anything to tweak its tail. That's what he's like, this bull of a man with the eyes of a bull and the strength of a lion: and it's his own father that's destroyed him, like a fish swallowing its young! The teachings of the eternal *śāstras* show the Twice-Born their duty: if only you had observed them instead of exiling your dutiful son! A woman's first refuge should be her husband, your majesty; the second her son, the third her kinsmen, and no fourth exists. But you're no refuge for me; Rāma's gone to the forest – I can't follow him there. You've destroyed me utterly.'

56.1–6 Sadly the king brooded over the harsh words of Rāma's angry, sorrowing mother; the mighty Lord of the Earth was rendered impotent by Kausalyā's grief on top of his own grief for Rāma. Burning with the double grief he replied: 'Kausalyā, most humbly I beg your forgiveness. You are always tender; even to strangers you are never unloving. A husband, deserving or not, is the god on earth of women who know what's right. You are a queen, you always do what's right, you are an example to the whole world. Even in your sorrow you ought not to say such hurtful things to me when I have been so badly hurt.'

At the desolate king's doleful words, Kausalyā's tears poured 56.7–15
out like rain gushing from a spout. In a gesture of respect to the king she clasped her hands above her head like a lotus, weeping, fearful and agitated, and blurted out her reply: 'Forgive me, I beg you, fallen to the ground with my head at your feet. Your majesty, your plea is hurtful to me, and you shouldn't be the one to do me any harm. In this world and the next, no woman is a proper wife if she has a praiseworthy, wise husband who has to plead with her. You're right, I know you are: I do know what's right; it was being so tormented by sorrow for my son that made me speak so. Sorrow does away with fortitude, sorrow does away with learning, sorrow does away with everything; there's no enemy to equal sorrow. A blow from an enemy's hand can be endured better even than a very slight sorrow. Today it's now the fifth night of Rāma's life in the forest, and sorrow has so done away with my joy that it might as well be five years. For thinking about him just adds to the sorrow in my heart, like the rushing rivers swell the ocean's great waters.'

While Kausalyā was speaking these soothing words, the sun's 56.16–17
rays lost their power and night approached. Then the king, overwhelmed as he was by sorrow, drew comfort from Queen Kausalyā's words and succumbed to sleep.

When night was over, early next day the heralds arrived at 59.1–13
the king's quarters and his staff, mostly women and eunuchs who were experienced at waiting on him in the correct fashion, approached as usual. At the set hour, according to rule, those trained in the art of bathing him brought golden pitchers of

water scented with yellow sandal. Other women, mainly girls, brought him auspicious objects, food and utensils. Then the women of the Lord of Kosala's bedchamber assembled to rouse their master; trembling and seized by apprehension for the king's life, they were already quivering like grass-tips in the breeze when the trembling women saw the king and knew for certain that the calamity they suspected had indeed occurred. Then the shapely women raised a loud cry of distress, like she-elephants in the forest when their leader has been ousted from his place. The noise of their shrieking roused Kausalyā and Sumitrā to sudden wakefulness. They looked at the king and touched him, then Kausalyā and Sumitrā both screamed 'Oh! my lord!' and collapsed on to the ground. The Kosala princess writhed about on the floor, smearing herself with dust, her brightness dimmed like a star fallen from the firmament. Fright and confusion, an agitated throng, everywhere a tumult of wailing, kinsmen in an agony of anguish, all joy suddenly blotted out; the palace of the Lord of Men presented the very image of gloom and distraction now that he had reached the end of his allotted span.

60.1–11 Heaven-bound, the king looked like a fire that had gone out, like the sea emptied of water, like the sun robbed of its radiance as Kausalyā gazed at him, her eyes full of tears and haggard under her twofold sorrow. As she cradled the king's head, she declared to Kaikeyī: 'You can be satisfied now, Kaikeyī, and enjoy the kingdom unhindered. You malicious mischief-maker, to throw over the king in pursuit of your one aim! With Rāma gone and my husband now in heaven, I'm left with no will to live. It's just as if I'd been dumped on the wrong road by a caravan. Does the woman exist who would want to live after she'd thrown over her husband, her own deity? Who but Kaikeyī, who has abandoned all morals? A glutton will go for anything and not bother about the consequences – he'll lust after a thistle.[9] Kaikeyī has destroyed the Rāghava dynasty at the prompting of a hunchback. Janaka will be as distressed as I am when he hears that Rāma and his wife have been exiled by the king's perverse decree. My handsome Rāma has gone away in danger of his life, and poor Sītā isn't used to hardship;

she'll shrink from the hardships of the forest, will the princess of Videha. When she hears the fearful calls of the wildlife at night she'll be bound to cling to the Rāghava in terror. The thought of Vaidehī will overwhelm the old man: his children are few, and this sorrow will kill him.' At this piteous lament the waiting-women folded her in their arms and led away the brokenhearted Kausalyā.

The ministers appointed to act as regents placed the Lord of 60.12–17
the World in a vat of sesame oil and took over the royal duties: in their judgement it was not right to perform the king's cremation in the absence of a son. They stood guard over the Lord of the Earth, and the women set about bewailing his death when they heard what the Lord of Men's attendants had done. They flung their arms pitiably in the air; tears flooded from their eyes and streamed down their faces; sorrow lacerated them, they mourned the stricken king. Ayodhyā was like a night stripped of stars, a wife bereft of her husband; without its noble king, the destitute city lost its lustre. With its people choked by sobbing, its womenfolk wailing, its squares and courtyards deserted, it lost all radiance.

Night passed, the sun rose, and the regents and Twice-Born 61.1–3;
gathered and went to the assembly-hall where Twice-Born and 62.1–3
ministers each made a speech before Vasiṣṭha, the excellent royal chaplain. Vasiṣṭha considered the suggestions put forward by the assembled allies, ministers and brāhmans, and gave his reply. 'Bharata is blithely staying with his brother Śatrughna in Rājagṛha, his uncle's family seat. Swift messengers must go at once with fast horses to fetch those heroic brothers. What are we waiting for?'

Hearing that all agreed with him that messengers should be 62.4–9
sent, Vasiṣṭha directed: 'Siddhārtha, Vijaya, Jayanta, Aśoka, Nandana: kindly approach, all of you, and listen while I tell you what you must do. I command you to ride quickly to Rājagṛha city on fast horses and give Bharata this message from me: "The chaplain and all the counsellors present their compliments and ask you to return in haste; your presence is required on urgent business." But you must conceal your grief when you get there, your Honours, and not tell him about this

calamity that has befallen the Rāghavas, Rāma's expulsion and his father's death. Hurry and collect silk garments and fine ornaments to take for the king and Bharata, then set off.'

62.9–14 Vasiṣṭha dismissed the envoys, and they set off in haste, crossed the Gaṅgā at Hastinapura and travelled west, reaching the Pañcāla region by way of the Kuru jungle. At speed they crossed the clear waters of the divine Śaradaṇḍā river, teeming with people and all sorts of birds, then reached the divine wishing-tree called Nikūla, which they saluted before reaching the city of Kuliṅgā. After that they arrived at Abhikāla by way of Tejobhibhavana, then went through the central Bāhlīkas and past mount Sudāman, catching sight of Viṣṇu's Footstep and the rivers Vipāśā and Śālmalī. The envoys made rapid and direct progress, and reached the excellent city Rājagṛha with their mounts exhausted by the lengthy journey.

63.1–7 The very night when the envoys were entering the city, Bharata had an unpleasant dream. It came just as night was turning to dawn, and was so unpleasant that it left the emperor's son feeling extremely distressed. His genial companions noticed his distress and tried to raise his spirits by telling stories in the assembly-hall, some playing soothing music while others danced or performed all kinds of dramas and comedies. Bharata the noble Rāghava did not cheer up at the jokes his genial companions were cracking in the assembly, so one of his group of companions, a particular friend, asked Bharata why he was not enjoying himself in the company of his friends, and Bharata told him the reason.

63.7–17 'I'll tell you why I'm so upset. I saw my father in a dream. He was dirty, his hair was wild, and he was falling off a mountain-peak into a pond of filthy cowdung. I saw him swimming in that cowdung pond, drinking sesame oil from his cupped hands; he seemed to be laughing again and again. Then he ate some rice and sesame, and time after time he would bow his head and plunge into the sesame oil until it was smeared all over his limbs. I also dreamed that I saw the ocean dried up, the moon fallen to earth, a blazing fire suddenly go out. The earth split open and all the trees withered. Even the mountains collapsed in smoke. Then he was dressed all in black, slumped on an iron throne, with swarthy women jeering at him. And then the worthy man was rushing off to the south, red garlands and unguents about him, in a chariot drawn by donkeys. That's the sight that terrified me during the night: I or Rāma or the king or Lakṣmaṇa is going to die. When a dream shows a man being carried off in a vehicle drawn by donkeys, smoke will soon be seen rising from his funeral pyre. That's why I'm gloomy and can't return your courtesy. My throat feels parched, my mind feels unhinged, and I hate reacting like this; I don't know what's wrong.'

While Bharata was telling his dream, the envoys were cross- 64.1–4
ing the impassable moat on their tired mounts and entering the pleasant city of Rājagṛha. They were received courteously by the king and prince, and bowed to the king's feet, then delivered their message to Bharata: 'The chaplain and all the counsellors present their compliments and ask you to return in haste; your presence is required on urgent business. Here is a gift for the king worth twenty crores, your highness, and another worth fully ten crores for your uncle.'

Bharata accepted it all, returned the envoys' courtesies and 64.5–9
attended to their wants, then in his concern for his family he asked them, 'Is my father, King Daśaratha, in good health? and is Rāma well, and noble Lakṣmaṇa? Wise Rāma's mother, noble Kausalyā, dutiful, virtuous and judicious – is she well? What about our middle mother, virtuous Sumitrā, birth mother of Lakṣmaṇa and heroic Śatrughna – is she well? My mother too, Kaikeyī, always selfish and quick-tempered, angry and self-opinionated – is she well?'

The envoys' reply to noble Bharata's words was prudent: 64.10–13
'Those for whose welfare you wish are well, you tiger of a man.' At this assurance Bharata told the envoys he would seek the Mahārāja's permission to leave at their urgent request; then the prince turned to his grandfather Aśvapati to pass on the envoys' urgent message. 'Your majesty,' he said, 'the envoys are urging me to return to be with my father, but I'll come back here whenever you like.'

The king his grandfather graciously replied to Bharata's 64.14–16
words by kissing the Rāghava's head. 'Go, my dear boy, with

my leave. Kaikeyī is blessed with a good son in you. Please give my best wishes to your mother, my hero, and to your father, my good wishes, too, to the chaplain and the other leading Twice-Born, and to those great bowmen, your brothers Rāma and Lakṣmaṇa.'

64.17–23 After these courtesies, the Kaikeya gave wealth to Bharata: excellent elephants, patterned blankets and hides, two thousand gold ornaments and sixteen hundred horses was the wealth bestowed by Kekaya in honour of Kaikeyī's son; in addition, Aśvapati hurriedly appointed reliable ministers of proven ability to act as Bharata's travelling-companions. His uncle Yudhājit gave him valuable presents: choice elephants from the Irāvata and Indraśiras mountains, and fast donkeys with fine bridles, and presented him with some huge sabre-toothed hounds, bred in the palace, strong and bold as tigers. Bharata took leave of his grandfather and uncle, mounted his chariot and set off, followed by servants whirling along in over a hundred chariots drawn by camels, oxen, horses and donkeys, with Śatrughna at his side.

[*On his return to Ayodhyā, Kaikeyī immediately tells Bharata of Rāma's banishment and Daśaratha's death. He is shocked and angrily rejects the throne.*]

70.1–5 Kaikeyī's son Bharata was tortured by his sorrow, but the sage Vasiṣṭha, that most eloquent orator, begged the illustrious prince to rise above his grief and perform the overdue rites to send the king on his final journey. Vasiṣṭha's words restored Bharata's composure and recalled him to his duty. He ordered all the funeral rituals to be performed, but when Daśaratha was lifted from the sesame oil, his face yellowed by the immersion, and his brokenhearted son saw the Lord of the Earth laid on the earth as if asleep, he laid him on a jewel-encrusted couch and wept over him.

70.6–9 'Why did you take this decision while I was away, your majesty? Why did you banish virtuous Rāma and mighty Lakṣmaṇa before I could return? What will become of you, Mahārāja, now you have forsaken a people already grieving over the loss of that lion of a man, Rāma, their tireless champion? And who is going to safeguard the wellbeing of this city of yours, my dear father, now you have gone to heaven and Rāma has taken refuge in the forest? Losing you, glorious king, the widowed Earth has lost her Lord and her glory; the city is like the night sky without the moon.'

The great sage Vasiṣṭha again addressed mighty Bharata 70.10–22
as he lamented, dejected in spirit, asking to have the funeral rituals for the Lord of the People duly completed without delay. Bharata thanked Vasiṣṭha for his words and agreed, urging on the whole company of priests, chaplains and teachers. Then the sovereign's sacred fires were formally brought from the fire-hall and taken by the priests and officiants. The lifeless king was lifted onto a bier borne by sobbing, distraught attendants, while people scattered gold, silver and all kinds of garments along the road in front of their lord, and others brought sandalwood, aloe, resin, pine-, cherry- and cedarwood to build a pyre. Next the sacrificial priests applied a variety of perfumes, and then had their monarch placed on the centre of the pyre, offered libations to the fire and muttered the formulae over him while *sāman* singers sang the hymns prescribed by the treatises. When his wives arrived from the city in order of precedence, borne on litters and vehicles, and escorted by elders, the sacrificial priests solemnly walked in the inauspicious direction* around the king as he lay on the fire, followed by the agonized wives, Kausalyā at their head. Then arose from the women a clamour that might have come from a flock of cranes, so pitiably did they wail a thousand times in their torment; weeping and hysterical, lamenting over and over again, the ladies alighted from their vehicles on the bank of the Sarayū.

When the ten days of ritual impurity had passed, the prince 71.1–3
purified himself, and on the twelfth day he had the memorial rites performed. He gave jewels, wealth and abundant food to brāhmans, with numbers of spotless goats and hundreds of cows; slave men and women, vehicles and mansions were conferred on brāhmans in memory of the king by his son.

At dawn on the thirteenth day, the mighty Bharata was mad 71.4–9
with sorrow and could not get his words out for crying. He went to the cremation ground to purify himself, then stood at

the foot of his father's pyre and indulged his grief: 'Dear father, you entrusted me to my brother Rāghava, but by exiling him to the forest you have abandoned me to the void. Father, you have abandoned Kausalyā. Now she has no lord, her support should be her son, the son exiled to the forest. Sire, where are you?' Gazing at the ashy circle of burnt bones, all that was left of his father's body, he groaned and crumpled, sinking to the ground at the dismal sight, like Śakra's standard toppling over as it is being erected.

71.10–20 The ministers all rushed to the true-hearted Bharata, like the sages rushing to Yayāti fallen when his time had expired. Seeing Bharata overwhelmed by sorrow, and remembering the Lord of the Earth, Śatrughna too fell senseless to the earth. Beside himself like a madman, he mourned in anguish as one by one he called to mind his father's good deeds. 'How irresistible, how overwhelming, is the surging sea of our sorrow! It's Mantharā that's to blame for getting that boon for that crocodile of a Kaikeyī!' he ranted. 'Bharata's young and delicate, and you've always indulged him, yet you've left him to mourn! Father, my honoured father, where are you now? It's you that provide us all with our food and drink, our clothes and ornaments – who will do that for us now? If the earth doesn't dissolve when you, its noble, virtuous king, are wrenched away, the Dissolution won't dissolve it! My life's not worth living with my father gone to heaven and Rāma taking refuge in the wilderness! I'll immolate myself in the flames. Ayodhyā, ward of the Ikṣvākus, will be desolate for me without my father and my brother. I won't go back. I'll go off and be a forest ascetic.' Hearing them both lamenting and witnessing their grief distressed all the attendants even more, as Śatrughna and Bharata writhed about on the ground, cast down and wearied, like a pair of bulls with broken horns.

71.21–5 Their father's chaplain, the learned Vasiṣṭha, remained composed; lifting Bharata up, he declared, 'All creatures are subject to three pairs of opposing states:[10] they cannot be avoided, so it does not befit you to behave in this manner.' Sumantra helped Śatrughna up and comforted him, reminding him of the truth that all who are born must die. Once more erect, like Indra's standard braving rain and sun, the two tigers of men each radiated glory as, with mournful words, they wiped the tears from their reddened eyes, prompted by the ministers to complete the filial rituals.

When they were ready to return, Śatrughna, younger brother to Lakṣmaṇa, talked things over with the anguished Bharata. 'Rāma can shelter any creature in distress, let alone himself. He's a man of integrity, yet he's been exiled to the forest by a woman. And then there's our Lakṣmaṇa: he's strong and enterprising. If only he'd acted to restrain our father, Rāma would be a free man now. He should have worked out a sensible way of restraining the king earlier on, when he saw him going astray and coming under the influence of a woman.' 72.1–4

So said Śatrughna, Lakṣmaṇa's younger brother. At that moment, out of the front gate appeared the hunchback, adorned all over with ornaments, anointed with essence of sandalwood and dressed like a queen, all trussed up with fancy girdles and belts like a monkey on a string. A gatekeeper noticed the cause of so much trouble and seized the hunchback mercilessly, identifying her to Śatrughna. 'That's the woman, the evil, malicious woman that got Rāma sent to the forest and drove your father to death. Do what you think fit with her!' 72.5–8

Steadfast Śatrughna was horrified to hear these words. 'She's the one who has devastated all my brothers, and my father as well,' he told all her companions from the inner apartment. 'Let her taste the fruit of her evil deed!' With these words he laid violent hands on the hunchback in the midst of her companions. The palace rang with her screams, and the whole crowd of companions fled in all directions in terror of Śatrughna's anger. 'The way he's going, he'll absolutely destroy us all,' all her companions agreed. 'Let's go to Kausalyā for refuge. She's kind, generous, virtuous and distinguished; we're sure to be safe with her.' Pugnacious Śatrughna, eyes ablaze, then dragged the screaming hunchback Mantharā hither and thither along the ground, scattering her fancy gear over the floor, till the splendid palace was brighter even than before, bespangled with her jewels like the autumn sky. With her still in his clutches, the brawny bull of a man then angrily berated 72.9–19

Kaikeyī with harsh words, until she fled to her son for protection, so terrified was she of Śatrughna, and so wounded by his painful words.

72.20–24 Bharata took notice. 'The weaker sex, above all creatures, should not be killed,' he told the angry Śatrughna. 'Be patient. I would kill this evil, base Kaikeyī myself if it weren't that law-abiding Rāma would condemn me for matricide. If the Rāghava learned that even this hunchback had been killed, that virtuous man would certainly never speak to either of us again.' Lakṣmaṇa's younger brother Śatrughna listened to Bharata and forsook his anger; he let Mantharā go, and she fell groaning in anguish at Kaikeyī's feet, weeping pitifully.

73.1–5 As the fourteenth day dawned, the regents gathered and addressed Bharata. 'Our revered leader Daśaratha has gone to heaven. His eldest son Rāma has been exiled; so has the mighty Lakṣmaṇa. Today you, most glorious prince, should become our king; if we are left without a leader, only luck will prevent the kingdom going to rack and ruin. Preparations for your consecration are complete, Rāghava prince, and your people and the leading businessmen all await you. Deign to become king, Bharata, of the great realm of your fathers, and have yourself consecrated our guardian, you bull of a man.'

73.6–13 Bharata did reverent honour to all the consecration equipment, but his reply to all the people was steadfast: 'Your Honours ought not to be addressing me in this way, for you know that the custom of our dynasty is for kingship to devolve upon the eldest son. Rāma is the firstborn; my brother will become Lord of the Earth, and it is I who shall live in the forest for nine years plus five. Marshal our great and mighty regular army for me to go and bring my eldest brother the Rāghava back from the forest. As for all this consecration equipment you have gathered together, I shall put it at the head of the procession as I go to find Rāma in the forest. There and then I will consecrate that tiger of a man and place him at the head of a procession to bring him back, like a sacrificial fire brought back from the sacrifice. I will not give my mother what she wants, this woman who doesn't come within sniffing distance of a true mother! I will be the one to live in the impenetrable forest, and it's Rāma who'll be the king. Send workmen to clear a road and even it out, and appoint guards to scout out the way.'

Hearing the prince speak in favour of Rāma, all the people 73.14–15
answered with unparalleled joy, 'May lotus-decked Śrī attend you for being willing to yield the earth to the king's first-born.'

'If I can't get the prince to come back from the forest, then I 76.17–20
too will live there in the forest like noble Lakṣmaṇa, but I really will use every means in my power, in front of all you good, honourable gentlemen, to make him come back,' continued honest Bharata in his devotion to his brother. He then instructed shrewd Sumantra, who was standing nearby, 'Off you go quickly, Sumantra; issue my command for the rapid organization of my expedition, and muster an ample force.'

At noble Bharata's command, Sumantra joyfully and gladly 76.21–6
ordered all that he had been instructed. Subjects and army commanders alike were delighted at the news of an expedition to bring back the Rāghava. Then in house after house the soldiers' wives were all delighted to hear of the expedition's departure and hurried their husbands on. Generals chivvied the entire force: horses, speedy ox-carts, swift chariots and infantry. In the midst of his counsellors, Bharata saw that the force was ready, turned to Sumantra, and asked for his chariot to be brought at once. Delighted to receive Bharata's command, he took charge of the chariot with its team of choice horses, and came forward.

Bharata promptly stood up, jumped into the splendid chariot 77.1–7
and set off at once in his eagerness to see Rāma. In front rode all the counsellors and chaplains, their horse-drawn carriages rivalling the Sun's chariot, and nine thousand elephants, properly caparisoned, followed Bharata, pride of the Ikṣvāku dynasty, as he set out. Sixty thousand chariots and archers with varied weapons followed the illustrious prince Bharata as he set out. Cavalry numbering one hundred thousand followed the illustrious Rāghava prince Bharata as he set out. Kaikeyī, Sumitrā and illustrious Kausalyā travelled in a splendid equipage, all delighted to be going to bring back Rāma, and groups

of noblemen reminisced about Rāma and Lakṣmaṇa, delighted to be setting out to see them.

77.8–18 'When shall we see Rāma, cloud-dark, broad-shouldered, undeviating and steadfast, dispeller of all the world's sorrows? The mere sight of the Rāghava will scatter our sorrows, like the shades of night driven from our world by the rising sun.' Such was the optimism of the delighted citizens as they set out, chattering and hugging each other. All the rest of the people, prominent citizens and businessmen, the whole populace, were delighted to be going for Rāma. Respected, learned brāhmans in ox-carts flocked in their thousands to follow Bharata on his journey. All were well dressed, all wore clean clothes, all were burnished with unguent, as their vehicles all trailed off after Bharata, a joyful and delighted host following Kaikeyī's son.

77.18–22 The host of Bharata's followers stopped, and Bharata saw that they had reached the purifying waters of the Gaṅgā. 'Have my army encamp anywhere it sees fit,' he shrewdly instructed all his ministers. 'First thing tomorrow, when we have rested, we shall cross over this mighty river. Meanwhile, I wish to perform the water-offering in memory of the departed Lord of the Earth.' The assembled ministers assented to his words and directed each individual to select his own place to camp.

78.1–9 The king of the Niṣādas observed their banners as they encamped alongside the river Gaṅgā. 'A huge force has appeared here,' he hastily told his kinsmen. 'It's as big as the sea! I've racked my brains, but I can't think what it's doing here. There's a chariot sporting a stout standard with a *kovidāra* on it. Is it here to capture us river folk? Is it here to kill us? It must be Kaikeyī's son Bharata, here to kill Daśaratha's son Rāma, that his father exiled from the kingdom. But Rāma son of Daśaratha's my master as well as my friend; for his sake arm yourselves and take up position on the bank of the Gaṅgā. All the river folk that forage for meat, roots and fruit must be recruited to take up position along the Gaṅgā and guard the river. And deploy five hundred boats, each garrisoned with a hundred armed young fishermen,' he ordered rapidly. 'But if I can be sure that Bharata will be well disposed to Rāma, this fortunate army shall cross the Gaṅgā today.' With these words

Guha, overlord of the Niṣādas, took some fish, meat and wine and went to meet Bharata.

The foremost hereditary charioteer observed his approach, and informed Bharata with deferential courtesy: 'Here, with a thousand kinsmen about him, is a chief who is wise in the ways of Daṇḍaka Forest, and an old friend of your brother. So, Kākutstha, admit to your presence Guha, overlord of the Niṣādas; he's bound to know where Rāma and Lakṣmaṇa are.' Bharata's reply to Sumantra's welcome speech was, 'Admit Guha at once!' 78.10–13

Guha was delighted to be called forward with his kinsmen. Approaching Bharata, he invited him to treat the place as his own pleasure-garden. 'You have taken us by surprise,' he explained, 'but we fishermen all welcome you to our family: live here as one of us. We Niṣādas have brought you roots and fruit we have gathered, and fresh and dried meat, and all sorts of forest food. Your army will feed well, I trust, and spend the hours of darkness here; we shall be honoured to supply whatever they desire so that tomorrow you and your army may go on your way.' 78.14–17

Bharata listened, and shrewdly made the Niṣāda overlord Guha a politic, reasoned reply: 'My friend, I am sure you must have satisfied my elder brother's deepest desire by paying such willing honour to an army like mine.' Then glorious, triumphant Bharata went on to ask Guha, the overlord of the Niṣādas, 'Which of these paths would I do best to take for Bharadvāja's hermitage, Guha? This area is dense, and the Gaṅgā bank is impassable.' 79.1–4

At the prince's sensible enquiry, Guha saluted respectfully. 'River folk shall go with you,' said that denizen of dense forests. 'They will be alert and armed with bows, your Royal Highness, and I shall accompany you in person. I do hope you aren't going with ideas of harming ever-zealous Rāma; the size of your army almost arouses my suspicions.' 79.5–7

Bharata, spotless as the clear blue sky, replied gently to Guha: 'May such an evil day never come! You've no need to suspect me, for the Rāghava's my eldest brother, and like a father to me. I'm going to fetch Kākutstha back from his life 79.8–10 in the forest. You mustn't think any different, Guha; it's the truth I'm telling you.'

79.11–13 His face lit up at hearing Bharata's brave words, and he replied in delight: 'What a fortune is yours! There's no one to equal you in the whole world, no one who would willingly give up a kingdom that had fallen into his lap. Your fame is certain to circulate for evermore throughout all the worlds for wanting to rescue Rāma from his wretched state.'

79.14–20 As Guha and Bharata were talking, daylight faded and night came on. The prince saw to it that the army camped for the night after enjoying Guha's hospitality, then he and Śatrughna bedded down. Thoughts of Rāma arose to overwhelm noble Bharata with sorrow, matchless, virtuous and guiltless though he was. The Rāghava was tormented by an inner burning, like a tree scorched by a forest fire but blazing within. Sweat streamed from all his limbs, produced by the fire of his sorrow, like the Himālaya streaming with snow-melt when scorched by the sun's rays. A mountain with its rocks and caverns all made of gloomy care, its minerals all groans, its groves all despair, its peaks all sorrow and weariness, its wildlife all delusion, its bamboos and plants all made of torment: by such a huge mountain of melancholy was Kaikeyī's son overwhelmed.

80.1–24 Guha, denizen of dense forests, then sang the praises of noble Lakṣmaṇa to the incomparable Bharata. 'Lakṣmaṇa would stay on watch, with his fine quivers and his bow ready strung, to keep close guard over his brother, even though I told him, "Friend, I have had this comfortable bed got ready for you. Lie down and rest comfortably on it, pride of the Rāghavas. My people are all used to roughing it, but you're used to a life of ease; we'll keep awake to guard him, dutiful though you are. No one on earth is dearer to me than Rāma. Don't worry. Would I tell you a lie? He's favoured me with the chance to gain fame throughout the world, and great merit, and mere wealth too. I'm the one to guard my dear friend Rāma as he sleeps beside Sītā, my bow in my hand and my family all around. I'm always roaming about in this forest, and there's nothing I don't know about it. We could get the better of even the biggest regular army." That's what we told noble

Lakṣmaṇa, but his eyes were fixed only on his duty, and he won us over. "How", he asked, "can I possibly sleep while Dāśarathi is lying on the ground beside Sītā? How can I take any pleasure in life? He can't be conquered in battle by all the gods and anti-gods put together, but just look at him now, Guha, resting beside Sītā on the grass. It took great mortification and all sorts of trouble to produce him, and he's the only one of Daśaratha's sons to compare with him. With him gone off, the king won't survive for long: the earth must soon be widowed. Today the exhausted women will have given up all their weeping and wailing, and the king's apartment will no longer be filled with their clamour. As for Kausalyā and the king, and my mother too – I can't imagine them lasting the night. Even if thought of Śatrughna keeps my mother alive, the sorrowing Kausalyā, who gave birth to this hero, will be destroyed. Destroyed will be my father, unable to achieve his oft-expressed desire to appoint Rāma to the kingship. And when the time comes that they've got what they wanted, it's those evildoers who will purify my dead father the king with all the funeral rituals. My father's capital has lovely squares and buildings, its highways are well planned, its mansions and palaces abundant; it's ornamented with every jewel, crowded with elephants, horses and chariots, ringing to the sound of trumpets; it's crammed with everything good, it's teeming with happy, prosperous people, it's crammed with parks and gardens, and there are plenty of assemblies and fairs: and they'll be the ones to stroll at ease round my father's capital! If only we could be back there at ease, with him fit and well and his integrity intact, and the time completed!" So the night passed, with this noblest of princes lamenting as he stood on guard. When the spotless sun rose, they both matted their hair,* and I showed them this place on the bank of the Bhāgīrathī where they could cross easily.'

Listening to Guha's far-from-comforting report, Bharata 81.1–10
began to brood on the disturbing words he had heard. Gentle he was but bold, broad-shouldered and built like a lion; his eyes were the shape of lotuses, he was soft, he was attractive; he drew a deep and heartbroken breath, then a moment later

suddenly collapsed like an elephant struck in the heart by goads. Śatrughna was nearby. He caught the swooning Bharata in his arms and wept aloud, faint himself and emaciated by sorrow. All Bharata's mothers rushed up, thin from fasting, miserable and emaciated by the calamity that had befallen their lord. They wept around him as he lay on the earth, but it was Kausalyā who went to him and wrapped him in her heart-broken embrace like a cow doting on her calf. The miserable woman, overcome with grief, questioned Bharata through her tears: 'My son, I do hope there's no illness attacking your body, now that the survival of this royal family rests with you. It's the sight of you, my son, that's keeping me alive, with Rāma gone off with his brother and King Daśaratha passed away. You're the only one we have left to lead us. I do hope you've not had bad news of Lakṣmaṇa, or of my son, my only son who's gone off to the forest with his wife.'

81.11–12 The illustrious prince revived after a moment and reassured Kausalyā, wept and asked Guha, 'Where did my brother spend the night? Where did Sītā? And Lakṣmaṇa? What bed did he sleep on, and what had he eaten? Tell me, Guha.'

81.13–21 In answer, Guha the Niṣāda overlord told Bharata what hospitality he had offered to Rāma, his loved and loving guest. 'I brought all sorts of food and a lot of provisions and different fruits for Rāma to eat, but the truly valiant Rāma refused it all. He would not accept it, in accordance with *kṣatriya* customs. "It is not for us to accept gifts, my friend," the noble prince explained, your majesty, "only to give them." The illustrious Rāghava drank some water Lakṣmaṇa brought him, otherwise kept up a fast, and Sītā too. Lakṣmaṇa used the rest of the water for a libation, as the three of them performed the twilight ritual with hushed voices and concentrated minds. After that Saumitri quickly gathered up some sacrificial grass for the Rāghava and made him up a comfortable bed with it. Rāma lay down with Sītā on the well-made bed; Lakṣmaṇa bathed their feet and left them. This is the root of the *badam*-tree, and this is the very same straw that Rāma and Sītā lay on together that night.'

82.1–26 Bharata listened to all that he said, then he and his counsellors went up to the *badam*-root and viewed Rāma's bed, and he told all his mothers, 'Here did that noble man lie down on the earth for the night; this is the imprint of his body. Daśaratha, the opulent, the wise, fathered him in an opulent dynasty: Rāma shouldn't have to sleep on the earth. Once he's lain on a pile of fine counterpanes covered with quilts of hide, how can that tiger of a man lie on the bare ground? This is unheard of anywhere in the world! I can't believe it's true! I must be going out of my mind! I can only think that it's a dream. It's certain, Time must be the gods' strongest weapon for Rāma Dāśarathi to have to make his bed like this on the earth; and lovely Sītā too, his beloved, born of the king of Videha and daughter-in-law to Daśaratha, for her to have to make her bed on the earth! This is my brother's bed, for the hard bare ground all around has been disturbed, and the grass has been bruised by his limbs. I think this must have been the bed Sītā slept in, wearing her ornaments, for here and there I can see flecks of gold sticking to it. Quite obviously Sītā snagged her shawl, for there are threads of shining silk caught here. Maithilī really must enjoy sharing her husband's bed for the poor little thing, frail as she is, not to feel it a hardship. He was born in a line of universal monarchs, he's universally bountiful, universally popular, but he's given up the incomparable kingdom he loved; with his lotus-dark complexion, his red eyes, his attractive appearance, with pleasure as his portion and adversity unearned, how can the Rāghava make his bed on the earth? Vaidehī has certainly fulfilled her role by following her husband to the forest, but we don't know which way to turn without this noble prince. The world seems empty to me and rudderless now, with Daśaratha gone to heaven and Rāma off to the wilderness. Yet even with him living in the forest, no one so much as thinks of attacking our rich realm; the long arm of his heroism is our safeguard. The capital is defenceless. Its guardrooms have been emptied, its horses and elephants are unharnessed, the city gates stand open, the garrison's unmotivated, it's unprovisioned, it's unprotected, it's in a poor way. Even so, our enemies are not threatening to devour it: it might as well be food laced with poison. But from today on I'll be the one to sleep on grass or even on the bare earth, just living on fruit and roots, matting my hair and wearing bark cloth. For his sake I'll be happy to live out the rest of the time in the forest to release him from his promise: he won't be found false. Śatrughna shall stay with me, living there for the sake of my brother, while that noble man shall protect Ayodhyā with Lakṣmaṇa beside him. The Twice-Born shall consecrate Kākutstha in Ayodhyā. This is my heart's desire: if only the gods would make it come true!'

83.1–2 After spending the night there on the bank of the Gaṅgā, Rāghava Bharata rose early and called out to Śatrughna, 'Up you get, Śatrughna! Why are you still lying down? Hurry up, for goodness sake, and fetch Guha, overlord of the Niṣādas! He'll get the army across.'

83.3 'I am awake,' replied Śatrughna to his brother's summons. 'I'm not asleep, I'm just thinking about our noble brother.'

83.4–5 While these two lions of men were still talking, Guha came up and respectfully greeted Bharata: 'I trust you spent a comfortable night on the riverbank, Kākutstha, and that everything was in order for your army?'

83.6–7 Recognizing the affection in Guha's words, Bharata replied as Rāma would have wished: 'We passed the night in comfort, your majesty; you have indeed honoured us. We would now like your fisher fleet to ferry us across the Gaṅgā.'

83.8–9 When he heard what Bharata wanted, Guha hurried off back to his town and told his kinsmen. 'Get up!' he called, 'for goodness sake do wake up and launch the boats, so we can ferry the army across!'

83.10–21 At these words they jumped up and hurriedly collected together five hundred boats from all around, as commanded by the king. Some were marked out by *svastika* signs and carried great bells; they were fine, good-looking, flag-bedecked, well-built craft, trimmed to the wind. Then Guha brought alongside a *svastika*-marked boat, ringing with joyful sounds, festive and covered with a pale woollen awning. Bharata went on board with mighty Śatrughna; so did Kausalyā, Sumitrā and the king's other wives. The chaplain embarked at the head, then the brāhman elders, after them came the king's wives, and finally the waggons and provisions. As men fired the camp, plunged into the ford, and stowed the gear, the hullabaloo rose to the highest heaven, but the flag-bedecked boats carrying the people on board flew rapidly along with fishermen in charge. Some were laden with women, others with horses, others again carried whole equipages of great value. When they had reached the further shore and discharged the people, they were turned round and put through a number of manoeuvres by the fisher folk. Pennanted elephants waded across under the urging of their mahouts, their pennants making them look like beflagged mountains. While some went by boat, others crossed on rafts, or clung to pots and pitchers, and others swam across. The fishermen saw this well-favoured army across the Gaṅgā, and at the Maitra moment it set out for the exalted Prayāga forest.

When Bharadvāja's hermitage came into view a *krośa* away, 84.1–13
the bull of a man halted the whole force and went on himself with his counsellors. As he thought proper, they went on foot, leaving behind sword and insignia, in simple linen clothes, led by the chaplain. On seeing Bharadvāja, the Rāghava halted the counsellors and went forward after the chaplain. When the great and glorious ascetic Bharadvāja saw that it was Vasiṣṭha, he jumped up from his seat and hastily called to his pupils for water to greet a guest, and when Bharata saluted him he realized that Vasiṣṭha's companion was the son of Daśaratha. As was proper, he greeted them both with water for head and feet and then offered them fruit, enquiring successively about the health of the family, about Ayodhyā, the army, the treasury, the allies and the counsellors. He knew Daśaratha had passed away, and so did not name the king. Vasiṣṭha and Bharata asked him about his physical welfare, and about his fires,* trees, pupils, animals and birds. The great ascetic Bharadvāja gave a positive reply to each question, then, out of the affection binding him to the Rāghavas he asked Bharata, 'What is your purpose in coming here, now that you are the ruler of the kingdom? I am not clear in my mind about it: explain it all to me. That slayer of enemies, born to Kausalyā to increase her joy, has been banished to the forest along with his brother, and his wife, for a lengthy stay; his father ordered that illustrious

prince to live here in the forest for a full fourteen years, but the orders came from his wife. Surely you have no wish to harm this guiltless man and his young brother so that you can enjoy the kingship unhindered?'

84.14–18 Bharadvāja's question brought tears to Bharata's eyes, and his voice faltered with pain as he replied. 'It crushes me that your Honour should even think such a thing of me. Don't expect me to do wrong! Don't reproach me like this! It was not by my will that my mother demanded for me what she did. I take no personal pleasure from it and I refuse to profit from her demand. It's as a suppliant that I've come after that tiger of a man, to take him back to Ayodhyā and there throw myself at his feet. Now you know my intention in coming here, I beg you to be gracious, honoured sir, and let me know where Rāma, Lord of the Earth, is now.'

84.19–21 Bharadvāja graciously replied to Bharata, 'You tiger of a man, such conduct towards your elder, such self-denial, such integrity befits one born in the dynasty of the Rāghavas. I do know what is in your heart of hearts. It was for your greater glory that I asked you to confirm it. Your brother is living on the great mountain Citrakūṭa. Tomorrow you shall go there; but today stay here with your counsellors. You are very wise, and know how to fulfil desires; grant me my wish.'

86.1–3 When night was over and Bharata and his entourage had again been hospitably entertained, he happily approached Bharadvāja. The sage had performed his fire oblation, and when he noticed the respectful salute of that tiger of a man, Bharadvāja asked Bharata, 'I trust the night has passed pleasantly for you here among us? Have your people been satisfied by our hospitality? Do tell me, sinless man.'

86.4–8 As the sage, most glorious of the glorious, emerged from the hermitage, Bharata greeted him respectfully, bowed and sat down. 'I have stayed here in comfort, reverend sir,' he replied, 'and my whole army and their animals likewise; my ministers too; we have all had our wishes gratified by you to the highest degree. All our travel-weariness has gone, we've been well fed and well lodged, even including the servants; we have all lived here in comfort. Nevertheless, I must take leave of your reverence, excellent sage. Look on me with a friendly eye, righteous sage, as I set off to find my noble and righteous brother in his hermitage. Will you show me the way, and tell me how far it is?'

Glorious Bharadvāja, that great ascetic, noting Bharata's eagerness to see his brother, answered his question. 'Bharata, mount Citrakūṭa with its lovely glens and groves lies two and a half *yojanas* into the unpeopled forest. The river Mandākinī flows towards its northern flank, hidden by flowering trees amid lovely flowering groves. Between that stream and mount Citrakūṭa is your brother's leaf-hut, my son; that is where they live. Direct your army, with its mass of elephants, horses and chariots, to take the road to the south and south-west, commander blessed by fortune; then you will see the Rāghava.' 86.9–13

When the emperor's wives heard of their departure, they left the vehicles they were entitled to travel in and clustered round the brāhman. Trembling, wasted and miserable, Kausalyā and Queen Sumitrā then bowed down to the hermit's feet. Kaikeyī, her plans thwarted, despised by all the world, bowed down to him in her shame, circumambulated the holy sage and stood dejectedly not far from Bharata. Then steadfast Bharadvāja asked Bharata, 'Rāghava, I should like to know which of your mothers is which.' 86.14–18

Righteous Bharata saluted and answered Bharadvāja's question gracefully: 'This lady, your reverence, visibly so downcast and spare through fasting from her sorrow, is yet my father's chief queen, the divine Kausalyā, who bore that tiger of a man, him of the lionlike tread, Rāma, just as Aditi bore Dhātṛ. The lady standing to her left, clinging despondently to her arm, looking like the fast-fading flowers on a *karṇikāra*-branch from the forest depths, that queen is mother to those godlike princes, both every inch a valiant hero, Lakṣmaṇa and Śatrughna. And this is the one at whose doing the two tigers of men have left here in peril of their lives, at whose doing King Daśaratha, bereft of his son, has gone to heaven; this is Kaikeyī, power-mad, cruel and malicious, no noble though she looks like one; this is she whom I see as the root of all my troubles; this is my 86.19–26 mother.' Sobs choked his voice as he spoke; his eyes were copper-hued, his sighs incessant; the tiger of a man was like an angry snake.

86.27–8 Wisely, the sage Bharadvāja replied to Bharata's outburst with reassuring words: 'Don't hold it against Kaikeyī; this exile of Rāma's will end happily.'

86.29–35 At that Bharata made ready to go, saluted, circumambulated him and took leave, then ordered his army to harness up. The multitude then harnessed all those divinely gilded horse-chariots and jumped in, so eager were they to set out. With their pennants and golden girths, elephant cows and bulls thundered as they set out, like clouds at summer's end. Carriages of all sorts, large and small, but all of great value, set off too, with the infantry on foot. Headed by Kausalyā, the women rode off in superb conveyances, joyful at the prospect of seeing Rāma. A fine palanquin, gleaming like the newly risen sun, had been made ready for Bharata and his entourage; he mounted it and set off in majesty. The host was a throng of elephants, steeds and chariots, like a towering cloud, as it started off, turned southwards and plunged through the forests with their teeming wildlife.

87.1–5 As that bannered array swarmed along, the elephant lords in their forest homes, *musth*-maddened, were agitated and fled with their herds. All around could be glimpsed bears, and herds of chital and nilgai along the forest tracks, as well as on the mountains and by the rivers. Daśaratha's righteous son was pleased to be setting out in the midst of his entire army; huge and thunderous, like the surging sea, noble Bharata's army spread over all the land like monsoon-clouds in the sky, so that for a long time the earth was lost to view beneath its covering of speedy chargers and tuskers.

87.6–20 When they had gone a long way and their mounts were tired, the glorious Bharata said to his excellent counsellor Vasiṣṭha, 'From the looks of it, we must have reached the place Bharadvāja told us about; it's just as I heard it described. This is mount Citrakūṭa, there's the river Mandākinī, and there in the distance, dark as a cloud, we can see the forest. Already my mountain-like elephants are pressing the lovely flanks of mount

Citrakūṭa. The boughs on the mountain-slopes are shedding their blossom like dark rain-laden clouds shedding their waters at summer's burning end. Śatrughna, look at the mountain, the haunt of *kinnaras*, yet now thronged on all sides by horses like crocodiles in the sea. Herds of deer have been startled into flight like clouds streaking across the autumn sky before the wind. The trees covering their heads with fragrant garlands of flowers from their cloud-dark limbs are like men of the south. This forest, once silent and dread, might now be Ayodhyā, so crammed is it with people. Dust raised by our animals' hooves hangs in the air, blotting out the sky, until the wind speeds it on its way as if to please me. Śatrughna, look how fast the chariots and their steeds are racing through the forest in the hands of their master charioteers! Look at those lovely peacocks running in terror to this mountain-sanctuary for birds! This place, home to ascetics, seems to me absolutely delightful, a real stairway to heaven. There are lots of beautiful chital stags with their does in the forest, looking as if they're dappled with petals. Good! Let soldiers go off and search the woodland till they find those tigers of men, Rāma and Lakṣmaṇa.'

At Bharata's command, armed warriors plunged into the 87.21–3
forest and saw smoke. They reported back to Bharata that they had seen a plume of smoke, and added, 'There's no smoke without men present: the two Rāghavas must certainly be here. But then again, it may not be the two heroic princes, those tigers of men, that are here; it may be other people, ascetics, who are Rāma's equals.'

Bharata listened to their reasoned report, then the indomi- 87.24–6
table hero instructed all his troops: 'Wait here at the ready. You need go no further. I will go on by myself, just with Sumantra and our *guru*.' At this command everyone on all sides halted, while Bharata fixed his gaze upon the plume of smoke.

As Rāma was sitting there the dust and clamour of the army 90.1–6
accompanying Bharata rose clearly to the heavens. Meanwhile *musth*-maddened elephant lords, frightened by the loud noise, were agitated and ran away with their herds. The Rāghava

heard the noise raised by the army, and noticed that the elephants were all taking flight. Remarking their flight and hearing the din, Rāma said to Sumitrā's glorious son, the fiery Lakṣmaṇa: 'Lakṣmaṇa, you credit to Sumitrā, listen! look! I can hear a loud noise, like the crashing of terrible thunder. Maybe some king or notable is in the forest, roaming around hunting, or maybe it's something else, a wild beast perhaps. You ought to investigate, Saumitri: find out the truth of it all without delay.'

90.7–10 Lakṣmaṇa hurriedly climbed a flowering *sāl* tree and scanned every direction, examining the east in particular. Craning his neck, he caught sight of the great army with its crowd of chariots, horses and elephants and its watchful infantry. He called out to Rāma and told him about the army with its many horses and elephants, and its chariots gaudy with standards. 'Put the fire out,' he advised his noble brother, 'and make Sītā hide in a cave. String your bow and get your arrows and armour!'

90.11 Rāma, that tiger of a man, answered Lakṣmaṇa, 'Well then, Saumitri, whose army do you think it is?'

90.12–25 Lakṣmaṇa's furious reply to Rāma's question was enough to burn the army to ashes: 'It's obvious!' he declared. 'It's Kaikeyī's son Bharata that's coming to kill us both! He's had the consecration performed and now he wants to enjoy the kingdom unchallenged. I can see gleaming on his chariot that great majestic standard with the tall trunk and branches of its *kovidāra* device. There are men mounted on their favourite horses that can go as fast as they like, and elephant-riders gleefully resplendent. Let's get our bows!' he urged his heroic brother. 'Let's go to the mountain for safety; better still, let's take our stand here, arms at the ready. If only we could get hold of the *kovidāra*-standard in battle! If only I could see Bharata! It's because of him that this calamity has befallen you, Rāghava, and Sītā, and me! Sir, hero, Rāghava: you've been driven out of an enduring kingdom, and the enemy who's the cause is close by. I'll kill Bharata for that! I can see nothing wrong in butchering Bharata, Rāghava, not I! There's no law against getting rid of someone who has struck the first blow.

With him dead, you can rule the whole earth. Today let Kaikeyī's lust for the kingdom bring her the excruciating sight of me killing her son in battle, like an elephant smashing a tree. Then I'll kill Kaikeyī, and her entourage, and her family: today the earth can be freed of this great stain! You've been honourable, and I've been reining in my anger and shame, but today I'll vent them on the enemy host like a fire eating up tinder. Today I'll riddle the bodies of our enemies with my honed arrows and sprinkle Citrakūṭa forest with their blood. Beasts of prey can drag around the elephants and horses, arrows embedded in their hearts, and the men I've slain too. At least, I won't have been wasting my bow and arrows in this great forest: it will be no waste to kill Bharata and his army, that's for sure.'

But Rāma calmed Lakṣmaṇa Saumitri's impetuous passion 91.1–9
with these words: 'Why would we need a bow, or a sword and shield, if it's wise Bharata himself, the great archer, who's arrived? The time's ripe for Bharata to want to see us; he'd never dream of hurting us. What harm has Bharata ever done to you, or threatened you with, for you to suspect Bharata now today? There are to be no harsh or unkind words from you to Bharata, for to treat Bharata unkindly would be the same as speaking unkindly to me. Could sons kill their father, no matter how hard-pressed they were? Saumitri, how could a brother kill his brother, his own flesh and blood?[11] If it's the kingdom that's worrying you, I'll tell Bharata when I see him, "Give him the kingship." For if I say that to him, Lakṣmaṇa, Bharata's sure to say, "Certainly offer him the kingship."' At this rebuke from his charitable, generous brother, Lakṣmaṇa hung his head for shame.

Seeing Lakṣmaṇa so crestfallen, the Rāghava went on, 'It's 91.10–14
my belief that this mighty prince has come here to see us. Or else he's thought what life in the forest is like, and has come to take my Vaidehī back home to the luxury she's accustomed to. There, my hero, we can see that pair of excellent, fast thoroughbreds, horses that gladden the mind and equal the wind for speed. There's the colossal elephant called Śatruṃjaya swaying at the head of the army, our wise father's ancient

mount.' All-conquering Lakṣmaṇa then climbed down from the top of the *sāl* and stood meekly beside Rāma.

91.15–16; 93.1–7 On Bharata's orders not to disturb the area, the army set up camp all around the mountain. The Ikṣvāku army spread out over the mountain slopes for a *yojana* and a half as it settled down with its host of elephants, steeds and chariots. While the army was settling, Bharata eagerly ushered Śatrughna along to see his brother. Instructing the sage Vasiṣṭha to bring his mothers quickly, he hurried on ahead in his affection for his older brother. Sumantra followed as well, hard on the heels of Śatrughna, his thirst for a sight of Rāma equalling Bharata's. On they went, until, in that haven of ascetics, Bharata saw a leaf-hut, piles of flowers and felled logs, and large amounts of dung left by wild animals and buffaloes, stacked among the trees ready for the cold weather.[12] Going forward, the mighty, glorious Bharata said in delight to Śatrughna and the ministers on all sides:

93.8–12 'It's my belief we have reached the place Bharadvāja told us about: it's my belief the river Mandākinī isn't very far from here. Up there some bits of bark have been tied: Lakṣmaṇa must have put them there so he could recognize the path in the dusk and avoid this track made on the mountain-side by elephants trumpeting their defiance at each other with their tusks raised. There in the forest we can see the dense smoke from the fires that ascetics seek to maintain perpetually. Here my delighted eyes will see that tiger of a man, the noble Rāghava, living like a great sage out of respect for his father.'

93.13–16 Rāghava Bharata carried on a little way towards Citrakūṭa and reached the Mandākinī. 'That tiger of a man is sitting on the ground,' he said to his companions, 'content with his hero-posture, a sovereign reduced to the wilderness. It's a pity I was ever born! It's because of me that the Lord of the World, the glorious Rāghava, has been afflicted, and has given up all his hopes and is living in the forest. The whole world reviles me for it! But now I can fall at the feet of Rāma and Sītā again and again, and implore their forgiveness.'

93.17–28 As Daśaratha's son was lamenting in this way, he saw through the trees a large leaf-hut. It was holy and attractive, thatched with many leaves from *sāl*, palmyra and *aśvakarṇa* trees, spacious and strewn with soft *kuśa* grass like an altar at a sacrifice. Bows like Śakra's weapon adorned it, powerful, gold-backed, springy, all-conquering bows; arrows like the sun's rays adorned it, ferocious, quiver-borne arrows, their points ablaze, like serpents adorning Bhogavatī; a pair of swords enriched it, swords with silver sheaths, and a pair of shields adorned it, shields studded with gold, along with patterned, gold-ornamented arm- and finger-guards. That hut would no more be attacked by enemy forces than a lion's den by deer. In Rāma's dwelling Bharata could see an altar, spacious and holy, sited north-east, with a blazing fire. A moment later, sitting in the cottage, crowned with a mat of hair, Bharata saw his elder brother, Rāma. It was Rāma he saw, seated nearby, clad in black-antelope skin and bark-fibre garments; irresistible as fire, lion-chested, broad-shouldered, lotus-eyed, the merit-seeking master of the sea-girt earth, broad-shouldered, was sitting there with Sītā and Lakṣmaṇa like eternal Brahmā on the *kuśa*-strewn bare earth. The sight overwhelmed glorious Bharata with pain and confusion, and he ran to him; Bharata was Kaikeyī's son, but he was righteous.

In a voice smothered by sobs, he lamented in torment at the 93.29–35
unbearable sight, and stoutly declared, 'My elder brother is worthy to be honoured in the assembly by his subjects; here he sits honoured by forest animals. Once my noble brother was accustomed to be clad at immense cost; here his duty leads him to be clothed in deerskin. This Rāghava used to sport all sorts of colourful flowers; how can he bear this load of matted locks? A man who should be heaping up merit by duly performing sacrifices is pursuing merit by mortifying his flesh. Expensive sandalwood paste used to coat that noble prince's limbs; how can he let them be coated by grime? And it's because of me that Rāma has had to exchange his wonted pleasure for this pain! Oh, why must I live to be such a monster, so despised by the world!'

Sweat streamed from Bharata's lotus of a face at this mourn- 93.36–9
ful lament, and he fell in tears before Rāma's feet. In the

torment of his sorrow, the mighty prince Bharata uttered one mournful cry, 'Noble brother!' and could say no more. Sobs choked his throat at the sight of illustrious Rāma; he called out 'Noble brother', and could speak no more. Śatrughna too wept and did obeisance to Rāma's feet. Rāma embraced them both, then he too burst into tears.

96.1–3 Vasiṣṭha was eager for a sight of Rāma, and set off to escort Daśaratha's wives to the place. The queens made slow progress as far as the Mandākinī, where they saw the place where Rāma and Lakṣmaṇa bathed. Kausalyā's mouth was dried up and full of sobs as she spoke mournfully to Sumitrā and the king's other women:

96.4–5 'So just ahead there is the place in the forest their restless zeal has beaten down as they go to bathe, with no lord and driven from their kingdom. Sumitrā, it's from here that your son Saumitri never tires of fetching water himself in the service of my son.'

96.6–12 Her beautiful eyes fell upon a cake of *badam*-flour offered for their father on the south-pointing* *kuśa* grass. Noticing what Rāma had left on the ground in his sorrow for his father, Queen Kausalyā said to all Daśaratha's women: 'See what the Rāghava has offered as the prescribed due for his father, the noble Rāghava, lord of the Ikṣvākus! That's not what I think is the right food for that noble, godlike king; he's been used to the best of everything. He was like great Indra on earth, he used to enjoy all that the wide world could offer, all nature's resources were his to command: how can he enjoy a *badam*-cake? Nothing in the world could give me greater pain than to see opulent Rāma with only *badam*-flour to offer to his father. The sight of Rāma's offering to his father of a *badam*-cake is enough to make my heart burst a thousand times over with sorrow!'

96.13–20 Her fellow wives offered her comfort in her torment, then went on until they saw Rāma in the hermitage, looking like an immortal fallen from heaven. At the sight of Rāma forsaken by all comforts, his tormented mothers burst into loud tears, wasted by their sorrow. Rāma rose and, true to his word, that tiger of a man bowed low to the dainty feet of all his mothers, while the beautiful-eyed women wiped the dust from his back with their dainty, gentle, soft hands. Saumitri gazed sadly upon all the mothers, then he followed Rāma in greeting them all affectionately and unhurriedly. All the women treated him in the same way as they did Rāma: he was Fortune-favoured Lakṣmaṇa, he was born of Daśaratha. Sītā sadly clasped the feet of her mothers-in-law, then stood before them, her eyes filled with tears. As if she were her own daughter, Kausalyā folded the anguished woman in her motherly arms, so emaciated and disconsolate was she from her life in the forest.

'What has the daughter of the king of Videha,' she asked, 'the daughter-in-law of Daśaratha, the wife of Rāma, done to deserve such privation in the desolate wilderness? When I see your face, Vaidehī, looking like a heat-scorched lotus, like a faded blue water lily, like gold shrouded in dust, like the moon molested by clouds, then sorrow sears me, blazing in my heart like an all-consuming fire kindled by your calamity.' 96.21–3

While his tormented mother was speaking, the Rāghava, Bharata's elder brother, reached Vasiṣṭha and saluted his feet. Rāma comforted his devoted younger brother, then he and his brother Lakṣmaṇa began to question him. 96.24;97.1

'I'd like you to tell us why you've come here wearing matted hair, bark cloth and skins. Why have you abandoned the kingdom and come here dressed in black-antelope skins, your hair matted? You must tell us all about it.' 97.2–3

Kaikeyī's son reached out eagerly towards the noble Kākutstha and responded deferentially to his questions. 'Our mighty father did a grievous wrong in exiling his noble son,' he declared. 'Now sorrow for his son has weighed him down, and he has gone to heaven. It was under coercion from a woman, my victorious brother, from my mother Kaikeyī, that he dishonoured himself by performing this heinous crime. That woman, the mother who bore me, now a widow wasted by grief at not getting the kingdom she hungered after, will fall into a terrible hell. I have come here as your slave. It's for you now to gratify me, and be consecrated for the kingship, like 97.4–15

Indra the Bountiful. You should show favour to all the subjects and to our widowed mothers who have come out here to you, and accept the kingdom which is yours by right of succession and by right of your own person. Grace us with your presence and fulfil your friends' desires. Relieve the Earth of her widowhood, make her whole with you as her Lord, like an autumn night with the pure hare-marked moon. With our heads bowed low we beseech you, these ministers and I: be gracious to me, your brother, your disciple, your slave! You tiger of a man, you can't ignore the whole time-honoured ancestral council.' With these words the sobbing Bharata, Kaikeyī's mighty son, again threw himself at Rāma's feet, groaning again and again like a rutting elephant.

97.15–23 Rāma embraced his brother Bharata. 'Your breeding, your force of character, your distinction, your constancy,' he said, 'all make it impossible for a man of your stamp to use foul means to gain a kingdom! I recognize no fault in you, mighty warrior, not the least one, so it's not for you to revile your mother so childishly. You should set an example of proper behaviour, and pay to your mother just as much respect as you would to our father, esteemed by the world for knowing what was proper. You're a Rāghava: for my part, when I was told to go to the forest by my upright mother and father, how could I do otherwise? You're to have the world-renowned kingdom of Ayodhyā, I'm to live in bark cloth in Daṇḍaka Forest. The Mahārāja publicly ordained this apportionment. Now glorious Daśaratha has gone to heaven. People the world over looked up to that righteous king: you should comply with his decree and enjoy whatever of his gifts falls to your lot. For my part, my sweet brother, for fourteen years I shall take refuge in Daṇḍaka Forest and enjoy what falls to my lot from my noble father.

99.2–16 'It's fitting that you should have spoken in this way, you who were born by Kaikeyī as a son to Daśaratha, the best of kings. Long ago, brother, when our father married your mother, the prodigious bride-price he promised your grandfather was that the kingdom should go to you. Then, during the war between the gods and the anti-gods, that mighty king,

Lord of the Earth, was pleased by your mother, and gratefully gave her a boon. Subsequently your illustrious and beautiful mother reminded the best of men and claimed two boons: kingship for you, you tiger of a man, exile for me. The outcome of the boon-giving, bull of a man, was that I was enjoined by him, by Father, to live for fourteen years in the forest. My lot is this desolate forest, along with Lakṣmaṇa and Sītā; I will allow no one to deflect me from maintaining the integrity of our father. You too sir ought by your assent to maintain the integrity of our sovereign father: be consecrated immediately. For my sake, Bharata, discharge the obligation of our lord the king. You know what's right: save our father, and delight your mother. Dear brother, we are taught that long ago illustrious Gaya, sacrificing to his ancestors at Gayā, sang, "It is because a son saves his father from the hell called Put that he is called a 'son',[13] or because a son protects his ancestors. Desirable is it to have many sons, accomplished and learned, so that one among them might journey to Gayā." All the royal sages are in accord. You are the king's choice, so it's for you, prince paramount, to save our father from hell. Go to Ayodhyā, Bharata, my hero, with Śatrughna as your companion, and gratify the subjects and all the Twice-Born, while I, your majesty, go with Vaidehī and Lakṣmaṇa without delay to Daṇḍaka Forest.'

High-minded Bharata was pained by Rāma's reply to him. 103.12–15
Instantly he ordered the charioteer, 'Be quick, driver, spread me some *kuśa* grass, here on the bare ground. I'm going to sit here and face out my noble brother until he gratifies me. So long as he refuses to return, I shall fix my gaze and take no food, lying in front of the hut, like an indigent brāhman.'* Then he realized that Sumantra had eyes for Rāma alone, so he fetched a covering of *kuśa* grass himself, and spread it on the ground in despair.

Glorious Rāma, prince yet supreme sage, asked him, 'Dear 103.16–18
brother, what am I doing to incur such an assault? A brāhman is quite entitled to put pressure on people by taking up a fixed position, but assaults of this kind are not the practice for men consecrated to rule. Give up this cruel vow. Get up, you tiger

of a man, and go straight back to that excellent city, Ayodhyā: you're a Rāghava.'

103.19 Bharata remained seated. Seeing all around people from town and country, he asked, 'Why don't you put my noble brother right?'

103.20–21 His subjects answered their generous prince, 'We acknowledge that Rāma Rāghava is talking correctly to Bharata Kākutstha, for the distinguished prince is standing by his father's promise, so we certainly cannot deflect him.'

103.22–3 Rāma acknowledged their words and went on, 'Your well-wishers have an eye for what's right. Listen to what they say. Consider it properly, Rāghava, now that you've heard all the pros and cons. Stand up, mighty brother; touch me, then touch water.'*

103.24–6 Bharata stood up. He touched water, then declared, 'Listen to me, men of the council, advisers and guildsmen: I have not petitioned my father for the kingship, nor have I instructed my mother to do so. I admit that the noble Rāghava is very wise. But if someone has to live in the forest to keep our father's word, then I am the one who will live for fourteen years in the forest.'

103.27–32 Rāma the righteous was taken aback by the sincerity of his brother's words. Surveying his subjects, he told them, 'Neither Bharata nor I can cancel any transaction – any sale, pledge or purchase – made during his lifetime by my father. I cannot cheat about living in the forest: that would be abhorrent. Kaikeyī's request was apt and my father's action correct. Bharata is steady, I know; he defers to his elders. Everything will turn out well, for this noble prince will keep faith. When I come back from the forest with my worthy brother I shall become supreme Lord of the Earth. Kaikeyī claimed a boon from the king, and I have carried it out to absolve my father, the lord of the world, from wrongdoing.'

104.9–13 Bharata's whole body crumpled. With hands joined in supplication he again pleaded with the Rāghava in a faltering voice. 'Kākutstha, you should be doing what your mother and I are begging for; it's your royal duty to continue our family tradition. I can't safeguard this huge kingdom on my own; nor can I gratify its loyal populace. You're the one our family and soldiers, our allies and our friends are longing for, like farmers longing for Parjanya. You will secure the kingdom on your return, Kākutstha; you have the wisdom and the power to protect the world.'

Bharata had assented. He fell at his brother's feet, pleading 104.14–20
with Rāma with heartfelt passion. Clasping his swarthy, lotus-eyed brother to his bosom, Rāma himself sobbed like a frantic goose as he replied, 'It's your praiseworthy character that's led you to this instinctive resolve. My dear brother, you emphatically have got the power to protect the earth. Take advice from ministers, friends and learned counsellors and you'll be able to have even the greatest deeds performed. Lakṣmī would leave the moon, Himālaya would shed its snow, the sea would exceed its confines before I would transgress my father's command. It was your mother who brought this about for you, but whether she acted out of ambition or greed, don't you entertain the same ideas and behave like your mother.' Kausalyā's son blazed like the sun in splendour as he spoke, and his face shone like the new moon.

'Noble brother,' Bharata said to him, 'place your feet on 104.
these gold-ornamented sandals: they are what shall dispense 21–2;
welfare to the whole world.' The glorious tiger of a man 105.1
stepped on to the sandals, then took them off and handed them to noble Bharata. Bharata placed his head beneath them,* then joyfully mounted the chariot with Śatrughna at his side.

Headed by Vasiṣṭha, Vāmadeva, resolute Jābāli and all the 105.2–6
most revered counsellors, they set off eastwards towards the lovely river Mandākinī and then circumambulated the great mount Citrakūṭa, observing its wealth of beautiful sparkling minerals. Bharata and his army then pressed on along its flank, and not far from Citrakūṭa Bharata saw the hermitage where lived the sage Bharadvāja. The wise pride of his family got down from his chariot when he reached Bharadvāja's hermitage and bowed low to his feet.

Bharadvāja was delighted. 'My dear boy,' he said to Bharata, 105.7–8 'you have done what you had to do. You have met Rāma.' With these words the perspicacious Bharadvāja greeted Bharata.

105.8–14 Bharata, devoted to duty, replied to Bharadvāja. 'Both his *guru* and I begged him, and the steadfast Rāghava was highly gratified, but told Vasiṣṭha, "My father's command was fourteen years, and I shall observe my father's command to the letter." With great wisdom Vasiṣṭha the practised orator answered the eloquent Rāghava's words with weighty advice. "Be pleased in your great wisdom to consign these gold-emblazoned sandals to work the welfare of Ayodhyā in your place." On Vasiṣṭha's advice the Rāghava stood up, faced the east and handed me these gold-adorned sandals as emblems of sovereignty. With leave from Rāma, that noblest of men, I am returning, returning to take the symbolic sandals to Ayodhyā.'

105.15–17 Noble Bharata's fine speech was answered by an even finer speech from the sage Bharadvāja. 'It is not to be wondered at, you tiger of a man, supreme exponent of virtue and integrity, that nobility should abide in you like rain in a crater. Your mighty father Daśaratha will live on in a son like you, righteous devotee of duty.'

105.18–24 After respectfully saluting the noble sage for his words, bowing to touch his feet and preparing to take his leave, glorious Bharata repeatedly circumambulated Bharadvāja and set off with his counsellors for Ayodhyā. The army with its vehicles, waggons, horses and elephants turned around and trailed after Bharata. They crossed the holy, wave-garlanded Yamunā, and then all gazed again upon the auspicious water of the river Gaṅgā. When he had seen his family across its lovely, abundant waters, he led his army into lovely Śṛṅgaverapura, and beyond Śṛṅgaverapura Bharata could make out Ayodhyā. Tortured by sadness he said to his driver, 'Look at Ayodhyā, driver, desolate, lustreless, a joyless jumble, muted and miserable.'

109.1–4 When they had all left, the Rāghava took thought and found many reasons why living there no longer satisfied him. 'This is where I saw Bharata, and our mothers, and the citizens; I grieve over them constantly, and the memory haunts me. Besides, the place has been churned up where the noble prince's camp was pitched, and fouled by the dung from the horses and elephants. So I'm going somewhere else.'

With these thoughts the Rāghava set out, with Vaidehī and 109.4–8
Lakṣmaṇa. When the illustrious prince arrived at Atri's hermitage, he honoured the sage, and the blessed Atri in turn received him like a son. He personally ordered hospitality for them, and prepared everything nicely; Saumitri and fortune-blessed Sītā he set at ease. Knowing what was proper, the most excellent benevolent sage invited his aged, respected wife to join him and then considerately asked that fortune-blessed ascetic, virtuous Anasūyā, to look after Vaidehī.

'When the world was burned up by an unremitting drought 109.9–13
for ten years,' he told Rāma, 'that virtuous ascetic produced roots and fruit and set the Gaṅgā rolling by the force of her severe asceticism and the restraint that adorns her. She practised great austerities for ten thousand years, my dear man, with vows to be free of envy: she alleviated disasters, and swiftly made one night last for ten nights to achieve some purpose of the gods. She will be another mother to you, sinless man. Let Vaidehī approach her: all creatures respect that illustrious old woman; she never angers.'

The Rāghava assented to the sage's suggestion, and gave 109.14–16
pious Sītā excellent advice. 'Princess, you've heard what the sage has said. Step forward at once and gain benefit from the ascetic Anasūyā, whose deeds have brought her renown throughout the world. Step forward at once and give the ascetic the due greeting.'

Sītā heard what he said. Eager to help the Rāghava, Maithilī 109.17–21
went up to Atri's pious wife, a feeble old woman, wrinkled and hoary, her whole frame constantly trembling like a plantain in a gale. Demurely Sītā greeted the blessed Anasūyā, her husband's votary, and told her her name. Vaidehī was delighted to greet the spotless ascetic; showing her respect, she enquired after her health. Observing how correctly the blessed Sītā was conducting herself, she addressed her kindly and gladly:

'How good it is that you are so attentive to what is right! 109.21–8
How good it is, exalted Sītā, that you have given up family,

status and wealth to follow Rāma, cast adrift in the forest. Women who cherish their husband, in the city or in the wild, for better or worse, achieve the pinnacle of worldly acclaim. Women of breeding set their lord up as their supreme deity, even if he is evil, lustful or penniless. Try as I may, Vaidehī, I cannot see a relative superior to him, in every situation bringing benefit as imperishable as an act of austerity. But they are bad wives who do not understand rights and wrongs in this way, whose hearts are swayed by desire, and lord it over their husbands. Women of that sort, Maithilī, slaves to depravity, injure morality and incur disgrace. But women like you, full of merit, who have experienced the best and the worst the world can offer, will take their place in heaven as paragons of virtue.'

THE FOREST

[*Further into the forest they reach another hermitage.*]
A group of sages assembled. Versed in virtue as they were, they 3,5.6–18
petitioned Rāma, that supreme pillar of virtue, himself well versed in virtue. 'You are a great warrior, you are head of the Ikṣvāku dynasty, you are Lord of the Earth like Indra the Bountiful is of the gods; you are famed throughout the three worlds for your glory, for your prowess, for your devotion to your father; integrity and virtue abound in you. We have come to you as suppliants, noble, right-minded, virtuous lord; be so good as to allow us to petition you. It would be very wrong, sir, for a king to exact a tax of one sixth and yet not to protect his subjects like sons. It is by taking more care of them than of his own life – more than of his sons, who are dearer even than his own life – Rāma, it is by always remaining on guard and protecting all who live in his land that he gains long-lasting, eternal fame and at the last reaches Brahmā's abode, there also to be honoured. A king who protects his subjects righteously benefits from one quarter of the great merit accruing to a sage who lives on roots and fruit. You, Rāma, are lord of this great company of hermits, most of us brāhmans, yet we are being persecuted by *rākṣasas* as if we had no lord. Come and see the bodies of many a devout sage slain by savage *rākṣasas* all over the forest. Massive carnage is being inflicted on those who live by the river Pampā and along the Mandākinī and on those who make their home on Citrakūṭa. We cannot endure the terrible injury being done to the forest ascetics by these ruthless *rākṣasas*, so we have come to you for protection and refuge. We are losing our lives to the night-walkers. Rāma, protect us.'

5.19–20 Hearing of the hermits' sufferings, virtuous Kākutstha declared to all the ascetics, 'You have no need to petition me: I am at the command of the suffering. Fortune has led me here, sirs, to help you achieve your purpose. This stay of mine in the forest will bear much fruit. I am willing to fight and kill the ascetics' enemies, the *rākṣasas*.'

6.1–6 The Twice-Born took the heroic Rāma, with his brother and Sītā, to Sutīkṣṇa's hermitage. The journey was long and he crossed rivers in full spate before a huge mountain came into sight, like a great lofty cloud. Then with Sītā the two Rāghavas, champions of the Ikṣvākus, penetrated a forest abounding in different trees, a fearful forest with many flowers and fruits and trees. In a lonely part Rāma saw a hermitage adorned with garlands of bark, and politely addressed the ascetic Sutīkṣṇa who was sitting there, grown old in austerities, with dirt-encrusted hair. 'I am Rāma, your reverence; I have come to visit you. Give me your greeting, great sage, versed in virtue and valiant for truth.'

6.7–11 When he saw Rāma, that supreme pillar of virtue, he enfolded the hero in his arms and replied: 'You are welcome indeed, heroic Rāma, supreme pillar of virtue; now that you have arrived the hermitage seems to have its lord. It is because I have been expecting you, illustrious hero, that I have not ascended to the world of the gods, leaving my body behind on the earth. I heard that when you were turned out of your kingdom you went to Citrakūṭa. When Indra Śatakratu, king of the gods, came here he declared that I had won all worlds by my pious deeds.[1] Those regions are frequented by gods and sages and have been earned by my penance. By my grace you may enjoy yourself there with your wife and Lakṣmaṇa.'

6.12–14 Like Indra Vāsava speaking to Brahmā, Rāma replied calmly to the great sage, who blazed forth in the fierceness of his austerities and integrity. 'Great sage, it is for me to win those worlds for myself. What I wish for from you is that you point out somewhere where we can live in the forest. The noble Śarabhaṅga Gautama declared your reverence to be skilled in every way and devoted to the welfare of all creatures.'

6.15–17 The world-renowned great sage was overwhelmed by joy at Rāma's words, and sweetly replied: 'Enjoy this excellent hermitage, Rāma; it is thronged with groups of sages and always supplied with roots and fruit. Herds of deer come to this hermitage, illustrious prince; they wander about and are attracted to return without fear.'

At the great sage's words, Lakṣmaṇa's elder brother set an 6.18–20
arrow to his bow and firmly declared, 'Most eminent sir, I should kill any herds of deer that came with a keen arrow, brilliant as a lightning-bolt. That would compromise you, sir. What could be worse than that? I don't envisage staying long in this hermitage.'

After these words to his benefactor, Rāma carried out the 6.21;
twilight ritual; when he had performed the evening rite, he 7.1–9
prepared his lodging there. Honoured by Sutīkṣṇa's welcome, Rāma and Saumitri spent the night there and woke at daybreak. Rising at the proper time, the Rāghava and Sītā washed in cool lotus-scented water. Rāma, Lakṣmaṇa and Vaidehī duly offered the appropriate worship to Agni and the gods in the forest, the ascetics' refuge, then, purified, watched the sun rise. They approached Sutīkṣṇa with these courteous words: 'Pleasant has been our stay with you, sir, honoured by your honourable self; we now beg leave to depart, for the sages are hurrying us on. We are anxious to see the whole group of hermitages of the pious sages living in Daṇḍaka Forest. Along with these excellent sages, ever dutiful and chastened by their austerities like smouldering fires, we wish to take our leave. We should like to set off before the sun blazes forth its unbearable heat too fiercely like a nouveau riche flaunting his ill-gotten gains.' With these words the Rāghava, together with Saumitri and Sītā, saluted the sage's feet.

The excellent sage raised the pair as they clasped his feet, 7.10–16
embracing them tightly, and replied affectionately: 'Go in safety, Rāma and Saumitri, with Sītā following you like a shadow. Heroic prince, you will see the home of these Daṇḍaka Forest ascetics, their lives uplifted by penance; it's a lovely hermitage. You will see flowering forests with their harvest of fruit and roots, their herds of peaceful deer and flocks of tame birds, their ponds and lakes with clumps of blossoming lotus

and their calm waters disturbed only by ducks. Your sight will be charmed by mountain torrents and attractive forests filled with the clamour of peacocks. Go there, good Saumitri; go there, my lord; and when you have seen it, do come back to my hermitage.'

7.17–19; 10.26–7 Kākutstha and Lakṣmaṇa assented to this suggestion, circumambulated the sage and prepared to leave. Large-eyed Sītā handed the two brothers their exquisite quivers, their bows and their gleaming swords. Rāma and Lakṣmaṇa strapped on their elegant quivers, picked up their twanging bows and emerged from the hermitage to set off. After their tour the glorious, righteous Rāghava returned with Sītā to Sutīkṣṇa's hermitage, to be honoured on his arrival by the sages. There Rāma, conqueror of his foes, stayed for some time.

10.28–32 Once during his stay at the hermitage, when Kākutstha was sitting near the great sage, he politely said to Sutīkṣṇa, 'Sir, storytellers are always telling me that Agastya, that holiest of sages, lives in this forest, but the forest is so vast that I don't know what part this wise sage's holy hermitage is in. With your blessing, sir, I should like to go with my younger brother and Sītā to pay my respects to the sage Agastya. In my heart I long to be able to attend in person on him, the best of sages.'

12.1–8 'Rāma, I'm so very pleased, Lakṣmaṇa, I'm overjoyed', said Agastya, 'that you and Sītā have come to visit me. You are a prey to weariness and exhaustion after your tiring journey. Janaka's daughter Maithilī is clearly wilting, for she is very delicate and a stranger to hardships; it's her affection for her husband that has compelled her to come to the forest with its innumerable privations. Rāma, do make sure that Sītā enjoys her stay here, for she's done something very difficult in following you to the forest. Pride of the Raghus, since the world began it's been the nature of women to be loyal in easy circumstances but to desert when the going gets rough. Women are by nature capricious as lightning, sharp-tongued as swords, fast as Garuḍa and the wind. This wife of yours, though, is free from those faults: she is as praiseworthy and exemplary as the goddess Arundhatī. Victorious Rāma, you will be an ornament to this place while you stay here with Saumitri and this Vaidehī.'

The Rāghava acknowledged his words with a respectful gesture and courteously replied to the resplendent sage, 'Fortunate am I and favoured, for a pre-eminent sage, a granter of boons, to be delighted with me, my brother and my wife for our merits. Only point out to me some well-watered, thickly wooded spot where I can erect a hermitage to live in ease and comfort.' 12.9–11

At Rāma's words the excellent, righteous sage thought for a moment, then wisely gave this wise reply: 'Two *yojanas* from here, sir, is Pañcavaṭī, a charming, renowned spot, well provided with roots, fruit and water, the haunt of many animals. If you go there with Saumitri, erect a hermitage and enjoy yourself, you can keep your father's command to the letter. For your whole history, spotless man, has been revealed to me by the power of my austerity and my affection for Daśaratha. Your desire, discerned by me through my austerity, is close to my heart, and I have given my word that you shall live here with me in the forest of austerities. That is why I advise you to go to Pañcavaṭī, for it's a pleasant part of the forest which Maithilī will enjoy. Rāghava, this estimable place is not too far away, near the Godāvarī; Maithilī will enjoy it. It is well supplied with roots and fruit, mighty man, and teeming with flocks of all sorts of birds; it's remote, it's holy and it's attractive. Your lordship has your wife with you: you will be able to guard her if you live there, Rāma, and protect the ascetics too. *Madhūka* trees mark out that forest, heroic prince; to the north of it you will come to a fig tree, then, if you climb the bare flank of the neighbouring mountain, you will see the perpetual blossoms of the grove known as Pañcavaṭī.' 12.12–22

Rāma and Saumitri thanked the honest sage Agastya for his advice, and begged his leave to depart, which was granted. They prostrated themselves at his feet, and left the hermitage for Pañcavaṭī with Sītā. 12.23–4

When they reached Pañcavaṭī, thronged with deer and various wild animals, Rāma said to his glorious brother Lakṣmaṇa, 'We've arrived at the place the great sage told us about, the flowering forests of Pañcavaṭī, my dear brother. Have a good 14.1–5 look all over the forest. You know what you're about: what site shall we decide on for a hermitage, that Vaidehī can enjoy, and you and I as well, Lakṣmaṇa? A suitable place would be close to a water supply; it should be where the forest's attractive – and the water's attractive too – with fuel, flowers, *kuśa* grass and water nearby.'

14.6–7 At Rāma's words, Lakṣmaṇa respectfully replied to Kākutstha, while Sītā looked on, 'Kākutstha, I should defer to you even if you lived for a hundred years, so it's for you to command me in this beautiful place.'

14.8–19 The radiant prince was delighted with Lakṣmaṇa's words and grasped his hand. Rāma chose a place provided with all they needed, went up to the beautiful hermitage-site, clasped Saumitri's hands in his and said to him, 'Here's a level area, charming and shaded by flowering trees; dear brother, do build us a suitable hermitage here. Not far away we can see that lovely lotus pool – it's adorned with lotuses, with sweetly scented, sunlike lotuses. There's the lovely Godāvarī, as the devout sage Agastya described it, shaded by flowering trees, filled with wildfowl, adorned with *cakora* birds and teeming with herds of deer – they're quite close, not too far off. We can see fine mountains, brother dear, resounding to the calls of peacocks. They're very high, criss-crossed with valleys, and covered with blossoming trees; in some places they're flecked with outcrops of gold, silver and copper, so that they glint like boldly painted elephants! Here it's holy, here it's pure and abounding with wildlife; Saumitri, this is where we'll live.'

14.20–27 At Rāma's words, Lakṣmaṇa, that mighty slayer of hostile heroes, quickly built his brother a hermitage. The hut was spacious and made of leaves bonded with mud on to firm uprights, with rafters of long bamboos, and it was skilfully decorated. The handsome Lakṣmaṇa then went to the river Godāvarī, bathed, picked some lotuses and came back with some fruit. He made an offering of flowers and duly pronounced a blessing, then showed the completed hermitage to Rāma. The Rāghava looked over the shady hermitage with Sītā and was highly delighted by the leaf-hut. In his delight he threw his arms around Lakṣmaṇa and spoke with heartfelt affection.

'Well done, mighty brother! What you have achieved deserves the hug I've given you. My righteous father lives on in you, Lakṣmaṇa, his thoughtful, grateful, right-minded son.'

With these words to Lakṣmaṇa, the fortune-conferring 14.28–9
Rāghava settled into that place of abundant fruit, at ease and master of himself, and for some time the righteous man lived there attended by Sītā and Lakṣmaṇa like an immortal in heaven.

One day, when they had bathed, Rama, Sita and Saumitri 16.1–11
returned from the banks of the Godāvarī to their own hermitage. On their arrival at the hermitage the Rāghava performed the morning rite and entered the hut with Lakṣmaṇa. Seated inside the hut with Sītā, mighty Rāma was resplendent as the Moon with Citrā as he and his brother Lakṣmaṇa told stories. As Rāma sat there, engrossed in the storytelling, a certain *rākṣasī* happened to come to that spot; she was sister to the *rākṣasa* Daśagrīva, Śūrpaṇakhā by name. As she passed she saw Rāma sitting there like one of the Thirty Gods: with his lion-chest, his powerful arms and his lotus-petal eyes, tender by nature, noble in character, he was every inch a king. Rāma was dark as a blue lotus, he rivalled Kandarpa in splendour, he was the equal of Indra, and the sight infatuated the *rākṣasī*. Pot-bellied was she while he was slim-waisted, her eyes were hideous while his were shapely, her hair copper-coloured but his beautiful, she was misshapen and he well proportioned, her voice was harsh and his melodious, she was a vicious crone while he was a gentle youth, her words were devious but his were frank, she was wicked but he was proper, she was repulsive and he attractive: yet that ugly *rākṣasī* was seized by lust and spoke to the handsome Rāma: 'What are you doing in this *rākṣasa*-infested place, wearing your hair matted like the ascetics do, but carrying a bow and arrows, your wife at your side?'

In answer to the *rākṣasī* Śūrpaṇakhā, the high-principled 16.12–16
conqueror began to tell her everything. 'There was a king called Daśaratha who was equal to the Thirty in valour. I am his eldest son; my name is Rāma, and I am well known to all. This is my devoted younger brother, Lakṣmaṇa, and this is

Vaidehī my wife, the famous Sītā. At the command of my royal father, who was coerced by one of my mothers, I have come to live in the forest to further righteousness and pursue it. Now I should like you to introduce yourself. Please tell me who you are, of what family and why you are here: tell me everything.'

16.17–24 Hearing this the *rākṣasī*, tormented by passion, replied, 'Listen Rāma, and I'll tell you everything. I am a *rākṣasī*, and can assume any form. My name is Śūrpaṇakhā and I roam about in the forest alone, terrorizing everyone. The chief of the *rākṣasas*, Rāvaṇa by name, is a brother of mine; so is mighty Kumbhakarṇa, sunk in perpetual sleep; another, Vibhīṣaṇa, is righteous, and shunned by other *rākṣasas*; and my brothers Khara and Dūṣaṇa are famous for their bravery in battle. Never mind them, Rāma; it's you I have sought out to be my exalted husband; I was smitten by love before ever I saw you. Be my husband for ever! Why bother with Sītā? She's ugly and deformed and not worthy of you. But I'm suited to you – consider me your wife. I'll devour that ugly, unchaste, gaping, pot-bellied mortal woman, and that brother of yours. Then, my beloved, you shall roam the Daṇḍakas with me, and see the mountain-peaks, and all the woods.'

16.25; Hearing this, eloquent Kākutstha prepared a mocking reply
17.1–5 for the wild-eyed *rākṣasī*. Rāma smiled, then spoke to the lovelorn Śūrpaṇakhā in gentle, inviting tones: 'Madam, I am already married: this is my dear wife. A woman like you would find the existence of a rival galling. But my younger brother here is honourable, attractive and handsome, and he's not married; the hero's name is Lakṣmaṇa. He's an attractive young bachelor, eager to find a wife. A man of such character will make you a fitting husband. Enjoy my brother as your husband without a rival, lady with the beauteous eyes and shapely hips, like the sun in its splendour enjoys mount Meru.'

17.6–7 At Rāma's words the infatuated *rākṣasī* abandoned him at once and said to Lakṣmaṇa, 'I cleave to you, a man of such character, as your fair-skinned wife; you shall roam freely with me throughout the Daṇḍakas.'

17.8–12 Hearing the *rākṣasī's* words, Sumitrā's smooth-tongued son Lakṣmaṇa smiled and replied in the same vein to Śūrpaṇakhā:

'But I am subservient to my noble brother. Why should you, fair as the lotus, want to become the wife – the slave – of a slave? Become this wealthy nobleman's junior wife. Then you can rejoice in your success, with your beauteous eyes and flawless complexion, for he'll desert that ugly, unchaste, gaping, pot-bellied hag of a wife so he can possess you. What man of discrimination would abandon your beautiful figure, your fair complexion and shapely hips, in favour of mortal women?'

The gaping, pot-bellied *rakṣasī* did not see the joke and 17.13–16
thought Lakṣmaṇa's words sincere. Crazed with lust, she told Rāma, that invincible warrior, as he sat in the hut with Sītā at his side, 'It's out of regard for this ugly, unchaste, gaping, pot-bellied hag of a wife that you don't value me! I'm going to devour this mortal woman, now, while you watch! Then, with no rival, I shall roam freely with you.'

Her eyes blazed as she spoke, and she pounced in a frenzy 17.17–20
upon her doe-eyed rival, like a great meteor attacking Rohiṇī. Her attack was like the noose of Death, but wrathful Rāma overpowered her with great strength, and told Lakṣmaṇa, 'Good Saumitri, never try joking with cruel, uncivilized people. Just look at Vaidehī, she's half dead! You'd better mutilate this ugly, unchaste, lascivious, big-bellied *rākṣasī*, you tiger of a man.'

At these words the mighty Lakṣmaṇa angrily drew his sword 17.21–4
and cut off her ears and nose[2] while Rāma watched. Shorn of her ears and nose, the savage Śūrpaṇakhā dashed back through the forest, shrieking raucously. Spattered with blood, the misshapen, savage *rākṣasī* was roaring and bellowing like a monsoon cloud; the fierce-faced *rākṣasī* scattered gore on all sides as she ran into the great forest, roaring and clutching at herself.

The *rākṣasa* Khara flew into a rage when he saw his sister 18.1–9
lying there, blood-spattered and disfigured. 'Who has brought you to this deathly state?' he demanded, 'You, so full of strength and courage, who wander about freely and change your shape at will? What god, *gandharva*, ghost or noble sage has had the strength to mutilate you? There's no one that I know of in the world capable of crossing me, apart from great Indra, the Thousand-eyed Punisher of Pāka. I'll seek out his

life-breath this very day with mortal arrows, like a *sārasa* separating out milk mixed in water to drink.[3] Whose foaming red gore shall the earth drink up when I have slain him in battle, my arrow piercing his vitals? Birds shall flock to the battlefield to tear the flesh from his corpse and devour it in delight – but from whose body? Not gods nor *gandharvas*, not *piśācas* nor *rākṣasas* will be able to save that wretch when I have laid him low in warfare. When you've had time to collect your wits, you must tell me what villain has overpowered you in the forest.'

18.10–16 The rage in her brother's words prompted Śūrpaṇakhā to declare through her tears, 'There were two of them. They were young and handsome, they were dainty, they were powerful, their eyes were like huge lotuses, and they were dressed in bark cloth and black-antelope hides; each could rival the king of the *gandharvas*, each was every inch a king. I can't work out whether they were gods or mortals. And I could see a young woman between them – she was handsome and slender waisted, with an array of ornaments. It's that slag's fault – that pair's companion – that I've been brought to this state, as if I were wanton and had no one to protect me. When that pair and their whore have been killed in combat, I want to drink their foaming blood. To drink her blood and theirs on the battlefield, that's my greatest wish, and I'm looking to you, brother dear, to fulfil it.'

18.17–20 In response, the furious Khara gave orders to fourteen mighty, Deathlike *rākṣasas*. 'Two men, carrying weapons but dressed in bark cloth and black-antelope hides, have brought a trollop into the wild Daṇḍaka Forest. Kill them and that slut, then come back and my sister will drink their blood. Go quickly, *rākṣasas*, and destroy that pair by your own prowess; you'll fulfil my sister's dearest desire.'

18.21; With these orders the fourteen *rākṣasas* set off with her, like
19.1–5 clouds driven by the wind. When they reached the Rāghava's hermitage, savage Śūrpaṇakhā showed the *rākṣasas* the two brothers and Sītā. They could see mighty Rāma sitting in the hut alongside Sītā Vaidehī and Lakṣmaṇa. The Rāghava saw them arrive with the *rākṣasī*, and said to his glorious brother

Lakṣmaṇa, 'Stay here a moment, Saumitri, close to Sītā; I'll kill those creatures approaching along the path with her.' Lakṣmaṇa respectfully assented to what sagacious Rāma had said.

The righteous Rāghava strung his great gold-adorned bow and said to the *rākṣasas*, 'We are two sons of Daśaratha, the brothers Rāma and Lakṣmaṇa. We have come with Sītā to the Daṇḍaka wilderness, to live as restrained and dutiful ascetics on fruit and roots in Daṇḍaka Forest. Why are you hostile to us? At the request of the sages I have taken up bow and arrows in the forest to kill you wicked, evil-minded creatures. Be content to halt there and don't creep forward. If you value your lives, you night-walkers, turn back.' 19.6–10

The fourteen spear-wielding *rākṣasas*, red-eyed and raucous, savage slaughterers of brāhmans, replied in rage to the words of Rāma, his voice well modulated, his eyes fringed with red, exulting in his unheard-of valour. 'We shall vent on you the anger of our most noble master, Khara: this day we shall snatch from you your life's breath in battle. How will you be able to stand your ground in combat, one against our many, let alone put up a fight? In our hands, these clubs, spears and javelins will put an end to you, to your valour, and to that bow you are holding.' 19.11–15

So saying, the fourteen enraged *rākṣasas* rushed at Rāma, weapons and swords uplifted. They hurled their spears at the invincible Rāghava, but Kākutstha split all fourteen spears with as many gold-adorned arrows. Next, resplendent in his great rage, the Rāghava seized fourteen radiant, whetted bolts, grasped his bow, took aim at the *rākṣasas* and discharged the arrows like Indra Śatakratu does the thunderbolt. Gold-notched, well-feathered,[4] blazing and adorned with gold, they rivalled in splendour great meteors in the sky. Their impetus drove them through the *rākṣasas*' breasts till they emerged bloodstained and sank into the ground with a sound like a thunderbolt. Pierced to their hearts, the *rākṣasas* fell to the ground like trees torn up by the roots, gory, disfigured, lifeless. 19.16–22

Seeing them fallen on the ground, the *rākṣasī* was crazed 19.23–4;
with anger and terror. Again Śūrpaṇakhā uttered a fearful roar, 20.1–5

shrieked wildly and hurried back to Khara. Once more she fell before him in distress, her blood partly congealed like resin on a creeper. Seeing Śūrpaṇakhā returned after this reverse, and again prostrate before him, Khara declared in a clear, angry voice, 'I've sent those heroic blood-guzzling *rākṣasas* about your affair – what are you moaning about now? They are ever devoted, loyal and attached to me, bent on killing, not being killed; they wouldn't fail to do my will. I want to know why you're back, writhing on the ground like a snake, and clamouring for protection. How can you bewail like someone who hasn't got a protector while I'm here to protect you? Get up, get up; don't be afraid, and give over despairing.'

20.6–18 Khara's words soothed the dread *rākṣasī*. She brushed a tear from her eye and told her brother, 'You did send those fourteen savage *rākṣasa* heroes to kill the Rāghava and Lakṣmaṇa for me; their spirits were up and they were armed with spears and javelins, but Rāma has pierced their vitals with his arrows and killed them all in battle. Seeing Rāma's great deed and those mighty warriors laid low in an instant has overwhelmed me with terror. I've come back to you for refuge, night-walker, fearful, trembling, downcast, and seeing perils on all sides. I'm sunk in a vast sea of sorrow inhabited by crocodiles of despair and wreathed with waves of horror – why won't you rescue me from it? Those flesh-eating *rākṣasas* who followed where I led have been butchered by Rāma's sharp arrows. If you've any compassion for me or for those *rākṣasas*, night-walker, if you've any power or might against Rāma, eradicate this thorn of the *rākṣasas* living in Daṇḍaka Forest. If you won't kill my enemy Rāma this very day, I'll breathe my last without hesitation before your eyes. I can't imagine you being able to stand your ground in a battle with Rāma and his bow. You'll not be the hero you think yourself, the valour you parade will be false, if you can't kill those two humans, Rāma and Lakṣmaṇa. Clear out of Janasthāna quickly, you and your companions. What's the use of your staying here, you faint-hearted coward? You'll quickly be overcome by Rāma's valour; you'll be annihilated. This is Rāma, Daśaratha's dauntless son! And the one who disfigured me is his indomitable brother!'

Śūrpaṇakhā's rant made the harsh hero Khara speak even more harshly before the assembled *rākṣasas*. 'Your contempt arouses unparalleled anger in me, irresistible as the salt sea surge,' he brayed. 'My valour sets no store by this short-lived mortal: today Rāma will draw his last breath, slain for his own crimes. Stop sobbing! Don't get so worked up! I'm the one to dispatch Rāma and his brother to Yama's realm. Today, my *rākṣasī*, you shall drink Rāma's warm, red blood as he lies at his last gasp on the ground, a victim of my axe.' Delighted to hear these words fall from Khara's lips, the imbecile again praised her brother as the best of *rākṣasas*. 21.1–6

Scolded by her one minute and praised the next, Khara then said to his general, Dūṣaṇa by name, 'Marshal fourteen thousand reckless *rākṣasas* loyal to me, general. They must be steadfast in battle, the colour of black clouds, savage and vicious; they must delight in gratuitous violence; they must be zealously ferocious, proud as tigers, gaping-jawed and powerful; they must stop at nothing. Get my chariot ready quickly, with my bows and glittering arrows, and my swords; and sharpen every spear. I have decided to lead the noble Paulastyas into battle myself to slay that villain Rāma by my prowess.' 21.7–12

Even as he was speaking, Dūṣaṇa brought for his inspection a great sun-coloured chariot harnessed with fine greys. It looked like mount Meru's peak, ornamented with refined gold, golden-wheeled, spacious, with a pole made of beryl; on all sides appeared fish, flowers, trees, mountains, golden suns and moons, and auspicious stars and flocks of birds; it was decked with his standard and swords, adorned with bells and harnessed with fine horses. Into that chariot stepped vengeful Khara. 21.13–16

Seeing him in the chariot, the ruthless *rākṣasas* formed up round him and the mighty Dūṣaṇa. From his stance on the chariot, Khara surveyed the *rākṣasa* host, the archers with their terrible shields, weapons and standards, and gave the order, 'March!' The *rākṣasa* army with their terrible shields, weapons and standards marched rapidly out from Janasthāna, raising raucous roars. In their hands they grasped dreadful-looking weapons, mallets, javelins, pikes, keen axes, swords, discuses, 21.17–22 glittering lances, spears, terrible maces, enormous bows, clubs, scimitars, pestles, bolts. Loyal to Khara, fourteen thousand ferocious *rākṣasas* marched out from Janasthāna.

21.23–5; 22.1–17 Seeing the onrush of those ruthless *rākṣasas*, Khara moved his chariot into the lead; obedient to Khara's command, the charioteer whipped up the greys adorned with gold, and the chariot of triumphant Khara raced along, till every direction rang with the din. As they marched on, a huge turbulent cloud, tawny as a donkey, showered a rain of blood down upon that savage force, an evil portent. The swift horses drawing the chariot stumbled for no reason on a level, flower-strewn part of the highway. A dark, blood-bordered halo, like a ring of fire, began to blot out the sun. Then a hideous, huge-bodied vulture came and perched on the upraised, gold-shafted standard, clawing at it. The raucous, flesh-eating wildlife that ranged Janasthāna region each uttered their discordant calls. Inauspicious for the fiends, fierce jackals hurled fearful howls into the blazing sky. The heavens were obscured by terrible thunderclouds like riven mountains, raining blood. Deep gloom descended, hair-raising and horrific, till nothing could be seen clearly in any direction. An untimely twilight glowed like wet blood and savage beasts and birds cried out in Khara's path. Fierce-faced jackals, ever bringers of doom in war, howled before the force, their muzzles belching flame. Clouds like clubs surrounded the sun; the great planet Rāhu eclipsed the sun, though it was not the nodal time. The wind blew strongly, the sun lost its lustre and stars flickered like fireflies though it was not night. Pools, the haunt of fish and birds, had their lotuses shrivelled; trees were stripped of flowers and fruit on the instant; clouds of tawny dust were thrown up without any wind; mynahs started shrieking '*vīcīkūcī*'. Crashing meteors hurtled frighteningly down upon the earth, setting its mountains, forests and woods reeling; standing bellowing in his chariot, Khara felt his left arm throb. Khara understood. His voice dried up, his eyes filled with tears as he watched it all, his forehead began to ache; fool that he was, he did not turn back.

22.18–24 Khara laughed at the horrendous portents he saw occurring, and addressed all the *rākṣasas*: 'My courage is such that I care as little about the fearsome portents that are occurring as a strong man does about weaklings. I could even tumble the stars out of heaven with my sharp arrows; my anger can make Death subject to the rule of dying. That I should turn back before my sharp arrows have slain this Rāghava who exults in his might, and his brother Lakṣmaṇa too! *That* I could not endure. My sister's desire to drink their blood shall be satisfied; disaster awaits Rama and Lakṣmaṇa. Never before have I been defeated in war. I declare this before you all without falsehood. When my anger is up I could kill the king of the gods in battle, even if he were riding Airāvata in rut and wielding his thunderbolt, so why not this pair of mere mortals?'

The *rākṣasa's* huge army were immeasurably delighted to 22.25–33
hear this bombast, for they were snared in Death's noose. Khara's chariot dashed him along at the head of his army, prompting the *rākṣasas* to dash along all the more recklessly. Twelve great heroes surrounded Khara as he led the charge: Śyenagāmin, Pṛthugrīva, Yajñaśatru, Vihaṃgama, Durjaya, Karavīrākṣa, Paruṣa, Kālakārmuka, Meghamālin, Mahāmālin, Sarpāsya and Rudhirāśana, while four generals, Mahākapāla, Sthūlākṣa, Pramāthin and Triśiras, brought up the rear with Dūṣaṇa.

As audacious Khara reached the hermitage, Rāma and his 23.1–12
brother noticed the portents. At the sight of those fearful, hair-raising portents that bode disaster for men he told Lakṣmaṇa, 'Look at these doom-laden portents, mighty brother, welling up all around for the ruin of *rākṣasas*. There are ragged clouds, raucous and donkey-grey, careering about the sky, showering blood. All my smoking arrows are twitching, Lakṣmaṇa, and my gilded bows too, rejoicing at the prospect of war. To judge by the cries of the birds ranging the forest, some danger, some hazard to our lives, has arisen. I'm sure there's going to be an almighty battle; the throbbing in my arm proclaims it repeatedly. Victory is close for us, and defeat for our enemy, my hero; I can see it in your steady, shining face. Slaughter awaits anyone who goes to war without the light of battle in his eyes, Lakṣmaṇa. Nevertheless, a

prudent man hoping for success but fearing misfortune should take precautions for the future, so keep your bow and arrows to hand and take Vaidehī to find refuge in an inaccessible mountain cave screened by trees. You're not to disobey this command; swear by my feet,* then go without delay, my boy.'

23.13–16 At Rāma's words, Lakṣmaṇa picked up his bow and arrows and took refuge with Sītā in an inaccessible cave. Once Lakṣmaṇa and Sītā were inside the cave, Rāma exclaimed, 'Well now, I'm ready,' and donned his coat of mail. Adorned with that fiery coat of mail, Rāma blazed out in the darkness like a smokeless fire; as he took up a heroic stance there, grasping his great bow and seizing his arrows, he filled all regions with the sound of his bowstring.

23.19–27 Then an army of fiends, growling and terrible with their armour, weapons and standards, broke cover on all sides, roaring like lions, bellowing at one another, twanging their bows, yelling and blaring and beating their drums till the hullabaloo filled the forest, frightening the beasts of prey living there into stampeding to a quieter spot without a backward glance. Armed to the teeth, the host surged forward, creeping up on Rāma like the swelling sea. The skilful warrior Rāma cast his eye all around and observed that Khara's army was eager and ready for battle. Drawing arrows from his quiver, he bent his dread bow and summoned up intense anger for the slaughter of all *rākṣasas*, anger which made him as hard to look at as the blazing Doomsday Fire. Seeing him cloaked in splendour, the forest deities trembled, as in his anger Rāma looked like the frenzied Śiva about to destroy Dakṣa's sacrifice.

24.1–9 As Khara approached the hermitage with his company, he saw Rāma the warrior angrily grasping his bow. At the sight he flourished his ready-strung, harsh-sounding bow and urged his charioteer on towards Rāma. Obedient to his order to urge on the chariot, the charioteer whipped up the horses towards where mighty Rāma stood alone, brandishing his bow. Seeing him attack, the night-walkers all closed ranks in escort round him, bellowing mightily, till Khara, riding his chariot amid the fiends, looked like Lohitāṅga risen amid the stars. Then all the furious night-walkers rained their many weapons down on the invincible Rāma with his dread bow – iron hammers, pikes, darts, swords and axes – as the raging *rākṣasas* joined battle with Rāma. The *rākṣasa* troops swooped on Kākutstha Rāma with the force and din of thunderclouds in their eagerness to kill him in battle, showering Rāma with arrows like great clouds raining in torrents on the king of mountains.

Encircled by these fierce troops of *rākṣasas*, the Rāghava looked like the Great God amid his troops of attendants on festal days. With his arrows the Rāghava blocked all the weapons loosed on him by the fiends, like the sea absorbing the inflow of rivers. With his limbs pierced by these terrible weapons, Rāma still trembled no more than a great mountain at a host of blazing lightning bolts. Rāma was wounded in every limb and smeared with blood, so that the Rāghava now looked like the sun obscured by sunset clouds. Gods and *gandharvas*, *siddhas* and matchless sages then despaired at the sight of one man encircled by many thousands. 24.10–14

Then raging Rāma arced his bow and fired off sharp arrows by the hundred and thousand. Unwavering arrows, heron-feathered, hard to avoid, hard to suffer, like the noose of Death in battle, Rāma loosed them playfully. Playfully loosed by Rāma against the enemy army, the arrows snatched the life-breath from the *rākṣasas* like nooses tied by Time. Flying through the air and tearing through the *rākṣasas'* bodies, those arrows bathed in blood till they shone with the splendour of blazing fires. Countless the arrows that flew from Rāma's bent bow, savagely snatching the life-breath from the *rākṣasas*: bows, crests of standards, armour, heads, arms complete with hands and ornaments, thighs like elephants' trunks, by the hundred and by the thousand the arrows sliced them off for Rāma in his battle. 24.15–20

The night-walkers raised a terrible howl of torment as the supple shafts, spiked and sharp-pointed, tore into them. With whetted arrows piercing their vitals, that tormented army was no more comforted by Rāma than a dry forest is by fire. Some of the night-walker heroes, terrible in their might, frenziedly hurled pikes, swords and axes at Rāma, but the mighty-armed Rāghava warded off their weapons with his arrows, to sever 24.21–8; 25.22–3 their necks and take away their lives in battle. Tormented by the arrows, the remaining night-walkers rushed in their dismay to Khara for protection, but Dūṣaṇa rallied and reassured them all, then rushed furiously at Kākutstha, like Death at Rudra. Sheltering behind Dūṣaṇa they were delivered from their dread; all turned back and rushed at Rāma wielding *sāl* trees, palmyras and rocks. Again there began a prodigious, hair-raising battle, tumultuous and ferocious, between Rāma and those *rākṣasas*, until the fourteen thousand ruthless *rākṣasas* were all slain by a single human foot soldier, Rāma. Out of that whole army there remained only the warrior Khara and the *rākṣasa* Triśiras – and Rāma, exterminator of enemies.

26.1–5 Khara was setting out against Rāma, but the *rākṣasa* general, Triśiras by name, came forward and said, 'It's brave of you, but give up this recklessness! Deploy me, and you'll see mighty-armed Rāma laid low in battle. It's the duty of all *rākṣasas* to slaughter Rāma, and I swear to you in truth, my hand on my weapon, that I will slaughter him. Either I bring about his death in battle, or he mine in the struggle. Set aside your battle-zeal and be a spectator for a moment. Either you'll go back to Janasthāna rejoicing at Rāma's fall, or if I fall you can renew hostilities with Rāma.'

26.6–12 Triśiras gratified Khara with his readiness to die; permission to go and fight being granted, he ventured out against the Rāghava. Triśiras was like a three-peaked mountain as he rushed his shining horse-drawn chariot into battle with Rāma, he was like a great cloud pouring out torrents of arrows and thundering with the noise of a dampened kettledrum. The Rāghava noted his approach, and prepared his bow to receive the *rākṣasa* Triśiras, flourishing his sharp arrows. Then began a tumultuous great conflict between Rāma and Triśiras, like that between a lion and an elephant, both were so immensely strong. Rāma was struck on the forehead by three of Triśiras' arrows; indignant and angry, he furiously declared, 'So, this valiant *rākṣasa* hero is so strong that his arrows feel like flowers as they strike my forehead; now it's your turn to receive arrows shot from my bowstring.'

26.13–20 With these furious words he angrily hurled at Triśiras' breast fourteen arrows, venomous as snakes. In his glory he felled the four swift steeds with four close-jointed arrows; with eight arrows he felled the charioteer on the driving-box; and with one arrow Rāma cut down the upraised standard. As the night-walker leapt from his wrecked chariot, Rāma pierced him to the heart with arrows, and he lost consciousness. In his rage that man of boundless resource lopped off the *rākṣasa's* three heads with three sharp, speedy arrows. The night-walker was agonized by Rāma's arrows; vomiting blood, he fell to the ground, his heads falling after him. Then those *rākṣasas* surrounding Khara, defeated when the rest were killed, remained no longer but fled like deer frightened by a tiger. Seeing them flee, Khara turned in fury and rushed at Rāma himself, like Rāhu at the Moon.

Seeing Dūṣaṇa and Triśiras slain in combat, Khara too was 27.1–16
filled with dread at the sight of Rāma's prowess. He saw that Rāma, single-handed, had slain the invincible, mighty *rākṣasa* army, and even Dūṣaṇa and Triśiras: he saw his troop all but exterminated, yet the demented *rākṣasa* Khara attacked Rāma, as Namuci did Indra Vāsava. Khara drew back his powerful bow and launched bloodthirsty bolts at Rāma, venomous as angry snakes. Twanging his bowstring repeatedly and displaying his weaponry with skill, the chariot-borne Khara carved out a path with his arrows. Rāma, the great chariot-warrior with the huge bow, saw him and filled every direction with arrows, invincible arrows like sparkling fires, making the sky impenetrable, as if he were Parjanya with his rain. Everywhere was a press of arrows, the surrounding space was crammed with the arrows Khara and Rāma were shooting, the sun was blotted out, invisible through the curtain of arrows as they fought together in their eagerness to kill each other. Rāma was struck in the battle by supple shafts, spiked and sharp-pointed, like an elephant struck by goads. All creatures watched the *rākṣasa*, at the ready on his chariot, bow in hand like Death gripping his noose, bold as a lion, pacing like a lion, yet Rāma trembled no more at the sight than a lion at a puny deer. Then Khara hurtled his great sunlike chariot towards Rāma in the fray, like a moth towards a flame. In a display of dexterity he

shot through Rāma's bow and arrow at the handgrip, then furiously seized another seven arrows splendid as Śakra's thunderbolt, and struck him in the fray on his armour; struck by the well-jointed arrows Khara sent, that cuirass fell to the ground from sun-splendid Rāma.

27.17–22 Stung into anger by the arrows in all his limbs, Rāma the Rāghava shone in combat like a blazing, smokeless fire. Then Rāma the foe-crusher strung another great deep-roaring bow to make an end of his enemy, and rushed towards Khara, wielding the fine huge Vaiṣṇava bow a great sage had presented to him. Raging in the fray, Rāma severed Khara's standard with gold-notched, close-jointed arrows, shattering the imposing golden standard and bringing it to the ground like the sun at the command of the gods. Khara was infuriated. He knew the vulnerable points and pierced Rāma's limbs to the quick with four arrows; he was like an elephant pierced by lances.

27.23–8 Rāma was incensed by the many arrows shot from Khara's bow and streaking his limbs with blood. That supreme bowman, that champion archer gripped his bow and defiantly sent off six selected arrows, striking him on the head with one, then on the arms with two, and on the chest with three half-moon-headed arrows. After that, glorious in his anger and eager to kill the *rākṣasa*, he seized thirteen sunlike, whetted bolts, sliced through Khara's yoke with one, his four horses with four and his charioteer's head with a sixth; with three the mighty hero smashed the triple pole, with two the axle, and Khara's bow and arrow with his twelfth arrow; and with the thirteenth thunderbolt of an arrow, Indra's equal, the Rāghava, ripped and tore Khara open with savage mockery.

30.1–3; 31.1–21 Then Śūrpaṇakhā again thundered and roared like a cloud to see the fourteen thousand ruthless *rākṣasas* slain by Rāma alone, and Dūṣaṇa, Khara and Triśiras slaughtered. At the sight of Rāma performing a deed so difficult for others, she fled in extreme terror to Laṅkā, Rāvaṇa's realm. The miserable Śūrpaṇakhā spoke harsh, angry words in the midst of the court to Rāvaṇa, to him who makes the world cry out: 'You're so besotted in the enjoyment of your lusts, you're so self-willed, so unbridled! You don't appreciate the terrible danger that's arisen! It demands your attention! A king addicted to vulgar pleasures, hedonistic and greedy as a funeral fire, arouses no respect in his subjects. A king who puts off shouldering his responsibilities in person is destroyed: himself, kingdom and responsibilities too. A king employing no spies, or unapproachable, or not independent, is widely shunned, like river mud by elephants. Kings who don't safeguard the independence of their realms remain obscure, like mountains growing under the sea. How can you rule in such a haphazard way, employing no spies in your struggle against the self-controlled gods, *gandharvas* and *dānavas*? Kings are no better than commoners, you supreme conqueror, if their spies, treasury and policy are not under their control. It's because kings see everything that's going on a long way off through their spies that rulers are called far-sighted. It's my belief you haven't got any spies. You're surrounding yourself with common companions, so you don't realize your own subjects are being destroyed, and Janasthāna too. Rāma, single-handed, has slain fourteen thousand ruthless *rākṣasas*, and Khara and Dūṣaṇa as well. That tireless Rāma has freed the sages from fear, made the Daṇḍakas safe and violated Janasthāna. But you're so greedy, Rāvaṇa, so besotted, so abject, you don't realize the danger that's arisen in your realm. In bad times no one runs to a king who's irritable, niggardly, besotted, haughty and deceitful. In bad times even his own people will kill a king who's overweening, unapproachable, conceited and wrathful. If he doesn't discharge his obligations or take proper heed of danger he quickly falls from his kingdom in misery, like chaff. Dry sticks can be put to good use, so can clods, so can dust, but rulers ousted from their position are of no use. Even a capable one is useless when he's ousted from his kingdom, like cast-off clothes or a bruised garland. To last for long a king needs to be wary, omniscient, disciplined, grateful, law-abiding. To be honoured by his subjects a king must be awake via the organs of the state even when his own eyes are fast asleep; his pleasure and displeasure must be clear. But you, Rāvaṇa, lack these qualities, you simpleton, and no spies have reported to you the enormous slaughter of *rākṣasas*.'

32.1–3 Then in the midst of the court Rāvaṇa angrily interrupted the angry Śūrpaṇakhā's strident complaint, asking, 'Who is Rāma? What's his courage made of? What does he look like? How strong is he? What's his purpose in venturing into the impenetrable Daṇḍaka Forest? What weapon did Rāma kill the *rākṣasas* with, and Khara in the battle, and Dūṣaṇa, and Triśiras too?'

32.4–11 In answer to the *rākṣasa* lord, the *rākṣasī*, crazed with anger, began a systematic description of Rāma. 'Rāma son of Daśaratha has long arms and broad eyes; he wears bark cloth and black-antelope hides, but he's as handsome as Kandarpa. He draws a gold-bound bow like Śakra's, and hurls blazing bolts venomous as snakes. I couldn't see mighty Rāma as he chose his fierce arrows, or fired them off, or bent his bow in the battle; but I could see that army being mown down by storms of arrows like fine corn mown down by storms of Indra's bolts. Fourteen thousand ruthless *rākṣasas* slaughtered by the sharp arrows of that one foot soldier, and in half a moment more, Khara and Dūṣaṇa too! The sages have been made free from fear, the Daṇḍakas have been made safe. I'm the only one left that managed to escape; noble, learned Rāma baulked at killing a woman.

32.12–23 'He's got a glorious brother, heroic Lakṣmaṇa, who's loyal and devoted to him, and just as brave and accomplished: he's easily roused, an invincible conqueror, bold, intelligent and powerful; he's Rāma's right-hand man, he's ever his second self. Rāma has a splendid broad-eyed wife; he's married to Sītā Vaidehī, and she's got curvaceous hips and a slender waist. Never before on earth have I seen goddess, *gandharvī*, *yakṣī*, *kinnarī* or mortal woman with such a figure. A man embraced by the joyful Sītā as his wife would bask in a better life than Indra Puraṃdara has in all the worlds. She's compliant, a paragon of beauty and unrivalled in shapeliness on earth. She'd be just the wife for you, and you'd be just the husband for her. I'm prepared to bring you this woman with the wide hips, this woman with the full, raised breasts, this woman with the fair face, to be your wife. Gaze on that Vaidehī today, on her face like the full moon, and you'll be smitten by Manmatha's arrows. If desire to possess her as your wife is welling up in you, then take prompt steps toward the conquest. Slaughter this cruel Rāma living in his hermitage, *rākṣasa* lord, and you'll benefit these *rākṣasas* too. When you've killed him and warlike Lakṣmaṇa with your sharp arrows you'll be at liberty to enjoy Sītā to the full, with her protector dead. If my suggestion is agreeable to you, Rāvaṇa, lord of the *rākṣasas*, act on it without delay!'

Hearing Śūrpaṇakhā's hair-raising story the lord of the 33.1–38
rākṣasas decided what to do, dismissed his counsellors and went out. He went in secret to his coach-house and ordered his charioteer to get his chariot ready, then journeyed to the opposite shore of that Lord of Rivers, the Ocean, where, in a holy, solitary, pleasant forest-hinterland he saw a hermitage. There he could see an abstemious *rākṣasa* called Mārīca, clothed in black-antelope hide, with matted hair and wearing bark cloth. Rāvaṇa approached that *rākṣasa*, and after the due courtesies, exercised his powers of persuasion.

'My dear Mārīca, listen to what I'm going to tell you. I'm in 34.1–20
trouble and you're my last hope in my trouble. You know Janasthāna? Where my brother Khara, and brawny Dūṣaṇa, and my sister Śūrpaṇakhā, and the glorious man-eating *rākṣasa* Triśiras and a lot more tried and tested night-walkers, *rākṣasa* warriors, make their homes under my authority in the great forest to hinder the sages from performing their duties? Fourteen thousand ruthless *rākṣasas* there were, tried and tested warriors, loyal to Khara. Well, this mighty force, on the alert in their Janasthāna home, went into battle against Rāma, and this Rāma, with his battle-fury aroused but never a harsh word being spoken, so busied his bow with arrows that the fourteen thousand ferociously stalwart *rākṣasas* were slain by the sharp arrows of that human foot soldier! Khara was killed in battle; Dūṣaṇa fell; Triśiras was killed, and the Daṇḍakas liberated from fear. That Rāma's a disgrace to the *kṣatriyas*, so his angry father banished him and his wife, and it's him that's slain that army. He's not got long to live! This dissolute, brutal, cruel, foolish, greedy, self-indulgent, unprincipled, immoral, sadistic brute, relying solely on his superior nature,

with no provocation, here in the forest, disfiguring a sister of mine! He's cut off her ears and nose! His wife Sītā's fit to be the daughter of a god; I'm going to snatch her away from Janasthāna, and you're going to help me. With you to help me, my hero, with you and my brothers to back me I wouldn't think twice about fighting all the gods together. So do help me, *rākṣasa*, for it lies in your power. There's no one to equal you in bravery, in battle and in spirit. That's why I've come to see you, night-walker; listen while I tell you what you're to do to help me. Turn yourself into a golden deer dappled with drops of silver and wander about at this Rāma's hermitage in front of Sītā. When she sees you in the form of a deer, there's no doubt Sītā will tell her husband and Lakṣmaṇa to go and catch it. Then, while those two are away and the place is empty, I'll make off with Sītā with no one to disturb my pleasure, as Rāhu does with the Moon's radiance. Making off with his wife will weaken Rāma, so I'll easily be able to attack him afterwards, with confidence and a contented heart.'

34.21; Noble Mārīca's mouth dried up when he heard this tale
35.1–7 about Rāma. He was terrified. Mārīca was very astute and when he heard what the *rākṣasa* ruler had to say, he used his eloquence to dissuade the lord of the *rākṣasas*. 'Your majesty, yes-men are ten a penny; one who'll tell you, for your own good, what you don't want to hear is one in a million. You're not aware of Rāma's great heroism and elevated nature, that's obvious – you rule haphazardly and employ no spies. He's like great Indra and Varuṇa put together! May all turn out well, my lord, for all *rākṣasas* on earth; may Rāma not be provoked into ridding the world of *rākṣasas*. May it not be that Janaka's daughter was born to put an end to your life, and may no great disaster occur because of Sītā. Now that you have become lord of Laṅkā, licentious and unbridled as you are, may the city not be destroyed together with you and the *rākṣasas*; for an ill-disposed king of your sort, licentious, dissolute and ill-advised, destroys his own people and realm with himself.

35.8–22 'He's not been cast adrift by his father, and he's not the least unrestrained; he's not greedy, he's not dissolute, and he's not a disgrace to the *kṣatriyas*; he lacks none of the virtues, he's a growing joy to Kausalyā! He's not cruel, he's eager to benefit all. He saw that Kaikeyī had taken advantage of his father's integrity and righteously assented to become a forest-wanderer. To satisfy the wishes of Kaikeyī and of his father Daśaratha he renounced both the kingdom and its delights and went into Daṇḍaka Forest. Rāma is not brutal, sir, he's not ignorant, he's not self-indulgent. It's a lying rumour and you shouldn't repeat it. Rāma is righteousness personified, virtuous and truly brave; he's the king of the whole world, like Indra Vāsava is of the gods. How do you expect to lay violent hands on his Vaidehī? She's guarded by her own glory, brilliant as the sun. The Rāma-flame flares up quickly: it's irresistible, it's fuelled by battle-bows and swords, its blazing maw is agape with his bow, its rays are arrows – arrows! Keep out of it! That hero will put up with nothing! The bows and arrows he bears can destroy whole armies of enemies! Don't abandon your kingdom, your happiness, your own dear life, sir; don't go too far and challenge Death in the form of Rāma. The lord of Janaka's daughter is boundless in his glory. She has entrusted herself in the forest to Rāma's bow, and you're not capable of carrying her off. Slender-waisted Sītā his wife is dearer to him than life, and she's as constant in her devotion to him as flame is to a burning fire. What's the point of executing this vain plan of yours, king of the *rākṣasas*? If he sees you in battle, your life's over; life, happiness and kingdom are all too easily lost. Consult all your most virtuous ministers, chiefly Vibhīṣaṇa, before reaching your decision; consider its strengths and weaknesses, its defects and advantages; work out realistically your own strength and the Rāghava's, and decide where your advantage lies before doing what's best.

'At one time I too used to roam the earth in my boldness. I 36.1–12
was like a mountain. I had the strength of a thousand elephants. Like black clouds I spread terror through the world, wearing my earrings of refined gold and my diadem; armed with my mace, I wandered through Daṇḍaka Forest, feasting on the flesh of sages. The righteous sage Viśvāmitra was so terrified of me that he went in person to King Daśaratha to ask, "Let steadfast Rāma here protect me at the nodal time from Mārīca,

your Majesty, for I'm overwhelmed by terrible fear." Righteous King Daśaratha then replied to the request of the distinguished sage Viśvāmitra: "The Rāghava is a child! He's twelve years old, and he's untrained in weaponry, but I'll take my army and I'll kill your enemy at your request, excellent sage." At these words the sage replied to the king, "Against this *rākṣasa* no other power on earth is adequate except Rāma. Child though he is, he is glorious and capable of punishing him. Give me Rāma, and I will go. My blessing on you, destroyer of foes." At these words Viśvāmitra the sage was given the prince; he went to his own hermitage in delight, and consecrated himself for his sacrifice in Daṇḍaka Forest. Then Rāma stood guard over him, flexing his decorated bow. Rāma was a handsome, swarthy, beardless boy with fine eyes, dressed in nothing but one garment; bow in hand, tonsured, garlanded with gold and lighting up Daṇḍaka Forest with his own blazing glory, he was like the newly risen infant moon.

36.13–19 'Then, wearing my earrings of refined gold, like a thundercloud in my arrogance, relying on the power of a boon I'd been granted, I approached that hermitage. He saw me as I burst in with weapon upraised, but was unruffled by the sight and strung his bow. In my delusion I despised the Rāghava as a mere boy, and rushed recklessly at that altar of Viśvāmitra's. It was then he let fly an arrow, a sharp foe-crusher, that struck me and hurled me a hundred *yojanas* into the sea. I was battered into unconsciousness by the force of Rāma's arrow as it flung me along and plunged me into the ocean depths. When at last I recovered consciousness, sir, I made my way towards the city of Laṅkā. That's how I escaped, while my companions were cut down by tireless Rāma, a child untrained in weaponry. If you make war on Rāma despite my warnings, you'll swiftly meet with a terrible disaster; you'll be destroyed.

37.1–14 'That's how I managed to escape my battle with him, but now listen to what happened next. Unabashed at my treatment, I entered the Daṇḍaka wood accompanied by two *rākṣasas* in the form of deer. I roamed about in Daṇḍaka Forest as a great deer with blazing tongue, huge body and sharp horns, a mighty meat-eater. I was ferocious beyond measure, Rāvaṇa, and I wandered about harassing the ascetics at their fire-offerings, their bathing places and their sacred trees. I slaughtered the ascetics as they performed their duties in Daṇḍaka Forest; I drank their blood and devoured their flesh, then, drunk with blood, I roamed through the Daṇḍaka wood, brutally eating sages' flesh and terrorizing the forest-dwellers. While I was wandering in Daṇḍaka Forest in defiance of the right, I came across Rāma; he was now an ascetic resorting to right, with distinguished Vaidehī and the great warrior Lakṣmaṇa, an abstemious ascetic beneficent to all. I despised mighty Rāma now he had come to the forest – thinking him no more than an ascetic – so remembering our earlier hostility I rushed upon him in my rage in my guise of a sharp-horned deer, recklessly eager to kill him, as I remembered that fight. He drew back his bow with might and let fly three arrows, sharp foe-crushers, swift as birds or the wind. These terrible thunderbolts of arrows, bloodthirsty and close-jointed, flew all three together. Knowing Rāma's power and the fear I had felt before, I slyly dodged and was saved, but both *rākṣasas* were killed. Rāma's arrow missed me, and I managed to save my life.

'That's why I now wander about here as a disciplined, stead- 37.14–19
fast ascetic. For in tree after tree I see Rāma, clothed in bark and black-antelope hides, grasping his bow, like Death, noose in hand. In my fear, Rāvaṇa, I can even see thousands of Rāmas. This whole forest seems to me to have turned into Rāma. I can see Rāma in any deserted spot, king of the *rākṣasas*. I see Rāma coming at me in my dreams and start up out of my wits. Names beginning with r, Rāvaṇa, from rubies to rickshaws,[5] strike terror in me, I'm so terrified of Rāma. It's my opinion, I who know his might, that war with him is out of the question for you. Fight a battle with Rāma, *rākṣasa*, or don't, but if you want to see me again, tell me no more tales about Rāma.'

Like a suicide refusing medicine, Rāvaṇa refused Mārīca's 38.1–19
advice, apt and fitting though it was. Spurred on by Time, the lord of *rākṣasas* made a harsh, inappropriate reply to Mārīca's salutary, beneficial admonition. 'Indeed, Mārīca, your inept advice will bear no more fruit than seed sown in a desert. Your

speeches can't dissuade me from fighting Rāma. He's dissolute, he's foolish, and above all he's human, for he's abandoned friends, kingdom, mother and father, and come hotfoot to the forest at the word of a common woman. Sītā's dearer than life to the man who killed Khara in battle; I'm going to snatch her in your presence, and that's that. I've made up my mind about it, Mārīca, I've set my heart on it, and all the gods and anti-gods and Indra put together can't deflect me. When I consult you in planning an enterprise, you should give your advice on its defects and advantages, problems and methods. But when consulted by a king, a shrewd counsellor with an eye to his own welfare should reply with respect. Advice given to a monarch should be uncontentious, soft-spoken and cautious, elegant, advantageous and courteously phrased. But a dissenting speech devoid of deference, Mārīca, even if the content is salutary, is unwelcome to a king who deserves deference. In their infinite industry, kings display the five aspects of Agni, Indra, Soma, Yama and Varuṇa: fervour, heroism, gentleness, compulsion and mercy, so rulers deserve honour and respect in every situation. But you don't acknowledge what's right; you've fallen into mere delusion. It's your depravity that makes you receive me with such harsh words. I'm not asking you about the merits and demerits of this scheme, *rākṣasa*, nor about its suitability for me: your lordship will be so good as to help me achieve it. When you've turned yourself into a golden deer dappled with drops of silver and enticed Vaidehī, then you may go where you please. But when Maithilī sees you as a magic golden deer, her wonder will be roused and she'll tell Rāma to catch it quickly. With Kākutstha and Lakṣmaṇa gone off I'll carry away Vaidehī with no trouble, like Thousand-eyed Indra did Śacī. When you've finished your job, go off where you like, *rākṣasa*. I'll give you half my kingdom, honest Mārīca. Off you go, good sir, on the best path for achieving my objective. When I've got hold of Sītā without a fight by deceiving the Rāghava, I'll come back successfully with you to Laṅkā. You are going to do this job, even if I have to force you. No one prospers who stands out against a king.'

39.1–19 Mārīca the night-walker rudely rebutted the imperious commands of the *rākṣasa* overlord: 'What criminal has taught you how to destroy your children, country, companions, and yourself, night-walker? What criminal resents your comfort, your majesty? Who has directed your steps towards the door of Death? It must be that some cowardly enemies are seeking your injury and destruction by a stronger person, night-walker. What low-down, raving adviser has given you this advice? He wants you to bring destruction on yourself, night-walker. Rāvaṇa, your ministers have escaped the execution they certainly deserve for not restraining you by every means from venturing on this wrong path, for a hedonistic king bent on an evil path should at all times be restrained by honest ministers; but you're not being restrained as you require. Night-walker, best of victors, it's by their master's grace that ministers achieve probity, prosperity and pleasure, fame too; but Rāvaṇa, in misfortune all that becomes futile, and their master's faults bring disaster on others. Probity and triumph, excellent conqueror, are rooted in the king; that's why a ruler should be protected in all situations. A kingdom can't be defended, night-walker, by bad temper, nor by petulance and licence, and ministers who advise such conduct are driven with him to destruction, like chariots smashed on uneven ground by feeble drivers. Many are the good men the world over, practised in the discipline of righteousness, who are destroyed along with their fellows through the fault of others. Subjects with an irritable, contentious master to protect them prosper no better, Rāvaṇa, than sheep with a jackal. With you, Rāvaṇa, as their harsh, headstrong, unbridled king, all *rākṣasas* are doomed to destruction. You are on your way to meet this dreadful end, like the Crow with the Palm Tree;[6] what's the point of getting yourself and your army destroyed? That Rāma will kill me, but then before long it's you he'll kill. I shall welcome death from an enemy like this. Consider me slain just by the mere sight of Rāma, and rest assured that you and your family will be slain if you lay hands on Sītā. If you carry off Sītā from the hermitage with my help, then that will be the end of you, me, Laṅkā and the *rākṣasas*.'

*

41.1–5 The shapely lady was picking flowers when she caught sight of him with his golden, silver-adorned flanks; she too shone like burnished gold, and her figure was perfect. She cried out in delight to her husband, and to Lakṣmaṇa standing on guard; in response that pair of tigers of men, Rāma and Lakṣmaṇa, looked all around until they saw the deer. Lakṣmaṇa was suspicious at the sight and said to Rāma, 'It's my belief that deer is the *rākṣasa* Mārīca. Kings taking their pleasure at the chase have been slain by his foul deceptions in the forest, Rāma; he can change his shape at will.'

41.8–20 Sītā's mind was seduced by the masquerade. In her delight she rejected Kākutstha's opinion, smiled sweetly and begged, 'Prince, that delightful deer captivates my heart! Do bring it us for a pet, my hero! Here at our hermitage we have lots of pretty deer wandering about together, and we've got handsome, powerful yaks and *sṛmaras* wandering about too, my hero, and bears, and herds of chital and monkeys, and *kinnaras* as well. But your Majesty, no deer like this incomparable deer has ever been seen before; it's so splendid, so tame, so sparkling! It's flecked with jewelled spots! Its limbs are dappled and variegated! It's gleaming like the moon, and lighting up the whole forest! Oh, how lovely! how graceful! what a beautiful, melodious voice! That marvellous dappled deer wellnigh enslaves my heart. If you manage to catch that deer alive, it will be a source of wonder and astonishment to ornament the inner apartments when we go back to live in your kingdom at the end of our stay in the forest. This divine deer will astonish Prince Bharata and my mothers-in-law, my hero. If you don't manage to catch that supreme deer alive, you tiger of a man, it will make me a glossy pelt; I'd love to sit on that creature's golden skin spread over a *kuśa* grass cushion, if you'll kill it for me. It's thought shockingly improper for women to be so impulsive, but I'm wonder-struck by that creature's beauty!'

41.21–48 The Rāghava was fascinated by that golden-coated beast with its horns of fine gems, its hue like the rising sun and its splendour like the path of the stars, so when he'd heard what Sītā had to say and examined the marvellous deer, the delighted Rāghava said to his brother Lakṣmaṇa, 'Lakṣmaṇa, look how

Vaidehī's yearning for this deer. Its beautiful appearance means that it won't outlive the day. There's no deer to equal it in the Nandana forest nor in the shelter of Caitraratha, Saumitri, so how could there be one on earth? Sleek or ruffled, the glossy layers of hair, dappled with drops of gold, are gleaming on that deer. Look at its tongue, blazing like the tip of a flame, flickering out of its mouth as it pants, like lightning from a cloud! Who is there that wouldn't be bewitched by that incomparable deer with its mouth of sapphire and crystal and its belly of conch and pearl? Whose mind wouldn't be carried away with wonder at the sight of this heavenly bejewelled form, radiant as gold? Lakṣmaṇa, kings take their bows to hunt in the great forest and kill deer for meat as well as sport. Wealth can also, with resolution, be amassed in the great forest; various minerals too – gems, jewels and gold. But in this one place, Lakṣmaṇa, the entire wealth of the world – as much as Śukra's – is overflowing! There's everything you could think of! Practical men, expert in political science, term it "expediency" when an ambitious man pursues his goal without deflection. Slender-waisted Vaidehī shall sit beside me on the magnificent golden skin of that jewel of a deer; it's my belief that neither plantains nor *priyaka* fruit, not saddle cloth nor sheepskin could compare with its feel. This handsome deer and the divine star-ranger – star-deer and earthly deer: both deer are alike divine. You arm yourself, ready to guard Maithilī diligently: that's your job; we must always take good care of her, pride of the Raghus. I'm the one to kill or else capture this deer. While I hurry off to bring the deer, Saumitri . . . oh, Lakṣmaṇa, just look how Vaidehī's yearning for that deer skin! Its matchless coat means that deer shall today be no more! You stay on the alert in the hermitage with Sītā, while I kill the chital with a single arrow; once it's slaughtered, Lakṣmaṇa, I'll take the hide and be straight back.'

With these instructions to his brother, the glorious pride of 42.1–11
the Raghus strapped on his golden-hilted sword, picked up his triple-curved bow – an ornament in itself – and bound on two quivers; then the bold warrior set out. Mārīca noticed him leave, and in terror he vanished and reappeared, deluding the

king into hurrying on, wearing his sword and carrying his bow; he could see the deer ahead of him, radiant of form. Bow in hand he kept glimpsing it as it slipped away just out of bowshot, gradually decoying him away in the great forest. Timorous and bewildered, it seemed to fly along, visible in one part of the forest, invisible in the next, like the disc of the autumn moon surrounded by broken clouds. One moment he could see it clearly, the next moment only glimpse it far away. This appearing and disappearing drew the Rāghava away. Kākutstha grew exasperated at being led on against his will, and paused in his weariness on some grass in the shade; then the deer showed itself among some wild deer close by. Glorious Rāma saw it and resolved to kill it. Setting an arrow to his unyielding bow and drawing it back with might, the mighty man fired upon that deer a blazing missile, Brahmā-made, glowing like a blazing snake.

42.12–16 The supreme arrow struck the deer that was Mārīca with the force of a thunderbolt, piercing him to the heart. The arrow was agonizing. High as a palm tree he leapt, then crashed to the ground, roaring a terrible roar with his dying breath. Recognizing that his time had come, Mārīca abandoned his fictitious body, and cried out as he died, imitating the Rāghava's voice: 'Sītā! Lakṣmaṇa!' Mortally wounded by that matchless arrow, Mārīca gave up the form of a deer and as he expired went back to his own colossal *rākṣasa* form. Slain by that arrow he became again a *rākṣasa* with fangs, adorned with colourful bangles and all sorts of ornaments, and garlanded with gold.

42.17–21 At the sight of the dreadful-looking *rākṣasa* fallen to the ground, Rāma remembered Lakṣmaṇa's warning, and his mind flew to Sītā. 'This was a *rākṣasa*, and he died screaming loudly, "Sītā! Lakṣmaṇa!" How will Sītā react at the sound? What sort of a state will mighty Lakṣmaṇa get into?' Righteous Rāma's hair bristled at the thought. Then was Rāma gripped by acute fear born of despair that the deer he had slain was a *rākṣasa* in disguise, and of hearing that scream; killing another chital and hastily butchering it, the Rāghava set off back towards Janasthāna.

Sītā recognized that cry of anguish from the forest. It sounded like her husband. 'Go and find the Rāghava,' she told Lakṣmaṇa. 'I can never ignore violent screams from a voice in agony – my heart, my whole being won't let me! Your brother's crying out in the forest – you must rescue him! Quick, hurry to your brother. He needs your help. He must have fallen into the power of *rākṣasas*, like a bull among lions!' But he remembered his brother's orders and would not go, despite her entreaties. This angered Janaka's daughter. 'Saumitri,' she told him, 'you're more like your brother's foe than his friend. Not to search for your brother in this situation! You want Rāma dead so you can get me, Lakṣmaṇa. I believe you're pleased at his trouble. You've no affection for your brother. That's why you're staying here so calmly, shutting your eyes to your brilliant brother. For as long as I'm still here, if your master's in trouble, what's to hinder you having your way with me?' Sītā Vaidehī was overwhelmed by sobs and grief as she spoke, fearful as a widowed deer. 43.1–9

'My lady, my beautiful lady,' replied Lakṣmaṇa, 'there's no one among gods and men, among *gandharvas* and birds, among *rākṣasas*, *piśācas* and *kinnaras*, animals too, and ferocious *dānavas*, who could fight a battle against Rāma; he's the equal of Indra Vāsava! None can kill Rāma in battle. You shouldn't say such things. I daren't leave you alone in this forest without the Rāghava. His might is proof against the mighty, even against the three worlds combined, even including their lord and the immortals. Set your heart at rest; stop distressing yourself; your husband will soon come back from killing that outstanding deer. That was clearly not his voice; nor was it any of the gods. It was conjured up by that *rākṣasa*, like the city of the *gandharvas*. Noble Rāma confided you, entrusted you to me, handsome Vaidehī, and I daren't abandon you here. We've earned the enmity of these night-walkers, good madam, by killing Khara and devastating Janasthāna. All sorts of *rākṣasas* shout out in the great forest for the pleasure of making mischief. Dismiss it from your mind, Vaidehī.' 43.10–18

She bridled at Lakṣmaṇa's words and her eyes reddened. Her 43.19–24
retort to the truthful Lakṣmaṇa was harsh. 'Ignoble, cruel man,

your base behaviour is a disgrace to your family! I believe you see me as the object of your pleasure, and that's why you're talking like this. It's no surprise that such evil should occur in half-brothers like you, cruel and ever sly. It's because of me that you alone are trailing after lone Rāma in the forest; either that, or you've been secretly employed by Bharata. I have devoted myself to my husband Rāma, with his dark-blue lotus complexion and his lotus-shaped eyes; so how could I desire a common person? I'll tell you this, Saumitri: before your eyes I'll draw my last breath sooner than live even another moment on earth without Rāma.'

43.25–31 Sītā's harsh words were enough to make his hair stand on end, but Lakṣmaṇa replied calmly, with a respectful gesture towards Sītā. 'I will venture to say no more; your ladyship is like a goddess to me. Improper speech is not unusual among women, Maithilī. It's the natural disposition of females, and it's seen the world over: women are loose, capricious, peevish mischief-makers. Let all the forest-dwellers bear witness how harshly you spoke to me when I told you the truth. Shame on you for suspecting me like that, when I was just obeying my elder brother's order. You'll very soon be the worse for it, you and your womanish, spiteful nature! I will go after Kākutstha. May all go well with you, my beauty, and may the forest deities unite to protect you, my lovely. Terrible are the omens appearing before me: I only hope I shall come back to see you and Rāma together.'

43.32–5; Janaka's sobbing daughter was overwhelmed by her tears,
44.1–2 but made a trenchant reply to Lakṣmaṇa's words: 'Lakṣmaṇa, without Rāma I'll jump into the Godāvarī, or else hang myself, or hurl my body from a precipice, or drink poison, or leap into searing flames, but not even with my foot will I touch a man other than the Rāghava,' she screamed at Lakṣmaṇa in her misery. Weeping bitterly, Sītā beat her breast. The Rāghava's younger brother was enraged at being spoken to so harshly by her. Anxious to find Rāma, he set out without more ado. That was the opportunity Daśagrīva had been waiting for; in the guise of a mendicant he quickly strode up to Vaidehī.

46.2–18 'Fair-skinned lady, I am half-brother to Vaiśravaṇa; my name is Rāvaṇa, if you please, the mighty ten-necked one! Gods and *gandharvas*, *piśācas*, birds and snakes all flee from me in fright, as people always do from Death. That half-brother of mine, Vaiśravaṇa, had some quarrel with me, but I attacked him in my anger and defeated him in battle. It was fear of me that drove him, Naravāhana, in distress from his own wealthy home to live on excellent mount Kailāsa, while I, my dear lady, heroically commandeered his handsome chariot that can fly of its own volition, Puṣpaka by name, to carry me around the sky. When my rage is roused, Maithilī, the mere sight of my face makes Śakra lead the gods into terrified flight. Wherever I take up my position, the wind scarcely ventures to blow, and the sun's hot rays turn cold in fear. Wherever I am, wherever I go, the leaves on the trees stop rustling, rivers check their waters from flowing. On the further shore of the sea my fair city, Laṅkā by name, like Indra's Amarāvatī, is filled with formidable *rākṣasas*. It's a beautiful city, encircled by a gleaming white rampart, with golden courtyards and archways of beryl, thronged with elephants, horses and chariots, resounding with the sound of trumpets, adorned with orchards dense with trees bearing every kind of fruit you could wish for. Use your intelligence, Princess Sītā, and live there with me; you'll forget the lot of human women. You'll enjoy pleasures human and divine, fair-skinned lady, and you'll not remember human Rāma: his life's over! He's the eldest son, but his heroism's so feeble that he was sent off into the forest when King Daśaratha installed his favourite son. Why bother about that Rāma, now he's been expelled from his kingdom, broad-eyed lady? He's a wretched ascetic, out of his mind! The lord of all the *rākṣasas* has come here of his own accord, driven by desire, pierced by Manmatha's arrows: don't reject me! If in your shyness you reject me, you'll suffer the same agony that Urvaśī did when she kicked Purūravas.'[7]

Angry Vaidehī's eyes blazed at these words, and she replied harshly to the lord of the *rākṣasas* in the wilderness, 'Vaiśravaṇa is a god reverenced by all beings! How can you claim him as your brother and yet harbour such a vicious desire? All the *rākṣasas* are doomed to perish, Rāvaṇa, with such a harsh, 46.19–22 malicious, dissolute king as you. You might abduct Indra's wife Śacī and survive, but if you make off with me, Rāma's wife, your life's at an end.'

47.1–4 When powerful Daśagrīva heard what Sītā had to say, he clapped his hands and took on an immense form, then renewed his threats to Maithilī. 'I think you were too distraught to realize just how mighty and mettlesome I am. I could stand in the sky and lift up the earth in my arms, I could drink up the ocean, I could slay Death in battle, I could bring the sun to a halt with my sharp arrows, I could shatter the earth. You madwoman, I can take on any form at will, I can give you any pleasure you like; look on me as your husband.'

47.5–10 With these words angry Rāvaṇa's fiery, tawny-edged eyes reddened and Vaiśravaṇa's younger brother suddenly cast off his benign mendicant's guise, again assuming his true form as Rāvaṇa, a form like that of Time itself, turning into a majestic ten-faced night-roamer with bright red eyes, earrings of burnished gold, carrying bow and arrows. Rāvaṇa, colossal lord of the *rākṣasas*, threw off his disguise as a mendicant, regained his own thundercloud form, red-clad, eyes reddened from rage, and confronted Maithilī, that jewel of a woman, Maithilī of the black hair and the sunlike splendour, robed and adorned.

47.11–15 'If you want a husband famed throughout the three worlds,' said Rāvaṇa, 'entrust yourself to me, shapely lady; I'm the right husband for you. Bind yourself to me for ever! I am worthy of your love and praise. Never, dear lady, will I ever do anything to displease you. Give up your affection for this human. Direct your affection at me! Rāma's been deposed from his kingdom, he's accomplished nothing, his life will soon be at an end: what advantage do you see in attaching yourself to him? You're out of your mind, though you think yourself so wise. To give up kingdom, family and friends to live in this forest infested with wild animals, all at the word of a woman! He's a fool!' Such abuse was not what the courteous Maithilī deserved.

47.15–22 Then Rāvaṇa sprang on Sītā, like Budha seizing Rohiṇī in the sky, grabbing the lotus-eyed Sītā by the hair with his left hand and by the thighs with his right. He looked like a mountain-peak, sharp-toothed and mighty-armed; he looked like

Death; the forest deities fled in terror, tormented by the sight. There then appeared Rāvaṇa's great, divine chariot, gold ornamented, wrought by magic, rumbling raucously like the asses that drew it. Abusing Vaidehī with loud, harsh words, he lifted her on to the chariot, clasping her to his side. In Rāvaṇa's grip the illustrious Sītā was wrung with anguish; 'Rāma!' she screamed and screamed, but Rāma was far away in the forest. As the lust-smitten Rāvaṇa bore her away against her will, she squirmed about in his grip like the snake king's wife, then shrieked at the *rākṣasa* ruler as he carried her off through the sky; she might have been tortured out of her mind or into madness.

'Oh, Lakṣmaṇa! You're strong, and eager to please your 47.23–35
elder brother! Don't you know I'm being carried off by a shape-changing *rākṣasa*? Rāghava, did you give up life, happiness and wealth to do what was right, only to see me carried off against what's right? You are ever on the offensive to punish the lawless; aren't you going to trounce this evil Rāvaṇa? But the wicked don't reap the reward of their deeds immediately: you can look to Rāma to end your life with some dreadful disaster. Oh, how happy Kaikeyī and her family will be now for me to be carried off, me, the rightful wife of that glorious, right-minded prince! Janasthāna, I call on you and your blossoming *karṇikāra* trees: be quick and tell Rāma, "Rāvaṇa is making off with Sītā!" Prasravaṇa Mountain, hail to you with your garlands and peaks: be quick and tell Rāma, "Rāvaṇa is making off with Sītā!" Godāvarī River, hail to you with your calling geese and *sārasas*: be quick and tell Rāma, "Rāvaṇa is making off with Sītā!" You forest deities dwelling in its different trees, I salute you: tell my husband I've been carried off! Whatever creatures are living here, even the flocks of animals and birds, I seek your aid: all of you tell my husband that the woman he loves more dearly than his own life is being carried off – "Sītā is helpless in Rāvaṇa's grip!" When the mighty hero learns about me, he'll deploy his power and rescue me even from the grip of Death!'

Jaṭāyus was asleep when he heard the noise, looked round 48.1–2
quickly and saw Rāvaṇa and Vaidehī; he was a supreme bird,

sharp-beaked, mountainous and glorious. From his perch in a tall tree he made a courteous speech:

48.3–27 'Daśagrīva, I am the mighty king of vultures, steadfast in ancient lore and probity. Jaṭāyus is my name. Rāma son of Daśaratha, the equal of great Indra and Varuṇa, is king of the whole world and devoted to the welfare of the worlds. The shapely woman you are trying to carry off is the glorious rightful wife of that Lord of the Earth; her name is Sītā. How could a king rooted in right lay hands on the wife of another? The wife of a king in particular deserves protection, mighty hero. Abjure your odious intention of laying hands on the wife of another. The wise do not lay their behaviour open to censure, but protect the wives of others from molestation as they would their own. Delight of the Paulastyas, questions of business or pleasure that are beyond the scope of the regulations are resolved by the learned with reference to justice and to the king. A king embodies justice and desires; he's the fount of all material possessions. Justice, for good or ill, is rooted and grounded in the king. How have you secured dominion, *rākṣasa* hero, when you are so evil-natured and capricious? It's like an evil-doer obtaining a celestial chariot! A nature rooted in desire cannot be cleansed, and no one can maintain his integrity for long when he lives among the evil-natured. Neither in countryside nor city has mighty Rāma's rectitude given you cause for offence: why then cause offence to him? Khara was wrong to have gone to Janasthāna for the sake of Śūrpaṇakhā; if tireless Rāma killed him, then just tell me what Rāma did wrong to justify you in making off with the wife of that Lord of the Earth in your clutches? Let go of Vaidehī at once, or his terrible eyes will blaze with fire to burn you up, like Indra's thunderbolt did Vṛtra. You don't realize that you've caught a poisonous snake in your skirt, and you can't see the noose of Time fastened round your neck. A man should not try to carry a burden that will floor him, good sir, and should not bite off more than he can chew. Who would engage in conduct discreditable or notorious, or a public scandal, to the destruction of his body? It's sixty thousand years since I was born, Rāvaṇa, and I rule my ancestral kingdom the way it should be done. I am old, and you are young; you have armour, a bow and arrows and a chariot. But despite all that you'll not get away with carrying off Vaidehī. With me looking on, you can't make off with Vaidehī in your grasp, any more than the revelation of the eternal Veda can be grasped by rational logic. Fight, if you're a hero! Halt a moment, Rāvaṇa, and you'll lie dead on the ground like Khara before you. Rāma is used to killing *daityas* and *dānavas* in warfare, and in a battle with you, even in his bark clothes, he'll soon kill you. But what can I do now, with the two princes far away? You are certain to die of fright of that pair very soon, you villain. As long as I'm alive you won't carry off this lovely Sītā with her lotus-petal eyes: she's Rāma's beloved consort! I've no option but to act to please noble Rāma, and Daśaratha too, even at the cost of my life. Halt! Daśagrīva, halt a moment! Rāvaṇa, see here! I will welcome you to a battle as long as life remains to me, Rāvaṇa. It's my wish to knock you off that excellent chariot like a fruit from its stalk.'

Eyes reddened with anger, and with earrings of burnished 49.2–15
gold, the Lord of *rākṣasas* rushed impetuously upon the Lord of Birds, initiating in that great forest a tumultuous conflict between them as if between two gale-driven clouds in the sky. The stupendous battle that broke out between the vulture and the *rākṣasa* might have been between two great mountains, winged and garlanded. Then the mighty warrior showered the vulture king with shattering shafts, supple, spiked and sharp-pointed; the mesh of arrows shot by Rāvaṇa in that battle found their mark in Jaṭāyus, lord of sky-rovers. Over and over again the gallant champion bird tore open his limbs with his sharp-clawed feet, until the exasperated Daśagrīva, eager to rid himself of this attacker, drew out ten arrows, dreadful as the rod of Death. The great warrior fired off those terrible, unerring, sharp-whetted, stone-ground arrows and split open the vulture, but the sight of Jānakī sobbing on the *rākṣasa's* chariot drove away all thought of the arrows from the glorious winged chief as he rushed at the *rākṣasa*, using his feet to smash his pearl-bejewelled bow with its arrow fixed. Then the glorious winged chief used his wings to shatter

Rāvaṇa's blazing, fiery shield, and with violent power destroyed his divine asses, clad in gold armour, *piśāca*-faced and speed-endowed though they were; the fine great triple-poled chariot, mottled with gems and gold, unstoppable and brilliant as fire he wrecked, together with its fans and its parasol[8] like a full moon. Bow broken, thrown from his chariot, horses and charioteer alike killed, Rāvaṇa fell to the ground, clasping Vaidehī to his side.

49.18–27 Unabashed, and clasping Janaka's daughter to his side, he set off, but the vulture king Jaṭāyus swooped down on him. 'Rāvaṇa, you fool,' he cried, 'it's Rāma's wife you're carrying off! His arrows are certain to fall like a thunderbolt to annihilate the *rākṣasas*. You are gulping down a draught of poison as if you were thirsty for water, you, your friends, family, ministers, army and followers! Idiots like you who don't understand the consequences of their actions soon perish, just as you're sure to perish. You're ensnared in Time's noose, like a fish that's taken the fatal bait; where will you go to escape it? The two Kākutstha Rāghavas are invincible, Rāvaṇa; they'll never tolerate your violation of their hermitage. Heroes don't act like you, committing a crime the whole world condemns, then skulking away like a thief. Fight, if you're a hero! Halt a moment, Rāvaṇa, and you'll lie dead on the ground just like your brother Khara. If ever a man at the point of death brought about the destruction of his soul by a reckless sin, that's what you're doing now. What man would commit an act with such evil consequences, even if he were the blessed overlord of the worlds himself, the eternal Brahmā?'

49.28–37 With these fine words the heroic Jaṭāyus swooped violently on to the back of the *rākṣasa* Daśagrīva. Clutching at him with his sharp claws he tore him to shreds all over, perched on him like a mahout on a rogue elephant. He tore at him with his claws, he stuck his beak into his back, he wrenched out his hair; claws, wings and mouth were his weapons. The *rākṣasa's* lips quivered at the repeated torment meted out by the king of the vultures and he shook with rage. Tormented and crazed with anger the heroic Daśagrīva clasped Vaidehī to his left side, slapping at Jaṭāyus with his palm, then let go of Sītā in fury and belaboured the vulture king with his fists and feet. Then ensued a brief battle between those two matchless heroes, the chief of the *rākṣasas* and the winged paragon, until Rāvaṇa drew his sword and sliced off wings, feet and flanks of Rāma's stubborn champion. The ferocious *rākṣasa* cut off his wings at a stroke, and the vulture slumped to the ground, wounded to death.

Seeing him fall to earth drenched in blood, Vaidehī rushed 49.38;
up to Jaṭāyus in as much distress as if he were one of her own 51.1–2
family. Janaka's daughter Maithilī quailed in terror, grief-stricken and horrified to see him fallen to the ground. The *rākṣasa* chief's eyes were ferocious as he pulled her away; hers were red with anger and tears as she sobbed out a piteous appeal.

'Have you no shame, ignoble Rāvaṇa? It's the act of a thief, 51.3–24
to run off with me when you knew I'd been left on my own! It was you, wasn't it, you villain, in the form of a deer, who lured my husband away by trickery so that you could make off with me? You coward! What outstanding bravery, not to proclaim your name and fight a battle to win me! That shows you're the worst of *rākṣasas*. Aren't you humiliated to do such a dastardly deed – sneaking off with another man's wife behind his back, you wretch? You may pride yourself on your audacity, but men the world over will tell tales about this scandalous, brutal, utterly disgraceful deed of yours. What heroism! What character! So much for all you told me about yourself! Conduct like yours casts a worldwide slur on your family. What can I do when you're rushing me away so fast? Stop a minute and you'll not move another step alive! As soon as those two princes catch sight of you, you won't live a moment more – not even if you've got your army with you! You'll be no more able to bear the touch of their arrows than a forest bird can bear the touch of a blazing fire. Be sensible, I beg you! I beg you, Rāvaṇa, let me go! If you don't, my husband will be so enraged that he and his brother will pulverize you for attacking me. Whatever it is you hope to gain by laying violent hands on me, you've no hope of getting it, for I'd not venture to go on living for long in subjection to an enemy if I couldn't see my godlike

husband. You certainly can't recognize what's for your own good or what will help you, just like a dying man seeking out what will do him harm. You're like all those who hasten their death by refusing what will help them, but I can see you've got Time's noose knotted around your neck. For you not to be afraid in such a terrifying situation, you ten-faced *rākṣasa*, you must be seeing golden trees.* You really are looking at the dread river Vaitaraṇī flowing with streams of blood through its fearful forest with swords for leaves, Rāvaṇa. You'll see a silk-cotton tree* with flowers of refined gold and beautiful beryl all over, yet barbed and studded with iron thorns. You, you pitiless creature, you won't be able to last long after you've dealt such a blow to my noble husband, just as if you'd drunk poison. You, Rāvaṇa, bound in the inexorable noose of Time, where can you go to find sanctuary from my noble husband? He has killed fourteen thousand *rākṣasas* in battle in the mere twinkling of an eye, and without his brother too! The Rāghava hero is mighty and skilled in all weaponry; how could he fail to kill you with his sharp arrows for carrying off his beloved wife?' These bitter reproaches, and more, Vaidehī poured out in a piteous lament, overwhelmed by grief and terror as Rāvaṇa clasped her to his side.

52.1–4 Vaidehī could see no one to protect her from capture. Then she saw five bulls of *vānaras* standing on a mountain-peak, and into the middle of them the broad-eyed Maithilī with the shapely hips dropped her gold-coloured silken shawl and fine ornaments, thinking they might tell Rāma about her; Daśagrīva was too agitated to notice her action in taking off her garment and ornaments, and throwing them down into their midst, but the tawny-eyed bulls of *vānaras* observed the screaming broad-eyed Sītā quite clearly.

52.5–11 The *rākṣasa* lord passed beyond Pampā and headed towards the city of Laṅkā, grasping the weeping Maithilī. Rāvaṇa was delighted to be carrying her off – she who was to bring about his own death – as if he were clasping a sharp-toothed venomous snake to his bosom. He flew quickly through the sky like an arrow shot from a bow, past forests, rivers, mountains and lakes. When he reached the everlasting abode of Varuṇa, home of whales and crocodiles, refuge of rivers, he crossed the ocean. Varuṇa's abode churned its waves and held back its fish and serpents in agitation at Vaidehī's abduction; *cāraṇas* in the sky above gave tongue and *siddhas* proclaimed, 'This will be the end of Daśagrīva.' Yet Rāvaṇa still made for the city of Laṅkā, clasping the struggling Sītā to his bosom, her beauty his own death.

When he reached Laṅkā city with its well-built roads, 52.12–14
Rāvaṇa Daśagrīva produced Sītā like the anti-god Maya producing his magic, and gave orders to some fierce-faced *piśāca* women:

'No one, man or woman, is to visit Sītā without my auth- 52.14–16
ority. It is my wish that she be given whatever pearls, gems, gold, garments and ornaments she may desire. No one who values her own life shall utter an uncongenial word, whether deliberately or from negligence, to Vaidehī.'

With these instructions to the *rākṣasīs*, the mighty lord of 52.17–18
the *rākṣasas* left his private apartment. While he was considering his next move, he caught sight of eight valiant flesh-eating *rākṣasas*. Seeing them, the valiant *rākṣasa*, deluded by a boon he had been granted, praised their might and courage, then went on:

'Be quick and arm yourselves with all your weapons and 52.19–27
hurry away to Janasthāna. Khara's late haunt is now "the place of the slain". You are to take up your quarters in Janasthāna, empty now the *rākṣasas* have been killed, relying on your strength as heroes and rising far above any fear. That huge force I stationed in Janasthāna under Dūṣaṇa and Khara, it's been slaughtered by Rāma's arrows in a battle. I have kept my anger in check up to now, but it is mounting beyond control and begetting intense, savage enmity towards Rāma. I'm determined that I shall requite my enemy's hostility, and I won't sleep until I've killed that enemy in combat; but killing Rāma, that murderer of Khara and Dūṣaṇa, will bring me the satisfaction that wealth brings to a beggar. You, good sirs, are to live in Janasthāna and submit accurate reports on Rāma's

activities; all night-walkers are to exercise vigilance and exert themselves to kill the Rāghava. I have often proved your might in battle: that is why Janasthāna has been assigned to you.'

53.1–13 Weak-minded Rāvaṇa considered that in issuing these instructions to the eight ferocious and powerful *rākṣasas*, he had done all that was necessary, and his thoughts returned to Vaidehī. Afflicted by Kāma's arrow, Rāvaṇa hurried back into his pleasant palace to see Sītā, but when he entered the living-quarters, the *rākṣasa* overlord saw Sītā sitting amid the *rākṣasīs*, given over to grief. He showed Vaidehī all over the marvellous building, and then the evil Rāvaṇa put a proposition to Janaka's daughter.

53.17–35 'Sītā, my dear, become my wife, and you'll be mistress over all these many thousands of women in my entourage. Come now! What's the point of you wishing for anything else? Agree to my proposal. Possess me in my passion! Do grant me this grace! Laṅkā here is surrounded by sea for a hundred *yojanas*; all the gods and anti-gods and Indra put together couldn't slight it. There's no one to equal me in heroism throughout all the worlds, not among gods, *yakṣas*, *gandharvas* nor sages. What is Rāma to you, ousted from his kingdom, a miserable ascetic, his life all but over, such a puny man? Take me, Sītā, a husband worthy of you. Youth is fleeting. Don't be coy, but take your pleasure here with me. Don't set your heart on seeing the Rāghava again, my beauty. Who could possibly manage to reach here, Sītā, even if his wishes had chariot-wheels?' With this proposition to Janaka's daughter Maithilī, Daśagrīva sealed his fate, thinking, 'She's mine!'

54.1–19 Vaidehī was racked by grief, yet fearlessly placed a blade of grass between them[9] as she replied to Rāvaṇa's proposition. 'A king called Daśaratha, immovable in his defence of what is right, and renowned for keeping to his pledged word, had a son, the Rāghava, Rāma by name. He is righteous, famed throughout the three worlds, mighty and good-looking. He's my husband and my deity. He was born in the Ikṣvāku line. He's got shoulders like a lion, he's glorious, and he and his brother Lakṣmaṇa will put an end to your life. If he were present to see you lay violent hands on me – on me! – you'd be lying killed in battle like Khara in Janasthāna. Those *rākṣasas* hailed as ferocious in form and might all lose their venom when confronted by the Rāghava, like snakes before Garuḍa. Gilded arrows shot from his bowstring will batter your body like waves on Gaṅgā's banks. Maybe you can't be killed by gods or anti-gods, Rāvaṇa, but after committing such an outrage you won't escape alive from him. The powerful Rāghava will bring an end to what's left of your life, a life with as much security as an animal's at the sacrificial stake. If Rāma were to see you, *rākṣasa*, the fury of his fiery eye would shrivel you up at once and exterminate you today. He could destroy the moon in the heavens, he could knock it down to earth, he could dry up the ocean: he could rescue his Sītā! When your prosperity's gone, your senses are gone, your reason is gone, your life's gone, your deed will have reduced Laṅkā to widowhood. You will see no happy ending to this evil deed of yours, snatching me away to separation when I should be at my husband's side in the forest. Now my godlike, many-splendoured husband must display his fearless valour, living in an empty Daṇḍaka. He will rain arrows on you in a battle to strip your body of your arrogance, your strength, your heroism, your vainglory. Whenever Time ordains a destruction of creatures, it achieves its object by driving the doomed to madness. Now you've molested me your time is up, you low-down *rākṣasa*, for you, for the *rākṣasas* and for your harem to be slaughtered. I'm like an altar erected at the centre of a sacrifice, encircled with ladles and other implements, worshipped by the Twice-Born with their *mantras*, that may not experience the polluting touch of a *caṇḍāla*. You may imprison this shell of a body, or have it killed. I don't care about preserving my body nor even my very life, but *rākṣasa*, I refuse to draw upon myself the censure of the world.'

After this vehement repudiation of Rāvaṇa, Vaidehī Maithilī 54.20–21
lapsed into silence, but when he heard Sītā's vehement, horrifying words, he replied with a speech calculated to terrify Sītā.

'Listen to my vow, Maithilī. I'll give you twelve months, my 54.22
proud beauty. If by that time you refuse to yield to me with a

sweet smile, then my cooks shall chop you into minced meat for my breakfast.'

54.23–4 With this dire threat, Rāvaṇa – who could make his foes roar – angrily instructed some *rākṣasīs*: 'I want some ugly, fierce-looking, flesh-and-blood-eating *rākṣasīs*! They'll soon take away her pride.'

54.25–6 Ugly and fierce-looking indeed were those who saluted at these words and closed around Maithilī; fierce-looking too was King Rāvaṇa, stamping his feet as if he would convulse and rend the earth.

54.27–8 'Maithilī is to be taken to the middle of the *aśoka* grove,' he commanded. 'There she's to be concealed and guarded with you surrounding her. By ferocious threats alternating with kindness you are all to subdue Maithilī to my will like a wild she-elephant.'

54.29–31 At Rāvaṇa's orders the *rākṣasīs* encircled Maithilī and went off to the *aśoka* grove. It was full of all the fruit trees she could wish for, all kinds of flowers and fruit, and home to ever-twittering birds, but Janaka's daughter Maithilī's whole body felt only sorrow: like a doe to tigresses she could but submit to the *rākṣasīs*.

55.1–9 When Rāma had killed Mārīca, that shape-changing *rākṣasa* trotting about in the form of a deer, he quickly turned back in his tracks. As he hurried along in his eagerness to see Maithilī a jackal yelped savagely behind him, setting his hair on end with its vicious cry. Alarmed by the jackal's cry, he thought, 'That jackal's shriek sounds really ominous to me. I hope all's well with Vaidehī, and that *rākṣasas* are not feasting. That shriek Mārīca uttered in the form of a deer – what if Lakṣmaṇa heard it and recognized it – what if he took it to be me? If Saumitri heard the shriek and then left Maithilī – and she would send him at once! – he'll be coming here after me. *Rākṣasas* eager to kill Sītā must have gathered together, and that's why Mārīca became a golden deer and lured me away! That's why he shouted, "Lakṣmaṇa, I've been hit!" when he'd led me far away until my arrow killed him and he turned into a *rākṣasa*. I do hope those two are all right, now I've left them alone in the forest: Janasthāna has made the *rākṣasas* my enemies. I've noticed a lot of terrible omens today.'

The thought that he had heard a jackal shriek, and had been 55.10–15
decoyed by a *rākṣasa* in the form of a deer, sent Rāghava Rāma back to Janasthāna in alarm. Wildlife clustered, calling ferociously and shunning the noble man in his misery and worry. After these dreadful omens the Rāghava then caught sight of a melancholy Lakṣmaṇa coming along, and soon Lakṣmaṇa and Rama met: gloom joined with gloom, sorrow with fated sorrow. Then the older brother reproached Lakṣmaṇa for coming, deserting Sītā in that unpeopled, *rākṣasa*-infested wilderness; the pride of the Raghus took hold of Lakṣmaṇa by the left hand* and in his pain spoke words that wounded despite their outward mildness:

'Oh, Lakṣmaṇa, my dear brother, you'll answer for what 55.16–18
you've done, deserting Sītā and coming here! I hope it turns out well! My hero, I've no doubt at all, Janaka's daughter's been slaughtered, perhaps even devoured, by *rākṣasas* wandering about in the forest, I've seen so many inauspicious signs. Oh, Lakṣmaṇa, if only we could find Sītā unharmed!'

At the sight of Lakṣmaṇa coming miserably through the 56.1–17
wilderness without Vaidehī, Daśaratha's righteous son exclaimed: 'Where is she, Lakṣmaṇa, the woman who followed my steps to Daṇḍaka Forest? Vaidehī, the woman you've deserted by coming here? Where is she, the woman who shared in my sorrow when I was ousted from the kingdom to go running miserably around the Daṇḍakas: slender-waisted Vaidehī? Where is she, you hero, the woman I can't live without even for a moment, my comrade through life: Sītā, truly a deity's daughter? Lakṣmaṇa, I wouldn't covet the lordship of heaven or earth without her, Janaka's burnished golden daughter. Is she still living, Vaidehī who is dearer than my own life? Dear brother, my exile won't all have been for nothing, will it? Saumitri, with you away and me dead because of Sītā, won't Kaikeyī be pleased at getting what she wanted? Poor Kausalyā! With her son dead will she have to wait politely on Kaikeyī – her son, kingdom and purpose secured? My only thought is to get back to the hermitage and find Vaidehī still

alive. If that virtuous woman is gone, gone will be my life, Lakṣmaṇa. If Vaidehī, the laughing Sītā, doesn't greet me when I get back to the hermitage, Lakṣmaṇa, I shall be destroyed. Lakṣmaṇa, tell me whether Vaidehī is alive or not, or if your carelessness has let her be devoured by *rākṣasas*, poor thing! She's frail, young and unused to suffering; Vaidehī must be in the depths of despair to be separated from me. Even you were frightened by that cunning spiteful *rākṣasa* shouting out "Lakṣmaṇa", and I can imagine Vaidehī being terrified when she heard that cry like my voice and sending you off at once to find me, but losing sight of Sītā in the forest was quite the wrong thing to do; you've given the cruel *rākṣasas* an opportunity to take their revenge. The flesh-eating *rākṣasas* are mourning the death of Khara. Those savages will kill Sītā, I've no doubt. Oh, what a terrible mess I'm mired in, victorious hero, but what can I do about it now? We shall find that this is what's happened, I'm afraid.'

56.18; With thoughts like these about shapely Sītā, the Rāghava
57.1 hurried Lakṣmaṇa back to Janasthāna. Rāma, pride of the Raghus, was tormented by sorrow, and on the way he repeatedly asked Saumitri why he had left the hermitage.

57.2–4 'Why have you left Maithilī behind and come away, when I had left her confidently in the forest with you? I was perturbed to see you coming, Lakṣmaṇa, with Maithilī left behind, and feared the worst. My left eye throbbed, so did my arm and heart when I saw you, Lakṣmaṇa, in the distance on the path, with Sītā left on her own.'

57.5–18 These words deepened Lakṣmaṇa Saumitri's gloom, favoured though he was by Fortune, and he replied to the gloomy Rāma: 'It wasn't my own idea to leave her and come here; it was her harsh words that drove me to come and find you. A sound reached Maithilī's ears like her noble husband calling out "Oh! Sītā, Lakṣmaṇa, save me!", and when she heard that anguished cry, Maithilī was beside herself with terror. "Go! Go!" she wept in her tenderness for you. Time and again Maithilī urged me to go, but I answered her with words full of confidence in you. "I can't see any *rākṣasa* frightening him. Calm down. It's not what you think. Somebody was imitating him. How could that noble man stoop to utter such a degrading word as 'save me'? Sītā, he could even save the Thirty Gods! For some reason someone or other is mimicking my brother's voice: it's out of character for him to shout, 'Lakṣmaṇa, save me!' Madam, don't get wrought up like inferior women do. Stop acting so weak; pull yourself together and don't be frightened. In the three worlds there's not a man born – or not yet born – who could fight a battle against the Rāghava and win." That's what I told Vaidehī, but she was distraught. She burst into tears, and her reply was cruel: "You wicked man, you have set your heart on me! But even if you succeed in getting rid of your brother you won't succeed in getting hold of me. It's in collusion with Bharata that you're trailing after Rāma, and that's why you won't help him when he's crying out for you so. You've been following us on my account as an undercover enemy, hoping the Rāghava would give you a chance; that's why you won't help him." It was this accusation from Vaidehī that drove me from the hermitage, furious, my eyes ablaze, my lips trembling with anger.'

Rāma was tormented by Saumitri's account, and replied, 57.19–23
'My dear brother, you have done wrong to come here without her. You left, sir, at an angry word from Maithilī, when you know how capable I am of warding off *rākṣasas*! I am not pleased with you for coming here: you, leaving Maithilī, because you heard a cross word from an angry woman! It was utterly ill-judged of you to yield to your temper and let Sītā's provocation make you disobey my order. There lies the *rākṣasa* that lured me away from the hermitage in the form of a deer, slain by my arrow.'

Rāma raced back. As he lurched along he felt a throbbing 58.1–3;
below his left eye and he began to tremble. Conscious of these 59.1–2
repeated portents of disaster, he cried out, 'If only Sītā is safe!' Desperate to see Sītā, he burst into the hut. It was empty. Panic seized him. Rāma searched all around, but the hermitage was empty, the leaf-hut deserted, the seats scattered. There was no Vaidehī to be seen. Daśaratha's son Rāma threw up his beautiful arms and screamed.

'Lakṣmaṇa, wherever is Vaidehī? Where has she gone? 59.3–10

Saumitri, who has carried her off? My beloved, who has devoured you? Sītā, if you're just hiding behind a tree for a joke, that's enough of your joke. Be good to me! I'm in such distress. Sītā, dear wife! Your playfellows, the baby animals that trust you, are wondering why you have abandoned them. Their eyes are clouded with tears. If Sītā has been captured it will arouse grief in me great enough to kill me, and my father the Mahārāja is certain to see me in the Otherworld. "What are you doing coming into my presence without completing the time you promised at my command? Shame on you, you selfish, ignoble liar!" That's what my father's certain to say to me in the Otherworld. You've left me here a miserable, feeble wreck, burnt up by grief and broken-hearted, like a crook who's lost his reputation. You've left me, my beauty! Where have you gone, my lovely? If I'm deserted by you I'll end my own life!'

59.11–12 With this lament Rāma the Rāghava searched frantically for Sītā, grief-stricken at not finding Janaka's daughter. Rāma son of Daśaratha was like an elephant wallowing in a great bog, clasping at Sītā but sinking back, till Lakṣmaṇa became anxious for his health and spoke to reassure him.

59.13–16 'Don't despair, mighty brother; let's both exert ourselves. The forest is full of pretty hollows, my hero. Maithilī loves wandering about in the woods. She's crazy about the forest. She may have gone off into the forest; she may be in some flowery lotus pool; maybe she's gone to the river with its hordes of fish and water birds, or maybe Vaidehī wants to frighten us, you bull of a man, and she's hiding somewhere in the wood to test us. Your majesty, we'll set to quickly and search for her, we'll ransack the whole forest for Janaka's daughter.'

59.17–20 Lakṣmaṇa's friendly words calmed Rāma, and he and Saumitri began the search. The two sons of Daśaratha searched for Sītā throughout forests and mountains, streams and lakes, slopes, caves and mountain-peaks; they searched everywhere, but nowhere did they come across her. They searched the whole mountain, then Rāma said to Lakṣmaṇa, 'Saumitri, I cannot see Vaidehī here on the lovely mountain.'

59.21–2 Lakṣmaṇa was consumed with anguish as he wandered about

Daṇḍaka Forest, but assured his brilliant, glorious brother, 'You are clever enough to get back Maithilī, Janaka's daughter, just like mighty Viṣṇu won back the earth when he bound Bali.'

The Rāghava's mind was plunged in grief and he answered 59.23–4
heroic Lakṣmaṇa's words in a miserable voice. 'You're so clever, but we've ransacked the whole forest, its blossoming lotus pools, this mountain and its many hollows and waterfalls. I can't find Vaidehī, and she's dearer to me than my own life!'

Wretched, grief-stricken, haggard at Sītā's capture, as he 59.25–9
sobbed out his thoughts, Rāma was momentarily overcome by panic. In the torment of his misery he uttered a long, loud groan and sank down in a swoon, mind and body overcome by pain. Over and over again lotus-eyed Rāma sighed; over and over again his sobs choked him as he cried out, 'Oh my darling!' Lakṣmaṇa, dutiful and affectionate as he was, tried to soothe him with respectful words and gestures, but the words that fell from Lakṣmaṇa's lips could not stop him crying out again and again at not seeing his beloved Sītā.

Then his eye seemed as if it would burn up the ground in his 60.22–4,
frenzy when he caught sight of the track of a huge *rākṣasa*. His 32
heart in a turmoil, Rāma peered at the footprints of Sītā and the *rākṣasa* and declared to his dear brother: 'Look, Lakṣmaṇa, here are scraps of gold broken off Vaidehī's ornaments, and bits of her garlands; and that war-chariot with its battle standard, resplendent and brilliant as a blazing fire, but abandoned and smashed – whose is it?'

Then in his torment, haggard at Sītā's capture, Rāma was 61.1–3
ready to destroy the worlds like the Doomsday Fire. With rapid breaths he inspected his bow, already strung, as eager for the kill as Rudra was for the beast at Dakṣa's sacrifice. Lakṣmaṇa had never seen Rāma so angry; his mouth dried up as he respectfully gave his advice.

'You have always been gentle and restrained; you've 61.4–15
delighted in the welfare of all creatures. You shouldn't let anger make you untrue to your nature. The moon has its grace, the sun its radiance, the wind its motion, the earth its endurance; just as immutable is your unsurpassable glory. I don't know who this war-chariot belongs to, or the weapons or equipment,

or who smashed them, or why. This place has been churned up by hooves and wheels, and splattered dreadfully with blood: a battle has taken place here. You are eloquent, your highness, but this trouble has been caused by only one person, not even by two, and I can see no sign of a large force. For the deed of an individual you ought not to destroy the worlds. Rulers of the earth act with restraint and composure; the punishment they inflict is proportionate. All creatures flock to you, their supreme refuge. Whoever would think it good for you to lose your wife, Rāghava? Rivers, oceans, mountains, gods, *gandharvas* and *dānavas* can no more bring themselves to injure you than good people can a consecrated sacrificer. It's the one who has carried off Sītā that you should pursue with your bow, your majesty; I'll back you up, and supreme sages will support you. We'll all ransack sea, mountains, forests, every dreadful cave there is, pools and mountain streams. The worlds of gods and *gandharvas*, together we'll ransack them all until we come upon the abductor of your wife. And if the Thirty Gods themselves cannot be persuaded to give back your wife, then, Lord of Kosala, you shall act as the occasion demands.'

62.1–2 Rāma was consumed by grief and mourned as if he had nowhere to turn, distraught and unable to think for sorrow, but Lakṣmaṇa Saumitri kept on clasping his feet,* and after a moment he was roused by his consolation.

62.3–20 'Rāma, it took great asceticism and good deeds for King Daśaratha to be granted you;[10] it was like the immortals getting hold of the ambrosia. Indeed, it was separation from you that caused the Lord of the Earth to join the gods, so attached was he to your virtues, as we heard from Bharata. Kākutstha, if you can't bear the sorrow that's been inflicted on you, then what ordinary man, what weak character, will be able to bear anything similar? If in your distress, sir, you burn up the worlds with your splendour, then where, you tiger of a man, can your tormented subjects turn for peace? It's the way of the world. Nahuṣa's son Yayāti had succeeded in reaching the same world as Śakra but misfortune struck him down. Even the great sage Vasiṣṭha, our father's chaplain, had a hundred sons born to him in a day, but then they were killed. Steadfast lord, even the Earth has been known to tremble – that goddess, universally revered mother of the world. Even the gods from Śakra downwards experience fortune and misfortune, so we hear, so you ought not to panic, you tiger of a man. You are a blameless hero, and you ought not to grieve like any ordinary man, even if Vaidehī has been captured or done to death. Men of your stamp, Rāma, don't grieve however great the calamity; they always understand reality and don't despair. A great man like you should think it over realistically and rationally; sagacious men use their acumen to discriminate benefit from bane. If you don't examine and weigh up the good and bad points of your actions – unless you do this – you won't get the results you're hoping for. You're the one, my hero, who's taught me this so many times before, for could anyone, even Bṛhaspati himself, teach you anything? You are so wise that even the gods find it hard to understand your intelligence. Grief has stupefied your intellect, but I'm reawakening it. Call to mind values divine and human – and your own gallantry, bull of the Ikṣvākus! It's your enemies you must exert yourself to kill. What's the use of universal destruction, you bull of a man? It's that evil enemy that you must identify and then destroy.'

Despite his seniority, the Rāghava was astute enough to 63.1–3
accept the value of Lakṣmaṇa's cogent advice. Mighty Rāma checked his overwhelming wrath and leaned on his glittering bow, asking Lakṣmaṇa, 'What shall we do, my boy? Lakṣmaṇa, where shall we go? Work me out some plan for finding Sītā.'

Lakṣmaṇa replied to the agonized Rāma: 'What you must 63.4–7
do is ransack Janasthāna. It's full of *rākṣasas*. It's thick with all sorts of trees and creepers, there are mountain fastnesses, caves and valleys, a lot of fearful hollows crammed with herds of all kinds, the homes of *kinnaras* and the haunts of *gandharvas*. You should search them systematically along with me. People like you, bull of a man, noble and gifted intellects, stand firm against troubles like mountains in a violent gale.'

All this talk made the wrathful Rāma fit a razor-sharp arrow 63.8–12
to his bow and range about the whole forest with Lakṣmaṇa until he saw fallen to the ground a mountainous bird, a superlative paragon bathed in blood. It was Jaṭāyus. The sight of his

mountain-like form made Rāma declare to Lakṣmaṇa, 'That's who's eaten Sītā Vaidehī; no doubt about it. It's obvious this is a *rākṣasa* that wanders about the woods in the form of a vulture, and it's resting after devouring broad-eyed Sītā. I'll kill him with my fierce blazing arrows. They never miss.' So saying, the furious Rāma fitted a razor-sharp arrow to his bow and rushed towards the vulture as if he would shake the ocean-girt earth.

63.13–18 The bird, however, spoke to Rāma son of Daśaratha in a feeble voice, vomiting foaming blood. 'The woman you're searching for in the great forest – like a healing herb though you're healthy – that queen, and my own life too – Rāvaṇa has taken them both. I saw the queen, Rāghava, after you and Lakṣmaṇa had left her alone; Rāvaṇa was carrying her off, but he was too strong for me. I went to Sītā's aid, and knocked Rāvaṇa to the ground. I smashed his chariot and parasol in the fight. This broken bow is his. This shield is his. That war-chariot is his, Rāma, wrecked in the fight. When I was exhausted Rāvaṇa sliced off my wings with his sword, then caught hold of Sītā Vaidehī and flew up into the sky. Don't kill me. The *rākṣasa*'s killed me already.'

63.19–20 Rāma and Lakṣmaṇa wept with relief to hear the news of Sītā and embraced the vulture king. Rāma was saddened to see him gasping for breath, alone in that remote wilderness, and said to Saumitri:

63.21–5 'Exile from the kingdom, my home the forest, the loss of Sītā, the death of this bird – such bad fortune as mine would even burn up fire! If I were to cross the whole wide ocean, the Lord of Rivers, now, my bad fortune would be certain to blast it dry! Of all the creatures in this world, fixed or moving, there's not an unluckier than I, I who gained the great earth only to find myself enmeshed in misfortune! It's my calamitous fortune that's left this friend of my father, the aged king of the vultures, lying dead on the ground.' He repeated this over and over again, then, moved by affection for their father, the Rāghava and Lakṣmaṇa stroked Jaṭāyus.

64.1–7 The sight of the vulture violently hurled to the ground testified to his loyalty. Rāma said to Saumitri, 'It's clear that it was exerting himself on my behalf that got this bird struck down in a battle with the *rākṣasa*; that's why he's gasping his life away. There's still some life in his body, Lakṣmaṇa; he's not speaking, but he's gazing around in confusion. Jaṭāyus, if you can still speak, tell us about Sītā, I beg you, and tell us how you were struck down. Why did Rāvaṇa carry off Sītā? What have I done to him? Is it in response to some provocation by me that Rāvaṇa has carried off my darling? What did her captivating moonlike face look like? What did Sita say then, you excellent bird? How strong is this *rākṣasa*? What does he look like? What is he capable of? Where does he live, my friend? Do answer my questions.'

Jaṭāyus mournfully fixed his eyes on Rāma, who was 64.8–14
lamenting ceaselessly, and whispered feebly, 'Rāvaṇa king of the *rākṣasas* called up many magic storms and gales and carried her off through the sky. When I was exhausted the night-walker sliced off my wings, sir, then caught hold of Sītā Vaidehī and set out towards the south. I'm beginning to choke and my sight is failing, Rāghava. I can see golden trees hairy with cuscus-grass. The moment when Rāvaṇa made off with Sītā is the one when an owner can expect to regain promptly any wealth he loses then – it's called the Vinda moment – but he didn't realize that, Kākutstha. He'll soon perish, like a fish that's taken the hook. So you mustn't be anxious about Janaka's daughter. You'll soon kill that *rākṣasa* in battle and be able to enjoy yourself again with Vaidehī.'

While the clear-sighted vulture was still talking to Rāma, 64.15–18
blood and flesh spurted from his dying mouth. Gasping, 'the very son of Viśravas, Vaiśravaṇa's brother . . .', the Lord of Birds gave up his life. Rāma was still pleading with him, 'Tell me, please tell me', while the vulture's life ebbed from his body and fled to the sky. His head jerked to the ground, his feet sprawled out, his frame convulsed and he fell to the earth.

Rāma was overcome with sorrow to see the vulture red-eyed, 64.19–28
lifeless and motionless as a mountain, and spoke sadly to Saumitri. 'This bird has lived for many years undisturbed in the *rākṣasas'* home, roaming about in Daṇḍaka Forest. Now he lies slain, at the end of a long life; Time is indeed inexorable.

Look at this vulture, Lakṣmaṇa, our champion. He went to Sītā's aid, and has been killed by Rāvaṇa's superior might – and for my sake! This Lord of Birds has given up his life, renouncing his great ancestral vulture kingdom for my sake. Even among the lower orders, Saumitri, there is virtue, merit, heroism, support. My dear warrior, as a cause for grieving Sītā's abduction comes nowhere near the murder of that vulture for my sake. This Lord of Birds is due as much respect and honour from me as his glorious majesty, King Daśaratha. Bring some logs, Saumitri; I'll kindle fire and cremate the vulture king. It was for my sake he met his end. The lord of the bird world shall be lifted on to the pyre by me. He's been murdered by that cruel *rākṣasa*, Saumitri, and I'm going to cremate him.'

64.31–5 With these words Rāma lifted the Lord of Birds on to the blazing pyre and devoutly cremated him with the sorrow due to one of his own family. Then heroic Rāma went into the forest with Saumitri and killed some plump gazelles to spread around the bird. Glorious Rāma selected some of the gazelle-meat, cut it up and offered it to the bird on the lovely green turf. Rāma promptly muttered for him all the going-to-heaven *mantras* prescribed by the Twice-Born for a dead human, then the supreme king's two sons went to the Godāvarī river and both performed the water-ritual for the vulture king.

65.1–8 After the Rāghavas had performed his water-ritual they then set out towards the west to search the forest for Sītā. Bows, arrows and swords in hand, the two descendants of Ikṣvāku turned southwards along an untrodden path beset with bushes and trees, screened by curtains of creepers, impassable, dense and dread, but the mighty pair hurried through that huge, terrible forest on their journey south. When the Rāghavas had gone three *krośas* beyond Janasthāna they plunged fervently into the dense Krauñca Forest. It was thick as billowing clouds, seeming to bristle with pleasure at the lovely colourful flowers and flocks of wildlife filling it on all sides. Eager to find Vaidehī but haggard at Sītā's capture they searched that forest, pausing only here and there, until the splendid Lakṣmaṇa, upright, virtuous and pure, respectfully warned his brilliant brother:

65.9–11 'My arm is throbbing steadily, my mind seems agitated and the signs I can see are mostly unpropitious, so be on your guard, noble brother, and take my words to heart; to me these are the portents of impending trouble. That bird called the *vañculaka* is shrieking terribly as if to warn us about a mortal battle.'

As they continued to ransack the whole forest, suddenly it was rent by a loud noise, its serried ranks pounded by an onrush of wind; the noise swelled throughout the forest until it seemed to fill the sky. Looking to see what had caused the noise, Rāma and his younger brother discovered where a huge broad-chested *rākṣasa* was lurking, and ran up. Kabandha stood before them. He was enormous. He had no head or neck, but a face in his belly; his mountainous size was increased by mounds of bristles until he looked like a terrible black cloud, and his voice was like thunder. His single, penetrating eye was in his chest; it was large and broad, with long tawny lashes. He was continually licking his maw with its huge teeth, and devouring ferocious bears, lions, deer and elephants. Each fearsome arm was a *yojana* long; he was waving them about and seizing all kinds of bears, flocks of birds, and deer in his hands. This was who barred the path the brothers had embarked on, dragging several stag chieftains towards him and tearing them apart. Seeing Kabandha, huge, vicious, fearsome, his arms wrapped around him, scarce a *krośa* away, they started back, but the strong-armed monster reached out, stretching his interminable arms, and crushed both Rāghavas in his violent grip; their swords, their stout bows, their acute courage, their powerful arms, all the brothers' great might became useless as they were dragged along. 65.12–23

Mighty Kabandha, that supreme *dānava*, interrogated them. 'Who are you bull-chested men with your great swords and bows? You are welcome food for me in this place of dread. Tell me your objective: why have you come here? The place you have reached is my haunt; I am tormented by hunger here and you are going into my mouth; you may be like sharp-horned bulls with your bows and arrows and swords, but you'll find it hard to escape from there with your lives.' 65.24–6

Rāma's mouth ran dry on hearing evil Kabandha's words, 65.27–30 and he lamented to Lakṣmaṇa, 'We've gone from one trouble to a worse, heroic brother, and now here's a calamity that'll kill us and stop us rescuing my darling! Look, tiger of a man, you and I are both bewildered by these calamities; no creature can bear the weight of his fate, Lakṣmaṇa. When their time is up, even warriors on the battlefield collapse like embankments made of sand, however great their strength, however skilful their weaponry.'

66.1–2 Seeing the brothers Rāma and Lakṣmaṇa standing enmeshed in all his coils, Kabandha asked, 'Why stand there when you can see I'm tormented by hunger, you bulls of *kṣatriyas*? Fate has marked you out for my food and you're as good as dead.'

66.3–4 Lakṣmaṇa was overwhelmed with pain at his words but drew confidence from his prowess; his response was swift and apt. 'Before this vile *rākṣasa* can seize us both, let's be quick and cut off his massive arms.'

66.5–8 Then the two Rāghavas seized the right moment, took their swords and vigorously severed his arms at the shoulder: Rāma, on the right, quickly cut off the right arm with his blade, while the warrior Lakṣmaṇa sprang up on the left. Arms severed, the mighty monster crashed down; earth, air and every direction resounded with a noise like a storm-cloud. At the sight of his sliced-off arms and steeped in torrents of blood the miserable *dānava* asked the heroes, 'Who are you?'

66.9–12 In answer the mighty Lakṣmaṇa, favoured by Fortune, declared to Kabandha, 'This is Kākutstha, the famous heir of the Ikṣvākus, Rāma by name, and I am his younger brother Lakṣmaṇa. Although his splendour is godlike, he's been living in the unpeopled wilderness. His wife has been carried off by a *rākṣasa* and we have come here in search of her. But then who are you? Why are you writhing about in the forest on broken legs, a mere torso, your blazing mouth in your chest?'

66.13–15; Lakṣmaṇa's words reminded Kabandha of something Indra
67.1–6 had told him and he replied in delight, 'Welcome, you two tigers of men! Fortunate indeed am I to see you! Fortunate am I to have had my arms cut off by you! I'll tell you truly about the sin that gave me this deformed frame. Listen, you tiger of a man. Mighty Rāma, powerful, valiant man, I used to have

an unimaginable body, famous throughout the three worlds; I was as beautiful as Soma, as Śakra, as Sūrya! But then, Rāma, I took on this huge shape to terrify the world and began to terrorize the sages here in the forest. In that guise I harassed a great sage called Sthūlaśiras as he was gathering all kinds of forest fare, and in his anger he uttered a dreadful curse on the body he saw me in: "May you be condemned to remain in that cruel form!" I implored the angry sage to put a term to the curse, and, although I had brought the curse on myself, he replied, "When in the unpeopled wilderness Rāma cuts off your arms and cremates you, then shall you regain your own body, huge and handsome."

'Lakṣmaṇa, you can recognize in me a being resplendent 67.7–17
with grace, a son of Danu. It was Indra's anger on the battlefield that gave me this form. I had gratified the Grand Father by fierce asceticism till he granted me long life; then delusion gripped me. "I have been granted long life," I thought, "so what can Śakra do to me?" With that idea in my head I attacked Śakra in battle. He hurled his hundred-forked lightning bolt at me and drove my head and legs right into my body, but at my entreaty did not dispatch me to Yama's realm. "The Grand Father's words shall be true," he told me. "But how can I live for a very long time?" I asked. "My legs and head and face have been smashed by your thunderbolt, so what shall I do for food?" Śakra then gave me arms a *yojana* long and provided me with a sharp-toothed mouth in my belly. This is the only way for me to feed, using my long arms to collect up lions, elephants, deer and tigers roaming in the forest. But Indra told me, "When Rāma and Lakṣmaṇa cut off your arms in combat, then shall you go to heaven." That's you, Rāma, and I'm thankful. Rāghava, no one but you can kill me, according to what the great sage truly said. Bull of a man, when I've been purified by fire I'll be your ally, with you heart and soul: you'll see.'

With Lakṣmaṇa listening, the righteous Rāghava made this 67.18–23
appeal to the Danu. 'My splendid wife Sītā was carried off by Rāvaṇa when I was away from Janasthāna with my brother, unconcerned. But I know this *rākṣasa* only by name, not by

sight. Tell me, do, about who has taken Sītā and where to! If you really do know, you'll be doing a great favour to anyone in a grief-stricken, leaderless turmoil.'

67.24–31 The Rāghava spoke persuasively, but the Danu was a canny speaker and made a judicious reply to Rāma's words. 'I don't have divine knowledge, and I don't know Maithilī, but when I've been cremated and restored to my real form I'll be able to tell you someone who does know her. Until I'm cremated, your majesty, it's impossible for me to know anything about that mighty *rākṣasa* who's captured your Sītā, because when I brought upon myself a form abhorrent to the world, Rāghava, that disabling curse destroyed my intellect. However, before the Sun drives his weary horses home, Rāma, cast me into a pit and cremate me with due ceremony, for if you cremate me properly in a pit, pride of the Raghus, I'll tell you about someone who will know that *rākṣasa*. You should enter into an alliance with him in the customary way, Rāghava. He's slight of valour, but he'll organize help for you. There's nothing in the three worlds that he doesn't know, Rāghava, for he used to roam all over the worlds for another reason.'

68.1–7 At Kabandha's words those two heroic Lords of Men found a mountain gully and kindled a fire, and Lakṣmaṇa soon had a pyre well alight with great blazing brands. On all sides it blazed out, and Kabandha's huge body was like a lump of *ghī*, the blubber cooking out of it as the fire gently burned. Suddenly the pyre shook. Suddenly, as if a smokeless fire had been kindled, a mighty figure leapt up in delight, clad in stainless garments and a divine garland, all his limbs ornamented. In a gleaming, glorious, goose-drawn carriage stood Kabandha, radiating his great splendour to the ten Directions; from the air he told Rāma:

68.7–21 'Listen, Rāghava, to how you can really get Sītā back. My good friend, you must have an ally. I've thought it over, but I can't see you being successful if you don't get one. Listen, Rāma, while I tell you. There's a *vānara* called Sugrīva who's been thrown out by his angry brother Vālin, a true Son of Śakra; he's a self-controlled hero, and he's living with four *vānaras* on Ṛśyamūka, the excellent mountain on the lovely shore of Pampā. Go straight there now, Rāghava, and make a comrade of him; make common cause with him before the fiery flame. Don't look down on Sugrīva: he's the *vānara* leader, he will repay a favour, he's a shape-changer, he's heroic, and he's looking for an ally. You two could carry out the thing he wants done, but whether he gets his wish or not he'll do what you need. He's the son of Ṛkṣarajas, and he roams around Pampā, a true Son of the Sun but suspicious after the injury done him by Vālin. Lay down your weapon at once, Rāghava, and plight true comradeship with the monkey that lives on Ṛśyamūka and roams its forest. That elephant of a monkey's skilful and he's thoroughly acquainted with all the places in the world where those cannibals live. There's nothing hidden from him in the world, Rāghava, victorious hero, nothing under the sun's thousand scorching rays. He'll search rivers and spreading mountains, hill forts and hollows; he and his *vānaras* will find your wife. Sītā will be grieving at being separated from you, Rāghava, but he'll send out mighty *vānaras* to search every direction for her.'

Sensible Kabandha went on to tell Rāma more that he needed 69.1–32
to know if he was to recover Sītā. 'Rāma, this is the path you want: its blossoming trees will point you westwards and entrance you with their appearance: there are *jambūs*, *priyālas*, jackfruits, different sorts of figs, ebonies, *aśvatthas*, *karṇikāras*, mangoes and others. Climb them or else shake them hard to make their fruit fall to the ground; eat it as you go – it'll taste like ambrosia! Journey on through lovely regions, from mountain to mountain, from forest to forest, you heroes, until you reach the lake called Pampā. It's pebble-free and calm, Rāma, with level bathing places and no duckweed but lots of sand, and it's decked out with lotuses and water lilies. Geese, coots, cranes and ospreys wander about there on Pampā's waters, Rāghava, and utter their melodious calls. They're lovely, and they aren't shy of the sight of men, for they're not used to killing; they're fat as lumps of *ghī* and you shall shoot these birds with your arrows, Rāma Rāghava, and eat them – and the fine fish there in Pampā, carp, crooked-nosed and reed fish. Your loyal Lakṣmaṇa shall catch you some plump ones,

take off the skin and fins to leave just the backbone, and cook them for you on an iron grill. When you've eaten your fill of Pampā fish on the flowery grass, Lakṣmaṇa shall then draw some sweet lotus-scented water, pleasant and cool, pure and clear as crystal or silver, for you to drink from a lotus leaf. If you gaze at the cool water of Pampā you'll lose your grief, Rāghava, amid the piles of blossom, the *tilakas*, the *naktamālakas*, the lotuses and the water lilies. There's no man there to put their garlands on. Some well-conducted sages used to be there, the pupils of Mataṅga. They brought such heavy loads of forest produce for their *guru* that drops of sweat streamed from their bodies to the ground, and these garlands were born from the heat of the sages' mortifications; sprung as they are from drops of sweat, they do not perish, Rāghava. An attendant of theirs still lives there, Kākutstha; she's a nun, very old, and actually a Śabara woman but so steadfast in merit that when she sees your universally honoured godlike form she will go to heaven. Then if you go to the west bank of Pampā, Kākutstha, you'll see hidden away the site of a first-rate hermitage. No elephant can attack that hermitage, nor the wood either, by ordinance of the sage Mataṅga. You'll enjoy yourself in comfort in that forest, Rāma; it looks like Nandana, it could be the forest of the gods, with so many birds scattered about. Blossom-decked Ṛśyamūka lies to the east of Pampā. It's high and steep, and guarded by elephant calves; it was Brahmā of yore who raised it up. If a man lies down at the top of that mountain, Rāma, and dreams of wealth, when he wakes up he'll obtain it. But no wicked sinner can climb it, for *rākṣasas* will surprise him in his sleep and carry him off, and Mataṅga's forest-rangers, the elephant calves, will be heard trumpeting their war cries, Rāma, as they sport in Pampā. Matchless elephants roam about singly, cloud-grey and violent, spattered with streaks of blood from their battles. They drink the pure, cool, eternal water, then the forest-rangers turn and plunge once more into the forest. Rāma, on that mountain a great cavern is manifest; it's blocked by a boulder, Kākutstha, and difficult to enter. At this cave's eastern entrance is a large lake with cool water; it's delightful, with many roots and fruits, and it's surrounded by all sorts of trees. That's where Sugrīva lives with four *vānaras*, but sometimes he stations himself on the peak of the mountain.'

As Kabandha finished his instructions to them both, to Rāma and to Lakṣmaṇa, he blazed powerfully forth in the sky with his garlands, sunlike in splendour. Before Rāma and Lakṣmaṇa set out they spoke to the distinguished Kabandha standing there in the sky, wishing him well, and he replied, 'May your journey be successful.' Then Kabandha took leave of the delighted pair and set out. 69.33–5

The king's two sons turned west and set out on the route to Pampā indicated by Kabandha. Rāma and Lakṣmaṇa could see trees with honey-like fruits covering the mountains as they went to find Sugrīva. The two brothers, pride of the Raghus, paused on the mountain flank, then those Rāghavas made for the western shore of Pampā. When they reached lotus-filled Pampā's western shore they saw the Śabarī's lovely hermitage. They arrived at the hermitage, really lovely among its many surrounding trees, looked around and went up to the Śabarī. The Perfected Woman saw them, stood up and greeted them respectfully, grasping the feet of Rāma and of Lakṣmaṇa the wise. 70.1–6

Rāma then addressed the disciplined nun: 'Doubtless you have overcome your problems; doubtless your ascetic power is increasing; doubtless you can control your anger and your diet, so rich is your ascetic power; doubtless you have observed all the prescribed conduct; doubtless your mind is content; doubtless you are reaping the reward of obedience to your *gurus*, honey-tongued woman?' 70.7–8

At Rāma's questions, that Perfected ascetic whom the Perfected honoured, the aged Śabarī, came up close to Rāma and told him, 'When you reached Citrakūṭa those on whom I was waiting were taken up from here to heaven on carriages unequalled in splendour, and those right-knowing, distinguished great sages told me, "Rāma will come to your most holy hermitage. You must receive him as a guest, and Saumitri with him, then the sight of him will allow you to go to the excellent worlds of eternity." So, you bull of a man, I've been 70.9–13 gathering for you all kinds of forest produce that grows on Pampā's shores, you tiger of a man.'

70.14–15 So said the Śabarī. This Śabarī had never been excluded from learning, so the Rāghava rightly replied: 'I have heard direct from a Danu the truth about your noble masters' power; I should like to see it for myself, if that seems good to you.'

70.16–24 Hearing the words that fell from Rāma's lips, the Śabarī showed them both round that great forest. 'See, pride of the Raghus, this is Mataṅga's famous forest, billowing like clouds and thronged with wildlife. This is the bathing place, blessed by *mantras*, where my holy *gurus* made *mantra*-conforming oblations. This is the westward-facing altar where those I respected so highly made their offerings of flowers, their hands trembling from weariness. See, best of the Raghus, even today the power of their austerities makes the altars, unequalled in radiance, light up every direction with their splendour. By thought alone they could bring the Seven Seas together here, for fasting had made them so faint and weak they could not go there. Here on the trees they hung out their bark-fibre clothes after they had bathed, but in this place they still have not dried, pride of the Raghus. You have now seen the whole forest and heard all that I have to tell, so with your approval I wish to leave my body. It's my wish to go to join those holy sages whose hermitage this was, and whose attendant I was.'

70.25–7 The Rāghava's face lit up with delight – Lakṣmaṇa's too – as he heard that most righteous speech and replied, 'Go, with my leave!' When Rāma gave his permission she offered herself into the sacrificial fire and was gone to heaven with a fiery aura. To the holy place where sport those sages made great by their extreme discipline, there, by the power of her own meditation, went the Śabara woman.

KIṢKINDHĀ

Rāma went with Saumitri to the lake, his mind in a whirl, and gave way to grief. The sight of the teeming lotuses, water lilies and fish set his senses quivering with delight; desire seized him, and he cried out to Saumitri: 4,1.1–2

'Saumitri, look at Pampā's lovely wood! It looks as if it's growing from the tops of mountains, so mountainous are its trees! But I'm weighed down by care and tormented by grief: there's Bharata's trouble and now the capture of Vaidehī! The forest floor gleams green with dark and light patches, carpeted with flowers from the trees. Saumitri, it's the season of balmy breezes, frenzied desire, fragrance – spring, begetter of blossom and fruits on trees. Look, Saumitri, how fair are the forests, decked with flowers! They're like clouds, raining down flowers in floods! In the pretty glades the ground is strewn with flowers fluttering down from the woodland trees, wafted by the breeze. A gentle breeze blows sandal-cool through honey-fragrant forests buzzing with bees. Amid the fair, flower-girt, pleasing summits, whole chains of mountains flaunt their great trees. Look at these *karṇikāras* all around, with their flowery heads covered in gold: they're like men in yellow clothes! Saumitri, this bird-proclaimed springtime fans the flames of my grief, bereft as I am of Sītā! I'm overwhelmed by grief, and Manmatha's tormenting me! The *kokila* is raising its voice and calling in delight, and the moorhen calling out in rapture from a pretty forest waterfall makes me grieve, Lakṣmaṇa, gripped as I am by Manmatha. His bees have brought joy to all sorts of birds, Saumitri; sweetly they sing as they sport with their mates in flocks of their own kind. Saumitri, when I think of 1.3–46 my doe-eyed wife I'm tormented by grief – and now by this cruel springtime breeze blowing through the forest. Manmatha's overwhelming me and the flocks of peafowl displaying to their mates on the mountainsides are augmenting Manmatha's might. Lakṣmaṇa, look how that peahen's dancing attendance on her mate, the cock, as he's dancing on the mountain-side. She's suffering from Manmatha! That peacock has certainly not had his beloved stolen by a *rākṣasa* in the forest. It's very hard for me to have to live without her in the springtime. At the end of the winter the forests are enriched by a mass of blossom. Look, Lakṣmaṇa, how fruitless for me is that blossom. Flocks of enraptured wildfowl are calling out to each other, their muffled cries making me mad with desire. Sītā must be grieving like me in her captivity – my dark darling with her lotus-petal eyes and sweet voice! This breeze gently wafting the flowers feels cool, but to me it's like a fire when I think of the woman I yearn for. When she was lost, then this winged ranger of the skies sang out; now that crow is calling in delight from its perch on a tree. The winged sky-ranger kept watch over Vaidehī then; now it shall lead me to my broad-eyed beauty's side. Lakṣmaṇa, look how the birds in the blossom-capped forest trees are cooing out their impassioning song. Saumitri, see glittering Pampā – we can glimpse it through the trees – its water's radiating lotuses like the rising sun! That's Pampā with its still water, crammed with water lilies and lotuses – blue and red – strewn with geese and coots, and always crammed with sheldrake, its lovely banks and glades graced by herds of elephants and deer in search of water. Lakṣmaṇa, the sight of those lotus-ball petals reminds me of the eyeballs of Sītā! The captivating breeze blowing clouds of lotus filaments from the forest depths is sighing like Sītā! Saumitri, see on the mountain-side to Pampā's south the wonderful flowery shaft of a *karṇikāra*. That king of a mountain is enriched with so many minerals that the dust blown up from it by the wind is multi-coloured. Everywhere, Saumitri, the mountain-slopes are ablaze with beautiful flame-trees, flowers all over their leafless limbs, indeed the hillsides are flecked all over with their flowers, they're carpeted red and yellow all over! Saumitri, see the woodland bringing forth its flowers after the end of winter; now it's the flowering season, the trees are vying with each other with their blossom. Saumitri, see too the cool water, choking with lotuses, covered with sheldrake, home to coots, filled with water hens and cranes and the haunt of boar and deer: Pampā is resplendent with cooing birds! The joy of all these birds enflames my yearning as I remember my dark darling, her moon-bright face and her lotus-eyes. See! on the glittering slopes the bucks are accompanied by their does, but I remain desolate without doe-eyed Vaidehī.'

So did he mourn, his mind overcome by his grief, as he gazed 1.47
there at the bright and gleaming waters of lovely Pampā.

Sugrīva noticed Rāma and Lakṣmaṇa, those noble brothers 2.1–6
with their fine warlike weapons, and grew alarmed. When he saw how mighty they were he was not reassured; the monkey became very frightened and his spirits sank. He thought it over and considered it from all sides, but righteous Sugrīva and all his followers were highly suspicious. So suspicious was Sugrīva, lord of the monkeys, at the sight of Rāma and Lakṣmaṇa that he told his companions, 'Vālin has obviously sent this pair to that inaccessible forest, to roam about here disguised in bark clothes.'

A glance at the two supreme bowmen sent Sugrīva's com- 2.7–11
panions scurrying from the mountain-side to another lofty peak. These leaders ran to their bull of a leader, and the apes in the *vānara* chief's guard clustered round him. Up narrow tracks they went, leaping from mountain to mountain, their momentum making the peaks shudder. In their flight, all the mighty monkeys smashed blossoming trees clinging to the fastness, and all the excellent apes startled deer, wild cats and tigers as they came leaping on all sides towards that great mountain.

When Sugrīva's companions had all assembled on the Lord 2.12–13
of Mountains and clustered round the Chief of the Monkeys, they stood and saluted. Hanumān eloquently addressed the timorous Sugrīva, who was terrified by the thought that Vālin might harm him.

2.14–17 'Bull of a *vānara*, you've fled with your mind in a turmoil from savage, grim-faced Vālin, but I can't recognize him here. My dear sir, you're afraid of some evil from your older brother, but evil-natured Vālin is not here. There's nothing to frighten you that I can see. Shame on you! It's plain to see you're just a monkey bounding around, too light-minded to stand firm on anything. You've been gifted with intelligence and understanding: act according to the circumstances! A king who acts without judgement can't tell others what to do.'

2.18–26 Sugrīva heard all Hanumān's reasonable advice; his reply to Hanumān was yet more reasonable. 'They have strong arms and broad eyes, and they're carrying bows and arrows and swords. Who wouldn't be terrified to see this pair? They look like sons of a god! It's my suspicion that these excellent warriors are agents of Vālin. Kings can call on many confederates: they're not to be trusted. A man should watch out for enemies operating under cover, for the untrustworthy attack the trusting at their weak points. Vālin is shrewd and practical; far-sighted kings eliminate their enemies, and it's for ordinary men to discover them. Monkey, you're just an ordinary person: you can go and investigate them – the clues in their behaviour, their appearance, the way they talk. Assess what mood they're in: are they well disposed? Gain their confidence with repeated courteous remarks and gestures. Act as my frontman, bull of an ape; you, ask the two bowmen why they have come into this forest. Monkey, from their words and behaviour you must judge their intentions: are they, in your opinion, honourable?'

2.27; At the command of the King of Apes, that true Son of the
3.1–3 Wind resolved to go after Rāma and Lakṣmaṇa. Learning what noble Sugrīva wanted, Hanumān leapt over to the two Rāghavas from mount Ṛśyamūka. When he arrived, that truly valiant, excellent *vānara*, the mighty Hanumān, approached them with courteous words. The *vānara* changed his own form into that of a mendicant and addressed the heroes with due deference:

3.4–21 'Fair-skinned, steadfast ascetics, equal to royal sages or gods, why have your Honours come to this region? As you glance all around at the trees growing on Pampā's bank you are startling the herds of deer and other forest wildlife; your golden lustre brightens the river's bright waters. Who are you, so bold, so resolute, to be wearing bark? Lionlike your gaze, lionlike your mighty courage, my heroes; like Śakra's bow are the bows you both grasp in your powerful arms; intrepid as the best of bulls, you are majestic, handsome, glorious bulls of men; like the trunks of elephants are your arms. This Lord of Mountains shines with your splendour! You are worthy to be kings, you could be taken for immortals: why then have you come here? You are warriors, your eyes are like lotus petals, yet you wear your hair matted into a mound; you are warriors, both alike come here from the world of the gods, as if sun and moon had chanced to fall to earth. You are warriors with broad chests, men in the guise of gods; lionlike your shoulders, great your spirit, like rutting bulls are you. Your arms, long and well developed, are like clubs: they're fit for adornment with every kind of ornament – so why are they bare of ornament? You're a pair who could protect this earth – ocean, forests, lovely Vindhya and Meru and all – that's my opinion! These glittering, gilded bows of yours, smooth and glittering with grease, flash like Indra's lightning bolts. Your magnificent quivers are all filled with sharp arrows the like of lethal serpents, dread and blazing. These two estimable swords, long and ornamented with refined gold, sparkle like sloughed snakes. Won't you answer my questions when I'm talking to you like this? There's a certain *vānara* lord, the righteous Sugrīva by name. This hero has been ill-treated by his brother, and roams the world in sorrow. I have come on the orders of noble Sugrīva, king of the *vānara* chiefs: I am the *vānara* named Hanumān. Sugrīva the righteous wishes to make an alliance with you both. Let me introduce myself: I am his minister, a *vānara* Son of the Wind. I can assume any form I choose and go wherever I choose, and I've come here from Ṛśyamūka disguised as a mendicant out of desire to please Sugrīva.'

With these words from Hanumān the eloquent to warlike 3.22–3
Rāma and Lakṣmaṇa – eloquent themselves – he said no more. Majestic Rāma's face lit up to hear his speech, and he said to his brother Lakṣmaṇa standing beside him:

3.24–5 'This is a companion of the Ape Lord approaching me – that noble Sugrīva, that I so want to meet. Talk to him, Saumitri, with honeyed words: he's an ape, but he's Sugrīva's companion and he's an eloquent warrior, well disposed to us.'

4.1–2 Those sweetly spoken words delighted Hanumān as he realized the stranger had come out of need, and his mind flew to Sugrīva. 'Noble Sugrīva's coming into his kingdom is about to be realized with the arrival of this person in need; that need is as good as met.'

4.3–4 Hanumān, the bull of a monkey, was highly delighted and used his skill at speaking to question Rāma in reply. 'What is your purpose in coming with your younger brother to the fearsome forest, girdled by Pampā's woods, impenetrable and teeming with every kind of savage animal and deer?'

4.5–16 When he heard these words, Lakṣmaṇa was urged by Rāma to introduce him as noble Rāma, son of Daśaratha. 'A king called Daśaratha was glorious and devoted to doing right; his eldest son, Rāma by name, is world-famous as a refuge for all creatures, a hero faithful to his father's command. This is he, the most distinguished of Daśaratha's sons. He was banished from his kingdom and came to live here in the forest with me; glorious in his self-control, he was accompanied by his wife Sītā, just as the glorious sun is by its radiance at the dying of the day. I am his junior, Lakṣmaṇa by name. I've been led to serve him because of his distinction: he's appreciative but shrewd, yet sovereignty has been snatched from him and he has taken refuge in the forest. A shape-changing *rākṣasa* carried off his wife in a deserted place, but which *rākṣasa* it was that captured his wife we don't know. A certain Danu, a true Son of Śrī but cursed to *rākṣasa* form, told us of Sugrīva, the competent lord of the *vānaras*, "That hero will know who has captured your wife." When he'd told us that, the brilliant Danu went happily to heaven. I've told you truly all you asked, for Rāma and I have come to Sugrīva for protection. The man who once upheld the world, dispensing wealth and earning glory unparalleled, seeks the aid of Sugrīva, in the expectation that Sugrīva and his lords will be gracious to grief-stricken, heart-broken, supplicant Rāma.'

When Saumitri had sobbed out his pitiful tale, eloquent Hanumān replied, 'Men like you will be received by the lord of the *vānaras*, gifted as you are with wisdom, your anger checked, your senses under control. It is by good fortune that you come to see him! He too has been driven out of his kingdom and is in conflict with Vālin; his wife's been seized in the forest, he's been terrified, he's been violently ill-treated by his brother. Sugrīva himself, a true Son of the Sun, and the rest of us, will give you our aid in your search for Sītā.' 4.17–20

Hanumān spoke these gentle words in sweet tones, then said to the Rāghava, 'Let's go to Sugrīva.' 4.21

Righteous Lakṣmaṇa duly honoured Hanumān for his words, then declared to the Rāghava, 'We've found him! and he has a need too, as this delighted ape, this true Son of the Wind, tells us! Your need is met, Rāghava! That doughty Hanumān, that Son of the Wind, can't be telling an untruth; his face and features are calm and it's clear he's delighted at the news.' 4.22–4

Then Hanumān Son of the Wind wisely led the Rāghava heroes to the king of the monkeys, going from Ṛśyamūka to mount Malaya. Hanumān then announced the two Rāghava heroes to the king of the apes. 4.25; 5.1

'It is Rāma who has come, accompanied by his brother Lakṣmaṇa! Rāma the intelligent, steadfast in his courage, truly valiant! Rāma born of the Ikṣvāku race, son of Daśaratha, renowned for righteously upholding his father's commands! While this noble was living a life of discipline in the forest, a *rākṣasa* carried off his wife, and he has come to you for support. That king was a man of integrity, who gratified the sacrificial flame with *rājasūyas* and *aśvamedhas* and gave away cows as sacrificial fees hundreds and thousands of times, protecting the earth with his austerity. It's his son Rāma who's come to you for support on account of his wife. These brothers Rāma and Lakṣmaṇa wish to enter into alliance with you, sir; you should receive and honour them, for they are both most worthy of respect.' 5.2–7

Sugrīva was delighted and relieved to hear Hanumān's words. Shaking off his terrible fear of the Rāghava, Sugrīva 5.8–12 the monkey lord assumed a most becoming human form and greeted the Rāghava with pleasure. 'Sir, this true Son of the Wind has told me all about your excellent qualities, how you are schooled in righteousness, courageous, and kind to all. My lord, it is the utmost privilege and benefit that you wish for friendship with me, a *vānara*. If this friendship please you, here is my hand on it; clasp hand in hand and let the bargain be sealed.'

5.13–18 Hearing Sugrīva's well-phrased speech, Rāma delightedly pressed hand into hand and cordially embraced him as a friend. The warrior Hanumān changed back from a mendicant into his own form, kindled a fire with a pair of sticks, honoured the pure flame with flowers when it blazed, then placed it between them with joyful care. Sugrīva and the Rāghava circled the blazing fire to inaugurate their friendship. Then those two, monkey and Rāghava, could not have enough of gazing at each other, so great was their delight. Illustrious Sugrīva made a wholehearted promise to Daśaratha's all-wise son, Rāma.

6.1–10 'Rāma, Hanumān, my companion and best of my counsellors, has told me why you've come to the deserted forest and how, while you've been living in the forest with your brother Lakṣmaṇa, Janaka's daughter, your wife Maithilī has been carried off by a *rākṣasa*, who sought his opportunity then snatched her away in tears from you and prudent Lakṣmaṇa after killing the vulture Jaṭāyus. I will soon release you from the sorrow born of separation from your wife. I'm the one to bring her back to you, like the once-lost Vedic scriptures. Whether she's in the world below or the world above, I'm the one to fetch her and return her to you, victorious warrior. Believe my words, mighty Rāghava, and forsake your grief: I am bringing your darling to you. I realize it must have been Maithilī I saw being carried off by an evil *rākṣasa*: no doubt of it! She was incoherently shrieking out "Rāma! Rāma! Lakṣmaṇa!" and writhing about in Rāvaṇa's grip like the serpent queen. She saw me standing with four others on a mountain-side and dropped her shawl and fine ornaments. These we gathered up and kept, Rāghava. I'll fetch them; you ought to recognize them.'

Hearing Sugrīva's glad tidings, Rāma cried, 'Fetch them quickly, my friend! What are you waiting for?' 6.11

At these words, in his eagerness to please the Rāghava, Sugrīva plunged at once into a hidden cave in the mountain and brought out the shawl and fine ornaments. Saying, 'Look, here they are!' the *vānara* showed them to Rāma, who took the garment and fine ornaments, clouded with tears like the moon with mist. Tears welling up out of love for Sītā overwhelmed him. 'Oh my darling!' he cried out as he lost his composure and fell to the ground. Again and again he pressed that perfect ornament to his heart, his sighs deep as a snake's raging in its hole. His tears flowed unchecked. Noticing Saumitri at his side he began a sorrowful lament: 6.12–17

'Lakṣmaṇa, look at the shawl and jewels Vaidehī's cast off from her body to the ground as she was being carried off. This jewel was definitely dropped by Sītā on to the grassy earth as she was being carried off: I recognize its shape. Sugrīva, tell me where you saw her, dear to me as my life! Where was that horrific *rākṣasa* taking her? Where does he live, that *rākṣasa*, my tormentor? Because of him all *rākṣasas* shall meet destruction at my hands! He's opened the gates of Death to end his own life, so greatly has he enraged me by capturing Maithilī!' 6.18–22

The *vānara* Sugrīva was overcome by sobbing at Rāma's sorrowful words; making a respectful gesture he replied through his sobs: 'I know nothing about the evil *rākṣasa's* lair, nor his capability or strength, nor his low-bred lineage. But this I pledge in all truth, victorious hero: I will make such an effort that you'll get Maithilī back. Stop grieving! I will take swift steps to secure your happiness: killing Rāvaṇa and his horde will vindicate my manliness. Don't let weakness overcome you! Remember your natural composure. It's not right for a man like you to be so irrational. I too have incurred great distress by having my wife seized, but I'm not grieving, I'm not losing my composure. I'm only a common *vānara*, but I'm not grieving over her. You, sir, are noble – and self-controlled too – so you have all the more reason to be resolute. It's for you to restrain your falling tears with composure, and not abandon that resolve which is the guiding principle of those who pursue 7.1–13 true integrity. A resolute man draws on his inner resources and doesn't get discouraged by distress or difficulty or deadly fear. It's a foolish man who's always lapsing into frailty; he's bound to sink under his sorrow like an overladen ship in the water. I'm saluting you respectfully, and begging you with deference: be a man and don't give grief a chance. Those who lapse into sorrow never find happiness; their brilliance is dimmed, so you mustn't grieve. I'm not giving you orders, I'm speaking out of friendship: it's in your own interest! Out of respect for that friendship you should stop grieving.'

7.14–15 The Rāghava was comforted by Sugrīva's gentle words. His face was wet with tears, but at Sugrīva's words he wiped it with the edge of his robe and pulled himself together: he was Lord Kākutstha. He embraced Sugrīva and replied:

7.16–22 'Sugrīva, you've done everything that it's right and proper for a dear, kind friend to do. At your prompting I'm myself again, my friend. Such friendship is hard to find even in a relative, especially at a time like this. Even so, you should be getting on with the hunt for Maithilī and that base, ferocious *rākṣasa*. What must I do? Tell me that with confidence, and I'll promise to do it; I give you my true word.' Sugrīva and his *vānara* companions were thrilled to hear the Rāghava's promise.

8.1–10 The *vānara* Sugrīva was so delighted by the promise that he cried to Rāma, Lakṣmaṇa's senior, 'I must certainly be a favourite of the gods and blessed with every virtue for you, sir, to be my friend! With you to help me I could even win the kingdom of the gods, let alone my own kingdom! Friends and family alike will certainly commend me, Rāghava, for securing a born Rāghava as my ally, with the fire as witness. You will gradually come to recognize me as a fitting friend for you, but I can't begin to list all the virtues of your character. Noble, generous people like you are to the highest degree unwavering in their affection, like self-controlled people in a resolve. To the righteous, the silver and gold, the clothes and the ornaments of the righteous are common property: the highest gain is a friend, rich or poor, miserable or happy, perfect or imperfect.

The sight of affection like that will lead a man to lay down wealth, happiness or life itself for the sake of a friend.' Rāma agreed with Sugrīva's welcome words witnessed by wise Lakṣmaṇa, another Indra Vāsava in fortune.

Seeing that Rāma and mighty Lakṣmaṇa were still standing, 8.11–15
Sugrīva looked all round the forest until the Lord of the Apes saw a nearby *sāl* tree in full flower, covered with small leaves and buzzing with bees. Sugrīva broke a well-flowered branch full of leaves off the *sal* and spread it out, sitting down on it with the Rāghava. Seeing them seated, Hanumān too tore a branch off the *sāl* and courteously invited Lakṣmaṇa to sit. The delighted Sugrīva addressed Rāma deferentially in a soft, sweet voice, his words filled with joy.

'For my part, I've been badly treated by my brother, so that 8.16–18
I roam this lovely mount Ṛśyamūka, weighed down by fear and in utter misery from the seizure of my wife. I live here in terror, in the depths of dread, my thoughts in a whirl, injured by my brother Vālin, Rāghava, and at enmity with him. You give security to all the world: do take up my cause. I've no one to turn to, and I'm weighed down by fear of Vālin.'

With a gentle smile illustrious Kākutstha, who knew what 8.19–23
was right and was devoted to doing right, answered Sugrīva: 'The fruit of friendship is aid; injury is the mark of an enemy. This very day I will kill the captor of your wife. These feathered arrows of mine are sharp-edged and very swift: they're the product of Kārtikeya's forest. They are gilded and trimmed with heron feathers, well jointed, their points well honed: they're like angry snakes, they're like great Indra's thunderbolt. That enemy in the guise of a brother, that cause of your torment, you'll see that Vālin laid low by my arrows, like a shattered mountain!'

Commander-in-Chief Sugrīva was immeasurably delighted 8.24–7
to hear the Rāghava's words. 'Well said, well said!' he cried. 'Rāma, I was overwhelmed by sorrow. Sorrow-oppressed people should turn to you, sir. With you as my friend, I can pour out my plaint. You have become my friend, valued above life itself – I swear it in all truth – you gave me your hand –

the fire was witness! The alliance we have formed gives me confidence to speak out: the grief possessing my mind is constantly burning me up!'

8.28–30 These words were enough; tears dimmed his eyes, tears choked his voice, and he could say no more. But in Rāma's presence Sugrīva resolutely stemmed the flood of tears suddenly bearing down on him like a river in full spate. The illustrious *vānara* checked his tears, wiped his fine eyes, sighed and continued his tale to the Rāghava.

8.31–9 'Some time ago, Rāma, Vālin unseated me from my own kingdom, slandered me and drove me out by force. He seized my wife, who is dearer to me than life itself, and imprisoned my friends. Rāghava, the wretch has made efforts to destroy me, and many times have I killed *vānaras* in his employ. Even when I saw you, Rāghava, it was anxiety on this score that made me afraid to approach you myself, for every alarm frightens me. These have been my sole companions since then, led by Hanumān, as I eke out my hard-lived existence. These affectionate monkeys protect me on all sides: when I go they go with me and when I stay they stay. In short, this is my tale, Rāma. Why spin it out? My eldest brother Vālin, renowned for his manliness, is my enemy. His destruction would end my troubles at once; my happiness – indeed my life – depend on his destruction. I've told you how to end my sorrow, Rāma; I'm tormented by sorrow, and in good times or bad a friend can always rely on a friend.'

8.40–43 Hearing what he said, Rāma told Sugrīva, 'I wish to hear the true reason for this enmity. When I have heard what caused your enmity, *vānara*, and thought over the pros and cons, I will at once procure your happiness. Strong indignation is welling up in me to hear how disgracefully you have been treated; my heart is agitated like waters at the onslaught of the rains. Tell me in glad confidence while I string my bow, for when my arrow is released your enemy will be destroyed.'

8.44–5 So spoke noble Kākutstha. Sugrīva was immeasurably delighted, along with the four *vānaras*. His face full of joy, Sugrīva began to explain to Lakṣmaṇa's elder brother the true cause of his enmity.

'My victorious elder brother, Vālin by name, used always to be high in our father's esteem, and in mine, too. On our father's death he, as the eldest, was installed in the kingship by the counsellors as the supremely honoured Lord of the Monkeys, and while he was ruling our great ancestral kingdom, I remained at all times as obedient to him as a servant. Between Vālin and the eldest son of Dundubhi, the illustrious Māyāvin by name, there had once been a notorious, fierce quarrel over some woman. One night while everyone was asleep, Māyāvin came to the gate of Kiṣkindhā, roaring in rage, and challenged Vālin to fight. Hearing that hideous roaring as he slept, my brother Vālin couldn't contain himself but dashed out at once. His wives and my obedient self tried to prevent him from rushing out in anger to kill that champion of the anti-gods, but the mighty *vānara* shook us all off and ran on, with me rushing after him, driven by my affection for Vālin. The sight of my brother and me coming in the distance struck terror into the anti-god, and he ran off quickly, so we increased our pace to catch up with his timorous flight, with the rising moon illuminating the chase. The anti-god bolted into a deep cleft in the earth, constricted and hidden in the grass. We ran up quickly and stopped; Vālin was angry and perplexed to see his foe enter the cave, but instructed me, 'Sugrīva, you stay here at the cave entrance on the alert while I go in and fight and kill my enemy.' Despite my entreaties when I heard his instructions, he made me swear by his feet, my lord, then went in. A full year elapsed after he went into the cave, with me standing at the entrance the whole time. When my brother didn't come back I decided he must be dead; in my fondness for him I feared the worst but didn't know what to do. A long time later I was greatly distressed to see red blood come foaming out of the cave. I could hear the sound of anti-gods roaring and the shouts of my respected brother struck down in battle. These signs convinced me that my brother had been slain, so I blocked the cave entrance with a rock the size of a mountain, sorrowfully made a water offering and returned to Kiṣkindhā, my friend, strenuously concealing what had happened. Nevertheless, the counsellors heard about it and consecrated me publicly. 9.1–20

9.21–4; 10.1–6 'While I was duly ruling the kingdom, Rāghava, Vālin returned. He had killed his enemy, that anti-god chief! When he saw that I had been consecrated, rage reddened his eyes, he bound my counsellors and he uttered a stream of vituperation. I was quite capable of punishing my evil brother, Rāghava, but respect for him restrained me. I welcomed him with the honour due to his nobility, but his joyless heart spoke no greeting. My wish was to smooth things over and calm my furious brother, so eaten up with anger was he on his return. "Fortune has brought you back safe! You have killed your enemy!" I exclaimed. "My lord, I have no lord but you alone, you who delight the lordless. This many-ribbed parasol is like the risen full moon: take it and the fan[1] that I am holding out to you. It is you who are king, now perpetually to be accorded the homage I have been receiving. The kingdom has been held in trust for you: I restore it to you. Most respectfully do I entreat you by your head, gentle conqueror, not to be angry with me. When the counsellors resident in the city met me, they forced the kingship upon me, lest the vacancy should invite conquest."

10.7–25 'That *vānara* requited my gentle words with insults, crying out "Shame on you!" and much more of that sort. He called together the subjects and the honoured counsellors, and addressed this accusation to me in the midst of my friends. "You know that Māyāvin, that huge, vicious, belligerent, wicked anti-god, challenged me one night. When I heard his roar, I rushed out from the royal palace, followed quickly by this most ruthless brother. Through the darkness the giant saw I had a companion; terror gripped him at the sight of the two of us running towards him and he fled, running at top speed, and bolted into a cavern. When I discovered he was inside that huge, monstrous cave, I told my cruel-faced brother, 'I can't go back to the city without killing him. You keep watch at the cave entrance; I'll kill him myself.' Confident he would stay, I went in with difficulty, and then a year elapsed while I searched, but my dauntless courage enabled me to spy out that terrifying enemy, and I killed the anti-god and his family. As he lay groaning on the ground, a stream of blood came gushing out of his mouth and filled that winding cave. I had overcome my enemy, Dundubhi's audacious son, but found my exit, the mouth of the cave, blocked! I shouted out 'Sugrīva!' again and again, and was devastated to get no answer, but I battered my way out with kick after kick and so managed to come back. That's why I'm enraged with this cruel Sugrīva, who has forgotten all brotherly affection and sought the kingdom for himself." So said that *vānara* Vālin. When his fury abated he turned me out in just a single garment. Rāghava, not only did he exile me, he seized my wife, and fear of him has sent me roaming the forests and seas of the whole earth, mourning the seizure of my wife, until I reached this lovely mountain, Ṛśyamūka, which for a special reason is out of Vālin's reach. I've given you a lengthy and complete account of our enmity. Rāghava, you can see what misfortune has befallen me, though I am guiltless. Do be gracious to me, valiant protector of the world, and punish Vālin for this fearful persecution.'

Sugrīva had right on his side: knowing where his duty lay, 10.26–9
his glorious hearer told him with a smile, 'These sharp unerring arrows of mine, like the sun, shall fall in fury on that vicious Vālin. That evil Vālin, that scandalous abductor of your wife, shall live only until I catch sight of him. My own experience tells me that you are sunk in a sea of sorrow. I will bear you across and you shall obtain your heart's desire.'

Rāma's words cheered Sugrīva and gave him courage; he 11.1–6
paid homage to him and told the Rāghava, 'You, I'm sure, when roused to anger could burn up the worlds like the sun at Doomsday, tearing bodies open with your blazing, sharp arrows. Listen attentively to what I can tell you about Vālin's courage and might and resolution, then work out what to do next. Before sunrise, his strength restored, Vālin strides from western to eastern ocean, from southern to northern. He climbs to the mountain-tops and even hurls great peaks violently into the air, staunchly catching them again. To demonstrate his strength, Vālin has made short work of smashing all kinds of forest trees full of sap.

'A buffalo called Dundubhi, splendid as Kailāsa's peak, was 11.7–13
courageous and strong as a thousand elephants. Deluded by pride in his valour and the possession of a boon, this ill-natured

giant approached the Ocean, Lord of Rivers, and issued a challenge to the billowing waves, the source of gems, the Great Sea, to do battle with him. Then up rose the righteous mighty Ocean, your majesty, and replied to the anti-god, who was hastening to his doom. "I have not the power to do battle with an expert warrior such as you; listen, and I will name one who will do battle with you: the King of the Mountains in the great forest, the ascetics' chief sanctuary, father-in-law to Śiva, clad with caves and torrents, replete with gorges and waterfalls, renowned by the name Himavān! A duel with him would give you unparalleled satisfaction."

11.14–24 'Realizing that the Ocean was afraid, that pre-eminent anti-god shot off to Himavān's forest like an arrow from a bow. Dundubhi then pelted the ground with the mountain's own snowy rocks huge as elephant lords, and bellowed until cloud-white Himavān, cool and pleasant to behold, stood on the very summit and addressed him. "Dundubhi, you cleave to what's right: it's not for you to torment me, for I know nothing of warfare. I'm the refuge of ascetics." Hearing what the wise King of the Mountains said, Dundubhi's eyes reddened with rage and he replied, "If you are incapable of fighting or paralysed by fear, then tell me who will do battle with me today. I want a fight!" When righteous Himavān heard that unprecedented demand he grew angry and eloquently told the pre-eminent anti-god, "A glorious *vānara* of great wisdom called Vālin, equal to Śakra in might, lives in peerless, splendid Kiṣkindhā. He's a knowledgeable and expert warrior, and he's the one to give you a duel great as Indra Vāsava's with Namuci. Go straight to him if you want a fight now. He's a difficult warrior to vanquish in feats of arms."

11.24–30 'Rage possessed Dundubhi when he heard Himavān's words and he went off to Kiṣkindhā, Vālin's city. He had the form of a terrifying, sharp-horned buffalo, looking like a huge monsoon cloud full of rain in the sky. When he came to the gate of Kiṣkindhā, mighty Dundubhi bellowed like a kettledrum, shaking the earth, smashing down the neighbouring trees, pawing up the ground with his hooves and arrogantly scouring the gate with his horns like a tusker. Vālin heard the noise from inside his private apartment and dashed out irritably, surrounded by his wives as the moon is by stars. Vālin, lord of all the apes that roam the forest, enquired of Dundhubi in moderate tones and clearly spoken words, "Why are you obstructing the city gate and bellowing? I know you. Look to your life, mighty Dundubhi!"

'The words of the wise *vānara* lord made Dundubhi's eyes redden with rage, and he replied: "A warrior like you shouldn't be prattling away in the presence of women! You should be doing battle with me! Then I'll know how strong you are. Either that, or I'll check my rage for tonight, *vānara*, and you can indulge yourself to your heart's content until dawn. Killing someone who's drunk, or making love, or asleep, or powerless, or led astray by passion like you, is everywhere rated as bad as procuring an abortion." 11.31–4

'He sent all the women away, led by Tārā, then laughed in rage and spoke slowly to that supreme anti-god: "Don't dismiss me as drunk, unless you're afraid to fight! If I'm drunk, it's with battle-frenzy!" 11.35–6

'With these words he angrily threw off a golden garland his father, great Indra, had given him and prepared to do battle. Seizing the mountainous Dundubhi by the horns, Vālin felled him and roared loudly. The life was squeezed out of Dundubhi in that fight to the death; as he fell, blood spurted from his ears, and his great corpse lay lifeless on the ground. 11.37–9

'Impetuously Vālin picked up the inert carcass in his arms and with one heave flung it for a *yojana*. As he was hurled violently along, drops of blood falling from his mouth were blown by the wind towards Mataṅga's hermitage. When the sage saw those spots of gore falling he pronounced a great curse upon Vālin for throwing them there: "Let him not come here on pain of death." 11.40–42

'He went to see the great sage and humbly begged for mercy, but since then fear of the curse has made that monkey refuse to approach lofty mount Ṛśyamūka, or even to look at it, Lord of Men, so I've been roaming this great forest with my 11.43–6 counsellors, free from worry, knowing that he can't come here. You can see the huge, mountainous heap of bones that he hurled here, glorying in his might. That's Dundubhi.

11.47–9 'Here are seven spreading *sāl* trees with drooping branches; it's as much as Vālin can manage to shoot an arrow right through one of them, although I've told you clearly, Rāma, that his might is unmatched. How will you be able to kill Vālin in a fight, your majesty? If you could split these *sāls* with a single arrow, then, sir, I would know you to be a mighty warrior, capable of killing Vālin.'

11.50–52 Hearing what noble Sugrīva had to say, the mighty Rāghava lifted Dundubhi's body playfully with his toe and kicked it for ten *yojanas*. Sugrīva's response to seeing the body kicked was pointed: in front of Lakṣmaṇa he told Rāma, 'The body was fresh, fleshy and full of moisture when it was thrown before, my friend; now, Rāghava, it's fleshless and light as straw. That makes it impossible to compare your strength and his.'

12.1–11 When he heard Sugrīva's well-turned speech, glorious Rāma grasped his bow to reassure him. Taking his dread weapon and a single arrow, he deigned to aim at the *sāl* trees, and shot; the noise of his bowstring filled every direction. The gold-adorned arrow released by his might pierced the seven *sāls* on the mountain-top and disappeared into the earth, travelled for a moment below ground then quickly burst out again, emerging at great speed to re-enter its own quiver. The bull of a *vānara* was amazed to see the seven *sāls* pierced by the impact of Rāma's arrow, and bowed his head with its dangling ornaments to the ground; with the utmost pleasure Sugrīva humbled himself before the Rāghava. Delighted by the deed he declared to the warrior standing before him, Rāma the right-minded supreme exponent of all weaponry, 'You could kill all the gods in battle with your arrows, Indra included, you bull of a man; how much more Vālin, my lord! Kākutstha, who could withstand you in the forefront of battle, when you can rip open seven great *sāls*, the mountain and the earth with a single arrow? This day is my sorrow fled, this day do I experience extreme pleasure at making a friend of you, great as Indra or Varuṇa! Please me this very day, Kākutstha, I humbly implore you, by killing Vālin, that enemy in the guise of a brother!'

Sugrīva looked so delighted that Rāma embraced him and, with Lakṣmaṇa's approval, very shrewdly replied, 'Let's leave here at once and go to Kiṣkindhā. You must lead the way. When you get there, Sugrīva, challenge Vālin, that sham of a brother.' 12.12–13

They all hurried off to Vālin's city of Kiṣkindhā and halted in the dense forest, concealing themselves in the trees. Sugrīva girded himself and roared horribly to challenge Vālin, rending the air with the violence of his roars. Hearing his brother's roar, mighty Vālin rushed out, angry and infuriated; it was as if the setting sun had risen again. Then ensued a tumultuous battle between Vālin and Sugrīva, dreadful as the celestial one between the planets Budha and Aṅgāraka. Crazed with rage the brothers fought, striking each other with slaps like thunder-claps and punches like thunderbolts. Rāma, bow at the ready, stared at the two warriors: they were like the twin gods, the Aśvins, so like each other that he could not distinguish Sugrīva from Vālin, so the Rāghava decided not to loose his death-dealing arrow. 12.14–20

While he hesitated, Vālin gained the advantage; finding no support from his lord, the Rāghava, Sugrīva fled to Ṛśyamūka, exhausted, bleeding from every limb, battered and disabled. Vālin chased him furiously as far as the great forest, but when he saw him go into that forest, Vālin was afraid of the curse and, mighty as he was, he turned back, shouting, 'You've got away!' The Rāghava and his brother, and Hanumān too, joined the *vānara* Sugrīva in the forest. 12.21–4

When Sugrīva saw Rāma and Lakṣmaṇa coming he asked with downcast eyes, miserable and shamefaced, 'What did you mean by telling me to challenge him and demonstrating your prowess, then getting me killed by my enemy? You should have told me the truth then and there, Rāghava, that you weren't going to kill Vālin, and then I shouldn't have stirred from here.' 12.25–7

The Rāghava replied to noble Sugrīva's plaintive, pitiful words, 'Sugrīva, my friend, listen to me, and dispel your anger. The reason I didn't shoot my arrow was that you, Sugrīva, and 12.28–35

Vālin look just like one another in ornament, dress, size and bearing. *Vānara*, I could detect no difference between you in voice, splendour, appearance, prowess or words. That was why, excellent *vānara*, I could not loose my foe-destroying, irresistible arrow: I was confused by the similarity of your appearance! But very soon you'll see Vālin writhing on the ground. I'll dispatch him from your fight with a single arrow. What you must find, *vānara* lord, is some way I can recognize you in the course of your duel. Lakṣmaṇa, pick some of these beautiful elephant-flowers and hang them round noble Sugrīva's neck.'

12.36–8 Lakṣmaṇa picked some of the luxuriant, mountain-born elephant-flower blossoms and hung them round his neck. The creeper round his neck made him glow with glory, like a twilight cloud garlanded by egrets. Rāma's promise reassured him, and he radiated beauty as he went with Rāma to Kiṣkindhā, stronghold of Vālin.

14.1–6 They all hurried off to Vālin's stronghold of Kiṣkindhā and halted in the dense forest, concealing themselves in the trees. Stout-necked Sugrīva gazed all around the woods; his beloved woodland fired him with fury and in the midst of his attendants he uttered a dreadful roar and issued his challenge, rending the air with the violence of his roars. Sugrīva looked like the rising sun, he had the gait of a haughty lion after Rāma's demonstration of his prowess: 'We have arrived,' he said. 'Ape-deterrent snares on all sides, burnished gold gateways, standards and siege-engines in abundance: this is Kiṣkindhā, Vālin's city! A bramble bears its fruit in due season: now, hero, the time is ripe for your promise to slaughter Vālin to be fulfilled.'

14.7–17 At Sugrīva's words the Rāghava, that righteous crusher of enemies, then replied: 'Sugrīva, this so-called elephant-flower singles you out for recognition, as the sun in the firmament is distinguished from its garland of constellations. *Vānara*, by me you shall today be rid of your fear of Vālin's enmity, by the loosing of a single arrow in your struggle. Sugrīva, show me your enemy in the guise of a brother, and Vālin lies writhing in the dust, slain! If I set eyes on him and he returns alive, then, sir, you may turn round at once and reproach me for my wrongdoing. Before your eyes I pierced seven *sāls* with an arrow: that tells you that today Vālin will meet a violent death at my hands. I've never yet told a lie, valiant prince, even under duress, so eagerly do I yearn for what's right; and in no circumstances will I utter one. I will make my promise bear fruit, like Indra Śatakratu with his rain on the rice sprouting in the field: cast aside your doubts! So, Sugrīva, shout out a challenge to gold-garlanded Vālin that will make that *vānara* rush out. If it's you that's attacking him, Vālin will think he's already won and will brag about his victory; he relishes a fight and nothing will stop him rushing out from the city. Warriors will not tolerate being attacked by their enemies in war, but trust to their prowess, especially within sight of their womenfolk.'

In response to Rāma's words, tawny-gold Sugrīva then 14.18–20
roared out a roar harsh enough to rend the whole air, terrifying cows with the din, shorn of their glory like women violated by a sinful king huddling together, stampeding wild animals like battle-wounded steeds and dashing birds to the ground like planets whose merit is exhausted.*

From inside his private apartment Vālin heard noble Sugrīva 15.1–5
roaring and lost his temper with his brother. Intoxication vanished in a flash when he heard that world-harrowing roar, and tremendous rage seized him. Vālin was radiant as the rising sun,[2] but when wrath took command of his body he was suddenly stripped of his radiance, as if the sun had been blotted out. In his anger Vālin was like a blazing fire; with his terrible teeth he gleamed like a lake displaying its open lotus flowers and stalks. At the sound of that intolerable noise the ape jumped up hastily, his feet thudding down as if they would rend the earth.

Tender Tārā was fearful and upset; in a demonstration of 15.6–23
affection she flung her arms round him and advised him prudently: 'Come, come, heroic ape! Anger is flooding over you like a river, driving you from your bed! Get rid of it quickly, like a garland you've worn. I don't think you should rush straight out: listen and I'll tell you why I'm holding you back. He's attacked you angrily once before and challenged you to

fight. He attacked, but you beat him and put him to flight. For him to come back and challenge you again makes me feel suspicious, when you've defeated him so emphatically and put him to flight. The arrogance and spirit of his bellowing, and the fervour of his shouting, are of no slight concern. I don't think this Sugrīva has come here on his own; he's bellowing because he's got some stout helper to rely on. That *vānara* Sugrīva is shrewd by nature, and certainly canny too: he won't have brought a companion without testing his prowess. My hero, a little while ago I heard Prince Aṅgada talking. I'll tell you what he said. It's to your advantage. It's that famous Rāma that's helping your brother! He's a fierce fighter who won't yield to hostile force, he blazes like the Doomsday Fire! He's a tree to shelter the good, the prime support of the unfortunate, a refuge for the afflicted – he alone is glorious! He's blessed with knowledge and understanding but content to obey his father: like a mountain of minerals, he's a whole heap of virtues! So it's not for you to oppose that noble, matchless Rāma in warfare: he's unassailable! Heroic ape, I'm going to make a suggestion and I don't want you to take it amiss; just listen, and then do as I say. I'm telling you for your own good. Consecrate Sugrīva as Young King straight away, if you please! Your glorious majesty, don't make war on your brother – he's stronger than you! It's my belief you'd be better off banishing your enmity far away and being on terms of friendship with Rāma and goodwill with Sugrīva. You should cherish this *vānara*, your younger brother; when all's said and done, he's your own flesh and blood. If you wish to please me and want to do me good, I beg and pray you to act upon my word.'

16.1–8 While she was still speaking Vālin reviled moonfaced Tārā and replied, 'My beauty, why should I put up with that rabid bellowing by my brother, especially when he's my enemy? You are timid, but unvanquished warriors don't retreat from battle; for them, intolerable harassment is worse than death. I cannot endure that weak-necked Sugrīva bellowing out his passionate hunger for battle. Don't worry about me because of the Rāghava. He knows what's right, and he knows what's happened, so why should he do me any harm? Go back with the women. Why follow me any further? You've demonstrated your affection for me, Tārā, and proved your devotion. It's for me to meet Sugrīva and fight. Stop worrying! I'll rid him of his arrogance, but I won't kill him – I swear that to you on my own life – so wish me victory and turn back. I'll be back when I've fought that brother and taught him enough of a lesson.'

Tārā had spoken kindly, but now she embraced Vālin and 16.9–10
circumambulated him in the auspicious direction, weeping softly, then pronounced a blessing with victory *mantras* and went with the women into the private apartments, in a turmoil of sorrow.

With Tārā back with the women in her own quarters he 16.11–14
issued angrily from the city, hissing like a great snake. Hissing vehemently in his great fury, majestic Vālin cast his eyes all round, eager to spy out his enemy, until he saw, tawny-golden, well-clad, dauntless as a blazing fire, Sugrīva. Remarking Sugrīva's resolute stance, Vālin flew into a rage and hitched his garment tightly round him.

'My fist is clenched tight: I'll lay its fingers on you so hard 16.18
they'll put an end to your life!' shouted Vālin.

Sugrīva's angry reply to Vālin was, 'It's my fist that shall fall 16.19–24
on your head and put an end to your life!' but as he rushed forwards in fury he received a blow that set the blood bursting from him like mountain springs. Then with a mighty heave Sugrīva completely uprooted a *sāl* tree and struck Vālin a body blow like a thunderbolt on a high mountain, sending Vālin reeling under the devastating force of that *sāl* like a heavy-laden boat sinking in the sea. Each displayed dread, vigorous might and the momentum of Garuḍa, each was puffed-up and ferocious to behold; they were like the sun and moon in the sky. Humiliated by Vālin, his strength ebbing, Sugrīva's resentment at Vālin fuelled his agility.

Then the Rāghava set to his bow an arrow like a poisonous 16.25–6;
snake, and shot the great shaft into Vālin's chest. Cut down by 19.2
its force, Vālin fell to the ground. His limbs had been shattered by rocks, he had been battered by trees and overcome by Rāma's arrow: his life was drawing to an end and he swooned.

Tārā his wife heard Vālin, that tiger of a monkey, being 19.3–7 struck down in battle by the impact of the arrow shot by Rāma. Hearing her husband's horrible, agonizing death she was terrified and rushed out with her son from the extensive mountain fastness. When the *vānaras* who attended Aṅgada saw Rāma with his bow, powerful as they were they fled in terror. When she saw frightened apes rushing headlong away like deer scattered from the herd when the leader is killed, she ran to them in her distress; they too were distressed, and as terrified of Rāma as if his arrows were pursuing them. She addressed them all:

19.8–9 'You *vānaras*, attendants of that lion of a king, why have you deserted him in terror and fled in confusion? Is it because brother has been struck down by savage brother to gain the kingship, with Rāma attacking him from afar, shooting his arrows from a distance?'

19.10–16 The shape-changing monkeys all made the same prompt response to the words of the monkey's wife: 'You have a living son! Turn back and safeguard your son Aṅgada! Death in the form of Rāma has struck Vālin down and is leading him away. Vālin has been laid low as if by a thunderbolt, by arrows that smashed like thunderbolts right through the trees and rocks he was hurling. This whole troop that charged forward has fled; we scattered when that tiger of a monkey, splendid as Śakra, was killed. Get warriors to protect the city and have Aṅgada consecrated. The monkeys will be loyal when Vālin's son takes his place. Do you really think this is a good place to stay, charming lady, with *vānaras* almost at our gates? Forest-roamers? We're in a turmoil of fear about these relations of ours; wives or not, they're destitute and predatory.'

19.17–19 True to herself, the lady only smiled sweetly when she heard that, and called after the speakers, already some way off: 'Why should I be bothering about my son, or the kingdom, or myself, while my husband, that distinguished lion of a monkey, is perishing? That noble lord has been laid low by an arrow sent by Rāma; my place is at the soles of his feet.'

19.20–28; 20.1–3 So saying she ran on in tears, haggard with grief and mournfully beating her head and breast with her arms. She roamed on until she saw her husband lying on the earth: he could kill *dānava* lords, who would not turn tail in a battle; he could hurl lordly mountains like Indra Vāsava with his gales and massed banks of booming clouds can hurl thunderbolts; his valour had equalled Śakra's, now he was like a cloud emptied of its rain; his roar had been fearsome above all roars; that hero struck down by a hero was like the king of beasts killed by a tiger for its prey; he was like a sacred tree universally reverenced with banners and railing, destroyed by Garuḍa to get at a snake. She saw Rāma standing there, his ample bow grounded, and Rāma's younger brother, her husband's younger brother too, but she ran past them to reach her battle-slain husband; when she saw him she collapsed on the ground, distressed and hysterical. As if in a trance she picked herself up again, wailing, 'Noble prince!' and wept to see her lord fast in the fetters of Death. Sugrīva heard her screeching like an osprey and was seized by pangs of despair to see Aṅgada there. Seeing him on the ground, struck down by the death-dealing arrow shot from Rāma's bow, beautiful moonfaced Tārā reached out and clasped her husband in her arms, realizing that Vālin, proud as an elephant, had met his death in that arrow. Tārā's mind was tormented by grief and suffering as she wept over that *vānara* lord, great as Indra, now like a tree uprooted.

'Why won't you speak to me, you hero above all others, you 20.4–20
monkey-champion, so ferociously courageous in battle? My heart's breaking, I'm not reproaching you now. Get up, you tiger of an ape, and enjoy your beautiful bed! Peerless kings like you don't lie on the ground. It seems you're too much in love with the Earth, Lord of the Earth, it's her you're holding in your arms in death in preference to me. There's an end to what we all used to enjoy in your company in the sweet-scented woods – you too, from time to time! Now that you are departing this life, great lord of lords, I am joyless, hopeless, sunk in a sea of sorrow. My heart must be very hard, to see you laid low on the earth and not to burst into a thousand pieces in a torment of sorrow. What have you gained, monkey overlord, by seizing Sugrīva's wife and exiling him? You were mad to revile me, *vānara* lord: I acted for the best, I gave you helpful advice, I wanted to do you good. It's Time that's

bringing your life to an end, that's certain; that's what has forced you into Sugrīva's clutches in spite of yourself. Life as a widow is miserable and tormented by sorrow; mine has always been abundantly free from sorrow, but now I shall spend it husbandless. And spirited Aṅgada, so cosseted in every ease and luxury, how will he fare when his uncle is out of his mind with rage, I wonder? – Son, hard though you'll find the sight, take a good look at your righteous father, my dear. – You must reassure your son and give him your instructions, then kiss him on the head before you embark on your final journey. Rāma has done a monstrous deed in killing you, but it was to fulfil his promise to Sugrīva here. – You'll get what you want, Sugrīva; Rumā shall be yours. Don't worry, you can enjoy the kingdom; your enemy, your brother, has been punished. – Why won't you give me a kind word in reply to my lament? Lord of the *vānaras*, just look at all these fine wives of yours!'

20.21; Hearing her lament, those *vānarīs* all around clustered about
22.1–2 the miserable Aṅgada and wailed in their melancholy. With life ebbing away and breathing feeble, Vālin looked all around, then fixed his gaze on Sugrīva standing before his son; speaking to victorious Sugrīva the monkey lord with affection in his clear voice, he said:

22.3–16 'Sugrīva, please don't blame me for the wrong I did while I was in the grip of mental delusion dragging me inexorably along. Dear brother, I don't think we were both destined to be happy at the same time, for the friendship expected of brothers has come to naught. Kingship over these forest-dwellers is now yours, and you can see that I'm on my way to the land of the dead. I'm fast leaving life, kingdom and great splendour, but with my fame high and unimpeached. Since I am in this plight I will tell you where your duty lies, heroic king, though it will not be easy. Look at Aṅgada: he deserves some enjoyment, he's been brought up to comfort; he's not a childish boy but his face is awash with tears as he sprawls on the ground. My son is dearer to me than life itself. Look after him like your own son, and don't let him want for wealth of any sort after losing me. You are Lord of the Monkeys; you should provide for him and look after him in all things, and shield him from harm in my place. Tārā's glorious son is your equal in courage; he will take the lead in slaughtering those *rākṣasas*. He'll march boldly into battle and accomplish fitting exploits, will Aṅgada, this dashing, refined son of Tārā. And Suṣeṇa's daughter here is in every way thoroughly competent to assess subtle matters and all kinds of portents. Any course of action she approves may be pursued with confidence, for no opinion of Tārā's will be found false. What the Rāghava requires of you should be carried out without hesitation, for it would be wrong not to do so and if you treated him with disrespect he would injure you. I entrust this divine golden garland to you, Sugrīva, the seat of lofty Śrī, lest she forsake it at my death.'

The brotherly affection of Vālin's words stripped Sugrīva of 22.17–18
his joy and made him wretched again, like the Constellations' Lord when engulfed by the Devourer. Pacified by Vālin's speech, his fatigue gone, he duly accepted the golden garland as he was bidden.

When Vālin had handed over the golden garland and was 22.19–23
about to become a ghost, he caught sight of his son standing there, and said affectionately to Aṅgada, 'Now you must adjust yourself to the present situation. Take the rough with the smooth, accepting equally pain and pleasure in their turn, but be submissive to Sugrīva's will. I have always cosseted you, mighty son, but Sugrīva will not think well of such behaviour. Don't associate with anyone except his allies, never with his enemies, victorious prince, but control yourself and seek your master's benefit: be submissive to Sugrīva's will. Too much deference and too little deference are both great faults: so avoid them both, and cultivate a happy medium.'

So saying, his eyes contorted by agony from the arrow, he 22.24
bared his fearsome teeth, and gave up his life.

Sugrīva was tormented by grief; while his garments were still 25.1–3
wet,[3] the monkey ministers clustered around him and waited on him. Then they went up to Rāma the mighty, the tireless, and all stood before him with heads bowed like the sages round Brahmā. Hanumān, a true Son of the Wind, his face like the

rising sun, looked like a mountain of gold as he respectfully spoke:

25.4–7 'It is by your Honour's favour, my lord, that this great ancestral *vānara* kingdom, so hard to win, has been conferred on Sugrīva. With your Honour's leave, he will enter the goodly city with his supporters and make all necessary arrangements. He will bathe in the various prescribed perfumes and herbs and single you out for special honour with jewels and garlands. Be so good as to go from here to that pleasant mountain fastness, and rejoice the *vānaras* by the consecration of their lord.'

25.8–10 So said Hanumān, but the Rāghava, that slayer of doughty enemies, replied wisely and eloquently to Hanumān: 'Hanumān my friend, for fourteen years I shall observe my father's command and enter neither village nor city. Let the bull of a *vānara* Sugrīva enter that divinely opulent fastness, and let that hero at once be sprinkled as king according to rule.'

25.11–15 After these words to Hanumān, Rāma advised Sugrīva, 'My hero, you should also sprinkle Aṅgada here as Young King. This is the first of the rainy months, Śrāvaṇa, the start of the monsoon; the designated four months of rain have begun, my friend. This is no time for enterprises. You should enter your fine city, my friend, while I shall reside on this mountain along with Lakṣmaṇa. This can be my pleasant mountain fastness, my friend: it's spacious and airy, it's got ample water and ample lotuses and water lilies. When Kārtika comes, you should exert yourself so that Rāvaṇa can be killed: that will be our opportunity, my friend. You must go to your own home, consecrate yourself to the kingship and make your friends rejoice.'

25.16–19 So with Rāma's leave the bull of a *vānara* Sugrīva entered into Kiṣkindhā, the lovely city Vālin had watched over. Thousands of *vānaras* welcomed the *vānara* lord on his entry and swarmed all around him in delight. At the sight of the Lord of the Ape-hordes all the citizens with one accord bowed their heads and prostrated themselves. Sugrīva their hero greeted his subjects and bade them all rise, then the mighty monkey entered his brother's comfortable private apartments.

25.20–34 When Sugrīva came out again his companions consecrated that bull of a *vānara*, as the immortals did Thousand-eyed Indra. They brought him his gold-adorned white parasol and a magnificent pair of gleaming fans with gold handles,[4] jewels of all kinds, and every sort of seed and plant and sprig and blossom from sap-laden trees; gleaming garments too and white ointment, and fragrant garlands culled from earth and water, with divine sandalwood paste and many different perfumes; golden unhusked grain, millet, honey, *ghī* and curds; a tiger-skin and a pair of boar-skin sandals. Sixteen lovely damsels joyfully approached bearing unguent, and yellow and red pigments. When the bulls of brāhmans had been gratified at the proper time with the prescribed gems and garments and food, people well versed in the *mantras* offered a *mantra*-purified oblation into the blazing fire, strewn around with *kuśa* grass, and with numerous *mantras* installed the supreme *vānara* facing the east upon a gorgeous throne on a pedestal of gold, spread with fine cloths and beautified with glittering garlands, upon the splendid palace roof. Water drawn from rivers, streams and holy fords all around and collected from all the oceans was placed, pure and auspicious, in golden jars; using auspicious bull's horns and golden pitchers according to the rules laid down by the great sages and the ritual texts, Gaja, Gavākṣa, Gavaya, Śarabha, Gandhamādana, Mainda and Dvivida, Hanumān, Jāmbavān and Nala, bulls of *vānaras*, sprinkled Sugrīva with clear, fragrant water as the *vasus* did Thousand-eyed Indra Vāsava, and all the bulls of *vānaras*, thousands of them, noble and joyful, acclaimed Sugrīva's consecration.

Sugrīva, that bull of an ape, then embraced Aṅgada and 25.35–7
carried out Rāma's suggestion, consecrating him Young King, at which the noble monkeys cheered their approval and honoured Sugrīva. Pleased and prosperous people were everywhere: emblazoned with banners and standards, Kiṣkindhā city rejoiced in its mountain fastness.

With Sugrīva consecrated and the *vānara* withdrawn to his 26.1–8
retreat, Rāma went with his brother to mount Prasravaṇa. Resounding with tigers and deer, swarming with fierce-roaring lions, overgrown by all kinds of bushes and creepers, thronged

with trees and home to bears, *vānaras* and langurs and to wild cats, the mountain was like a towering cloud and was always supplied with pure water. It was at the summit of that mountain that Rāma and Saumitri selected an extensive, spacious cave for their lodging place, and there that the righteous Rāghava settled with Lakṣmaṇa among the many picturesque caverns and arbours on mount Prasravaṇa. Rāma, though, could take no pleasure at all from living on that pleasing, well-provided crag as his memory dwelt on his captive wife, dearer to him than life. At night as he lay in bed, especially when the moon was rising in the east, sleep eluded him. Kākutstha's mind was overwhelmed by weeping for the grief welling up in him. In his grief, he could never shed his sorrow. His brother Lakṣmaṇa shared his pain and offered a word of consolation.

26.9–14 'Stop fretting so! You're a warrior, and shouldn't give way to grief. You know that a low spirit reduces anyone's chances of success. You, sir, carry out all earthly observances; you, sir, are devoted to the gods; you're devout, righteous and resolute; you're the Rāghava! Without resolve you won't have strength to fight and kill any enemy, especially that crafty *rākṣasa*. Root out every bit of your grief; cultivate a firm resolve; then you'll root out that *rākṣasa* and his retinue. You're so strong you could even topple the world complete with its oceans, forests and mountains – how much more Rāvaṇa! Your courage is asleep, but I'm arousing it, like a fire smouldering in its ashes when it's time for the oblations to blaze out.'

26.15–18 The Rāghava courteously acknowledged that Lakṣmaṇa's well-meaning words were appropriate and replied to his affectionate comrade, 'Lakṣmaṇa, you've said everything there is to be said by a fond, affectionate well-wisher who holds fast to what's true and courageous. I'm rid of the grief that will wreck all my efforts. My spirit has never given way in feats of valour: I will rouse it to courage. Now that the rains have come I can wait till autumn, but then I shall destroy that *rākṣasa*, and his country, and his hordes.'

26.19–22 Lakṣmaṇa was delighted to hear Rāma's words. Saumitri, joy of his friends, replied, 'Now you've gone back to being Kākutstha. Now you've acknowledged your own courage you should live up to it. Your words are typical of you and your renowned dynasty. So, you tiger of a man, endure these rains that have arrived by thinking about how to punish your enemy. You're the Rāghava!'

Rāma's thoughts were with lotus-petal-eyed Maithilī. His 29.21–37;
mouth ran dry as he remarked to Lakṣmaṇa, 'Prince, it's high 30.8
time for a royal expedition, and I've seen nothing of Sugrīva or of any preparations. The four months of the rains have passed, dear brother, but for me tormented by grief at not being able to see Sītā they've felt more like a hundred rainy seasons. I'm bereft of my darling, I'm grief-stricken, I've been robbed of my kingdom, I'm in exile, but now he's king, Sugrīva shows me no sympathy, Lakṣmaṇa. You must go to Kiṣkindhā and give a message from me to that bull of a *vānara*, that besotted Sugrīva addicted to his vulgar pleasures. You should be tactful and avoid hard words, but tell Sugrīva that he has exceeded the time limit.'

When his older brother had explained exactly what he 30.9–33
wanted, that bull of a man, that slaughterer of enemy heroes, the warrior Lakṣmaṇa went into the city like the blazing Doomsday Fire or an enraged lord of snakes; Aṅgada approached him in terror and despair. Eyes copper-coloured with rage, the renowned prince ordered Aṅgada, 'Young man, give Sugrīva this message about my arrival: "Destroyer of your enemies, Rāma's younger brother has come to have audience with you. He is seething with rage at his brother's distress. Lakṣmaṇa is at your door."'

Aṅgada was filled with anguish at what he heard from 30.34;
Lakṣmaṇa. He went up to his father and said, 'Here comes 31.1–2
Saumitri!' Sugrīva and his courtiers heard what Aṅgada had to say, and the news that Lakṣmaṇa was enraged made him leap from his seat, though he retained his composure. He thought out reasons, serious and trivial, then, since he knew how to seek advice and how to take it, he consulted his wise counsellors.

'I have neither said nor done anything wrong. I wonder why 31.3–8
the Rāghava's brother Lakṣmaṇa is angry? Enemies of mine are always on the lookout for opportunities to be hostile, and

they've filled the younger Rāghava's ears with reports of faults I've not committed. Meanwhile let your Honours all exert your brains and work out some rational explanation, thorough but measured. It's certainly not that I'm frightened of Lakṣmaṇa or even of the Rāghava: it's just that having an ally enraged inappropriately gives rise to uneasiness. It's easy enough to strike up a friendship but harder to maintain it; sentiments are fickle and even a trivial matter can cause a rift in cordiality. That's why I'm frightened of noble Rāma in case I can't repay the help he gave me.'

31.9–21 That bull of an ape Hanumān replied to Sugrīva's words in the midst of the *vānara* counsellors with a conjecture of his own. 'It is not at all surprising, Lord of the Ape-hordes, that you have not forgotten the welcome assistance and great friendship with which he favoured you. To please you, the heroic Rāghava banished your fear and killed Vālin, though he was Śakra's equal in might. No doubt it's from injured affection that the Rāghava has dispatched Lakṣmaṇa, furtherer of Fortune. You are usually the most punctilious person, but you have not noticed the season: auspicious autumn has begun. The *saptacchadas* are dark with blossom; the clouds have vanished, leaving the sky and its planets and stars spotless; in every direction, streams and lakes are tranquil. Bull of an ape, do you not realize that the time for action has arrived? Clearly Lakṣmaṇa thinks you negligent; that's why he's come. The noble Rāghava is distressed by his wife's capture, so you should reconcile yourself to harsh words brought from him by an intermediary. You've offended him, and I don't see what else you can do but propitiate Lakṣmaṇa with hands clasped in submission. A king's appointed counsellors are under an obligation to speak for his own good; that's why I have made bold to give you my considered opinion. If the Rāghava raises his bow in anger he can subjugate the world – gods, anti-gods and *gandharvas* too! You should remember his previous assistance with gratitude: it's not good to enrage him when you'll only have to placate him again. Bow your head to him, your majesty, you, your son, and your companions, and keep your promise to him, submissive as a wife to her husband.'

Then at Rāma's command Lakṣmaṇa, that slayer of hostile warriors, entered the terrible fastness of Kiṣkindhā. When the huge, powerful apes on guard at the gate saw Lakṣmaṇa they all stood up and saluted, but the apes were frightened to see Daśaratha's son snorting with anger and kept away from him. The majestic prince gazed at the great fastness, jewel-built, jewel-encrusted and divine, charming with its blossoming woods, crowded with mansions and palaces, adorned with markets of all kinds, adorned with flowering trees bearing every fruit one could wish for, its beauty set off by shape-changing *vānara* sons of gods and *gandharvas* lovely in their divine garlands and garments, its highways joyful with fragrant sandalwood, aloes and lotuses, and with sweet-scented wine and mead. The many-storeyed palaces stood firm as mounts Vindhya and Meru, and the Rāghava could see there pure mountain streams. Aṅgada had a lovely house; so did Mainda and Dvivida, Gavaya, Gavākṣa, Gaja and Śarabha. Along the king's highway Lakṣmaṇa could see the imposing, lordly dwellings of all these noble monkey lords, gleaming like white clouds, garlanded divinely, rich with goods and grain, bejewelled with women. Then he saw the lovely residence of the *vānara* lord; it was difficult of access, encircled by a white mountain, like great Indra's seat, and adorned with gleaming turrets like Kailāsa's peaks. He saw flowering trees bearing every fruit one could wish for, and handsome, cloud-dark trees bestowed by great Indra bearing divine flowers and fruit, cool, shady and captivating. Around the splendid, divinely garlanded entrance with its gateways of burnished gold stood powerful apes, sword in hand. 32.1–17

Mighty Saumitri entered Sugrīva's charming palace unhindered, like the sun entering a great cloud. Once inside the seven courtyards with their many vehicles and benches, the righteous prince saw the extensive, heavily guarded private apartments; on all sides it was beautified by gold and silver couches and many fine benches covered with costly cloths. As he entered he could hear the continual sweet sound of mingled strings and singing, every word, every syllable in harmony. In Sugrīva's palace the mighty prince saw many different women 32.18–26 exulting in their youth and beauty. At the sight of these high-born ladies with their necklaces of glittering garlands, absorbed in plaiting fine garlands and adorned with every possible adornment, and of Sugrīva's attendants, resplendent in their livery, content but not self-satisfied, Lakṣmaṇa looked all around until he saw Sugrīva, who was seated glorious as the sun on a golden throne covered with costly cloths; in his divine garlands and garments, divine ornaments glittering on his limbs, he looked like a god, like invincible great Indra.

33.1–5 Sugrīva was agitated to see that bull of a man Lakṣmaṇa come in unhindered and angry. Seeing that Daśaratha's son was snorting with anger, almost ablaze with splendour in his distress at his brother's misfortune, the ape chief left his golden seat and sprang up just like great Indra's lofty, much-adorned standard. As Sugrīva sprang up, the women sprang up after him, Rumā at their head, like stars crowding after the full moon in the firmament. With reddened eyes, majestic but deferential, he swayed, then stood there, firm as a great wish-granting tree.

33.6–18 Lakṣmaṇa angrily addressed Sugrīva, standing with Rumā at his side surrounded by the women like the moon by the stars: 'A king gains worldwide honour if he is of good lineage, compassionate, self-controlled, grateful and truthful. But a king who persists in doing wrong, dishonouring a promise to allies and supporters! Could anyone be more malign? A lie concerning a horse destroys a hundred, a lie concerning a cow a thousand, while a lie concerning a man destroys teller and family.[5] One who has achieved his object but is ungrateful and does not repay his friends, Lord of Leapers, is universally condemned to death. Monkey, mark this verse, respected the world over; it was sung by Brahmā in anger at the sight of ingratitude: "Expiation has been enjoined by the good for one who kills a brāhman, for one who drinks liquor, for a thief, or for one who has broken a vow; but there is no expiation for an ingrate."[6] You are a low-born, ungrateful liar, *vānara*, for achieving your own object but not repaying Rāma. Rāma achieved your object for you, *vānara*, so now you should be anxious to return the favour by exerting yourself in the search for Sītā. Rāma did not realize that you were a snake roaring like a frog, attached to vulgar pleasures and false to your promises! It was by distinguished Rāma's doing, that compassionate, noble prince, that you obtained the kingship of the apes, evil and ill-intentioned as you are. If you don't acknowledge tireless Rāma's action, you will go straight away to join Vālin, killed by his sharp arrows: the path Vālin took at his death is not too narrow for you. Keep your pledge, Sugrīva! Don't follow Vālin's path.'

Lakṣmaṇa Saumitri's splendour blazed forth as he spoke, 34.1–22
but it was moonlike Tārā who replied. 'Lakṣmaṇa, you should not say such things! The Lord of the Apes here should have to listen to no harsh words, from your mouth in particular. Indeed Sugrīva is not ungrateful, nor is he a deceitful, cruel liar, my lord, and the monkeys' lord is no fraud. This heroic monkey, Sugrīva, certainly has not forgotten the aid lent him by Rāma; another such fighter would be difficult to find, my lord. By Rāma's grace Sugrīva has attained fame and perpetual kingship over the monkeys, victorious warrior; he has also gained Rumā and me. Before then he could get no comfort at night, but now that he has gained the ultimate pleasure he is like the sage Viśvāmitra, and doesn't realize how time has passed. You know Lakṣmaṇa, when the great sage Viśvāmitra, righteous though he was, was besotted with Ghṛtācī, he thought ten years was one day. If such a punctilious timekeeper as glorious Viśvāmitra didn't realize how time had passed, how could an ordinary person? Rāma should be patient with one whose carnal appetite has left him exhausted but with his desire still not sated. Lakṣmaṇa, you sir shouldn't immediately give way to fury like a common person without investigating the matter. People of integrity like you, bull of a man, don't give way to fury without thought! You know what's right: I earnestly entreat you for Sugrīva's sake to give up this furious passion. It's my belief that Sugrīva would throw us over, Rumā and me, and the ape kingdom – goods, grain, wealth and all – just to please Rāma. Sugrīva will kill Rāvaṇa in battle and reunite the Rāghava with Sītā like the hare-marked Moon with Rohiṇī. There must be millions and millions of *rākṣasas* in Laṅkā.

These *rākṣasas* are hard to overcome and can change shape at will, but unless they're killed there'll be no killing Maithilī's captor, that Rāvaṇa! You won't be able to kill that wicked Rāvaṇa without help, Lakṣmaṇa, particularly from Sugrīva. That's what Vālin said, and that Lord of the Apes knew what he was talking about! I've no definite knowledge myself, I'm just telling you what I heard from him. Bull-like apes have already been dispatched to call up large numbers of *vānara* ape chiefs for warfare in your cause. Those indomitable champions are needed to ensure the success of the Rāghava's mission: that's why the Ape-lord has not yet set out. But Saumitri, this is the very day set by Sugrīva for all those mighty *vānaras* to arrive. Today thousands of crores of bears and hundreds of langurs will muster around you. Throw off your anger, victorious prince. Kākutstha, there'll be many crores of monkeys blazing in splendour!'

35.1–4 Saumitri's natural gentleness prompted him to accept Tārā's courteous, right-minded words, and once the speech was accepted the Lord of the Ape-hordes shed his terror of Lakṣmaṇa like a wet garment. Tearing the many strands of the glittering garland from his neck, Sugrīva, lord of the *vānaras*, was free from dissipation. Sugrīva the supreme *vānara* rejoiced and spoke courteously to fearsome, mighty Lakṣmaṇa.

35.5–11 'Majesty, fame and perpetual kingship over the monkeys were lost to me, Saumitri, but by Rāma's favour I have them all back. Heroic, victorious prince, who could repay the prowess shown by this king, so famous for his deeds? The righteous Rāghava will get Sītā back and kill Rāvaṇa by his own glory; I shall be no more than a helper. What help can I be to a man who can shoot an arrow through seven great trees and a mountain, and then into the ground? Lakṣmaṇa, when the rattle of his bow shakes the earth and its mountains, what does he need with assistants? Bull of a man, I'll organize a force to accompany the Lord of Men as he goes to kill his enemy Rāvaṇa and his followers. If I have committed any trespass by taking his goodwill for granted, please forgive your servant: no one is faultless.'

35.12–20 Noble Sugrīva's words mollified Lakṣmaṇa and his reply was kind. 'Lord of the *vānaras*, my brother has an excellent protector – and a courteous one too – with you, Sugrīva, to look after him. Whether because of your might, Sugrīva, or because of your unsullied character, you are worthy to enjoy the unsurpassed glory of the kingship of the monkeys. There is no doubt that with you, Sugrīva, to help him, majestic Rāma will soon kill his enemies in battle. Sugrīva, you have made a speech fitting and appropriate to your upright nature, grateful and steadfast in battle. Who else in a position of power other than my senior brother and you, supreme *vānara*, would acknowledge his faults? You and Rāma are alike in valour and might, bull of an ape; the gods have sent you to be our helper for evermore. Do come at once, though, my hero, and we'll go together to soothe your friend in his distress at the capture of his wife. And I ask you to overlook the harsh words I spoke to you in response to Rāma's heartbroken lament.'

At noble Lakṣmaṇa's words, Sugrīva issued instructions to 36.1–15
his minister Hanumān standing at his side. 'Those who are stationed on the peaks of the Five Mountains – Mahendra, Himālaya, Vindhya, Kailāsa and pale-peaked Mandara; those on the mountains on the edge of the Western Ocean, sparkling all around with the hue of the rising sun; also those bulls of apes on the mountain abode of the sun that resembles a cloud at twilight, they who are sheltering among the *padma* trees and palmyras of the fearsome forest; those too who bound about on mount Añjana, equal to tuskers in strength and black as collyrium clouds; those bright golden *vānaras* who live in caves of realgar on the flanks of Meru or shelter on mount Dhūmra; and those with the hue of the rising sun who drink mead and wine as they bound about with fearful impetus on mount Mahāruṇa; those too in the vast, delightfully fragrant forests, and on the forest margins frequented by ascetics: summon them at once, each one of them, all the *vānaras* on earth! Dispatch *vānaras* straight away with all the standard inducements and gifts. Swift messengers have already been sent out by me but you should send out more apes to hurry them up. At my command, any self-indulgent *vānaras* who string things out are to be brought here at once, and on my orders any who are

not here within three days are to be executed for malicious non-observance of their king's command. At my command, lions of monkeys – a hundred thousand crores of them – are to set out in all directions, steadfast in implementing my decree. At my command supremely terrible monkeys are to set out, blotting out the sky in their mountainous clouds. At my command every *vānara* scout is to scour the earth and speedily fetch all the apes.'

36.16–26 When he heard the *vānara* king's words, the Wind's true son dispatched valiant *vānaras* in all directions. On the instant the apes sent out by their king took to the path of birds and light where Viṣṇu strode; in oceans, mountains, forests and streams these *vānaras* chivvied all other *vānaras* for Rāma's sake. Hearing the order of the supreme king, Sugrīva, fatal as Death himself, *vānaras* mustered out of fear of Sugrīva. Three crores of them, black as the collyrium mountain, came leaping swiftly down towards the Rāghava; ten crores sporting on that marvellous mountain where the sun sets[7] came down from it glowing like burnished gold; from Kailāsa's peaks came thousands of crores of *vānaras* splendid in lionlike manes; of those who had resorted to living on fruit and roots on Himālaya there arrived a thousand thousand crores; in haste flew in thousands of crores of thousands of crores of Vindhya *vānaras*, dread in demeanour and deed as Aṅgāraka; countless were those who dwelt on the shore of the Milk Ocean or who lived on coconuts in the *tamāla* forest; from forests and thickets and streams they hurried: as if it would swallow the sun, the *vānara* host arrived.

36.27–33 Those heroic *vānaras* who had gone to hasten all the *vānaras* saw the mighty trees of the Himālaya mountain, that pleasant, excellent mountain which once used to glow with divine, pleasing sacrifices to the Great God that delighted the minds of all the gods. There the *vānaras* saw roots and fruits in superabundance sweet as ambrosia, lovely fruit and roots born of the food of the gods; anyone eating it once is satisfied for a month. The fruit-eating leaders of ape troops gathered those divine roots and fruit, together with divine plants, and as they went the *vānaras* took fragrant flowers from the sacrificial sanctuary to give pleasure to Sugrīva. When all the ape chiefs had called up all the *vānaras* on earth they hurried off at the head of their troops.

Quickly – in a moment – those nimble troop leaders reached 36.34–6
Kiṣkindhā where Sugrīva the *vānara* was, and the *vānaras* presented him with all the herbs, fruit and roots they had brought, with these words: 'We have all scoured the earth's mountains, oceans and forests and all the *vānaras* attend you at your command.'

Sugrīva, overlord of the monkeys, was delighted to hear their 36.37;
report, and accepted all their tribute with pleasure. When all 37.1–2
the tribute had been brought forward and presented, he dismissed all the *vānaras* politely; with the dismissal of those heroic apes, their task accomplished, he felt that he and the mighty Rāghava had already achieved their objective.

Lakṣmaṇa delighted the chieftain of all the *vānaras*, the 37.3
fearsome, mighty Sugrīva, with a courteous invitation: 'May it please you to set out from Kiṣkindhā, my friend.'

Lakṣmaṇa's words were nicely put, and Sugrīva was happy 37.4
to hear them. 'Very well, let us go!' he replied. 'I must adhere to your command.'

So saying to Fortune-favoured Lakṣmaṇa, Sugrīva dismissed 37.5–10
Tārā and the other women, then called loudly for the ape chiefs. The apes came as soon as they heard his shout, and when they arrived the king in his sunlike splendour instructed the *vānaras* to make his palanquin ready at once. When they heard what he said the apes zealously prepared his handsome palanquin, and when he saw it was ready the *vānara* lord said to Saumitri, 'Get in at once, Lakṣmaṇa.'

With these words Sugrīva climbed beside Lakṣmaṇa into the 37.11–16
golden, sunlike vehicle, borne by many apes. A white parasol was held above his head, gleaming fans were waved all around, conches and kettledrums were sounded and bards sang his praises as Sugrīva set out, possessed of unsurpassed regal pomp. Sword in hand, many hundreds of ferocious *vānaras* escorted him to where Rāma was waiting. When in his splendour he reached Rāma's beautiful home, he and Lakṣmaṇa got down from the palanquin and he approached Rāma with a submissive gesture, his deferential pose copied by the *vānaras*.

37.17–23 Rāma was pleased with Sugrīva when he saw that great army of *vānaras* like a pool of budding lotuses. When the lord of the apes bowed his head to the Rāghava's feet, he raised him up again, embracing him with affection and esteem. With his arms around him he graciously invited him to sit down; then, seeing him seated on the ground, Rāma spoke. 'A true king, heroic, supreme ape, is one who can always distinguish between duty, profit and pleasure,[8] and seek each in due season; but one who abandons duty and profit to seek pleasure is like someone who goes to sleep in a treetop, and wakes up when he falls out. However, a king who is intent on killing his enemies and delights in collecting allies – who concentrates on his duty – will enjoy the fruits of all three aims. The time to exert yourself has come, destroyer of your foes; you should be making plans in consultation with the apes, Lord of the Monkeys.'

37.24–33 Rāma's words were answered by Sugrīva: 'Mighty prince, it is by your grace that I have recovered my lost majesty, fame and perpetual kingship over the monkeys. Anyone who failed to repay a favour granted by you, your majesty, exalted conqueror, and by your brother, would bring disgrace on the world. Victorious warrior, these *vānara* chiefs have assembled in their hundreds, bringing with them all the earth's mighty *vānaras*. Alert warrior bears also and langurs, Rāghava, fearsome to behold and familiar with wildernesses and forest fastnesses, and shape-changing *vānara* sons of gods and *gandharvas* escorted by their own troops are on the march, Rāghava. Warriors are leaping along in the midst of hundreds, and of hundreds of thousands, and crores, and myriads, and millions, ravager of your foes; *vānaras* will come, your majesty, with tens of millions and with hundreds of millions and with thousands of millions and with billions, tawny chiefs of ape troops too with hundreds of billions and with trillions, bold as great Indra, steadfast as Meru and Mandara, from their homes on Vindhya and Meru. They will rally to you, kill Rāvaṇa the *rākṣasa* and his supporters in battle and rescue Maithilī.'

38.1–7 As Sugrīva spoke, his arms raised in submission, Rāma the supreme upholder of what is right embraced him and replied, 'It's as natural for such a ravager of your foes as you to repay his allies as it is for Indra to shower the earth with rain, or for the sun with its thousand rays to free the sky of darkness, or for the moon to cleanse the earth with its beams, my friend. So it's natural, Sugrīva my friend, for me to acknowledge your favour and your ever-welcome words. With you as my comrade to aid me, I shall triumph over all my enemies in battle; do please give me your assistance, my ally and supporter. That base *rākṣasa* has brought about his own destruction by seizing Vaidehī; it's like Anuhlāda deceiving Śacī, daughter of Puloman. In a short time I shall kill that Rāvaṇa with my sharpened arrows like Indra Śatakratu did Śacī's arrogant father."[9]

Meanwhile, dust was being kicked up to blot out the hot, 38.8–36
intense brilliance of the thousand-rayed sun in the sky, dust that carried confusion and alarm in every direction till the earth tottered, mountains, forests, groves and everything, and the entire ground disappeared as there leapt along countless monkeys, mountainous, sharp-toothed and mighty, covering it in the twinkling of an eye with chiefs of ape troops and their hundred-crore hordes of thunderous shape-changing mighty apes from rivers, mountains and oceans. Other forest-wanderers came too: *vānaras* the colour of the rising sun or creamy as the moon, some the colour of lotus filaments, or white ones from their home on Meru. Then appeared a glorious *vānara* warrior Śatabali by name, surrounded by ten thousand crores. Next appeared Tārā's heroic father, brilliant as a golden mountain, with several tens of thousands of crores. Then came Hanumān's father, majestic Kesarin, accompanied by many thousands of *vānara* battalions; he glowed like a lotus filament, his face was like the rising sun, he was wise, he was a superlative *vānara*, he was the foremost of all *vānaras*. Gavākṣa, mahārāja of langurs, terrible in his valour, could be seen amid a thousand crores of *vānaras*. Dhūmra arrived; that slaughterer of enemies had with him two thousand crores of bears of fearful impetus. A great warrior chief called Panasa brought three crores, wild as great mountains. A gigantic chief, dark as a mound of collyrium, Nīla, could be seen surrounded by ten crores. The might-filled chief Darīmukha approached Sugrīva with a thousand crores, and the mighty twin sons of

the Aśvins, Mainda and Dvivida, could be seen with a thousand crores of crores of *vānaras*. Gandhamādana then arrived, followed at his back by a thousand and a hundred thousand crores of apes. Next came Aṅgada, the Young King, his father's equal in prowess, in the midst of a million millions and a thousand billions, followed at a distance by star-splendid Tāra, an ape of fearsome prowess with five crores of apes. Indrajānu, a heroic ape chief, arrived with the eleven crores he commanded. Then like the rising sun arrived Rambha, surrounded by a myriad and a thousand and a hundred, and the intrepid mighty *vānara* chief Durmukha arrived with two crores. Like Kailāsa's peak in the midst of a thousand crores of *vānaras*, dreadful in their valour, came Hanumān. Nala of great prowess brought a hundred crores, a thousand, and a hundred tree-dwellers. Śarabha, Kumuda, Vahni – the *vānara* Rambha too – these and many other shape-changing *vānaras* swarmed over the entire earth, mountains and forests as they leapt along, as they leapt around Sugrīva, leaping and bellowing like billowing clouds round the sun and presented themselves with all their equipment to the *vānara* overlord Sugrīva, bowing their heads with a joyful hullabaloo. Other high-ranking *vānaras* assembled in the customary manner, saluted Sugrīva and stood respectfully before him. Sugrīva quickly presented all these bulls of *vānaras* to Rāma, saluted respectfully and gave an appropriate address.

43.1–6 It was to Hanumān in particular that Sugrīva set out his objective, confident in that ape's supreme ability to achieve his aim. 'Bull of an ape, I see nothing that can stand in your way, on earth or in the air, in the sky, in the abode of the gods, or in the waters. You know all the worlds with their anti-gods, *gandharvas*, *nāgas*, men and gods, their oceans and mountains. Great monkey hero, you have all the penetration and speed, the fierceness and gentleness of your father the wild Wind. Indeed, no creature as splendid as you is to be found on earth, so it's for you to bring about a way of rescuing Sītā. You are experienced in proper procedure, Hanumān: in you reside strength, wisdom and valour, and you know how to take the right action at the right time and place.'

When the Rāghava understood that it was Hanumān who was to be entrusted with the task, he pondered what he knew about Hanumān. 'The Lord of Apes here has every confidence that Hanumān will achieve his aim; Hanumān too is quite sure of his ability to accomplish his task. For him to be chosen on account of his deeds and sent out by his master ensures that the task will be fruitful.' 43.7–9

The mere sight of the ape, so full of resolve, was enough to delight his glorious heart and mind, as if his purpose was already achieved. In his pleasure, the ravager of his foes gave him a ring that the princess would recognize, for it was decorated with the mark of his own name. 'Excellent ape, this token will see to it that Janaka's daughter will not take fright at you, but will realize you are a messenger from me. Your resolution, heroic ape, your valour and integrity, and your commissioning by Sugrīva all tell me I shall be successful.' 43.10–13

The excellent ape took it and touched it to his head;* then the champion bowed to his feet, saluted and leapt off. 43.14

In recognition of their lord's stern command, the bulls of apes set off, swarming over the earth like locusts while Rāma stayed there on Prasravaṇa with Lakṣmaṇa awaiting the end of the month fixed for locating Sītā. The heroic ape Śatabali set out at once for the pleasant northern region guarded by the king of the mountains, while the ape chief Vinata went towards the east. The monkey Son of the Wind, an ape chief, accompanied by Tāra, Aṅgada and others went to the south, home of Agastya, but to the dread west, guarded by Varuṇa's zeal, went Suṣeṇa, tiger of an ape and lord of leaping folk. When the king had duly dispatched his chief monkey commanders in all directions he gladly relaxed and rejoiced. 44.1–7

Acting on the king's orders the *vānara* chiefs all rushed off in their designated directions. Calling and crying out as they leapt, jumping and running went the champion leapers, bellowing that they would rescue Sītā and kill Rāvaṇa. 44.8–9

'I'm the one to find Rāvaṇa and kill him in single combat! I'll pulverize him! Janaka's daughter's trembling and exhausted now, but I'll carry her off!' 'You others can wait here, sirs. I'll be the one to carry Jānakī back on my own from the very 44.10–14

Underworld!' 'I'm the one to scatter the trees!' 'I shall tear open mountains!' 'I shall tear open the earth!' 'I shall convulse the oceans!' 'I shall leap hundreds and hundreds of *yojanas*, you may be sure!' 'Well, I'll leap hundreds and hundreds more!' 'Nothing will stop me on land or sea, on mountains or in forests or even in the middle of the Underworld!'

44.15 In the presence of the king of apes so spoke each *vānara*, exulting in his might.

45.1 When the *vānara* chiefs had gone, Rāma asked Sugrīva, 'How, sir, do you know so much about the whole round world?'

45.2–17 Sugrīva humbly replied to Rāma: 'If you will listen, bull of a man, I will tell you the story in all its detail. When Vālin chased Dundubhi, the *dānava* in the guise of a buffalo, towards mount Malaya, the buffalo plunged into a cave on Malaya and Vālin followed him inside Malaya, anxious to kill him, while I unassumingly kept to my appointed station at the cave entrance. When a year had elapsed and Vālin had not emerged I was astonished to see the cave filled with gushing blood, and grief for my brother poisoned me until I reached the obvious conclusion that my senior had been killed. In despair for his life, I blocked the cave entrance with a mountainous boulder so that the buffalo would be unable to get out and would perish, then went to Kiṣkindhā. The extensive kingdom was conferred on me; Tārā too became mine in addition to Rumā, and my companions and I lived there undisturbed. Vālin then came back after killing that bull of a *dānava*, and fear compelled me to give him the kingdom, he being my senior. Evil-natured Vālin's passions were aroused to wish to kill me, and he pursued me angrily as I fled with my ministers. That Vālin set me and my companions running till I could see many rivers, forests and cities; in fact the earth was as clear to me as the surface of a mirror, as the circle traced by a fire-brand, or as a cow's footprint. First I went eastwards, then I sought refuge in the south, and after that, fearful of danger, I went to the west, but when I arrived in the north Hanumān said, "Your majesty, now I remember! In this group of hermitages Vālin lord of the apes was once cursed by Mataṅga: if Vālin entered it, his head would shatter into a hundred pieces! We can live there happily and untroubled." So, prince, when Vālin reached mount Ṛśyamūka he kept out for fear of Mataṅga. Your majesty, that was how the whole round world unfolded before my eyes until I reached my hiding place.'

As directed, the monkey chiefs sped off to all the places the monkey king had indicated they should search for Vaidehī: lakes and streams, hiding places and open spaces, cities, swamps and mountains were all ransacked until the *vānara* chiefs had searched every region specified by Sugrīva, mountains, forests, woods and all. Intent on reaching Sītā, the *vānaras* all searched through the day and gathered on the ground at night. Each day at nightfall the *vānaras* found seasonal fruit trees in the area and then slept. 46.1–5

On the day after a month had elapsed, the monkey chiefs went despondently to meet the king of the monkeys at Prasravaṇa. Mighty Vinata arrived with his companions after searching as directed in the east, but had not seen Sītā. Then came the great monkey hero Śatabali with his army, after searching all the north. Suṣeṇa and his *vānaras* had searched the west before assembling at the end of the month and returning to Sugrīva, who was stationed on Prasravaṇa peak, seated beside Rāma. When they had arrived and saluted, they reported to Sugrīva: 46.6–10

'Mountains, forests, cities, rivers right down to the edge of the ocean, also peoples, have all been searched; hiding places have all been searched according to your instructions, also extensive bushes smothered with thick creepers have been searched; gigantic creatures have been located and have been eliminated; dense areas have been searched repeatedly.' 46.11–13

The monkey Hanumān had set off with Tāra and Aṅgada for the region appointed by Sugrīva. He advanced a considerable distance with all the monkey champions, searching the hiding places and thickets of Vindhya: peaks and swamps, lakes and lofty trees, mixed groves and tree-girt mountains – however hard all those heroic *vānaras* combed that region they could find no trace of Janaka's daughter Sītā Maithilī. Intrepidly they moved from place to place, living off roots and all kinds of 47.1–22 fruit as they combed, but the area was extensive and hard to search, with its caves and thickets. When they left that area, the indomitable ape chiefs all plunged into another impassable region: here trees were barren of fruit, flowerless, devoid of leaves; here lakes were without water and roots scarce; here were no buffaloes, no deer and no elephants, no tigers nor birds, nor any other forest creatures; in the lotus pools on the tableland here were glossy-leaved lotuses blossoming, spectacular and fragrant, yet bereft of bees. There was a great sage called Kaṇḍu, eminent, truthful, rich in austerities but extremely irascible; his observances had made him unassailable, but his son, a ten-year-old child, perished in that wilderness. The great sage was angered that he had lost his life there, and righteously cursed the entire forest land to become shelterless, impassable and empty of wildlife. Even so they rigorously searched its wooded edges, its mountain hollows and its river sources, but though they carried out Sugrīva's wishes nobly, there too they could find no trace of Janaka's daughter or of her captor Rāvaṇa either. Then when they had come to a dreadful area overgrown with creepers and bushes they saw a savage, sinful anti-god. When the *vānaras* saw that mountainous monster standing there like a cliff, they all girded themselves tightly at the sight. For his part the brute roared, 'You're done for!' and rushed furiously towards all the *vānaras* with his fists tight clenched, and attacked them violently. Vālin's son Aṅgada assumed him to be Rāvaṇa and slapped him with his hand. This blow from Vālin's son felled the anti-god to the ground, spewing blood from his mouth; it was as if a mountain had been overturned. When life had left him the *vānaras* triumphantly searched widely in every hiding place on that mountain. Again they scoured the woodland, and then they all plunged into yet another even more fearful mountain hiding place. After a further wearisome search they tumbled out and sat down at the root of a solitary tree, a despondent group.

48.1–10 Then weary Aṅgada gently rallied all the *vānaras* with words of great wisdom: 'Forests, mountains, rivers, fastnesses and thickets, caves and mountain hiding places all around –

together we've ransacked them all. We've not laid eyes on Jānakī, nor on that *rākṣasa* who has captured divinely beautiful Sītā. A great deal of our time has been spent, and Sugrīva is a fierce taskmaster. My lords, you must scour the whole place. Shake off the lethargy and disappointment welling up in you – sleep too – and search till we find Janaka's daughter Sītā. This very day you forest-dwellers must search forests and fastnesses; shake off your weariness and search this whole forest again. We're bound to see the fruit of our labours! No more giving way to melancholy! We've no business so much as to close our eyes! Sugrīva's an impatient king, *vānaras*, and his punishments are harsh. We must always beware of him, and of noble Rāma. I'm telling you this for your own good; act on my suggestion if you agree with it, or else make a better one, *vānaras*.'

Hearing what Aṅgada had to say, Gandhamādana replied in 48.11–14
a low voice weary with thirst and exertion. 'Aṅgada's proposal is certainly apt, well-meant, and also in our interests. Let's do as he says. Let's once more hunt mountains and glens, caves as well, deserted woods and mountain torrents, everywhere noble Sugrīva directed. Let everybody search every forest and mountain fastness.'

The mighty *vānaras* stood up again and roamed through the 48.15–21
Vindhya forests enveloping the southern region. The *vānaras* climbed a majestic mountain, silvery as an autumn cloud with its peaks and caves, then the champion apes searched a pleasant *lodhra* forest and *saptaparṇa* forests in their eager hunt to set eyes on Sītā. Strong though they were, they were exhausted when they reached its summit, but they could not find Rāma's beloved queen, Vaidehī. The apes scrutinized the mountain and its many glens, then climbed down, looking everywhere till they reached the ground exhausted and distraught. They stood for a moment, then sank down at the root of a tree, but a moment later they had revived their spirits and recovered a little from their exhaustion, and were again straining to hunt through the whole southern region.

Hunger and thirst were assailing them when, exhausted and 49.7,
parched, they noticed a cavern set about with creepers and 30–31;
trees. The gallant and glorious *vānaras* were scouring the cave 50.1

on all sides when a woman appeared nearby. The sight struck them with terror, for she was an ascetic dressed in bark and black-antelope skins, emaciated from fasting and seeming to blaze with splendour. Hanumān very wisely explained to that illustrious ascetic, who was seeking merit clad in bark and black-antelope skins:

50.2–8 'We have been driven into this gloomy cave by exhaustion, hunger and thirst; we are altogether worn out. We came into this great cleft in the earth in the hope of finding something to drink, but we have seen so many different marvels that we feel perplexed, bewildered and confused. There are trees here, golden as the rising sun, their roots and fruit pure and luscious; there are golden mansions and silver houses, their windows burnished gold and their lattices studded all over with gems: whose are they? Whose power created these golden blossoming fruit trees, holy and fragrant, and these golden lotuses born in the spotless water? How is it that golden fish are swimming there alongside turtles? Do please tell us about yourself and your position; whose austerities have brought this about? We are all completely ignorant.'

50.9–19 At Hanumān's words, the merit-seeking ascetic, devoted to the welfare of all creatures, replied to Hanumān: 'A glorious bull of a *dānava*, a magician called Maya created all this golden forest by magic. Once upon a time he was appointed architect to the *dānava* chiefs, and it was he who created this wonderful, heavenly golden residence. He had practised asceticism in the great forest for thousands of years and had been granted a boon by the Grand Father: all the wealth of Uśanas. Lord of everything he could wish for, he had all this built and then lived at ease in this great forest for a while, with the *apsaras* Hemā as his partner, till Indra Puraṃdara attacked him and killed that bull of a *dānava* with his thunderbolt and Brahmā gave this marvellous forest and golden dwelling to Hemā to enjoy in perpetuity to her heart's content. I am Svayaṃprabhā, daughter of Merusāvarṇi, excellent *vānara*, and I watch over Hemā's residence. My dear friend Hemā is skilled in dance and song, and she has given me the privilege of watching over her lovely home. What do you want? Why are you here? This forest is unassailable: how did you cross the wild places and find it? These roots and fruits are good to eat; eat them and drink some water, then please tell me all.'

When the ape chiefs were all revived, the merit-seeking 51.1–2
ascetic with the focused mind spoke to them: 'If eating the fruit has dissipated your weariness, *vānaras*, and if I'm not intruding, I should like to hear your story; please tell it.'

Hearing her request, Hanumān, that true Son of the Wind, 51.3–17
began to tell her honestly and truthfully. 'The glorious Rāma Dāśarathi, king of all the world, equal to great Indra and Varuṇa, entered Daṇḍaka forest with his brother Lakṣmaṇa and his wife Vaidehī. Rāvaṇa forcibly carried off his wife from Janasthāna. It's that king's friend, a heroic *vānara* called Sugrīva, the king of the *vānara* chieftains, who has sent us out to the southern region – where Agastya roams and Yama rules – in company with these chief *vānaras* under the leadership of Aṅgada. All of us jointly have been exhorted to hunt for the shape-changing *rākṣasa* Rāvaṇa and for Sītā Vaidehī. We all searched the whole southern region until we were starving and exhausted, and clustered round the roots of a tree, pale-faced and brooding, sunk so deep in a sea of thought that we could see no way out. Then as we glanced all around we saw a great hole hidden by creepers and trees and shrouded in gloom. Birds were flying out from there, geese damp with water, spraying drops from their wings, and ospreys, and *sārasas* too. "Hooray! Let's go in!" I told the monkeys. The urgency of their master's task led them all to the same decision: "Let's go! Let's go inside!" They took firm hold of each other's hands then tumbled and scurried down into this gloom-obscured hole. That's our mission and that's why we're here. We came to you miserable and famished. We were burdened by our hunger, but now we've fed on the roots and fruit you gave us in accordance with the laws of hospitality. Tell us what we *vānaras* can do to repay you for saving us all from starving to death.'

After the *vānaras*' words, all-knowing Svayaṃprabhā gave 51.18–19
her answer to the *vānara* chiefs. 'It's my pleasure, daring *vānaras*. No one need reward me for doing what's right.'

Hanumān replied to the irreproachable ascetic's pleasant 52.1–5 and creditable words. 'You are our last resort, merit-seeker: noble Sugrīva set us a time, and we passed the limit while we were wandering about in this cavern. Please will you help us get out of this dreadful hole? We've exceeded Sugrīva's command! Our lives are up! Do save us all! We're afraid we're in danger from Sugrīva. We've got a huge task ahead of us, merit-seeker, and that task won't get done by staying here.'

52.6–8 The ascetic replied to Hanumān's request, 'Once in here I think you would find it hard to get out alive, but I can release you by the power built up by my ascetic observances. Close your eyes, all you bulls of *vānaras*; no one can get out unless their eyes are closed.'

52.9–11 Anxious to be on their way, in delight they all pressed their tapering fingers over their tightly closed eyes, then she released the noble *vānaras* from the hole, hands covering their faces, in no more than the twinkling of an eye. When the *vānaras* had all escaped from that strait, the pious ascetic spoke to reassure them:

52.12–13 'There is the Vindhya mountain, majestic and thick with trees and creepers; there is mount Prasravaṇa; and there are the mighty waters of the ocean. I wish you success as I go to my dwelling, bulls of *vānaras*.' So saying Svayaṃprabhā disappeared into that glorious cavern.

52.14–18 Then they saw Varuṇa's dread abode, the boundless ocean, roaring and turbulent with its terrible waves. Knowing they had exceeded the month their king had set as their limit while they were searching the mountain fastness created by Maya's magic, those lords seated themselves among the trees in full bloom at the foot of the Vindhya mountain and deliberated. When they saw how heavily laden with flowers were the tips of the springtime trees, covered with hundreds of creepers, they began to fear danger. They told each other that spring was under way, and collapsed on the ground: the time for them to fulfil their orders was gone.

52.19–27; That monkey with shoulders like a lion or a bull and long
54.11–15 brawny arms, Aṅgada, the sagacious Young King, spoke. 'We all set out at the command of the king of the monkeys. Apes, the month was up while we were stuck in that hole. Why won't

you wake up to that fact? Now that the time fixed by Sugrīva himself is over, the only thing all we forest-dwellers can do is sit here and fast to death. Sugrīva is harsh by nature, and now that he's secured his status as ruler he won't condone our having gone off and breached his command. He will certainly do something drastic if he gets no news of Sītā. That's why sitting here in a fast is the right thing for us to do now, abandoning our sons and wives and wealth and homes; if we go back from here the king will have us all executed. It's better for us to die here than suffer a dishonourable slaughter. It wasn't Sugrīva who wanted me to be consecrated Young King; I owe my consecration to that Lord of Men, tireless Rāma. The king is already confirmed in his hostility towards me; his mind is made up. When he sees my shortcoming he will have me punished with a cruel death. How could my friends bear to watch me suffer such a calamity in my prime? I am going to sit here at this holy seashore and fast to death. You should take leave of me, all you *vānaras*, and go home, but I will not go to the city, that I promise you. I am going to sit here and fast to death. It's better for me to die. You must greet the king for me, my junior father Sugrīva, lord of the *vānaras*, and enquire after his health. Mother Rumā too should be wished well, and her health enquired about, and you should particularly console my mother Tārā. The poor thing is tender by nature and fond of her son; she is bound to give up her life when she hears I have perished here.'

After this long speech Aṅgada took leave of his elders weep- 54.16–19
ing despondently and seated himself on the ground on some *kuśa* grass. To see him seated there made the bulls of *vānaras* shed hot tears from their sorrowful eyes. They heaped blame on Sugrīva and praise on Vālin, then closed ranks around Aṅgada and decided they would all sit down and fast to death. Those bulls of monkeys recognized the resolve of Vālin's son. They sipped water, then seated themselves on the northern shore, all huddled together facing east on stalks of *kuśa* with its tips to the south.*

While the apes were engaged in their fast to death, there 55.1–5
came to the part of the mountain tableland where they were

sitting a long-lived bird called Saṃpāti. He was king of the vultures, famed for his manly might, Jaṭāyus' glorious brother. As he stepped out of a hollow in the great Vindhya mountain, he saw the apes seated there and gloated, 'In this world a man is certain to gain his allotted portion! At last my appointed sustenance has arrived. I shall eat these *vānaras* as they die one after another.' So said the bird when he caught sight of the monkeys.

55.6–15 Aṅgada was extremely distressed to hear the voracious bird's words, and said to Hanumān, 'Look, Yama Lord of Death has arrived here in person; Sītā was a pretext to bring catastrophe on the *vānaras*. We have not performed Rāma's task or carried out our king's instruction; now this unexpected catastrophe has suddenly befallen the apes. You've heard all about the deed Jaṭāyus did, how the king of the vultures wanted to help Vaidehī: so you see we can all do something pleasing to Rāma, even if we've been born as animals, even if it means giving up our lives as we are doing. We have worn ourselves out for the Rāghava's sake; we have abandoned our lives; we have taken refuge in the wilderness; yet we have not found Maithilī. But happy is the king of the vultures to have been killed in combat with Rāvaṇa! He is free of fear of Sugrīva and has reaped the ultimate reward. The destruction of Jaṭāyus and of King Daśaratha and the capture of Vaidehī have put the apes at risk; Rāma and Lakṣmaṇa's stay in the forest with Sītā; the murder of Vālin by the Rāghava's arrow; the killing of the *rākṣasas* as well – not one escaping Rāma's wrath; all this evil has resulted from granting Kaikeyī her boons.'

55.16–21 When the sharp-billed vulture heard the words issuing from Aṅgada's mouth, he cried out loudly, 'Who is this talking about the death of my brother Jaṭāyus? I'm beside myself to hear it! He was dearer to me than my life. Why should there have been a battle between a *rākṣasa* and a vulture in Janasthāna? Today's the first time for a long while that I've heard my brother's name. My younger brother was judicious and his bravery commendable: I should like to hear how he can have died, you bulls of *vānaras*. My brother Jaṭāyus lived in Janasthāna, so how was my brother a friend of Daśaratha, whose beloved eldest son Rāma is dear to his elders? My wings have been so burnt up by the sun's rays that I can't move about, but I should like to come down from this mountain, victorious heroes.'

The ape chiefs did not trust what they heard him say; despite 56.1–4
its grief-stricken tones, they were alarmed about what he might do. As they sat there fasting to death, the fearsome sight of the vulture convinced the monkeys that he would devour them all, and that if he did devour them while they sat fasting to death they would achieve their object quickly and successfully. Then all the bulls of *vānaras* made their decision and helped the vulture down from the top of that mountain-peak. Aṅgada then explained to the bird:

'My grandfather, Ṛkṣarajas by name, was a glorious Lord 56.5–19
of the *vānaras*, a ruler of the earth. Two righteous sons were born to him, both irresistible as a flood, Sugrīva and Vālin. Vālin, my father, famed throughout the world for his deeds, became king. Glorious Rāma Dāśarathi, king of the whole world, great chariot warrior of the Ikṣvākus, came into the Daṇḍaka Forest with his brother Lakṣmaṇa and his wife Vaidehī too; he was following the righteous path, devotedly carrying out his father's decree. Rāvaṇa forcibly carried his wife off from Janasthāna. Jaṭāyus the vulture king, ally of Rāma's father, saw Sītā Vaidehī being carried off through the sky. He brought Rāvaṇa down from his chariot and set Maithilī on the ground, but he was old and exhausted and Rāvaṇa killed him in combat. That's how the vulture was defeated by Rāvaṇa's superior strength; he's gone to his ultimate reward, his funeral rites duly performed by Rāma. Then the Rāghava made an alliance with my father's noble brother, Sugrīva, and killed my father, for Sugrīva and his associates were hostile to my father. When he'd killed Vālin, Rāma had Sugrīva consecrated and established him in the kingdom as Lord of the *vānaras*, king and commander-in-chief. That's who sent us out; we've been directed by Rāma to hunt here, there and everywhere, but we've discovered no more of Vaidehī than of the radiant sun at night. We scoured Daṇḍaka Forest scrupulously, then made the mistake of going down a deep hole in the ground, a cavern

created by Maya's magic. While we were searching it, the month that the king had set as the time limit was up. We've carried out the instructions of the king of the monkeys, but we're all sitting here fasting to death from fear at having exceeded the limit set. If we go back Kākutstha will be angry, Sugrīva and Lakṣmaṇa too, and life will be over for us all.'

57.1–7 The *vānaras* had abandoned life. Hearing their pitiful story the vulture sobbed loudly and replied to the *vānaras*, 'You tell me Jaṭāyus has been killed in battle by Rāvaṇa's superior strength: *vānaras*, he was my younger brother. I must bear the news, for now, old and wingless as I am, I can do nothing to avenge my brother. Once upon a time, around the time Vṛtra was slain, he and I competed in flying towards the blazing rays garlanding the sun. We went wheeling through the sky with the utmost speed, but when the sun reached its zenith, Jaṭāyus grew faint. I saw that the sun's rays were tormenting my brother so, moved by affection at his great distress, I shielded him with my own wings. My wings were burned, excellent *vānaras*, and I fell on to Vindhya; living here I could get no news of my brother.'

57.8–10 Hearing what Jaṭāyus' brother Saṃpāti said, the Young King Aṅgada shrewdly replied, 'If you're Jaṭāyus' brother and you heard what I said, tell us, do you know the lair of this *rākṣasa*? If you know that short-sighted lord of *rākṣasas* Rāvaṇa, whether he's nearby or far away, do tell us!'

57.11–32 True to his nature, Jaṭāyus' glorious older brother delighted the *vānaras* with his reply. 'Monkeys, I'm a vulture with burnt wings and my prowess is spent, but I'll do all I can to help Rāma with my words alone. Old age has robbed me of my glory, and my life is hanging by a thread: my immediate task is what I can do for Rāma. I saw a lovely young woman, adorned with every ornament, being carried off by that evil Rāvaṇa. The beauty was screaming "Rāma, Rāma! Lakṣmaṇa!", squirming about and throwing down her ornaments. Her gorgeous silks lit up the sombre *rākṣasa* like sunrays on a mountain-top, or like lightning against a cloud. Her calling to Rāma makes me think that must have been Sītā. Let me tell you about this *rākṣasa's* lair. The very son of Viśravas,

Vaiśravaṇa's brother, that *rākṣasa* called Rāvaṇa lives in the city Laṅkā. Laṅkā is a charming town built by Viśvakarman on an island in the sea a full hundred *yojanas* from here. That's where Vaidehī is living, silk-clad but miserable, imprisoned in Rāvaṇa's private apartments, closely guarded by *rākṣasīs*. This Laṅkā is protected by sea on all sides, but you'll find King Janaka's daughter Maithilī there; go to the coast, and a full hundred *yojanas* beyond you'll land on the sea's southern shore and there you'll find Rāvaṇa. Hurry off there! Bound along quickly, monkeys! My insight tells me it's certain you'll come back when you've seen it all. Drongos and other grain-feeders take the lowest paths; the second is for those that scavenge the ritual offerings and peck fruit on the trees; the third is for hawks, cranes and ospreys; the fourth for eagles; the fifth for ordinary vultures; the sixth path is for graceful, youthful geese, bold and powerful; but the highest is the course of Vinatā's sons. Bulls of *vānaras*, we were all born as Vinatā's sons, but a deed was committed that condemned us to be carrion-eaters. My sight is such that from where I stand I can make out distant Rāvaṇa and Jānakī, for we also have divine Garuḍa's eyesight. Our innate inheritance and the prowess demanded of us by our diet, *vānaras*, have developed in us an unfailing ability to see for more than a hundred *yojanas*. Our nature requires us to seek sustenance from afar, while those that fight with their feet[10] find their sustenance right at their feet. You must find some way of leaping over the salt sea; but when you've found Vaidehī you can go back with your mission accomplished. I should like you, sirs, to help me down to Varuṇa's abode, the ocean, so that I can make the water offering for my noble brother, now he's gone to heaven.'

The *vānaras* then were filled with the greatest vigour. They 57.33–4
led Saṃpāti with his burnt wings to the place on the shore of the Lord of Rivers and Streams, then brought the Bird Lord back again, delighted at the information he had given them.

When the king of the vultures had told his story, the monkeys 63.1–8
leapt up in a happy crowd, bold as lions, and roared. Hearing Saṃpāti's information about where Rāvaṇa lived, the joyful apes went to the ocean, eager for a glimpse of Sītā. When they

got there, the mighty warriors saw it spread out before them like a complete reflection of the wide world. The *vānara* chiefs reached the northern edge of the southern sea and halted there; elephants of monkeys they were, but their hearts sank to see it crammed with all kinds of great ugly creatures with gaping jaws and enormous bodies playing about in the water, its waves in one place seeming asleep but playful in another and covered with mountainous breakers somewhere else; with its crowds of *dānava* lords from the depths of the Underworld it was hair-raising. The *vānaras* gazed at the ocean and suddenly they all lost heart: it would be as hard to cross as the sky, and they asked themselves how it could be done.

63.9–11 The ape chief saw that the sight of the ocean had depressed the army, and rallied the apprehensive apes. 'We'll have no despondency. Despondency is a grave offence. Despondency kills a man as easily as an angry snake kills a child. Anyone in the grip of despondency now that it's valour that's required will be stripped of his energy and fail to achieve his goal.'

63.12–15 When that night had passed, Aṅgada and the senior *vānara* apes assembled and held another consultation. The *vānara* host with its standards clustering round Aṅgada was resplendent as the army of *maruts* stationed around Indra Vāsava. Who could stiffen the nerve of this *vānara* host, who but Vālin's son or Hanumān? Majestic, victorious Aṅgada saluted the senior apes and the army, then made a speech that came straight to the point.

63.16–20 'Who has splendour enough to cross the ocean today? Who will enable foe-conquering Sugrīva to keep his word? Which of you heroic monkeys would leap a hundred *yojanas* and free all these chiefs from dread? Whose grace will allow us to leave here content, with our mission accomplished, and again see wives, sons and homes? Whose grace would let us approach Rāma, mighty Lakṣmaṇa and mighty Sugrīva with delight? If any of you apes is capable of leaping the ocean, let him of his bountiful generosity free us here and now from fear.'

63.21 No one said anything in reply to Aṅgada's speech. The whole army of apes remained motionless.

63.22–3 Aṅgada, chief of the apes, again addressed his apes: 'My lords, mightiest of the mighty, you are steadfast in valour, born of distinguished families and recipients of repeated honours: nothing hinders any one of you from going at any time. Declare your ability at leaping, each of you bulls of monkeys.'

When they heard Aṅgada's words, all the *vānara* chiefs in turn then stated how far each could go: Gaja, Gavākṣa, Gavaya, Śarabha, Gandhamādana, Mainda and Dvivida, Suṣeṇa and Jāmbavān. 64.1–2

Said Gaja, 'I could leap ten *yojanas*.' Gavākṣa declared, 'I will go twenty *yojanas*.' The *vānara* Gavaya then told the other *vānaras*, 'But monkeys, I will go thirty *yojanas*.' Then the *vānara* Śarabha told the *vānaras*, 'I will go forty *yojanas*, definitely.' But Gandhamādana, that very splendid *vānara*, claimed, 'I will definitely go fifty *yojanas*.' Mainda the *vānara*, however, then told the other *vānaras*, 'I'll venture to leap more than sixty *yojanas*.' Very splendid Dvivida then countered, 'Seventy *yojanas* is what I'll do, without any doubt.' But that outstanding ape Suṣeṇa declared to all the leading monkeys, 'I would leap eighty *yojanas*, you bulls of monkeys.' 64.3–9

While they were making these assertions, the oldest among them, Jāmbavān, praised them all but countered, 'Once we too were expert leapers but now we are past our prime. However, this task cannot be ignored, even by one as far-gone as I am; the monkey king and Rāma are both resolved on it. I will tell you how far Time has restricted me to going nowadays: I will go ninety *yojanas*. There's no doubt about that.' 64.10–13

Jāmbavān then resumed, and told all the ape chiefs, 'Certainly my ability to leap is not what it used to be. Indeed, of old at great Bali's sacrifice I was able to circumambulate eternal Viṣṇu while the triple-strider was striding. I'm old now and my ability to leap has waned, but in my youth no one could rival my power. That's all I reckon I could manage nowadays, and that's not enough to accomplish this task successfully.' 64.14–17

Aṅgada spoke next; his sagacious reply was calculated to inspire. First he praised the great monkey Jāmbavān. 'For my part, I will go the whole hundred *yojanas*, but whether I should be able to return I cannot be sure.' 64.18–19

The ape chief Jāmbavān made him an eloquent reply. 'You 64.20–27 are supreme among apes and bears, and your ability to leap is well known. Your Honour is certainly capable of leaping a hundred *yojanas*, or a thousand, and of returning, but you are not required to do so. My son, a commander deploys others; on no account is he to be deployed himself. Best of leapers, you have all these troops to deploy. Your Honour, in your position as our commander we must protect you like a wife. An army's commander is its wife: that's the way things are, you scorcher of your foes. And so, my son, we must always safeguard you like a wife, your Honour. Besides, your Honour is the very root of this mission, victorious prince, and the root of any enterprise must be safeguarded: that's the tactic employed by those who are experienced in matters of policy, for when the root is whole, the benefits are obtained – flowers, fruit or whatever. Your Honour is truly valiant, and your wise and intrepid character is the basis on which the success of our mission depends, scorcher of your foes. You are not only our leader but the son of our leader, excellent monkey; with your support, your Honour, we shall be capable of accomplishing our goal.'

64.28–32 The great monkey Aṅgada son of Vālin again replied to Jāmbavān's astute advice, 'But if I don't go, and neither does any other bull of a *vānara*, then we shall certainly have to proceed with the fast to death, for if we go back to the wise Lord of the Apes without carrying out his order, I can't see us keeping our lives. That ape has mercy at his command, but rage much more so. If we transgressed his orders we would return to our destruction. Your Honour understands the position, so work out some other way of accomplishing our goal.'

64.33–4 Aṅgada's retort drew from the heroic bull of a leaper Jāmbavān a further reply. 'Heroic Aṅgada, there is nothing lacking for the task. I will encourage the one who can bring the mission to a successful conclusion.'

BEAUTY

[It is Hanumān who makes the leap, aided by his ability to increase his size at will. When he arrives in Laṅkā he searches for Sītā at night time in the Palace, at first mistakenly thinking he has found her asleep among Rāvaṇa's women.]

The great monkey dismissed that idea then pulled himself together and had another thought about Sītā. 'Separated from Rāma, that beautiful woman would not like to sleep or eat, and she wouldn't wear ornaments, or indulge in drink, or let another man near her, even if he were the Lord of the Gods, for there's no one to equal Rāma even among the Thirty. This is somebody else.' 5,9.1–3

With that conclusion he roamed about in the drinking-hall. The tiger of a monkey saw that the drinking-hall was stocked with everything that the noble *rākṣasa* lord could wish for in his residence, and he saw that the drinking-hall was set with joints of venison, buffalo and pork. On broad golden dishes the tiger of a monkey saw half-eaten peacocks along with jungle fowl; boar and rhinoceros marinaded in savoury curds; desserts and all kinds of liquor and different eatables; assortments of confectionery too, bitter, savoury and sweet; meats skilfully prepared and spread out in that drinking-hall; various divine clear wines and spirits distilled from sugar and mead, from flowers or from fruit, each flavoured with different aromatic spices. The floor sparkled with a carpet of heaped-up garlands and was covered with golden water pots, crystal vessels and other water pots of alluvial gold. There the monkey saw in silver and gold jars an abundance of choice wines; golden, gem-studded and silver vessels full of liquor were seen 9.3–33 by that great monkey. The drinks he saw in one place were half-finished, in another they had been completely drunk, in another they had not been started. As he wandered about he noticed an assortment of food here, drinks served out there, half-eaten scraps everywhere, sometimes broken water pots, sometimes overturned jars, sometimes garlands jumbled among water and fruit. All around a breeze was wafting various scents, cooling sandalwood, sweet tasting liquor, garlands and flowers of all sorts, sandal for bathing and mingled perfumes; the Puṣpaka Palace was fragrant in that perfumed breeze. The great and glorious monkey viewed everything without exception in Rāvaṇa's private apartment, but Jānakī was nowhere to be seen.

9.34–6 He pondered deeply, apprehensive and alarmed about what was proper. 'Peering into the private sleeping-quarters of somebody else's wives! Surely I'm committing a shocking breach of propriety! Spying on another person's wives was not my intention, yet I have been looking at this bevy of somebody's wives.'

9.37–42 As he once more fixed his mind on his one goal, another thought occurred to the wise *vānara* to guide his actions. 'Granted, I've seen all Rāvaṇa's wives unawares but my mind is none the worse for that. It's the mind that causes the senses to be stimulated in good situations and in bad, and mine is well adjusted. It's no use my searching for Vaidehī anywhere else. If you're serious about looking for a woman, always look among women. Search for any creature among its own kind. If it's a young woman you've lost, don't look for her among deer. My mind has been pure all the time I've been searching this private apartment of Rāvaṇa, but I've not found Jānakī.'

9.43; 10.6–14 Heroic Hanumān viewed daughters of gods and *gandharvas*, *nāga* girls too, but still he could not find Jānakī. 'I've seen the whole private apartment, I've seen Rāvaṇa's wives, but I've not seen the virtuous Sītā. I've exerted myself in vain. When I go back all the *vānaras* will crowd round me, and just what are they going to ask? "Hero, tell us what you've done over there!" What shall I say if I've not seen Janaka's daughter? They'll certainly undertake a fast to death because we've overstayed the time limit. When I'm back across the ocean what will old Jāmbavān and Aṅgada both say, and all the *vānara* host? Fortune grows from not despairing, the highest happiness comes from not despairing: I will keep on exploring where I haven't explored so far. Not despairing always drives on every undertaking. Whatever a person undertakes, that's what brings it to fruition. So it's for me to bestir myself to make a supreme effort without despairing and explore any areas under Rāvaṇa's control that I've not seen yet. I've already searched drinking-halls, I've searched flower-houses and picture galleries too, and gaming rooms and pleasure-garden pathways, and mansions, thoroughly.' Checking them all off, he began to extend his search.

He jumped up, he jumped down, he stood still, he ran about, 10.15–25 he opened gates, he broke down doors, he went in, he went out, he bounded along, he leapt upwards: the great monkey roamed through the whole area. In Rāvaṇa's private apartment there was no space so much as a hand's breadth that the monkey did not enter. Alleys within the ramparts, platforms around sacred trees, pits, lotus pools: he scanned them all. There Hanumān saw every kind of deformed, distorted *rākṣasī*, but not Janaka's daughter. There Hanumān saw fine *vidyādhara* women unequalled in the world for beauty, but not the Rāghava's darling. There Hanumān saw slinky *nāga* girls with faces like the full moon, but not slender Sītā. There Hanumān saw *nāga* girls whom the *rākṣasa* lord had violently abducted, but not the joy of Janaka. Despite all his might the mighty Hanumān Son of the Wind could not see her, and the sight of the other fine women cast him down; Hanumān Son of the Wind descended from the palace with thoughts grief-stricken and began to deliberate.

'Laṅkā has been utterly ransacked in an effort to please 11.3–45 Rāma but I've had no sight of Vaidehī Sītā's lovely frame. Pools, tanks,[1] lakes, streams too, and rivers, shores, forest margins and inaccessible mountains: the whole earth's been ransacked, yet I can't see Jānakī. Saṃpāti king of the vultures described seeing Sītā here in Rāvaṇa's realm, but I can't see her myself. I think that at the time when the *rākṣasa* had snatched

Sītā and was hurriedly flying upward to escape Rāma's arrows, he might have dropped her. Or else I think that while the noble lady was being carried off on the path frequented by the *siddhas*, it was her heart that failed when she spied the ocean. Or I think the force of Rāvaṇa's legs and arms squeezed the life out of this noble, broad-eyed lady. Or definitely, as they were climbing higher and higher over the ocean Janaka's daughter struggled free and fell into the sea. Could it be that poor friendless Sītā has been devoured by Rāvaṇa because she preserved her honour against that wretch? Or else the dark-eyed innocent will have been gobbled up by the *rākṣasa* lord's evil wives. Or I think she's imprisoned in Rāvaṇa's palace, feebly lamenting and lamenting like a caged mynah. Rāma's slender wife with the lotus-petal eyes was born in the family of Janaka: how could she submit to Rāvaṇa's authority? Rāma loves his wife, and I can't tell him that Janaka's daughter's been murdered or killed or has died. It would be wrong for me to make such a report; it would be wrong for me not to make the report. Whatever am I to do? It looks to me a difficult path to tread. If I go back to the *vānara* lord's city without seeing Sītā, then what will become of my mission? What's Sugrīva going to say, or the ape council, or Daśaratha's two sons when I get back to Kiṣkindhā? And if I do go back and make Kākutstha the very painful report that I've not found Sītā, then he'll give up on life. It'll kill him to hear the bad news about Sītā, so harsh, savage, cruel, searing, so agonizing! Wise Lakṣmaṇa is extremely devoted to him; seeing him so miserably breathing his last will kill him too. When he hears that his two brothers have perished, Bharata too will die, and seeing Bharata dead will kill Śatrughna. And learning that their sons are dead will be the death of their mothers, Kausalyā, Sumitrā and Kaikeyī, no doubt about it. When the monkey lord Sugrīva sees what's happened to Rāma he'll meet his end out of gratitude and loyalty. Rumā will be despondent, troubled, miserable, joyless, wretched and weighed down by grief for her husband, and will give up her life; Tārā too, weighed down by her grief over Vālin and wasted by sorrow, will not survive the king's death. Then there's young Aṅgada: how can he carry on his life after the death of his mother and father and the calamity to Sugrīva? That glorious monkey king has been so indulgent with his appeasement, rewards and honours that the *vānaras* will lay down their lives. Never again will those elephants of monkeys congregate in forests, mountains or valleys and sport there; weighed down by their master's calamity, they will congregate in the heights with their wives, sons and ministers and throw themselves from the cliff tops. When I arrive, dreadful, I think, will be the wailing, and the destruction of the Ikṣvāku line, and the destruction indeed of the forest-dwellers. I certainly will not leave here for the city of Kiṣkindhā. I shall build a pyre somewhere with ample roots and fruit and water at the ocean shore, kindle a fire and throw myself into it. Or I will sit still and duly perfect myself, then crows and beasts of prey can eat my body: I believe the sages countenance this method of departure. If I can't find Jānakī I will enter the waters in the prescribed fashion, or else I'll become a disciplined ascetic living beneath the trees. Unless I see that dark-eyed lady, I will not stir from here.'

Thoughts such as these overwhelmed the *vānara*. He had 11.51
not found Sītā. Grief and brooding overcame him, and he racked his brains.

[*Hanumān finally identifies Sītā in the grove of aśoka trees, but hides and watches when Rāvaṇa approaches, surrounded by a bevy of beauties.*]

In her captivity she was miserable, joyless and wretched; 18.1–33
Rāvaṇa made his proposition in honeyed, elegant phrases. 'Your legs are as shapely as elephants' trunks, yet when you see me you hide your breasts and stomach as if you're afraid and want to make yourself invisible. My broad-eyed beauty, I desire you: grant me your favour, my dear. Every part of your body is praiseworthy and altogether ravishing. Here are no men, no shape-changing *rākṣasas*, Sītā, and you can dismiss any lurking fear you're harbouring about me! Granted, certainly, timid woman, it's customary for *rākṣasas* to take other men's wives or carry them off violently, but even so I will not touch you against your will, Maithilī, however fervently Desire is coursing through my body. You need have no fear of me

here, lady; trust me, my dear, and show me your affection by your action. Don't be so set on grieving! Your single plait,[2] your sleeping on the ground, your brooding, your soiled clothes, your fasting out of season – they're not right for you. Pretty garlands, sandalwood and aloes, clothing of every kind, divine ornaments, choice wines, conveyances and couches, singing, dancing, music: take them, Maithilī, and then take me! You are a jewel of a woman; don't let yourself go like this. Ornament your limbs! Now you've captivated me you should make yourself worthy of me, shapely woman. Your youth is in full bloom but it is passing, and when it is past, like a swift-flowing stream it will not come back. I think Viśvakarman, designer of all, halted when he had formed you, for you have no rival for your beauty, lovely woman. What man who had possessed you in your youthful beauty, Vaidehī, would look further, even the Grand Father himself? You moonfaced lady, wherever on your body my eye rests it is kept enchained, stately woman. Become my wife, Maithilī. Abandon this delusion. Become the Chief Queen of all my many excellent women. Bashful creature, whatever treasures I have forced from the worlds are all yours, and this kingdom, and so am I. For you I will conquer the whole earth with its garlands of cities and present it to Janaka, you tease. I can't see anyone in this world who can match my strength. Look at my immense heroism: it's unchallenged in battle. In more than one battle, gods and anti-gods have crumbled before me; their standards have been trampled, their forces could not stand against me. Let me arouse your desire. Reward yourself today in the best possible way and have brilliant ornaments hung on your body. How good it would be to see your beauty suitably adorned. My shy lovely, if you'll behave as you should and be kind to me, you shall enjoy all the delights you desire; you'll have drink and pleasures, and you'll be able to make gifts – the earth and all its riches if you like! You can make merry with me in all confidence and order me about boldly; your relations too shall make merry under my protection, if you will make merry with me. Now you've seen how prosperous, how majestic, how glorious I am, darling, what do you want with bark-clad Rāma in your good fortune? Rāma's been stripped of his glory and given up conquest to wander in the forest observing vows and sleeping on the bare ground. I don't even know if he's still alive. Rāma won't so much as manage to see you, Vaidehī: you'll be like the moon hidden by egret-heralded monsoon clouds. In any case the Rāghava would be no more able to rescue you from my clutches than Hiraṇyakaśipu was his Kīrti from Indra's clutches. Your smile is lovely, your teeth are lovely, your eyes are lovely; your teasing timidity captivates my mind – you're like Garuḍa with a snake! The sight of you, clad in soiled silk, gaunt and unadorned though you are, stops me taking my pleasure from my own wives. Jānakī, you can assume power over all the many excellent women I have living in my private apartments. My women are the finest in the three worlds, my raven-tressed beauty, but they shall attend on you like the *apsarases* on Śrī. You with the lovely forehead and shapely hips, all the gems and wealth of Vaiśravaṇa and all the worlds are yours to enjoy to your heart's content – and with them, me. My lady, not for ascetic power, not for strength, for prowess, wealth, splendour, and not for reputation can Rāma compare with me.'

Sītā was distressed to hear the fearsome *rākṣasa's* speech, 19.1–3
and replied miserably, hesitantly, in tones of misery. Poor shapely Sītā wept and trembled in the torment of her grief as she thought about the one object of her devotion, her husband. She placed grass between them,[3] smiled sweetly and replied.

'Turn your thoughts away from me; it's on your own kind 19.3–4
that you should let your thoughts dwell. You are no more worthy to woo me than a sinner to aspire to merit. The family I was born into is great; pure is the family I was taken into to have a sole husband. It is unthinkable that I should commit such a contemptible act.'

With these words to Rāvaṇa, glorious Vaidehī turned away 19.5–29
from the *rākṣasa* and went on: 'As the wife of another I am not a proper wife for you. You'd do well to observe the law of morality; you'd do well to follow the example of virtuous people. Other people's wives are to be protected like your own, night-walker. Set yourself up as a model and enjoy the favours

of your own wives. One who is unsatisfied with his own wives, with a roving eye, fickle and deceitful, pursues other men's wives to his own perdition. Whether it's because you have no decent men around you, or whether you don't follow the advice of decent men, spoken wisely for your own good, you are being led astray. When an intemperate king arises who delights in disorder, prosperous countrysides and cities go to rack and ruin. Laṅkā here may be flooded with heaps of gems, but led by you it will soon be destroyed, and it will be your fault alone. People gloat when a wicked person with no foresight is struck down by his own deeds, Rāvaṇa, so those you have injured by your wickedness will be delighted and tell you, "It's a good thing that this disaster has befallen you, fearsome as you are." I can no more exist without the Rāghava than its radiance can without the sun: I cannot be seduced by power or wealth! When I have once had the honoured arm of the world's protector around me, how could I seek the arms of anyone else? I belong to that Lord of the Earth alone, just as wisdom belongs to a ritually purified, spiritually awakened brāhman. The best thing for you, Rāvaṇa, would be to restore me in my sorrow to Rāma, like an elephant cow longing for her elephant chief in the forest. If you want to maintain your position and avoid a dreadful death, the right thing to do is to make an ally of Rāma, that bull of a man. Someone like you might dodge the divine thunderbolt, for a long time you might escape Death, but not the Lord of the World, the Rāghava, in his wrath. You'll hear the twanging of Rāma's bow roaring like a thunderbolt hurled by Indra Śatakratu. Soon well-jointed shafts marked out as Rāma's and Lakṣmaṇa's shall rain down on this place like blazing-mouthed snakes, slaughtering *rākṣasas* all over the city; devastation will drop with the heron-feathered bolts. With the impetus of his assault Rāma, a mighty second Garuḍa, will exterminate those great snakes, those *rākṣasa* lords, like Vinatā's son does serpents. My all-conquering husband will speedily rescue me from you, as with his three strides Viṣṇu did Śrī from the anti-gods. This sin was all you could manage, *rākṣasa*, in response to the defeat of the *rākṣasa* horde that turned Janasthāna into a "place of the slain". It was when those brothers, that pair of lions of men, were absent foraging that you entered the hermitage and captured me. No one could be more vile! If you'd got so much as a sniff of Rāma and Lakṣmaṇa you'd have been like a cur before a pair of tigers: you couldn't have withstood their gaze. For you to defeat that pair in battle is as impossible as for Vṛtra's one arm to overcome Indra's two. Like a drop of water disappearing in the sun, your life will shortly be snatched from you by the arrows of Saumitri and of Rāma, my lord.'

The *rākṣasa* overlord heard the harshness of Sītā's words, 20.1–6
and made the lovely Sītā an unlovely reply: 'Giving in to women only lets them dominate us. Our fair words are always met with contempt. My mounting passion for you is bridling my anger as a good charioteer does his galloping steeds on the open road. Passion leads men astray: whoever it fastens on is sure to grow soft and tender-hearted. That's why I haven't had you killed, my beauty, though you deserve death and dishonour for your devotion to that sham ascetic. Maithilī, every harsh word you address to me merits a cruel death.'

After these words to Vaidehī, Rāvaṇa the *rākṣasa* overlord 20.7–9
was overcome by the vehemence of his wrath; he then continued to warn Sītā, 'I shall observe the two months' grace I set for you, my beauty, but then you shall share my bed. If after two months you still reject me as a husband, they can get their hands on you in the kitchen for my breakfast.'

The broad-eyed daughters of gods and *gandharvas* were 20.10–12
dismayed to see Jānakī being threatened by the *rākṣasa* lord; as the *rākṣasa* threatened, they encouraged Sītā with movements of lips, eyes or faces, emboldening Sītā to address to Rāvaṇa overlord of the *rākṣasas* an edifying speech attesting to her courageous nature.

'You obviously have no one who cares for you enough to 20.13–22
hold you back from this despicable behaviour. Who apart from you in the three worlds would set his sights on me, even only in his mind, when I'm the wife of a righteous man as much as Śacī is of her lord? Vile *rākṣasa*, where will you fly to escape the boundless might of Rāma now that you have spoken evil to his wife? It's like an exultant elephant encountering a hare

in the forest: Rāma's the tusker and you, you wretch, you're reminiscent of the hare! But you, you're not ashamed to stand here hurling abuse at the Lord of the Ikṣvākus, just so long as he can't see you. These cruel eyes of yours, ugly, murky and sallow – why haven't they fallen to the ground for staring at me, you uncouth creature? Why has your tongue not shrivelled up, you villain, for talking to me, to me the wife of that righteous man, me the daughter-in-law of Daśaratha? Daśagrīva, I have the power to reduce you to ashes, but in the absence of any such instruction by Rāma, and to conserve the fruits of my asceticism, I will not burn you up. I can't be sundered from sagacious Rāma, so this course of events must have been decreed in order to bring about your death; that's obvious! How could Vaiśravaṇa's warrior brother with all his armies lure away Rāma to rob him of his wife?'

20.23–8 When he heard what Sītā had to say, Rāvaṇa overlord of the *rākṣasas* rolled his cruel eyes and glared at Jānakī. Like a thundercloud he looked; his arms and neck were stout, his nature and gait were leonine; he was majestic, his tongue was blazing and his eyes were savage; his tall frame quivered to the tip of his headdress; he was perfumed and glittering with garlands; he was clad in red wreaths and raiment, in ornaments and burnished bracelets; he was tightly girt in a great blue-black girdle like the snake wound around Mandara to churn out the ambrosia; a pair of earrings the colour of the rising sun adorned him, like the red shoots and flowers of a pair of *aśokas* on a mountain, as Rāvaṇa glared at Vaidehī with rage-reddened eyes, hissing at Sītā like a serpent as he spoke.

20.29 'Since you refuse to abandon that wretched pauper, I'm going to rid myself of you now like the might of the sun dispelling the shades of morning.'

20.30–35 So said Rāvaṇa, the king who made his foes roar, to Maithilī; then he gave orders to all the savage-looking *rākṣasīs*. 'All you *rākṣasīs* must co-operate at once in bending Sītā Jānakī immediately to my will. Use threats and blandishments[4] – use inducements, rewards or anything to provoke a rift – violence even, but turn Vaidehī round.'

20.36–7 The *rākṣasa* lord repeated his orders over and over again, beside himself with lust and fury, then as he was roundly threatening Jānakī the *rākṣasī* Dhānyamālinī hurried up and threw her arms round Daśagrīva with inviting words.

'Have some fun with me, great king; what's this Sītā to you? 20.38
Lusting after an unwilling woman brings torture to the body, but delightful pleasure awaits one whose desire is aroused by a willing woman.'

The *rākṣasī's* words diverted the monster; Daśagrīva and his 20.39–40
entourage of daughters of gods, *gandharvas* and *nāgas* returned to his lovely residence, the palace whose colour rivalled the blazing sun.

Rāvaṇa, the king who made his foes roar, had finished speak- 21.1–4
ing to Maithilī and gone away, leaving all the *rākṣasīs* with their instructions. When the *rākṣasa* lord had left and gone back to his private apartment those savage-looking *rākṣasīs* rushed to surround Sītā; crazed with anger, the *rākṣasīs* came up to Sītā and carried on taunting her in harsh tones: 'Sītā, don't you think it would be a fine thing to be the wife of noble Rāvaṇa Daśagrīva, that most excellent Paulastya?'

A *rākṣasī* called Ekajaṭā with infuriated copper-coloured 21.5–8
eyes then spoke up, telling wasted[5] Sītā, 'You see, the fourth Prajāpati, son of Brahmā's mind – one of the six Prajāpatis – is the famous Pulastya, and Pulastya's glorious, mind-born son is the great sage called Viśravas. His splendour equals a Prajāpati's, and Rāvaṇa, he who makes his foes roar, you broad-eyed beauty, is his son. You are worthy of becoming a wife of this *rākṣasa* lord. You are loveliness through and through. Why won't you accept what I'm telling you?'

Then a *rākṣasī* named Harijaṭā put in a word. She had eyes 21.9–19
like a cat's, and she rolled them in fury. 'The king of the gods – indeed all Thirty-Three gods – has been defeated by that *rākṣasa* lord, and you are worthy of becoming his wife! He exults in his heroism, he's a warrior who never turns tail in battle, he's mighty, he's utterly heroic: why refuse to become his wife? Mighty King Rāvaṇa will desert his beloved, much prized wife, the most blessed of us all, and turn to you. Rāvaṇa will abandon the thousand women abounding in his jewel-decked private apartment and turn to you. He who has more

than once warred against deities and defeated *nāgas*, *gandharvas* and *dānavas* in battle, he has drawn near to you. What reason can you have for refusing to become a wife of the opulent lord of the *rākṣasas*, noble Rāvaṇa, you shabby little woman? The sun dare not scorch him nor the wind blow on him: why won't you yield to him, you with your lozenge-shaped eyes? Out of fear of him trees drop showers of blossom, mountains and clouds bestow water at his whim; you with the smooth brow, why will you not make up your mind to accept your role, my beauty, and be wife to the king of the sons of Disorder, to Rāvaṇa, king of kings? It's in your interest, my lady, it's in your interest, my beauty; it's the truth I've told you. Take our advice, you with your sweet smiles, or it'll be the end of you.'

22.1–4 They came right up to Sītā, those hideous *rākṣasīs*; cruel they were, and cruel the hurtful words they spoke: 'Sītā, why won't you consent to live in the all-entrancing private apartment with its costly couches? It's only because you're a human that you think so much of being the wife of a human. Stop dwelling on Rāma; you'll never belong to him. It's being human, lovely innocent, that makes you yearn for that Rāma, that miserable failure, turned out of his kingdom, that human.'

22.5–7 As Sītā heard the *rākṣasīs'* words her lotus-like eyes filled with tears and she replied, 'What you are all telling me is universally condemned, and such offensive conduct finds no support in my mind. He may be poor, he may have been turned out of his kingdom, but my husband must retain my respect.'

22.8–11 Sītā's speech brought forth from the anger-crazed *rākṣasīs* the harsh threats Rāvaṇa had demanded. Concealed in the *śiṃśapā* tree Hanumān the monkey listened in silence as those *rākṣasīs* menaced Sītā, crowding all around her trembling form, furiously licking their fiery, pendulous lips with gusto. In their great frenzy they snatched their battleaxes, crying, 'She does not deserve Rāvaṇa the *rākṣasa* overlord as a husband.'

22.12–14 The abuse from the fearsome *rākṣasīs* drove the fair-faced lady nearer to the *śiṃśapā*, wiping away a tear till, overwhelmed by sorrow, Sītā stood surrounded by *rākṣasīs* beneath the *śiṃśapā*, wasted, her face downcast, her clothes filthy, menaced on all sides by the fearsome *rākṣasīs*.

Then Vinatā spoke up; she was a fearsome-looking *rākṣasī*, with frenzied form, gaping maw and pot belly. 'Sītā, up till now you've given ample proof of your affection for your husband, but excess always leads to disaster, gracious lady. You've carried out your duty as a human. Well done! I'm pleased! Now you must carry out my salutary advice, Maithilī. You must enjoy Rāvaṇa, the lord of all the *rākṣasas*, as your wedded lord. He is valiant and handsome as Indra Vāsava, lord of the gods; he is adroit and generous, and speaks kindly to all. Give up that wretched human Rāma, and give yourself to Rāvaṇa. Anoint your body with divine unguents, Vaidehī. Adorn it with divine ornaments. From this very day you shall be mistress of all the worlds. You'll be like Agni's queen Svāhā, or Indra's Śacī, my lovely. What do you want with Rāma, that doomed wretch, Vaidehī? If you refuse to follow my advice, we will all gobble you up this instant.' 22.15–22

Another one called Vikaṭā raised an angry fist above her sagging breasts, bellowed and said to Sītā, 'Maithilī, you are very ill-natured! We've been kind and gentle enough to put up with a lot of uncongenial talk from you, but you refuse to benefit from our opportune advice. You've been brought to the far side of the ocean, where other people will find it hard to follow; you're in the dread private apartments of Rāvaṇa, Maithilī. You're confined in Rāvaṇa's palace, close guarded by us; not Indra Puraṃdara in person can rescue you. Profit by my good advice, Maithilī. You've shed enough tears. Give up pointless grief and enjoy pleasure and delight. Climb out of this constant depression. Sītā, have fun with the *rākṣasa* king to your heart's content. You shy girl, you know how fleeting is women's youth; you should take your pleasure before it passes, and roam in pleasant parks and mountain groves with the *rākṣasa* king, you with the enticing eyes. You shall have seven thousand women at your beck and call, fair lady. You must enjoy Rāvaṇa, lord of all the *rākṣasas*, as your wedded lord, or else I will tear out your heart and eat it, Maithilī, if you won't do exactly as I've said.' 22.23–32

22.33–5 Then a cruel-looking *rākṣasī* named Caṇḍodarī brandishing a long spear spoke up: 'When I saw this woman Rāvaṇa had brought, with the eyes of a tremulous deer and breasts shuddering in terror, an immense craving welled up in me: I yearned to eat her liver, spleen, lights, heart and veins, chitterlings and brain.'

22.36–7 The *rākṣasī* named Praghasā then suggested, 'Let's strangle this pitiless woman; what are we waiting for? Then we can tell the king, "This human woman is dead," and no doubt he will tell us to eat her.'

22.38–9 A *rākṣasī* called Ajāmukhī replied, 'Then we must all share. I don't like squabbling.'

22.40–41 Then a *rākṣasī* named Śūrpaṇakhā said, 'I certainly agree with what Ajāmukhī has said. Let's send at once for some wine to drive away all our cares. When we've obtained some human meat we can dance the Nikumbhilā.'

22.42 Sītā was the equal of a daughter of the gods, but such threats from the savage *rākṣasīs* broke down her resistance and she wept.

23.1–3 While the uncouth *rākṣasīs* were pouring out their cruel taunts, Janaka's daughter wept, but in the depths of her fear clear-minded Vaidehī countered the *rākṣasīs'* words in a voice choked with sobs. 'It is not right for a human to become the wife of a *rākṣasa*. You can devour me, all of you, but I will not do as you say.'

23.4–10 Sītā was the equal of a daughter of the gods, but in the torment of her grief and with the *rākṣasīs* crowding round her she could find no refuge from Rāvaṇa's threats. Sītā was like a doe cut off from the herd and harassed by wolves; she shuddered intensely and seemed to shrink into herself. She grasped a spreading branch of the blossoming *aśoka* for support[6] as her mournful, broken heart flew to her husband. Floods of tears bathed her ample bosom; her gloomy thoughts could not plumb the depths of her sorrow. She quivered like a plantain in a gale, and toppled over; fear of the *rākṣasīs* drained the colour from her face. Her shudders so agitated Sītā's long, thick plait that it looked like a writhing serpent. Moaning in the torment of her grief, out of her mind with sorrow, Maithilī uttered a tormented, tearful lament.

'Oh, Rāma!' came again and again from the grief-tormented beauty. 'Oh, Lakṣmaṇa! Oh, my mother-in-law Kausalyā! Oh, Sumitrā! It's true what they say; learned people attest it: "Death will not come to a woman or to a man until it is time," if I can remain alive here in my sorrow, tormented by these cruel *rākṣasīs*, even for a moment in the absence of Rāma. What a wretch I am! How small my store of merit! I shall perish as if I'd been cast adrift, as if I were a heavy-laden boat on the open sea battered by the onslaught of the wind. In the power of these *rākṣasīs*, if I can't see my husband I'm bound to subside under my sorrow like a bank eroded by the water. People prosper from the sight of my lotus-petal-eyed protector; his gait is that of a bold lion, but he's courteous and resourceful. Torn away from sagacious Rāma, for me it's every bit as hard to cling to life as it would be if I'd swallowed a bitter poison. What kind of evil did I do in a previous life to bring this savage, grinding grief upon me? In the depths of my great grief I want to put an end to my life; guarded as I am by these *rākṣasīs*, I shall never see Rāma again. If only I weren't a human! If only I weren't a captive! That's what's preventing me deliberately ending my own life.' 23.11–20

At these words the girl's face swam with tears; Janaka's daughter hid her face and began to lament. She grieved like a madwoman or a drunkard, thrashing about on the ground like a colt, as if reason had deserted her. 24.1–2

'The shape-changing *rākṣasa* carried me off by force from the Rāghava's watchful care; I screamed at Rāvaṇa's violence. In the power of these *rākṣasīs* with their savage threats, and brooding as I am in a torment of sorrow, life for me is more than I can bear. Not wealth, not ornaments, not life itself have any purpose for me if I have to live among *rākṣasīs* without Rāma the chariot warrior. Shame on me for being so vile, so sinful as to preserve my life even for a moment when I've been forced apart from him: how wicked I am! How can I have any desire for life or happiness without my beloved, the 24.3–25 sweet-spoken lord too of the whole ocean-girt earth? Let my body be chopped up, let it be devoured even; I abandon it. In any case, I could not long survive the sorrow of being parted from my beloved. I would not touch Rāvaṇa so much as with my left foot;* how much less would I feel desire for that despicable night-walker? He can't understand rejection! He can know nothing of himself or of his race to rely on his savage nature in an attempt to win me over. He can slice me, he can skewer me, he can chop me up or have me roasted over a blazing fire, but I will not wait on Rāvaṇa, so why keep chattering on about it so? The Rāghava is famed for his wisdom, reason and tenderness, but I suspect that this disastrous misfortune of mine has turned his righteousness to ruthlessness. Single-handed he destroyed fourteen thousand *rākṣasas* in Janasthāna, so why hasn't he come to me when I'm held captive by that cowardly *rākṣasa* Rāvaṇa? My husband is certainly capable of killing Rāvaṇa in battle. Rāma killed that bull of a *rākṣasa* Virādha in a fight in Daṇḍaka Forest, so why hasn't he come to me? Granted, it's difficult to attack Laṅkā here in the middle of the sea, but nothing can stand in the way of the Rāghava's arrows. His wife has been carried off by a *rākṣasa*, and he's yearning for her, so what can be the reason why steadfast Rāma hasn't come to me? I suppose Lakṣmaṇa's older brother can't know where I am, for would that glorious man tolerate the offence knowingly? The one who knew what happened and might have told the Rāghava about my capture – the king of the vultures, that is – he was cut down in battle by Rāvaṇa; it was a great deed Jaṭāyus performed when he came forward despite his age and engaged Rāvaṇa in a duel. If the Rāghava did know where I'm eking out my existence, he would immediately clear the world of *rākṣasas* with his arrows, in his anger. He would devastate the city of Laṅkā; he would dry up the great sea; he would destroy the fame and name of that vile Rāvaṇa. Then in house after house the *rākṣasīs* whose lords have been killed will surely have more to weep for than I. Rāma and Lakṣmaṇa will search out Laṅkā and do away with the *rākṣasas*: no enemy that pair sees can survive for another moment. Before long this Laṅkā will look like a cremation ground: its roads will be choked with smoke from the pyres and swarming with hordes of vultures. Before long I shall get what I'm longing for. Your crime calls down calamity on you all.'

The *rākṣasīs* were crazed with anger at Sītā's fierce riposte. While some hurried off to report to Rāvaṇa, other savage-looking *rākṣasīs* crowded round Sītā and repeated their harsh words, words that had one point only, a point that it was pointless to pursue: 'Well then, base-born Sītā, since you're determined to come to a bad end, *rākṣasīs* shall today feast on your flesh to their hearts' content.' 25.1–3

The aged *rākṣasī* Trijaṭā had been asleep; when she saw how Sītā was being menaced by that rabble she spoke up. 'Eat yourselves, you rabble, for you won't feast on Sītā: she's the beloved daughter of Janaka and the daughter-in-law of Daśaratha. I've just had a horrifying, hair-raising dream about the annihilation of the *rākṣasīs* and the ascendancy of her husband.' 25.4–6

The anger-crazed *rākṣasīs* all took fright at Trijaṭā's words and begged Trijaṭā to tell them about the dream she had had that night. When she heard the words falling from these *rākṣasīs'* lips, Trijaṭā told them about her timely dream: 25.7–9

'The Rāghava, mounting a divine aerial carriage made of ivory and harnessed to a thousand steeds . . . Sītā standing on a white sea-girt cliff, reunited with Rāma like its radiance with the sun . . . next I saw the Rāghava mounted on a four-tusked elephant huge as a mountain . . . he was advancing with Lakṣmaṇa . . . then the prince himself, white garlanded, white clad, was riding with Lakṣmaṇa on a chariot drawn by white bulls . . . eight in the yoke . . . with him Lakṣmaṇa his brother and Sītā his wife. Again, now it was Rāvaṇa I could see, fallen to earth from the Puṣpaka chariot, black-clad, shaven-headed, being dragged along by a woman . . . then dispatched to the southern region on an ass-drawn chariot . . . red-garlanded, red-smeared . . . he's been plunged into a mire of mud . . . a red-clad wench, dingy, mire-smeared, has Daśagrīva by the throat, dragging him to the region of Yama . . . a boar is setting out for the southern region with Daśagrīva . . . a dolphin with 25.10–25

Indrajit . . . a camel with Kumbhakarṇa. Next, a din of singing and music, arisen from a carousing crowd of *rākṣasas*, red-garlanded, red-clad . . . this lovely Laṅkā city with its jostling steeds and chariots . . . I saw it toppled into the sea, its towers and gateways smashed . . . all the *rākṣasa* women guzzling sesame oil, cavorting and laughing raucously in a Laṅkā smothered by soot . . . Kumbhakarṇa and the rest, all these bulls of *rākṣasas* had put red garments on and plunged into a lake of cowdung.

25.26–37 'Away with you! Get lost! The Rāghava's rescuing Sītā; all the *rākṣasas* will share in the destruction his immense wrath will wreak. The Rāghava loves and admires the wife who vowed to stay beside him in his life in the forest: he won't tolerate her being threatened or reviled. So that's enough of cruel words from you; we should make peace. I think it would be best for us to appeal to Vaidehī, for such a dream about her in her distress foretells that she will be freed from her great distress and attain the highest bliss. You've threatened her, *rākṣasīs*, but now appeal to her. Why go on talking? The Rāghava bodes dire peril for the *rākṣasas*, but Janaka's daughter Maithilī would be capable of safeguarding us *rākṣasīs* from all peril if we fell at her feet in propitiation. What's more, there's not the slightest sign of anything ominous to be detected anywhere on this broad-eyed lady's body: her suffering has merely drained her of colour. I believe it was because her suffering was unmerited that this lady took her stand in the sky. Vaidehī will achieve her objective, I can see: the destruction of the *rākṣasa* lord and victory for the Rāghava. I can see one of her broad, lotus-petal eyes quivering: that's a portent that she will hear something to bring her great happiness. So, too, one of kind Vaidehī's arms – the left one – is trembling spontaneously, its hairs quivering with anticipation, and her left thigh, matchless, shapely as an elephant's trunk, is throbbing: that points to the Rāghava standing before her, it seems.'

28.1–2 Valiant Hanumān could hear Sītā, Trijaṭā and the *rākṣasīs*' abuse quite clearly. The queen seemed like a goddess in Nandana as he watched, and aroused conflicting thoughts in the *vānara's* mind.

'I've been the one to locate the woman searched for in all directions by many thousands and myriads of monkeys, and I've observed as much as a well-trained spy moving about under cover could about the strength of the enemy – and about the distinctive features of the *rākṣasas*; the city's been spied out, and so has the might of the *rākṣasa* overlord Rāvaṇa. Now I ought to encourage this wife as she yearns to see her incomparable, universally compassionate husband. This woman with a face like the full moon had seen no suffering, but now she can see no end to her suffering: it's for me to comfort her. To leave without comforting this queen when her mind is overwhelmed with grief would be to leave reprehensibly, for this glorious Princess Jānakī would see no hope of rescue and would give up on life after I'd left. The mighty hero with the face like a full moon is also anxious to see Sītā and needs to be reassured. But it's impossible to talk to her in the presence of these night-roamers. How ever am I to manage it? I'm in a dilemma. If I don't reassure her somehow or other before the end of the night, there's no doubt she'll give up her life. And if Rāma asks me what message Sītā's sent him, how shall I answer unless I talk to his slender-waisted wife? If I hurry back from here without a message from Sītā, Kākutstha might even be so angry he would burn me up with his searing glance. In any case, there will be no point in allying my master to Rāma's cause, and bringing his army here. What I'll do is wait here until the *rākṣasīs* give me an opportunity to comfort her gently in her many tribulations; I'm tiny, and anyway I'm a *vānara*. But if I launch into a polished speech like a brāhman, Sītā will think I'm Rāvaṇa and take fright. I must talk in ordinary language that she can understand; there's no other way I can console this blameless lady. Jānakī here has already been terrified by the *rākṣasas*; when she notices my appearance and words she will be even more terrified. That broad-eyed lady is astute; she would assume me to be the shape-changing Rāvaṇa and would scream out in panic, and Sītā's scream would immediately summon a mob of ferocious, weapon-wielding Deathlike *rākṣasīs* with ugly faces who would surround me on all sides and make all possible efforts to kill or 28.3–36 capture me: they would be worried and alarmed to see me scurrying through the twigs, branches and trunks of these magnificent trees. Then the *rākṣasīs* would summon the *rākṣasas* employed by the *rākṣasa* lord in the *rākṣasa* palace, and they would fall on me with spears and arrows and swords and all sorts of weapons in their hands; the onslaught of their attack would be appalling and would put me into a frenzy, but annihilating the whole *rākṣasa* army would leave me unable to get back to the far side of the ocean; I should be captured and her chance of rescue would be lost, and the mission entrusted to me by Rāma and Sugrīva would be wrecked. Jānakī lives concealed and guarded by *rākṣasas* in this trackless land surrounded by the ocean, and with me slaughtered or captured in a battle with the *rākṣasas* I can't see anyone else being able to help Rāma achieve his goal; racking my brains, I can think of no other *vānara* who could leap over the great hundred-*yojana* sea if I am killed. Granted, I'm capable of killing even thousands of *rākṣasas*, but then I wouldn't be able to reach the other side of the ocean. Warfare can be deceptive, and I have to be certain; it's not sensible to take uncalculating risks. That's the big problem about my talking to Sītā: how can I be certain she will hear my words without taking fright?'

28.40–43 Shrewdly Hanumān pondered, then made his decision: 'Tireless Rāma is her own relative and on that relative her thoughts always dwell; singing his praises won't alarm her. I'll string together some well-merited compliments about learned Rāma, finest of the Ikṣvākus. I'll let her hear it all spoken in a sweet voice. I'll put it all together in a way that will win her trust.'

29.1–8 After going over all these conflicting thoughts, the great monkey uttered a sweet speech that Vaidehī could hear: 'There was a king called Daśaratha. He owned chariots, elephants and steeds; he was pious and upright; great was his fame, great his glory; harming none was his constant care; he was generous, compassionate, truly brave, and he was the head of the Ikṣvāku dynasty; endowed with prosperity, he conferred prosperity; he was every inch a king, his glory was widespread, he was a bull of a king, famed to the four corners of the earth; fortunate himself, he bestowed fortune. His beloved eldest son, Rāma by name, has a face like the lord of the stars; he is discerning, he is the most excellent of archers; he watches over his own conduct, he watches over his people's conduct, he watches over the life of the world and over good order, and he triumphs over his enemies. To keep a promise made by his aged father, the hero set out with his wife and brother to roam the forest. News of the slaughter he had wrought in Janasthāna as he was hunting there in the great forest, and that Khara and Dūṣaṇa had been killed, induced the irascible Rāvaṇa to abduct Jānakī.'

So saying, the bull of a *vānara* halted. Jānakī was transported 29.10–11;
with amazement at what she heard, and the woman with the 30.1–2
lovely curled locks timidly raised her hair-framed face to look into the *śiṃśapā* tree. Her mind in a whirl, she peered between the branches and hidden there she spied the courteous, soft-spoken monkey. Beautiful Maithilī glimpsed the excellent ape's modest stance, and thought, 'I must be dreaming.'

With a gesture of the utmost deference, Hanumān, that 31.1–10
splendid Son of the Wind, addressed Sītā in a sweet voice: 'Who are you, blameless lady with eyes as broad as lotus petals, standing clad in worn-out silk, supporting yourself against the branch of a tree? Why are there tears of grief flowing from your eyes like drops scattered from lotus petals? Who are you, radiant lady, which of the gods or anti-gods, *nāgas*, *gandharvas*, *rākṣasas*, *yakṣas* or *kinnaras*? Who are you, beautiful lady, which *rudra*, which *marut*? Shapely lady, which *vasu* are you? To me you look like a goddess. Are you excellent, goodly Rohiṇī, supreme star but snatched away from the Moon and expelled from the heavens? Surely it can't be that you are the virtuous Arundhatī, dark-eyed lady, and that you've angered your husband Vasiṣṭha in a moment of anger or madness? The characteristics I discern in you make me think you must be the chief queen of some sovereign, the daughter of some king. Could it be that you are Sītā, carried off by force from Janasthāna by Rāvaṇa? Answer me, I beg you.'

Vaidehī was delighted to hear his speech with its kind words 31.11–27
about Rāma, and replied to Hanumān still perched in the tree: 'I am indeed Sītā, daughter of the noble Janaka of Videha; I am the wife of the wise Rāma. For twelve years I enjoyed every

human pleasure; all I could wish for was heaped upon me in the Rāghava's palace. Then in the thirteenth year, the king and his advisers undertook to consecrate the pride of the Ikṣvākus for the kingship, but while they were preparing to sprinkle the heir of Raghu, one queen, Kaikeyī, declared to her husband, "Day after day I will not drink, I will eat no food; if Rāma is consecrated it will bring an end to my life. Your excellent majesty, unless you intend to go back on the promise you made when you were pleased with me, have the Rāghava go to the forest." The honourable king remembered that he had offered the queen a boon, and swooned when he heard Kaikeyī's horrible, cruel words. But the venerable king was firm in his pursuit of integrity, and, weeping, asked his glorious eldest son to give up the kingship. That majestic prince valued his father's integrity more highly even than the consecration, and assented with heart as well as voice. Rāma's courageous pursuit of integrity values giving more highly than receiving; he couldn't say an unkind word to save his life! All his costly robes – gloriously he abandoned them! His hope of the kingship – he renounced it! Me he entrusted to his mother, but I set out at once to roam the forest in front of him. Without him I couldn't live happily even in heaven. Right in front went Saumitri, so distinguished, so popular with his friends, his tree-bark garments gracing him in his resolve to accompany his elder brother. Our sole thought, our unshakable resolve, was to keep our lord's command as we three entered the impenetrable, unexplored forest. While that heroic paragon was living in Daṇḍaka Forest, I – his wife! – was carried off by the evil *rākṣasa* Rāvaṇa; as for my life, he's given me another two months' grace, but after that two months I shall live no longer.'

32.1–4 Misery overwhelmed her, but the account of her misery drew further words of comfort from Hanumān the ape chief. 'My lady, I am here at Rāma's command, and as his messenger. Rāma is well, Vaidehī, and he wants to know if you are well. My lady, Rāma Dāśarathi, well versed in Brahmā's missile and in the Vedas – indeed an expert in the Vedas – wants to know if you are well. Illustrious Lakṣmaṇa too, your husband's beloved attendant, greets you respectfully; he is tormented by grief.'

Moonfaced Sītā gasped to see his respectful demeanour and replied sweetly to the *vānara*: 'If you are that master of illusion Rāvaṇa himself and this is an illusion you have created to increase my torment, that's just not right. But if you are a messenger arrived from Rāma, then blessings on you! I beg you, excellent ape – for news of Rāma is so welcome to me – recite to me my darling Rāma's virtues, gentle *vānara*, and you'll captivate my heart like the current does a river bank. Oh what a sweet dream this is! After my long captivity, to see a forest-dweller like this sent by the Rāghava! If only I could see my hero, the Rāghava, with Lakṣmaṇa, even in a dream, I would bear up; yet even my dreaming has been loathsome. But I don't think this can be a dream, for no good can come of seeing a *vānara* in a dream,[7] yet good has come to me. Can it just be because my thoughts are in turmoil? Perhaps it's a fleeting delusion, or perhaps I'm going out of my mind; or maybe it's a mirage. But then it can't be madness, nor yet delusion that looks like madness: I'm aware of the reality of my condition and of this forest-dweller too.' 32.13–23

Considering it thoroughly from all angles, and knowing that *rākṣasas* could take on any form at will, Sītā concluded that he must be the *rākṣasa* overlord; when she had reached that conclusion, Janaka's slender-waisted daughter Sītā made no reply to the *vānara*. Hanumān, Son of the Wind, understood what Sītā was thinking and framed welcome words to raise her spirits: 32.24–6

'In splendour he is like the sun, like the moon he is loved the world over, like divine Vaiśravaṇa he is king over the whole world; valorous as far-famed Viṣṇu, with a voice as sweet and true as Vācaspati, he is as handsome, as well blessed, as majestic as Kandarpa incarnate; he is the world's champion chariot warrior, venting his wrath where required: this is the noble prince, this is he whose sheltering arms safeguard the world. But that one in the form of a deer who lured the Rāghava away from the hermitage, then carried you off in the wilderness – he'll get his reward, you'll see! The one who will soon do battle with Rāvaṇa and kill him with arrows like blazing brands fired in fury, that hero, that's who has sent me to your presence as 32.27–39 his messenger. He is tormented by pain at being parted from you, and he wants to know if you are well. Glorious, mighty Lakṣmaṇa, that growing joy to Sumitrā, sends his respectful greetings too and wants to know if you are well. Rāma's ally, my lady, the *vānara* called Sugrīva, king of the *vānara* lords, also wants to know if you are well. Rāma thinks of you constantly, and so do Sugrīva and Lakṣmaṇa. Fortune has kept you alive, Vaidehī, in the clutches of these *rākṣasīs*. Before long you shall see Rāma, and Lakṣmaṇa the chariot warrior, amid crores of *vānaras* – Sugrīva too with his measureless might. I am Sugrīva's minister, the *vānara* called Hanumān, and I've got into Laṅkā by leaping over the great sea: I've used my mettle to trample on evil Rāvaṇa's head, and I've come to see you. My lady, I'm not what you imagine. Forget that suspicion and believe what I'm telling you.'

38.1–11 When she heard what the noble Son of the Wind said, divinely beautiful Sītā realized it would benefit her to reply. '*Vānara*, I'm delighted to see you! You bring such welcome news, I'm like the earth refreshed by rain on its half-grown grain. To help me fulfil my longing to enfold that tiger of a man in my arms gaunt with grief, most excellent of all the apes, do me this kindness . . . there's something Rāma will recognize . . . "the shaft you shot in your anger that put out one of that crow's eyes . . . the *tilaka* you painted on my cheek with realgar when my *tilaka* got rubbed off – surely you remember that! A hero like you . . . comparable to great Indra and Varuṇa . . . how can you bear Sītā to live a captive among *rākṣasas*? I've kept this heavenly hair-jewel carefully . . . gazing at it in my affliction lets me rejoice as if it were you, my blameless husband . . . I'll send you this majestic pearl. I shan't be able to go on living with this all-consuming grief . . . but for your sake I'll endure the unbearable pain and heart-rending words of these ferocious *rākṣasīs*. For one month I'll cling to life, my enemy-conquering husband; but without you I can't survive beyond a month, my prince. This *rākṣasa* king is fierce and his leering disgusts me; if I heard that you were coming to grief I could not survive for a moment."'

38.20–22 Janaka's daughter, miserable, her eyes brimming with tears, addressed her swift messenger in a voice choking with sobs, and his spirits rose. 'If you please, Hanumān, assure that lion-like pair of brothers, Rāma and Lakṣmaṇa, and Sugrīva, his ministers, and everyone, that I am unharmed. Then see to it that the mighty Rāghava gets me out of this dire, water-bound captivity.'

As the *vānara* made ready to go, she praised him with 39.1–10
expressions of admiration, but on leaving the area he thought, 'Now I've seen the dark-eyed lady there's still one small part of my mission left. The three forms of diplomacy are out of the question, but a fourth tactic remains.[8] If someone finds himself able to accomplish more than he's been commanded to do, without detriment to his main mission, he has an obligation to do so. Even a very limited task can't be accomplished by one tactic alone; to accomplish a mission successfully you have to recognize its complexity. Here is a fine grove belonging to that brute; it could be Nandana, it's so attractive to spirit and senses alike with its mass of different trees and creepers. I will destroy it like wildfire; Rāvaṇa will be incensed when it's wrecked.'

Then the Son of the Wind, furious as the Wind, called up his 39.13–15
dreadful might and set about kicking down the trees with his powerful legs. Heroic Hanumān wrecked the Girls' Grove with its mass of different trees and creepers made merry with ardent birdsong. Dreadful to behold was that grove with its trees smashed, its tanks split open and its hilltops ground to dust.

The clamour of the birds and the sound of splintering trees 40.1–5
bewildered and terrified all Laṅkā's inhabitants. Stampeding animals and birds squealed in alarm and terror, and there appeared signs portending evil to *rākṣasas*. Roused from sleep, the ugly *rākṣasīs* saw the shattered grove and that hero, the great monkey, but when the mighty monkey with the noble character and enormous strength saw them, he assumed a huge form that brought terror to the *rākṣasīs*. The sight of the mountainous *vānara* with his enormously powerful body set the *rākṣasīs* questioning Janaka's daughter:

'Who is he? Whose son? Where's he from? What's he come 40.6–7
here for? Why have you been talking to him? Don't be afraid

to tell us, you broad-eyed lovely. Why was he talking to you, you dark-eyed beauty?'

40.8–10 Virtuous Sītā, lovely in every limb, replied, 'What means do I have of telling one *rākṣasa* from another when you can take on any form you like? You're the ones who should know who he is or what he'll do: it takes a snake to see a snake's feet,[9] that's certain. I'm frightened of him as well and I don't know him: whoever is he? I just assume he's some shape-changing *rākṣasa* that's arrived here.'

40.11–12 Vaidehī's words sent the *rākṣasīs* scurrying off, some to report to Rāvaṇa while others remained at their post. Those ugly *rākṣasīs* who found Rāvaṇa began to tell him about the terrible misshapen *vānara*.

40.13–21 'Your majesty, a monkey of terrible form has been talking to Sītā in the middle of the *aśoka* grove; he's standing there with dauntless spirit. We've asked deer-eyed Sītā Jānakī repeatedly who the ape is but she won't tell us. He may be Indra Vāsava's envoy, or an envoy of Vaiśravaṇa, he may even have been sent by Rāma yearning to discover Sītā, but that amazing creature has obliterated your girls' enchanting grove, with its teeming flocks of different birds. There's no area that he's not destroyed; only where Sītā Jānakī is has he not destroyed, but we can't tell whether that's from fatigue or in order to protect Jānakī – but then, how would he feel fatigue? He must have been protecting her: he's saved the flourishing *śiṃśapā* tree that Sītā was standing under, with its rich canopy of beautiful twigs and leaves. It's for you to ordain a savage punishment for this savage monster for talking to Sītā and destroying this grove. Who could address Sītā – your intended – without forfeiting his life, Lord of *rākṣasa*-hordes?'

40.22–35 The *rākṣasīs*' words acted on Rāvaṇa Lord of the *rākṣasas* like oblations offered into a fire: he blazed up, eyes rolling with rage. The potentate ordered some *rākṣasas*, as powerful as himself though just retainers, to go and arrest Hanumān. Eighty thousand vigorous retainers sped off from the palace, armed with cudgels; a fearsome sight with their paunches and fangs, stalwart and belligerent, all were avid to capture Hanumān. The monkey was perched on a gateway when they reached him; like moths rushing towards a flame they fell upon him. Splendid, majestic, mountainous Hanumān pounded the ground with his tail, roaring lustily till the tumultuous din struck them with terror and dread. They gazed at Hanumān as he towered over them like a cloud at twilight, but their master's command stiffened their nerve and the *rākṣasas* fell upon the monkey from all sides with fearsome, glittering weapons. With the warriors completely surrounding him, he reached for the fearsome iron beam barring the gate, wrenched it free with all his might and belaboured the night-roamers. Like Vinatā's son gripping a wriggling snake, the heroic Son of the Wind roamed about with it in the sky. That hero, that true Son of the Wind, struck down the *rākṣasa* retainers; then the hero resumed his position on the gateway, thirsting for a fight, while some *rākṣasas* who had escaped the terrible scene reported to Rāvaṇa that all the retainers had been killed.

Blazing forth with splendour till he looked like mount Pāriyātra, inviolable Hanumān then violated the platform around the lofty sacred tree. Hanumān Son of the Wind grew to enormous stature and slapped his arms in defiance till the sound filled Laṅkā, tumbling the birds out of the sky as the tumultuous slapping assaulted their ears. Then he bellowed out: 41.3–5

'Victory to Rāma the all-powerful, and to Lakṣmaṇa the mighty! The Rāghava will secure victory for King Sugrīva! I am the servant of Kosala's lord, tireless Rāma! I am Hanumān Son of the Wind, slayer of hostile hordes! A thousand Rāvaṇas could not counter me in battle as I hurled rocks and trees by the thousand. I've devastated the city of Laṅkā, I've paid my respects to Maithilī, and now I've achieved my objective I shall leave before any of the *rākṣasas* can blink an eye.' 41.6–9

These words he hurled at those stationed around the sacred tree from his stance on its tip. Then the bull of an ape roared a fearsome bellow to terrify the *rākṣasas*; high in the sky the majestic monkey called out: 41.10, 15

'Noble, powerful *vānara* chiefs like me have set out by the thousand in obedience to Sugrīva's instructions. Sugrīva will arrive with hundreds, and with hundreds of thousands, with 41.16–18 crores and with myriads to pulverize you all. Incurring the hostility of the noble Lord of the Ikṣvākus has brought annihilation on you, on the city of Laṅkā and on Rāvaṇa.'

42.1–18 On the orders of the lord of the *rākṣasas*, Jambumālin, powerful son of Prahasta, set out, bow in hand. With his prominent fangs and the red garlands and garments he was wearing, with his wreaths and flashing earrings, his huge size, his rolling eyes and his fury, he was indomitable in battle. His huge bow was the like of Śakra's bow, with flashing arrows and a noise like the crash of a thunderbolt as he flexed it with vigour, until suddenly every corner of the sky in all directions resounded with the din of the flexing of that bow, but when the impetuous Hanumān saw him coming on his ass-drawn chariot he roared eagerly. As the great monkey Hanumān was standing on the pinnacle of the gateway, mighty Jambumālin struck him with sharpened arrows: the monkey chief's face he wounded with a half-moon tip, his head with an eared-tip, and with ten bolts his arms. Struck by the arrow, his face glowed like a full-blown autumn lotus touched by a ray of sunlight. The great monkey was annoyed at being hit by the *rākṣasa's* arrows. Close by he saw a gigantic boulder, wrenched it up on the instant and hurled it with all his might – that mighty monkey – but the furious *rākṣasa* warded it off with ten arrows. Hanumān was emboldened by rage at seeing that tactic fail; he uprooted a spreading *sāl* tree, and brandished it heroically. When mighty Jambumālin saw the mighty monkey brandishing the *sāl* tree, he launched arrows in abundance, piercing the *sāl* with four and the *vānara* with five in the arm, one on the chest and ten on the breastbone; his body was filled with arrows and rage came over him. Then he picked up that same beam and whirled it violently around. Possessed by violent might, violently he whirled the beam and brought it down on Jambumālin's huge chest. Then his head was no more, nor his arms nor his knees nor his bow, chariot or horses; even his arrows could be seen no more. The force of the blow laid Jambumālin the chariot warrior dead on the earth, limbs and ornaments ground to dust. The news that Jambumālin as well as the mighty retainers had been killed angered Rāvaṇa; his eyes reddened with rage.

Rāvaṇa showed no emotion at the news that the noble 44.1–3
vānara had killed his counsellor's son, but hit on a further plan. Daśagrīva issued instructions to five generals, Virūpākṣa and Yūpākṣa, Durdhara the *rākṣasa*, Praghasa and Bhāsakarṇa. These warriors were experienced leaders, swift as the wind in battle, and intent on capturing Hanumān.

'Generals, advance! Each of you take a large supporting 44.4–14
force with steeds, chariots and elephants. This monkey has got to be punished. It is imperative you proceed with caution when you come upon this forest-dweller and employ tactics appropriate to the terrain and the hour. It's my belief he's no mere monkey, to judge by his exploits. He's some great being with a large supporting force, for sure; alternatively he's been created by Indra, by the power of his asceticism, specifically with us in view, because you and I together have roundly defeated the gods, anti-gods and great sages, and the *nāgas*, *yakṣas* and *gandharvas*. It's only to be expected that they'll ordain some calamity for us. This is it, there's no doubt about that. You'll have to employ force to capture him. Don't despise the mighty savage for being an ape, my lords. I've seen apes who are nimble and extremely brave: there's Vālin and Sugrīva, there's Jāmbavān – he's very strong – there's General Nīla and the rest, especially Dvivida, but not even they have such a fearsome gait, such splendid might, such ingenuity, such strong resolution, such ability to change shape. You must recognize him as some great being assuming the form of a monkey: you'll have to exert a great effort, but make sure you secure him. Granted, not the three worlds – Indra, gods, anti-gods and humans included – are sufficient to withstand your lordships in battle; nevertheless, a shrewd tactician who wants to win a battle should take every care to safeguard himself, for success in warfare can never be guaranteed.'

On receiving these instructions from their master they all 44.15–19
jumped to it, quick and powerful as a blazing fire. The warriors marshalled an ample force of chariots, rutting elephants and

swift steeds, with every kind of sharp weapon and all necessary troops, then spied the great fiery monkey, wreathed in the brilliance of his own splendour like the rays of the rising sun. He was standing on the gateway. Great was his energy, great his character, great his might, great his ingenuity, great his determination, great his stature, great his strength; but when they saw him, they took up positions all around him and all fell upon him from all sides with every kind of terrible weapon.

44.20–26 Like lotus petals falling on his head were the golden tips of the five gleaming sharp iron arrows that Durdhara loosed at him. Then, warlike and mighty, Durdhara advanced on his chariot, bow at the ready, and showered him with hundreds and hundreds of arrows. As he rained down arrows from the sky the monkey baulked him like the wind dispatching a rain cloud at the end of the monsoon. Under Durdhara's harassment the Wind's Son then increased his roaring and raised his battle-frenzy. Suddenly the ape leapt up high and crashed down hard on Durdhara's chariot like a lightning-strike on a mountain, slaughtering its eight horses, wrecking the chariot-pole and axle, and hurling Durdhara lifeless to the ground.

44.27–30 The sight of him stretched out on the ground fired Virūpākṣa and Yūpākṣa with frenzy and the indomitable pair of champions sprang into the attack, springing up abruptly to the mighty monkey's station in the clear sky and each striking him on the chest with his hammer. That mighty creature repulsed the frenzied pair's onslaught, then, gallant as Garuḍa, the *vānara* Son of the Wind leapt back to earth, ran to a *sāl* tree, tore it up by the roots and killed both those *rākṣasa* warriors.

44.31–5 When he realized that the bold *vānara* had killed those three, energetic Praghasa attacked the ape with vigour, and belligerent Bhāsakarṇa angrily snatched up a pike; shoulder to shoulder the pair confronted the glorious tiger of a monkey and harried the monkey champion, Praghasa with a sharp-pointed javelin and Bhāsakarṇa the *rākṣasa* with the pike. They wounded his limbs till his fur ran with blood, enflaming the *vānara* till he blazed like the rising sun. Heroic Hanumān, that elephant of a monkey, tore off a mountain-peak complete with its deer, beasts of prey and trees, and slaughtered both *rākṣasas*.

With the five generals eliminated, the *vānara* annihilated the remainder of the army. Horse after horse, elephant after elephant, warrior after warrior, chariot after chariot the monkey destroyed, like Thousand-eyed Indra did the anti-gods. The roads were jammed with the corpses of elephants and chargers and with broken-axled chariots, and the earth was strewn with slain *rākṣasas* on all sides. 44.36–8

[*Rāvaṇa next sends his son Indrajit to attack. Indrajit succeeds in capturing Hanumān by supernatural means and takes him before Rāvaṇa.*]

Yellow-eyed, he stood before mighty Rāvaṇa; he who makes the world roar looked at him and flew into a great rage. The king's eyes were copper-coloured with rage as he addressed his excellent counsellor Prahasta with ominous, weighty words that went straight to the point: 'Interrogate this evil creature about his origin, his business and what he means by destroying the grove and threatening the *rākṣasīs*.' 48.1–3

When he heard Rāvaṇa's instructions, Prahasta made a speech. 'Be reassured, honoured sir; monkey, you have no need to feel alarm. Even if it be Indra who has sent you to Rāvaṇa's abode, you can declare the truth. Fear not, *vānara*; you will be released. Whether you be sent in this goodly guise to this our city by Vaiśravaṇa, Yama or Varuṇa, or even as an envoy from victory-wishful Viṣṇu – for your *vānara* appearance is belied by your preter-*vānara* powers – *vānara*, give an immediate accurate account and you will be released (albeit that utterance of a falsehood will forfeit your life), in particular an account of your purpose in penetrating Rāvaṇa's abode.' 48.4–9

In reply the excellent ape told the *rākṣasa* commander-in-chief: 'I do not come from Śakra, Yama or Varuṇa; I have made no alliance with wealth-bestowing Vaiśravaṇa, and I have not been dispatched by Viṣṇu. I come here as a *vānara*; that is my true race. Admittance to the *rākṣasa* lord's presence is difficult to obtain, so I destroyed the grove to secure an audience with the *rākṣasa* king. Then these mighty *rākṣasas* arrived spoiling for a fight and in sheer self-defence I had to engage them in combat. Not even gods or anti-gods can bind me with their missiles or fetters; this is a boon I was granted 48.10–1[illegible] by the Grand Father. In my wish to see the king I submitted to the force of a missile; the missile could not hold me but I submit to the *rākṣasas'* force. Let it be known that I am the envoy of the Rāghava of measureless might, and let my lord listen to my salutary message.'

49.1–34 The ten-faced king's spirit was roused, but with spirit unruffled the excellent ape fixed him with his gaze and made a speech of great significance. 'Lord of the *rākṣasas*, I am here at your court by order of Sugrīva. The Lord of Apes sends you fraternal greetings. Hear the advice of your brother monarch, the noble Sugrīva; his words are rooted in right and in expedience, apt both here and in the hereafter. There was a king named Daśaratha, rich in chariots, elephants and steeds. To the world he was like the father of a family, in radiance he was equal to the Lord of the gods. Pleasure flowed from his regal, powerful eldest son, but at his father's command he left to enter Daṇḍaka Forest; the path of righteousness was his refuge, in company with his brother Lakṣmaṇa and his wife Sītā too. Rāma is his name, and great is his glory. Sītā his wife, daughter of noble Janaka, king of Videha, was devoted to her husband. She disappeared in the forest. The prince and his younger brother hunted for the queen until they reached Ṛśyamūka and met Sugrīva, who promised him he would organize a search for Sītā. In return Rāma promised Sugrīva kingship over the apes; the prince killed Vālin in battle and established Sugrīva in the kingdom as Lord of the hosts of apes and bears. True to his promise, Sugrīva threw himself into the hunt for Sītā, and the Lord of Apes dispatched apes to every region. Hundreds, thousands, millions of apes are hunting for her in all directions, on earth and in heaven: some are a match for Vinatā's son, others are like the Wind; powerful and swift, those heroic apes can move around without hindrance. For my part, I am Hanumān, true Son of the Wind. For Sītā's sake I even hastened to leap over the hundred-*yojana* sea and have come here in the hope of finding her. You, my lord, understand both what is right and what is expedient; you have reaped great benefits from asceticism. It is not for you to hold captive someone else's wife: you are too wise. Intelligent people like your lordship do not persist in deeds that run counter to right and are fundamentally prejudicial and injurious. Who, even among the gods and anti-gods, can withstand arrows fired by Lakṣmaṇa consequent upon the wrath of Rāma? Your majesty, not anywhere in the three worlds can anyone be found who could prosper after injuring the Rāghava. Ponder this advice, beneficial in all three eras[10] and bound up with expedience as well as morality: have Jānakī restored to the Lord of Men. I have seen that the queen is here: I have accomplished the almost impossible. It is for the Rāghava to determine what happens next. I have seen that Sītā is engulfed in grief; you do not understand that in your clutches she is like a five-tongued serpent,[11] impossible even for immortals and anti-gods to deal with, any more than the strongest constitution can stomach food laced with poison. It is not proper for you to throw away the store of merit you gained by your distressing asceticism: your whole life is at stake! My lord, you are relying on the invulnerability against gods and anti-gods resulting from your asceticism, and with good reason. But Sugrīva is neither a god nor an anti-god; nor is he a human, a *rākṣasa*, *gandharva*, *yakṣa* or serpent. The Rāghava, your majesty, is human, and Sugrīva is Lord of the Apes, so how, your majesty, will you preserve your life? The fruits of immorality are incompatible with the acquisition of merit. We reap what we sow; virtue triumphs over vice. My lord, it is clear that up till now you have reaped the reward of your righteousness; just so, you will swiftly reap the reward of this sin. The slaughter in Janasthāna has already been brought to your attention; now that the slaughter of Vālin and the alliance of Rāma with Sugrīva have also been brought to your attention, you should pay attention to your own welfare. It is true that I can destroy Laṅkā on my own – steeds, chariots and elephants – but the decision belongs elsewhere, for with the hosts of apes and bears to witness, Rāma has vowed that he will exterminate the enemies who have molested Sītā. Not even Indra himself would prosper after injuring Rāma: how much less someone like you! In that Sītā whom you now regard as your captive you should see Time's Night of Destruction for all Laṅkā. The noose of Time in the shape of Sītā is around your neck. Free yourself! Consider your own interest!'

50.1–4 Rāvaṇa was beside himself with anger when he heard the noble *vānara's* words, and ordered his execution. Vibhīṣaṇa did not concur with evil Rāvaṇa's order to execute one who had declared himself an envoy; he adhered to the rules of proper conduct, and when he learned that the angry *rākṣasa* overlord had embarked upon that course, he pondered what he ought to do and came to a decision. Deferentially he sought to placate his belligerent elder brother, eloquently addressing him with words conducive to his good.

50.5–13 'Your majesty, doing away with this monkey would breach convention; custom and practice the world over would condemn it as unworthy of a hero like you. Nor can I see any advantage in killing this monkey. It is on those who sent this monkey that your retribution should fall. Good or bad, this person is but the emissary of others. An envoy following his master's orders in connection with his master's business is inviolate. Furthermore, your majesty, if you kill him, I can't see any other creature here who could go flying back to the other side of the ocean. You can conquer hostile forts; you don't need to bother killing him. You should direct your energies towards Indra and the gods, my lord.'

51.1–4 Hearing his speech with its apt and timely advice, mighty Daśagrīva replied to his brother, 'You've spoken the truth, my lord. The killing of an envoy incurs denunciation. I must find some other form of punishment short of death. Now, the most desirable ornament of a monkey is his tail . . . I'll have his set alight at once. When it's burning, I'll have him released, so his family and friends, relations and comrades, can all gaze on his miserable state, his body maimed and disfigured.'

51.5 The *rākṣasa* lord issued an order: '*Rākṣasas* are to parade him through all the city thoroughfares with his tail ablaze.'

51.6–9 Obedient to his instructions the rage-envenomed *rākṣasas* bound the tail with cotton rags. While his tail was being bound, the great monkey swelled up like a fire when it spreads to dry kindling in a forest. It was soaked with sesame oil and set alight, but he felled those *rākṣasas* with his blazing tail, so consumed was he with fury and indignation; his face glowed like the rising sun.

The savage *rākṣasas* crowded round and bound him more 51.10–14
tightly, but the excellent heroic ape made a resolution befitting the occasion. 'The *rākṣasas* have no power over me even when I'm bound, that's true. I could snap my bonds, leap up again and kill them, but I need to see Laṅkā by daylight. I couldn't make out the layout of the citadel clearly by night. Let the *rākṣasas* heap more bonds on me and set my tail alight to their hearts' content; it won't bother me.'

The *rākṣasas* seized him and set off in delight, but that great 51.15–18
monkey, that sublime bull of a monkey, remained impassive. The savage *rākṣasas* paraded him through the city, making it resound with the din of conches, drums and their own hullabaloo, while the monkey surveyed its enclosed courtyards and well-planned squares, its highways crammed with houses, and its crossroads.

When the tip of Hanumān's tail was blazing, the ugly-eyed 51.20–21
rākṣasīs told the queen the dreadful news. 'Sītā, that monkey with the copper-coloured face who was talking to you is being paraded about with his tail ablaze.'

Those cruel words affected Sītā as much as her own abduc- 51.22–3
tion. Vaidehī burned with anguish and turned to the sacrificial flame, anxious for the great monkey's welfare; devoutly the broad-eyed lady approached the sacrificial flame:

'If I am obedient to my husband, if I have performed aus- 51.24–8
terities, if I am my husband's one true wife, become cool for Hanumān. If my wise lord retains any tenderness towards me, or if any shred of my auspiciousness remains, become cool for Hanumān. If that righteous man recognizes my virtue and my longing to be with him, become cool for Hanumān.'[12] Then the steady fire flared up, its sharp-tipped flames pointing to the right as if to assure the fawn-eyed lady that it would be gentle towards the monkey.

With his tail alight, the *vānara* wondered, 'Why is this 51.29–30 blazing fire not burning me all over? It's obviously burning fiercely but yet it's causing me no pain. It's as if winter had arrived and settled on the tip of my tail.'

51.35–8 Then the glorious Son of the Wind scattered the crowd of *rākṣasas* and bounded on to the city gate, lofty as a mountain-peak. With aplomb he threw off the mountainous size he had assumed and reverted in an instant to being tiny enough to escape from his bonds; once he had broken free, the majestic monkey went back to looking like a mountain. Surveying the scene, he noticed the iron-bound beam barring the gate, snatched it up and again battered all the guards, that mighty Son of the Wind.

52.1–5 Pleased with his work, the monkey looked round at Laṅkā with mounting determination and wondered what more he should do. 'Now then, what is there left for me to do here that could produce more agony for the *rākṣasas*? So far I've laid waste the grove, killed some leading *rākṣasas* and wiped out a division of the army; it just remains to destroy the citadel. The citadel destroyed would be worth the effort it took, and a little exertion would bring a fitting reward for my labours. There's a fire blazing on my tail; it's only right I should satisfy it with these lovely houses.'

52.6–13 The great monkey Hanumān with his blazing tail was like a cloud flashing lightning as he roamed the roofs of Laṅkā, kindling a conflagration the like of the flaming Doomsday fire. The intense vigour of the mighty fire was fanned by the wind. Like the Doomsday fire it blazed ever more fiercely as the wind drove the burning flames into the houses. Down they go, those great gem-studded palaces, pearly and jewel-built, with their golden lattices! The palaces collapsed to the ground in ruins, like the residences of *siddhas* falling from heaven when their merit expires. He saw a stream of different ores mingled with diamonds, coral, beryl, pearls and silver flowing from a palace, but Hanumān was no more sated by his slaughter of *rākṣasa* lords than fire is by sticks and straw.

52.17; Once the ape champion had set the whole of Laṅkā alight,
53.1 the great monkey doused the fire in his tail in the sea, then gazed at the blazing ruins of Laṅkā city with its hordes

of terrified *rākṣasas*. A thought then struck Hanumān the *vānara*.

'I've undermined the whole purpose of my mission! Burning down Laṅkā has not protected Sītā. Surely my mission was all but accomplished, but I was carried away by anger and I've completely wrecked it. Jānakī must have perished, for it looks as if no part of Laṅkā has escaped burning: the whole city has been reduced to ashes. If I've wrecked my mission by my own stupidity, I'm ready to forfeit my life here and now. Shall I jump into the fire? Or perhaps into the Mare's Head? Or should I present my body to the sea-creatures? How could I appear before the Lord of Apes alive – or those two tigers of men – when I've wrecked the whole mission? My reprehensible rage has certainly demonstrated what all three worlds know: the monkey nature is fickle. Shame on my headstrong, unbridled, irresponsible nature that misled me into not safeguarding Sītā even when I was master of the situation! If Sītā has perished, those brothers will both perish, and when they perish Sugrīva and his family will perish too. Bharata is upright and devoted to his brother; when he hears the news, how will he be able to survive, or Śatrughna either? With the annihilation of that most righteous Ikṣvāku dynasty all their subjects will no doubt be harrowed by a torment of grief. By giving way to this reprehensible rage, I've stripped myself of prosperity and squandered all I've gained from virtue and prudence! It's clear I've destroyed the world!' 53.5–16

While he was musing in this way, well-recognized omens appeared before his eyes and he had second thoughts. 'On the other hand, that paragon of grace and beauty is safeguarded by her own radiance! She won't have perished: fire can't harm fire. The purifying power shouldn't touch that upright man's wife! His radiance is unbounded, and her own behaviour keeps her safe. It was certainly Rāma's power and Vaidehī's good deeds that kept the fire from burning me at the height of the blaze. She's Rāma's darling, and a goddess to Bharata and his other two brothers: how could she perish? Everywhere fire is the immutable master; its function is to burn. If it can't burn my tail, how could it burn that noble lady? Her asceticism, her 53.17–2 integrity, her faithfulness to her one husband are such that she could even burn up fire; fire will not burn her.'

53.24–6 As Hanumān was reflecting on the queen's many virtues, he heard words uttered by noble *cāraṇas*: 'Oh who could withstand what Hanumān has done, loosing ferocious fire throughout the *rākṣasa* realm! This city Laṅkā has been burnt, watch-towers, ramparts, gateways and all, but Jānakī has not been burnt. This is a marvel! We're truly amazed!'

53.27 Hanumān now saw the meaning of the omens; the force of his reasoning and the sages' words relieved him.

5.18–19; The energetic monkey landed, huge as a mountain, on mount
59.2–6 Mahendra's tree-thronged peak, to the delight of all the bulls of *vānaras* who rushed up and crowded around noble Hanumān. With that Son of the Wind at their head, all the bulls of monkeys left the summit of Mahendra and bounded happily along. They were like rutting elephants, huge as Meru and Mandara, seeming to blot out the sky with their enormous, powerful bodies and to uplift with their gaze Hanumān, praised by all for his presence of mind, might and speed. Now they knew that the Rāghava's goal and their master's highest renown were assured, they felt they had achieved their objective and were elated by the success of their mission. All the wise creatures were anxious to tell the good news, all were eager for battle, all were determined to lend Rāma their assistance.

9.7–11; The forest-dwellers bounded along – bounded up into the
60.1 sky – then came to a grove filled with trees and creepers, the equal of Nandana, known as the Honey Orchard. This enticing spot was Sugrīva's private preserve, and no one was allowed to damage it; it was in the constant care of Dadhimukha, the noble monkey chief Sugrīva's maternal uncle. When they reached the extensive orchard, so dear to the *vānara* lord's heart, the *vānaras* grew highly excited, and in their delight at seeing the great Honey Orchard the honey-golden *vānaras* begged the prince for mead. That champion ape, that bull of a *vānara* Hanumān, told them, 'Enjoy the mead, *vānaras*, with a clear conscience.'

60.2–3 When he heard Hanumān's command, the ape leader

Aṅgada reacted indulgently, 'The apes may drink the mead. Now that he has accomplished his mission I should be obliged to grant a request from Hanumān even if it were wrong. How much more in a case like this!'

The delighted *vānaras* applauded and praised Aṅgada as 60.4–12
they heard the words falling from his lips. Praising that bull of a *vānara* Aṅgada, all the *vānaras* rushed like a river in full spate to the Honey Orchard. They overcame the wardens with violence made the more savage by the leave granted them when they saw it and by the news about Maithilī, and entered the Honey Orchard, where they bounded about in a mob, raining hundreds of blows on the forest-wardens stationed at the Honey Orchard. They picked up vats of mead in their arms and joined in smashing them while some consumed the contents. When the honey-golden ones had drunk their fill, some threw the mead around, drunkenly showering each other with the dregs of mead, while others stood holding on to branches, or, dead drunk, collapsed among the tree roots, scattering the leaves. Some bounded about gleefully, intoxicated out of their minds with mead, throwing punches at each other, while others staggered around. Some poured out abuse, others grew happily maudlin; other apes passed out on the ground, drunk on the mead.

Dadhimukha's servants, whose job was to guard the mead, 60.13–1
scattered in all directions, victims of the wild *vānaras* dragging them about by their knees and mooning at them. They fled in panic to Dadhimukha and told him, 'The Honey Orchard has been vandalized with Hanumān's permission; they've dragged us about by our knees and mooned at us!'

Dadhimukha the *vānara* forest-warden was angry to hear of 60.16,
the damage to the Honey Orchard but calmed the apes. 'Never 28–32
mind them! Let's go to where our stout-necked master, Sugrīva the *vānara*, is waiting with Rāma. We'll report Aṅgada's whole offence to the king. When he hears our report he'll be indignant and have those *vānaras* executed, for noble Sugrīva has treasured his divine, ancestral Honey Orchard, where even the gods are prohibited. Sugrīva will order the execution of all these *vānaras* and their comrades; their thirst for mead has put

an end to their lives. These criminals deserve death for infringing the king's commands; his displeasure and resultant rage will bear the fruit we want.'

60.33–7 When mighty Dadhimukha had said this to the forest-wardens he leapt up and set off at once surrounded by the forest-wardens. In the twinkling of an eye the forest-dweller reached the wise *vānara* Sugrīva, Son of the Sun. Seeing Rāma and Lakṣmaṇa as well as Sugrīva, he leapt down from the sky and came to rest on a level patch of ground. After alighting with his squad of wardens, the Head Warden, that heroic ape Dadhimukha, with a sorrowful countenance saluted with great humility and prostrated himself at Sugrīva's auspicious feet.

61.1–2 The bull of a *vānara* was perturbed to see the *vānara* prostrating himself, and said, 'Stand up, stand up! Why have you fallen at my feet? Have no fear, my hero, but tell me the truth.'

61.3–10 Reassured by noble Sugrīva, Dadhimukha rose and gave a well-considered report. 'The orchard hitherto prohibited by Ṛkṣarajas, by yourself, your Majesty, and by Vālin too, has been ransacked by *vānaras*. They were challenged and resisted by these forest-wardens, of course, but paid no heed. They are feasting and drinking the mead, some throwing the dregs about while others are guzzling. When challenged they all just scowled, and those raging bulls of *vānaras* affronted those who were barring their way to the orchard even more by assaulting them. The superior numbers of those warlike *vānaras* with their rage-reddened eyes utterly overwhelmed my tawny bulls of *vānaras*: some they punched, others they kneed; they dragged them about as they liked, they mooned at them. They've assaulted these heroes with you, their lord, standing idly by: indeed they're vandalizing the whole Honey Orchard to their hearts' content.'

1.11–12 Foe-conquering Lakṣmaṇa shrewdly asked the bull of a *vānara* Sugrīva what the complaint was about. 'Your majesty, why has this *vānara* forest-warden come here? What information has he brought? Why did he make such a sorrowful report?'

1.13–23 At noble Lakṣmaṇa's questions, Sugrīva made Lakṣmaṇa this eloquent reply. 'My lord Lakṣmaṇa, the monkey hero

Dadhimukha has reported that *vānara* heroes headed by Aṅgada are drinking my mead. They would not be doing such a thing if they had failed in their mission. Taking over the orchard means that the *vānaras* have accomplished their task. It's clear that they've discovered the queen, and it can only be Hanumān who's done it! No one else could bring success to this mission but Hanumān! In Hanumān, that bull of an ape, astuteness, determination, courage and learning combine to ensure the success of a mission. With Jāmbavān to guide, Aṅgada to command and Hanumān to execute, the mission could have no other outcome. It must be those heroic bulls of apes headed by Aṅgada returning from searching the southern region who are vandalizing the Honey Orchard; the *vānaras* have got into that Honey Orchard on their way back and made free of it, causing havoc throughout the grove, driving the wardens away and kneeing them. That's the welcome news brought by this notably valiant ape Dadhimukha. Sītā is found, mighty Saumitri! It's obvious! That's why all the *vānaras* are drinking mead on their way back. The famous forest-dwellers certainly wouldn't be wrecking that divine, god-given orchard, you bull of a man, if they'd failed to find Vaidehī.'

Righteous Lakṣmaṇa and the Rāghava were thrilled to hear 61.24–6
the welcome tidings falling from Sugrīva's lips. Rāma and illustrious Lakṣmaṇa were absolutely thrilled by Dadhimukha's account, and Sugrīva too was thrilled. Then Sugrīva replied to the forest-warden. 'I am pleased, dear uncle,' he said, 'for them to enjoy the orchard now they have accomplished their mission. Success demands and receives indulgence.'

At Sugrīva's words the monkey Dadhimukha was delighted. 62.1–5
He saluted the Rāghava, then Lakṣmaṇa and Sugrīva, with reverence. After bowing to Sugrīva and the two mighty Rāghavas, he leapt up into the sky with his escort of *vānara* warriors and hurried back the way he had come, landed back on earth and went into the orchard. As he entered the Honey Orchard he saw the ape chiefs, no longer pissed but all insolently pissing mead. The hero approached them with a gesture of great deference and joyfully addressed Aṅgada with conciliatory words:

62.6–11 'Dear nephew, don't be vexed that these wardens barred your way; it was through ignorance that they took offence and refused your Honours admittance. As Young King you are the mighty owner of this orchard. Their earlier error was an act of folly that your Honour should overlook. I went to your uncle, blameless prince, and reported the arrival here of all these forest-roamers; he was delighted to hear that you and these ape chiefs had arrived, and took no offence on hearing of the damage to the orchard. Your uncle King Sugrīva, lord of the *vānaras*, told me with delight to send you all to him at once.'

62.12–16 When he heard Dadhimukha's conciliatory speech, Aṅgada the champion ape replied appropriately. 'Ape chiefs, victorious warriors, I imagine Rāma will have heard the news; we shouldn't be dallying here with our mission accomplished. Now we've drunk our fill of mead and we've rested, forest-roamers, it only remains for us to return to Sugrīva, my superior. I will implement your joint recommendation, ape chiefs. I defer to you, my lords. Young King I may be, but it is not for me to order you about; it would ill become me to treat you with disrespect, you who have accomplished your mission.'

62.17–21 Hearing Aṅgada speaking as he always did, the forest-dwellers responded with joy in their hearts. 'Who but you, your majesty, you bull of a *vānara*, would talk like that? All who wield power are intoxicated by it and think only of themselves. Your words are just typical of you, but of no one else. Your modesty proclaims a blessed and prosperous future for you. We are indeed all ready to go at a moment's notice to Sugrīva, that ever-constant lord of ape heroes. Without your leave we apes can't put one foot in front of another to go anywhere, and that's the truth we're telling you.'

62.22–4 Even as they spoke Aṅgada replied with the words 'Agreed! Let's go!' and leapt up off the ground, his leap followed by all the ape chiefs leaping up too until they blotted out the sky like flames flung up from a sacrifice. After their sudden skyward bound the tempestuous leapers roared, their great roar sounding like storm-driven clouds.

62.25–30 While they were waiting for Aṅgada to arrive, Sugrīva lord of the *vānaras* spoke to lotus-eyed Rāma, who was still tormented by grief. 'Take heart, I beg you! They've found the queen! There's no doubt about it, otherwise they wouldn't possibly come back with our time limit overstayed. The Young King, the monkey commander mighty Aṅgada, would not enter my presence with his mission bungled. Even if they did venture to return with their mission unaccomplished, his face would be downcast and his spirit overwhelmed by confusion: that monkey lord would not damage my ancestral Honey Orchard, the preserve of my forefathers, unless he had something to celebrate. Kausalyā is blessed in her child, Rāma: your vows will be rewarded, so take heart! It's clear that they've discovered the queen, and it can only be Hanumān who's done it!'

Then, close by in the sky he heard a joyous clamour of 62.34–40
forest-dwellers approaching Kiṣkindhā, glorying in Hanumān's achievement and bellowing as if to announce their success. When he heard the monkeys' din, the monkey chief uncurled his tail and stretched it out with delight. Eager to see Rāma, the apes arrived and fell in behind Aṅgada and the *vānara* Hanumān. Led by Aṅgada, those delighted and joyful heroes landed close to the ape king and the Rāghava. Mighty Hanumān bowed his head, then informed the Rāghava that the queen was a prisoner but unharmed. Glad Lakṣmaṇa gazed admiringly at glad Sugrīva: his faith in this Son of the Wind's success was vindicated. But it was on Hanumān that the admiring gaze of the enemy-slaying Rāghava rested as he rejoiced in gladness.

They went off to the varied woodland on mount Prasravaṇa, 63.1–5
bowed their heads to Rāma and mighty Lakṣmaṇa, and formed up behind the Young King. When they had paid their respects to Sugrīva they began to report the news about Sītā: her imprisonment within Rāvaṇa's private quarters, the *rākṣasīs'* threats, her utter devotion to Rāma, and the time limit imposed on her – all this the apes reported with Rāma looking on. When he heard that Vaidehī was unharmed, Rāma asked in reply, 'Where is Queen Sītā and what are her feelings about me? Tell me everything about Vaidehī, *vānaras*.'

63.6–7 When they heard Rāma's questions the apes urged Hanumān forward while Rāma looked on. He knew everything there was to tell about Sītā, and when he heard their words Hanumān Son of the Wind gave a well-expressed account of his discovery of Sītā.

63.8–25 'In my desire to find Sītā Jānakī I went hunting for her and I jumped over a sea one hundred *yojanas* wide. There on the southern shore of the southern sea lies evil Rāvaṇa's city, Laṅkā. There I found the virtuous Sītā in Rāvaṇa's private quarters, lovely for you, Rāma, living for you, her trust in you. I saw her surrounded by *rākṣasīs* being threatened every moment, and guarded by hideous *rākṣasīs*: she's in his girls' grove. Your virtuous queen, a stranger to suffering, is meeting suffering imprisoned in Rāvaṇa's private quarters and close confined by *rākṣasīs*. She's done her hair in a single plait; she's miserable, and she thinks constantly of you; her bed is on the ground and her body is as pale as a lotus pool covered in snow; she utterly repudiates Rāvaṇa and is resolved to die. Kākutstha, the queen's mind dwells on you, and I have managed to discover her. I won her confidence, blameless tiger of a man, by relating little by little the renown of the Ikṣvāku dynasty. Then I talked to the queen and explained the whole business. She was overjoyed to hear of the alliance between Rāma and Sugrīva. She perseveres strictly in propriety and in devotion to you. That is how I saw the blessed pride of Janaka, practising severe austerity out of devotion to you, you bull of a man. She told me something by which you would recognize her identity, an event involving a crow that took place on Citrakūṭa in your presence, astute Rāghava. "Son of the Wind," said Jānakī to me, "you should tell that tiger of a man Rāma all that you have seen here without exception. And as you are speaking with Sugrīva listening, you should give him this: I have guarded it carefully. It's my majestic hair-jewel that I've guarded with great care for your sake. And remember the realgar *tilaka*," she said. "I'll have this majestic pearl brought back to you. Gazing at it in my troubles makes me rejoice as if I were looking at you, blameless man. Son of Daśaratha, I will cling to life for a month, but more than a month I cannot survive in the power of the *rākṣasas*." That's what Sītā told me, her body wasted and her doe-like eyes staring from her imprisonment in Rāvaṇa's private quarters; but she is persevering in her duty. Now that I've given you a full account, Rāghava, you should work out some means of crossing the ocean depths.'

At Hanumān's words Rāma son of Daśaratha pressed the jewel to his heart and wept, along with Lakṣmaṇa; the sight of that magnificent jewel filled his eyes with tears. Wasted by grief, the Rāghava spoke to Sugrīva: 64.1–2

'I'm like a cow overflowing from maternal love for her calf;[13] the sight of this peerless pearl is making my heart do the same. This peerless pearl was given to Vaidehī by my father-in-law at the time of our marriage, its lustre enhanced by being pinned on her head. This gem of a pearl is her most treasured heirloom, presented by wise Śakra as a mark of his gratification at a sacrifice. The sight of this magnificent jewel makes me think I can see before me my father, and the lord of Videha too, my friend. This is the jewel that adorns my darling's head. Seeing it here and now almost makes me believe I've got her back. 64.3–7

'Good sir, tell me again and again what Sītā Vaidehī said! Shower me with a stream of words, like water to revive my fainting spirit! But Saumitri, what could give me greater pain than the return of this gem of a pearl without Vaidehī? Vaidehī can cling to life for a month: what a long time! My friend, I feel I can't live for another moment without my dark-eyed lady. Do show me the way to where you found my beloved! I can't stand idle for an instant now I've heard your news. How is my shapely lady bearing up among the savage *rākṣasas*? They'll terrify her, she's so very timid! She must be like the clouded autumn moon when it's only just becoming visible: her face won't be radiant in the midst of those *rākṣasas*. What did Sītā say, Hanumān? Tell me the truth. That's what will keep me alive, like medicine for a sick man. What did my shapely beauty say? What sweet words could my sweet wife utter, snatched away from me? Tell me, Hanumān!' 64.8–15

Such were the words of the noble Rāghava. Hanumān reported to the Rāghava everything that Sītā had said. 'Queen Jānakī told me in detail about something that happened once 65.1–7 on Citrakūṭa that you would remember, you bull of a man. You'd been sleeping contentedly together. Jānakī was the first to get up. Suddenly a crow swooped down and clawed her between her breasts. Later, you elder brother of Bharata, you were asleep on the queen's lap when, so says the queen, the bird again startled her, flew back and again clawed her – badly, she says, so that you were woken up by a trickle of her blood. The queen says she woke you up from your contented sleep to find her being repeatedly molested by a crow, you who can burn up your enemies! When you saw her clawed between her breasts you hissed like an enraged poisonous snake and asked:

65.8 '"What has clawed you between your breasts, my timid wife? Who is playing with an enraged snake, its mouth agape?"

65.9–17 'You looked round and at once spotted the crow standing in front of her with blood on its sharp claws. This crow, she says, was a splendid bird, a son of Śakra, swifly ranging over the earth with the speed of the wind. Your eyes rolled with rage, then, mighty warrior, in your great wisdom you passed a savage sentence on the crow. You plucked a blade of *kuśa* grass from your couch and infused it with the Brahmā-missile. It blazed like the Doomsday Fire, and flared up towards the bird as you hurled the blazing *kuśa* blade at the crow. That blazing *kuśa* pursued the crow as, abandoned by its father and all the gods and great sages, it sped through the three worlds finding no one to save it. It sought your protection and fell to the ground, Kākutstha. You took pity and gave it your protection, saving it from the death it deserved; you were aware that a missile may not be fired to no purpose, Rāghava, so it put out the crow's right eye. The crow paid homage to you, Rāma, and to King Daśaratha; you then released it and it went back home.

65.18–23 '"You", she says, "are the foremost expert in missiles, and you are powerful and upright, so why don't you use missiles on the *rākṣasas*, Rāghava? Not *nāgas* nor *gandharvas* either, not anti-gods nor *marut* hordes are able to confront you, Rāma, and withstand you. You're a warrior; if you're at all concerned about me you'll kill Rāvaṇa in battle at once with well-whetted arrows. Again, Lakṣmaṇa's a champion who can exterminate his enemies: Rāghava, why doesn't he act on his brother's command and save me? Those two tigers of men are both as splendid as Wind and Fire, invincible even to the gods; why are they neglecting me? I must have committed some grave offence for that pair to ignore me when they have the power to exterminate their enemies."

'When I heard the pitiful words Vaidehī was sobbing out to me, I answered the noble lady: "My lady, Rāma hides his face out of grief over you, I swear it by the truth; and Rāma is so overwhelmed by his pain that it distresses Lakṣmaṇa too. But one way and another I've found your ladyship; now is not the time to grieve! This moment shall mark the end of your sorrows, lovely lady. Those two princes, both of them tigers of men and slayers of enemies, are determined to find you. They'll reduce Laṅkā to cinders. The mighty Rāghava will kill ferocious Rāvaṇa and his family in battle and take you back to his own city, that's certain. But if you could give me something Rāma would recognize that would cheer him up, please let me have it." 65.24–9

'She looked round in every direction, mighty prince, then fetched this superb hairpin out of her clothing and gave the jewel to me. For your sake, Raghu chief, I took the divine jewel, then bowed my head low to her to hurry off back. As I increased my size and she saw that I was resolved to leave, Janaka's fair-skinned daughter's face filled with tears; her sobs choked her in her misery as she begged: 65.30–32

'"Hanumān, those two lionlike princes, Rāma and Lakṣmaṇa, and Sugrīva and his ministers too, wish them all well from me; but then do please devise some way that the mighty Rāghava can rescue me from the sea of the sorrow of my captivity." 65.33–4

'Then the queen honoured me with further instructions, agitated by her love for you, you tiger of a man, and concern for me. "You should suggest all sorts of ways to Rāma Dāśarathi that he can fight and kill Rāvaṇa and get me back quickly. Or stay here another day if you think you should, you heroic foe-crusher. You can rest in some hideaway, and leave tomorrow. And your presence in my unhappy lot, *vānara*, would give me a moment's respite from my burgeoning sorrow. 66.1–15

When you've gone, valiant ape, even though you'll be coming back again, I'm not sure I can survive – really not sure. Not being able to see you would grieve and torment me even more; sorrow would beget overwhelming sorrow, I'm so worn out, so beset by sorrow. And I'm still assailed by one doubt, heroic monkey, a very big one, that's certain, and it's this: what about the apes and bears, your comrades? How will those armies of apes and bears – how even will the excellent king's two sons – ever get over the ocean? It's so hard to cross! Only three creatures would be able to leap this ocean: Vinatā's son, Vāyu or you, blameless monkey; so tell me what plan you can devise to achieve such a difficult objective – you're such an expert tactician, heroic monkey! Granted, you slayer of warlike foes, you could accomplish this task on your own, and your might would become legendary as a result, but it would bring glory on Rāma if he and the army he's mustered were to fight and kill Rāvaṇa and take me in triumph back to his own city. The Rāghava should not be like that cowardly *rākṣasa* who snatched me away from that hero in the forest by deceit. Kākutstha should make Laṅkā swarm with his troops, he should crush the hostile troops and then he should release me. That would befit him! It's for you to devise some means for the noble warrior-hero to display his valour."

66.16–28 'When I heard her calculated, courteous, well-reasoned words I then made a further reply. "My lady, the monkey chief Sugrīva, commander of the hosts of apes and bears, has espoused your cause with integrity and determination. Under his command lie courageous apes of power and integrity, swift as thought; upwards, downwards, sideways, nothing can impede their progress. Limitless is their might, and they do not shrink from great deeds. Many a time have these well-endowed, powerful *vānaras* flown around the whole earth, following in the wake of the wind. The forest-dwellers there are either my superiors or my equals: there is no one inferior to me in Sugrīva's presence. If I can reach here, how much more will those mighty ones manage? Envoys are chosen not from the best people, but from the remainder. So give up your anguish, my lady, and dispel your distress. Those ape chiefs will make it to

Laṅkā with a single bound. Like the sun and moon rising the two lions of men will come to you riding on my back, blessed lady. At Laṅkā's gate soon will you see that enemy-slayer, the lionlike Rāghava, and Lakṣmaṇa wielding his bow. Soon will you see mustering the heroic *vānaras* who fight with claws and teeth, like tusker chiefs, brave as any lion or tiger. Before long will you hear the din of monkey chiefs rumbling like mountain clouds on the slopes of Laṅkā's Malaya. And soon will you see the Rāghava, triumphant over his enemies, his forest-life at an end, consecrated in Ayodhyā, together with you."'

WAR

6,1.1–15 Rāma was filled with joy to hear Hanumān's well-phrased words and replied: 'Hanumān has completed a momentous mission, hard to accomplish on earth; no one else in the world could even contemplate performing such a thing. Other than Hanumān I can see no one who could cross the ocean, apart from Garuḍa and Vāyu. Laṅkā city is well guarded by Rāvaṇa, and even gods, *dānavas* and *yakṣas*, *gandharvas*, *nāgas* and *rākṣasas* would not be able to take it; if anyone were bold enough to get in, who would get out alive? Who could penetrate the *rākṣasa* defences of that unassailable place unless he had power and courage to equal Hanumān? Hanumān has done Sugrīva a great service, using his innate might and equally great valour. A servant who performs with zeal a difficult task assigned him by his master achieves acclaim, but a servant employed by a king who does not apply all the diligence at his command to perform an assignment is reckoned worthless. Hanumān has performed the task allotted to him without becoming distracted, and that has pleased Sugrīva. His devotion to duty in discovering Vaidehī has today rescued the race of Raghu – myself and mighty Lakṣmaṇa especially. But it increases my grief, wretch that I am, that I am unable to make a fitting recompense to this bearer of good news: I have reached such a state that all I have left to give to this noble is this embrace. The search for Sītā has gone well up to now, it's true, but my heart fails again when I think about the ocean. How will the troops of apes ever get over to the southern shore of the sea? Its mighty billows are so hard to cross! I may have received good news about Vaidehī, but what about getting the apes to the other side of the sea?'

With this response to Hanumān, Rāma the mighty destroyer of his foes, distraught with grief, became lost in thought. 1.16

As Daśaratha's son Rāma lamented his woes, majestic Sugrīva spoke to dispel his sorrow. 'Why are you distressing yourself, heroic prince, just like any ordinary person? You shouldn't behave like this. Drop your distress, like an ungrateful man would a friend. I can't see any reason for you to be distressed, Rāghava, now you've received the news and know where your enemy is lurking. You are resolute, erudite, intelligent and learned, Rāghava. Get rid of this wrong-headed way of thinking, like a self-controlled man would a mere golddigger! We will leap the crocodile-infested sea! We will scale Laṅkā! We will kill your enemy! If a man is indecisive, despairing and bowed down by grief, his plans come to nothing and he meets with disaster. We ape chiefs are all heroic and capable; we are resolute enough even to walk through fire to help you. I am delighted to know them and I have absolute confidence that my valour will enable me to kill your enemy and rescue Sītā. Rāghava, you should organize the construction of a causeway to give us a sight of the *rākṣasa* king's city; once we've seen Laṅkā city perched on the top of Trikūṭa you can consider Rāvaṇa killed in battle from the mere sight. As soon as a causeway's been constructed in the sea leading to Laṅkā and all the army has crossed over, you can consider him as good as defeated. These shape-changing apes are heroic fighters, your majesty, so you can banish all indecision from your mind – it would wreck all your objectives. Grieving robs a man of heroism in this world. The present task calls for boldness in the execution: be sensible and pluck up your courage with vigour. Grieving leads to defeat or death, and wrecks all the objectives of noble human heroes like you. You are highly intelligent, you are erudite on all subjects and you have allies like me; it's for you to defeat your enemy. Rāghava, I can't see anyone in the three worlds who could withstand you and your bow in a battle. Your mission will not fail if you entrust it to the *vānaras*: 2.1–21 soon will you cross the everlasting sea and behold Sītā. Stop wallowing in grief. You are Lord of the Earth: rely on rage! A wrathful warrior strikes terror into weak and feeble ones. You have come to us to help you cross the fearsome sea, the rivers' lord. You've got a good brain: use it! These shape-changing apes, these heroic fighters, will quell the foes with showers of rocks and trees. We must prepare to face Varuṇa's abode somehow or other. What's the point of carrying on talking? My lord, complete victory will be yours!'

3.1–5 Kākutstha listened to Sugrīva's speech and accepted its cogency like the skilled strategist that he was, then addressed Hanumān. 'Whether I exert myself to build a causeway or I dry up the ocean, I shall be well able to get across that ocean somehow. How many fortresses are there on well-fortified Laṅkā? Tell me. I want to know everything as if with my own eyes, *vānara*: size of the garrison, how the gates have been fortified, what defensive works there are on Laṅkā, the *rākṣasas'* domestic buildings. You've reconnoitred Laṅkā: in your own time make an accurate and realistic report, utilizing all your skill.'

3.6–32 At Rāma's words Hanumān Son of the Wind, that excellent speaker, replied to Rāma, 'Listen while I give a detailed report on the disposition of the fortification works: how Laṅkā city is defended and how it is protected by its garrison; Laṅkā's great prosperity and the perils of the ocean; the distribution of the forces flooding everywhere, and the numbers and types of vehicles. Laṅkā is contented and joyful, extensive and thronged with rutting elephants; it's filled with chariots and teeming with hordes of *rākṣasas*. It has four gateways, wide and huge; the gates are firmly attached and fitted with massive bolts. On the ramparts are enormous, powerful engines for fighting off an enemy invasion. Dreadful murderous iron-spiked contrivances stand ready beside the gates, built by the *rākṣasa* hordes. The great golden rampart is proof against attack and is studded on the inside with jewels, coral, beryl and pearls. All around are dreadful welcoming moats of cold unfathomed water replete with crocodiles and fish. They are crossed at the gateways by four lengthy bridges with many huge engines of war firmly embedded there; these engines protect the bridges against the arrival of a hostile army, scattering them into the surrounding moats. One bridge, Rāma, strongly built to be indestructible, is adorned with many a golden pillar and dais where Rāvaṇa can stand, bellicose, vigilant and surrounded by the trappings of power, to review his troops. Laṅkā city is self-sufficient and fearsome: not even the gods can reach it by any of the four means of access – rivers, mountains, forest or constructed. It stands, Rāghava, on the further shore of the wide ocean, without even access by boat through the uncharted waters. This impregnable city has been built on a mountain-top; with its teeming steeds and tuskers it rivals the city of the gods. Laṅkā will be extremely hard to conquer. Furthermore, evil Rāvaṇa's city of Laṅkā is adorned with beams and catapults and siege engines of all types. Ten thousand *rākṣasas* are drawn up at the western gate; all are armed with pikes, all are indomitable, all are champion swordsmen. At the southern gate one hundred thousand *rākṣasas* are drawn up in a four-square formation; these too are unsurpassed warriors. One million *rākṣasas* are assembled at the eastern gate; all are expert in all weaponry, all bear shields and swords. There are ten million *rākṣasas* drawn up at the northern gate, warriors on chariots, warriors on horses, well born, well respected. But at the central keep are drawn up one hundred times one hundred thousand invincible fiends and whole crores of *rākṣasas*. I have smashed the bridges, emptied the moats, burned Laṅkā city and demolished the ramparts, so by whatever route we cross Varuṇa's abode we *vānaras* can consider Laṅkā city as good as destroyed. Aṅgada, Dvivida, Mainda, Jāmbavān, Panasa, Nala, Nīla the commander too – do you need me to mention the rest of the army? – they will leap over to Rāvaṇa's great city with its ramparts and houses; they will bring back Maithilī. You should quickly order the whole force to muster for this purpose, and when you are satisfied that the moment is right, dispatch it.'

In Laṅkā the lord of the *rākṣasas* addressed all the *rākṣasas*, 6.1–18
his head bowed a little from shame at the sight of the dreadful, terrifying deed performed by noble Hanumān as if he'd been

Śakra. 'Not only has Laṅkā, my impregnable fortress, been slighted and penetrated by this mere *vānara*, but Sītā Jānakī has been discovered. The palace has been slighted, the sacred tree too, leading *rākṣasas* have been killed and the whole city of Laṅkā has been fouled by Hanumān. What am I to do, good sirs? What is the immediate need? Advise me as to the best and most practical action. Wise statesmen declare victory to be rooted in strategy. That's why I am seeking your advice, mighty *rākṣasas*, with regard to Rāma. There are three sorts of people in the world: high-, low- and medium-rated, all with their merits and faults, as I shall state. One who determines policy in consultation with well-disposed, capable advisers, with allies too, or with affectionate relations as well, then embarks on a course of action and exerts himself in accordance with his fate, he is highly rated. The one who considers a matter alone, makes up his mind on its merit alone, and performs the deeds alone, he is middle-rated. But one who undertakes a deed without determining the merits and demerits and without regard to his fate, just thinking "I'll do it", he is rated lowest of all. Just as there are always these three categories – highest, lowest and middle – so too advice can be rated high, low or medium. What is rated the best advice is produced when counsellors have reached a consensus and are satisfied that it is in line with the prescriptions of the ritual texts. Where counsellors are swayed by many opinions before again reaching a consensus in determining a matter, their advice is traditionally rated medium. Where each remains adamant and completely rejects other opinions, and no viable consensus can be reached, that is rated the worst advice. So you, my lords, who are excellent counsellors, you must deliberate well and advise me plainly what is the most beneficial course of action for me to follow. Rāma is approaching Laṅkā city surrounded by thousands of *vānara* warriors to lay siege to us. It's perfectly clear that the Rāghava will cross the sea easily with his characteristic energy, together with his younger brother and a supporting force. Give me advice about the best course of action for my city and army when he arrives with the *vānaras* to carry out his intention of besieging us.'

Thus addressed by the lord of the *rākṣasas*, those powerful *rākṣasas* all answered the *rākṣasa* lord Rāvaṇa with deference. 'Your majesty, our army is huge and abundantly equipped with maces, spears, lances, pikes and javelins. What reason is there for your lordship to experience despondency? You caused devastation and vanquished Vaiśravaṇa even though he was dwelling on Kailāsa's peak surrounded by numerous *yakṣas*. That powerful Protector of the World, priding himself though he did on his comradeship with the Great God, was defeated in furious combat by you, your lordship; when you had stemmed the tide of *yakṣas*, struck them down and routed them, you brought this chariot back from Kailāsa's peak. Out of fear of you, and anxious for an alliance with you, bull of a *rākṣasa*, the *dānava* lord Maya gave you his daughter for a wife. The *dānava* lord Madhu, Kumbhīnasī's darling, puffed up with courage and unassailable though he was, was fought and conquered by you. *Nāgas* have been defeated by you, mighty lord, after they fled to Rasātala: Vāsuki, Takṣaka, Śaṅkha and Jaṭin have been brought under your sway. For a year, mighty lord, despite their trust in a boon, you battled against those unassailable powerful heroes, the *dānavas*. Whether they relied on their own power or resorted to magic, crowds of them were brought under your sway, foe-crushing overlord of the *rākṣasas*. In your might, you fought and defeated Varuṇa's sons, heroic and powerful though they were, and supported by an entire army. Yama's army is like the sea, with Death's sceptre for the sharks and islands of silk-cotton trees for adornment, yet you dived in and gained a famous victory that fettered Death, delighting all the worlds by your well-fought fight. The earth was crowded with heroic *kṣatriyas* – forests of them – each rivalling Śakra in valour, but you have battered and killed them, your majesty;[1] they were very difficult to defeat, but the Rāghava exerting all the prowess at his command is no match for them in combat. Your majesty, the havoc wrought by this low wretch is beneath your notice; you really should banish it from your heart. You're the one to kill the Rāghava.' 7.1–16

Then Prahasta, a *rākṣasa* dark as a thundercloud and a heroic general, saluted and spoke: 'If gods, *dānavas*, *gandharvas*, 8.1–5 *piśācas*, birds and serpents are impotent, what can *vānaras* do in a battle? It's because we were confident and complacent that Hanumān deceived us all, or that forest-wanderer would not have left here living as long as I was alive. I will wipe out *vānaras* from the whole of the sea-girt earth, mountains, forests and woodland: just give me the order, my lord. I will organize measures to counter that *vānara*, night-roamer. No harm shall come to you as a result of your crime.'

8.6–8 Then spoke the *rākṣasa* Durmukha, highly indignant: 'This assault on us all is not to be endured, and more particularly the humiliation of the city and your private apartment: the lord of the *vānaras* has attacked the majestic lord of the *rākṣasas*! Alone will I strike them down, I will repel the *vānaras* whether they are in the fearsome ocean, or the sky, or even Rasātala.'

8.9–11 Then Vajradaṃṣṭra, furious and mighty, picked up his horrific mace, stained with flesh and blood, and spoke: 'Why bother with this miserable wretch Hanumān, when we are confronted by formidable Rāma, with Sugrīva and Lakṣmaṇa too? Today will I alone kill Rāma with my mace, Sugrīva and Lakṣmaṇa too, rout the army of apes, and return.'

8.12–13 Then Kumbhakarṇa's heroic son, the warrior Nikumbha, in great fury addressed Rāvaṇa who makes the worlds roar: 'You my lords can stay here clustered round the Mahārāja. I will be the one to kill the Rāghava and Lakṣmaṇa on my own.'

8.14–16 Then spoke up a mountainous *rākṣasa* called Vajrahanu, again and again licking his lips with his tongue in his anger: 'Your lordships can go about your business as you please without anxiety. I'm the one who will, on my own, gobble up all the leaders of this army of apes. On my own will I kill Sugrīva and Lakṣmaṇa, Hanumān and Aṅgada too, and that battle-elephant of a Rāma.'

9.1–6 Then Nikumbha, Rabhasa, powerful Sūryaśatru, Suptaghna and Yajñakopa, Mahāpārśva, Mahodara and formidable Agniketu, the *rākṣasa* Raśmiketu, splendid Indrajit – Rāvaṇa's mighty son – also Prahasta, Virūpākṣa, powerful Vajradaṃṣṭra, Dhūmrākṣa too and Atikāya and even the *rākṣasa* Durmukha seized maces, javelins, darts, spears, pikes, battleaxes, bows and arrows and long, sharp swords and sprang up. All these furious *rākṣasas* seemed to blaze with splendour as they assured Rāvaṇa, 'Today will we slaughter Rāma and Sugrīva, Lakṣmaṇa too, and that wretch that violated Laṅkā, Hanumān.'

Vibhīṣaṇa restrained all those belligerents and made them 9.7–20
resume their seats, then saluted respectfully and made a speech. 'Sir, authorities have laid down the appropriate occasions for the use of force when someone cannot achieve his objective by any of the three regular means.[2] Force will succeed, sir, against one who is unwary, preoccupied or struck down by Fate, if it is employed in a proper manner and with circumspection. But how can you think of attacking one who is on the alert, avid for victory, supported by an army, imperturbable and indomitable? Who could conceive that Hanumān would leap the dreadful sea, lord of rivers and streams, to perform an almost impossible deed? Night-roamers, those forces are immeasurable and heroic; hasty contempt for such opponents is utterly inexpedient. As for the offence formerly committed against the king of the *rākṣasas* by Rāma, occasioning the abduction of his illustrious wife from Janasthāna: if Khara could be overcome and struck down by Rāma in battle, then it behoves those who remain alive to safeguard their lives to their utmost ability. For that reason Vaidehī poses a great threat to us. She has been abducted, she should be released. There is no advantage in pursuing this dispute. There is no point in us pursuing senseless hostility against this righteous hero. Let Maithilī be returned to him. Before his arrows tear apart the city with its elephants, with its horses, with its multitudes of gems, let Maithilī be returned to him. Before the ferocious, huge, formidable ape army storms our Laṅkā, let Sītā be given back. If the wife Rāma dotes on is not yielded voluntarily, Laṅkā city and all the *rākṣasa* heroes will perish. I entreat you as your brother: follow my advice. I'm speaking to your advantage and for your own good: let Maithilī be returned to him.'

Destiny drove Rāvaṇa to reply harshly to Vibhīṣaṇa's sound, 10.1–11
well-reasoned advice. 'One should set up home with a rival or an angry poisonous snake sooner than live with one who

professes friendship while serving the enemy. I know the ways of relations in all the worlds, *rākṣasa*: relations always glory in the misfortunes of their relations. If the head of a family is an effective, learned and law-abiding hero, *rākṣasa*, his relations disdain and despise him. Relations are to be feared for constantly gloating over each other's troubles and dreaded for their murderous hypocrisy. There's a proverb once current among the elephants of the Padmavana, verses they sang when they spied men with nooses in their hands; listen while I recite them. "Not fire, not weapons, not nooses can terrify us; it is ferocious relations intent on their own interests that terrify us. It is they who are certain to betray the method of capturing us."[3] We all know that of all the perils there are, the peril from members of our own family is the worst. We look for choice food to cows, for restraint to brāhmans, for fickleness to women, for danger to relations. That is why, dear brother, you are envious of my position in the world, that I was born to be sovereign[4] and have triumphed over my enemies. Anyone else who spoke like that, night-roamer, would meet his end that very moment. You disgrace our family! Shame on you!'

10.12–13 At that harsh reply to his apt advice, Vibhīṣaṇa sprang up, mace in hand, joined by four *rākṣasas*. Out of the sky glorious Vibhīṣaṇa spoke in fury to his brother, the *rākṣasas'* overlord.

10.14–20 'Your majesty, you are my brother: you may say what you wish to me, but I will not put up with these cruel lies of yours. Ten-faced king, only undisciplined people in the grip of Time will not accept prudent advice from a well-wisher. Your majesty, yes-men are ten a penny; one who'll tell you, for your own good, what you don't want to hear is one in a million. It's not my desire to witness you, bound in Time's inexorable noose, perish like a blazing hut. It's not my wish to see you slain by Rāma with sharp, gilded arrows like blazing fires. However powerful a warrior may be, however skilled in weaponry, when Time overtakes him on the battlefield he'll collapse like an embankment made of sand. Use any means at your disposal to defend yourself, the city and the *rākṣasas*. I wish you well! I'm going. Be happy without me.'

11.1–5 After these harsh words to Rāvaṇa, Rāvaṇa's junior fled in an instant to the place where Rāma and Lakṣmaṇa had arrived. From the ground the *vānara* lords spied him in the sky like mount Meru and brilliant as flashing lightning. When Sugrīva lord of the *vānaras* and the other indomitable *vānaras* saw him and his four companions, he wisely reflected, and after a moment's thought told all the *vānaras* and Hanumān their leader his conclusion: 'Look, there's a fully-armed *rākṣasa*, with four other *rākṣasas*! They're coming to kill us, that's certain!'

When the leading *vānaras* heard Sugrīva's words they all 11.6–7
grasped *sāls* and rocks, crying, 'Your majesty, give the command at once for us to slay these villains! We'll batter them and lay them lifeless on the ground.'

During this exchange Vibhīṣaṇa reached the northern shore 11.8–9
and halted in the sky. From his station in the sky Vibhīṣaṇa, great and very wise, saw Sugrīva and the rest and called out to them in a loud voice:

'The wicked *rākṣasa* Rāvaṇa is lord of the *rākṣasas*. I am his 11.10–15
younger brother. My name is Vibhīṣaṇa. He killed Jaṭāyus and carried off Sītā from Janasthāna; she is imprisoned against her will, miserable and closely guarded by *rākṣasīs*. Again and again I gave him this advice, supported by reasons and any number of arguments: "Very well, have Sītā returned to Rāma." But as if it had been medicine to the perverse, Rāvaṇa refused this salutary advice; he was in the grip of Time. He abused me roundly and scorned me like a slave, so I have abandoned my sons and my wives too, and come to seek asylum with the Rāghava. Announce me quickly to the noble Rāghava, the whole world's refuge; tell him Vibhīṣaṇa has arrived.'

Hearing those words enraged the volatile Sugrīva and in 11.16–20
front of Lakṣmaṇa he told Rāma, 'My lord, Rāvaṇa's younger brother, named Vibhīṣaṇa, with four other *rākṣasas*, is seeking asylum with you. It's Rāvaṇa who's dispatched him, this Vibhīṣaṇa, you can be sure. You're the best person to judge what's proper, but I think the proper thing to do is to arrest him. This *rākṣasa* is designing and sly: he has come to abuse your confidence, Rāghava, and attack you covertly with his

cunning. You should have him and his companions suffer condign punishment. This is Vibhīṣaṇa, this is savage Rāvaṇa's brother: execute him.'

11.21–2 With these furious words to well-spoken Rāma the outspoken commander-in-chief fell silent, but on hearing Sugrīva's opinion the mighty Rāma declared to the apes led by Hanumān standing alongside:

11.23–4 'You have heard, my lords, the cogent arguments about Rāvaṇa's younger brother advanced by the king of the monkeys: but in distressing matters it is proper to consult any upright, wise and capable comrade with one's interests constantly at heart.'

11.25–8 Each was eager to help, and at this invitation each gave Rāma his own unstinted, courteous advice. 'There is nothing in the three worlds that you do not know, Rāghava. It redounds to your credit that you should value our friendship enough to ask us, for you are a hero of unfailing integrity, righteous, steadfast, circumspect, heedful yet prepared to trust your comrades. Let all your companions therefore individually, one by one, present their considered, practical opinions, rationally reached.'

11.29–33 Aṅgada was the first to respond to the invitation; the proposal the astute ape addressed to the Rāghava was that Vibhīṣaṇa be investigated. 'His arrival from your enemy's presence inevitably gives rise to suspicion; we should not rush to put our trust in Vibhīṣaṇa. Sly-minded people conceal their true nature, prowling around and attacking through any chink in the defences. He might turn out to be a heavy liability. We must weigh up the factors on both sides before coming to a conclusion about him: if found worthy he should make a compact with us, if unworthy he should be sent packing. If the disadvantages are great we should have no hesitation in rejecting him, but if many benefits become apparent we should conclude a compact, your majesty.'

11.34–5 Śarabha had been thinking hard, and his suggestion was to the point. 'Tiger of a man, you should immediately assign someone to spy on him. When an intelligent spy has been assigned to investigate him in proper fashion we can reach a verdict in due form.'

Jāmbavān was cautious; he pondered the teachings of the *śāstras* and made his views known in clear and unambiguous terms: 'Vibhīṣaṇa has arrived inopportunely. He has come from the lord of the *rākṣasas*, our evil, sworn enemy. Everything about him arouses suspicion.' 11.36–7

Mainda was experienced in discriminating between good courses of action and bad; his thoughtful response was well expressed and more judicious: 'Vibhīṣaṇa is indeed Rāvaṇa's brother. Lord of champions, you should have him interrogated gently and patiently, then when you've established his character, bull of a man, you'll be able to make a judgement about whether he is driven by vice or virtue.' 11.38–40

The advice proffered by Hanumān, that erudite leading minister, was mild, apt, sweet and agreeable. 'Bṛhaspati himself is not a more excellent speaker than you, my lord: your advice is perfect, you are practical, your expression is faultless. Your majesty, I shall speak not for the sake of speaking, not out of rivalry or a sense of superiority, not to please myself, Rāma, but because the gravity of the situation demands it. In your ministers' advice, both for and against, I detect a problem, for their proposals are inappropriate. We cannot determine his ability without setting him some task, but I deem the immediate imposition of a task to be unsound. Your ministers' advice as to the suitability of dispatching spies is also inappropriate: the proposal has no purpose. You were told, "Vibhīṣaṇa has arrived inopportunely"; that topic I wish to address. Listen while I present my opinion. 11.41–7

'His arrival here is most opportune. Shifting one's loyalty from one person to another can either be a vice or indeed a virtue. You should at once turn his earnest enterprise to your advantage. He has witnessed your endeavour and Rāvaṇa's sin; he has heard about the killing of Vālin and consecration of Sugrīva; and he wants the kingship. That is his chief reason for coming here, and if due weight is attached to it, then a compact with him becomes appropriate. I have spoken to the 11.48–59 best of my ability in support of the *rākṣasa's* honesty, but it is for you to evaluate all you have heard, for your wisdom is supreme.'

12.1–3 Indomitable Rāma listened calmly to the words of the judicious Son of the Wind and responded to his advice. 'I too wish to express my opinion about Vibhīṣaṇa. You are all right-minded, my lords, so I wish you to listen to it all. I would in no way reject anyone, even if he were flawed, who came to me in the way of a friend: the righteous would never condemn such behaviour.'

12.4–7 When Sugrīva lord of the monkeys heard Rāma's words he was impelled by friendship to answer Kākutstha: 'You know what is right, you jewel in the crown of lords of the world! What is there to be wondered at that you should speak nobly, you who are pure and behave with propriety? I know in my heart that Vibhīṣaṇa is pure; I've examined it from every angle, from what I can infer as well as by using my own judgement. So let him join us at once on equal terms, Rāghava; Vibhīṣaṇa is very perceptive, so let him enter the circle of our advisers.'

12.8–21 When Rāma had deliberated on what he had heard from Sugrīva, he replied most graciously to the bull of an ape. 'What does it matter whether this night-roamer is utterly lawless or not? He can do me no harm, no not the slightest. Worldwide there are *piśācas*, *dānavas*, *yakṣas* and *rākṣasas*, but I could kill them with my fingertip if I wished, lord of the ape armies. It's been handed down that a pigeon honoured an enemy that had sought refuge with it, and offered it its own flesh.[5] If a pigeon could accept as a suppliant the one who had taken its wife, *vānara* chief, how much more should a man of my calibre? Listen to the homily recited of old by that supreme sage the soothsayer Kaṇḍu, son of the sage Kaṇva; it's highly moral: "Enemy-burner, one should not kill an enemy with hands raised in submission, when he is wretched and begging for mercy and asylum. Humiliated or overweening, a foe seeking asylum from strangers should be protected by the scrupulous, heedless of his own life. Should dread, delusion or desire drive him not to afford him all possible protection, then this crime attracts worldwide condemnation. If he stands idly by, offering no protection while one who has sought asylum from him perishes, all the protector's merit perishes with the victim."[6] That's why it would be so wrong in this case not to extend our protection to those who have sought it; it would debar us from heaven, it would sully our good name, and it would sap our strength and morale. It is much more appropriate for me to carry out Kaṇḍu's worthy precept: may the deed be accounted righteous, may it bring renown, may heaven be its reward. I give sanctuary from all creatures to any who surrender and pledge their loyalty to me: that I vow. Bring him here, ape lord; I grant him sanctuary, whether he be Vibhīṣaṇa, Sugrīva, or Rāvaṇa himself.'

Granted immunity by the Rāghava, Rāvaṇa's delighted 13.1–3
younger brother bowed and leapt to earth from the sky along with his loyal followers. Righteous Vibhīṣaṇa and the four *rākṣasas* then fell at Rāma's feet and claimed sanctuary. Vibhīṣaṇa's words to Rāma were meritorious and apt, but now exultant too:

'I am Rāvaṇa's younger brother, but he has treated me with 13.4–6
contempt. My lord, I have come to seek sanctuary with you, who grant sanctuary to all. I have renounced Laṅkā, friends and wealth; to you, my lord, I surrender the kingdom, along with my life and welfare. I am willing to aid you wholeheartedly in killing *rākṣasas* and attacking Laṅkā; I am willing to join your army.'

Rāma embraced Vibhīṣaṇa as he was speaking, and happily 13.7–8
said to Lakṣmaṇa, 'Fetch some water quickly from the sea and consecrate this sagacious Vibhīṣaṇa as king of the *rākṣasas*; I will grant him my blessing and you will confer honour on him.'

Hearing this, Saumitri carried out Rāma's command and 13.9–10
consecrated Vibhīṣaṇa king before the leading *vānaras*, a demonstration of Rāma's goodwill that at once set the monkeys cheering loudly and crying 'Bravo! Bravo!'

Hanumān and Sugrīva both asked Vibhīṣaṇa, 'How are we 13.11–12
to cross the abode of Varuṇa, the indomitable sea? By what method can we venture on to the lord of rivers and streams,

and speedily transport us all, with the army, over Varuṇa's abode?'

13.13–14 Vibhīṣaṇa knew the correct way to answer this question. 'A king of the Rāghavas should appeal to the Ocean for support. It was Sagara who excavated this huge expanse of water, so that expanse of water ought to do what his kinsman Rāma needs.'

13.15–16 It was in the Rāghava's nature to value tradition and he approved of the suggestion made by the shrewd *rākṣasa* Vibhīṣaṇa, but as a formality that splendid expert in due form smiled at Lakṣmaṇa and at Sugrīva lord of the apes and consulted them.

13.17–18 'Lakṣmaṇa, I like Vibhīṣaṇa's suggestion. Tell me whether you like it as well – you and Sugrīva. Sugrīva is always erudite, and you, sir, are a shrewd judge of advice. Reflect on the matter, both of you, then give me your opinions.'

13.19–22 The reply the heroes Sugrīva and Lakṣmaṇa both made to this request was seemly. 'Rāghava, you tiger of a man, why should we not agree with the beneficial suggestion Vibhīṣaṇa has just made? Unless a causeway is constructed across this savage sea, Varuṇa's abode, not even gods, anti-gods or Indra himself could reach Laṅkā. The hero Vibhīṣaṇa's suggestion should be put into practice just as he said. We've taken up enough time. The Sea must be won over.'

13.23; 14.1–3 Hearing this, Rāma installed himself on the *kuśa* grass strewn on the seashore like the fire of sacrifice on the altar. Three nights passed with Rāma sleeping on the *kuśa*-strewn ground, intent on his observances, but the Sea was slow to show himself to Rāma, even though Rāma invoked him with due devotion. Then the corners of Rāma's eyes grew red with anger at the Sea, and he remarked to Fortune-favoured Lakṣmaṇa, who was standing by his side:

14.4–13 'Lakṣmaṇa, just see the arrogance of the dastardly Sea, not appearing when he's invoked! Serenity, patience, uprightness and fair words – the qualities good people exhibit – are interpreted by the unprincipled as weakness. The man the world honours is boastful, corrupt, headstrong, impetuous, lashing out on all sides. It's not peace-making that wins renown,

Lakṣmaṇa, it's not peace-making that wins glory in this world or victory in battle. This very day, Saumitri, shall you see the watery haunt of crocodiles crammed with writhing crocodiles shot through by my shafts. You shall see me pierce arching fishes, sea-elephants' trunks and serpents' coils. This very day in a great battle my arrows shall dry up the sea with its network of conches and pearl-oysters, fish and crocodiles. Just because I am patient, the haunt of crocodiles dismisses me as impotent. Patience is no use with people like that! Saumitri, bring me my bow, and my venomous snakes of arrows! This very day in my anger I shall daunt even the indomitable sea. Varuṇa's abode with its teeming waves is bounded only by the shores: my arrows shall force it back from its boundaries.'

At the end of this speech Rāma seized his bow, eyes dilated 14.14–20
in fury, formidable as the blazing Doomsday Fire. The world shuddered at his arrows as he bent back his dreadful bow and loosed a savage broadside like Indra Śatakratu with his thunderbolts. Those superlative arrows struck panic into the sea-serpents as they blazed their way into the water with irresistible might, whipping up a great turbulence among its swordfish and crocodiles, and a terrifying howling gale. Suddenly the sea became garlanded with strings of towering conch- and oyster-crammed waves and spume-crested breakers. Mouths blazing, eyes blazing, snakes were in turmoil, *dānavas* too – heroic though they were – in their Underworld haunt, and the swordfish- and crocodile-infested waves of the King of Rivers swelled in their thousands to rival Vindhya and Mandara.

Then from the depths of the sea, like the sun rising over the 15.1–3
great Meru mountain, Ocean himself arose; serpents blazed fire from their jaws as the Sea itself appeared. Smooth as beryl, adorned with gold, red garlanded, red clad, eyes like lotus petals, Ocean approached; the mighty lord announced himself, then with a deferential gesture spoke to the Rāghava, who was still brandishing his arrows.

'Rāghava my friend, earth, wind, ether, water and light pur- 15.4–10
sue their ordained path according to their immutable characteristics. My nature is to be fathomless and impossible to traverse:

it would be a perversion if I could be forded, or so I believe. Prince, not lust nor greed nor fear would make me hold back my crocodile- and swordfish-infested water, but I will tell you what I will submit to, Rāma: no crocodiles shall attack while the army is crossing. This Nala here is the glorious Son of Viśvakarman; his father has passed on to him a talent for construction, my friend. This *vānara* is very determined: let him build a causeway across me. Him I will tolerate for his resemblance to his father.' With these words, Ocean disappeared.

15.10–13 Then Nala stood up, an excellent *vānara* of great strength, and addressed Rāma. 'In reliance on my father's talent I will build a causeway across Varuṇa's broad abode. It was the truth the great Sea told you: Viśvakarman did grant my mother a boon on Mandara. I am a true Son of Viśvakarman: I take after him, though I would not proclaim my talents unbidden. I agree that we bulls of *vānaras* should build a causeway this very day.'

15.14–24 Then at Rāma's command the joyful ape leaders all around descended in their hundreds and thousands on the great forest, where these *vānaras*, these mountainous bulls of the monkey hordes, demolished the mountains, dragging them into the ocean. As they hurled the mountains in, the water was convulsed with the violence and whipped up to the sky, then gradually retreated. Across the middle of the lord of rivers and streams Nala built the great causeway ten *yojanas* broad and a hundred *yojanas* long; the uproar was tumultuous as the boulders and mountains plummeted into that great sea. The causeway Nala constructed across the crocodile-haunted ocean gleamed full of majestic promise as the path of Svātī across the sky, until gods, *gandharvas*, *siddhas* and supreme sages assembled in the sky in their eagerness to gaze upon that wonder. The monkeys leapt and bounded about, cheering at that inconceivable, unbearably astonishing marvel, as creatures of all kinds viewed the causeway constructed across the ocean.

15.25–31 With great energy the thousands of crores of *vānaras* built the causeway across the ocean until they reached the further shore of the sea. The grand causeway was wide and well constructed, imposing and well packed with beaten earth; it gleamed like a hair-parting in the ocean. Then Vibhīṣaṇa and his companions took up position on the further shore of the sea, mace in hand, to ward off opposition. Majestic Rāma, bow in hand, with Lakṣmaṇa alongside, led the army; Sugrīva accompanied the righteous man. Some monkeys marched along the middle, some on the edges, some missed their footing, some fell into the water, some flew through the air like birds. The hullabaloo of the fearsome ape army as it crossed masked the fearsome din arising from the sea. When the *vānara* army had crossed Nala's causeway and reached a part of the shore well supplied with roots, fruit and water, the king had them set up camp.

Rāma Daśaratha's son and his army now being on his side of the ocean, majestic Rāvaṇa spoke to two of his ministers, Śuka and Sāraṇa. 'The ocean is proof against passage, but the whole *vānara* army has crossed it! Rāma has constructed a causeway across the ocean: that's unprecedented! I can't believe a causeway has possibly been constructed across the ocean! In any case, I need to have a count made of this *vānara* army. My lords, you are to infiltrate the *vānara* army under cover and ascertain precisely its size and capability, the identity of the leading monkeys and the advisers of Rāma and Sugrīva, the formation of the vanguard and the identity of the monkey champions, the design of the causeway across all the ocean waters and of these *vānara* nobles' encampment, the determination, valour and weapons possessed by Rāma and by dauntless Lakṣmaṇa, and the identity of this *vānara* army's commander. As soon as you've established that with accuracy, you are to return.' 16.1–8

With these instructions the *rākṣasas* Śuka and Sāraṇa disguised themselves as apes and infiltrated the *vānara* army, but Śuka and Sāraṇa could not manage to count that tremendous, unimaginable *vānara* army occupying peaks, caves and defiles, seashores, forests and woodland: whether crossing, already across or still anxious to cross, whether encamped or still in the process of encamping, that enormous host was making a fearful din. 16.9–12

16.13 Vibhīṣaṇa was smart enough to see through their disguise, took Śuka and Sāraṇa prisoner and reported to Rāma, 'Victor over enemy fortresses, two spies have turned up from Laṅkā.'

16.14–15 They trembled at the sight of Rāma and lost all hope of life; in their terror they surrendered humbly and confessed, 'Sir, pride of the Raghus, Rāvaṇa sent us both here to gain intelligence about your whole army.'

16.16–21 Their words amused Daśaratha's son Rāma, who rejoiced in the welfare of all creatures. 'When you've seen the full extent of the army, inspected it thoroughly and completed your task as instructed, you may return without hindrance. Go back to Laṅkā, my lords, and report my exact words to the *rākṣasa* king, Vaiśravaṇa's junior:[7] "In keeping Sītā captive from me you are relying on your army. You may display that army and your confederates as much as you wish, but tomorrow you will see Laṅkā city – ramparts, gateways and *rākṣasa* army – swiftly desolated by my arrows. Tomorrow, like the wielder of the thunderbolt, Indra Vāsava, launching his thunderbolt against the *dānavas*, I will unleash my fierce wrath; tomorrow, Rāvaṇa, will you feel its weight." '

16.22–8 With these instructions the *rākṣasas* Śuka and Sāraṇa went back to Laṅkā and reported to the *rākṣasa* overlord. 'We were taken prisoner by Vibhīṣaṇa, *rākṣasa* lord, and taken before boundlessly mighty Rāma; he was entitled to order our execution, but magnanimously he released us. There are four bulls of men there, skilled in weaponry, determined and valiant, like Protectors of the World come together – Rāma Dāśarathi the glorious, Lakṣmaṇa, Vibhīṣaṇa and Sugrīva the splendid, who rivals great Indra in valour. Even if all the *vānaras* stood idly by, they would be able to tear up Laṅkā city and overturn it, ramparts, gateways and all. Rāma is of such stature and his weapons so fearsome that he could destroy Laṅkā city on his own, with the other three standing idly by. The army under the care of Rāma and Lakṣmaṇa, and of Sugrīva too, is proof even against all the gods and anti-gods.'

17.1–3 Sāraṇa's report was well meant and did not spring from cowardice, but King Rāvaṇa retorted to Sāraṇa, 'I will not return Sītā, not if gods, *gandharvas* and *dānavas* should require me, not from fear of all the world. You sir, you've been terrified by the apes. You've quite lost your nerve, and that's why you recommend returning Sītā. What opponent would ever be able to defeat me in a battle?'

With these harsh words Rāvaṇa the imperious overlord of the *rākṣasas* then climbed to the top of his snow-white palace, tall as many palmyras; Rāvaṇa was anxious to see for himself. With the pair of spies at his side, Rāvaṇa surveyed sea, mountains and forests, and was beside himself with fury when he saw the whole earth round about swarming with monkeys. King Rāvaṇa gazed at that limitless, untold host of *vānaras* and asked Sāraṇa: 17.4–6

'Identify the warriors to me. Who are the strongest among the *vānara* chiefs? Who are the most intrepid of all, and form the vanguard? Whose advice does Sugrīva follow? Who are the overall commanders? Give me a full report, Sāraṇa! Which are the principal monkeys?' 17.7–8

In answer to the *rākṣasa* lord's demand, Sāraṇa identified the chief forest-dwellers as far as he knew them. 'That *vānara* standing roaring in front of Laṅkā, surrounded by a hundred thousand officers, whose hullabaloo is throbbing through all Laṅkā – ramparts, gateways, mountains, forests and woodland: he stands in the vanguard of noble Sugrīva, lord of all monkeys. This commander is the warrior called Nīla. 17.9–12

'The one with the warlike threatening gesture who is pacing about on the ground opposite Laṅkā, repeatedly snarling with anger, mountainous but wiry as a lotus filament, continually thumping his tail on the earth in fury as if he would make the ten Directions resound with the noise of that tail: that is Aṅgada. Sugrīva king of the *vānaras* has consecrated him Young King, and he's challenging you to fight. Those bulls of apes on their feet with sinews stiffened, growling, roaring, snarling with anger, invincible, savage, ferocious, ferociously courageous – eight hundred thousand and a thousand crores of them: they are his sandal-painted followers. He boasts of crushing Laṅkā with his own battalion. 17.13–18

'Silvery Śveta with his troop is terrifyingly valiant; that astute *vānara* is a hero famed throughout the three worlds. He 17.19–20 answered Sugrīva's summons with alacrity, and now the *vānara* is going around positioning the *vānara* army and rallying the troops.

17.21–2 'There's one who once used to roam the lovely tree-covered mountain called Saṃkocana on the bank of the Gomatī; he's the ruler there, and he's called Kumuda, the commander of a thousand times a hundred thousand followers.

17.23–4 'The one with the long shaggy tail covered with hairs many yards long, copper-coloured, yellow, cream and white: he does terrible deeds, and he's exultant in his anger. He is Caṇḍa, and he's spoiling for a fight; he boasts of crushing Laṅkā with his own battalion.

17.25–7 'The one with a long mane like a tawny lion, fixing Laṅkā in his gaze as if he'd like to burn it down with his eye: your majesty, he is hereditary ruler of the dark Vindhya mountain and goodly mount Sahya. That commander is called Rambha. Thirty hundred thousand ape officers cluster around him, following him to crush Laṅkā with their might.

17.28–30 'Then there's one who's pricking up his ears and always snarling: he doesn't shrink from death or retreat from the foe; his strength is great and he's banished fear. Your majesty, that is the hereditary ruler of lovely mount Sālveya; that mighty commander is called Śarabha, your majesty, and as his mighty lieutenants he leads forty hundred thousand rovers.

17.31–4 'There's one standing out among the *vānara* warriors like Indra Vāsava among the gods; he's like a great cloud blotting out the sky and he's making a terrible din like the drums of monkey lords spoiling for a fight: that's the commander called Panasa; he can never be conquered, and his territory is matchless mount Pāriyātra. At his command that excellent commander has fifty hundred thousand lieutenants with troops in proportion.

17.35–6 'Then that ornament of the dread army bounding along the seashore, himself brilliant as a second sea: that commander is called Vinata; he's as mountainous as Dardara, and he drinks from the beautiful river Parṇāśā.

17.37 'Krathana, leader of a troop of sixty hundred thousand monkeys, is challenging you to battle.

'And that *vānara* showing off his realgar-coloured coat: he's called glorious Gavaya, and he's hurling angry defiance at you, backed by seventy hundred thousand. He boasts of crushing Laṅkā with his own battalion. Those are the commanders – the outstanding commanders: they are invincible, ferocious and mighty, they can change shape at will, and they are beyond anyone's ability to count.' 17.38–40

When Sāraṇa had concluded his report to the *rākṣasa* overlord Rāvaṇa, Śuka ran his eye over the whole force and made his own report. 'Look at them standing there like great rutting elephants, like Gaṅgā banyans, like Himālayan *sāls*! Your majesty, their might is irresistible and they can change shape at will; they are like *daityas* and *dānavas*; in battle-strength they equal the gods. Sugrīva's comrades number nine plus five plus seven thousand crores, and a thousand billion and a hundred trillion in addition, shape-changing apes born of gods and *gandharvas*, always at his call in Kiṣkindhā. See the godlike pair of youths standing there: they are Mainda and Dvivida, and both are unequalled in battle; Brahmā allows them to eat ambrosia. They boast of crushing Laṅkā in violent battle. 19.1–7

'The one you can see standing there like a rutting elephant, who would be capable even of convulsing the sea when his anger is aroused, that is the *vānara* who gained access to Laṅkā, to Vaidehī, and to you, my lord. You have seen that *vānara* before; look, he's come back. Renowned Hanumān, Kesarin's eldest son, is celebrated as a Son of the Wind; it was he who leapt the ocean. That shape-changer, that powerful, handsome ape champion, can no more be resisted than the lordly, inexorable Wind. It's said that as a child he watched the sun rise and wanted a drink, so thinking to himself in youthful pride of his strength, "I'll capture the sun; I refuse to die of starvation," he made a journey of three thousand *yojanas*, but when he still could not reach the god whom even gods, sages and *dānavas* find it utterly impossible to approach, he fell down again on to the mountain where the sun rises. Tough though the monkey's jaws are, when he fell on the rocky surface one jaw was cracked: that's why he's called Hanumān. I know all about this ape from previous encounters; his power, grandeur and splendour 19.9–17 are beyond description. He boasts that he'll crush Laṅkā by his own unaided might.

19.18–21 'The swarthy, lotus-eyed hero nearby is the Ikṣvāku chariot warrior, world renowned for his courage, who upholds morality, who does not transgress what's right, who is well versed in Brahmā's missile and in the Vedas – indeed an expert in the Vedas – who could pierce the sky with his arrows and even split mountains open, who is wrathful as Death, who is valiant as Śakra, and whose wife Sītā was carried off from Janasthāna by you: that is Rāma, your majesty, and he is advancing to do battle with you.

19.22–5 'That broad-chested one on his right, brilliant as burnished gold, with copper-coloured eyes and dark curly hair: that is his brother Lakṣmaṇa. He's dear to him as his own life, proficient in diplomacy and warfare, and skilled in all the ritual texts; impetuous, invincible, victorious, valiant, shrewd and mighty, he's Rāma's right-hand man, ever his second self. He pays no heed to his own life in the service of the Rāghava. He boasts that he will certainly kill all the *rākṣasas* in battle.

19.26–7 'There at Rāma's left side, where he has found asylum, surrounded by a troop of *rākṣasas* stands King Vibhīṣaṇa, consecrated by his majestic protector to rule Laṅkā. In his fury against you, he is advancing to do battle.

19.28–33 'And the one you can see standing in the middle, immovable as a mountain: that is the unconquered master of the lords of all monkeys. By his might, his renown, his wisdom, his knowledge, his birth, he stands out among monkeys like Himālaya among mountains. Kiṣkindhā, hidden among dense trees, inaccessible among mountain fastnesses, is where he lives together with his principal commanders. His golden garland glistens, bedecked with a hundred lotuses; Lakṣmī, desire of gods and men alike, resides there. Rāma presented Sugrīva with this garland, with Tārā and with the hereditary kingship over the monkeys after killing Vālin, so, with a thousand crores and a hundred billion, Sugrīva lord of the *vānaras* is advancing to do battle.'

20.1–4 The sight of the ape commanders Śuka had listed, of his own brother Vibhīṣaṇa standing beside Rāma, of Rāma's intrepid right-hand man Lakṣmaṇa, and of Sugrīva, terrifyingly valiant king of all the *vānaras* rather perturbed Rāvaṇa; when Śuka and Sāraṇa finished their report he grew angry and furiously berated those stout warriors with cutting words, his voice choking with rage.

'For courtiers to make statements displeasing to their king, 20.5–13
who has power to punish or reward, is not at all in keeping with their dependent status. It is certainly inexpedient for you two to praise hostile enemies in that way when they are advancing to do battle. By not grasping the central tenet of the treatises on kingship that should rule your lives you have been honouring your teachers, instructors and elders in vain. Either that, or you have not taken in and understood the full significance of what you have learned. With stupid courtiers like you to serve me, it's only good luck that keeps me alive! Why aren't you afraid for your lives to speak harsh words to me, whose tongue has the power to decree either good or ill? Trees may survive a forest fire, but blackguards incurring the censure of the king don't survive his retribution. I would kill these two villains for praising the enemy if it weren't that their past record of support inclines my anger to clemency. Out of my sight! Get out! I don't want to kill you. I remember what you've done for me in the past. This pair are dead to me now they've forgotten my favours and turned their backs on me.' Humiliated by his tirade, Śuka and Sāraṇa saluted Rāvaṇa, wished him victory, and slunk away.

Daśagrīva told Mahodara, who was in attendance, to find 20.14–16
him at once some spies expert in strategy. Spies were hastily produced at the king's command; they presented themselves, saluted and acclaimed him with hopes of victory. These spies were reliable, intrepid warriors in whose loyalty Rāvaṇa had confidence, so the *rākṣasa* overlord issued his instructions.

'Go and reconnoitre: what does Rāma intend to do? Who 20.17–19
are his favourites and intimate advisers? How does he sleep, how does he wake? What other plans does he have? When you have thoroughly verified everything, you are to return without

delay. When a well-informed sovereign has gained intelligence through espionage, he will overcome his enemy's attack without difficulty.'

20.20–23; 21.1–2 The spies were delighted to accept their orders. They circumambulated the *rākṣasa* lord, then went to find Rāma and Lakṣmaṇa. They went in disguise to mount Suvela, where they saw Rāma and Lakṣmaṇa, but Vibhīṣaṇa the righteous lord of *rākṣasas* saw the *rākṣasas* standing there, surprised them and took them prisoner; they were groaning and dazed when they arrived back in Laṅkā after suffering at the hands of the nimble, valiant *vānaras*. The spies then briefed Laṅkā's overlord about Rāma's encampment on mount Suvela with his dauntless host. This report from the spies of the arrival of Rāma's mighty force rather perturbed Rāvaṇa and he addressed Śārdūla:

21.3–4 'You are downcast, night-roamer, and you do not have your accustomed colour: have you perhaps suffered at the hands of our angry enemies?' Nervous and fearful, tigerlike Śārdūla responded feebly to the *rākṣasa* tiger's demand.

21.5–13 'Your majesty, it's impossible for you to spy on those bulls of *vānaras*: they are valiant and mighty, and the Rāghava watches over them. Nor is it possible to open talks with them; there's no question about that. Mountainlike *vānaras* guard all approach routes. I was identified when I had scarcely penetrated the host, before I had been able to gain any intelligence; I was set upon by numerous assailants and practically torn to shreds. I was kneed, punched, bitten and slapped, and paraded around by the incensed mighty apes; then after I had been paraded everywhere I was taken before Rāma's council, panic-stricken, my senses failing and with all my limbs streaming with blood. The apes were battering me though I begged for mercy, but the Rāghava rescued me and by some chance I've managed to survive. Rāma has filled in the ocean with mountains and rocks, he's reached the gate of Laṅkā, and he's taken up position with his weapons: he's deploying the Garuḍa formation, flanked on all sides by apes. Now he's released me he's advancing with great power on Laṅkā itself. Quickly, before he reaches the rampart, you must act in one of two ways:

either offer to return Sītā with all speed, or mount a stout counter-attack.'

Rāvaṇa overlord of the *rākṣasas* burned with indignation to 21.14–15
hear Śārdūla's recommendation. 'I will not return Sītā, not if gods, *gandharvas* and *dānavas* should fight me, not from fear of all the world.'

After this initial reaction, mighty Rāvaṇa went on, 'You sir, 21.16–18
you've observed the army. Which of these monkeys are the leading warriors? What are they like, these indomitable *vanaras*? How effective are they? Whose sons and grandsons are they? Give me an accurate report, *rākṣasa*, then when I know their strengths and weaknesses I will take the offensive. It is imperative to size up the opposition before engaging battle.'

At Rāvaṇa's command that outstanding spy Śārdūla began 21.19–35
laying his report before Rāvaṇa. 'First, your majesty, there is the son of Ṛkṣarajas, who will be very hard to defeat in battle; next there is Gadgada's son, the renowned Jāmbavān, whose son devastated the *rākṣasas* single-handed. Then there's Suṣeṇa, sir: he's the righteous, heroic Son of Dharma; and Soma's son, your majesty, the monkey Dadhimukha. There's Sumukha and there's Durmukha, and there's the *vānara* Vegadarśin: he was begotten by Brahmā, definitely Death in the form of a *vānara*. There's General Nīla himself, Son of the Sacrificial Fire, and there's the Wind's son, renowned as Hanumān. There's Aṅgada, a dauntless, mighty youth, grandson of Śakra, there's a pair, Mainda and Dvivida, mighty offspring of the Aśvins, and there are five Sons of Death equal to Time that puts an end to all: Gaja, Gavākṣa, Gavaya, Śarabha and Gandhamādana. There are Śveta and Jyotirmukha, Sons of the Sun, and there's Varuṇa's son, the monkey Hemakūṭa. There's Viśvakarman's son Nala, a heroic, outstanding monkey, and ten crores of heroic *vānaras*, glorious sons of gods, thirsting for battle – I can't even begin to list the remainder. And then there's that youth with the brawn of a lion who killed Dūṣaṇa, Khara and Triśiras: the son of Daśaratha! He's killed Virādha and Death-like Kabandha. There's no one in the world to equal Rāma in valour. Who on this earth could recite the virtues of

Rāma, who killed so many *rākṣasas* in Janasthāna? Righteous Lakṣmaṇa too, that bull elephant: not even Indra Vāsava could survive being the target of his arrows. Even the *rākṣasa* champion, your brother Vibhīṣaṇa, is there: he's had Laṅkā city conferred on him, and he's devoted himself to furthering the Rāghava's cause. That's all I can tell you about the *vānara* army encamped on mount Suvela: it's for you, my lord, to direct the consequential action.'

22.1–3 So the king's spies made their report in Laṅkā about the Rāghava's encampment on mount Suvela with his dauntless host. This report from the spies of the arrival of Rāma's mighty force rather perturbed Rāvaṇa and he addressed his courtiers: 'The counsellors are to assemble at once, *rākṣasas*, for all to deliberate diligently now the time has come for us to make our plans.'

22.4–7 When they heard his command, the counsellors came running and he discussed the situation with his *rākṣasa* courtiers, at once seeking their advice about the best course of action; then, unbowed, he dismissed the court and entered his private apartments, summoned Vidyujjihva, an expert in powerful magic, and went to Maithilī's quarters. The *rākṣasa* overlord said to the cunning Vidyujjihva:

22.7–8 'We will use magic to deceive Sītā Janaka's daughter. Magic me a head of the Rāghava, night-roamer, bring it and a big bow and some arrows, and come with me.'

22.9–12 The night-roamer Vidyujjihva assented to these instructions, pleasing the king, who presented him with a jewel. Then Vaiśravaṇa's mighty junior went to the *aśoka* grove and saw the miserable woman suffering such unmerited misery: she was sitting on the ground, head bowed, wrapped up in her grief, her thoughts fixed on her husband, consigned to the *aśoka* grove and closely surrounded by fearsome *rākṣasīs*. He crept up on Sītā, exultantly announced himself and brazenly addressed Janaka's daughter.

22.13–15 'Khara's killer, the Rāghava, the husband in whose favour you recoil from my advances, has been killed in battle. I have completely severed your root and humbled your pride. This misfortune of yours, Sītā, will make you become my wife. Worthless, deluded woman, you think you're so clever, but you've lost your purpose in life! Listen, Sītā, while I tell you about your husband's death; it was terrible as the death of Vṛtra.

'The Rāghava arrived at the edge of the sea surrounded by a vast army led by the *vānara* lord: he was going to kill me! Rāma encamped with his vast army when he reached the sea's southern shore as the sun was setting. The army was fatigued by the march when it arrived and was stood down; at midnight, when it was sleeping securely, spies made an initial reconnaissance, then that army of Rāma's and Lakṣmaṇa's was destroyed at night by my vast army led by Prahasta. Repeatedly the *rākṣasas* rained down on the *vānaras* javelins, maces, swords, discuses, great iron bars, skeins of arrows, pikes, gleaming cudgels, staves, lances, darts, discuses and clubs. Then at a stroke Prahasta, broadsword in hand, violently severed Rāma's head as he slept. Vibhīṣaṇa jumped up, but was surprised and captured; Lakṣmaṇa and all the monkeys were scattered in all directions; Sugrīva, overlord of the monkeys, lies with his fine neck broken;[8] Hanumān lies with his jaw smashed, struck down by *rākṣasas*. Then Jāmbavān fell to his knees, felled like a tree, killed in the battle, riddled with spears. That pair of *vānara* bulls, Mainda and Dvivida, died screaming, shrieking and groaning, spattered with blood. Cut in two by a sword, Panasa the foe-crusher crashed to the ground like a *panasa* tree. Darīmukha is lying in a ditch riddled with bolts, and mighty Kumuda is moaning, cut down by arrows. Aṅgada is a fallen anklet; when the *rākṣasas* reached him, they riddled him with arrows and felled him to the ground spewing blood. Apes have been crushed, some by elephants, some by squadrons of chariots; they have been laid low and shredded like clouds by a boisterous wind. Others have been struck from behind as they fled in panic, *rākṣasas* pursuing them like lions after great elephants. Some have plunged into the ocean, some have taken to the sky, and bears and *vānaras* alike have climbed into trees. On ocean shores, on mountains, in forests, many are the 22.16–34 tawny-eyed apes the hideous-eyed *rākṣasas* have killed. And so your husband and his army have been slain by my army; here, streaming blood and encrusted with dust, is his head.'

22.35–6 Then Rāvaṇa, invincible lord of the *rākṣasas*, instructed a *rākṣasī* in Sītā's hearing, 'Fetch the savage *rākṣasa* Vidyujjihva, the one who brought the Rāghava's head from the battle.'

22.37–9 Then, carrying that head and the bow, Vidyujjihva stepped forward and bowed his head to Rāvaṇa, and King Rāvaṇa said to his constant companion as he stood there, Vidyujjihva of the lolling tongue, 'Place the head of Dāśarathi before Sītā at once, so that the wretched woman can clearly see what her husband has come to.'

22.40–42 On these orders the *rākṣasa* threw down before Sītā the head she loved to look at, and quickly vanished. Rāvaṇa threw down in addition the great gleaming bow famed throughout the three worlds, telling Sītā, 'Here is your Rāma's bow, bowstring and all; Prahasta brought it back during the night after he had killed that mortal.'

[*Sītā is taken in and mourns, but after Rāvaṇa has left to confer with his advisers a friendly rākṣasī called Saramā tells her she has been tricked by magic.*]

25.1–2 At Saramā's speech the distressed, swooning woman recovered like the earth when watered by the sky. Out of friendship her friend was anxious to comfort her; realizing the time had arrived for a well-timed offer, she smiled and suggested,

25.3–4 'Black-eyed lady, I would make bold to go in secret to Rāma myself and give him a message from you to tell him you are well, and then to come back. Not the Wind, not even Garuḍa can follow my path when I course through the vault of heaven.'

25.5–11 Sītā replied sweetly to Saramā's offer in a soft voice still faint from her earlier grief. 'You are capable of reaching the heavens or even Rasātala. I know you could achieve the impossible for my sake. If you are determined to do something to please me, I should like you to go after Rāvaṇa and let me know what he is doing, for cruel Rāvaṇa, he who makes his enemies roar, bewilders me with his magic power, the villain, just as if I had drunk alcohol. He has me threatened all the time, he has me menaced repeatedly by the savage *rākṣasīs* perpetually guarding me. I'm in a turmoil of suspicion and I'm not in command of my mind, I've been in such a turmoil of terror about him since I've been in the *aśoka* grove. If you could bring me a full report of the discussion, or even what they decide, that would do me a very great favour.'

Sītā's plea was met with caresses and a tender reply from Saramā, her voice choked with sobs: 'If that is what you wish, Jānakī, that is what I'll go and do; I'll be back when I'm in possession of your enemy's intention: you'll see.' 25.12–13

With these words she went off and got close to Rāvaṇa, and heard what that *rākṣasa* was discussing with his counsellors. When she had heard what the unyielding villain had resolved, she hurried back to the *aśoka* grove, went in and saw Janaka's daughter watching out for her like Śrī with a withered lotus. When tender-hearted Saramā got back, Sītā hugged her with great affection and sat her down. 'Sit down comfortably', she said, 'and tell me in detail all this villain Rāvaṇa's plans.' 25.14–18

As Sītā trembled, Saramā replied with an account of all the deliberations of Rāvaṇa and his counsellors. 'Vaidehī, the *rākṣasa* lord's mother made a strong plea for your release, supported by the senior counsellor Aviddha: "Do homage to the Lord of Men, and give Maithilī back to him. You've seen the prodigious feat he performed in Janasthāna, and how Hanumān leapt the ocean to see her: that should be enough for you! What other man on earth could have fought and slaughtered those *rākṣasas*?" His mother and the senior counsellors persisted in their pleas, but he's as incapable of letting go of you as a miser is of his wealth. He'll not bring himself to let you go till he's been killed in battle, Maithilī: that's the decision of this savage and his ministers. He is obdurate in his determination, so eager is he for death. Fear won't make him release you as long as he's unvanquished in battle: nothing will, short of the total annihilation of the *rākṣasas*, himself included. By whatever means, Rāma will kill Rāvaṇa in battle with his honed arrows and take you back to Ayodhyā, you black-eyed beauty.' 25.19–26

Meanwhile, the earth-shaking din of drums and conches 25.27;
could be heard throughout the armies: that noise of mingled 26.1–4

drums and conches heralded the advance of Rāma, the Rāghava, the mighty conqueror of enemy citadels. Hearing the noise, Rāvaṇa lord of the *rākṣasas* took thought for a moment, then looked at his courtiers; mighty Rāvaṇa then addressed the whole court, his voice resounding throughout the counsel chamber. 'My lords, I've listened to all you've had to say about the crossing of the ocean, about his prowess, and about the huge force Rāma has assembled; but I also know how truly valiant your lordships are in battle.'

26.5–10 Then a very wise *rākṣasa* called Mālyavān, Rāvaṇa's mother's uncle, responded to his declaration: 'Your majesty, that king who controls his instincts with wisdom and exercises statesmanship long reigns sovereign and triumphs over his enemies. His empire increases by the contracting of alliances, or the waging of war on his enemies, as occasion requires to promote his own interests: a weaker or equal king should contract an alliance – an opponent should not be underrated – but a stronger may make war. Hence, Rāvaṇa, I recommend contracting an alliance with Rāma. Sītā is the object of the operation: let her be restored to him. Gods, sages and *gandharvas* alike are all desirous of victory for him. Let there be no hostility with him; be pleased to contract an alliance with him.

26.11–20 'Now the blessed Grand Father created two opposing parties, gods and anti-gods, supporters respectively of *dharma* and *adharma*:[9] the noble gods are recognized as being on the side of *dharma*, Rāvaṇa, and the *rākṣasas* and anti-gods of *adharma*. When it was the Kṛta Age, *dharma* devoured *adharma*; now it is Tiṣya, *adharma* is devouring *dharma*. By rampaging around the worlds attacking *dharma* and promoting *adharma* you've in fact been lending strength to our opponents. That snake *adharma* has battened on your recklessness till it is we who are being devoured and the cause of the gods that is being advanced; it is tipping the balance in favour of the gods. Self-indulgent and self-willed, you have aroused great trepidation among the fire-pure sages, whose power is as irresistible as a blazing fire. These Twice-Born are intent on promoting *dharma* by their asceticism and holiness, continually offering every kind of the most excellent sacrifices, together with oblations duly offered into the fires, and with recitation of the Vedas. Vedic chants arose from them when the *rākṣasas* were overcome, scattered in all directions like thunder in the hot season. The smoke rising from the fire-oblations of fire-pure sages pervades the ten Directions and strips *rākṣasas* of their energy, and the fierce asceticism performed in all those holy regions by those who are committed to their vows commits the *rākṣasas* to torment.

'I foresee the destruction of all the *rākṣasas*, so many differ- 26.21–30
ent awesome portents have I seen. Dreadful clouds are braying thunder and terrifying all Laṅkā with showers of hot blood. Weeping steeds are shedding tears. Standards have toppled and faded, losing their wonted lustre. Wild beasts, jackals and vultures keep on invading Laṅkā in packs, their horrific shrieking echoed in people's dreams by the mockery of sombre women with white teeth pillaging their homes. In the houses dogs are devouring the *bali* offerings. Cows are giving birth to donkeys, mongooses to rats. Cats are mating with leopards, boars with bitches, and *kinnaras* even with *rākṣasas* and men. Pigeons are roaming about, pale, red-footed birds, dispatched by Time to destroy the *rākṣasas*. Squabblesome mynahs, caught and tethered, are flying around in the houses screaming "*vīcī-kūcī*". Time, in the person of a dun-dark, gaping-jawed, hairless monster, is on the prowl, inspecting everyone's house in turn. These and more are the evil omens springing up.'

But the ten-faced villain was in thrall to Time and he would 27.1–2
not accept Mālyavān's beneficial advice. Anger overcame him: his brow contorted into a scowl and his eyes rolled with resentment as he declared to Mālyavān:

'I will not listen to your speech, since you have gone over to 27.3–13
the enemy. You may have meant well, but your words are detrimental and vicious. Rāma has been cast out by his father to live in the forest; he's a miserable mortal who's had to turn to monkeys for aid; what do you think he can do on his own? I am lord of the *rākṣasas*, I strike terror into the gods; in what way do you think me inferior? There is no feat of arms in which I am inferior. I suspect you are envious of my courage

or have sided with the enemy and that's why you're berating me; maybe it's the enemy that's put you up to it. What scholar who has studied the treatises in depth would direct harsh words at a well-established potentate, unless an enemy had put him up to it? I've brought Sītā here from the forest, like Śrī without her lotus; what fear could make me give her back to the Rāghava? In a few days you shall see me slay the Rāghava – Sugrīva and Lakṣmaṇa too – surrounded by crores of *vānaras*. Of whom shall that Rāvaṇa be afraid, he against whom not even the gods can withstand a duel? I would be broken in two rather than bow before anyone. This is an innate flaw in my character; there's no changing one's natural disposition. But if against all the odds Rāma has managed to build a causeway across the sea, is it any wonder that fear should grip you? This Rāma may have crossed the sea with the *vānara* army, but he shall not go back alive, I promise you; and that's the truth.'

27.14–15 Mālyavān was crestfallen when he realized the rage and fury with which Rāvaṇa spoke, and said not another word; after praising the king with the customary good wishes for victory, Mālyavān took his leave and went to his own quarters.

27.16–21 Rāvaṇa consulted his ministers and deliberated with them, then the *rākṣasa* took unparalleled steps to improve Laṅkā's security. The *rākṣasa* Prahasta he appointed to the eastern gate and the valiant pair Mahāpārśva and Mahodara to the southern; then to the western gate he appointed his son Indrajit, a powerful magician, surrounded by many *rākṣasas*. Appointing Śuka and Sāraṇa to the northern gate of the city, he told the counsellors, 'I'll be there in person.' At the central keep he established with numerous *rākṣasas* Virūpākṣa, a *rākṣasa* of great courage and prowess. With this disposition of his forces around Laṅkā the bull of the *rākṣasas* thought his goal was achieved. He was in the grip of Fate.

28.1–3 The king of men and the king of *vānaras*, the monkey Son of the Wind, Jāmbavān king of bears, the *rākṣasa* Vibhīṣaṇa, Vālin's son Aṅgada, Saumitri, the monkey Śarabha, Suṣeṇa and his heirs Mainda and Dvivida, Gaja, Gavākṣa, Kumuda, Nala and Panasa too assembled when they had reached enemy territory, and made their plans.

'From here we can see Laṅkā, the city watched over by Rāvaṇa; even the gods together with anti-gods, *nāgas* and *gandharvas* would find it hard to conquer. Let us consider carefully the best means of achieving our goal, for the *rākṣasa* overlord Rāvaṇa is always on his guard here.' 28.4–5

As they were talking in this way, Rāvaṇa's younger brother Vibhīṣaṇa made a speech that was urbane and to the point: 'My ministers Anala and Śarabha, Sampāti and Praghasa, are back from an expedition to Laṅkā city. They all became birds and penetrated the enemy army, surveyed what disposition has been ordered, and returned. Listen, Rāma, while I tell you in detail all they report about the dispositions evil Rāvaṇa has made. Prahasta has been sent to the eastern gate and taken up position there with his force, and the valiant pair Mahāpārśva and Mahodara are at the southern. Indrajit, Rāvaṇa's son, is stationed at the west gate, surrounded by a large number of *rākṣasas* wielding spears, swords, and bows; but at the northern gate of the city, with many thousands of fully-armed *rākṣasas*, Rāvaṇa has stationed himself. At the central keep, with a great force of *rākṣasas* equipped with pikes, swords and bows, is stationed Virūpākṣa. My ministers all observed these various defensive arrangements in Laṅkā and then returned with speed. There are one thousand elephants in the city, ten thousand chariots, twice ten thousand horses and a full crore of *rākṣasas*, night-roamers selected by the *rākṣasa* king to be ever valiant, powerful and death-dealing in battle. Each single fighting *rākṣasa* is drawn from a pool of one thousand thousand, your majesty.' 28.6–18

Vibhīṣaṇa augmented his counsellors' report from Laṅkā, 28.19–23
telling lotus-petal-eyed Rāma, 'Now Rāma, when Rāvaṇa made war on Kubera there went forth sixty hundred thousand *rākṣasas*, in prowess, courage, energy, sturdiness of character and arrogance the equals of evil Rāvaṇa. In this situation you must not be carried away by fury, nor is it my wish to frighten you: I am urging you to unleash your wrath, for you have prowess enough to overcome even the gods. My lord, you have the support of an army strong in all four divisions; deploy the *vānara* host and you will pulverize Rāvaṇa.'

28.24–34 While Rāvaṇa's younger brother was still speaking, the Rāghava was issuing his instructions for the slaughter of his enemies. 'At the eastern gate of Laṅkā it is that bull of a *vānara* Nīla who should take on Prahasta, accompanied by a large number of *vānaras*. At the southern gate Vālin's son Aṅgada accompanied by a large force is to attack Mahāpārśva and Mahodara. Hanumān, that superlative Son of the Wind, is to put the western gate under pressure and gain entry with a large monkey force. But as for that savage who takes pleasure in hurting groups of *daityas* and *dānavas*, noble sages too, relying on the power granted him by his boon to roam all the worlds tormenting their inhabitants – as for that *rākṣasa* lord, him I am resolved to kill myself. Together, Saumitri and I will put the city's northern gate under pressure and lead the host to Rāvaṇa. The central keep shall be for the mighty lord of the *vānaras*, and Jāmbavān king of the bears and also the *rākṣasa* lord's younger brother. Furthermore, the apes are not to take on human form when fighting. In this war let us adopt this means of identification for the *vānara* army: *vānaras*, distinguish yourselves by keeping to your natural form. Just we seven will fight the foe as humans: I, of course, along with my very mighty brother Lakṣmaṇa, and also my five comrades – Vibhīṣaṇa and the others.'

28.35; 29.1–2 With these instructions to Vibhīṣaṇa about the successful achievement of their objective, Rāma judiciously came to a conclusion: the decision to ascend Suvela. Once he had taken the decision, endorsed by Lakṣmaṇa, to climb Suvela, Rāma turned to Sugrīva and to Vibhīṣaṇa, the night-roamer who was virtuous and dependable, whose counsel was right and proper, and addressed them in a loud, clear voice.

29.3–7 'Come on! We're going to climb Suvela, this lord of mountains, this store of a hundred ores! This night we'll camp there and inspect Laṅkā, lair of that depraved *rākṣasa* who has brought down death upon himself by carrying off my wife! The deliberate act of that evil *rākṣasa* is a crime against morality, against propriety, and against family values! My mounting anger at the crime of this villain, notorious as the worst of *rākṣasas*, will be demonstrated when I slaughter the *rākṣasas*.

It takes one individual caught in the noose of Time to commit a crime, but that wicked sin can bring destruction on the whole family.'

After this consultation Rāma set off to climb the glittering slopes of Suvela and camp there, filled with anger towards Rāvaṇa. Alert and brandishing his bow and arrow, Lakṣmaṇa followed at his back, relishing a deed worthy of his superlative prowess. After him climbed Sugrīva and his ministers, then Vibhīṣaṇa. Hanumān, Aṅgada, Nīla, Mainda and Dvivida too, Gaja, Gavākṣa, Gavaya, Śarabha, Gandhamādana, Panasa and Kumuda as well, and Hara and the commander Rambha: these and many other fleet, mountain-roaming *vānaras*, imbued with the force of the wind, climbed up Suvela behind the Rāghava in their hundreds. They had not been climbing long when, from all over, they were able to see the city on the summit, apparently hanging from the sky: goodly Laṅkā with its fine gateways was visible to the ape chiefs, adorned with superb walls and thronged with *rākṣasas*, the swarthy night-roamers looking to the ape champions like a further wall standing on top of the high ramparts. At the sight, while Rāma gazed, all the *vānaras* there and then let out loud roars in their eagerness to fight the *rākṣasas*. Then the sun sank down, reddened by the twilight, leaving the dark shades to be lit up by a full moon. 29.8–17

The *rākṣasas* went to Rāvaṇa's palace and reported that Rāma and the *vānaras* were besieging the city; the night-roamer's anger flared at the news of the siege of the town. He repeated his instructions, then climbed to the top of his palace and saw Laṅkā with its mountains, forests and groves surrounded on all sides by countless troops of battle-hungry apes. As he gazed at the *vānaras* swallowing up the whole earth, he pondered hard how they could be destroyed. After a great deal of thought Rāvaṇa regained his resolve and looked wide-eyed at the Rāghava and the hordes of apes. 32.1–5

As the lord of *rākṣasas* watched, these hosts successively scaled Laṅkā in their desire to please the Rāghava. Ready to lay down their lives for Rāma's sake, the copper-faced, golden-hued monkeys attacked Laṅkā with a battery of *sāls*, 32.6–13 palmyras and rocks, pounding gateways and lofty palace-roofs alike with trees, mountain-tops and their fists. The *vānaras* filled in the clear waters of the moats with dust and with mountain-tops, with straws and with logs, then commanders of companies a thousand strong, companies of a crore, and others with companies a hundred crores strong, led the leap to Laṅkā; huge as tuskers the leaping monkeys trampled the golden gateways, smashed barbicans tall as Kailāsa's peak, leapt here, leapt there, roaring as they leapt at Laṅkā, 'Victory to Rāma's supreme strength and to Lakṣmaṇa's great might! Victory to King Sugrīva, ally of the Rāghava!'

32.14–24 With such shouts and roars the shape-changing monkeys hurled themselves at the Laṅkā rampart. Vīrabāhu, Subāhu and the forest-roamer Nala charged the rampart, then these ape commanders established a bridgehead there and quickly set up their headquarters. Accompanied by ten crores, Kumuda besieged the east gate and heroically took up position there in triumph with his apes. Accompanied by twenty crores, the monkey warrior Śatabali reached the south gate, besieged it and heroically took up position there. Accompanied by sixty crores, the ape Suṣeṇa, father of Tārā, went to the west gate, besieged it and heroically took up position there. With Sugrīva, lord of the apes, Rāma and Saumitri won through to the north gate, besieged it and heroically took up position there. Accompanied by a crore, Gavākṣa the enormous dreadful-looking langur heroically took up position beside Rāma. Accompanied by a crore of bears of ferocious vigour, Dhūmra the foe-crusher heroically took up position beside Rāma. Accompanied by his alert comrades, mighty Vibhīṣaṇa, mace in hand and fully equipped, heroically took up position there. Gaja, Gavākṣa, Gavaya, Śarabha and Gandhamādana encircled the ape army protectively.

32.25–32 Rage coursed through Rāvaṇa's whole being; hurriedly the *rākṣasa* lord ordered a sortie by his entire army. At Rāvaṇa's urging his gleeful troops poured out like waves in the great ocean, constantly replenished; before all were out, *rākṣasas* were engaging *vānaras* in a battle fierce as that between gods and anti-gods of old. With blazing maces, with spears, pikes and axes they lashed out savagely at the *vānaras*, boasting of their mighty deeds. The gigantic *vānaras* violently counter-attacked the *rākṣasas* with trees and mountain-tops, claws and teeth, while from up on the rampart other fearsome *rākṣasas* were piercing them on the ground with javelins, swords and pikes. The *vānaras* on the ground were enraged; up leapt monkeys, felling *rākṣasas* standing on the rampart. The tumultuous, prodigious battle that broke out between *rākṣasas* and *vānaras* was a mire of flesh and blood.

Great was the ferocity of the battle that raged as the noble 33.1–15
vānaras fought the *rākṣasas*. With standards flaming like fire and exquisite armour, *rākṣasa* tigers set out on horses with golden chaplets and on chariots shining like the sun. The savage *rākṣasas* made all ten Directions resound with their cries of victory for Rāvaṇa, but that host of shape-changing *rākṣasas* was attacked by a large force of *vānaras* just as eager for victory. As *rākṣasas* confronted *vānaras*, duels developed: the glorious *rākṣasa* Indrajit fought against Vālin's son Aṅgada, like Andhaka against Tryambaka; Saṃpāti, always irresistible in battle, against Prajaṅgha; against Jambumālin the *vānara* Hanumān joined battle; Rāvaṇa's younger brother, the frenzied *rākṣasa* Vibhīṣaṇa, met violent Mitraghna in battle; mighty Gaja encountered the *rākṣasa* Tapana; glorious Nīla fought against Nikumbha; Sugrīva lord of the *vānaras* met Praghasa; majestic Lakṣmaṇa met Virūpākṣa in battle; dauntless Agniketu and the *rākṣasa* Raśmiketu, Suptaghna and Yajñakopa too were taken on by Rāma; Vajramuṣṭi by Mainda and Aśaniprabha by Dvivida – these ferocious *rākṣasas* were taken on by the champion monkey pair; the fierce *rākṣasa* warrior Pratapana, an indomitable fighter, battled against vehement Nala; powerful Suṣeṇa, that great monkey, that renowned Son of Dharma, fought against Vidyunmālin; and other fearsome *vānaras* plunged time and again into single combat with many *rākṣasa* opponents.

Great was the battle, tumultuous and horrifying, between 33.16–34
rākṣasas and *vānara* heroes as they strove for victory; from the bodies of apes and *rākṣasas* streamed rivers of blood, bearing along rafts of corpses through hair instead of weeds. Like Indra

Śatakratu with his thunderbolt, infuriated Indrajit clubbed Aṅgada, the hero who could cut through hostile armies, but the glorious, indomitable monkey Aṅgada pounded his chariot's carcass of glittering gold, his horses and charioteer too. Saṃpāti was hit by Prajaṅgha with three arrows, then hit Prajaṅgha with an *aśvakarṇa* tree in the heat of the battle. Mighty Jambumālin, mounted on his chariot, furious in the fray, wounded Hanumān on the breastbone with a chariot-spear, but Hanumān Son of the Wind attacked his chariot, rapidly smashing it and the *rākṣasa* too with the flat of his hand. Though wounded in the limbs with his sharp arrows, Gaja battered the swift-handed *rākṣasa* Tapana with a fist like a mountain-top. Praghasa seemed to be swallowing up armies, but the *vānara* ruler Sugrīva cleaved him with a *saptaparṇa* tree and killed him. Lakṣmaṇa harassed Virūpākṣa with a shower of arrows, then killed the dreadful-looking *rākṣasa* with a single shaft. Dauntless Agniketu and the *rākṣasa* Raśmiketu, Suptaghna and Yajñakopa wounded Rāma with arrows, but with four dread battle-arrows like blazing flames Rāma angrily severed the heads of all four. Vajramuṣṭi, cut down by a violent blow from Mainda's fist, collapsed to the ground like a city watch-tower, chariot and horses too. Dvivida, whose touch was like a thunderbolt, struck down Aśaniprabha with a mountain-peak within sight of all the *rākṣasas*. Nikumbha, though, was battling against Nīla; his sharp arrows tore into that dark collyrium-like mound like sunbeams into a cloud, then that swift-handed night-roamer Nikumbha attacked again, ripping Nīla open with a hundred more arrows and sneering, until Nīla, a second Viṣṇu in battle, retaliated by slicing off the heads of Nikumbha and his charioteer with a chariot-wheel.

33.43–5 Terrible was the fighting taking place with arrows, swords and maces, with spears, lances and javelins. The ground was littered with chariots and war horses, shattered and smashed, with slain elephants in rut, with *vānaras* and *rākṣasas*, with broken wheels, axles, yokes and poles; headless corpses of *vānaras* and *rākṣasas* lay heaped up in all directions. The conflict was as tumultuous as the battle between the gods and the anti-gods, and packs of jackals stood by.

Even as the *vānaras* and *rākṣasas* were fighting, the sun went home to mount Asta and night came on to snatch away lives. Then *vānaras* and *rākṣasas*, staunch in their mutual hostility, ferocious and desperate for victory, embarked on a night battle. With cries of 'You're a *rākṣasa*!' from apes and 'You're an ape!' from *rākṣasas*, they cut each other down in the battle in that fearsome gloom. 'Strike! Tear apart! Come on! Why are you running away?' Such was the tumult of shouts ringing out through the gloom. Black *rākṣasas* were visible through the gloom from the gleaming of their golden armour, like imperious mountains with forests and grass alight. In that impenetrable gloom frenzied *rākṣasas* fell furiously upon the monkeys to devour them; but they, fearsome too in their rage, leapt at the horses with their golden chaplets and flame-like pennants, tearing them apart with their sharp teeth, clawing and digging their teeth into elephants, mahouts, chariots, flags and standards, beside themselves with anger. Lakṣmaṇa and Rāma too struck down the foremost *rākṣasas*, visible or invisible, with arrows like venomous serpents. The dust kicked up from the earth by the horses' hooves and stirred up by the chariot-wheels clogged the ears and eyes of the fighters. As the savage, horrifying battle raged, rivers of blood spurted out and gushed along, and there arose a prodigious banging of drums, tabors and cymbals mingled with the blaring of conches and pipes. Horrible was the din from weapons, from *vānaras*, and from the groans of dying *rākṣasas*. The battleground was strewn with an offering, not of flowers but of weapons; it was unrecognizable and impassable, churned to mud by streaming blood. That night that bore away apes and *rākṣasas* was as terrible as the inexorable Night of Time that bears away all beings. 34.1–15

Then in that fearsome gloom, the gleeful *rākṣasas* attacked Rāma with showers of arrows giving out as they fell an angry roar like the turbulent crashing of the seven seas. In the mere blink of an eye, with six arrows honed and blazing like flames, Rāma struck down six of those night-roamers: Yajñaśatru the invincible, Mahāpārśva and Mahodara, Vajradaṃṣṭra the giant, and the pair Śuka and Sāraṇa, wounded to the quick by the flood of Rāma's arrows, slunk away from the battle at their 34.16–23 last gasp. Then the all-powerful warrior made every direction round about bright with his arrows, their shafts glittering with gold and blazing like flames; the *rākṣasa* warriors who had remained to face him rushed forward but were destroyed like moths by a fire. The well-feathered, gold-notched shafts he shot in their thousands made the night bright as if with autumnal fireflies.

34.24–6 Then that frightful night was made more frightful by the screaming of *rākṣasas* and the bellowing of apes. The abundant ravines of mount Trikūṭa seemed to howl with the hullabaloo as it swelled all around. Gigantic langurs no less dark than the gloom enfolding them choked the life from night-roamers with their arms.

34.27–30 Aṅgada was determined to kill his opponent in the duel and quickly struck down Rāvaṇi's charioteer and horses, but Indrajit, horses slain, charioteer slain too by Aṅgada, abandoned his chariot and used his magic skill to make himself invisible. Once that evil Rāvaṇi had made use of the boon Brahmā had granted him and vanished, Rāvaṇi, that unscrupulous warrior, invisible in his frenzy, let fly honed arrows flashing like lightning, until the furious *rākṣasa* had wounded Rāma and Lakṣmaṇa in all their limbs with his savage, serpentine shafts.

35.1–10 Powerful, majestic Prince Rāma commissioned ten *vānara* commanders to find out where he had gone: Suṣeṇa's two heirs, that bull of a monkey Nīla, Vālin's son Aṅgada, bold Śarabha, Vinata, Jāmbavān, mighty Sānuprastha, Ṛṣabha and Ṛṣabhaskandha were the ones selected by the foe-slayer. The delighted apes brandished fearsome trees, then all took to the sky to search the ten Directions, but Rāvaṇi countered their ferocious onslaught with his even more ferocious arrows, handling his fine missile with expertise. Wounded and bleeding from his bolts in their fierce onslaught, the *vānaras* could no more see him in the darkness than the sun hidden behind clouds. All-conquering Rāvaṇi drove his arrows into Rāma and Lakṣmaṇa, piercing them all over to the quick until those heroic brothers, Rāma and Lakṣmaṇa, had their whole bodies swathed in the venomous arrows of the furious Indrajit. Blood poured from their veins till both looked like flame-trees in bloom. Then the invisible Rāvaṇi taunted the brothers, his eyes reddened at the edges and his body like a heap of powdered collyrium.

'Not even Śakra Lord of the Thirty can see or get near me 35.11–12
when I become invisible to fight, so how could you two? Rage completely encompasses me: I'm dispatching you to Yama's realm.'

So saying he transfixed virtuous Rāma and Lakṣmaṇa 35.13–25
with sharp arrows, shouting in exultation. Dark as a heap of powdered collyrium, he flourished his broad bow and savagely released more and more arrows in that great battle. He knew the vulnerable points of Rāma and Lakṣmaṇa, and into those vulnerable points the warrior plunged his sharpened arrows, yelling repeatedly. In the heart of the battle, in no more than the twinkling of an eye, both were bound in chains of arrows, unable to see what was happening. Wounded all over their bodies, arrowheads embedded in them, they tottered like two of great Indra's standards broken free from their ropes. Wounded to the quick and weakened, the heroic great archers toppled: those Lords of the Earth fell to the earth, that bed of heroes, where those heroes lay streaming with blood, distressed and crushed, their whole bodies encased in arrows. Not one of their limbs was left unwounded save their fingers, down to their hands no part was not slashed or immobilized by the unerring arrows. Struck down by that savage shape-changing *rākṣasa*, they streamed blood as if it were water from two Prasravaṇas. Rāma was the first to collapse, wounded to the quick by the arrows of furious Indrajit, who had once even defeated Śakra; he sprawled on the bed of heroes, clutching his triple-curved, gold-adorned bow, now unstrung and split across the grip. When he saw that bull of a man Rāma collapse beneath the weight of arrows, then Lakṣmaṇa too lost hope of life.

The forest-dwellers keeping watch over heaven and earth 36.1–10
saw the brothers Rāma and Lakṣmaṇa wounded all over by arrows; his task accomplished, the *rākṣasa* ceased his storm like the god his rain. Vibhīṣaṇa and Sugrīva came up, and at once Nīla, Dvivida and Mainda, and Suṣeṇa, Sumukha and

Aṅgada, along with Hanumān, raised a lament for the two Rāghavas lying there motionless and still, scarcely breathing, streams of blood flooding over them, enmeshed in arrows, arrows for their beds. On the bed of heroes the heroes lay motionless, sighing like snakes, their strength sapped, the streaming blood making their bodies bright as burnished standards, their movements feeble. The commanders clustered round them, tears clouding their eyes. The sight of the fallen Rāghavas covered in a mesh of arrows harrowed Vibhīṣaṇa and all the *vānaras*. The *vānaras* searched the sky in all directions but could not see Rāvaṇi, hidden by magic means from the fray, but by magic means Vibhīṣaṇa was able to see him and spied his brother's son concealed by magic but standing at the ready; that warrior of unparalleled achievement, unrivalled in warfare and hidden by virtue of a boon, was visible to Vibhīṣaṇa.

36.11–16 Indrajit looked at the pair as they lay, and exulted at what he had done, boasting to the delight of the sons of Disorder, 'Rāma and his brother Lakṣmaṇa were strong enough to kill Dūṣaṇa and Khara, but my arrows have laid them low. All the gods, anti-gods and hosts of sages cannot help them escape their arrow-fetters. It is because of him that my father has been brooding and tormented by sorrow, and has not laid his body on his bed throughout the three watches of this night. It is because of him – this wretch who pulls everything up by the roots – that Laṅkā here has been churned up like a river in the rains, and I have struck him down. The might of Rāma, of Lakṣmaṇa, and of all the forest-dwellers is as barren as clouds in autumn.'[10]

36.17–19 With these words to all the *rākṣasas* thronging round him, mighty Rāvaṇi assailed all the *vānara* chiefs, distressing and terrifying them with floods of arrows, then sneered, '*Rākṣasas*, just look at those brothers, both of them caught in my savage arrow-fetters in front of their army!'

36.20–24 The *rākṣasas* who had been fighting by subterfuge were all astonished to hear his words; they rejoiced at the deed and all cheered and thundered like clouds. Learning that Rāma had been struck down they did honour to Rāvaṇi, and when they saw Rāma and Lakṣmaṇa motionless and not breathing they assumed they were dead. Consumed by delight, all-conquering Indrajit entered Laṅkā city, to the rapture of all the sons of Disorder, but the sight of Rāma and Lakṣmaṇa, their bodies, their limbs and every part buried beneath the arrows, overcame Sugrīva with fear.

Vibhīṣaṇa urged the miserable, terrified *vānara* lord with 36.25–8
his tearful face and grief-clouded eyes, 'Give up your terror, Sugrīva, and check your flowing tears. This is mostly the way with battles: victory cannot be guaranteed. If fortune has not entirely deserted us, heroic *vānara*, these brothers Rāma and Lakṣmaṇa will recover from their swoon. Pull yourself together and support me, *vānara*, for I have no one to turn to; those who are devoted to true righteousness have no need to fear death.'

So saying Vibhīṣaṇa wet his hand and washed Sugrīva's fine 36.29–30
eyes; when he had wiped the wise monkey king's face, he calmly gave him this timely advice:

'Lord of the monkey kings, this is no time to give way to 36.31–8
weakness. Too much emotion at this inopportune time will be fatal. Weakness brings failure to all enterprises, so rise above it and consider what would be best for the armies Rāma leads, or rather have Rāma protected as long as he remains unconscious, so that when the two Kākutsthas regain consciousness they will drive away our fear. To Rāma this is as nothing! Rāma won't surrender to death. Good fortune comes with difficulty to the dying, but will not desert him. So take courage yourself and encourage your own force, while I rally all the armies again. Rumours are circulating in ear after ear among the apes, you bull of an ape; their eyes are staring with fear and consternation; but when they see me hurrying around encouraging the troops, the apes will shed their terror like a used garland.'

When he had reassured Sugrīva, Vibhīṣaṇa lord of the 36.39–42
vānaras swiftly reassured the *vānara* host, but Indrajit the sorceror led his whole army back into Laṅkā city and went to his father. He greeted the seated Rāvaṇa respectfully and gave his father the welcome news that Rāma and Lakṣmaṇa had

been killed. Hearing of the fall of his enemies, Rāvaṇa sprang up in delight and embraced his son in the midst of the *rākṣasas*, kissed him on the head with satisfaction and questioned him; in answer to his father's questions he related all that had taken place.

37.1–4 When Rāvaṇa's son had gone back into Laṅkā, his mission accomplished, grieving bulls of *vānaras* formed up around the Rāghava and mounted guard: Hanumān, Aṅgada, Nīla, Suṣeṇa, Kumuda, Nala, Gaja, Gavākṣa, Gavaya, Śarabha, Gandhamādana, Jāmbavān, Ṛṣabha, Sunda, Rambha, Śatabali, Pṛthu. With their forces drawn up and on the alert, armed everywhere with trees, the *vānaras* scanned all directions, around and upwards: if even the grass moved they thought, '*Rākṣasas*!'

37.5–6 Rāvaṇa was delighted with his son; when Indrajit had taken his leave he sent for the *rākṣasīs* guarding Sītā. At his command the *rākṣasīs* including Trijaṭā attended on him, and the delighted *rākṣasa* lord gave the *rākṣasīs* their instructions:

37.7–10 'Tell Vaidehī that Rāma and Lakṣmaṇa have been killed by Indrajit. Put her in the Puṣpaka Chariot and show her them killed on the battlefield. It's this husband of hers she's been obstinately relying on in refusing to be mine: he and his brother have been exterminated in battle! Without hesitation, without trembling, without a backward glance, beautified with every ornament, Sītā Maithilī shall come to me! Today when she sees that Rāma, along with Lakṣmaṇa, has succumbed to Time in battle, her hopes will be overthrown and she will see no other way out.'

37.11–15 The *rākṣasīs* accepted evil Rāvaṇa's instructions; they went for the Puṣpaka Chariot; those *rākṣasīs* fetched the Puṣpaka Chariot; on Rāvaṇa's order they took it to Maithilī in the *aśoka* grove; on to the Puṣpaka Chariot the *rākṣasīs* lifted Sītā, plunged in grief for her husband. When Sītā was mounted, along with Trijaṭā, on the Puṣpaka Chariot, Rāvaṇa sent it round Laṅkā, now garlanded with flags and standards, and the delighted *rākṣasa* ruler had the news proclaimed around Laṅkā that the Rāghava and Lakṣmaṇa too had been killed in battle by Indrajit.

37.16–20 As Sītā went around in the carriage with Trijaṭā she saw all the host of fallen *vānaras*; she saw too the excited flesh-eaters and grief-stricken *vānaras* at the side of Rāma and Lakṣmaṇa. Then, lying on two mounds of arrows, unconscious, weighed down by arrows, Sītā saw Lakṣmaṇa, she saw Rāma; with their armour smashed, their bows shattered, wounded in every limb by arrows, the heroes were nothing but fallen columns of arrows. The sight of those heroic brothers, those bulls of men, tortured Sītā with the most agonizing grief, and she mourned pitiably.

Sītā, already pitifully wasted from grief, mourned most 38.1–14
pathetically to see her husband laid low beside mighty Lakṣmaṇa. 'Ignorant liars, all of them, now Rāma's been killed, those fortune-tellers who foretold I should bear sons and not be a widow! Ignorant liars, all of them, now Rāma's been killed, those who foretold I should be chief queen of a sacrificer and wife of an oblation-maker! Ignorant liars, all of them, now Rāma's been killed, those who declared my fortune was made when I became the wife of a heroic king! Ignorant liars, all of them, now Rāma's been killed, those Twice-Born astrologers who publicly labelled me auspicious! Each of my feet, certainly, bears the lotuses which are supposed to deck women destined with their kingly husbands for monarchy, and even without my lucky signs, search as I may I cannot discern in myself any of the signs which doom ill-omened women to widowhood. These lotuses, supposedly a true sign of a woman's fortune, have today become untrue for me now Rāma's been killed. With my fine, smooth, dark hair, my unjoined eyebrows, my shapely, hairless calves, my gapless teeth, my neat temples, eyes, hands, feet, ankles and thighs, my glossy rounded nails, my even fingers, my smooth, swelling breasts with their sunken nipples, my sunken, deep-set navel, my firm sides and chest, my pearly complexion and my soft body-hair, I was said to be provided with the twelve signs of good fortune. The tellers of girls' fortunes noted my gentle smile and my unblemished, well-coloured hands and feet with all the right barleycorn marks. And then my husband and I were to be consecrated by brāhmans into the monarchy . . . All the predictions of those skilled in divination have come to nothing.

38.15–21 'Those brothers, who cleansed Janasthāna, who crossed the immutable ocean when they heard news of me, to be killed in a puddle![11] Surely they would have employed their missiles from Varuṇa, from Agni, Indra, Vāyu, or even the Brahmā's Head missile, those Rāghavas! It must have been someone using sorcery to make himself invisible in battle that struck down Indra Vāsava's equals, Rāma and Lakṣmaṇa, those who should defend me in my defencelessness, for no enemy would escape from battle with his life once the Rāghava had set eyes on him, not even if he were swift as thought. Rāma lies beside his brother, fallen in battle: surely there is no greater force than Time, surely Fate is inexorable. I mourn not so much for my dead husband, or Lakṣmaṇa, or myself, or even my mother: it's for my poor mother-in-law. She will be constantly thinking that the vow has been completed, wondering, "When shall I see both Sītā and Rāma again, and Lakṣmaṇa?"'

38.22–33 The *rākṣasī* Trijaṭā replied to her lament: 'Don't despair, my lady; this husband of yours is alive. I'll give you good reasons that will convince you, my lady, that these brothers, Rāma and Lakṣmaṇa, are alive. Soldiers' faces don't become suffused with fury and battle-frenzy when their leader's been killed. Vaidehī, this divine vehicle called the Puṣpaka Chariot would not carry you if that pair had met their end. An army that loses a heroic leader loses its nerve and wanders about in battle as aimlessly as a ship that's lost its rudder on the water. This army though is not in disarray, nor is it panic-stricken; they're guarding the Kākutsthas vigorously, because it's magic that's overcome them in battle. These pointers to a happy outcome should fill you with confidence. Look, the Kākutsthas have not been killed. It's out of affection that I'm telling you this: I've never yet told an untruth and I never shall. Your comportment and courtesy have won my heart. These two cannot be defeated in battle by gods and anti-gods together, Indra included, I'm telling you straight, now I've seen their faces. And look carefully, Maithilī: there's a very important sign. Even though they're unconscious, Lakṣmī is definitely not abandoning either of them; usually when you look at the faces of men whose spirit and life are at an end, a horrible transformation occurs.

Daughter of Janaka, give up your sorrow and grief and delusion about Rāma and Lakṣmaṇa. Not still be alive? That's impossible!'

When Sītā Maithilī, truly a deity's daughter, heard her words she raised her hands and prayed that it might be so. But the Puṣpaka Chariot that moved as swift as thought was turned round, and poor Sītā was taken back into Laṅkā by Trijaṭā; she dismounted from the Puṣpaka Chariot along with Trijaṭā and was taken straight back to the *aśoka* grove by the *rākṣasīs*. 38.34–6

Moaning like hissing snakes, Daśaratha's blood-spattered sons were lying weighed down by the mass of savage arrows. Sugrīva and all the mighty *vānara* chiefs stood around the noble pair, plunged in the depths of grief. At that moment heroic Rāma, stalwart and steadfast, regained consciousness amid his arrow-fetters, but when he saw his bloodstained brother laid low, motionless and dismal looking, he uttered a sorrowful lament: 39.1–4

'What's the use of Sītā, what's the use of my life now I can see my brother lying defeated in battle? If I searched the world I could find another wife as good as Sītā, but not a brother as good as Lakṣmaṇa, my comrade-in-arms. If that growing joy to Sumitrā has met his end, then I will give up my life too in the sight of the *vānaras*. Whatever shall I say to Kausalyā, my mother? What to Kaikeyī? And how can I tell Sumitrā, his mamma, who is desperate to see her son? She'll be quaking and screeching like an osprey at losing her pet: how can I comfort her if I go back without him? How can I say to Śatrughna and illustrious Bharata, "He went with me to the forest, but I have come back without him"? Oh, Sumitrā will blame me, and I shan't be able to bear it. Here and now I give up on life, for I've lost the strength to live. Shame on me, ignoble sinner that I am! It's because of me that Lakṣmaṇa there is lying lifeless, fallen on to a bed of arrows. 39.5–12

'Lakṣmaṇa, you always comforted me when I was dejected, but now life has left you, you can no longer speak to me in my distress. Just now in the battle he struck down many *rākṣasas* to the ground, and now on that same ground he lies struck down by others. Lying on this bed of arrows, drenched with 39.13–21 his own blood, enmeshed in arrows, he's glowing like the sun setting on Asta. The arrows piercing his vitals prevent him looking around and the colour of his face bears silent testimony to the anguish he's in. Just as that radiant man followed me when I left for the forest, so indeed will I follow him to Yama's realm. He was always devoted to his beloved family, to me especially, and now it's my bad judgement that's brought him to this state: what a wretch I am! I can never remember hearing a harsh word from Lakṣmaṇa, or even an unpleasant one, not ever, even when that hero was roused to fury. Lakṣmaṇa who could fire off five hundred arrows in a single burst, who knew more about archery and missiles than Kārtavīrya, whose missiles could overcome the missiles of noble Śakra: he was used to a costly couch, but here he lies on the earth, struck down.

39.22–9 'I feel real burning shame about my vain rhetoric: Vibhīṣaṇa has not been made king of the *rākṣasas*. Sugrīva, it's time you went back; mighty Rāvaṇa would attack, your majesty, if he thought you no longer had me with you. Set Aṅgada to lead you, with your army and your comrades, Sugrīva, and re-cross the ocean by the same causeway. Hanumān has performed an action in this war that others would find hard to emulate; the king of the bears and the overlord of langurs have pleased me; Aṅgada, Mainda and Dvivida have done their duty; Kesarin and Saṃpāti have fought fiercely in the fray; Gavaya, Gavākṣa and Śarabha, along with Gaja and the rest, have been prepared to lay down their lives for my sake in this war. Sugrīva, men cannot escape their fate, but you, my lord Sugrīva, mighty conqueror, have done everything a comrade or friend possibly could in your anxiety to do what's right. My lords, bulls of *vānaras*, you have performed everything expected of a friend; now I give you all leave to go wherever you wish.'

39.30–32 As the *vānaras* all heard his lament their eyes grew dim and they shed streams of tears. Then Vibhīṣaṇa halted all the troops and hurried up to the Rāghava, mace in hand; seeing him rushing up, dark as a mound of collyrium, all the *vānaras* fled, thinking he was Rāvaṇi.

40.1 Then the glorious, mighty king of apes asked, 'Why is the army agitated like a boat being blown this way and that on the water?'

In answer to Sugrīva's question, Vālin's son Aṅgada replied, 'Can't you see Rāma and mighty Lakṣmaṇa? Both those noble heroic sons of Daśaratha are lying drenched in blood, enmeshed in arrows, arrows for their bed.' 40.2–3

Then Sugrīva lord of the *vānaras* told his heir Aṅgada, 'I don't think it can be for no reason; something must have frightened them. These despairing-looking apes have thrown away their weapons and are fleeing in all directions, eyes staring in panic; no one hides his shame, but without a backward glance they are dragging their fallen comrades along and leaping away.' 40.4–6

Meanwhile the warrior Vibhīṣaṇa, mace in hand, paid homage to Sugrīva and inspected the Rāghava. Sugrīva saw that it was Vibhīṣaṇa who had made the *vānaras* panic and told Jāmbavān king of the bears standing nearby: 40.7–8

'Here comes Vibhīṣaṇa. It's the sight of him that's terrified those bulls of *vānaras* into running away; they think he may be Rāvaṇa's son. Reassure them quickly in their panic. They've fled in all directions. Tell them it's Vibhīṣaṇa who's arrived.' 40.9–10

On Sugrīva's instructions Jāmbavān king of the bears halted the *vānaras'* flight, brought them back and calmed them. When they heard the bear king's voice and realized it was Vibhīṣaṇa, the *vānaras* all cast off their agitation and returned, but when Vibhīṣaṇa saw Rāma's body heaped with arrows, Lakṣmaṇa's too, that upright *rākṣasa* became distraught. He moistened his hand and washed their eyes, weeping and lamenting, his mind weighed down by grief. 40.11–14

'It's by duplicity that *rākṣasa* warriors have brought this stout-hearted, valiant, martial pair to this state! It's my brother's son, his wicked son, that villain, who has toppled these upright heroes with his crooked *rākṣasa* craft! Blood-spattered and shot through by arrows aplenty, they look like porcupines asleep on the earth. I hoped that seeking the protection of those heroes would bring me the paramountcy, but now those bulls of men have both lost consciousness they will lose their lives too. I'm still alive, but I'm ruined! I've lost the 40.15–19 kingship my heart desired and my enemy Rāvaṇa has achieved his aim and got everything he wanted.'

40.20–22 Sugrīva, the stout-hearted king of the apes, embraced Vibhīṣaṇa as he lamented, saying, 'You are righteous, and you will gain the kingship of Laṅkā; there's no doubt about it. Rāvaṇa and his son shall not hold on to sovereignty here. They are weighed down by arrows now, but the Rāghava and Lakṣmaṇa will recover from their swoon and together slaughter Rāvaṇa and his hordes in battle.'

40.23–5 When he had calmed and reassured the *rākṣasa*, Sugrīva turned to his father-in-law Suṣeṇa and told him, 'When Rāma and Lakṣmaṇa recover consciousness, you and the hordes of ape warriors are to take those enemy-subduing brothers back to Kiṣkindhā, while I kill Rāvaṇa and his son and family and rescue Maithilī like Śakra did his lost Śrī.'

40.26–32 Hearing that from the *vānara* lord, Suṣeṇa made a suggestion: 'A ferocious war arose between gods and anti-gods. The gods were experts in weaponry and directed their arrows with skill, but by dint of repeatedly making themselves invisible the *dānavas* overcame the gods, leaving them distressed and unconscious; their lives were ebbing away, but Bṛhaspati healed them with a combination of spells, *mantras* and herbs. You should immediately dispatch *vānaras* to the Milk Ocean to fetch those salves with all speed – Saṃpāti, Panasa and others – the apes know these two mountain herbs, Saṃjīvakaraṇī the divine and Viśalyā the god-created. Those two mountains – Candra one's called, and Droṇa – in the ultimate ocean, where the ambrosia was churned – that's where these eminent herbs are – those two mountains were ordained by the gods to bear those eminent herbs. Hanumān here, your majesty, he's the Son of the Wind, he's the one you should send.'

40.33–41 Just at that moment the water of the ocean was tossed about by gales and lightning clouds wild enough to shake mountains; all the island's lofty trees were uprooted by a great flapping of wings and plunged into the salt sea, their branches torn off; its inhabitants, the writhing serpents, took fright and its monsters all dived swiftly into its salty depths. Then, a moment later, the *vānaras* all saw mighty Garuḍa, Vinatā's son, blazing as a fire, and the arrows fettering the pair of mighty heroes turned back into snakes and fled when they saw him arrive. Seeing the Kākutsthas, the Bird saluted them and with his hands[12] stroked the moonlike brilliance of their faces. At the touch of Vinatā's son their wounds closed and their bodies quickly regained their colour and bloom; their power, heroism, might, vigour and resolve, their foresight, intelligence and memory – all their great qualities – were redoubled. Garuḍa helped them up, then delightedly embraced those heroes, each the equal of Indra Vāsava, to be told by Rāma:

'My lord, your beneficence has rescued us from the great 40.42–4
calamity inflicted on us by Rāvaṇi, and promptly restored our strength. Your lordship's presence is as welcome to my heart as would be that of my father Daśaratha or an ancestor. Who might your lordship be, with your handsome appearance and your divine garlands and unguents, clad in a spotless garment set off with divine adornments?'

Vinatā's splendid, mighty son, king of the birds, was gratified 40.45–54
and replied to him with eyes filled with delight. 'Kākutstha, I am Garuḍa, your comrade, your dear second self. I have come here out of solidarity with you both. Not the bold anti-gods nor the mighty *dānavas*, not even the gods and *gandharvas* with Indra Śatakratu at their head are able to release these terrible arrow-fetters devised by vicious Indrajit by the power of his sorcery. Those sharp-fanged venomous snakes, the off-spring of Kadrū, were turned into arrows by the power of that *rākṣasa's* sorcery and clung fast to you. Fortune is with you, righteous, truly valiant Rāma, you and your brother Lakṣmaṇa, that slayer of foes in battle, for when I heard the news I immediately rushed here out of affection for you both, as a mark of my comradeship. Now that you are free of these terrible arrow-fetters you must be constantly on your guard, for *rākṣasas* are all naturally duplicitous fighters, whereas your lordships are honourable heroes whose strength is your honesty. So be wary of *rākṣasas* in battle, for this is an example of ever-devious *rākṣasa* behaviour.'

So saying, the mighty Bird embraced Rāma and bade his 40.55–7
comrade an affectionate farewell: 'Rāghava my friend, you

who know what's right, you who treat even your enemies with kindness, I wish to take my leave: I am going back. With your waves of arrows you will strip Laṅkā of all but children and old people; you will kill your enemy Rāvaṇa and you will recover Sītā.'

40.58–63; 41.1–2 When the mettlesome Bird had finished speaking and freed Rāma from pain amid the forest-dwellers, he circumambulated and embraced him; then off into the sky like the wind went the heroic Bird. When the *vānara* chiefs saw the Rāghavas free of pain, they roared out lionlike roars and shook their tails, banging drums, beating tabors, blowing conches in delight and frisking around like before. Valiant *vānaras* by the hundred thousand ran to and fro uprooting every kind of tree to use as weapons, and formed up. Hurling out loud roars that terrified the night-roamers, the monkeys marched on Laṅkā's gates, eager for the fray, till the tumultuous hullabaloo bellowed by the bold *vānaras* reached the ears of Rāvaṇa and the *rākṣasas*. When he heard the uproarious booming he told his assembled counsellors:

41.3–5 'The thunderous din billowing from so many delighted *vānaras* must mean they have something to cheer about. There's no doubt about it, for the loud noise is churning up Varuṇa's abode – but the brothers Rāma and Lakṣmaṇa have been fettered by sharp arrows! This great clamour is enough to breed doubts in me.'

41.6–7 After telling that to his counsellors the *rākṣasa* lord turned to address the sons of Disorder attending him: 'Be quick and find out what has made all those forest-roamers so cheerful after they've been so mournful.'

41.8–11 Perturbed by his words they climbed the rampart and saw the army under the leadership of noble Sugrīva, but when they caught sight of the two Rāghavas on their feet, alive and well and liberated from the terrible arrow-fetters, the *rākṣasas'* spirits sank; with fear in their hearts they climbed down from the rampart and approached the *rākṣasa* lord with downcast faces. Looking miserable and choosing their words carefully, the night-roamers gave Rāvaṇa their unwelcome report, complete and accurate:

'The brothers Rāma and Lakṣmaṇa whom Indrajit fettered in the fray with arrow-fetters, pinioning their arms, can be seen on the battlefield freed from the arrow-fetters like elephants broken loose from their chains, intrepid as elephant lords.' 41.12–13

The powerful lord of the *rākṣasas* was overcome by vexation and alarm when he heard their report. With downcast face he mused, 'With great force Indrajit fettered that pair in the fray with dread, unerring, sunlike arrows, venomous as snakes, that he had been given as a boon. If my enemies have been released after being fettered by those missiles, I can see all my power being put at risk. The arrows may have incorporated the power of Vāsuki but they have turned out fruitless if my enemies have been restored to life in the battle.' 41.14–17

When he had spoken, hissing like a snake in his anger, he instructed a *rākṣasa* called Dhūmrākṣa, in the midst of the *rākṣasas*, 'You are to take a large force of ferocious *rākṣasas* and set forth to slaughter Rāma and the *vānaras*.' 41.18–19

The shrewd *rākṣasa* lord's command delighted Dhūmrākṣa, who saluted and left the monarch's palace. Once through the gate he told an officer, 'Quick! Hurry up the troops! Why delay? I'm eager to do battle!' 41.20–21

At Dhūmrākṣa's command the orderly officer assembled a force to carry out Rāvaṇa's order at the double. Dreadful-looking, mighty night-roamers bound on bells and roared in delight as they surrounded Dhūmrākṣa, carrying every kind of weapon: with spears and hammers in their hands, with clubs, javelins, staves, abundant iron pestles, maces, darts, quarrels, projectiles and battleaxes the dread *rākṣasas* set out, thundering like clouds. Others came in their armour on chariots adorned with standards and gold lattice-work: their asses had the faces of different creatures, their horses were supremely swift, their elephant chiefs were *musth*-maddened. Unassailable as tigers were those tigers of *rākṣasas* as they set out; Dhūmrākṣa brayed as he mounted a divine, gold-ornamented chariot harnessed to asses with the faces of wolves and lions. Stalwart Dhūmrākṣa laughed as he set out surrounded by *rākṣasas* for the western gate, the one assigned to Hanumān's charge, but as the dreadful, fearsome-looking *rākṣasa* set out 41.22–34 he was mobbed by savage fowls of the air; a terrifying vulture swooped down on to the chariot-head and skeins of scavengers swooped down to the standard's tip. Near Dhūmrākṣa a huge white torso drenched in blood fell to earth, shrieking horribly. The heavens rained blood and the earth quaked; a gale blew in tempestuous squalls with the noise of a thunderstorm, and a flood of darkness blotted out the light in every direction. The sight of these dread portents of doom for the *rākṣasas* appearing filled Dhūmrākṣa with alarm.

42.1–16 All the battle-hungry *vānaras* roared with delight when they noticed the *rākṣasa* Dhūmrākṣa setting out amid his dreadful uproar, and a tumultuous battle broke out with apes and *rākṣasas* belabouring each other savagely with trees, pikes and hammers. All around, fierce *vānaras* were cut down by *rākṣasas*, *rākṣasas* were brought to the ground with trees by *vānaras*, and enraged *rākṣasas* pierced *vānaras* with fearsome-looking arrows, sharp, heron-feathered, unerring. With dread clubs, javelins, cudgels, sharpened tridents and ferocious glittering iron maces the *rākṣasas* wounded the mighty *vānaras*, but resentment fuelled their courage and they acquitted themselves as if they had nothing to fear. Though arrows pierced their limbs, though pikes pierced their bodies, the ape chiefs snatched up trees and boulders. Fearful was the assault of the apes, roaring out their war cries again and again as they battered the fearsome *rākṣasas*; amazing was the ferocious battle with boulders and many-branched trees between *vānaras* and *rākṣasas*. Some *rākṣasas* were battered by triumphant *vānaras*; blood gushed from the mouths of those who were used to feasting on blood; some had their flanks sliced open; some were knocked into a heap by trees, some were pulverized by boulders, some were lacerated by teeth; with standards battered and broken, asses felled and chariots smashed, night-roamers were dashed down. Impetuous *rākṣasas* had their faces slashed by the sharp claws of fearsomely valiant *vānaras* leaping everywhere, till the smell of blood sent them swooning to the ground with wan faces and tousled locks. Other highly enraged *rākṣasas* of fearsome valour were laying into the apes, slapping them with the force of a bolt of lightning, but however impetuous their attack, the *vānaras*, more impetuous still, crushed them with fists and feet, with teeth and trees.

When that bull of a *rākṣasa* Dhūmrākṣa saw his army was 42.17–24
fleeing, he angrily set about butchering the battle-hungry *vānaras*. Some *vānaras* he pelted with darts till they streamed with blood; some he knocked to the ground with hammers; some he pounded with maces or gashed with javelins; some he struck with spears till they were reeling at their last gasp. Some forest-dwellers he hurled to earth drenched in blood, some he put to flight to be destroyed in battle by furious *rākṣasas*, some lay on their sides, their hearts cut through, some impaled on tridents had their entrails spilling out. Terrifying was the battle joined by ape- and *rākṣasa*-hordes with a multitude of weapons and with boulders and trees in profusion. Bow in hand, Dhūmrākṣa exultantly drove the *vānaras* in all directions from the fray with showers of arrows.

The Son of the Wind was enraged to see the army being 42.25–36
beaten and routed by Dhūmrākṣa; he snatched up a huge boulder and attacked. His eyes grew twice as red with fury and his strength equalled his father's as he hurled that boulder against Dhūmrākṣa's chariot. Seeing the boulder falling he frantically brandished his club and hastily jumped from his chariot to take his stand on the ground. The boulder shattered chariot, wheels, pole, horses, standard and bow as it fell to earth. With the chariot smashed, Hanumān Son of the Wind set about slaughtering *rākṣasas* with tree-trunks and branches; *rākṣasas* with blood pouring from gashes in their heads were pounded with trees and fell to the ground. With the *rākṣasa* army on the run, Hanumān Son of the Wind picked up a mountain peak and ran towards Dhūmrākṣa. Bravely Dhūmrākṣa brandished his club and ran vehemently at Hanumān, attacking him with a roar, then angrily and violently Dhūmrākṣa brought that many-spiked club down on Hanumān's skull. The ape with the power of the wind ignored the blow and the wound inflicted by that horrific club, and dropped the mountain-peak on to the middle of Dhūmrākṣa's head; his limbs tottered beneath the force of that mountain-peak and he crashed to the ground like a shattered mountain. When they saw Dhūmrākṣa slain,

the surviving night-roamers fled back to Laṅkā in terror, the monkeys continuing to slaughter them as they went.

43.1–2 When he heard Dhūmrākṣa was slain, Rāvaṇa lord of the *rākṣasas* spoke to an officer standing respectfully beside him: 'Straight away, send out some indomitable *rākṣasas*, ferocious and savage, under the command of Akampana; he is an expert in all weapons.'

43.3–10 Leading *rākṣasas*, fully armed, flocked to answer the officer's summons; fearsome were their eyes, fearsome their appearance. In his earrings of burnished gold, Akampana mounted his imposing chariot and set out, surrounded by the ferocious *rākṣasas*. Then, as he hastened furiously along, eager for battle, the horses pulling his chariot were struck by an unexplained listlessness. Though he rejoiced at the prospect of battle, his left eye began to throb, the colour drained from his face and his voice faltered. Brightness turned to gloom and a gale lashed them; the calls of birds and beasts took on a note of savagery and terror. He had the towering shoulders of a lion, he had the courage of a tiger, and he ignored these portents, pressing on to the battlefield; surrounded by his *rākṣasas*, the *rākṣasa* gave out a roar loud enough to shake the ocean.

43.11–27 The *vānara* host were terrified by the din, but grasped trees and boulders for weapons and stood their ground against the assault. With monkeys and *rākṣasas* alike utterly regardless of their lives in the service of Rāma and Rāvaṇa, the battle that broke out was savage. All the warriors were stalwart; apes or *rākṣasas*, all were mountainous and lusting to slaughter one another. A tremendous uproar arose as with valiant fervour they bellowed in anger at each other, and dreadful drab-coloured dust was kicked up in profusion by the apes and *rākṣasas* to hide all ten Directions. Creatures enveloped by this dust as if by billowing garments of pale silk could not distinguish one another on the battlefield. Standards, flags, armour, steeds even, weapons and vehicles: all were invisible in the pall. No shapes could be made out, but the tumult of their roars as they rushed together in that turbulent battle could be heard. Frenzied apes struck down apes in combat; *rākṣasas* too struck down *rākṣasas* in the gloom. Striking at friend and foe alike, *vānaras* and *rākṣasas* turned the mud-anointed earth wet with gore, sprinkling it with fountains of blood that laid the dust till the ground emerged again, corpse-strewn. With gusto, apes and *rākṣasas* were swiftly killing each other with trees and lances, rocks and darts, with clubs, with maces, with javelins. Fearsome were the exploits performed by mountainous apes as they fought in that battle, battering the *rākṣasas* with their mace-like arms, but the raging *rākṣasas* were armed with darts and javelins, and they replied by striking out at the apes with their vicious weapons. The apes returned to the charge with huge trees and huge boulders, heroically smashing their weapons and wounding the *rākṣasas*. At that point the frenzied ape warriors Kumuda, Nala and Mainda launched an unparalleled assault; it was child's play for these irresistible ape chiefs with their trees to devastate the *rākṣasas* in the face of their army.

When Akampana saw the exploit accomplished by the 44.1–2
vānara champions, he summoned up his ferocious battle-frenzy; the sight of his enemies' exploit sent anger coursing through his frame. He flourished his mighty bow and gave orders to his charioteer.

'Come on, charioteer! Be quick now and get my chariot 44.3–5
ready! A large force is slaughtering large numbers of *rākṣasas* in the fray! There before me stand mighty *vānaras* of fearsome physique, armed with trees and rocks. They may vaunt their prowess in battle, but it's my intention to slay them! Look at them, belabouring the whole *rākṣasa* army!'

Then from his chariot, drawn by speedy horses, that supreme 44.6–7
chariot warrior Akampana angrily pounded the apes with tangles of arrows. The *vānaras* were unable to resist, much less to fight back in that battle; broken by Akampana's arrows they all fled.

When mighty Hanumān saw that Death in the form of 44.8–24
Akampana had them in his grip, he came to his kinsmen's aid. The sight of that great monkey had all the heroic chiefs leaping up as one, crowding around and surrounding him in the fray. Hanumān's resolute demeanour reassured the ape chiefs and his strength gave them strength. Like great Indra's floods were

the arrows Akampana poured on to Hanumān, but he looked as immovable as a mountain, ignoring the floods of keen arrows falling on to his body as he concentrated with might and main on his objective, the killing of Akampana. Hanumān, splendid Son of the Wind, laughed, then made an earth-shaking rush at the *rākṣasa*, bellowing and blazing in his splendour till his figure became as unendurable as Agni's blaze. The wrathful bull of an ape realized he had no weapon and violently tore up a mountain; carrying that great mountain in one hand, the Son of the Wind let out a tremendous roar and whirled it around heroically, then rushed towards the *rākṣasa* lord Akampana like Indra Puraṃdara with his thunderbolt in his battle against Namuci. But when in the distance Akampana saw the mountain-peak being brandished, he shot it through with great crescent-headed arrows. Hanumān was maddened with rage to see the mountain-top in the sky shot through by the *rākṣasa's* arrows, shattered and fallen, but full of disdainful fury the ape found an *aśvakarṇa* tall as a high mountain and swiftly uprooted it. Picking up the *aśvakarṇa* with its huge trunk he laughed with the utmost pleasure and majestically whirled it in the fray as he ran forward, smashing down trees with the impetus of his legs, till in his fervent frenzy Hanumān split the earth open with his feet. Elephants and mahouts, chariots and chariot warriors, *rākṣasa* infantry: expertly Hanumān destroyed them. Seeing Hanumān snatching away their lives in the battle like an angry Death, the *rākṣasas* fled.

44.25–9 Heroic Akampana roared with anger when he saw how the furious onslaught was panicking the *rākṣasas*. Fourteen sharp body-penetrating arrows Akampana drove into valiant Hanumān. Transfixed by shower after shower of arrows, heroic Hanumān looked like a mountain bristling with trees, but uprooting another tree he made a supreme assault and swiftly smote the *rākṣasa* lord Akampana on the head. The *rākṣasa* fell down dead, struck down with the tree by that noble, wrathful *vānara* lord.

44.30–33 All the *rākṣasas* trembled like trees in an earthquake at the sight of the *rākṣasa* lord Akampana slain on the earth. The defeated *rākṣasas* all threw away their weapons and retreated in terror to Laṅkā, pursued by the *vānaras*; dishevelled and confused, unnerved, routed and groaning, their bodies running with sweat from the exertion, they fled. In their fear they pummelled each other to enter the city, all the time looking behind them in panic.

With the *rākṣasas* sheltering in Laṅkā, the powerful apes gathered and congratulated Hanumān. Gallant Hanumān too was delighted, and successively paid tribute to the deserving apes. The triumphant apes cheered themselves hoarse and dragged back there any *rākṣasas* still left alive. 44.34–6

The lord of the *rākṣasas* was truly angered by the news of Akampana's death, and he looked at his courtiers with some dismay in his face. He could see that Laṅkā city was guarded by hordes of *rākṣasas*, hidden behind numerous fortifications and garlanded with flags and banners, but Rāvaṇa lord of the *rākṣasas* was indignant to see the city under siege and gave a timely order to an experienced warrior, Prahasta. 45.1–4

'You are an expert in warfare, but I can see no way of releasing the city from the oppression of this severe siege except by battle. I or Kumbhakarṇa, Indrajit or Nikumbha, or you, Commander-in-Chief – all of us are capable of shouldering a burden of this nature. You're the one! Be quick about it! Select and assemble a detachment and make a victorious sortie against the forest-dwellers' position. A sortie by you will be sure to put the wavering ape army to flight when they hear the sound of *rākṣasa* lords roaring; wavering, undisciplined, irresolute *vānaras* will no more endure your roaring than elephants will the roaring of a lion. With that force routed, Rāma and Saumitri will have lost both their loyalty and their support, and will succumb to you, Prahasta . . . Better to meet trouble halfway than wait for it to come to us . . . Am I right or wrong? . . . What do you think would be best?' 45.5–11

At Rāvaṇa's words, General Prahasta replied to the lord of *rākṣasas* like Uśanas to the lord of the anti-gods. 'Your majesty, we and your experienced counsellors discussed this matter previously and a dispute arose between us as we debated together. I held it best to return Sītā, and that war would ensue from her non-return; it has transpired as predicted. I have ever 45.12–16 been honoured by you with gifts, distinctions and courtesies of many kinds; now the time has come, what would I not do to please you? I will not hold back my life, nor my sons, wives or wealth. Look on me! For your sake I am ready to offer up my life in battle.'

45.17–18 With this declaration to his suzerain Rāvaṇa, General Prahasta instructed the orderly officers standing before him, 'Quick! Bring me a large force of *rākṣasas*. Today let birds gorge on the flesh of woodland-dwellers slain on the battlefield by the velocity of my thunderbolts of arrows!'

45.19–23 On Prahasta's command, the orderly officers hastily drew up a force right there in the *rākṣasa's* palace, the *rākṣasa* warriors crowding Laṅkā in an instant with all their weapons, spiky as tuskers. As they were gratifying the fire with oblations and doing obeisance to brāhmans, a fragrant breeze wafted the scent of *ghī*, and the exuberant, battle-ready *rākṣasas* snatched up all sorts of consecrated garlands and put them on. Mailed and bow-wielding, the spirited *rākṣasas* bounded up to honour King Rāvaṇa, and formed up around Prahasta.

45.24–38 Prahasta then took leave of the king, beat his dread drum and mounted his divine chariot. It was ready and waiting, harnessed to swift-paced steeds and driven by an expert charioteer; it rumbled like huge clouds, it dazzled with the brilliance of moon and sun; it was protected by its serpent-standard and safeguarded by its stout rail; its frame was sturdy, its lattice-work was golden, and it seemed to be exulting in its splendour. That was the chariot he mounted when, given command by Rāvaṇa of the hastily assembled host, he sallied forth from Laṅkā. Then, as the general set out, there was heard a loud drumming like the sound of Parjanya, and a booming of conches. Forth from the eastern gate he sallied, around him arrayed a ferocious host the like of a herd of elephants. Forth sallied Prahasta in haste, wrathful and lethal as Time. The commotion of his sallying forth and the bellowing of his *rākṣasas* raised an echoing cacophony from all creatures in Laṅkā. Ferocious, carrion-feasting, blood-guzzling jackals spewing out flames and fire leapt into the cloudless sky and howled; a meteor fell from the air; a violent gale got up;

quarrelsome planets hid their light in anger, raining blood on him and spattering his vanguard; a vulture perched on top of his standard and looked to the south;* as the driver urged on the horses to plunge into the fray, the whip fell repeatedly from the charioteer's hand. Then in an instant his radiant Glory, who had attended his sallying forth, deserted him irretrievably: the horses stumbled on level ground.

As Prahasta sallied forth, vaunting his manly might, the army 45.39–41 of apes took up their weapons to launch a counter-attack; tremendous was the din raised by the apes as they broke down trees or snatched up heavy rocks. Both armies, *rākṣasa* hordes and forest-dwellers, were exhilarated: both fought with vigour, both were able, eager for the kill and belligerent. Ear-splitting was the din they made.

Then Nīla saw Prahasta standing on his chariot, pouring out 46.30–48 a flood of arrows and vigorously striking down the monkeys. Watching his terrible onslaught, the great monkey Nīla flew into a violent rage, snatched up a huge rock and attacked, swiftly hurling the rock at the battle-hungry Prahasta's head as he was fighting with a pestle in the fray; the terrible rock thrown by that monkey chief smashed Prahasta's skull to smithereens. Life, luck, spirit and senses all left him and he collapsed violently to the ground like a tree whose roots have been severed, blood streaming from his shattered head and pouring from his body like torrents from a mountain. Nīla had killed Prahasta, and his great, unwavering army now fled in dismay to Laṅkā.

Then glorious, heroic Rāma picked up his bow and caught 49.1–4 sight of Kumbhakarṇa, a diademed giant. When this mountain-like *rākṣasa* chief appeared, looking like Lord Nārāyaṇa when of old he strode across space – on seeing him, towering up like a rain cloud, ornamented with golden bracelets, the *vānara* army again fled. Rāma was astonished to see the army running away and the *rākṣasa* strength growing, and asked Vibhīṣaṇa:

'Who is that mountainlike, diademed, tawny-eyed warrior I 49.5–7 can see like a lightning cloud in Laṅkā? He's visible standing out on his own like a flagpole in the ground! Seeing him, all the *vānaras* are running away all over the place! Tell me, who is this giant? A *rākṣasa*? Or an anti-god? I've never seen anyone like him before!'

49.8–18 Vibhīṣaṇa knew all about him, and replied to the question Prince Rāma, untiring Kākutstha, had asked. 'Death has been defeated by him in battle; Indra Vāsava too. He is the mighty Kumbhakarṇa, a son of Viśravas. The Thirty were unable to kill scowling Kumbhakarṇa, powerful and armed with his pike; in their panic they thought he was Time. The other *rākṣasa* lords owe their power to some boon they've been given, but Kumbhakarṇa here's splendour and might are innate. As soon as this noble *rākṣasa* was born, he was famished and devoured many thousands of created beings, whose panic-stricken offspring sought protection from Śakra and told him what was happening. The din from wily Kumbhakarṇa's perpetual squalling further frightened the frightened earth. In fury against great Indra, lusty Kumbhakarṇa pulled a tusk out of Airāvata and struck Indra Vāsava on the chest. Vāsava staggered with the pain of Kumbhakarṇa's blow, and gods, brāhman sages and *dānavas* at once despaired.

49.19–20 'Śakra went with the created beings to Brahmā's abode, and told that Lord of Creatures about Kumbhakarṇa's depravity – how he was devouring the created beings and even assaulting the gods: "If he goes on devouring created beings like this the world will soon become empty."

49.21–3 'Hearing Vāsava's speech, the Grand Father of all the world summoned the *rākṣasas* and saw Kumbhakarṇa; the Lord of Creatures was frightened indeed when he had inspected Kumbhakarṇa. Brahmā gazed at him, sighed, and declared: "Paulastya engendered you to bring destruction upon the world, that's certain. From today onwards you shall lie like a corpse."

49.23–5 'Overcome by Brahmā's curse he collapsed in front of the Lord. Rāvaṇa was utterly bewildered and pleaded, "A mature golden tree is being cut down at harvest time. Prajāpati, it is not proper for you to curse your own progeny in this way, but your decrees cannot be unspoken; sleep he certainly must, but do determine a time for waking as well as for sleeping."

'Hearing Rāvaṇa's plea, Brahmā replied, "For six months he shall sleep, then for one day he shall wake." 49.26

'But this warrior, famished, roaming the earth with gaping maw for just one day would devour the worlds like a raging foe. It's because King Rāvaṇa has suffered a reverse and is so frightened of you that he's woken Kumbhakarṇa now. This warrior hero will sally forth famished and infuriated, no doubt, and will devour the *vānaras*. The apes have fled at the mere sight of Kumbhakarṇa; how will they stand against his battle-frenzy? Pass the word around all the *vānaras* that it's a machine that has reared up; if they believe that, the apes will lose their fear.' 49.27–31

The Rāghava listened to Vibhīṣaṇa's sensible, well-spoken words and then gave orders to General Nīla. 'Go, Son of Fire! Form up all the troops and take up your position. Secure all Laṅkā's gates, access roads and bridges. Stockpile mountain-tops, trees and rocks, and position all the *vānaras*, fully armed, boulders to hand.' 49.32–4

Nīla, commander of the ape army, that elephant of a monkey, instructed the *vānara* army in accordance with the Rāghava's orders. Then mountainous Gavākṣa, Śarabha, Hanumān, Aṅgada and Nala each picked up a mountain-top and went to his gate. 49.35–6

The tiger of a *rākṣasa* was quite drunk with sleep as he went along the king's highway, but his prowess was immense and he basked in glory. Thousands of *rākṣasas* crowded around that almost unconquerable warrior as he went, showered with flowers scattered down from the houses. Then the *rākṣasa* lord's delightful, spacious residence came into view, looking brilliant as the sun with its covering of golden lattice-work. When he reached his brother's dwelling, he burst into the courtyard and saw his agitated senior seated in the Puṣpaka Palace. Noticing his arrival, Daśagrīva jumped up in delight and brought him close. When he had resumed his seat on his 50.1–7 couch, mighty Kumbhakarṇa saluted his brother's feet and asked, 'What do you want?'

50.7–10 Rāvaṇa then leapt up ecstatically and embraced him. Embraced by his brother and greeted in due form, Kumbhakarṇa was honoured with a splendid, divine throne, but once seated powerful Kumbhakarṇa, eyes reddened with rage, addressed Rāvaṇa. 'Your majesty, what's your reason for waking me up to honour me? Tell me what it is you're afraid of. Who is to become a ghost today?'

50.11–18 Rāvaṇa's eyes began to roll as he explained to his angry brother Kumbhakarṇa beside him: 'You've been asleep for a long time now, mighty brother, in blissful ignorance of the threat posed by Rāma. This Rāma is a powerful son of Daśaratha, and along with Sugrīva and an army he's crossed the sea to eradicate us. Come and look! Laṅkā's forests and groves are just one sea of *vānaras*! They came easily over a causeway, and the *vānaras* have killed the foremost *rākṣasas* in battle. I can't see any means of destroying the *vānaras* in battle. Help me! My treasury's utterly depleted. It's up to you to save Laṅkā city – it's only got children and old people left. Mighty brother, for your brother's sake, carry out this difficult task. I've never appealed to anyone like this before, victorious warrior, but I'm fond of you and I rate you highly. Many are the times, bull of a *rākṣasa*, in fights between the gods and anti-gods, when you've defeated gods and anti-gods alike in battle array. There's not a stronger creature than you to be found anywhere.'

53.45–6; 54.1–2 Impelled by the power of Fate, Kumbhakarṇa went out. The mountainous *rākṣasa* jumped over the rampart and saw the stupendous *vānara* army massed like a bank of cloud; he uttered a roar loud enough to make the sea boom, to beget thunder, even to scatter mountains. Judging that their terrible-eyed attacker could be killed neither by Indra the Bountiful, nor by Yama, nor by Varuṇa, the *vānaras* fled.

54.3–6 But Aṅgada was the son of Vālin; when he saw their flight he called to Nala, Nīla, Gavākṣa and mighty Kumuda, 'Where are you going? You're as terrified and panic-stricken as common apes! You're forgetting yourselves, your deeds of valour, and your lineage! Come on friends! Turn back! What do you mean by safeguarding your lives? The *rākṣasa*'s not up to the fight. It's just scare tactics! The *rākṣasas* have put this giant up to scare us, but our valour will get rid of him. Come back, monkeys!'

With an effort they pulled themselves together and regrouped; from all quarters they returned to the battlefield, trees and mountains in hand. Their anger restored, the mighty forest-dwellers, like rutting elephants, belaboured Kumbhakarṇa with lofty mountain-peaks, with rocks, with blossom-tipped trees. He did not flinch from the blows. The rocks shattered into a hundred pieces when they fell on to his limbs, and the blossom-tipped trees splintered and crashed to the ground. Furious too, he used all his strength to pulverize the mighty *vānara* armies, like a fire raging through forests: many the bulls of *vānaras*, like crimson-blossomed trees, lying drenched in gore, tossed and hurled to the ground. Without a backward glance the *vānaras* leapt or ran, some jumping into the sea, some seeking safety in the air. In the face of the *rākṣasa's* murderous might, some warriors raced back along the very path that had brought them across the ocean, some to heights or hollows, their faces dismayed by fear; bears climbed trees or sought safety in mountains. Some dived into the sea, some hid in caves; some monkeys collapsed; some lost their resolve. 54.7–15

When Aṅgada saw that the *vānaras* were being broken, he called, 'Stand firm, monkeys! We're fighting! Come back! I can't see you finding any place to rest in the whole world if you break! Come back, all of you! What do you mean by safeguarding your lives? To throw away your weapons as you run, so as not to be hampered in your flight! How manly! Your wives will scorn you, and that's a living death. You've all been born in good families, prosperous and great, but you'll certainly be ignoble if you desert and run away. Where now is your proud, puffed up boasting in front of the assembled people? Cries of "coward" will ring in the ears of one who lives with reproach. Keep to the path prescribed by the virtuous; forget your fear! We may be struck down and lie expiring on the earth, we may be crushed in battle and attain the 54.16–24 unattainable world of Brahmā, or we may win renown by killing the enemy in combat: Kumbhakarṇa won't survive the sight of Kākutstha – he'll be like a moth flying into a flaming fire! But if we run for our lives we shall live disgraced. We are many: if we can be smashed by just one, our good name will perish.'

54.25–6 So urged heroic Aṅgada of the golden bracelet, but the fugitives answered that hero with reprehensible words: 'Terrible is the carnage caused among us by the *rākṣasa* Kumbhakarṇa. This is no time for making a stand. We're going. We value our lives.'

54.27–8 The sight of the dread *rākṣasa* with his dreadful eyes approaching sent all the *vānara* commanders scattering with no more ado in every direction, until Aṅgada's inducements and flattery persuaded his fleeing wrinkle-faced warriors to turn back.

56.1–5 When the *rākṣasas* saw that the noble Rāghava had killed Kumbhakarṇa, they reported the news to Rāvaṇa, lord of the *rākṣasas*. Rāvaṇa was tormented by grief to hear that mighty Kumbhakarṇa had been killed in the battle, and fell down in a faint. Devāntaka and Narāntaka, Triśiras and Atikāya were burdened by grief and wept to hear of the death of their uncle. Mahodara and Mahāpārśva were overwhelmed by grief to hear that their brother had been killed by tireless Rāma. When that bull of a *rākṣasa* Rāvaṇa had struggled back to consciousness, he gave vent to his sadness at Kumbhakarṇa's death.

56.6–18 'Alas, mighty Kumbhakarṇa, you've left me! You hero, you destroyer of enemy pride, you who single-handed tormented the hostile host, where are you gone? Now I am certainly lost! My mainstay is fallen, my right arm, my shelter from fear of gods and anti-gods! How could such a hero, murderous as the Doomsday Fire, capable of humbling gods and *dānavas*, how could he be killed in battle today by the Rāghava? A thunderbolt-strike would never trouble you – how can you have fallen asleep on the ground, hurt by an arrow from Rāma? Hordes of gods and sages gathered in the firmament are crowing with delight to see you slain in battle. This very day triumphant monkeys will be swarming in delight all over Laṅkā's impregnable gates. Kingship's nothing to me. What do I want with Sītā? I've no pleasure in life now Kumbhakarṇa's been torn from me. I must be the one to kill my brother's killer, the Rāghava, in battle; if not, death would be better for me than this purposeless life. This very day I shall follow where my brother's gone. I'll not endure life for an instant without my brothers. When the gods see me, their erstwhile scourge, they'll mock me. Kumbhakarṇa, how will I be able to conquer Indra, now you've been killed? Noble Vibhīṣaṇa's salutary advice comes back to me; it was ignorant of me to reject it, and it's to my shame that this savage slaughter of Kumbhakarṇa and Prahasta has fulfilled Vibhīṣaṇa's prediction. It's for banishing glorious, virtuous Vibhīṣaṇa that I'm reaping this grim harvest.'

[*In further fighting, Nikumbha's brother Kumbha is killed.*]

Nikumbha burned with rage to see his brother killed by 64.1–11
Sugrīva. Glaring at the lord of the *vānaras*, the warrior picked up his mace. It was enchained and girdled with garlands five fingers long, it was magnificent as a lordly mountain-peak, it was crowned with a golden fillet; adorned with diamonds and coral, fearsome as Yama's rod, it dispelled the *rākṣasas*' terror, in battle it was like Śakra's standard. Splendid Nikumbha whirled it with awesome might and bellowed from his gaping maw. Pectoral on his chest, bracelets on his arms, a pair of burnished earrings, glittering garlands – Nikumbha's ornaments and mace lit him up like lightning or like Indra's bow against a thunder-cloud, and the noble warrior's mace created a whirlwind raging around its tip, blazing and crackling like a smokeless fire. Viṭapāvatī city and its lovely *gandharva* dwellings, Amarāvatī too and all its dwellings, the hosts of stars, the constellations, moon and great planets – the whole sky shimmered at the whirling of Nikumbha's mace. Rage fanned Nikumbha's flames till, added to the splendour of his mace and ornaments, he became as hard to withstand as the fire that springs up at Doomsday. In their terror, *rākṣasas* and *vānaras* alike were unable so much as to tremble.

Baring his chest, however, mighty Hanumān confronted him. 64.11–23

Then the mighty *rākṣasa* used his mace-like arms to bring his sun-splendid mace down on that mighty monkey's chest: like a hundred shooting stars in the sky, the mace shattered and burst into a hundred fragments against the unyielding chest spread out before him. The great ape was no more ruffled by the mace – no more shaken by the blow – than a mountain by an earthquake, and that champion monkey Hanumān responded forcefully to the attack with a violent punch. The glorious, vehement hero with the valour of the Wind raised his fist and landed it vehemently on Nikumbha's chest; the hide burst, the blood flowed; lightning-like sparks flamed out from that fist. Nikumbha staggered beneath the blow but recovered enough to grab hold of mighty Hanumān. The inhabitants of Laṅkā uttered fearsome cries at the sight of Nikumbha dragging mighty Hanumān along, but even as Kumbhakarṇa's son was dragging him, the Son of the Wind punched him with the force of a thunderbolt and freed himself. Hanumān Son of the Wind then leapt to the ground and immediately laid into Nikumbha. Courageous and determined, he flailed at him, he pounded him, he took a gigantic leap and landed on his chest, seized him in his arms, grabbed him by the neck and tore off his dreadful, screeching head.

65.1–3 The news that Nikumbha had been killed and Kumbha also struck down kindled Rāvaṇa's resentment to a blaze. Beside himself with anger, beside himself with grief, the son of Disorder called upon Khara's son, broad-eyed Makarākṣa, urging him, 'Go, my son, I command you. Take a troop and kill the Rāghava; Lakṣmaṇa too, and the forest-dwellers.'

65.4–9 Hearing Rāvaṇa's words, Khara's son, boastful of his night-roamer heroism, replied in delight, 'Without fail!' He saluted Daśagrīva and circumambulated him, then ordered his chariot to be brought at once and the army quickly assembled. The night-roamer orderly officer marshalled vehicle and troops close by; the night-roamer circumambulated the chariot, mounted, and urged his charioteer to drive the chariot off immediately. Makarākṣa then addressed all the *rākṣasas*:

65.9–12 'All you *rākṣasas* are to precede me into battle. Noble

Rāvaṇa, king of the *rākṣasas*, has commanded me to kill both Rāma and Lakṣmaṇa in battle. Today, night-roamers, with my superb arrows I shall kill Rāma and Lakṣmaṇa, the monkey Sugrīva too, and the *vānaras*. Today with my spear-thrusts I shall set fire to the advancing host of *vānaras*, like a flame to dry kindling.'

In obedience to Makarākṣa's words, the assembled night- 65.13–20
roamers, all of them mighty and well armed, formed up around Khara's stout son; those stout shape-changing warriors, dreadful with their fangs, their yellow eyes and their wild hair, were trumpeting like elephants as they marched off in delight, making the earth shake. On all sides there swelled a din from thousands of conches, drums being beaten, growling and clapping, but suddenly the whip slipped and fell from the charioteer's hand; so too did the *rākṣasa's* standard. The steeds harnessed to the chariot lost all vigour and rhythm from their stride and plodded on with sorrowful, tear-stained faces. A harsh, biting, sand-laden gale was blowing as fierce, malicious Makarākṣa advanced. The audacious *rākṣasas* all observed the portents but paid no heed as they marched against Rāma and Lakṣmaṇa.

When the bulls of *vānaras* saw Makarākṣa advancing, they 66.1–7
all immediately leapt forward, ready for anything and eager for battle. The battle that broke out between monkeys and night-roamers was as stupendous and hair-raising as any between gods and *dānavas*: trees thudded, pikes were thrust, boulders and maces fell, as monkeys and night-roamers pounded each other. Night-roamers with spears and pikes and clubs and swords, with lances, javelins and darts, with flights of arrows on all sides, night-walkers with nooses, with hammers, with staves and other weapons of war made havoc among the lions of monkeys until, tormented by the floods of arrows from Khara's son, the *vānaras* all fled in bewilderment, burdened by fear. At the sight of the forest-dwellers running, lionlike roars arose from all the delighted *rākṣasas*: the *rākṣasas* were triumphant!

While the *vānaras* were fleeing all around, Rāma held the 66.8–9 *rākṣasas* at bay with a storm of arrows. When Makarākṣa the night-roamer saw that the *rākṣasas* were being impeded, anger flared up in him and he issued this challenge:

66.10–16 'Rāma, stand against me! I will fight a duel with you. I will snatch your life away from you with sharp arrows shot from my bow. That you can stand in front of me after killing my father in Daṇḍaka Forest! When I remember what you've done my rage increases. You evil-natured Rāghava, my whole body is on fire at not having met you then in the great forest. Fortune has brought you here to my sight, Rāma. Like a hunger-crazed lion lusting after another deer, so do I for you. Today the force of my arrows shall dispatch you to the realm of the King of the Dead to join those heroes you have slain. Why bother with a long speech? Listen to what I say, Rāma. Let the worlds in their entirety witness you and me on the battlefield. With missiles or with a club, in a great wrestling match with your two arms or by whatever means, engage in combat with me.'

66.17–19 When he heard what Makarākṣa had to say, Rāma son of Daśaratha retaliated derisively with ever more potent threats. 'In Daṇḍaka there were slain by me fourteen thousand *rākṣasas*, and Triśiras, and Dūṣaṇa too, besides your father. Evil *rākṣasa*, today with their sharp beaks and claws and fangs shall vultures, jackals and crows gorge on your flesh!'

66.20–37 At Rāma's words Khara's night-roamer son loosed floods of arrows towards the Rāghava on the battlefield, but with repeated storms of arrows Rāma splintered those gold-notched arrows, and they fell to earth by the thousand. Violent was the battle that ensued when the son of the *rākṣasa* Khara confronted the son of Daśaratha; strident the tones of string on wristguard heard ringing out over the battlefield from their bows as if from two clouds in the sky. Gods and *dānavas*, *gandharvas*, *kinnaras* and great *nāgas* all gathered in the sky in their eagerness to watch this wonder. The strength of each was redoubled with each wound, as blow was answered by blow on the battlefield: the *rākṣasa* splintered the floods of arrows loosed by Rāma in the contest, and with his arrows Rāma repeatedly splintered those loosed by the *rākṣasa*. Every single direction was inundated with arrows, and all around even the earth was lost to view. Then in his fury the mighty-armed prince snapped the *rākṣasa's* bow; next the Rāghava drove eight bolts through his driver; finally Rāma shattered the chariot with his arrows, throwing chariot and horses to the ground. Chariot gone, Makarākṣa the night-roamer took his stance on the ground. The *rākṣasa* stood on the ground holding in his hand a spear equalling the Doomsday Fire in splendour; it would terrify any creature. The night-roamer brandished that great blazing spear, then hurled it at the Rāghava in angry defiance, but as the blazing spear launched by the hand of Khara's son neared, the Rāghava sliced through it in the sky with three arrows; the force of Rāma's arrows cut that divinely gilded spear into pieces, scattering it over the earth like shooting stars. As they watched Rāma's amazing action in destroying that spear the heavenly creatures cheered; when the night-roamer Makarākṣa saw the spear destroyed, he raised his fist and shouted to Kākutstha to stand and fight. Rāma, pride of the Raghus, laughed to see him falling upon him, and fitted the Fire-missile to his bow. The missile struck. The *rākṣasa's* heart was violently torn apart by Kākutstha, and he fell dead. The sight of Makarākṣa's fall sent the *rākṣasas* all rushing back to Laṅkā, pursued by Rāma's arrows.

When all-conquering Rāvaṇa heard that Makarākṣa had 67.1–3
been killed, he angrily ordered his son Indrajit into battle. 'Rāma and Lakṣmaṇa are brothers of enormous prowess. You're a hero. Kill them. Visible or invisible, you are in every way their superior in power. You can triumph over Indra – and his martial exploits are unmatched – so how could you fail to find, confront and kill two men?'

When the lord of the *rākṣasas* had finished speaking, 67.4–15
Indrajit accepted his father's command; he then offered the prescribed oblation to the Fire at the sacrifice ground. Red-turbaned women, agitated *rākṣasīs*, attended Rāvaṇi at the fire-offering with swords and arrow-feathers, with fuel and *vibhītaka* nuts, with red garments and an iron ladle. He heaped arrow-feathers all around the fire, then seized a live, pitch-black goat by the throat.* The oblations were pleasing fuel, and the flames leapt up smoke-free as signs and tokens of victory. With

rightward-turning flames like refined gold, the fire blazed up of its own accord and accepted the oblation. With the oblation offered to the fire he gratified gods, *dānavas* and *rākṣasas*, then made his excellent, splendid chariot invisible and stepped on to it, splendid himself in that supreme carriage with its four steeds, sharp arrows and great bow mounted beside him. Beauty blazed and blazed out from ornaments of burnished gold. Secure in the possession of Brahmā's sunlike missile, mighty Rāvaṇi felt himself invincible. All-conquering Indrajit, oblation offered to the fire, invisibility conferred on him by *rākṣasa mantras*, emerged from the city, declaring:

67.16–17 'Today I shall fight and kill those two who became sham hermits in the forest, and present my father Rāvaṇa with an overwhelming victory. For me to kill Rāma and Lakṣmaṇa and strip the world of *vānaras* will give him exquisite pleasure.' With this boast he became invisible.

67.18–35 At Daśagrīva's urging, Indra's angry foe launched himself into the fray, ferocious with his ferocious bow and bolts. He saw the two heroic warriors in the midst of the *vānaras*, like triple-headed snakes firing off networks of arrows, concluded that they were the ones and strung his bow, inundating them with arrows like Parjanya the rain-maker. He took to the sky in his chariot, out of sight of Rāma and Lakṣmaṇa, and wounded them with sharpened shafts, but amid the onslaught of his arrows Rāma and Lakṣmaṇa fitted arrows to their bows and deployed their divine missiles; though, radiant as gods, they blotted out the sky with their curtains of arrows, the mighty pair could touch him neither with missiles nor with arrows. The majestic *rākṣasa* created a smokescreen that hid the sky and blotted out the surroundings, concealing himself behind mist and fog. Not a sound of bowstring on wristguard, nor of wheel-rim and hoof could be heard as he roamed about; there was no glint of his shape. In the gloomy clouds of darkness the mighty warrior rained down storms of bolts and arrows like a stupendous avalanche. Battle-frenzied Rāvaṇi used his boon to wound Rāma sorely in every limb with his sun-bright arrows, but when the two tigers of men were struck by his bolts, like mountains by torrents, they loosed off honed gold-notched arrows, heron-feathered, that flew into the sky, gashing Rāvaṇi as they flew and falling to earth sprinkled with blood. The two champions were pressed beyond endurance by the flood of arrows, but the two Dāśarathis shattered the falling shafts with any number of arrows, aiming their finest weapons at wherever they saw the arrows coming from, until Rāvaṇi the chariot warrior, darting about everywhere in his chariot and handling his weapons with agility, tore open the Dāśarathis with his sharp shafts: he wounded those heroic Daśarathis so sorely with his well-made gold-notched arrows that they looked as if they had turned into flowering flame-trees. No one knew where he was or what he looked like; his bow, his arrows, everything was as undiscernible as the sun when it plunges into a thundercloud, and apes fell to the ground by the hundred, wounded and struck lifeless.

Lakṣmaṇa grew furious and declared to his brother, 'I want 67.36
to kill every *rākṣasa*! I'm going to use Brahmā's missile!'

But Rāma replied to Fortune-favoured Lakṣmaṇa, 'You 67.37–40
shouldn't destroy the world for the sake of one *rākṣasa*. It's not right for you to kill non-combatants or fugitives, nor any who have surrendered, sought asylum, fled or been driven mad. We'll exert ourselves to kill him, mighty brother. We'll deploy venomous missiles of great impact, and when the *vānara* chiefs find that foul *rākṣasa* sorcerer with the invisible chariot, they'll pound him to death.'

When he realized what the noble Rāghava had in mind, he 68.1–6
avoided a confrontation and went back to the city, but Indrajit Paulastya remembered how those bold *rākṣasas* had been slaughtered. The brilliant warrior's eyes reddened with rage and he returned to the attack via the western gate, surrounded by *rākṣasas*, an intrepid bane of the gods, but at the sight of the heroic brothers Rāma and Lakṣmaṇa prepared to do battle, Indrajit displayed his magic. He magicked up a Sītā and set her on his chariot, surrounded by a large troop. Indrajit planned to slay her; the villain had determined he would delude everyone by killing this Sītā before the *vānaras'* eyes.

When the woodland-dwellers saw him advancing they were 68.7–13
infuriated; up they jumped, stones in hand, eager for the fight,

led by that elephant of a monkey Hanumān, who had snatched up an impossibly huge mountain-peak. Then he saw the Sītā on Indrajit's chariot. She was woebegone and miserable, her hair was in a single plait, her face was wasted with fasting, her only garment was worn out, she was unwashed. The Rāghava's darling, that dainty woman: her whole body was caked with dust and grime. For a moment he gazed at her, then concluded that she was Maithilī. Hanumān was dismayed, and sobs contorted his face. Seeing the Sītā there in the chariot, racked by grief, joyless and wretched, at the mercy of the lord of *rākṣasas*' son, he asked, 'What does he mean to do?'

68.13–15 Suspicion drove the great monkey and the *vānara* chiefs to attack Rāvaṇi, but seeing that *vānara* host, anger-crazed Rāvaṇi unsheathed his sword and grasped the Sītā by the head. As they looked on, Rāvaṇi struck the magic-created woman on the chariot. 'Rāma! Rāma!' she screamed.

68.16–21 Hanumān was disconsolate to see her seized by the hair and wept sorrowful tears. Then in fury the Son of the Wind spoke harsh words to the son of the *rākṣasa* suzerain. 'You may have been conceived in a *rākṣasa* womb, but you were born in a line of brāhman sages: shame on you, you villain, for even thinking of such a plan! You're a cruel, low-down, wicked, vile coward! This is not the act of a noble person! You've no pity! You're heartless! Maithilī has lost home, kingdom and Rāma's hand. What's she ever done to you that you want to kill her? You kill Sītā, and you've not long to live! A deed like that calls for death, and you'll get it at my hands! Then when you've lost your life, after death, you'll go to the worlds assigned to slayers of women – worlds abominated even by universally condemned criminals.'

68.22–4 While he was speaking, Hanumān was rushing furiously towards the *rākṣasa* lord's son with a company of armed apes, but as they attacked he beat back the heroic army of forest-dwellers with a fierce charge by his *rākṣasa* force. A thousand arrows caused the ape army to flinch, then Indrajit replied to the ape leader Hanumān:

68.25–8 'I'm going to kill Vaidehī today, and you're going to watch me. She's the reason you and Sugrīva and Rāma have come here. And when I've killed her, then I'm going to kill Rāma, and Lakṣmaṇa, and you, *vānara*, and Sugrīva, and that low-down Vibhīṣaṇa. Monkey, you may say it's wrong to kill a woman, but that's why I'm going to do it, because it will distress my enemies.'

So saying, Indrajit personally killed the weeping magic- 68.28–30
created Sītā with his sharp-edged sword, and that poor woman, that shapely beauty, collapsed to the ground, her body slashed in two.[13] With that woman slain, Indrajit told Hanumān, 'Look at Rāma's wife now, crushed by my fury!'

Indrajit was exultant at having killed her with his own broad- 68.31–2;
sword, and mounted his chariot bellowing raucously; the 69.1–2
bellowing resounding from his gaping maw as he regained the fortress reached the ears of the *vānaras* drawn up nearby. Hearing the fearsome roaring, loud as Śakra's thunderbolt, the bulls of *vānaras* glanced around and fled in all directions. Faces despairing, miserable and frightened they all scattered, but Hanumān Son of the Wind called out:

'Monkeys, why are you bounding away in despair, aban- 69.3–4
doning your resolution for the fight? Wherever has your courage gone? Follow me where I lead you into battle! It's not right for high-born heroes to retreat.'

These wise words from the Son of the Wind reassured them 69.5–14
and they furiously snatched up mountain-peaks and trees. The bulls of *vānaras* roared and fell upon the *rākṣasas*, surrounding Hanumān and following him into the thick of the fighting, where Hanumān, surrounded on all sides by these *vānara* chiefs, burned up the enemy host like a blazing sacrificial flame. In the midst of the *vānara* army, the gigantic monkey massacred *rākṣasas*; he was like Time, he was like Death, he was like Yama. Grief and rage possessed Hanumān as the great monkey hurled a huge rock at Rāvaṇi's chariot, but the charioteer saw it coming; his horses were responsive and he drove the chariot well away, preventing the rock from hitting Indrajit standing on the chariot beside the driver. Snatched up to no effect, it split open the earth and re-entered. Nevertheless, the fall of the rock threw the *rākṣasa* army into confusion. The woodland-dwellers roared into the attack in their hundreds. Enormous

vānaras of fearsome valour snatched up trees and mountain-tops and threw them into the midst of the enemy, and fierce-looking night-roamers writhed about on the battlefield beneath the heroic onslaught of these tree-wielding *vānara* warriors.

69.15–19 Then Indrajit surveyed the havoc the *vānaras* were causing his own army. Angrily he seized his weapons and went for his opponents, loosing floods of arrows from the midst of his own troops, demonstrating his prowess and killing many tigers of monkeys with pikes, clubs, swords, javelins and cudgels. The *vānaras* fought back against his followers in the fray: mighty Hanumān devastated the ruthless *rākṣasas* with *sāl* trunks and branches and with rocks, but when he had warded off the enemy army Hanumān ordered the forest-dwellers:

69.19–22 'Fall back! We can't overcome this force. We're losing our lives in our effort to please Rāma, but Janaka's daughter, the cause of the battle, has been killed. We should report this news to Rāma, Sugrīva as well, and then do whatever those two command.' When that leading *vānara* had issued this order he halted all the *vānaras* and gradually withdrew his troops in an orderly fashion.

69.23–5 When Indrajit observed Hanumān marching off to the Rāghava, he went to Nikumbhilā and made an offering to the Fire, and the fire on that sacrificial ground flared up and consumed the libation of blood ceremonially poured out by the *rākṣasa*. Wrapped in radiance like the sun at twilight, the fire rose fiercely, gratified by the offering of blood.

70.7–9 The glorious *vānara* rushed towards the ape army and sadly told Rāma his news. 'While we were fighting the battle, before our eyes Rāvaṇa's son – that Indrajit – killed the weeping Sītā. I saw her! I was so agitated and dismayed, destroyer of your enemies, that I've come to make my report to your lordship.'

70.10; When he heard his news, Rāghava fell to the ground like a
71.5 tree with severed roots, fainting with grief. Vibhīṣaṇa was devastated and grief-striken at the sight of Rāma laid low by anguish and asked, 'What's the matter?'

71.6–7 Lakṣmaṇa was overcome by sobs, but seeing Sugrīva and the *vānaras* with Vibhīṣaṇa at their head he told them, 'My friend,

Hanumān says that Indrajit's killed Sītā! When he heard that, the Rāghava fainted.'

As Saumitri spoke, Vibhīṣaṇa interrupted and addressed the 71.8–9;
dazed Rāma with words of encouragement. 'Sovereign lord, 72.8–10
what Hanumān told you in his distress is no more probable than for the ocean to run dry. That's my opinion! Stop grieving, your majesty! Don't distress yourself for nothing! Don't give the enemy the satisfaction of thinking you believe it! You'll have to act like a hero, pull yourself together, and keep up your morale if you're to rescue Sītā and kill the night-roamers. I'll tell you what to do, pride of the Raghus; just listen while I explain the best course. Well now, let Saumitri here lead a large troop to Nikumbhilā to challenge and kill Rāvaṇi.'

Vibhīṣaṇa's spirits rose again when he had made this sugges- 74.1–3
tion to Saumitri. He hurried off, bow in hand, to a forest close by; once inside, Vibhīṣaṇa showed Lakṣmaṇa what was going on. Rāvaṇa's glorious brother pointed out to Lakṣmaṇa a fearsome-looking banyan like a dark cloud.

'That is where Rāvaṇa's mighty son offers up an oblation of 74.4–7
living beings before going off to battle; then the *rākṣasa* becomes invisible to all creatures, kills his foe in combat and fetters them with his supreme shafts. With your sharp shafts you must deflect that mighty son of Rāvaṇa, chariot, horses and charioteer too, before he enters that banyan.'[14]

Saumitri agreed, and that splendid joy of his allies took up 74.7–9
his stance there, flexing his glittering bow, when Rāvaṇa's mighty son Indrajit appeared with his armour, sword and standard on his flame-coloured chariot. The splendid warrior called out to the unvanquished Paulastya, 'I challenge you to battle! Give me a fair fight!'

Seeing Vibhīṣaṇa there, Rāvaṇa's splendid son reflected on 74.10–16
what he had heard and reviled him: 'There you are, before my eyes, my father's brother born and bred. How can you do harm to his son, you, my uncle, a *rākṣasa*? You've no family feeling, no friendship, no breeding, you schemer! You don't measure up to the duties of a full brother! You're a disgrace! Decent people will grieve for you, you villain, and blame you for deserting your own kind and stooping to serve the enemy.

You're so weak-witted you don't know there's a huge difference between living with your own and dishonourably consorting with foreigners. The foreigners may be strong, your own people may be weak, but your own people are better, right or wrong. A foreigner is a foreigner. Such a lack of sympathy as yours for your own people – you alone could hold such a cruel attitude, younger brother of Rāvaṇa!'

74.17–26 Vibhīṣaṇa responded to his nephew's tirade: 'Don't you know my character, *rākṣasa*? Why are you getting above yourself? Stop talking so spitefully to your elder, you disreputable son of the *rākṣasa* lord. Even though I was born a *rākṣasa* in a family of savages, I have the best qualities of humans: my character is non-*rākṣasa*. I take no pleasure in cruelty, nor indeed do I take pleasure in immorality. My brother's so depraved, yet how could even he cast out his brother? Taking what belongs to someone else, laying hands on the wife of another, undue suspicion of well-wishers: any of these three sins ensures ruin. Ferociously slaughtering great sages, making war on all the gods, his arrogance, his rage, his belligerent and disagreeable nature: my brother's sins will destroy his life and his sovereignty, blotting out his good qualities like clouds over mountains. These are the sins that made me desert my brother, your father. Laṅkā, you, your father – they are nothing to me. You're arrogant, you're childish, you're wicked, *rākṣasa*, and you're in the grip of Time's noose. You can say what you like to me now, but calamity is on its way to you today, and then what will you say? You can't get into the banyan, vile *rākṣasa*. Now you've outraged the two Kākutsthas you've no longer to live. Fight a battle against that godlike man Lakṣmaṇa. You will be killed and go to serve the gods in Yama's realm.'

75.1–4 Maddened with fury, Rāvaṇi replied to Vibhīṣaṇa's words with a savage exclamation, then launched a violent attack. He looked like Time the Ender, standing brandishing weapons and sword on his great, well-adorned chariot with its team of black horses; the bow he wielded was huge – enormous, powerful, sturdy, fearsome. In fury he seized some foe-destroying arrows and told Saumitri, Vibhīṣaṇa and the tigers of *vānaras*:

'See my might! Today you will feel the weight of a merciless storm of arrows loosed from my bow in this battle, like rain pouring from the sky. Today the arrows I launch from my great bow shall rage through your bodies like fire in a heap of cotton. Today I shall dispatch you all to Yama's realm, impaled on sharp shafts, pikes, spears, lances and javelins. When I stand in battle like a thundering cloud, shooting out showers of shafts with my nimble hands, who will withstand me?' 75.4–8

No fear discomposed Lakṣmaṇa's features when he heard the *rākṣasa* lord's fulmination; he responded to Rāvaṇi with anger: 'Hard will it be for you, *rākṣasa*, to make good the boasts you've made; wise is the man whose actions fulfil his aims. The goal you've set yourself would be hard for anyone to reach: you'll never get there! You think you've reached your goal just by bragging about it, you villain! Your combat tactic of making yourself invisible befits a thief, not a warrior! I'm standing before you now, within reach of your arrows. Show your prowess! Or are your boasts just words?' 75.9–13

This challenge had mighty, all-conquering Indrajit grasping his fearsome bow and shooting off sharp shafts. The irresistible arrows he shot, venomous as snakes, fell like hissing serpents on Lakṣmaṇa. In that battle Rāvaṇa's irresistible son Indrajit wounded Fortune-favoured Saumitri with arrows of irresistible force, until glorious Lakṣmaṇa, his limbs shot through by arrows, drenched in blood, glowed like a smokeless fire. 75.14–17

Drawing close to examine what he had done, Indrajit bellowed uproariously and declared, 'Saumitri, these feathered, sharp-edged arrows I've loosed from my bow shall today take your life; they're death-dealing! Today let swarms of jackals, swarms of hawks and vultures descend upon you, lifeless, struck dead by me. Today that unwarlike warrior, that low-down, villainous Rāma, shall watch as I kill his devoted brother, slice through your armour, snap your bow and cut off your head: Saumitri, he'll see you on the ground, slain by me!' 75.18–22

Lakṣmaṇa's retort to the frenzied words of Rāvaṇa's savage son was well-judged and appropriate. 'Why are you boasting about a deed you've not yet done, *rākṣasa*? Do the deed: then I'll believe your boasts. I'm making no savage threats, I'm not 75.23–5 hurling abuse, I'm not bragging, but I am going to kill you. You watch me, cannibal!'

75.26–32 So saying, Lakṣmaṇa drew back to his ear five bolts, irresistible reeds, and drilled them into the *rākṣasa's* chest. Rāvaṇa's son was enraged to be struck by Lakṣmaṇa's arrows and wounded him in return with three well-directed shafts. There ensued a terrifying, tumultuous conflict between those two lions – the *rākṣasa* and the man – both lusting to kill each other in the battle, both powerfully built, both courageous, both bold and expert in weaponry and missiles, both invincible and matchless in strength and splendour; the great warriors fought like two planets in the sky. Like Bala and Vṛtra, or like two lions, the noble warriors fought that battle; both were unassailable. Many were the floods of arrows they gleefully poured out as they struggled, those two unyielding lions, the *rākṣasa* and the man.

76.1–4 Then the all-conquering Dāśarathi, angry as a hissing serpent, fitted an arrow and shot it at the *rākṣasa* lord; colour drained from the face of Rāvaṇa's son when he heard the sound of string on wristguard and he glared at Lakṣmaṇa. When Vibhīṣaṇa saw that Rāvaṇa's *rākṣasa* son's face was troubled, he told staunch Saumitri, 'I can see portentous signs about this son of Rāvaṇa, so hurry, mighty prince. He is weakening, I'm sure.'

76.5–8 Then Saumitri fitted arrows like tongues of flame and loosed those sharpened shafts at him like venom-laden snakes. When Lakṣmaṇa's arrows hit him with the force of Śakra's thunderbolt he swooned momentarily and lost control of his senses, but regained consciousness after a moment and came to. Then the warrior saw Daśaratha's warlike son standing on guard, and fell upon Saumitri with rage-reddened eyes, howling as he went:

76.9–12 'What, can't you remember our first battle, when my prowess had you and your brother writhing about in my fetters in that battle? That great battle, when I first knocked you senseless to the ground, you two and your escort, with shafts like Śakra's thunderbolt? If you insist on attacking me I can only think you've lost your memory, or else you clearly want to go to

Yama's realm. If my prowess wasn't apparent to you in the first battle, I'll demonstrate it to you today. On guard!'

So saying, he drove seven arrows into Lakṣmaṇa and ten 76.13–16
into Hanumān, savage-edged supreme shafts; then, his rage doubly aroused, the warrior impaled Vibhīṣaṇa with a hundred well-directed arrows. When Rāma's younger brother saw what Indrajit had done he dismissed it with disdain. 'That's nothing,' he said. No fear discomposed the features of Lakṣmaṇa, that bull of a man; he took ferocious arrows and fired them furiously at Rāvaṇi in the battle.

'That's not the way a warrior attacks in a battle, night- 76.17–18
roamer! These nice arrows of yours are gentle and ineffective. Warriors don't fight like that in a battle they want to win!' With these taunts he showered him with a storm of arrows.

Shattered by the arrows, his gold-adorned armour cascaded 76.19–33
to the chariot floor like a tracery of stars from the sky. The warrior Indrajit, like an enormous mountain, now had nothing left to protect him in the battle, and sustained wounds from the bolts. Continuously the pair panted as tumultuously they battled; their limbs were all slashed by arrows and completely drenched in blood. Those supreme missile-exponents went on deploying their missiles until they burdened the sky with arrows of every description, their shooting unerring, agile, versatile, exemplary. Fierce was the tumult raised both by man and by *rākṣasa*. A terrible slapping of bowstrings arose from each one of that ferocious pair, like the crashing of two clouds in the sky. The gold-notched arrows ricocheted bloodstained from their bodies in that battle, fell to earth and stuck in the ground. Arrows collided with well-sharpened shafts in the sky, smashing and shattering them by the thousand. The dreadful arrows piled up in the fray like piles of *kuśa* grass round two blazing fires at a sacrifice. The wounded bodies of those two nobles glowed like a silk-cotton and a flame-tree flowering leafless in the forest. Each desperate to defeat the other, Indrajit and Lakṣmaṇa kept up their tumultuous, fierce onslaught. Lakṣmaṇa struck Rāvaṇi in their struggle, Rāvaṇi struck Lakṣmaṇa: neither gave way to fatigue. Those energetic warriors with masses of arrows embedded in their bodies looked

spectacular, like mountains bristling with vegetation. Concealed behind their covering of arrows, their blood-drenched limbs all sparkled like blazing fires. A long time passed while they struggled, but neither succumbed to fatigue, neither lost his appetite for the battle.

77.1–6 Seeing the intensity with which man and *rākṣasa* were fighting, Rāvaṇa's heroic brother entered the field of battle, flexed his great bow in readiness and loosed sharp-pointed shafts at the *rākṣasas*, fiery shafts that fell as one, slicing through the *rākṣasas* like thunderbolts cleaving great mountains. Vibhīṣaṇa's followers were outstanding among *rākṣasas*: with pikes and swords and javelins they too cut down *rākṣasa* warriors in combat, but Vibhīṣaṇa stood out among his gleeful escort like a bull elephant among its young. Then that *rākṣasa* chief realized it was time to encourage the apes in their eagerness to fight the *rākṣasas* and made a well-timed speech.

77.7–14 'That lone warrior is the last one the *rākṣasa* lord can rely on; this is all that's left of his army. What are you waiting for, lords of the apes? Once this evil *rākṣasa*'s been killed in pitched battle, that's the whole army destroyed apart from Rāvaṇa. We've killed Prahasta the warrior, mighty Nikumbha, Kumbhakarṇa and Kumbha, Dhūmrākṣa the night-roamer, Akampana, Supārśva, Cakramālin the *rākṣasa*, Kampana and that spirited pair, Devāntaka and Narāntaka. You've slaughtered all those enormously powerful, elite *rākṣasas*, the work of your hands has brought you across the ocean: you can leap over this tiny puddle! *Vānaras*, this is the only one you have left to conquer: slain is every *rākṣasa* swaggering in his might that you've confronted. It would be improper for me to bring about the death of my father's son, but my brother's son I would kill: for Rāma's sake I would suppress all pity, only there's a tear clouding my death-dealing eye. It's for mighty Lakṣmaṇa here to silence him, and for you *vānaras* in a body to kill his escort.'

77.15–21 This encouragement from that most renowned *rākṣasa* cheered the *vānara* lords and they thumped their tails; the tigers of apes growled and growled, calling and screeching like peacocks at the sight of clouds. Supported by all his own troops, Jāmbavān assailed the *rākṣasas* with stones, claws and teeth, but the well-equipped, powerful *rākṣasas* fearlessly encircled the ruler of bears as he attacked; as Jāmbavān struck the *rākṣasa* host in the fray, so they struck him with arrows, keen axes, javelins, staves and lances, setting off a tumultuous conflict between apes and *rākṣasas*, as fearsome and clamorous as if they were gods and anti-gods. Hanumān too in fury tore out a *sāl* from a mountain, ran to the *rākṣasas* and massacred them by the thousand.

Indrajit battled violently against his uncle in the fray, then 77.22–8
again rushed at Lakṣmaṇa, that killer of enemy warriors. Lakṣmaṇa and the *rākṣasa* confronted each other with heroism in that battle, each smiting the other with storming floods of arrows, till the powerful, nimble pair disappeared repeatedly behind curtains of arrows, like the sun and moon behind clouds at the end of the hot season. So deft were the hands of those combatants that no movement could be seen as they picked up arrows, placed, bent their bows and shot, drew back and let fly, aimed and struck. With the entire sky blotted out by the curtains of arrows loosed by the vigour of their bows, no shapes could be made out. Hidden in that gloom, everything took on a more terrifying aspect. No wind blew; not a fire blazed. 'May all be well with the worlds!' intoned great sages; *gandharvas* and *cāraṇas* fled the scene.

Then Saumitri sent four arrows through that lion of a 77.29–37
rākṣasa's four black, gold-adorned steeds; as the charioteer struggled to regain control, with his next arrow that glorious Rāghava adroitly severed his head from his body. At the sight of his driver killed in battle, Rāvaṇa's son lost his stomach for the fight and despaired. The ape chiefs rejoiced to see the despair on the *rākṣasa's* face and congratulated Lakṣmaṇa, and four ape lords, Pramāthin, Śarabha, Rabhasa and Gandhamādana, launched an impetuous assault. With fearsome daring and tremendous heroism, the *vānaras* leapt up and suddenly fell upon his four champion steeds; the impact of those mountainous *vānaras* brought blood gushing from the horses' mouths. Steeds killed and chariot smashed, they rapidly leapt up again and returned to Lakṣmaṇa's side, but Rāvaṇi jumped

out of his chariot with its dead horses and overthrown driver and attacked Saumitri with a storm of arrows.

78.1–10 Horses destroyed, the mighty night-roamer Indrajit took his stand on the ground, infuriated and ablaze with splendour. Like two bull elephants in the forest the bowmen confronted each other with their arrows, desperately eager for the kill. *Rākṣasas* and forest-dwellers alike supported their own master in the struggle, pounding each other and attacking again and again. Taking aim, he rained down on Lakṣmaṇa with the utmost agility storms of arrows the equal of Indra Puraṃdara's storms of rain, but Lakṣmaṇa, that vanquisher of his foes, was unperturbed and warded off that irresistible hail of arrows poured out by Indrajit. Judging that he would be unable to pierce Lakṣmaṇa's armour, Indrajit dexterously wounded him on the forehead with three well-notched shafts, but despite the pain from the *rākṣasa's* arrows Lakṣmaṇa immediately returned his fire and wounded him with five arrows. Fearsome in their valour, the warriors Lakṣmaṇa and Indrajit struck each other with well-feathered arrows from their powerful bows, attacking and wounding one another in every limb with savage shafts; the two bowmen were intent on victory.

78.11–23 Vibhīṣaṇa's fury grew against the now horseless fighter and he fired off five arrows with the impact of thunderbolts at his chest, gold-notched shafts that met their mark, sliced open his body and emerged bloodstained like great scarlet serpents. Indrajit was enraged at his uncle; surrounded by his *rākṣasas* the mighty warrior selected a special arrow given him by Yama, but when powerful Lakṣmaṇa, of fearsome prowess, observed him fitting that great reed, he too selected an arrow, hard to overcome, hard even for gods and anti-gods, Indra included, to withstand: it had been given him while he slept by Kubera in person. Both arrows were supreme, both were put to excellent bows and drawn back by the warriors; both blazed with extreme radiance. Loosed from the bows, those well-feathered shafts lit up the sky as they smashed directly into each other in a violent collision. They had looked like great planets, but after their battle-collision they fell to earth in a hundred pieces. Lakṣmaṇa and Indrajit alike were taken aback and infuriated to see their arrows shattered in the fray: Saumitri in his fury seized a Varuṇa missile while dauntless Indrajit deployed a Rudra one, and there ensued between them a prodigiously tumultuous struggle. Celestial beings clustered round Lakṣmaṇa. Throughout that dreadful conflict, ringing with the dreadful cries of *vānaras* and *rākṣasas*, beings of all kinds graced the sky, awestruck: sages, ancestors, gods, *gandharvas*, Garuḍa and his snakes all gathered behind Indra Śatakratu to protect Lakṣmaṇa in that battle.

Then the younger Rāghava, the hero, set another excellent 78.24–31
arrow to tear through Rāvaṇa's son: its impact great as fire, well feathered, well proportioned, well fitted, well designed, gold-adorned, a body-destroying arrow, hard to avoid, hard to suffer, it filled the *rākṣasas* with fear as if it were a venomous serpent; the assembled gods held it in awe. Of old, in the war between gods and anti-gods, it had been used by the splendid, heroic lord Śakra with his team of bays to defeat the *dānavas*, and now Saumitri the champion set to his champion bow that champion arrow, unsurpassed in battle, the Indra missile. He set it, he drew back his bow, that cleaver of adversaries, bent by the bowstring; he was as irresistible as Time at the end of the world. He set it to his fine bow, he bent it, then Fortune-favoured Lakṣmaṇa spoke words to further his cause: 'If Rāma Dāśarathi is righteous, true to his word and unsurpassed in manliness, then kill Rāvaṇi.'[15]

With these words the warrior Lakṣmaṇa drew back the 78.32–7
unerring arrow to his ear and loosed it at Indrajit in the battle – the Indra missile, primed by Lakṣmaṇa, that slayer of hostile warriors. From Indrajit's trunk it tore his majestic head complete with helmet and flashing earrings, and fell to the ground. Blood-spattered, the great golden head lay on the ground for all to see, hewn from the shoulders of the *rākṣasa's* heir, and Rāvaṇa's son at once fell dead upon the earth, shattered along with his armour, helmet and bow. Then Vibhīṣaṇa and all the *vānaras* shouted with joy at his slaughter as the gods did at the slaying of Vṛtra, and the air was filled with the cheers of its populace, noble sages, *gandharvas* and *apsarases*.

When the great army of *rākṣasas* took in that he was fallen, 78.38–44 they fled in all directions, massacred by the triumphant apes. The *rākṣasas* all lost their nerve in response to the *vānara* slaughter, threw down their weapons and ran for Laṅkā; spears, swords and battleaxes, all their arms were cast aside in panic as the *rākṣasas* fled by the hundred in a rabble in every direction. Terrified, some were harried by *vānaras* until they reached Laṅkā, others jumped into the sea, yet others sought refuge on the mountain; not one among the thousands of *rākṣasas* remained once they had seen Indrajit lying slain on the battlefield. Just as when the sun goes to rest its rays disappear, so at his fall the *rākṣasas* were gone in all directions. Like the sun with its rays extinguished, like a fire put out, that brilliant warrior's life was over and done.

78.45–8 The world was filled with joy at the fall of the *rākṣasa* lord's son; with its enemy destroyed, its multifarious burdens were eased. Śakra the Blessed also, in company with all the bulls of gods, was filled with delight when that evil *rākṣasa* was slain. The pure waters and the sky rejoiced. *Daityas* and *dānavas* gathered when the one who had brought fear upon all the world was killed. All the assembled gods, *gandharvas* and *dānavas* proclaimed, 'Brāhmans may now wander without agitation or fear of pollution.'

78.49–53 The ape commanders were delighted at the battle and exulted at seeing that matchless bull, that son of Disorder, slain. Vibhīṣaṇa, Hanumān and the bear commander Jāmbavān exulted at the victory and congratulated Lakṣmaṇa. Their aim achieved, the monkeys growled and bellowed and roared as they crowded round Raghu's son to acclaim him. Thumping their tails and blurting out 'Lakṣmaṇa's won!' the *vānaras* raised their voices. With delight in their hearts the monkeys hugged each other and recounted all manner of tales of Rāghava exploits.

80.1–2 When Paulastya's courtiers had confirmed the rumour of Indrajit's slaughter, they reported to Daśagrīva with trepidation, 'Mahārāja, great is your splendour; while we were watching, your son was killed in battle by Lakṣmaṇa, assisted by Vibhīṣaṇa.'

83.1–5 Rāvaṇa could hear in family after family throughout Laṅkā the piteous lamentation of distressed *rākṣasīs*; heaving a long sigh he stood momentarily lost in thought. Then Rāvaṇa grew furious and took on a terrifying aspect: he bit his lip between his teeth, his eyes reddened with rage, he was as frenzied as the fire at Doomsday, and even the *rākṣasas* were frightened to look at him. The *rākṣasa* lord turned his blazing eye on some *rākṣasas* stammering in terror nearby – Mahodara, Mahāpārśva and the *rākṣasa* Virūpākṣa – and ordered, 'Send troops out at once under my command.'

Apprehensive at the king's command, those *rākṣasas* sum- 83.6–9
moned some unwavering *rākṣasas*; all the fearsome-looking *rākṣasas* assented, voiced their hopes for success, and assembled before Rāvaṇa. Rāvaṇa they honoured in due form, then with a respectful salute the chariot warriors all wished their master victory. Rāvaṇa was beside himself with fury and told Mahodara, Mahāpārśva and the *rākṣasa* Virūpākṣa with a sneer:

'Today from my bow shall I fire arrows like the Doomsday 83.10–20
blaze to dispatch the Rāghava and Lakṣmaṇa to the realm of Yama. Today shall I exact retribution for Khara, Kumbhakarṇa, Prahasta and Indrajit by slaughtering the enemy: not the air, not the regions around, not rivers, not even the ocean will be visible – all will be blotted out by the clouds of my arrows. Today like the sea shall my bow send forth successive waves of arrows to pulverize the troops of those leading *vānaras*. Today like an elephant shall I rampage through lakes of their troops, trampling their faces like full-blown lotuses decked with their filaments. Today in the battle shall *vānara* commanders adorn the earth, their arrow-studded faces looking like lotuses and their stalks. Today with the release of a single arrow in battle shall I tear open hundreds and hundreds of those bellicose apes who war with trees. Today by my slaughter of the enemy shall I wipe away the tears of those who have lost husband, brother or sons. Today shall I strew the earth with expiring *vānaras*, torn open by my arrows in the battle, till it well-nigh disappears. Today shall I glut jackals, vultures and all carrion-eaters with the arrow-vexed flesh of my foes. At once let my chariot be made ready, my bow be

brought, and let all remaining night-roamers accompany me into battle.'

83.21 At these words Mahāpārśva told the orderly officers in attendance, 'Hurry the troops along.'

83.22–5 The nimble orderlies raced round Laṅkā, furiously rounding up *rākṣasas* from house after house, and a moment later *rākṣasas* of fearsome valour tumbled out with a roar. Fearsome were their faces; many were the weapons in their hands – swords, javelins, pikes, clubs, pestles, ploughs, sharp-edged spears, great cudgels, darts, bludgeons and other fine weapons.

83.26–31 Then on Rāvaṇa's order four orderly officers rapidly summoned his chariot and charioteer, drawn by eight coursers; that divine chariot radiated its own brilliance, and Rāvaṇa seemed to be harrowing the earth with his unfathomable nature as he mounted. Mahāpārśva, Mahodara and invincible Virūpākṣa were ordered out by Rāvaṇa and mounted their chariots, delightedly raising a dreadful bellow fit to rend the earth with its noise, and set out lusting for victory. Finally the chariot warrior set out for battle, brandishing his bow, vigorous and supported by his army of *rākṣasa* troops, looking like deadly Time or Yama on his chariot with its fleet horses, and left through the gate closest to Rāma and Lakṣmaṇa's position.

83.32–7 Then the sun was stripped of its splendour and the regions all around were plunged into gloom; fierce birds called out and the earth quaked; blood rained down from heaven and the coursers stumbled; a vulture alighted atop his standard and jackals howled out their message of doom; his left eye twitched, his left arm throbbed, colour drained from his face and his voice grew hushed: signs arising to presage his death in combat as Daśagrīva the *rākṣasa* rushed out to battle. A meteor hurtled from the sky with a noise like thunder, vultures gave ominous calls that were echoed by crows, but Rāvaṇa thought nothing of all the grim portents around him and pressed on, madly seeking his own slaughter; he was in the grip of Time.

83.38–41; The sound of those noble *rākṣasas'* chariots mobilized the
84.1–4 *vānara* army too for battle, and a tumultuous struggle ensued between apes and *rākṣasas* as they angrily challenged each other in their desire for victory. Angrily Daśagrīva dealt great

destruction among the divisions of *vānaras* with his gold-adorned arrows: some of the wrinkle-faced warriors had their heads cut off by Rāvaṇa, others were struck down lifeless, some were run through, some had their heads cleaved, some had their eyes put out. Daśagrīva's arrows tore limbs from the apes, scattering them until the ground was covered. Unbearable was the impact of the arrows from the lone Rāvaṇa, and they could no more endure it than moths can a blazing fire; tormented by the sharpened shafts they fled, bellowing like elephants that have been caught in the flames of a fire and burnt. Rāvaṇa himself went about in the fray routing the monkey divisions with his arrows like clouds in a gale, rapidly devastating the forest-dwellers; before long the *rākṣasa* lord met with the Rāghava in combat.

Sugrīva saw that the monkeys had broken in combat and 84.6–12
were running away. He decided to enter the fray at once, assigning to his command post Suṣeṇa, a *vānara* warrior who was his equal; when he had been dispatched, Sugrīva took his stand in front of the enemy, armed with a tree. Beside and behind him the commanders all snatched up boulders too, and enormous trees of every description. The great Sugrīva roared out his great battle-cry, laying low in death some notable *rākṣasas*. The gigantic *vānara* lord flattened the *rākṣasas* like the wind does huge mountains at the end of an Era, raining a shower of boulders on the *rākṣasa* divisions like a cloud scattering hailstones over flocks of woodland birds. The storm of rocks hurled by the king of monkeys smashed the *rākṣasas'* heads and they collapsed like demolished mountains.

When the *rākṣasas* all around, broken, collapsing and 84.13–31
screaming, were being annihilated by Sugrīva, the *rākṣasa* Virūpākṣa, that irresistible bowman, yelled out his own name, jumped down from his chariot and sprang on to an elephant's shoulder. Riding that tusker, the chariot warrior Virūpākṣa bellowed a fearsome roar and charged the *vānaras*, firing fierce arrows at Sugrīva in the vanguard, rallying the shrinking *rākṣasas* and emboldening them. The monkey lord was angered by the wounds from the *rākṣasa's* sharp shafts; his anger thoroughly roused, he made up his mind to kill him. The heroic

ape tore up a tree in the struggle, leapt forward and bludgeoned his great elephant in the face with it, till Sugrīva's blows sent the great elephant reeling away a bowshot distance; it sank down trumpeting. The *rākṣasa* warrior hurriedly dismounted from the lurching elephant and faced up to his monkey adversary; nimbly he caught up a bull-hide shield and a sword and attacked Sugrīva, who stood ready to receive his threat. This enraged Sugrīva, who snatched up a boulder mighty as a cloud and hurled it towards Virūpākṣa. The bull of a *rākṣasa* saw the boulder coming and dodged, then boldly struck at him with his sword in his anger, shattering Sugrīva's armour with the sword in front of his troops and knocking him down with the force of that sword-blow. Back on his feet, the fallen monkey aimed at him a slap like a fearsome clap of thunder. Sugrīva's slap galvanized the *rākṣasa*: expertly recovering, he punched him on the chest. Sugrīva lord of the *vānaras* was even more enraged to see the *rākṣasa* had escaped his own blow, but the *vānara* spied an opening in Virūpākṣa's guard and furiously landed a powerful slap on his temple; his palm was like great Indra's thunderbolt, and the blow sent him drenched with gore to the ground, vomiting blood. Ugly-eyed Virūpākṣa could be seen weltering in foaming blood, eyes even uglier and rolling from rage. The monkeys gazed at their quivering, blood-spattered enemy thrashing about on his side and screaming piteously.

85.1–4 The armies were killing each other at such a rate in that great battle that they were like two lakes being dried up at the height of summer. Rāvaṇa overlord of the *rākṣasas* had double cause for wrath: the slaughter of his army and the death of Virūpākṣa. He saw his army diminishing, killed by wrinkle-faced monkeys; he observed the reversal of fortunes in that battle. Agitation overcame him, and he spoke to all-conquering Mahodara standing nearby:

85.4–5 'We're in a crisis, mighty warrior! My hope of victory rests on you. Now display your heroic prowess and kill the enemy army. The time has come for you to repay your master's bounty. May you fight well.'

85.6–7 Mahodara assented to the *rākṣasa* lord's command and plunged like a moth to the fire into the hostile host. Lustily the mighty warrior devastated the *vānaras*, at his master's command and urged on by his own boldness.

85.8–12
Sugrīva saw that the great *vānara* army was breaking in the battle and at once rushed towards Mahodara. The lord of apes snatched up a boulder, enormous, awesome, mountainous, and hurled it with all his might to kill him, but Mahodara was unruffled to see that irresistible boulder hurtling towards him, and shattered it with arrows. The *rākṣasa* shot the boulder into a thousand pieces with a flood of arrows and it fell to earth like a flock of squabbling vultures. Sugrīva was infuriated by the sight of the boulder being shattered, so he uprooted a *sāl* and threw it at the *rākṣasa* in the midst of the fray, only to have it riddled with arrows by that warlike conqueror of enemy forts.

85.13–18
Next in his anger he spotted a mace lying on the ground. That blazing mace he swung defiantly before him and battered his choice steeds violently with the mace tip. Steeds killed, the *rākṣasa* warrior Mahodara jumped down from that great chariot and angrily snatched up a club. Club and mace in hand, the two heroes confronted each other in battle, bellowing like bulls or like two thunder-clouds. With the mace the lord of apes struck the other's club, but the mace was shattered by the club and fell to the ground. Then from the earth the glorious Sugrīva snatched up an iron pestle, dreadful and adorned all over with gold; he brandished it, he threw it, but another club was hurled; they collided, they shattered, they both fell to the ground.

85.19–21
Then, with their weapons destroyed, those two closed with each other hand to hand, both radiating the energy and power of sacrificial flames. Again and again they struck each other and roared; blows from each other's palms laid both on the ground. Undefeated, the two heroes quickly sprang up and landed further blows, then grappled each other with their arms.

85.22–9
Finally Mahodara, that mettlesome *rākṣasa*, snatched up a sword that happened to be nearby, together with a shield. Sugrīva too, that even more mettlesome champion *vānara*, snatched up a huge sword that had been dropped along with a

shield. Then those two experts in battle-weaponry, rage coursing through their whole bodies, attacked each other with roars, gleefully wielding those swords in the fray. Rapidly they circled, each keeping the other on his right, both enraged, both intent on victory. Then malicious Mahodara, that mettlesome warrior, brought down his sword on the great shield, parading his heroism, but as he was raising the sword he had in his grip, with his own sword that elephant of a monkey lopped off his head, helmet, earrings and all. The *rākṣasa* lord's troops lingered there no longer when they saw him stretched headless on the ground, while the joyful ape who had killed him roared together with the *vānaras*. Daśagrīva grew angry; the Rāghava exulted.

86.1–4 When Mahodara had been killed, mighty Mahāpārśva harried Aṅgada's fearsome army with his arrows. On all sides heads were ripped from *vānara* chiefs' bodies like fruit from its stalk in a gale. The *rākṣasa* slashed the arms and shoulders of some *vānaras* with arrows and wrathfully transfixed others. The *vānaras* were tormented by Mahāpārśva with his storm of arrows; dejected, their faces fell, and they all lost heart.

86.5–23 When mighty Aṅgada saw that his troops were being worried and tormented by the *rākṣasa*, a tide of anger rose in him like the sea at full moon. The *vānara* leader snatched up an iron mace splendid as the sun's rays and brought it down violently on Mahāpārśva; Mahāpārśva was stunned by the blow and with his charioteer fell from the chariot to the ground, senseless. Then the glorious bear king, dark as a heap of collyrium, valiantly leapt out of his own cloudlike troop and angrily seized a huge, mountainous boulder; swiftly he battered the horses and smashed the chariot. But Mahāpārśva was very strong and regained consciousness after a moment. With many arrows he again wounded Aṅgada, with three arrows he hit Jāmbavān king of the bears on the breastbone, and he struck Gavākṣa with many shafts. Aṅgada was beside himself with anger to see Gavākṣa and Jāmbavān weighed down with arrows, and snatched up his dreadful mace. In his rage against that far-off *rākṣasa* he lifted the iron mace, splendid as the sun's rays, in both hands, whirled it violently and threw it; Vālin's son was intent on the death of Mahāpārśva. Hurled by that mighty monkey, the mace knocked bow and arrows out of his hand – the *rākṣasa's* helmet too. Vālin's mighty son rushed quickly up and slapped him furiously on the lobe of his ring-decked ear, but Mahāpārśva, brilliant, forceful and furious, picked up in one hand an enormous axe, oiled and polished, spotless, adamantine, tough; in his fury the *rākṣasa* was bringing it down on Vālin's son, but Aṅgada, enraged, dodged and caught the axe violently on his shield's left shoulder. Very angry and equalling his father in prowess, the heroic Aṅgada himself threw a punch like a thunderbolt. He knew the vulnerable area and aimed his fist beneath the *rākṣasa's* ribs up towards his heart with the force of Indra's thunderbolt; the violence of the blow burst the *rākṣasa's* heart and he fell dead to the ground. His fall to the ground dismayed his troops, and Rāvaṇa was overwhelmed with battle-fury.

[*The duel between Rāvaṇa and Rāma begins.*]

The destruction of his missile redoubled Rāvaṇa's anger, 88.1–12
and in his anger Rāvaṇa the very splendid *rākṣasa* overlord prepared to launch his next missile against the Rāghava, another awesome, Maya-made missile, the Rudra. Pikes and clubs and pestles, blazing and diamond hard, were streaking in all directions from his bow, and cudgels, nooses and flaming thunderbolts, varied and ferocious, were flying like winds at the end of an Era. That ultimate exponent of extreme weaponry, the radiant Rāghava, majestically destroyed that missile with his supreme *gandharva* missile. With frightful force wily Daśagrīva dispatched from his bow discuses, sunlike and huge, hurtling to every quarter and landing everywhere around; they set the sky ablaze as if they were the blazing sun, moon and planets, but with torrents of arrows the Rāghava splintered the glittering weapons coming from Rāvaṇa at the vanguard of his army, those discuses. When Rāvaṇa saw that his missile had been destroyed, the *rākṣasa* overlord wounded Rāma at all his vulnerable points with ten arrows, but though wounded by those ten arrows shot from his great bow by

glorious Rāvaṇa, the Rāghava did not waver; instead, the all-conquering Rāghava in great anger wounded Rāvaṇa with many arrows in all his limbs.

88.13–16 Meanwhile Lakṣmaṇa, that slayer of hostile heroes, the Rāghava's powerful junior, angrily laid hold of seven arrows, arrows of great impetus with which the glorious prince repeatedly pierced Rāvaṇa's standard with its human head. Next it was the head of his charioteer – a son of Disorder – that majestic, mighty Lakṣmaṇa shot off with an arrow, then with five sharpened shafts Lakṣmaṇa severed the *rākṣasa* lord's bow, although it was like an elephant's trunk.

88.17–27 Vibhīṣaṇa then sprang forward and clubbed Rāvaṇa's fine, black-cloudlike, mountainous horses. With the horses killed, vigorous Rāvaṇa leapt with vigour from the great chariot, incensed with anger against his brother. Then the mighty lord of *rākṣasas* used his great might to launch a spear fiery as a fiery thunderbolt at Vibhīṣaṇa, but before ever it arrived Lakṣmaṇa had sliced through it with three arrows, bringing a loud cheer from the battling *vānaras*. The spear was garlanded with gold, and it fell from the sky triply smashed, flashing and sparkling like a great shooting star. Next he seized a long spear that he thought would fare better. Even Time would find it hard to overcome this one with its blazing splendour; handled by evil, mighty Rāvaṇa it blazed up with frightful power, its radiance that of Śakra's thunderbolt. At this critical juncture, Vibhīṣaṇa was in danger of his life, but heroic Lakṣmaṇa ran rapidly to his aid, wielding his bow to rescue him; spear still in hand, Rāvaṇa was sprayed by a storm of arrows by Lakṣmaṇa the heroic. His courage gave way before the torrent of arrows spraying him, loosed by the noble prince; he saw that his brother had been rescued by Lakṣmaṇa, and he decided against the attack. Confronting Lakṣmaṇa, Rāvaṇa declared:

88.28–9 'All right, you braggart, you've rescued Vibhīṣaṇa, but the spear that's spared the *rākṣasa* shall fall on you! When I hurl this spear, my mace-like arms shall send it tearing through your heart, weltering in gore, and with it take your life.'

88.30–38 So saying, Rāvaṇa directed the spear at Lakṣmaṇa. It had eight bells, it boomed, it had been made by Maya's magic, it was unerring, it was lethal to foes, it radiated splendour, and with an infuriated bellow he hurled it. Fearsome was the power with which it was hurled. With a crash like Śakra's thunderbolt the spear flew violently towards Lakṣmaṇa in the thick of the battle. As the spear was about to fall, the Rāghava prayed, 'May all be well with Lakṣmaṇa! Go astray! Lose your force!' but with a great impact it pierced Lakṣmaṇa's chest, blazing and brilliant as the snake king's tongue. Driven far in by Rāvaṇa's force, the spear clove his heart. Lakṣmaṇa collapsed. When he saw Lakṣmaṇa in this state, the resplendent Rāghava close by was moved by affection for his brother and lost courage. Tears clouded his eyes, but after a moment's thought his wrath grew like the Doomsday Fire and the Rāghava, realizing that this was no time for despair, waged all-out war in his determination to slaughter Rāvaṇa.

Then Rāma gazed at Lakṣmaṇa, blood streaming down him 88.39–43
like snakes down a mountain, ripped open in the combat by that spear: so powerfully had Rāvaṇa hurled it that the efforts of even the best of the apes, harassed as they were by the floods of arrows from the *rākṣasa's* nimble hands, were insufficient to dislodge that spear. It had gone right through Saumitri and was stuck in the ground. Angrily, violently, Rāma grasped that awe-inspiring spear in his hands and broke it off, then pulled it out with vigour. As he was pulling the spear out, Rāvaṇa took advantage and poured down lethal arrows on all his limbs, but the Rāghava ignored the arrows and took Lakṣmaṇa in his arms, instructing Hanumān and Sugrīva:

'Stay here, *vānara* chiefs, and guard Lakṣmaṇa. The long- 88.43–54
desired time for me to display my valour has arrived. I yearn to kill this evil, malicious Daśagrīva like a *stokaka* yearns for the sight of clouds at the end of summer. This instant, *vānaras*, without delay, I promise you truly, you shall see the world without Rāvaṇa, or without Rāma. Losing the kingship, life in the forest, trailing around Daṇḍaka, the outrage against Vaidehī that caused that confrontation with the *rākṣasas*, and then the terrible calamity that I sustained, with the hellish grief it brought – today all shall be forgotten when I kill that Rāvaṇa in battle. It was on account of him that I assembled this army

of *vānaras*, killed Vālin in battle and then installed Sugrīva as king, it was on account of him that we crossed the sea and built a causeway across the ocean, and today I have set eyes on him in battle, that evil-doer. Now I've set eyes on him, this Rāvaṇa will die as surely as if I were a serpent darting venom from my eyes. Station yourselves at ease on the mountain-tops, invincible bulls of *vānaras*, and watch the battle – the one between me and Rāvaṇa. The three worlds with *gandharvas*, gods, sages and *cāraṇas* – today let them watch Rāma fight, let them see what makes me Rāma! As long as the earth endures, the worlds with their beings, animate and inanimate, gods too, shall tell of the deed I shall perform today.' With this declaration, Rāma attacked Daśagrīva with sharp, gold-adorned arrows, intent on battle.

88.55–8 Then Rāvaṇa too showered Rāma with blazing bolts and pestles like storms from a cloud. Arrow after arrow fired by Rāma and Rāvaṇa alike collided with a tumultuous crash. Tips ablaze, the arrows of Rāma and Rāvaṇa alike splintered and scattered as they fell from sky to ground. Prodigious was the noise of string on wristguard from Rāma and Rāvaṇa alike. All creatures took fright.

89.1–5 Tumultuous was the attack he launched at evil Rāvaṇa; he showered him with arrows, but then declared to Suṣeṇa: 'Lakṣmaṇa here, this hero, has been knocked to the ground by Rāvaṇa's onslaught. He's writhing about like a snake! It's breaking my heart! How can I find the strength to fight while I can see this hero drenched in blood? He's dearer to me than my own life, and my mind's in a turmoil! My brother here, this proud warrior, favoured by Fortune – if he's met his end how shall I enjoy life any more? I almost feel ashamed of my own vitality, my bow seems to be slipping from my hand, my arrows are falling short, I can't see properly for sobbing, I'm getting increasingly agitated, and I wish I was dead!'

89.6–8 The sight of his brother struck down by evil Rāvaṇa drove him to the utmost despair; his mind in a whirl, he lamented. 'I shouldn't be bothering with fighting or my life or with Sītā when I can see my brother Lakṣmaṇa slain in the dust of battle.

What do I want with kingship, what do I want with life? I can see no reason in fighting when Lakṣmaṇa here lies killed on the battlefield.'

Suṣeṇa the warrior spoke words of encouragement to Rāma. 89.8–12
'Lakṣmaṇa here, the mighty furtherer of Fortune, is not dead! His complexion is neither marred nor dark; it's not lost its glow. His face looks glowing and peaceful, the palms of his hands are like red lotuses and his eyes are quite clear. That's not the appearance of one whose life is over, your majesty. You're a victorious hero: don't despair, he's alive! He's just unconscious, sprawled on the ground; his breathing, and the regular beating of his heart tell you that.'

After these appropriate words to the Rāghava, Suṣeṇa issued 89.13–16
urgent instructions to Hanumān, who was standing nearby. 'Comrade, make haste from here to that mountain, the herb mountain, the holy one that Jāmbavān told you about earlier, heroic monkey. Fetch the sacred plant that frees from pain – it's called the Viśalyā herb and it grows on the southern peak – to revive the noble hero, Lakṣmaṇa.'

Unbounded was the strength of that Son of the Wind, and 89.18–21
he was determined to fulfil his commission. 'Right, I'll pick up the peak of this mountain and take him that, for if I go back without taking the Viśalyā herb, valuable time will be lost and great despair will arise,' thought mighty Hanumān, and he hurried back. 'I can't distinguish between these herbs, you bull of an ape, so I've brought the whole mountain-peak.'

The *vānara* chief Suṣeṇa congratulated the Son of the Wind 89.22–4
on his words, then uprooted and picked the herbs. When he had crushed some, Suṣeṇa, splendid leader of the *vānaras*, held the herb to Lakṣmaṇa's nose. Lakṣmaṇa smelt it, then that wounded slayer of hostile warriors got up from the ground, healed of his wounds and his pain.

The sight of Lakṣmaṇa on his feet filled the apes with joy 89.25–6
and they cheered Suṣeṇa, 'Bravo! Bravo!' 'Come here, come here!' cried Rāma the slayer of hostile warriors to Lakṣmaṇa and embraced him with deep affection, eyes clouded with tears.

When the Rāghava had embraced Saumitri, he said, 'Fortune 89.27–8 has brought you back from death before my eyes, you hero! Life, and Sītā, and victory – they were useless to me – what point would there be in living if you'd met your end?'

89.29–34 Lakṣmaṇa was still weak, and replied to the Rāghava's words in a feeble voice. 'You've once given your word, and a champion of integrity like you shouldn't be saying such things like any spiritless lightweight! You are irreproachable, and people of integrity don't break their word; keeping promises is the sign of a man of character. You are irreproachable, so stop acting so helpless on my account. Keep your word and kill Rāvaṇa today. When your enemy encounters your arrows he will live no longer than a great elephant in the sharp teeth of a roaring lion. For my part I want that villain killed straightaway, before the sun up there finishes its day's work and goes to its rest.'

90.1–4 When the Rāghava heard what Lakṣmaṇa said he shot savage shafts against Rāvaṇa at the head of his army. In return, from his stance on the chariot Daśagrīva struck Rāma with arrows like thunderbolts flooding ferociously down as if from a cloud, while Rāma assiduously wounded Daśagrīva in the battle with gold-adorned arrows like blazing fires. 'With the *rākṣasa* mounted on his chariot, Rāma on the ground is at a disadvantage in the battle,' cried gods, *gandharvas* and *dānavas*.

90.8–12 Then, there stood Mātali, charioteer of Thousand-eyed Indra, with chariot and goad, saluting Rāma with deference and explaining: 'The Thousand-eyed sends you this glorious, foe-destroying chariot to win you victory, heroic spirit, together with Indra's great bow, a fire-like cuirass, arrows like the sun's rays and a sharp, untarnished spear. Hero, mount this chariot and kill Rāvaṇa the *rākṣasa*, with me, Rāma, as your charioteer, as great Indra did the *dānavas*.' At this invitation Rāma responded courteously, circumambulated the chariot and mounted; his splendour lit up all the worlds.

90.13;
92.1–9 Then ensued a marvellous contest, a horrific chariot-duel between Rāma the mighty and Rāvaṇa the *rākṣasa*. The braggart warrior Rāvaṇa was infuriated to be harassed in the battle by the angry Kākutstha. Rage blazed from his eyes as he

heroically brandished his bow and furiously launched an almighty onslaught against the Rāghava. Rāvaṇa poured out thousands of streams of arrows like a cloud in the sky, and filled the Rāghava with arrows like a pond, but though skeins of arrows shot from his bow in that battle filled him, the Kākutstha wavered no more than an immovable great mountain. As if they were sunbeams that steadfast hero welcomed those skeins of shafts, warding them off with his own shafts. Then in his fury the nimble night-roamer fired off thousands of arrows into the noble Rāghava's chest, and blood streamed from Lakṣmaṇa's senior in that battle till he looked like a huge flame-tree flowering in a forest. The impact of the arrows infuriated Kākutstha too; brilliant as the Doomsday sun, he radiated power as he seized his shafts. Rāma and Rāvaṇa alike were so infuriated with each other that arrows blotted each from the sight of the other as they fought.

Then Rāma, heroic son of Daśaratha, was overwhelmed with 92.10–22
anger. He mocked Rāvaṇa and addressed him with contempt: 'Knowing no better than to make off with my wife from Janasthāna against her will doesn't make you a hero! You're the least of all *rākṣasas*! You made off with Vaidehī by force when I had left her on her own in her wretched forest-existence, so you think: "What a hero I am!" You abuser of other people's wives, you hero, you act like a low-down scoundrel towards defenceless women, so you think: "What a hero I am!" You break all the bounds of propriety, you act without shame or valour, you snatch at death in your arrogance, and you think: "What a hero I am!" What a great exploit for a warrior surrounded by armies! That will bring praise and renown to a brother of Vaiśravaṇa! Today you are going to taste the terrible fruit of that great exploit, infamous and ill-advised, that your arrogance led you to commit. You villain, you believe you're a hero, and you've no shame over dragging Sītā away like a thief. If I'd been there when you laid violent hands on Sītā my arrows would have sent you lifeless to join your brother Khara, but now that fortune has brought you within my sight, you blackguard, my sharp shafts shall dispatch you today to Yama's realm. Today shall my arrows sever your head with its fiery

earrings: carrion-eaters can tear it to pieces and drag it away through the dust of the battlefield! You shall be thrown to the ground, Rāvaṇa: then vultures can swoop down on to your chest and thirstily gulp down the gore gushing from the wounds of my arrows. Today shall you fall lifeless, ripped open by my arrows: then birds can tear at your entrails like Garuḍas at snakes.'

92.23–30 So saying, Rāma the heroic conqueror of his foes showered arrows over the *rākṣasa* lord standing nearby. As Rāma lusted after his enemy's end his courage, his strength, his exultation at the battle and even the might of his missiles were doubled; the missiles of that sagacious warrior of great splendour all manifested themselves[16] and his agility increased with delight. Rāma recognized how auspicious were the signs accompanying him and pressed home his attack on Rāvaṇa to make an end of the *rākṣasa*. Daśagrīva was so demoralized at being struck by the masses of rocks from the apes and the storms of arrows from the Rāghava that he could not keep hold of his weapon or draw back his bow; his spirits sank and he could offer the hero no resistance. No arrow he could launch, not one of his weapons, was equal to its task in this battle; the hour of his death was upon him. However, the driver guiding his chariot was aware of the predicament; calmly he edged his chariot out of the fight.

93.1–9 Delusion enraged Rāvaṇa; impelled by the power of Fate, eyes red with anger, he turned on his charioteer. 'So I've lost my courage, I'm useless, I'm not a man, I'm timid and lightweight, I've no spirit, no drive, my magic's all deserted me, I've no missiles left – is that why you despise me, you scoundrel? You're acting according to your own lights! What do you mean by despising me and disregarding my wishes, withdrawing my chariot in full view of my enemy? You, you scum, have destroyed in a day the renown, heroism, splendour and credibility that I've built up over a long period. I was lusting after battle, but you've turned me into a nobody – and while an enemy who is celebrated for his courage and can appreciate deeds of valour was looking on! But if it's not your own stupidity that's making you drive the chariot away, you rascal, then that proves my suspicion: you've been got at by the other side. This does not look like the action of a friend who wishes me well: it's more like that of an enemy, and you're ill-advised to carry it out. If you're one of my retainers, or if you remember what I'm capable of, you'll turn the chariot round at once while my enemy's still there.'

The charioteer had meant well, and replied with tact and good advice to injudicious Rāvaṇa's harsh words. 'I'm not afraid and I'm not deluded; I've not been suborned by enemies and I'm not negligent; I don't lack affection for you and I've not forgotten how kindly you've treated me. It was in your interest and with affection welling from my heart that I performed the action that displeases you, hoping to do you good and safeguard your prestige. Great king, in this case you shouldn't be finding fault with me as mere scum, when I'm intent on your welfare and happiness. Hear me out, and I'll explain why I turned the chariot round in the battle like the incoming tide checking the flow of a river. You're exhausted by your great feats of war. I realized that, because I could detect no composure or joy in your face, heroic lord. And then there's these chariot steeds: they're worn out with pulling the chariot, and they're as miserable and weary of the heat as cows drenched by a downpour. A growing succession of portents has been vouchsafed to us, but all of them indicate doom. We must make allowance for place and time, and take account of omens like distress and exultation, weariness and the strength or debility of the chariot warrior. We must watch out for the humps and hollows in the ground, the rough places and the smooth, as well as the opportunity, and we must detect a weak point in the adversary. Advancing or retreating, standing or fleeing – all that is for the driver to determine from his stance on the chariot. It was because of your exhaustion, and that of these chariot-steeds, that I took the proper course of action to counter your terrible weariness. It wasn't to please myself that I drove the chariot away, heroic lord; I did it overflowing with affection for my master, mighty lord. Give the order, heroic conqueror, and I will do exactly as you say, with not a thought of disobedience.' 93.10–23

93.24–5 Rāvaṇa approved of the charioteer's words, and commended him repeatedly. He was eager for the fray, and ordered, 'Bring the chariot round to face the Rāghava, driver; Rāvaṇa will not retreat from a battle until he's killed his enemies.'

94.1–3 The king of men watched the headlong approach of the *rākṣasa* king's chariot. With its great standard it roared along, drawn by black horses, dreadful in its brilliance, plastered with banners like flashes of lightning, equipped with the armoury of an Indra and discharging rivers of arrows like a cloud made of rivers. When Rāma saw his enemy's chariot advancing like a cloud, with the crashing noise of a mountain being split apart under the impact of a thunderbolt, he addressed Mātali, charioteer of Thousand-eyed Indra.

94.4–7 'Mātali, see our enemy's chariot furiously approaching. He's attacking me again from the left.* It's clear he intends to kill me in battle. So take your stand with vigilance, and advance towards the enemy's chariot. I want to tear him to shreds, like the wind does a billowing cloud. Take the reins and apply yourself calmly and resolutely, with clear head and clear sight; hurry the chariot along at once. Of course it is not for me to direct you: you are accustomed to the chariot of Indra Puraṃdara. It's because my sole desire is to fight; I'm only reminding you, not instructing you.'

94.8–11 Expert charioteer of the gods, Mātali was delighted by Rāma's words and urged the chariot onwards. He approached Rāvaṇa's chariot from the left, discomforting him with the dust thrown up by the wheels, but he, eyes rolling and copper-coloured with anger, harassed Rāma approaching in his chariot with arrows, an attack that aroused his resentment until rage overcame his composure and he grasped the Indra-bow: great was its power in battle, and the radiance of its arrows equalled the sun's rays in splendour.

94.12–27 Great was the battle into which they plunged then as they squared up to each other like two proud lions eager for the kill. Gods, *gandharvas*, *siddhas* and supreme sages gathered to watch the chariot-duel, anxious for Rāvaṇa to be overpowered. Portents appeared, baneful and horrendous, signalling destruction for Rāvaṇa and victory for the Rāghava. Blood rained down from the heavens on to Rāvaṇa's chariot, intense whirlwinds blasted him from the left, a huge flock of sky-borne vultures swooped over his chariot wherever it went; in broad daylight Laṅkā was shrouded by a twilight glow red as a *japā* flower and it seemed as if the earth was ablaze; great meteors pernicious to Rāvaṇa demoralized the *rākṣasas* with their thunderous crashing, the earth quaked beneath Rāvaṇa, the *rākṣasas* felt their arms being held back as they attacked; the sun's rays falling on Rāvaṇa's body gleamed coppery, yellow, cream and white like mineral deposits on a mountain, furious jackals escorted by vultures vomited flames from their mouths as they peered into his face and howled inauspiciously; the *rākṣasa* king was blinded by the battle-dust swirled up by a contrary wind, Indra's dread thunderbolts with their unbearable din fell from a cloudless sky on his army all around, every area in every direction was shrouded in gloom and the sky disappeared behind a great dust storm; savage mynahs squabbling ferociously with savage squawks swooped down on his chariot by the hundred, his horses continuously shed fire and water in equal measure – sparks from their flanks and tears from their eyes. Many were the terrifying portents of this kind that arose, savage signs of annihilation for Rāvaṇa.

For Rāma though, sweet, auspicious signs sprang up on all 94.28
sides, presages of victory.

Savage was the momentous chariot-duel waged then by 95.1–7
Rāma and Rāvaṇa alike, a struggle to bring fear to the whole world. The *rākṣasa* army and the ape host both halted, weapons in hand, all hearts captivated and lost in utter amazement at the sight of man and *rākṣasa* fighting with might; their arms were engaged with their many weapons but their minds were amazed, and they stood watching the battle rather than attacking each other till the glittering armies looked like a painting, *rākṣasas* gazing at Rāvaṇa and *vānaras* at the Rāghava. The Rāghava and Rāvaṇa had both seen the omens, but both had made up their minds, both were resolute and resentful, both fought fearlessly. 'He must be defeated,' thought Kākutstha. 'He must be killed,' thought Rāvaṇa. Steadfastly they then displayed their whole stock of battle heroism.

95.8–12 Then Daśagrīva, wrathful and warlike, set arrows and shot them towards the standard mounted on the Rāghava's chariot, but those arrows fell short of the standard on Indra Puraṃdara's chariot, just touching its shaft as they fell to the ground. Then in his warlike wrath Rāma bent his bow and applied his mind to how he should retaliate. He aimed at Rāvaṇa's standard and loosed a sharpened shaft as insupportable as a great serpent that blazed with its own radiance. The arrow sliced through Daśagrīva's standard and fell to earth; splintered, Rāvaṇa's chariot standard fell to the ground.

95.13–20 Anger fuelled the fire in mighty Rāvaṇa when he saw his standard toppled and he blazed into battle, in thrall to rage, spewing out a great storm of arrows, arrows with which Rāvaṇa pierced Rāma's divine steeds, but despite their wounds the horses did not stumble or even waver; their hearts were as stout as if the blows came from lotus stalks. Rāvaṇa was even more enraged to see the tenacity of those horses and fired off a storm of arrows, along with clubs and maces, discuses and pestles, mountain-peaks and trees, pikes and axes too. Unwearied by the effort, he poured out that storm of magic weapons, and then thousands of arrows: great was the battle tumult of those different weapons, terrifying, horrific, its fearsome resonance hard to endure. Throughout the *vānara* host he shot them, quickly making the Rāghava's chariot and the air itself solid with arrows: Daśagrīva was firing at random.

95.21–6 Kākutstha watched the strenuous efforts Rāvaṇa was making in the fray and disdainfully aimed his sharp shafts, releasing those battle arrows by hundreds and thousands; Rāvaṇa's response to the sight was to cram the sky with his own arrows, till the gleaming arrow-storm they deployed seemed to create a second gleaming firmament of arrows. No arrow but met its target, none that exceeded its goal, none that was unproductive, of those arrows poured out in the battle between Rāma and Rāvaṇa. Without pause they fought; shots from both sides choked the sky with their floods of arrows. Rāma on Rāvaṇa's steeds, Rāvaṇa on Rāma's steeds, both scored hits, then they pounded each other blow for blow.

96.1–7 All creatures looked on with wondering minds as Rāma

and Rāvaṇa fought out their battle. Both took on a dreadful appearance as they tested their magnificent chariots to the limit in their determination to kill each other. The charioteers displayed the whole range of their driving ability, wheeling and charging, advancing and retreating. Rāma injured Rāvaṇa, and Rāvaṇa the Rāghava as their own momentum carried them forward and back; their superlative vehicles roamed over the field of conflict like two rain clouds as they shot their skeins of arrows. When they had demonstrated their many skills they again came to a halt and faced each other in the fray: yoke to chariot-yoke, face to horse's face, flag to flag they halted.

Four sharp shafts fired from Rāma's bow then induced 96.8–19
Rāvaṇa's four radiant horses to give ground. The night-roamer was overcome with rage at his horses giving ground and loosed sharpened shafts at the Rāghava, but the Rāghava, ripped open though he was by the powerful Daśagrīva, remained unmoved and was not even perturbed. The night-roamer bombarded the Thunderbolt Wielder's charioteer with arrows that crashed loud as thunderbolts, but the great impact of the arrows landing on his body did not disconcert or rock Mātali in the least. The Rāghava was enraged more by the assault on Mātali than on himself and repulsed his enemy with a storm of arrows: the warrior Rāghava fired arrows at his enemy's chariot in twenties, thirties, sixties, hundreds and thousands. The seven seas were stirred up by the commotion of clubs and pestles and maces and by the wake of the arrows. Then gods, *gandharvas*, *siddhas*, supreme sages and *kinnaras* and *nāgas* too offered a prayer: 'May all go well with cows and brāhmans; may the worlds endure for ever; may the Rāghava be victorious in battle against Rāvaṇa lord of the *rākṣasas*.'

Then Rāma set to his bow a razor-edged arrow like a venom- 96.20–24
ous snake and sliced off Rāvaṇa's majestic head with its flashing earrings. The three worlds saw the head fall to the ground, but then there stood Rāvaṇa complete with an identical head! Quick to react, quick to act, Rāma quickly sliced off Rāvaṇa's second head with his battle arrows, but no sooner was that head cut off than another appeared. That too was cut off by Rāma with arrows like thunderbolts. And so a whole hundred

of equally splendid heads were cut off with no result: Rāvaṇa's life remained intact.

96.25–7 Then the Rāghava, that growing joy to Kausalyā, that hero who was expert in all missiles, reflected on the many arrows he had employed. 'The one that killed Mārīca, the ones that killed Khara and Dūṣaṇa, and Virādha in Krauñca Forest and Kabandha in Daṇḍaka Forest – all these were arrows I could rely on in battle; so why are they ineffective against Rāvaṇa?'

96.28–31 The Rāghava thought hard but remained focused on the fight and rained a storm of arrows on to Rāvaṇa's chest. From his stance on his chariot Rāvaṇa, angry lord of the *rākṣasas*, then counter-attacked Rāma in the fray with a storm of clubs and pestles. Gods, *dānavas*, *yakṣas*, *piśācas*, *nāgas* and *rākṣasas* looked on while that great battle continued through the night: not by night or by day, not for an hour, not for a moment was there any pause in the battle of Rāma and Rāvaṇa.

97.1–2 Then Mātali suggested to the Rāghava, 'Heroic prince, why are you heedlessly not pressing home your advantage? Mighty lord, you should use the weapon of the Grand Father to bring about his death. The time of destruction ordained by the gods has now arrived.'

97.3–19 Prompted by Mātali's words, Rāma selected a blazing arrow like a hissing snake first given to the hero by the blessed sage Agastya; the gift of Brahmā, it never missed its mark in battle. Brahmā of measureless might had once fashioned it to aid Indra and had given it to the Lord of the Gods when he wanted to conquer the three worlds, imparting Wind to its feathering, Fire and Sun to its tip; Ether composed its shaft, Meru and Mandara its weights; beauty ever flamed forth from its gold-adorned notch; all beings had lent it their radiance, the sun had lent it its lustre; smoking like the Doomsday Fire, blazing like a venomous snake, it could shatter nimble troops of chariots, elephants and horses, it could batter down gates and barriers, mountains too; it was stained all over with gore, it was bathed in grease, it was very savage; diamond-hard and thunderous, savage in every conflict, terrifying all, fearsome as a hissing snake, in warfare it was a constant source of food for flocks of herons and vultures and packs of jackals and *rākṣasas*, a second Yama, inspiring terror, bringing joy to *vānaras* and despair to *rākṣasas*; its layers of feathering glistened and glittered with feathers from Garuḍa. That arrow, supreme in the worlds, destroying Ikṣvāku fear, effacing the fame of their foes to his own delight – that great arrow, uttering a *mantra* and reciting a Vedic precept, Rāma the mighty, the powerful, set to his bow. Wrathful, his whole attention concentrated, he drew back his bow to its fullest extent and fired that lethal arrow. Irresistible as a thunderbolt, loosed by arms with the power of a thunderbolt, unavoidable as Fate, it struck Rāvaṇa's chest. The colossal impact of that flying bolt annihilated the body and tore open the heart of evil Rāvaṇa; drenched with blood, the lethal shaft thudded into the ground, taking with it Rāvaṇa's life, then, wet with blood, the arrow flew quietly back to its own quiver, its task accomplished. Rāvaṇa was dead.

As life and breath left him, bow and arrows slid quickly 97.20–21
from the hand of the slain; life at an end, like Vṛtra slain by the thunderbolt, with a fearful crash the brilliant Lord of the sons of Disorder fell from his chariot to the earth.

When the surviving night-roamers saw him lying on the 97.22–5
ground they fled in all directions, panic-stricken that their leader had been killed; *vānaras* armed with trees fell on them, cheering at the sight of Daśagrīva's death and the Rāghava's victory. Harassed by the joyful *vānaras* they rushed in terror to Laṅkā, their mournful faces awash with tears at the killing of their protector, while the jubilant and triumphant *vānaras* cheered and proclaimed the victory of the Rāghava and the death of Rāvaṇa.

Then in the sky the Thirty Gods' kettledrum was heard softly 97.26–30
beating, and divine perfumes were wafted on a gentle breeze, beauteous rare blooms showered down from sky to earth, strewing the Rāghava's chariot, and in heaven were heard the melodious voices of noble deities cheering and praising the Rāghava. Great joy filled gods and *cāraṇas* too when ferocious Rāvaṇa, that terrifier of all the worlds, was killed. The killing of that bull of a *rākṣasa* brought contentment to Sugrīva and mighty Aṅgada, and gladness to the Rāghava.

When the *rākṣasīs* heard that Rāvaṇa had been killed by the 98.1–5 noble Rāghava, they came rushing out of the private apartments, haggard with grief, flinging themselves this way and that, writhing about on the ground in the dust with their hair unfastened, distressed and sorrowful as cows whose calves have been killed. They left by the northern gate with an escort of *rākṣasas* and entered the dreadful battleground to search for their slain lord. 'Noble prince!' they called, and 'Alas for our lord!' as they darted all over the blood-muddied ground amid the corpses lying in its lap. Their eyes filled with tears as grief for their husband overmastered them, and their cries were like the trumpeting of elephant cows whose herd-leader has been killed.

98.6–11 Then gigantic, heroic, brilliant Rāvaṇa came into view, slain, like a heap of dark collyrium on the ground. Suddenly finding their lord lying in the battle dust, they collapsed on his body like forest creepers torn from their support. Out of love for him they wept. One threw her arms around him, one clasped his feet, one hung from his neck, one threw up her arms and rolled about on the ground, one swooned at the sight of the corpse's face, one cradled his head in her lap as she wept at the sight of his face, blotting out his face with her tears like a lotus with mists. So distressed were they to see Rāvaṇa their husband slain on the ground that they wailed repeatedly from sorrow, and lamented again and again.

98.12–17 'The one who terrified Śakra, who terrified Yama, who dispossessed King Vaiśravaṇa of the Puṣpaka Chariot, the one who spread fear among *gandharvas*, sages and noble gods – that one lies killed in battle! Knowing no fear from anti-gods, gods or even *nāgas* – to him fear has come from a human. Not gods, *dānavas* nor *rākṣasas* could kill him, but he lies there killed in battle by a human footsoldier. Not deities, not *yakṣas*, not anti-gods either could kill him, but he has been sent to his death by one subject to death, like a person of no consequence.' So saying over and over again his wives wept and lamented again and again in the torment of their grief.

98.18–26 'It's because you refused to listen to your well-wishers, who always gave you good advice, that they and we have been cut down today just like you. When your dear brother Vibhīṣaṇa gave good advice, in your folly you humiliated and abused him, seeking your own death. If you had sent Sītā Maithilī back to Rāma this dreadful calamity would not have occurred to eradicate us wholly. Your brother would be content, Rāma would be back with friends and family, we would not be widows and your enemies would not be exulting. But your cruel and violent imprisonment of Sītā has brought down a threefold destruction – on you, us and the *rākṣasas* alike. Admittedly it's not your own desire that's been driving you, it's been divine will; all killings are ordained by the divine will. This slaughter of *vānaras*, of your *rākṣasas*, and of you yourself has come about by divine ordinance. Indeed, not wealth, nor desire, nor valour nor ignorance can check the working out of the divine will in the world once it has been set in motion.' Tears dimmed the eyes of the *rākṣasa* overlord's young wives and grief tormented them as they wailed like ospreys in their misery.

While the *rākṣasa's* girls were pouring out this lament, his 99.1–2
dear senior wife was gazing miserably at her husband. At the sight of Daśagrīva her lord killed by Rāma's unimaginable prowess, Mandodarī mourned in anguish.

'You are Vaiśravaṇa's mighty junior! Surely even Indra Pur- 99.3–13
aṃdara is afraid to confront you in your anger! Surely even those gods on earth the sages, glorious *gandharvas* and *cāraṇas* too, have scattered in all directions through fear of you! This Rāma is nothing more than a man, and he's defeated you in battle! Why don't you shrink back in shame, you, a king, a bull of a *rākṣasa*? You've trampled the three worlds underfoot, you're gifted with majesty and prowess, you're invincible – how could a human forest-dweller kill you? You operate in a sphere inaccessible to humans, you can change shape at will; it's not right that you should be destroyed in battle by Rāma! I can't believe what Rāma's done on the battlefield – how could he get through to you with your followers all around you? Of old you subdued the threefold world by subduing your appetites; now your appetites have taken their revenge and overcome you. Or it must be that Indra Vāsava has appeared in person in the form of Rāma and it's his magic that's taken you

unawares and destroyed you. That was no human that killed your brother Khara amid a host of *rākṣasas* in Janasthāna! Then when Hanumān intrepidly got into Laṅkā, a city even the gods can scarcely enter, that really unnerved us, but when I told you, "Don't antagonize the Rāghava," you took no notice, and this is what's come of it.

99.14–20 'Anyway, you bull of a *rākṣasa*, you'd no reason to lust after Sītā to the destruction of your sovereignty, your life and your own people, or to demean yourself by conceiving that evil deed, assaulting Sītā when you should have respected her as superior to Arundhatī or even Rohiṇī! Not in family, not in beauty, not in ability is Maithilī superior to me or even equal, but you were too besotted to notice. Death never occurs in any creature without a harbinger; Maithilī was certainly the harbinger of your death. Maithilī will make merry with Rāma free of sorrow, but for my sins I am plunged into a dreadful sea of sorrow. I used to make merry with you on Kailāsa, Mandara, Meru as well, and in the Caitraratha forest and all the divine pleasure gardens; I used to travel in fitting style in a carriage of unparalleled splendour; and now your death, my hero, has plummeted me from pleasure and enjoyment.

99.21–2 'My distinguished brother-in-law spoke the truth when he predicted, "The annihilation of the chief *rākṣasas* is at hand: this emotion-born disaster is springing from your lust and rancour." It is you who have robbed the *rākṣasa* race of its lord.

99.23–9 'You don't need my grief; your might and manliness are well known. But my feminine, emotional nature stirs me to compassion. You've gone to meet your reward, the fruit of your good deeds and bad. It's myself I'm grieving for in my sorrowful separation from you. Why are you lying there like a black cloud clad in yellow and fine bracelets, bathed in blood and your limbs sprawled about? You look as if you're asleep. Why won't you answer me in my grief and sorrow? I was born into a noble house, so why are you ignoring me? The mace you've been using to batter your foes in battle, like a thunderbolt from Indra the Thunderbolt Wielder: you always honoured it, with its sunlike radiance and the golden filigree adorning it. It cudgelled your enemies in the fray, but arrows have shattered it into a thousand splinters. Shame on me! A thousand splinters is what my sorrow-laden heart should have burst into when you met your end.'

Meanwhile Rāma had been telling Vibhīṣaṇa he should per- 99.30–31
form his brother's funeral rite and console the wives. Vibhīṣaṇa knew what was proper, and he brought his mind to bear on the suggestion he had heard; was it right? was it advantageous? Then he replied to Rāma's words:

'I'm not the right person to purify him: he abandoned all the 99.32–4
constraints of morality; he was cruel, vicious, deceitful, and he molested other people's wives. This Rāvaṇa was my enemy in the guise of a brother, always intent on doing harm, and though I should respect him as my elder he deserves no respect from me. Humans the world over, Rāma, will call me cruel, but when they hear what he was like they will all applaud me.'

Rāma was delighted by his answer, but that supreme up- 99.35–40
holder of morality replied persuasively to Vibhīṣaṇa's well-chosen words: 'I must yield to your wishes, for your support has brought me victory, but it is incumbent upon me to give you appropriate advice, Lord of the *rākṣasas*. Certain it is that this night-roamer clung to evil and deceit but in battle he was ever a glorious, mighty warrior. It's said that this noble, powerful Rāvaṇa who could make the worlds roar could not be defeated by the gods led by Indra Śatakratu. Death cancels out enmity. We've achieved our goal. Let me join you in performing his funeral rite. You know tradition lays down that the funeral ought to be carried out quickly, in due form and in your presence, mighty warrior. It will redound to your credit.'

Hearing the Rāghava's words, Vibhīṣaṇa made haste to 99.41–4
organize a decent funeral for Rāvaṇa. Vibhīṣaṇa performed the ordained cremation, then quieted the wives with repeated words of consolation. When all the *rākṣasīs* had gone back in, Vibhīṣaṇa approached Rāma and stood deferentially at his side, while Rāma, together with Sugrīva, Lakṣmaṇa and the whole army, exulted at the killing of the enemy, like Indra Śatakratu about Vṛtra.

When gods, *gandharvas* and *dānavas* saw that Rāvaṇa had 100.1–3 been killed they assembled, each in his own chariot, talking over the auspicious events: the dreadful death of Rāvaṇa, the prowess of the Rāghava, the dogged fighting of the *vānaras*, Sugrīva's advice and the loyalty and heroism of Lakṣmaṇa Saumitri – the illustrious beings talked them over and went back as they had come, rejoicing.

100.4–8 Then the illustrious Rāghava paid his respects to Mātali and sent back the divine chariot splendid as fire, lent him by Indra; dismissed by the Rāghava, Śakra's charioteer Mātali mounted the divine chariot and rose up to heaven. When the supreme divine charioteer had risen to heaven the Rāghava embraced Sugrīva ecstatically; after embracing Sugrīva he went to the encampment, saluted by Lakṣmaṇa and honoured by the ape chiefs. Finding stout-hearted Lakṣmaṇa Saumitri blazing with brilliance nearby, Rāma told him:

100.9–10 'Dear brother, consecrate Vibhīṣaṇa here king of Laṅkā; he has been loyal and devoted, and a great support to me. Dear brother, it is my dearest wish to see Rāvaṇa's younger brother Vibhīṣaṇa consecrated in Laṅkā.'

100.11–18 Saumitri concurred with the noble Rāghava's words and joyfully picked up a golden vessel; from that vessel at Rāma's command Saumitri sprinkled Vibhīṣaṇa king over Laṅkā in front of the *rākṣasas*. Vibhīṣaṇa of the pure heart was consecrated by that upright man, and his ministers and loyal *rākṣasas* rejoiced. The Rāghava and Lakṣmaṇa were overjoyed to see Vibhīṣaṇa consecrated in Laṅkā as lord of the *rākṣasas*. With the kingship in Rāma's gift conferred on him, Vibhīṣaṇa spoke reassuringly to his subjects, then stood beside Rāma, while the night-roamer citizens in their delight presented to him unhusked grain, sweets, parched rice and divine blossoms; that dauntless hero accepted the holy gifts and offered all their holiness to the Rāghava and to Lakṣmaṇa. Rāma could see that Vibhīṣaṇa had completed his task and achieved his objective; anxious to please him, he accepted it all.

100.19–22 Then the Rāghava addressed the mountainous hero standing respectfully beside him, the monkey Hanumān: 'My friend, with the permission of King Vibhīṣaṇa here, go to Rāvaṇa's palace, approach Vaidehī with decorum and tell her, chief of conquerors, that Sugrīva, Lakṣmaṇa and I are well, and that I have killed Rāvaṇa. When you have told Maithilī the good news and learned her wishes, lord of apes, be so good as to return.'

With these orders Hanumān Son of the Wind entered Laṅkā city to a warm reception from the night-roamers, rushed to Rāvaṇa's palace and saw her wasted like Rohiṇī parted from the Moon. Gently, humbly and deferentially he approached, greeted her and began to give her Rāma's message in its entirety. 101.1–3

'Vaidehī, all is well with Rāma – Sugrīva and Lakṣmaṇa too. He is asking after you. He has achieved his objective: the conqueror has killed his enemy. My lady, with the support of Vibhīṣaṇa and the apes and the guidance of Lakṣmaṇa, Rāma has killed Rāvaṇa. I've told you the good news, my lady, but what I have to share with you goes on: "Virtuous lady, your life is safe! By good fortune I've gained the victory. We've won the war, Sītā! You can rest content, your terrors at an end. Our enemy Rāvaṇa has been killed and Laṅkā here subjugated. I took no rest, so determined was I to win you back; to carry out my resolve we built a causeway across the sea. You've no need to worry about living in Rāvaṇa's palace, for I've placed the sovereignty over Laṅkā under Vibhīṣaṇa's control." There! You can breathe as easily as if you were living in your own house. He's on his way! He's overjoyed and eager to set eyes on you!' 101.4–11

Sītā jumped up at that message, her face shining like the moon, but she was too overwhelmed by delight to utter a word. When Sītā made no response the champion ape asked, 'My lady, why are you so thoughtful? Why won't you answer me?' 101.12–13

Sītā had clung steadfastly to what was right, and she was overjoyed at Hanumān's message. In a voice choking with delight she replied, 'The joyful news I've heard about my husband's victory has overwhelmed me with delight; just for a moment I'm speechless. However much I think about it, monkey, I can't find a suitable reward for telling me this good news. Dear *vānara*, I can't think of anything on earth to give you that could remotely compare with the good news you've 101.14–18 given me. Gold ornaments or ingots, jewels of any sort, kingship over the three worlds – none of them is fit to be mentioned!'

101.19–28 The monkey stood before Sītā Vaidehī in a deferential pose and replied to her words: 'Such kind words are just what you might be expected to say, so intent are you on your husband's pleasure and welfare, so eager for your husband's victory. Dear lady, your kind words mean more to me than any heaps of jewels or even the kingship of the gods. Besides, I really do feel I've been granted all good things – kingship of the gods and everything – when I can see Rāma standing victorious, his enemy slain. Those *rākṣasīs* with their vicious tales: that's the boon I beg from you. They are terribly vicious creatures, lovely lady, and I long to kill them by every possible means, fists, hands, feet, pounding them hard with my knees and tearing them with my teeth, devouring their ears and noses and tearing out their hair until their mouths are absolutely dry with terror at the heavy blows I heap on them. That's the kind of injuries I want to inflict on them, illustrious queen, slaughtering those who did you wrong.'

101.29–37 Janaka's illustrious daughter Vaidehī gave a pious reply to Hanumān's tirade: 'Who could be angry at slaves, reliant on their king for survival and bound to obey orders, *vānara* chief? It's the chance consequence of an earlier injustice and my own bad deeds that I've been suffering all this: one must reap what one has sown. It was the operation of Fate that ordained it was my lot to submit in my weakness to these slaves of Rāvaṇa. It was on Rāvaṇa's orders that these *rākṣasīs* threatened me; now he's been killed they won't threaten me, excellent *vānara*. The bear once chanted an ancient verse to the tiger. Listen to it, monkey, it's full of piety: "Do not return evil for evil. Their conduct is the ornament of the good. Keep to that tradition."[17] A noble person should show mercy to evil and to good, monkey, even to those who deserve death; no one is without sin. It would be wrong to punish shape-changing *rākṣasas* even for doing evil; it's their nature to take pleasure in harming the whole world.'

101.38–9 Thus admonished by Sītā, Hanumān gave a tactful reply to

Rāma's illustrious wife: 'Your splendour, my lady, befits the lawful wife of Rāma. With your permission I will return to the Rāghava.'

At Hanumān's words, Janaka's daughter Vaidehī said, 'I 101.40
desire to see my husband, excellent *vānara*.'

Hanumān, that splendid Son of the Wind, was overjoyed to 101.41–2
hear her request and answered Maithilī: 'Like Śacī did the Lord of the Thirty, noble lady, you shall gaze on Rāma and his full-moon face – Lakṣmaṇa too – secure among his allies, his enemy destroyed.'

With this promise to Sītā, radiant as Śrī herself, Hanumān 101.43;
rushed back to the Rāghava, bounded up to wise Rāma, that 102.1–4
supreme archer, and came straight to the point. 'Do receive Maithilī as your queen. She's been tormented by grief, and she is the reason we undertook this enterprise with its resultant success. Maithilī was overwhelmed by grief and she couldn't see for sobbing, but the news of your victory has brought her delight. Once I had reassured and encouraged her she told me, "I desire to see my triumphant husband, and Lakṣmaṇa."'

The message Hanumān had delivered plunged Rāma into a 102.5–7
deep reverie and that supreme pillar of righteousness gave way to tears. Long and passionately he sighed, gazing down at the earth, then spoke to Vibhīṣaṇa standing like a gigantic cloud nearby. 'Fetch Sītā Vaidehī here without delay, but first let her body be anointed with divine unguents and adorned with divine ornaments, and her head bathed.'

Vibhīṣaṇa raced into the private apartments to carry out 102.8–9
Rāma's instructions and roused Sītā and his own wives to action. 'Vaidehī, anoint your body with divine unguents and adorn yourself with divine ornaments! Then mount this vehicle, I beg you; your husband wants to see you.'

Then King Vaiśravaṇa, Yama the foe-famisher, great Indra the 105.1,3;
Thousand-eyed and Varuṇa who burns up his enemies all drew 108.1–2
near in their sun-splendid chariots. They reached Laṅkā city and approached the Rāghava. As the Rāghava stood respectfully bowing, great Indra, Punisher of Pāka, addressed him in great delight: 'Rāma annihilator of your foes, this vision of us

shall not be fruitless for you. I am delighted with you. Tell me your heart's desire.'

108.3–8 At this invitation Kākutstha bowed, his brother Lakṣmaṇa and his wife Sītā too, and he replied, 'If you have been pleased with me, lord of all the gods, I will beg you to grant this wish of mine, eloquent lord. In my cause valiant *vānaras* have been dispatched to Yama's realm; let them all be restored to life! It was to please me that they took no account of death; let us be reunited by your grace! That is the boon I choose. You who can bestow favours, I desire to see the langurs and bears free of pain and free of wounds, their might and manliness renewed. And wherever the *vānaras* roam, let there be luscious roots and fruit and limpid streams, even out of season.'

108.9–12 Great Indra showed his pleasure at what the noble Rāghava had said, and replied, 'Great is the boon you have sought, dear son, pride of the Raghus. The apes shall be made whole again as if they had awoken from sleep, and shall be reunited with friends, family, kinsmen and their own kind; all will be filled with rejoicing. Out of season, trees shall be spangled with blossom and fruit, great bowman, and rivers shall abound in water.'

108.13 All the *vānaras* whose bodies had been shattered by wounds again became sound and free from wounds, wondering, 'What has happened?'

108.14–16 The almighty gods all offered well-merited congratulations to Kākutstha and to Lakṣmaṇa on having achieved his goal, then said, 'Hero, leave here and return to Ayodhyā. Take leave of the *vānaras* and comfort Maithilī, whose devotion to you has brought her suffering. Seek out your brother Bharata, who is living like an ascetic out of sympathy for you, and have yourself consecrated. Your arrival will bring joy to your people.'

108.17–18 With these instructions the gods graciously took leave of Rāma and Saumitri and returned to heaven in their sunlike chariots. Kākutstha and his brother Lakṣmaṇa paid homage to the Lords of the Thirty, then gave orders to make camp.

109.1–3 It was a happy Rāma who got up after spending that night. Vibhīṣaṇa saluted the conqueror with deep respect, hailed his victory and announced: 'Baths await to anoint your bodies! There are garments and ornaments, divine sandalwood paste and garlands of many kinds, and lotus-eyed women – artists in adornment – are in attendance to bathe you becomingly, Rāghava.'

Kākutstha replied to Vibhīṣaṇa's words, 'Offer the bath to 109.4–7
the apes, their leader Sugrīva in particular. There's a righteous prince, mighty and famed for his integrity but refined and accustomed to comfort, who's suffering because of me: without Kaikeyī's upright son Bharata I set little store by baths or clothes and ornaments. I'm setting off straightaway on the path to Ayodhyā city; it's a long way and the path's very difficult.'

Vibhīṣaṇa responded to Kākutstha, 'Prince, I'll get you to 109.8–14
that city in one day! Bless you, the sun-splendid Puṣpaka Chariot's at your disposal! Rāvaṇa commandeered it forcibly from my brother Kubera, and now that vehicle, massive as a cloud, stands waiting. Your worries are at an end; that carriage will ferry you back to Ayodhyā. But if you owe me any favours, if you remember anything good about me, if in your wisdom you bear me any friendship, stay here a little while. You, your brother Lakṣmaṇa and your wife Vaidehī shall be honoured with everything you could wish for; then you can go, Rāma. Enjoy yourself just for a while, Rāma, you, your army and this host of your friends, and accept the hospitality I'm offering; it's your due, and it's all ready. It's out of respect and esteem and friendship that I'm begging you, Rāghava. I'm yours to command; I wouldn't dream of giving orders to you.'

In the hearing of the *rākṣasas* and all the *vānaras* Rāma 109.15–21
replied to Vibhīṣaṇa's speech. 'I would never refuse a request of yours, *rākṣasa* lord; only my heart is impatient to see my brother – he went out to Citrakūṭa to call me back and I turned down his humble entreaty – and there's Kausalyā, Sumitrā and illustrious Kaikeyī as well, and the lords, my friends, and the citizens and their families. Lord of the *rākṣasas*, do have the carriage brought to me quickly. How could I ever agree to remain here now my task is done? Vibhīṣaṇa, my dear friend, I am honoured, but let me go. You really mustn't be offended with me because I'm in such a hurry to take my leave.'

109.27; 110.1–2 Vibhīṣaṇa's reply to Rāma was to summon that matchless carriage, swift as thought, to be brought up to Rāma, and he stood waiting till he saw the flower-decked Puṣpaka Chariot drive up and halt nearby. Then with a deferential gesture the lord of *rākṣasas* humbly and courteously hastened to ask the Rāghava, 'What may I do?'

110.3–7 The Rāghava thought in a flash and, with Lakṣmaṇa's approval, made this affectionate suggestion: 'Vibhīṣaṇa, for the efforts they have made, requite the forest-dwellers with jewels and wealth and ornaments of all kinds. They took part in the siege and conquest of Laṅkā, *rākṣasa* lord; in their zeal they laid aside fear for their lives and never turned tail in battle. It lies in your gift to gratify these ape chiefs with the respect and rewards they deserve from your gratitude. Then they will understand that you can give as well as receive, that you are kind as well as glorious. That's my advice to you.'

110.8–10 At Rāma's suggestion Vibhīṣaṇa rewarded all the *vānaras*, distributing jewels and wealth among them; when Rāma had seen the chiefs rewarded with their jewels and wealth, he stepped into that matchless carriage, clasping to his side Vaidehī, glorious but bashful, along with his brother Lakṣmaṇa, that bold wielder of the bow.

110.11–15 From his stance on the carriage Kākutstha addressed heroic Sugrīva and all the *vānaras*, Vibhīṣaṇa the *rākṣasa* too: 'My lords, best of the *vānaras*, you have achieved the objective of the alliance. I give you leave to go wherever you wish. Victorious Sugrīva, ever anxious to do what was right, you have fulfilled all the obligations of a comrade or a friend, my lord; go back quickly to Kiṣkindhā escorted by your army. Vibhīṣaṇa, live on in Laṅkā as your own kingdom; I present it to you. Not even the heavenly beings with Indra at their head can overcome you. I will go back to Ayodhyā, my father's capital. I wish to take my leave. Farewell to you all.'

110.16–17 At Rāma's words the mighty *vānaras* and Vibhīṣaṇa the *rākṣasa* cried out with great respect, 'We wish to go to Ayodhyā; do take us all, sir! When we have witnessed your consecration ceremony and paid our respects to Kausalyā, then after a short time we will go back home, your highness.'

So entreated the *vānaras* and Vibhīṣaṇa. The majestic Rāghava knew they were right, and responded to their leaders Sugrīva and Vibhīṣaṇa, 'For me and mine to return to the city in the company of all your lordships will heap joy upon joy for me. Step into the carriage at once, Sugrīva, you and the *vānaras*, and you and your ministers get in too, Vibhīṣaṇa, lord of the *rākṣasas*.' 110.18–20

Then Sugrīva and his army, and Vibhīṣaṇa and his ministers, made haste and jumped quickly into that celestial Puṣpaka Chariot; when they had all mounted Kubera's lofty throne, the Rāghava gave the word and it leapt into the sky. Drawn by geese, the radiant carriage bore along, resplendent as Kubera, the joyful and triumphant Rāma. 110.21–3

Afterthoughts

... and so they lived happily ever after ... didn't they?

That, undoubtedly, was the expectation of the first tellers. But they had created a romantic idyll about their hero, so popular, so perfect, that generations of their successors were determined both to preserve it and to contribute to making it more perfect still, and that is why the reader who has known and loved the *Rāmāyaṇa*, maybe from early childhood, may by now be feeling a little cheated. Why are so many of the best-loved episodes of the story absent from this translation? It is because many of these cherished familiar components of the Rāma story (so familiar that the absence of some may even have escaped the reader's notice) are the creation of later generations.

As with the first stage, this process was a continuous one and the boundaries between subsequent stages should not be sharply defined. The inherited text was elaborated in three broad ways: by poetic embellishment, by attempts to explain matters now seen as difficult, and by the introduction of completely new episodes, until, by about the first century AD, these individual, often contradictory, oral contributions were compiled to swell the text to approximately double its length (represented by the text of the Critical Edition, *Ayodhyā* to *Yuddhakāṇḍa*). The new material conforms to later patterns of diction, style, vocabulary and verse forms, and also reflects the more developed material and social culture of its authors and their ethical outlook, but the story was now so popular that although a certain amount of the earliest text was evidently overwhelmed by the first elaborations, the compilers apparently felt unable to jettison any more or to alter the main lines of the narrative; inevitably, this situation led to tensions and even inconsistencies between the different textual layers.

From this second stage onwards the plot would have been so well known to the audience that any surprise element had long been lost, a situation that could lead to greater banality, as when Bharata's adoption of the ascetic life is not reserved until the end of the War Book, but narrated at its logical place towards the end of the Ayodhyā Book; in the hands of a sensitive poet, however, it was a situation that could be exploited to increase the pathos. A wistful description of winter put into Lakṣmaṇa's mouth is a highly successful lyrical passage typical of the *kāvya* style, expressive of the exiles' longing to return home, a passage of beauty in its own right, but a triumph of irony as well as artistry for an audience that knows the next *sarga* will bring Śūrpaṇakhā's calamitous arrival. Such insertions take many forms and are of varying poetic achievement: large-scale elaborations of the narrative high point – the abduction – detract neither from plot nor characterization; others, pedantic and obtrusive, may consist of nothing more than lists of trees, weapons, trades or characters' ancestors, showing off the redactor's knowledge without adding to the enjoyment or understanding of the audience. We may perhaps imagine some being delivered tongue-in-cheek by a wily performer anxious to tantalize his audience with his delaying tactics, perhaps hoping to secure some material inducement to move on to the next more exciting episode. A number more duels are introduced into the war, including an unlikely preliminary, inconclusive fight between Rāma and Rāvaṇa, spinning the tale out but detracting from the pace and variety of the original.

Many of the narrative additions are closely linked to the changing conceptions of the main characters, particularly Rāma. As is clear from the text translated, he was orginally seen as wholly human, and a warrior; his power was appropriately superhuman and fantastic, but not supernatural, and his actions were dictated, first by the original author's need to progress his story, and secondly by the warrior code. He did what was necessary to win his war, and he was admired for doing so. This admiration developed until he came to be seen as primarily a moral hero, and the ethics of some of his exploits are questioned and must be justified. The most notable example is the underhand means he adopts to kill Vālin, intervening unannounced into a private fight between the *vānara* brothers, an intervention that inadvertently evokes a slightly more sympathetic image of its victim and is even criticized in the *Mahābhārata*.

Events leading to Rāma's departure to the forest have been so elaborated that the storyline can no longer be determined with any certainty, but it is clear that a great need was felt to exonerate Daśaratha as far as possible from the charge of being harsh, unjust and feeble, if only to ensure that Rāma is of the noblest stock. Yet the king's decree cannot be eliminated from the well-known story. One attempt to absolve him of responsibility for his conduct appears first at this stage. The night of his death, the king recalls a curse laid on him by the helpless, blind, ascetic parents of a boy he had accidentally killed: he, like they, is to die grieving for his son. The boy is not named anywhere in the *Rāmāyaṇa*. The story spread to vernacular tales, often unrelated to the Rāma story, and developed many new features: in Buddhist versions the boy is resurrected and all ends happily; elsewhere, the boy (sometimes now called Yajñadatta, more often some variant of Śrāvaṇa) gains enormous merit by carrying his parents on a pilgrimage in a pair of paniers, and is now a major figure of Hindu culture, exemplifying filial devotion.

Around the first to third centuries AD brāhman rather than *kṣatriya* values came to dominate the text. The details of the process are not entirely clear, but seem to have involved a change to a new set of redactors; probably at this time the text was first committed to writing, although it continued to be presented orally. A new ending was added to the War Book, but most of the additional material was collected into two new framing books, the *Bāla* and *Uttarakāṇḍas* ('Childhood' and 'Further'), where issues of sovereignty and the ritual purity that now forms part of this concept come to the fore, ideas which introduced a harsh note to the romantic idyll. The nation's prosperity came to be seen as entirely dependent on the king's personal purity, a purity which extended to the wife who must share his role; if that wife were not wholly and rigorously pure herself, the nation would not prosper. The redactors knew that Rāma had welcomed back to his side a wife who had been physically touched by another male, who had spent several months in his power if not technically under his roof (even the earliest tellers had taken the precaution of keeping her out of doors, in the *aśoka* grove, during the monsoon), and their attempts to exonerate their hero from any possible taint make him seem harsh and uncaring, very different from the man who had been driven to distraction by her capture. First, he rejects her coldly when she appears before him after her liberation, and she is so distraught that she attempts to commit suicide in a fire, only to be safeguarded in the flames by Agni, god of fire and purity, and given back to Rāma with the assurance that he should accept her again. For a while Ayodhyā prospers under their happy and benevolent rule, but then the suspicions of the citizens oblige him to exile her once again, now pregnant (later versions of the tale introduce new devices to explain the unjust suspicions and divert blame from Rāma). This time Sītā does not return to him: after giving birth to twin sons, Kuśa and Lava, and bringing them up to the verge of manhood, when they are recognized by their father as his heirs, she calls on the Earth to vindicate her, and is swallowed up in a final demonstration of her purity, a poignant sacrifice of personal happiness to the wider national interest that echoes the opening of the romance.

The three younger brothers each conquers territory of his own. Each of the four brothers has two sons, and each scrupulously divides his kingdom between them. The loving unity that has always characterized the four princes is carefully preserved in the latter part of the Further Book; maybe its authors had seen too much of the consequences of royal family squabbles in real life.

The text translated in this volume tells us virtually nothing about Rāma's life before the beginning of the story: he is the eldest of four brothers, the only one of them to be married, and he has come to the aid of Viśvāmitra in a youthful encounter with Mārīca. It was mostly the poets of the Childhood Book who filled in the details. Lakṣmaṇa and Śatrughna must now be no longer older and younger brother respectively but twins, for all four brothers are born more or less simultaneously, and no longer just as a result of the private devotions of their parents but following elaborate rituals conducted by the sage Ṛśyaśṛṅga.

Mārīca's reference to an earlier encounter with Rāma is seized upon and expanded into a detailed narrative with many additional tales of mythical heroes loosely integrated into the framework. On this occasion the authors must take care to ensure that the youthful prince does not kill Mārīca, only frighten him away, for the *rākṣasa* must reappear later to help in the abduction of Sītā.

This episode then leads into an account of the marriage of all four princes (created out of a brief second-stage remark by Sītā to Anasūyā). Rāma wins Sītā by bending and breaking a huge bow that no one else has the strength to string, a common enough motif in heroic tales, and one which does not conflict with the earlier phases of the poem; but this is the first suggestion that his three brothers are also married, and in the same ceremony. In the first-stage narrative, Rāma's specific statement to Śūrpaṇakhā that Lakṣmaṇa was unmarried was part of a joke, but surely was not intended as a lie; and if Lakṣmaṇa had left his wife behind in Ayodhyā when he went to the forest, he gave no sign of missing her, nor Sītā of missing her sister.

Sītā was originally considered the natural-born daughter of Janaka, but in the Childhood Book she too is given a fantastic birth-story which has Janaka find her in a furrow. Even so, there are none of the wilder elaborations of this story found in later adaptations (such as the *Adbhuta* and *Ānanda Rāmāyaṇas* and some Jain versions, where she is the daughter of Rāvaṇa, destined to cause his downfall, or, in some Buddhist versions, even of Daśaratha).

Rāma the moral warrior hero was still portrayed as a human,

but a human who was being constantly aggrandized by his redactors. One way this was achieved was by associating him with various figures known from mythology, and a number of pre-existent tales were incorporated at this third stage, with only the most tenuous link to the plot or situation. Another way was to aggrandize his opponents and allies, the task of a large part of the Further Book, which recounts the earlier exploits first of Rāvaṇa and his family, then of Vālin and of Hanumān, again expanded out of stray remarks in the earlier stages. If Rāma can defeat opponents of such awesome might, he must be a very great man indeed, both physically and morally. In the older portions of the text he had been associated in comparisons with the martial Indra; now that god was increasingly becoming portrayed as morally degenerate, these were still retained despite the inappropriateness, but in the newer layers Rāma became increasingly compared to the rising figure of Viṣṇu, and at the conclusion of the War Book a chorus of gods declared him to be divine. Finally, a further account clumsily grafted on to his birth-story identified Rāma and his brothers as partial incarnations of Viṣṇu. The belief that Rāma was an *avatāra* of Viṣṇu is rare even in this third stage of development, found only here and in the brothers' final self-immolation, and is a development that sits uneasily alongside the many statements still retained in the earlier text stressing that Rāma is human, as well as the boon developed from hints in the first stage that Rāvaṇa cannot be killed by gods, only by a human; the taut logic that governed the creators of the Rāma story was of less concern to their successors than their desire to aggrandize Rāma. It was this desire that led to the change in genre undergone by the text at this point. It is no longer a romance concerning the private antagonism between one man and his lustful enemy, or even of national importance; it is a struggle of cosmic significance, with Rāvaṇa's exploits threatening the stability of the universe and the existence of the gods themselves, and the gods themselves must take a hand to remedy the situation. In Western terms, the romance has been transformed into an epic, and the abduction of Sītā is merely an excuse, or even opportunity, for Viṣṇu to intervene.

The other creation of this stage is the figure of Vālmīki (although there is still no suggestion of several legends later attributed to him: that he created Kuśa magically after thinking he had lost the baby Lava, that he had been a bandit, and that so strong were his powers of concentration that he allowed an ant-hill to grow up around him as he meditated). He appears at the beginning of the Childhood Book, invents the *śloka* metre in his grief at seeing a mating crane killed by a hunter (in fact the *śloka* is a development from an older, Vedic metre), and is commissioned by Brahmā to compose the story of Rāma in this metre. This he does mentally, then teaches it to Kuśa and Lava, who sing, before Rāma, what purports to be the rest of the text, a scene which is not explained until the middle of the Further Book, when Vālmīki gives the exiled Sītā sanctuary at his hermitage, where she gives birth to her sons and brings them up; it is their singing of his story that leads Rāma to recognize and acknowledge them as his sons. It has become conventional to refer to the Sanskrit text of the Rāma story as the Vālmīki *Rāmāyaṇa* (and to attribute some later, independent versions to his authorship), but there is no textual warrant to confirm this identification.

Committing the tale to writing in manuscripts that had to be frequently recopied led to further stages of elaboration in the development of separate but interlocking recensions from about the fourth century AD onwards. Passages in all seven books were elaborated and narrative insertions made by poets who adopted a process similar to that of the poets of the second stage, equally reflecting the diction, style and outlook of their own day; they filled out the story, but did not extend it to any great degree forward or backward. Large-scale alteration ended perhaps about the twelfth century; by this time Rāma the originally human hero had become widely recognized as God. After this time rare hints are introduced, sometimes in only a few manuscripts, of concepts such as *bhakti*, the saving grace of Rāma's name, and – rarest of all – *rāmacandra* as the name of the hero.

*

The successive generations of poets who adapted and transmitted the so-called Vālmīki *Rāmāyaṇa* were constantly limited and constrained not only by their own talent, outlook and interests, but by the now well-known outline and even details of the story they had inherited. Audience expectation and participation in oral presentations demanded elaboration of detail but would allow of no radical reinterpretation of the basic story. By contrast, those who from a relatively early date adapted the story or some of its episodes into different genres and languages, and for different religious or didactic purposes, felt less constraint, and it is to their works that we should look for many of the now most familiar aspects or episodes of the tale of Rāma.

The Purāṇas developed the religious implications of the *Rāmāyaṇa*, and at the same general period many works of classical Sanskrit literature were drawing on its literary aspects. The *Raghuvaṃśa*, 'The Dynasty of Raghu', by the most famous Sanskrit playwright and poet, Kālidāsa (*c.* fifth century AD), precedes his summary of Rāma's life with stories of four of his ancestors, and follows it with tales or names of twenty-four descendants from Kuśa onwards.

Kuśa and Lava and their recognition as true heirs of Rāma figure in a number of independent versions where their story is developed. Instead of being noticed because they sing the Rāma story at the horse sacrifice Rāma is preparing to celebrate, they establish their credentials by attacking the sacrificial horse's guards, and in some versions they defeat or even kill Rāma himself, who is then brought back to life by Sītā. Only sons of Rāma would be capable of defeating Rāma, so they must be Rāma's sons.

Understanding of Sītā is extended dramatically in the *Adbhuta Rāmāyaṇa* (perhaps fifteenth century) where she is viewed from a *śākta* perspective. She scornfully tells Rāma that his feat in killing Rāvaṇa is of little value while a much more powerful relative of the *rākṣasa* remains alive, and, when Rāma is overcome by this new enemy, promptly defeats him herself. This episode, which has its roots in a widespread unrelated traditional tale, is assimilated to the Rāma story in several different versions. In some the relative is named Mahīrāvaṇa; when he captures Rāma and Lakṣmaṇa and is about to sacrifice them to the Goddess, it is Hanumān who rescues them.

There are folk tellings in which Hanumān's status as a monkey god is greater than that of the human Rāma, but whether or not the cult that has seen the erection of ever more imposing modern temples to Hanumān owes its origin to some pre-existent, independent monkey deity, it has certainly been promoted by the *Rāmāyaṇa's* lovable ape. Hanumān's role had continued to grow from the quite modest early beginnings to considerably greater prominence in the later Vālmīki *Rāmāyaṇa*, and has continued to expand ever since. As a subordinate to the *vānara* leaders he could be portrayed with a heroic yet naive, impulsive charm inappropriate to his masters but calculated to lighten the tone of the poem and endear him to generations of audiences. Miniature painters delighted in capturing his pride in his devotion to Rāma, and a familiar image of him nowadays, particularly in bazaar paintings, represents him ripping open his chest to show that Rāma and Sītā are enshrined in his heart. It is all the more curious that the *Harivaṃśa* (a supplement to the *Mahābhārata* within which the life-story of Kṛṣṇa is embedded), though incorporating a large number of allusions to the *Rāmāyaṇa* and its characters, studiously ignores Hanumān.

Guarding Sītā (and therefore, by extension, Rāma) from pollution continued to be a major pre-occupation of authors who placed ever-increasing stress on bodily purity at the expense of purity of character, and by doing so wrecked the original authors' conception of the tale. Ever since the composition of the Further Book we have known that Sītā's terror and staunch resistance, and Rāma's agony, have been quite unnecessary: Rāvaṇa is under a curse not to rape her. But an important theological development appears in the *Kūrma Purāṇa*, where Agni creates – at Rāma's behest – an illusory Sītā before her abduction by Rāvaṇa, which has the purpose of safeguarding the real Sītā's purity until she is returned to Rāma in the fire-suicide episode after the battle. Because of its theological implications, this idea is taken over by the *Adhy-*

ātma Rāmāyaṇa, followed by Tulsīdās in his *Rāmcaritmānas*. The *Adhyātma Rāmāyaṇa*, which combines a strongly devotional belief in Rāma's saving grace with an Advaitin understanding of the world as mere illusion imposed on the unitary Absolute, is perhaps the best known of the sectarian recastings in Sanskrit, and has exercised a great influence on modern devotional interpretation of the Rāma story. In Hindi, Tulsīdās' *Rāmcaritmānas* (late sixteenth century) is most notable for his stress on the name of Rāma, which for him is the essence of the supreme deity and has immense saving power. For Tulsīdās, the state of *rāmarājya* (Rāma's ideal rule) was accessible to the individual in the degenerate age of the world in which we live through Rāma's saving name. It is the *Rāmcaritmānas* that has become in Hindi-speaking areas the text for the *Rāmlīlās* that was mentioned in the Introduction. Staged annually at the Daśahrā festival, this enactment of the story in dramatic form has obviously been a potent force in shaping the nature of popular religion. The extent to which each local community is involved in the organization and in the acting is noteworthy.

The earliest versions of the Rāma story in languages other than Sanskrit are Buddhist and Jain: the *Dasaratha Jātaka* of the fifth century AD (sometimes but wrongly held to be an independent version), and Jain versions which are essentially reductionist critiques of the story, absolving Rāma from the taint of killing even animals. The first version in a vernacular language is one of the major works of Tamil literature, Kampaṉ's *Irāmāvatāram* in perhaps the tenth century AD; it shows a clearly devotional, *bhakti*, approach to the story with something of the emphasis on the name of Rāma later to be seen most prominently in the work of Tulsīdās. In North India, the first major adaptation into a modern language was the version of Kṛttibās, probably composed early in the fifteenth century, to be followed by several other Bengali versions.

The spread of the Rāma story into the rest of Asia is both dramatic and early, and the extent to which it has become part of the local culture in its new homeland is marked. The spread of Buddhism carried versions of the tale to Central Asia and even China. Sculptural and inscriptional evidence indicates that it must have reached Indonesia by the seventh century AD, and the Old Javanese version dates from the early tenth century. There are multiple versions in Khmer, Laotian and Thai, and its popularity in Thailand is demonstrated by the adoption of the name Rāma by its rulers from the eighteenth century. In Malaysia, Muslim elements have been absorbed, and it has reached as far as Japan and even the Philippines. More recent movements of population have brought it to Britain, where individuals and communities have drawn on it to create or maintain a sense of identity. In the land of his birth, devotion to Rāma and his story are exemplified both by the enthusiastic yet pious reception of the adaptation televised in 1987–8, but also by actions performed in his name that would surely not be approved by the one who was gracious even to his enemies.

So yes, they have lived ever after, and clearly they will continue to live, but with what degree of happiness? That is for the reader to decide, but for us all to determine.

Note on the Text Translated

The lists in the later part of this Note employ the sigla for manuscripts used in the Critical Edition. The following abbreviations are used:

Crit. Ed. = Critical Edition (1960–75, see Further Reading).
Critical Notes = The notes on the text at the end of individual volumes of the *Rāmāyaṇa*, Crit. Ed.
MB 2002 = Mary Brockington, 'The rise and fall of Mārīca', in *Stages and Transitions: temporal and historical frameworks in epic and Purāṇic literature*, Proceedings of the Second Dubrovnik International Conference on the Sanskrit Epics and Purāṇas, August 1999, edited by Mary Brockington (Zagreb: Croatian Academy of Sciences and Arts, 2002), pp. 177–92.
RR = John Brockington, *Righteous Rāma: The Evolution of an Epic* (Delhi: Oxford University Press, 1985).
Skt Epics = John Brockington, *The Sanskrit Epics*, Handbuch der Orientalistik 2.12 (Leiden: Brill, 1998).
Söhnen = Renate Söhnen, *Untersuchungen zur Komposition und Gesprächen im Rāmāyaṇa*, Studien zur Indologie und Iranistik, 2 vols. (Reinbek: Verlag für orientalistische Fachpublikationen, 1979).

The text translated has been established according to a rigorous linguistic analysis of the Baroda Critical Edition, conducted by John Brockington. Details have been published in a series of articles which were then summarized in his book *Righteous Rāma*, where he went on to draw out the implications. He examined grammatical and stylistic features (formation and declensions of nouns and adjectives, verbal forms, use of tenses, etc.), noting the frequency with which each occurred in each *sarga*. The vocabulary, formulae (building blocks of composition, characteristic of an orally composed work), use of imagery and figures of speech were subjected to the same statistical analysis. It soon became apparent that some features occurred more frequently in some *sargas* than in others, and that similar features were clustered in these *sargas*. A number of these features were already known to be characteristic of the later, elaborate Classical style; others clearly pointed to the existence of a distinctive epic diction similar to that studied by earlier scholars of the *Mahābhārata*, but with significant differences.

The types both of verbal and of nominal forms used are less complex than they become by the second stage; the vocabulary is simple and well defined, and considerably less extensive than in the later parts of the text. Essentially simple, too, is the use of figures of speech: similes are much the commonest figure employed, but even their usage is noticeably more restrained than in later, more ornate, passages, with the imagery largely confined to the natural world and martial pursuits.

The relatively small number of verses in longer metres, either *triṣṭubhs* or other more elaborate lyrical metres, have been identified as forming part of the expansion in the second stage; mostly they are added at the end of *śloka sargas*, and betray their lateness by the variability with which they are added within the manuscript tradition, as well as by their narrative redundancy.

Five stages of development were identified: in terms of the Crit. Ed., the first two are the earlier and later *sargas* in the printed text of the five core Books 'Ayodhyā' to 'War' (*Ayodhyākāṇḍa* to *Yuddhakāṇḍa*); each stage represents around 35% of the Crit. Ed. text. Stage 3 is the framing Books 1 and 7 ('Childhood' and 'Further', *Bālakāṇḍa* and *Uttarakāṇḍa*), and perhaps the last few *sargas* of 'War' (the remaining three tenths). Stages 4 and 5 comprise those many passages found in the manuscript sources but not regarded as part of the constituted text by the Baroda editors and therefore printed in the critical apparatus, either as so-called *passages or in the Appendix.

The *sargas* identified as stage 1 (listed below as table A), with a few further refinements, form the base text for this translation. A number of verses or part verses have been omitted where it is felt that the manuscript evidence did not justify their inclusion by the editors of the Crit. Ed., who, in following the Southern recension, have sometimes given insufficient weight to the absence of a verse or passage in a group of Northern manuscripts (list B). The complete *sarga*, the smallest base unit practicable for meaningful statistical analysis, has always been recognized to be a clumsy and arbitrary unit, not least because there is no certainty that the division into *sargas* is original; equally, it is clear that some have been expanded, with earlier and later material interwoven. A number of passages in first-stage *sargas* have therefore been excluded for reasons discussed in *Righteous Rāma* (list C). Where expansions and elaborations have obscured the narrative thread, a few verses have where possible been translated from otherwise second-stage *sargas* to avoid interrupting the narrative flow (list D): none of the verses selected contains identifiably second-stage diction. Where this has not been possible, the translators have composed brief bridging passages, printed in italics within square brackets, to give the reader the necessary help. Variant readings adopted in the translation are also listed at the end of this Note.

In tabular form, the text translated comprises:

A) Complete sargas (śloka verses only)

2.31–45	3.5–7	4.1–12	5.9–11	6.1–3
48–56	12	14–16	18–25	6–17
59–60	14	19–20	28–32	19–22
62–4	16–24	22	38–42	25–9
70–73	26–7	25–6	44	32–45
76–84	31–2	31–8	48–53	49–50
86–7	34–9	43–8	59–66	54
90–91	41–3	50–57		56
93	46–9	63–4		64–9
96–7	51–2			74–8
99	54–7			83–6
103–5	59			88–9
109	61–70			92–101
				108–10

B) Individual verses or part verses excised as insufficiently supported by the manuscript evidence

2,41.29–33
2,56.2
2,93.4c–5b

3,41.6–7, 36–44b
3,47.26c–27b, 36
3,49.1, 16–17, 33
3,51.4ef (*as suggested in the Critical Notes*)
3,52.12c–13b
3,59.16ef
3,62.10–11

3,64.29–30
3,65.29ab
3,67.20cd, 21cd–22 (*also re-ordering as in Northern mss*)
3,68.5ab, 8–9
3,69.13–14ab

4,2.2
4,4.10ab
4,16.15–17
4,20.7
4,32.26ef
4,37.7cd
4,46.13ab
4,48.6, 22
4,57.13

5,9.4–9, 13c–14d, 15c–18b, 26–8, 31–32, 34ab, 44
5,10.15ab, 24
5,11.1–2, 6, 13–14, 19, 21, 32, 36, 38cd–40, 44, 46–50, 52–67
5,20.31–3
5,22.7a–d, 38cd, 39cd
5,24.26–49
5,25.11ab, 13–16
5,28.17cd, 25, 29ab, 36cd–39 (37–9 = 5,2.37–9)
5,29.2ef, 9
5,31.8
5,32.5–12, 15–16
5,38.12–20ab
5,40.27
5,41.1–2, 11–15ab
5,44.21
5,49.35
5,51.12–13ab, 17, 19, 27, 34
5,53.2–4
5,59.1, 12–13
5,60.17–27
5,62.8 (*as suggested in Critical Notes*), 30ef–33
5,64.15ef (*as suggested in Critical Notes*)

6,8.16ab
6,11.49–56b
6,14.21 (*also rare vocabulary*)

6,15.18
6,19.8
6,20.4ab
6,21.21ab, 28cd
6,26.31–2
6,28.11d–12a, 13ab
6,33.30–31, 35–42
6,35.12ab
6,43.5
6,45.2, 29, 31ab, 33cd
6,65.5cd–6ab
6,67.12c–13
6,68.17ab
6,78.6ef–7
6,83.25ab
6,88.6
6,89.16a–d, 17, 20cd
6,93.26
6,96.16–17, 20ab
6,99.20cd, 26ab, 31ef
6,101.6, 23–4
6,109.16

C) Passages considered for other reasons to be secondary expansions (amplifying or modifying the listing in Righteous Rāma*)*

2,31.1–12 *essentially a continuation of 2,1–30*
2,32.21 *breaks narrative continuity*
2,40.13–30 *rare vocabulary*
2,75 *and* 76.1–16 *repeat too much, destroying narrative logic; language and style are more elaborate*
2,77.12–15 *a list of tradesmen, cf. RR p. 66 §2 and Skt Epics p. 409*
2,82.5–8 *ornate description, typical of second stage*
2,92 *redundant; also absent from D4.5.7*
2,103.1–11 *continuation of second-stage sargas 100–102*
2,104.1–8 *cf. RR p. 212 §1; also Söhnen pp. 273–81, 285*

3,5.1–5 *an anomalous and clearly late list of various types of ascetics – in reality a continuation of 3.4*
3,14.15–18 *a list of trees, cf. RR p. 104 n. 29*
3,22.26–9 *cf. RR p. 212 n. 30*

3,36.20–27 *cf. MB 2002*
3,46.1 *out of place, also absent from Ś1, Ñ1 and D1–3*

4,1.35–40 *a list of trees, cf. RR p. 104 n. 29*
4,19.1 *conclusion of second-stage sargas 17–18*
4,32.10–11 *a list of vānara names not found elsewhere, also some signs of textual disturbance*
4,52.28–54.11b *a number of later features of language, especially vocabulary, reinforce the obvious incongruity of subject-matter*
4,58 and 62 *form a unit with 59–61 (stage 2); some less decisive signs of lateness than in those sargas*

5,51.31–3 *late vocabulary and incongruity of subject-matter*

6,15.16–17 *a list of trees, cf. RR p. 104 n. 29 (following verse, 6,15.18, omitted because of insufficient manuscript support)*
6,18 *intrusive development of sarga 17 in a more elaborate style; 17 is complete in itself and leads naturally into 19*
6,35.23 *list of weapons, see RR p. 142*
6,42.23 *elaborate metaphor with rare vocabulary*
6,51–2 *in a more elaborate style, with many rare words*
6,108.1a *belongs with 6,102–7 (stage 2)*
6,109.22–6 *elaborate description using many long compounds*

D) Passages from expanded sargas included to aid the narrative flow

2,23.1–7, 17–31
2,26.1–5, 10–14, 17–22
2,27.27–32
2,28.1–11
2,30.1
2,61.1–3

3,10.26–32
3,25.22–3
3,30.1–3 *(first stage in style)*
3,33.1, 4, 36–8
3,44.1–2
3,53.1–3, 13, 17–23, 35
3,58.1–3
3,60.22–4, 32

4,29.21, 31–3, 37
4,30.8–9, 31–4
4,49.7, 30–31

5,55.18–19

6,46.30, 43–8
6,53.45cd–46 *(cf. also 1153* / 1154*)*
6,70.7–10
6,71.5–9
6,72.8–10
6,80.1–2
6,90.1–4, 8–13
6,102.1–9
6,105.1,3

VARIANT READINGS ADOPTED IN THE TRANSLATION

2,23.30c *bharata* (with all but 3 mss)
2,41.15 *avidūrataḥ* for *vidūrataḥ*
2,60.2 reading *dvividha-* with most mss (cf. 1518*1)
2,86.12ab translated in the light of 2049*1
2,109.1b v.l. of Dt1, Ct adopted
2,109.23b dividing as *vā śubhaḥ*

3,35.9d reading *ahite* for *ca hite* (cf. vv.ll.)
3,35.12c reading *duḥśrutaṃ* (with majority of mss)
3,35.20 not adding 688* (as suggested in the Critical Notes)
3,36.6a v.l. 'twelve years' of all S mss (and Ñ1) adopted
3,43.35d *uraḥ prati°* for *udaraṃ pra°*
3,47.26a reading *na tu* for *nanu* (with 11 mss)
3,69.16a *teṣāṃ* for *tāni* (with most N mss)

4,31.20b reading *prasādyaḥ* for *-dya* (with N mss)
4,50.1a reading *atha tāṃ hanumān prājñaḥ* (with most NE mss)
4,57.29a *sauparṇa* for *sauvarṇa* (10 mss for *p*, 13 for *v*, 9 *other*)
4,63.11a reading *viṣādo yaṃ* for *viṣādo 'yaṃ*

5,44.1 plural replaced by singular in *pāda* a, following excision of *sarga* 43
5,50.6a reading *praviṣṭā* for *prahṛṣṭā* (with majority of mss)

6,17.27a reading *enaṃ* for *śataṃ* (for consistency with 17.30c, 34a, 37a, 39a)
6,28.12b reading *āsthito* for *āvṛto* (with N mss)
6,40.43b reading as N mss (*yathā ca prapitāmaham*)
6,44.22a read *ūru-* for *uru-* (with many mss, cf. 5,54.20a)
6,49.29 adopt N readings (futures – last also in M1.2)
6,78.6b read *vivyādha laghuhastavat* with all N mss
6,83.13a read *-mukhyānāṃ* for *-yūthānāṃ* (with majority of mss)
6,99.31a read *uvāca* for *praśritaṃ* with the N mss

Appendix 1
Rituals and greetings

The general character of the early *Rāmāyaṇa* reflects its origin as a product of the warrior aristocracy (*kṣatriyas*). By comparison with many other early works, rituals are rarely mentioned, apart from those closely connected with *kṣatriyas*. A new ruler is consecrated by sprinkling with water (the *abhiṣeka* ceremony) and by being presented with auspicious objects and symbols of sovereignty, including white parasols and fans, usually made from yaks' tails.

One particularly simple ritual, *saṃdhyā*, the twilight ritual of invocation to the deities with a few muttered verses, is performed at dawn and sunset by every individual belonging to the upper three classes or *varṇas*, so by *kṣatriyas* as much as brāhmans.

Funeral rituals featuring in the narrative involve cremation of the corpse, normally as soon after death as possible. The funeral pyre is lit by the nearest male relative (ideally, the oldest son), who subsequently makes an offering of a ball of rice (exceptionally, of other food); he and other mourners also make a water-offering, in which they commonly stand in a stream or river and pour water back into it from cupped hands.

Water plays an important part in purification customs, and the presence of a good supply with readily accessible places for ritual bathing is an essential for a hermitage site. Touching water is a solemn gesture guaranteeing a promise (cf. the Western custom of taking an oath by resting the hand on a sword or on the Bible).

Fire is another purifying element, significant because of its importance in sacrifices and other rituals. It is often personified as the god Agni, one of the most frequently invoked deities in the Vedic hymns. Properly qualified brāhmans maintain and tend their ritual fire, which may therefore be enquired about as a matter of politeness. A frequent ritual act consists of pouring *ghī* into the fire, which then blazes up brightly, but Indrajit also once makes a libation of blood into the fire. This is in conflict with the Vedic ritual practice, in which the animal victim was strangled and parts of the carcass burnt in the sacrificial fire. Another form of ritual offering (especially to malign deities and semi-deities) is a portion of food left on the ground for them to consume.

Many rituals involve the spreading of *kuśa*, a particular type of grass, on the ground where they are performed. Temple worship is unknown (though beginning to be mentioned by the second stage), but certain trees, either single specimens surrounded by a railing (*caityas*), or groves, have sacred value.

By due performance of the prescribed rituals, and in particular of ascetic observances, a stock of merit can be accumulated which secures a period in the realm of one of the gods (especially that of Indra), only for this exalted state to be reversed when the merit is exhausted. Other meritorious actions include immediate obedience to parental wishes. Truth is an important concept, regarded as having an inherent power by which events can be affected.

Brāhmans are also known as Twice-Born. At the transition from childhood to adulthood, males are invested with the sacred thread – worn diagonally from the left shoulder to the waist on the right – in a ceremony which is considered a second birth. Giving to brāhmans is another meritorious action, so much so that it is sanctioned by custom for brāhmans (only) to threaten to fast to death as a way to coerce someone else to grant what they want.

Many of the hermits whom Rāma and his companions meet in the forest are brāhmans, but some clearly are not and, while their lifestyle is simple, they have not abandoned all links with society (the later better-known pattern of the *saṃnyāsin*). Some are accompanied by their wives, they perform simple rituals and they are happy to welcome visitors to their hermitages. Their dress consists regularly of cloth made from bark and of animal skins; their hair is matted (*jaṭā*), originally no doubt simply from lack of attention but often symbolically done to mark adopting this way of life by piling up the hair into a kind of topknot and fixing it with tree sap.

A variety of persons and objects can confer auspiciousness on an undertaking; courtesans are regarded as auspicious but widows have not yet acquired the negative connotations of later times. Particular marks on the body are among the many manifestations interpreted as omens of good or ill fortune. Seeing golden trees or silk-cotton trees is a special presage of imminent death.

Directional symbolism plays an important role. Omens occurring on a man's left are regarded as bad and those on his right as good: the reverse for women. To clasp a man by the left hand is a sign of disfavour, and to approach a warrior from the left in battle seems tantamount to a challenge (as it was in Old Irish heroic tales). The south, the realm of Yama, is generally inauspicious, and a dream of a journey to the south is a gloomy portent. Circumambulation (*pradakṣiṇa*) is an action of great respect or reverence, performed in a clockwise direction (the term 'sunwise' would be more appropriate); the reverse direction is unlucky or a marker of inauspicious events such as funerals.

The normal form of greeting in the period of the *Rāmāyaṇa*, especially for an inferior to a superior, is the *añjali*, in which the cupped hands are raised to the level of the chest or even of the head; nowadays, when this gesture is used the hands are more often placed together, as in the common attitude of Christian prayer. We have not attempted to translate such gestures literally, but have substituted expressions like 'deferential gesture', 'respectfully' or 'salute', as appropriate to the context. Bowing could well go as far as clasping the feet of the respected senior person or even touching them with one's head, a gesture of the greatest respect, since the feet are regarded as the most impure and unworthy part of the body and the head by contrast as the purest. In developments of this, Bharata places Rāma's sandals on his head to take them back as the symbol of Rāma's authority, and Sītā declares that she would not touch Rāvaṇa even with her left foot. The word 'kiss' renders the so-called 'sniff-kiss', a greeting of particular affection involving sniffing at or smelling the head of another, especially one's child.

Arrivals and departures tended to be highly formalized. A visitor is announced by a servant, an ascetic's pupil or someone else of junior status and is commonly greeted by being offered various auspicious items, principally and sometimes solely water (indeed, in more recent times some of the other items would actually be placed in the water). Correspondingly, rather than simply saying goodbye, one would seek the permission of one's host before leaving, and might well make a clockwise circumambulation of him as a mark of respect.

Appendix 2
Genealogies

The families of Rāma, Sugrīva and Rāvaṇa
as they appear in the translation

Rāma and the Rāghavas

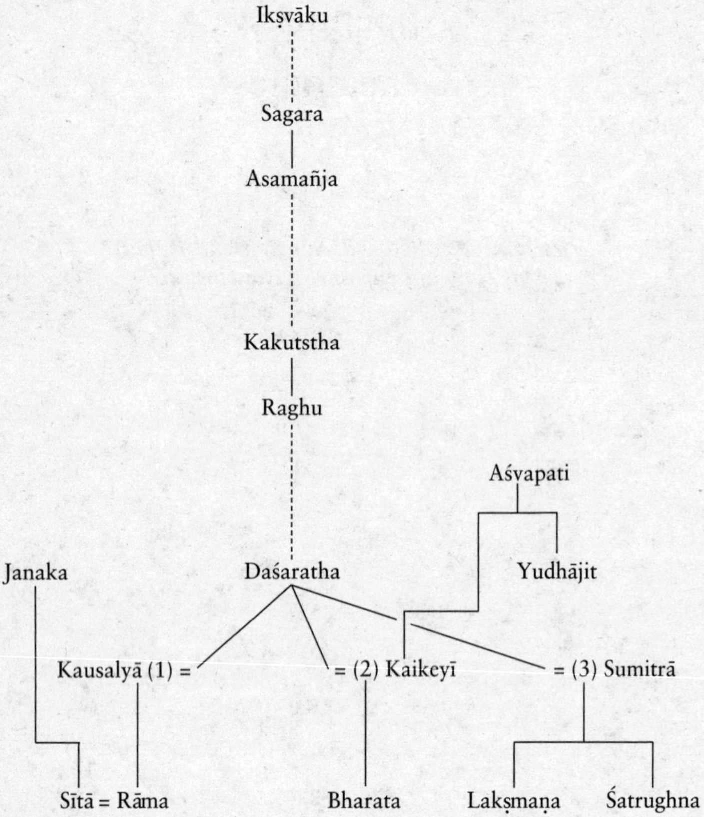

Sugrīva and the vānaras

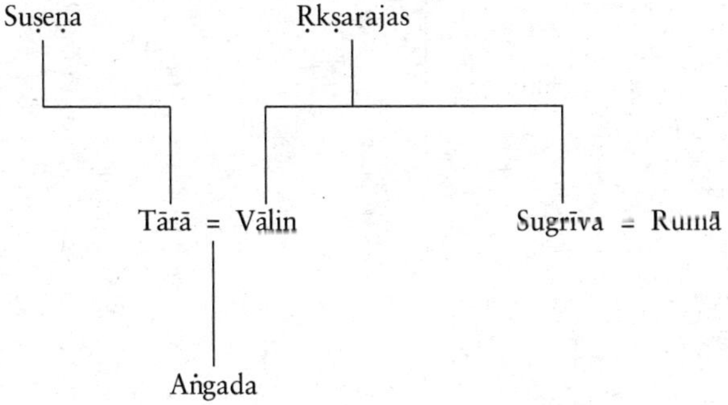

At 6,28.2 and 6,35.2 Suṣeṇa is also said to be the father of Mainda and Dvivida.

At 5,59.9 and 5,61.25 Dadhimukha is Sugrīva's maternal uncle.

Rāvaṇa and the rākṣasas

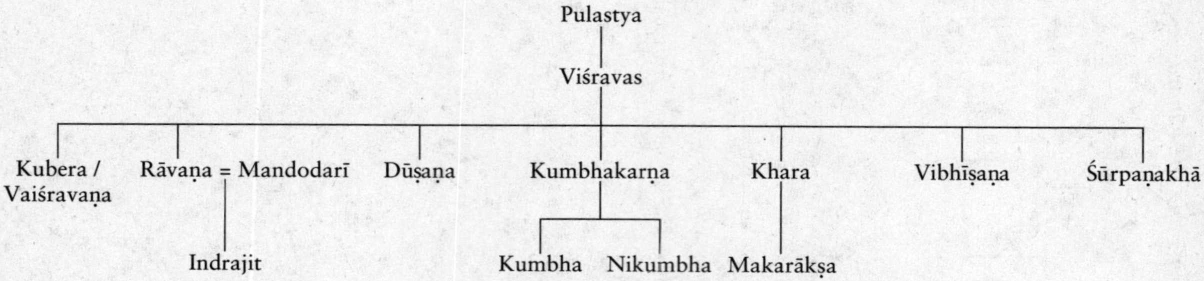

At 6,26.5 Mālyavān is the maternal great-uncle of Rāvaṇa; the relationship is not explained in detail until 7,25.23–4 (not translated).

At 6,56.3–4 Mahodara and Mahāparśva are said to be brothers of Kumbhakarṇa, and Atikāya, Devāntaka, Narāntaka and Triśiras are his nephews (specifically identified as sons of Rāvaṇa in passages added in the second stage).

Notes

Ayodhyā

1. *Some comes from a father ... worship her husband*: Proverb found also in the *Mahābhārata* (12,144.6) and in several later texts.
2. *if you resort to him*: Throughout Indian culture, it has been common for a weaker or inferior person to seek the protection and patronage of a stronger or superior person (including a deity) in what is often essentially a patron-client relationship. This is not a matter of temporarily seeking refuge, but involves a continuing relationship.
3. *broad-shouldered*: Literally, 'great-armed'.
4. *like lambs to the slaughter*: Literally, 'like cattle to a butcher'.
5. *goose*: The call of the wild goose (admired in India for its lofty, purposeful flight) is both musical and penetrating, especially its alarm call. Here and at 2,104.15 the comparison underlines the urgency of Rāma's words.
6. *It took mantras and mortifications and all sorts of trouble to produce him*: The text gives no explanation of what meritorious deeds Daśaratha performed to bring about the birth of such an outstanding son, either here, at 2,80.12 or at 3,62.3; the explanations provided by the later poets are mentioned in Afterthoughts.
7. *tonsured seer*: Literally, 'with skull-like head', which we take to mean that their heads have been shaved, although other interpretations are possible, including that they are white-haired through age. The usual hairstyle for brāhmans and hermits is to shave the head except for one topknot: *śikhin*, 'having a peak', as Rāma is described at 3,36.11, also translated 'tonsured'.
8. *sweet smile*: Literally, 'round teeth'.
9. *thistle*: Literally, 'snake-gourd' (*kiṃpāka*, *Trichosanthes*

palmata), a sour, indigestible fruit, as the Sanskrit name indicates.

10. *All creatures are subject to three pairs of opposing states*: Early Indian thought typically sees the world as made up of complementary opposites, such as pleasure and pain, gain and loss; the third pair here is no doubt life and death (or existence and non-existence).
11. *his own flesh and blood*: Literally, 'breath of himself', since the Indian tradition regards the breath (*prāṇa*) as being the life of anyone (as in the English 'vital breaths').
12. *dung . . . stacked . . . ready for the cold weather*: To be used for fuel.
13. *It is because a son saves his father from the hell called Put that he is called a 'son'*: An early etymology (a 'folk' etymology) for the word *putra*, 'son', which derives it from the root *trā*, 'to save', and a name for a hell, *Put*, occurring only in this context and evidently invented for the purpose.

The Forest

1. *won all worlds by my pious deeds*: In older Indian thought there are several heavenly realms above the earth which can be reached as a reward for one's religious and moral activities (especially asceticism).
2. *cut off her ears and nose*: Widespread traditional punishment for a loose woman.
3. *like a sārasa separating out milk mixed in water to drink*: The goose or, as here, the sarus crane is reputed to be able to drink only the milk from a mixture of milk and water.
4. *well-feathered*: There is some ambiguity about the term (*viśikha*). It could also mean 'very pointed' or, alternatively, either 'unpointed' or 'unfeathered', if the prefix *vi-*, which we have taken to mean 'well, very', has its more usual dissociative sense. We have also translated it 'well-feathered' at its other occurrences (6,34.23a; 6,78.9d,17b).
5. *rickshaws*: The text has *ratha*, 'chariot'.
6. *the Crow with the Palm Tree*: Fable not extant; the derivative expression ('like the Crow with the Palm Tree') elsewhere usually indicates an accidental coincidence but here seems to indicate something unexpected or unforeseen.
7. *the same agony that Urvaśī did when she kicked Purūravas*: The love story of the mortal king Purūravas and the *apsaras* Urvaśī

is found already in the Veda, although no extant version has anything precisely corresponding to this incident of Urvaśī insulting or spurning Purūravas.

8. *its fans and its parasol*: Symbols of sovereignty (as also at 4,10.3 and 4,25.21). The fan (*vyajana*, *cāmara*), which also functions as a fly-whisk, is usually made from a yak's tail. Both it and the parasol are white.

9. *placed a blade of grass between them*: Presumably as a symbolic barrier between them (as also at 5,19.3); cf. J. L. Brockington, 'Guarded by Grass: a Ramayaṇa motif and some Western parallels', *Indologica Taurinensia* 13 (1985–6), pp. 15–28.

10. *it took great asceticism and good deeds for King Daśaratha to be granted you*: See Ayodhyā n. 6.

Kiṣkindhā

1. *This many-ribbed parasol . . . the fan*: Symbols of sovereignty (as also at 3,49.14 and 4,25.21).

2. *rising sun*: Or 'setting' (the Sanskrit term *saṃdhyā* denotes both the morning and the evening twilight: dawn and dusk).

3. *his garments were still wet*: From making the water-offering at Vālin's funeral.

4. *gold-adorned white parasol and a magnificent pair of gleaming fans with gold handles*: Symbols of sovereignty (as also at 3,49.14 and 4,10.3). The subsequent items listed in this paragraph symbolize power or prosperity (and so in more general terms sovereignty).

5. *A lie concerning a horse destroys a hundred . . . teller and family*: Proverbial and somewhat elliptical; a parallel passage in the *Laws of Manu* (8.97–9) makes explicit that the numbers are the totals of his relatives that a liar destroys by his falsehoods.

6. *Expiation has been enjoined . . . no expiation for an ingrate*: Another proverbial saying, also found in the *Mahābhārata* (12,166.24; cf. 5,105.10) and in later texts.

7. *that marvellous mountain where the sun sets*: Elsewhere this mountain is named as Asta.

8. *duty, profit and pleasure*: These are the three traditional aims of life (*dharma*, *artha*, *kāma*), ranked in order of precedence; all may be pursued but *dharma* has priority.

9. *like Indra Śatakratu did Śacī's arrogant father*: This tale is obscure, as the varying explanations by the commentators reveal. The context suggests that there was some sort of collusion

between Anuhlāda, who as Hiraṇyakaśipu's son is a natural enemy of Indra, and Śacī's father, Puloman, but no such episode is actually extant.

10. *those that fight with their feet*: Cocks (the gamecock is descended from the Indian red junglefowl, *Gallus gallus murghi*).

Beauty

1. *tanks*: These are specifically bodies of water impounded for irrigation, rather than simply ornamental ponds.
2. *single plait*: This is a style worn by a woman whose husband is absent.
3. *She placed grass between them*: See The Forest n. 9 (on 3,54.1).
4. *threats and blandishments*: Literally, 'against the hair or with the hair'.
5. *wasted*: Literally, 'whose stomach was <flat as> the palm of a hand'.
6. *She grasped a spreading branch of the blossoming aśoka for support*: Although Sītā here clearly holds the branch for support (as his mother does on giving birth to the Buddha), it is interesting to note that a frequent motif in literature and in art is that of the *śālabhañjikā*, a young woman who coaxes a tree into bloom by grasping or more often kicking it. Is this episode a precursor of that motif?
7. *no good can come of seeing a vānara in a dream*: This appears to be a general popular belief, from which Sītā infers that the welcome outcome means that this is reality, not a dream.
8. *a fourth tactic remains*: The three forms of diplomacy are conciliation, gifts and creating dissension (as is spelt out in a longer verse added into the text here), while the fourth tactic is the use of force (cf. also 6,9.8).
9. *snake's feet*: There is a popular belief that in fact snakes do have feet (and legs) but only another snake can see them.
10. *three eras*: Past, present and future.
11. *like a five-tongued serpent*: This simile is usually applied to the warrior's hand grasping his weapon – the fingers corresponding to the heads of the snake (esp. cobra) – but here the point must be to highlight the degree of threat that Sītā poses.
12. *If I am obedient . . . become cool for Hanumān*: This is an example of the 'act of truth' in which someone affirms some truth about his or her self, especially one that is or should be characteristic, and uses the power inherent in the utterance to

achieve a particular goal. There is another example at 6,78.31.

13. *a cow overflowing from maternal love for her calf*: There is a general and ancient Indian belief that a cow's milk flows specifically at the sight of her calf.

War

1. *You caused devastation . . . you have battered and killed them, your majesty*: The quarrel with Vaiśravaṇa is the only one of these exploits to be recorded in the early part of the text; others, such as the conflict with Madhu, have been elaborated – with significant differences of detail – in later parts.
2. *three regular means*: Of diplomacy, i.e. conciliation, gifts and creating dissension; cf. Beauty n. 8 (on 5,39.2).
3. *There's a proverb . . . capturing us*: This saying seems unknown elsewhere.
4. *I was born to be sovereign*: Rāvaṇa is not being accurate here, since Vaiśravaṇa is his older brother, whom he ousted.
5. *a pigeon . . . flesh*: There are a number of versions of this tale, illustrating the virtue of generosity. A pigeon offers its own flesh to a hunter or a bird of prey which has already killed its mate. The best-known form is that of King Śibi (often alluded to with similar brevity, e.g. at *Mahābhārata* 3,199.6).
6. *the homily recited of old . . . perishes with the victim*: Parts of this homily are quoted in later anthologies as proverbial sayings but other early sources are lacking.
7. *Vaiśravaṇa's junior*: In referring to Rāvaṇa in this way Rāma seems pointedly to be insulting or taunting him (cf. n. 4 above on 6,10.10).
8. *Sugrīva . . . fine neck broken*: The passage from here up to *Aṅgada is a fallen anklet* is particularly rich in puns on the *vānaras'* names; details can be found in the Index / Glossary.
9. *dharma and adharma*: The connotations of *dharma* and its opposite are too all-encompassing here to allow one of our usual translations, especially since it carries overtones of the Vedic *ṛta*, the principle of cosmic order worked out also within human society.
10. *autumn*: Literally, 'at the end of the rains', by which time any clouds remaining are empty of rain.
11. *puddle*: Literally, 'cow-print', but so translated here and at 6,77.11 to underline the pejorative overtones, absent from the term's other occurrence at 4,45.12.

12. *hands*: Garuḍa is usually portrayed as having a bird's body but here is more fully anthropomorphic.
13. *slashed in two*: Literally, 'cut along the path of the sacred thread', that is, diagonally across the body, since at the transition from childhood to adulthood male brāhmans are invested with the thread which is worn diagonally from the left shoulder to the waist on the right.
14. *enters that banyan*: The aerial roots dropping from its branches gradually turn a single tree into a thick grove.
15. *If Rāma Dāśarathi is righteous . . . kill Rāvaṇi*: Another example of an 'act of truth', seen already at 5,51.24–7 (cf. Beauty n. 11).
16. *the missiles of that sagacious warrior of great splendour all manifested themselves*: The divine missiles earlier granted to Rāma, which are evidently envisaged as some kind of spell, become incorporated into his actual weapons.
17. *Do not return . . . that tradition*: Parallels to this verse are lacking, although it is clearly proverbial, as the style of our translation is intended to indicate and as Böhtlingk recognized by including it in his collection of Indian aphorisms, *Indische Sprüche* (2nd edn, 3 vols., St Petersburg: Commissionäre der Kaiserlichen Akademie der Wissenschaften, 1870–73).

Index / Glossary

Hemā *'golden', apsaras, partner of dānava Maya* 182
Hemakūṭa *'golden crested', vānara* 267
herbs, healing 292, 339
heron *(kaṅka,* Ardea cinerea *L. and* A. purpurea *Meyen)* 348
heron-feathered arrows 87, 145, 200, 296, 315
Himālaya *'abode of snow' (also Himavān 'possessing snow')*
site of hermitages 48, 67, 171–2, 263–4
Himavān *Himālaya personified esp. as father of Pārvatī, Śiva's wife*
refuses to fight Dundubhi 150
Hiraṇyakaśipu *'having golden garments', a daitya king* 199
honey *(madhu)* 26, 28, 163
Honey Orchard *(Madhuvana) part of Sugrīva's personal estate, wrecked by exultant vānaras* xv, xx, 230–35
horses *(ásva, turaga, turaṃga, vājin, haya)*
care for 19, 22–3
in battle 83 *etc.*
of Indra 346
of the Sun 130
stumbling or listlessness a portent of disaster 84, 298, 303, 311, 330
weep 31, 273, 311, 345
humour, irony, mockery xx–xxi, xxix, 65, 77–9, 88, 97, 108–9, 231–3, 304–6, 323, 339, 341
hunting
for food xv, 27, 101, 131
for sacrifice 28
for sport xv, 7, 22, 100–101
Hutavaha *'oblation-bearer'* = Fire

Ikṣvākus *dynasty to which Rāma belongs* 7, 9, 14, 19, 22, 42, 45, 60, 62, 71–2, 114, 123, 126, 128, 141, 187, 197, 202, 212, 214, 220, 229, 236, 264, 349
'pride of the Ikṣvākus' designates Bharata 31
'pride of the Ikṣvākus' designates Rāma 32
Indra *chief god of Vedic pantheon, warrior and thunder god, Protector of East*
visit to Sutīkṣṇa 72
carries off Śacī 98
enmity with Kabandha 128–9
defeated by baby Kumbhakarṇa 304
congratulates victorious Rāma, grants boon of restoring fallen *vānaras* to life and perpetually providing them with food 357–8
armed with thunderbolt 81, 108, 129, 182, 300, 349

invisibility *see* Indrajit
Irāvata *'possessing food', mountain famed for elephants* 40

Jābāli *counsellor of Daśaratha* 67
jackal *(gomāyu, śivā,* Canis aureus *L.)*
scavenger, portent of disaster 84, 99, 116, 273, 280, 302, 312, 321, 329–30, 345, 348
jackfruit *(panasa,* Artocarpus integrifolia *L. f.) evergreen tree with huge edible fruit* 131, 269
Jāhnavī *'daughter of Jahnu (an ancient sage)'*= Gaṅgā
Jain versions 366, 371
Jāmbavān *vānara chief, king of bears; meaning unknown*
senior member of party searching south, dissuades Aṅgada from attempting the leap to Laṅkā, knows who can accomplish it 191–2
strength known to Rāvaṇa 221
suspicious of Vibhīṣaṇa 253
Sītā told he has been killed 269
assigned to central keep 276
searches for invisible Indrajit 282
mounts guard over unconscious Rāma and Lakṣmaṇa 286
rallies *vānaras* 291
play on words with *jānu* 'knee' 269
son said to have devastated *rākṣasas* 267
also named at 163, 195, 233, 245, 325, 328, 334, 339
jambū (Syzygium cumini *(L.) Skeels (formerly* Eugenia jambolana *Lam.), jambolan or Black Plum) forest tree with edible fruit* 131
Jambumālin *'garlanded with jambu / jambū', rākṣasa*
son of Prahasta, killed by Hanumān 220
killed by Hanumān 279–80
Janaka *'progenitor', father of Sītā and king of Videha / Mithilā* xxvii, 36, 195–6, 198, 213, 236–7, 366
Janaka's daughter *(Janakātmajā) Sītā* 9, 12, 25–6, 74, 94–5, 103–4, 110, 111, 114, 116–17, 125, 142, 177, 179–80, 181, 189, 194–6, 206–7, 209–10, 213, 215–17, 224, 239, 268, 271, 289, 318, 356–7
Jānakī *'<daughter> of Janaka ('father')', Sītā* 3, 31, 109, 177, 181, 189, 194–5, 197, 199, 201–3, 211–13, 218, 225, 229–30, 236–8, 246, 271
Janasthāna *'place of people', a forest area* 82–4, 88, 91, 93–4, 102–3, 107–8, 113–15, 117–18, 126, 129, 183, 186–7, 208, 213, 225, 249, 251, 264, 268, 271, 288, 341, 352
called 'place of the slain' 113, 200

stages of transmission xxiii–xxvi, 373–4
standard 46, 58, 83–4, 86–7, 89–90, 121, 154, 163, 190, 198, 273, 279, 281, 284, 286, 296–8, 303, 311, 319, 330, 336, 344, 346
see also Indra
stars *(tārā, also jyotis, nakṣatra)* 36–7, 83–6, 101, 151, 166, 168, 213, 323
see also Svātī
star, shooting *(ulkā)* 310, 313, 336
also called meteor
stars, lord of *(tārādhipa) moon* 213
statecraft 29, 34, 44, 67, 69, 71–2, 74, 91, 94–5, 98–9, 108, 200, 217, 226, 246, 249–50, 252–5, 265, 272–4
staves *(daṇḍa, yaṣṭi)* 269, 295, 311, 325
Sthūlākṣa *'dim-eyed', rākṣasa companion of Khara* 85
Sthūlaśiras *'blockhead', an ascetic sage* 129
stokaka *(*Clamator jacobinus serratus *(Sparrman)) pied crested cuckoo, bird supposed to live on raindrops, migrant arriving with monsoon* 337
storytelling 77, 111, 338
Subāhu *'with good arms', vānara who charges ramparts* 278
Sudāman *'giving well', mountain in Bāhlīka* 38
sugar 193
Sugrīva *'with good neck', king of vānaras, son of Ṛkṣarajas and brother of Vālin (major items only)*
expelled by Vālin, wife seized, lives on Ṛśyamūka 130–33, 137–8, 141, 145–9, 178–9
Kabandha advises Rāma to form alliance with him 130–31
alarmed by appearance of Rāma and Lakṣmaṇa 137–8, 141
offers alliance with Rāma, pledges to search for Sītā 142–3
feared by Tārā, Aṅgada, Hanumān 155–6, 181, 184–6, 192
fights Vālin xix, 153–7
makes peace with dying Vālin, who invests him with his golden garland xix, 160–61, 264
musters *vānaras*, dispatches search parties 170–78
strength known to Rāvaṇa 221
realizes that wrecking of Honey Orchard proclaims success of Hanumān's mission 232–3
initially suspicious of Vibhīṣaṇa 251–2, 254
identified to Rāvaṇa by Śuka 264
Sītā told he has been killed 269
assigned to central keep, takes up position at northern gate, kills Praghasa 276, 278–80

Tiṣya *fourth and worst of the ages of the world (from presiding constellation)* 272
tonsure *see* ascetics
trident *(triśūla) weapon* 296
Trijaṭā *'triple braid', rākṣasī guard of Sītā*
dream presages doom for *rākṣasas* 209–10
takes Sītā to see apparently dead Rāma and Lakṣmaṇa, reassures her 286–9
Trikūṭa *'triple peak', mountain in Laṅkā* 243, 282
Triśaṅku *'triple peg', constellation (Southern Cross)* 14
Triśiras *'triple-headed', rākṣasa*
companion of Khara, killed by Rāma 85, 88–90, 92–3, 267, 312
nephew of Kumbhakarṇa 308
truth, integrity 3–5, 7, 24, 49, 52, 65–6, 72, 114, 141, 155, 168, 214, 229–30
act of truth 227, 327, 381–3
Tryambaka *'three-eyed', Śiva* 279
Tulsīdās *author of best-known Hindi version of Rāmāyaṇa* 371
Twice-Born *(dvija, dvijāti) term for brāhmans as having had a second birth at their investiture with the sacred thread* 16, 34, 37, 40, 52, 65, 72, 115, 126, 272–3, 287
twilight ritual *muttered invocation to the deities performed at dawn and sunset* 19, 21, 23, 25, 50, 73, 77

Underworld *(Pātāla)* 178, 190, 257
Urvaśī *'spreading wide', apsaras who married mortal king Purūravas* 105
Uśanas *ancient sage (identified with Śukra), preceptor of anti-gods, noted for his wealth* 301
Uttarakāṇḍa *see* Further Book

Vācaspati *'lord of speech', Vedic deity* 215
Vahni *'conveyer, fire', vānara* 176
Vaidehī *'daughter of king of Videha', Sītā* 3, 6, 10, 15, 17–18, 22, 25, 28, 30, 33, 37, 51, 59, 63, 65, 69–70, 73, 75–6, 78–80, 86, 92, 95, 97–8, 101, 103–5, 107–21, 123–6, 135–7, 143, 175, 179, 181, 183, 186–7, 189, 194–5, 198–9, 201–2, 205–6, 210, 212–14, 216, 218, 227, 229, 233, 235, 237, 239, 242–3, 249, 263, 271, 286, 288, 316, 337, 341, 354, 357, 359–60
Vainateya = Vinatā's son
Vaiṣṇava = of Viṣṇu 90

THE STORY OF PENGUIN CLASSICS

Before 1946 ... 'Classics' are mainly the domain of academics and students, without readable editions for everyone else. This all changes when a little-known classicist, E. V. Rieu, presents Penguin founder Allen Lane with the translation of Homer's *Odyssey* that he has been working on and reading to his wife Nelly in his spare time.

1946 *The Odyssey* becomes the first Penguin Classic published, and promptly sells three million copies. Suddenly, classic books are no longer for the privileged few.

1950s Rieu, now series editor, turns to professional writers for the best modern, readable translations, including Dorothy L. Sayers's *Inferno* and Robert Graves's *The Twelve Caesars*, which revives the salacious original.

1960s The Classics are given the distinctive black jackets that have remained a constant throughout the series's various looks. Rieu retires in 1964, hailing the Penguin Classics list as 'the greatest educative force of the 20th century'.

1970s A new generation of translators arrives to swell the Penguin Classics ranks, and the list grows to encompass more philosophy, religion, science, history and politics.

1980s The Penguin American Library joins the Classics stable, with titles such as *The Last of the Mohicans* safeguarded. Penguin Classics now offers the most comprehensive library of world literature available.

1990s The launch of Penguin Audiobooks brings the classics to a listening audience for the first time, and in 1999 the launch of the Penguin Classics website takes them online to a larger global readership than ever before.

The 21st Century Penguin Classics are rejacketed for the first time in nearly twenty years. This world famous series now consists of more than 1300 titles, making the widest range of the best books ever written available to millions – and constantly redefining the meaning of what makes a 'classic'.

The Odyssey continues ...

read more

PENGUIN CLASSICS

THE EPIC OF GILGAMESH

'Surpassing all other kings, heroic in stature,
brave scion of Uruk, wild bull on the rampage!
Gilgamesh the tall, magnificent and terrible'

Miraculously preserved on clay tablets dating back as much as four thousand years, the poem of Gilgamesh, king of Uruk, is the world's oldest epic, predating Homer by many centuries. The story tells of Gilgamesh's adventures with the wild man Enkidu, and of his arduous journey to the ends of the earth in quest of the Babylonian Noah and the secret of immortality. Alongside its themes of family, friendship and the duties of kings, *The Epic of Gilgamesh* is, above all, about mankind's eternal struggle with the fear of death.

The Babylonian version has been known for over a century, but linguists are still deciphering new fragments in Akkadian and Sumerian. Andrew George's gripping translation brilliantly combines these into a fluent narrative and will long rank as the definitive English *Gilgamesh*.

'This masterly new verse translation' *The Times*

Translated with an introduction by Andrew George

---

read more

PENGUIN CLASSICS

THE ANALECTS CONFUCIUS

'The Master said, "If a man sets his heart on benevolence, he will be free from evil"'

The Analects are a collection of Confucius's sayings brought together by his pupils shortly after his death in 497 BC. Together they express a philosophy, or a moral code, by which Confucius, one of the most humane thinkers of all time, believed everyone should live. Upholding the ideals of wisdom, self-knowledge, courage and love of one's fellow man, he argued that the pursuit of virtue should be every individual's supreme goal. And while following the Way, or the truth, might not result in immediate or material gain, Confucius showed that it could nevertheless bring its own powerful and lasting spiritual rewards.

This edition contains a detailed introduction exploring the concepts of the original work, a bibliography and glossary and appendices on Confucius himself, *The Analects* and the disciples who compiled them.

Translated with an introduction and notes by D. C. Lau

THE KORAN

'God is the light of the heavens and the earth . . . God guides to His light whom he will'

The Koran is universally accepted by Muslims to be the infallible Word of God as first revealed to the Prophet Muhammad by the Angel Gabriel nearly fourteen hundred years ago. Its 114 chapters, or *sūrahs*, recount the narratives central to Muslim belief, and together they form one of the world's most influential prophetic works and a literary masterpiece in its own right. But above all, the Koran provides the rules of conduct that remain fundamental to the Muslim faith today: prayer, fasting, pilgrimage to Mecca and absolute faith in God.

N. J. Dawood's masterly translation is the result of his life-long study of the Koran's language and style, and presents the English reader with a fluent and authoritative rendering, while reflecting the flavour and rhythm of the original. This edition follows the traditional sequence of the Koranic *sūrahs*.

'Across the language barrier Dawood captures the thunder and poetry of the original' *The Times*

Over a million copies sold worldwide.

Revised translation with an introduction and notes by N. J. Dawood

read more

PENGUIN CLASSICS

THE BHAGAVAD GITA

'In death thy glory in heaven, in victory thy glory on earth.
Arise therefore, Arjuna, with thy soul ready to fight'

The Bhagavad Gita is an intensely spiritual work that forms the cornerstone of the Hindu faith, and is also one of the masterpieces of Sanskrit poetry. It describes how, at the beginning of a mighty battle between the Pandava and Kaurava armies, the god Krishna gives spiritual enlightenment to the warrior Arjuna, who realizes that the true battle is for his own soul.

Juan Mascaró's translation of *The Bhagavad Gita* captures the extraordinary aural qualities of the original Sanskrit. This edition features a new introduction by Simon Brodbeck, which discusses concepts such as dehin, prakriti and Karma.

'The task of truly translating such a work is indeed formidable. The translator must at least possess three qualities. He must be an artist in words as well as a Sanskrit scholar, and above all, perhaps, he must be deeply sympathetic with the spirit of the original. Mascaró has succeeded so well because he possesses all these' *The Times Literary Supplement*

Translated by Juan Mascaró with an introduction by Simon Brodbeck

Penguin Classics

BUDDHIST SCRIPTURES

'Whoever gives something for the good of others, with heart full of sympathy, not heeding his own good, reaps unspoiled fruit'

While Buddhism has no central text such as the Bible or the Koran, there is a powerful body of scripture from across Asia that encompasses the *dharma*, or the teachings of Buddha. This rich anthology brings together works from a broad historical and geographical range, and from languages such as Pali, Sanskrit, Tibetan, Chinese and Japanese. There are tales of the Buddha's past lives, a discussion of the qualities and qualifications of a monk, and an exploration of the many meanings of Enlightenment. Together they provide a vivid picture of the Buddha and of the vast nature of the Buddhist tradition.

This new edition contains many texts presented in English for the first time as well as new translations of some well-known works, and also includes an informative introduction and prefaces to each chapter by scholar of Buddhism Donald S. Lopez Jr, with suggestions for further reading and a glossary.

Edited with an introduction by Donald S. Lopez, Jr

read more

PENGUIN CLASSICS

THE RUBA'IYAT OF OMAR KHAYYAM

'Many like you come and many go
Snatch your share before you are snatched away'

Revered in eleventh-century Persia as an astronomer, mathematician and philosopher, Omar Khayyam is now known first and foremost for his *Ruba'iyat*. The short epigrammatic stanza form allowed poets of his day to express personal feelings, beliefs and doubts with wit and clarity, and Khayyam became one of its most accomplished masters with his touching meditations on the transience of human life and of the natural world. One of the supreme achievements of medieval literature, the reckless romanticism and the pragmatic fatalism in the face of death means these verses continue to hold the imagination of modern readers.

In this translation, Persian scholar Peter Avery and the poet John Heath-Stubbs have collaborated to recapture the sceptical, unorthodox spirit of the original by providing a near literal English version of the original verse. This edition also includes a map, appendices, bibliography and an introduction examining the *ruba'i* form and Khayyam's life and times.

'[Has] restored to that masterpiece all the fun, dash and vivacity.'
Jan Morris

Translated by Peter Avery and John Heath-Stubbs

read more

PENGUIN CLASSICS

BEOWULF

'With bare hands shall I
grapple with the fiend, fight to the death here,
hater and hated! He who is chosen
shall deliver himself to the Lord's judgement'

Beowulf is the greatest surviving work of literature in Old English, unparalleled in its epic grandeur and scope. It tells the story of the heroic Beowulf and of his battles, first with the monster Grendel, who has laid waste to the great hall of the Danish king Hrothgar, then with Grendel's avenging mother, and finally with a dragon that threatens to devastate his homeland. Through its blend of myth and history, *Beowulf* vividly evokes a twilight world in which men and supernatural forces live side by side, and celebrates the endurance of the human spirit in a transient world.

Michael Alexander's landmark modern English verse translation has been revised to take account of new readings and interpretations. His new introduction discusses central themes of *Beowulf* and its place among epic poems, the history of its publication and reception, and issues of translation.

'A foundation stone of poetry in English' Andrew Motion

Translated with an introduction and notes by Michael Alexander